Alba Reborn

The Celtic Heaven Trilogy
Book One

A Celtic Path of Enlightenment
The Healing Power of the Heart
Celtic Lore and Cosmology

By Jill Rose Frew, Ph.D.

Dedication

This book, and my every breath, is dedicated to the cosmic Christ, the humble divine masculine of the Creator Sun, Who puts a bit of His Heart into every human and descends to live through the fears of this world and lift all worlds a little bit with His efforts on earth. In the Celtic pantheon, He is called Oghama, the masculine aspect of the Creator, the Beloved. It is His heart I felt every step of the way on my own spiritual path, behind every fear, no matter how intense. Each time, He was beaming gentle tenderness and waiting in silence for me to calm down and do my inner healing work, so I could embody another piece of His great Heart. Oh, I <u>love</u> the Goddess and the faeries and angels, too, as deeply as can be. But for me there has never been and will never be any being in any world to compare with the cosmic Oghama/Christ. And so I place all efforts of my life, from the smallest to the most involved, including this trilogy, on the altar of His love. You, my Oghama Heart, are the closest, dearest, most intimate and cherished partner of my life. I love You with everything in me, forever and a day.

From: The Candle of Vision, by A.E. (George Wm. Russell)

From: "Retrospect.": "As I walked in the evening down the lanes scented by the honeysuckle, my senses were expectant of some unveiling about to take place, I felt that beings were looking in upon me out of the true home of man. They seemed to be saying to each other of us, 'Soon they will awaken; soon they will come to us again,' and for a moment I almost seemed to mix with their eternity... The visible world became like a tapestry blown and stirred by winds behind it. If it would but raise for an instant I knew I would be in Paradise."

"All desire tends to bring about unity with the object adored...So did I feel one warm summer day lying idly on the hillside, not then thinking of anything but the sunlight, and how sweet it was to drowse there, when, suddenly, I felt a fiery heart throb, and knew it was personal and intimate, and started with every sense dilated and intent, and turned inwards, and I heard first a music as of bells going away, away into that wondrous underland whither, as legend relates, the Danaan gods withdrew; and then the heart of the hills was opened to me, and I knew there was no hill for those who were there, and they were unconscious of the ponderous mountain piled above the palaces of light, and the winds were sparkling and diamond clear, yet full of colour as an opal, as they glittered through the valley, and I knew the Golden Age was all about me, and it was we who had been blind to it but that it had never passed away from the world."

Table of Contents

6

Preface

In a very real sense, this trilogy is a true story, though it was woven from threads and hues of different centuries into the tapestry you will find on these pages. Virtually all the teachings that come through the druid, Coillore, are identical to the wisdom lessons I have learned on my own path of transformation during the past twenty-four years of my life. It has been a distinctly druid path and largely solitary, with inner guides and magical openings that were unrecognized by those around me. But my heart aches to reconnect with others who know and wish to share such things!

And the healing method used by Fìrinn and Soillse is precisely the same one I use myself every morning and evening. It's a very simple process, for once the ancient fears are brought into consciousness, just imagining them moving into the diamond light in the deep heart and releasing the contract to believe in those fears melts them into the highest light. I know it is powerful in its childlike way, for it has brought my consciousness through all the planes of the sensate, soul, spirit, logos, cherubim, diamond centerpoint, and Diamond Core realms in twenty-four years of daily meditations. During this long transformation process, I observed very specific stages of suffering and growth that appear to be the same for everyone, and that information is also woven into this trilogy. This revised version of Alba Reborn is identical to the first edition but has been updated to include many new regents and planes of light that were not included in the first book published in 2011. Please see the Appendices for a description of the planes of the Diamond Core and Celtic pantheon, the healing process, and the stages of growth on the path of life.

This story also rings true to me on a personal level, for I know I've lived on the Isle of Skye in the very places and times this tale takes place, the first century BCE. Whether I was queen of Skye, though, or high priestess of the temple of Isis in Egypt or the Child Heart temple of Atlantis or the Creator Sun, I prefer to leave within the mists of history. Such past life memories are best taken with a grain of salt, I find, and I value humility greatly. In this life, I am a very ordinary person, a psychologist, light healer, and author, in service to the One, Who I love from the depths of my heart. But my inner guides tell me many of the historical details are true and wish this thought to be included. The memories contained here are certainly the way the story unfolded during my many trips to the isles of Skye and Iona, my years of reading about Celtic life and spirituality, and my frequent meditations over the years to sense details of ancient Celtic times and culture. I know these pages contain memories from many levels of the descent and the Celtic realms of heaven as well, so it's difficult to say how closely the details may fit an actual historical lifetime. The characters are distinctly 1st century BCE, however, and any resemblance to people now living is purely coincidental. The guides spoken of in the story, too, Sebhia (sheveeya,) and Donardin (donarstin), are my own inner teachers and have taught me the uses of light and the laws of love in a similar way as described in this trilogy. And they are as well my brother and sister from my Creator Sun tuath (tooah, farm in modern use, but in this book meaning a family compound), beings of light who reside in the Creator Sun.

The planes of consciousness or ladder of light described in these books are hues of light that came into my aura and remained there for several weeks as I steeped in the experiences, trials, and healing work at each particular level. And when I completed each phase, each color moved out my root, and a new one took its place from above. Over the past twenty years, there have been 365 of these. These gradual openings all the way along have been both magical and tender, with synchronicities and small details of love that were exquisitely precise. It has been very, very clear the Great Heart walked alongside me every step of the way. The names and images of the regents of these planes are taken from the inner spirit beings who presented themselves to me at each particular level. Please do not be concerned that all world traditions are not represented at the diamond levels in Appendix One, for I am not familiar with all paths. I make no attempt whatsoever to say one tradition or one god or goddess is better or higher than another, for I'm certain all traditions have regent names for every one of the planes in the ladder of light. I wish I knew them all, but I do not, and have included only the very few that seemed clear to me. The list is by no means comprehensive for any tradition other than Celtic.

This Creator Sun is a small sun at the center of the cosmos that I often felt, and finally began to see with my inner vision a decade or so ago. It's a small dense star, dazzlingly bright, Home of the Creators, the White Tara and Oghama (ohama) (Magdalena and Christ). It is Their heart that pulses together and a bit apart forever, the heartbeat of the universe. Their pulsed union creates the clear diamond light that surrounds and supports all beings in all worlds, the love force. In the next decades and centuries, I believe the clear light on earth will be activating rapidly, so we'll finally feel and know here the intensity and ecstasy of love we were once created into at the very beginning, the creator love that is our birthright.

Many of the Celtic traditions contained here, too, came primarily through my meditations and inner guidance. During the fifteen years before I began meditating every morning, I read everything I could find on Celtic life and lore. But this research left me with more questions than answers, and the sense that all historical written works contained distortions and veils over the truth. It was only after I began meditating with inner druid guides that pieces of the puzzle began to move into place, and this happened very slowly with much inner clearing work all along the way to open new understandings. Certain details seem more connected to realms of light than the actual life of first century Alba, such as the sexual abstinence of the virgin year, a young woman's first sun cycle after the beginning of her moon time. When I was writing about that, I distinctly felt the Celtic realms of heaven overlighting me.

My guides tell me there are heavenly realms for eleven other major cultures on earth as well. I believe their holy traditions, which move forward the forces of light in ways we have yet to remember here, will be surfacing and becoming reestablished in native communities across the earth in future years. I feel a deep personal reverence for this sacred Celtic culture of light and have tried to maintain purity in my meditative sessions and during the writing of this trilogy. I have tried my best to hear and sift through all written historical and meditative details as carefully as possible, but I have no doubt there are mistakes contained in this work, as well as filters over revelations that God and Goddess are keeping for future times. I say this only to suggest that if a passage or message contained in this trilogy does not feel accurate to you, then perhaps it isn't. Let your own heart and your relationship with God/Goddess be your guide.

Finding names for all the god and goddess regents of the Celtic pantheon was particularly challenging, given that there are varied equivalents in all the Gaelic dialects of Ireland, Wales, Britain, Scotland, and France. The names as well as the spiritual understandings written here came through numerous meditations over many years, included only after I felt confident in their accuracy. Still, feel free to substitute other names that may feel better to you, if you like. Only pronouns associated with the Creators are capitalized throughout the text, for all others are lesser regents.

I wish, also, to thank my daughter, Heather MacKenzie, for doing the text graphics, and my Gaelic teacher, the late Donald MacDonald of Montreal, for helping me with the pronunciation and meanings of all Gaelic words throughout the books. These are in parentheses following the initial use of each one. (He did not wish to help with names. Possible errors there are all my own.) In Scottish Gaelic, every R is rolled and Ch is guttural. For the Ogham letters and many of the Celtic pantheon, I used the old Irish words. This was in order not to create more confusion and because Scottish Gaelic spelling would have changed the ancient sacred alphabet. Also, I chose to limit Scottish dialect to dialog, leaving it out of thoughts entirely, since dialect can make for challenging reading to some. And I italicized thoughts being transmitted telepathically from one person to another, but not those within a person's own mind.

Nearly all of the fear images described here came from my own spiritual journey over the past twenty-four years as well. In a very few cases, the content was changed in order to blend with the landscape of Scotland, or Alba, in the first century BCE and the lives of Fìrinn and Soillse. The reptilian energies from the star Maya in the Pleiades, the dark goddesses and gods, Ashtar and Malduk of Orion, and Isle/Isis and Taranis/Osiris of the Dragon/Death star, who block the Creator Sun, are powerful ancient beings who brought bucket loads of fear into my life for healing over the past ten years especially. And I believe they did, in fact, bring to earth the personal will force in separation from the One (Malduk, Osiris, Taranis) and the death force (Ashtar, Isis, Isle) just before the fall of Atlantis and long ago, when we descended out of the Creator Sun into the Dragon star, Draco. These are forces of darkness that have held humanity captive for eons, and they continue to block the revelation and love of the Goddess of Light, the White Tara and Her life force, and the Heart of the cosmic Christ, Oghama, and His gentle Will for good.

It is my hope that this trilogy will help awaken each reader's memory of his or her own captivity to fear. And I offer these teachings that have helped me so much as a way for each person to find his or her path to freedom from fear forever. This is a deeply held wish, and I place these knowings in your hands, each and every one of you, with tenderness and love. For I know in the depths of my heart that inner beliefs do, in fact, create our outer 'realities.' This means that, if everyone on the planet went through an inner fear-clearing process like Fìrinn and Soillse on these pages, all pain, all suffering of any kind, all the fear-based horrors we are currently collectively creating across our global stage, will disappear. This includes: illness, all forms of slavery, money and power driven economies, mental illness, war, child abuse, the various sexual distortions, murder, crime, and on and on. Should you choose to climb this ladder of light, you'll meet your own fears on the way Home. And every one will melt, simply and easily, in the diamond light of love as you embrace it in your heart. And every fear cleared will also cleanse the planet and the realms of the Otherworld a little bit. It will take everyone to bring forth the heaven that earth was always intended to become and to open the veils between worlds, so we can see and touch our brothers and sisters in our Creator Sun and star tuaths once more. I cannot describe in words the strength of my own wish to give Sebhia a hug!

The straight path can be intense, but if you are faithful in your promise to free yourself and persevere, the spirit world will ease and soften the way. About two-thirds of the way along on my own path, I realized the dark energies that kept showing up in my life were just as frightened of me as I was of them. And when I simply explained to them, right from the beginning, that I wished only to transmute them back into light and meant no harm, they calmed down immediately. My process became far easier after that. And then after a time as well, I began to notice that, as the shadow or demon form melted into light, a small cherub child always emerged out of the darkness. It became clear that even the darkest, most horrific beings, are simply wounded cherub children underneath.

I'm told within that all who succeed through this fear-clearing process will move through a portal my inner guides call the happily-ever-after. It is beyond this point, they say, that one's individual true love partner finally appears, that world service or one's highest destiny opens, and each person moves to a community of ancient family members, whose love is old and deep beyond measuring. These communities will reflect the Creator Sun tuath of every family, which are the light templates for the clan structure of; Alba (Scotland, the Tara and mother land), Albion (Britain, the Oghama and father land), Eire (Ireland, the child heart), Cymru (Wales, the virgin male land), and the outer Hebrides (the virgin female land), the United Kingdom. My guides say that each family, as well as each nation, has a sacred purpose before the King and Queen of Heaven. Those, too, will be surfacing through these sacred family communities of future days.

But most importantly, when an individual's inner channel to the Diamond Core is cleared, God and Goddess become one's own best Friend, Parent, Child, and eternal Beloved, all rolled into One. So, all that happens in one's own little world, daily work and small miracles of love, are cocreated within this divine eternal partnership. One lives forever in the wild and passionate freedom, intensity, and love of the Great Heart. The human true love partnership, I'm told, is a reflection of this mystical marriage within. And once begun, the heart's desires of both human true love partners are created through their personal sacred sexual process, precisely in the image of the Creators. Keep in mind, though, that divine union is primarily through the Heart. This, too, I believe, is the template of the future for all humanity, the Arthurian fulfillment, and will form the pattern of these beloved communities.

I would like to add one small correction to the story as it is told here, for my understanding is that our true love of light is actually our higher self, split off and held behind the veils during the fall of Atlantis. This higher self is our other half, the one who was and has always been our true love partner, since our original creation into light, described on the concluding page of Book Two. This means that our human true love is actually another individual, chosen for this role during our final earth lifetime to complete the fairy tale ending God and Goddess have decreed for each one of us, the happily-ever-after on earth. And there is only one person chosen for this final sacred matrimony and prepared over many, many lifetimes, to serve as priest or priestess of the Beloved stream from God/Goddess. But that human true love is not the one we unite with in realms of light, for that role is forever filled by our higher self. Because I felt this extra detail would add confusion to the story, I did not include it in Soillse and Fìrinn's relationship.

My heartfelt blessing goes out to each and every one who commits to and braves their way through this transformation process into freedom from fear. Hold onto your divine hearts, everyone, for love as we have never known it on earth is about to arrive! I mean radical love that accepts no imposters of any kind and will speak up whenever necessary to see that the laws of heaven are fulfilled, intense and simple love that nourishes our inner child hearts. It will create: true love partnerships, world service, simple family time, sensuality and love of the physical, a community of lifelong friends, spiritual intimacy with all forms of life, nourishment and security of both love and material resources, and peace: peace of mind, peace of heart, and peace of spirit. All these are ours for the living once we clear our own fears out of the way. If you wish to take our simple Zoom classes or workshops to assist you on your path, see Facebook.com/CelticHeavenCenter/

May the One Heart all across the universe be released from darkness as soon as possible, and may the happily-ever-after become a living reality for everyone across our exquisite and loving planet. We all do, indeed, sit at the same hearth fire in heaven. And now is the time to birth all our inner divine children and become one family on earth, too. Blessed be, each one, on your walk to freedom. My heart is with you.

With much love,
Jill Frew, Ph.D.,
December 10, 2017 Portsmouth, RI

Celtic Calendar
Fifteen 24-day moons,
with 5 intercessory days

Beithe (beetha)-Birch moon-December 23rd-January 15th

Luis (loois)-Rowan moon-January 16th-February 8th

Imbolc (imbolt)-February 5th (opens at sunset Feb. 4th)-the little girl impulse of the year

Nion (neeoon)-Ash moon-February 9th-March 4th

Fearn (feearn)-Alder moon-March 5th-28th

Alban Eilir (alaban ayleer)-Vernal Equinox-March 21st(sunrise), the little boy impulse

Saille (syeeya)-Willow-March 29th-April 21st

Huath (hooah)-Hawthorne moon-April 22nd-May15th

Bealltain (bealchen)-May 5th (opens at sunset May 4th)-the virgin girl impulse of the year

Duir (jooer)-Oak moon-May 16th-June 8th

Tinne (teenya)-Holly moon-June 9th-July 2nd

Alban Hefin (alaban hefeen)-Midsummer-June 21st(sunrise)- the virgin boy impulse of the year

Coll (cohl)-Hazel moon-July 3rd-26th

Quert (keerst)-Apple moon-July 27th-August 19th

Lughnasa (loonassa) -August 5th (opens at sunset Aug. 4th)-the mother impulse of the year

Muin (mwin)-Vine moon-August 20th-September 12th

Gort (gorst)-Ivy moon-September 13th-October 6th

Alban Elved (alaban ehlvet)-Autumnal Equinox-September 21st (sunrise), the father impulse

Ngetal (engehtahl)-Reed moon-October 7th-30th

Straif (stryeef)-Blackthorne moon-October 31st-November 23rd

Samhein (1) (sahven)-November 4th (opens at sunset on the 4th)-the grandmother impulse

Samhein (2)-November 24th-28th (opens at sunset on the 23rd)-New Year, the gratefulness celebration to the Goddess, the intercessory days

Ruis (rooey)-Elder moon-November 29th-December 22nd

Alban Arturan (alaban arstooran)-Midwinter-December 21st (sunrise), the grandfather impulse

The Seven Heavens and 16 Light Structures of the Diamond Core

7) The Diamond Core: 174 planes, gods and goddesses in beloved partnerships

> Creator Sun, Beloveds light structure
> (Death or Dragon Star, wisdom light structure, not permanent)
> Stillpoint Center, mind light structure
> Luckenbooth Realms, heart and virgin girl light structure
> Tìr Nan Òg, action and virgin male light structure
> Old Heart, mother light structure
> Sun of the Son, boy light structure
> Old Heart, father light structure
> Child Heart, girl light structure
> The Wizard Wheel, cosmic seventh chakra
> The Pineal Wheel, cosmic sixth chakra
> The Triple Spiral, cosmic fifth chakra
> The Holy Family, cosmic fourth chakra
> The Pillar Realms, cosmic third chakra
> The Circle of Eight, cosmic second chakra
> The White Pentagram, humanity first chakra

6) Diamond Centerpoint: 39 planes, lesser gods and goddesses

5) The Cherubim Realms: 10 planes, cherubim

4) The Logos: 14 planes, seraphim

3) The Spirit Realms: 66 planes, djinns (male fairies)

2) The Soul Realms: 44 planes, devas (female fairies)

1) The Sensate Realms: 18 planes, humans

Chapter One: Fìrinn

Once, two thousand years ago and more, a high chief and his queen ruled Skye, the largest of the Scottish isles. It was a rocky road they both walked to the crowning, but the two brought the light of God/Goddess to the clans the like of which none had seen before. And the path they traveled can teach us much in our own time, those who may need to reawaken their hearts again. In those Celtic days the hills burned with a wildfire of life, and the earth mother suckled all on her mountain breasts, people and creatures alike untamed in the sea wind's song. That was long before the terrors and the tiredness of our own days set in. So come, ladds and lassies, listen to the story of the mountain king and queen.

A tuath (tooah, farm or family compound) was a tribal village, consisting of a single family descended from one maternal great-grandmother, and it included the matriarch, her daughters with their families, and her unmarried sons to four generations. On the Isle of Skye, the clan of the deer lived just across the sea loch from where the castle Dunbheagan (doonvaygan) is today. They'd taken up residence in that valley 200 years before our tale takes place, which is in the first century BCE, as waves of Celtic folk set out from their Austrian homeland to people the western reaches of the earth.

The clan of the deer lived on a low hillside, well back from the sea loch, in the flat sculpted plain below the inland hills. Twenty-two huts were scattered below the chief's broch there, all perched on the rise just above the burn (the river Osdale). All the houses were small and round with stone foundations and wooden palisaded walls, no windows, and a single door. They were topped with thatch, each roof with a central smoke hole over the hearth.

The broch itself, a stone tower and home of the matriarch and her chief, was just a grand extension of a simple hut foundation, round again, but with the square stones of the hillsides piled in careful courses to ten meters. It had an outer wall and an inner one, too, with a meter space in between and stone steps anchored between them that allowed the men to climb to the top, unseen, and watch for intruders entering the bay.

Norse raiders had landed to the west along the same peninsula some decades before, capturing women and cattle of the clan of the pony and sailing off again in half a morning. And many other isles felt the talons of the raiders, too. So druids came to all tuaths after that, bringing plans for the brochs, the double circle, exactly the same as God/Goddess in the Creator Sun, that would call forth the most protection of the Sun Lord and the Queen of Heaven. The whole clan could fit inside their broch, and most of the cattle, too, with water and stores to stay well fed beyond the patience of any raiders.

Great-grandmother, Nuala (nooahla, lovely shoulders), the reigning matriarch, was the eldest woman of the deer tribe. Tall and lithe, with fine grey hair blowing round her shoulders, she and Frithe (freeya, deer forest or by road), her granddaughter, a red-headed sprite of a girl with eyes as green as the hills, went for a ramble late one sunny afternoon. It was warm, so neither needed a cloak at all, both dressed in their homespun shifts, grandmother with only a light woolen shawl. They went to the wee pond, fringed by plumed grasses, around the bay and over the hill, ever so peaceful in the gloaming of a summer's eve. The end of the Apple moon (August) it was, loveliest season of the year, and bright yellow gorse and purple heather colored the hillsides along the way.

But after they returned that night, great-grandmother slumped into her chair beside the hearth, quite suddenly, as she sipped her mead. She shuddered once and never breathed again, just as the stars were coming out. As plump cook began wailing, Frithe felt her heart fill with sudden coldness, and she ran howling to the hill where the Goddess face looked skyward from the mountaintop (MacLeod's table south, Dunbhegan). And there the lass sat till dawn, with her arms curled round her knees, sometimes whimpering, sometimes still as night.

After the rites of passage that opened the portal for great-grandmother to return to the Otherworld, the tribe needed a new matriarch. And it was Frithe, with her fiery hair falling in waves down her back, not two skyturns past her first moontime, who glowed with the Goddess light in the fire circle on the night of choosing. Folk were startled by that, for usually the Goddess chose the eldest in the tribe, the wise woman. But there were not many elders left after the coughing disease that swept through the clan in the spring, and none of those who remained were drawn to Goddess lore. So it was up a to slender girl of fourteen winters to hear the Goddess voice within and bring through Her wishes for them all. Wasn't that a fearsome responsibility for a lassie? For as everyone knew, disaster of Goddess wrath could result from wrongdoing. But Frithe had spent her growing years beside great-grandmother: clambering the forest nooks, learning all the women's lore there was to know, helping with ceremonies on sacred festival nights, and dancing with faery in the light of the crescent moon. And after she became matriarch, with her bare feet and hiked up skirts, the lass won the trust of the tribe within a moon or two. For her tongue was as honest as sunshine, and her sure inner sight saw the Goddess as clear as the sea loch on a summer's dawn.

And then, as soon as the moons of mourning passed, warriors began to arrive from as far as the mainland to vie for Frithe's hand, for the man who won her would become chief of the clan. But the lass only shook her waves of russet hair and walked away from them all, keeping her own silence whenever suitors were near. Ladd after ladd, in their fine teeth necklaces and fur cloaks, she sent to the winds again. Climbing the sea rocks alone, instead, Frithe called for great-grandmother's spirit to come, and they climbed the hills together once more.

But great-grandfather, ever gruffer without his queen, shaking his grizzled head and standing tall as an arrow in his deerskin chieftain robe, growled at the lass all the next summer about his age and the tuath's need for a chief. Still no one, even he, could force the mind of the matriarch, chosen by the cosmic matriarch herself. Frithe only turned her heel on him, too, when he shouted at her this way and threw back to him she was wed to the forest king. And that was that.

Finally, one and a half skyturns after great-grandmother's passing, late in the Rowan moon (February), great-grandfather had had enough. He sent to the druid isle, Iona, for spells to make the girl yielding before the fertility rites of spring. And it was Fitheach (feeuch, meaning raven) they sent, small, silent, and dark as he was. Two nights past the spring equinox, the druid landed below the tuath, climbing the rocks to the broch from his coracle in the bay.

Sitting by the fire in the yard outside the huts in his white druid robe, Fitheach watched Frithe silently for several days, waiting for the druid moon, sixth night past new, when the slivered crescent ripened with the girl goddess's power. And then at moonrise, he led Frithe to the standing stone in the hidden glen on the far side of the mountaintop. The druid's raven feather cloak held him in shadows, his eyes blacker than both, with only his dark furred arms visible in the firelight, as he bent over her. Chanting to sanctify her rulership, he spoke the rune that would prepare her for a consort. It was a feminine rite, and male druid was tampering with Goddess power to perform it. But Frithe felt great-grandmother hovering nearby, whispering that she herself would weave the spirit light of the spell into the lass and allow no harm. And then Fitheach dropped herbs from his pouch into the steaming brew over a low fire and handed Frithe the potion of the oak. Oak held the strongest of male powers, for its inner channel of light rose from the heartwood to the very throne room of the Creators, to Oghama, King of Heaven, the Beloved. It would fill Frithe with the need for action, and the heart's ache for partnership and service to the tribe. And then Fitheach brought her back to the burn below the broch and left her there, himself walking away in the pale light to his coracle before moonset. He was gone before Frithe could growl that he was a meddlesome fool. And then she wandered home in her own good time.

But the potion Fitheach gave her only made Frithe more unruly than ever. The Hawthorne moon (May) and Bealltain rites came and went as she combed the shores and forests alone in fern-stained feet. Through the summer till long past harvest, even into the dark moons of winter, she was off with a wildness in her eyes to match the sea eagles coursing closer to the hut circle in the winter-shortened days. And the chief, beside himself, sent for Fitheach again.

Moons later, a message came to great-grandfather, just a bit of scrolled birch from a passing trader marked with the sign of the raven.

"Wait one turning of the sun," the trader said, relaying the druid's message, "a warrior will come."

"She'd better be ready for him," great-grandfather grumbled into his mead.

The old chief, skinnier than ever with his wiry hair thinned to only a tuft above his ears, kept to the fire, huddled in his warmest furs, muttering, while the sea wind moaned over the high broch wall as the moons of winter, spring, summer, and fall circled past. In Celtic times, each skyturn ended at Samhein (2). It was the five-day passage between years (November 24th-28th). This was when the spirit debts of the passing skyturn were paid off at the insistence of the Goddess, and the Sun Lord, acknowledging Her rulership till Midwinter, all but disappeared.

A quarter moon later, deep in the night, a coracle washed up in the shallows of the loch below the tuath. It rocked in silence at the river mouth all night long, wrapped in winter's mist. Old Aedd found it the next morning, gone early to see if he could fish for his breakfast at all in the fog. And didn't he nearly jump out of his skin, for there was the curragh, holding a brooding ladd of nineteen winters, wrapped in furs and waiting for dawn, along with a clutter of corpses.

Great-grandfather came then, hustling down to the bay on his aged legs, his fur cloak wrapped tightly over his woolen tunic. With pinched mouth, he eyed the ladd, thinking suddenly of Fitheach. The boy was paler than most, tall and skinny, with a wild thatch of hair as brown as walnut stain and eyes to match, but he didn't look crazed with the fever, only hungry. He told them his name was Speireag (speerak, hawk), and he'd been off hunting the day the tribe ate the game that poisoned them. And he wore the tattoo of initiation, too, so by Brehon law, they had to take him in. It was forbidden to refuse hospitality to any folk of the tribes, least of all the hurt, hungry, or sick, else the Goddess would repay your own in kind. Besides, gods had visited before in the guise of a stranger, so the legends said.

While the boy gulped down stew and oatcakes in the broch, tribesmen gathered with wary eyes round the hearth. The ladd stuffed himself to bursting and warmed his backside near the flames a while, watching great-grandfather, and then hunched off into the shadows of the hall.

He still looked starved and filthy in his fur-lined buckskin breeks and fur jerkin when Frithe sauntered in to see what all the commotion was about. She turned to stare at the boy, huddled with his hands in the pockets of his breeks, just as if she'd known he'd be there. And she took in the likes of him, all up and down. Maybe it was the sadness in his eyes or the fierce refusal to give in to it that pried open her heart. Who can say? But from the moment she set eyes on that ladd, she rarely took them off. And t'was herself brought the water skins and hearthstones for his bath of welcome.

Life went on as usual through the cold winds of winter and the damp mists of summer, as the stars circled their way toward winter once again. And then one evening in the Blackthorne moon (November), Frithe found the old chief with his eyes gone vacant and his arms as still as the rocks of the broch. She laid his head in her lap then, crooning past moonset. And then she climbed clear up to the Goddess face and sat as silent as the hills again, before coming back to sit the death watch.

On the third night, they bore great-grandfather to the cairn of the ancestors, across the southeastern flatlands and over the ridge. Frithe walked alongside the bearers in her ceremonial doeskin robe under her heavy green woolen cloak, her eyes dry and burning. But beside the mounded cairn, the skirl of the pipes over the sea etched itself deeply into the fibers of Frithe's heart.

Sure an' wasn't it the coracle boy she chose for her consort, though the tribesmen sputtered about a chief so young, and the women left extra portions of meal at the standing stone all winter long. The ritual of the chief was set for the Vernal Equinox, for the tribe refused to hold a male rite of choosing during the dark moons of the Goddess.

And the boy-chief, as they called him, hardened like ice that whole winter long, for the ice queen ruled in his stead. The game the tribesmen found in the snowbound burrows was more bone than flesh. But it was then the hawk ladd's gift of the hunt emerged before them all, his aim sharp and true, his endurance the like of which none had seen before. So chief the ladd became, and then he and Frithe were wed on Bealltain Eve (May. 4th).

The next winter and one after their trothing, a boy child was born to Frithe, five days after the thankfulness celebration (Dec. 3rd). He was a plump wee babe with a thatch of red-brown hair, as if his Ma's and Da's had been mixed together. She named him Fìrinn na beinne mac Speireag (feereen nah benya mac speerak, truth of the mountains, son of Speireag), calling on the Goddess to write his name clearly in Her book of life as Frithe held the babe high, walking round the standing stone in her ceremonial robe. In her after-birth vision, Frithe saw the ladd grow to be chief of a clan himself or high king of the isle, perhaps. But to become chief, he'd have to win the hand of a matriarch who held the land right of her tuath. For the Celts knew that the earth is of the Goddess, Mother of all, and Her gifting of lands went to the women of each tribe, the ruling matriarch. Men were protectors of the land and the clans, and providers for the women as well, but never owners of either, for in those days, all served the Goddess. But for hundreds of years the world has forgotten those knowings and the Goddess Herself. And more's the pity, for Goddess power heals everything in sore need of love, and this, too, Frithe knew.

Chapter Two: Soillse

Soillse (sulsha, shining) sat in her small glass balcony, the one that opened off her bedroom and looked out over the woods, the river, and meadows of light that were her home in Paradise. She wore her cobalt linen robe over a long white dress, cinched with the braided girdle (belt) of a priestess, the robe that clung to her slim form and brought out the highlights of her fine ash brown hair. It was the Celtic realm she lived in, one of the twelve great cultures of the Creator Sun. She gazed out at the loveliness of the perpetual morning and smiled, but inside, her heart ached for Firinn, pure and simple.

She'd hoped to write today, to finish the chapter about the ladder of light through the lower realms. And she held the pen poised in her hand, but no words came. So she closed her eyes, took a deep breath, and pictured him again. Firinn had gone before her to earth this time, and as she sent her inner vision there, her smiled broadened. Nearly two in earth cycles, with his russet hair a tangle in the wind, he was trailing after his mother on the pebbles near the sea loch, dragging his fur blanket. His head felt full of wool and drowsy. Then he dropped onto the sand and began to cry. And suddenly, Soillse longed to move time forward, to make him into the man he would become and feel the love they'd share. But she could not. It was forbidden, and she didn't have the power, anyway. She opened her eyes and sighed. How was it possible to miss one warm male chest, two strong protective arms around her, and those dancing green eyes so much?

She'd risen early to help the virgin goddess of the Creator Sun, Maighdean (myjen, virgin), with the morning ceremony. And Maighdean, tall and fair-haired, stood with hands upraised below her temple, calling forth great swaths of light for all her priestesses to sweep out over the lower worlds to aid those still caught in the grip of fear. So Soillse went outside and joined them, walking quickly under the spreading beeches. But Soillse's heart wasn't full of love for those who suffered, as it should have been. And she spent some of her prayer time beaming tenderness to Fìrinn on earth, instead of those in deepest need. She was in her virgin form today, wearing the peach robes of the Maighdean order, with the white triple deer embroidered on it, for Soillse was of the clan of the deer. Around her, the priestesses chanted the song of the new dawn, and Soillse opened her mouth to sing, but her thoughts interrupted again. Three more moons and I'll go, then five more solar cycles, and we'll be together once more! Soillse's heart leaped at that and she smiled, but then she had to start the chant all over again. The goddess, so slender in her long robe with her blond hair falling like water down her back, came and held Soillse tight as they left the ceremonial circle.

"You'll be together soon," Maighdean breathed into Soillse's ear.

As she waited for the moons to pass, Soillse sometimes sent cherubim off on errands for Fìrinn. They placed that mother-of-pearl shell he found one day at the coral beaches with his Ma, across the loch from his tuath, and later the bluestone from the hills of Wales that washed up in the bay below the huts. It was forbidden to interfere, but Soillse couldn't help herself. The father gave her permission every time, and the bluestone was written into Fìrinn's future, so it was allowed. Quite a few things were delivered to Fìrinn this way by angel children, tiny miracles from her heart to his.

Finally, the morning before her descent to earth arrived, and Soillse sat at the large round table in the father's great hall. The wide twelve-sided room had high windows that looked out over the emerald fields of Paradise, the cosmic sea, and all the stars glittering in the great beyond. The Dagda (king/father god of the Creator Sun) held his hand on her head as Soillse bent over the life plan she was studying. He was tall and well built, wearing his long, old gold tunic and mustard tartan plaid (played, a long sash or length of cloth, often hung over the right shoulder and/or wrapped around the waist) and cloak of his clan, his eyes bursting with honest confidence that said he'd carried the responsibility of the cosmos for eons and done so successfully. His chest was large and shoulders broad, as a father's should be, his hair burnished gold. But the most noticeable thing about him was his kindly warmth and the wanting-to-grin feeling that always pervaded the room.

"There are passages here that might be too hard," Soillse said, pointing, "here, an' here." His eyes followed her finger.

"Hm, difficult," the father nodded. "So what are you thinking, child?"

"What if we add a vision to widen the inner beloved stream, there, on Fìrinn's first sea passage, instead o' the second, when he's so close to freedom. See? Right after his core woundin', the night before he lands in Carthage?" She put one finger on the scroll and looked up at the Dagda.

She was in her child form today, about the age of six in earth time, wearing the simple lilac shift of the Union of Child Hearts order, the robes she always wore on her little girl days. She was preparing for the dense human form she'd soon become, no more shape-changing into a full-grown priestess any time she felt like it. On earth, she'd have to be a little girl for a very long time.

"Ok," he said, nodding, "and where's the other one?" The sun of his great heart filled the room with a yellow glow, and her chest bubbled with laughter in his presence. This was always her response to him.

"Here," she said, pointing again, "the hardest days o' me adulthood, when the rape happens, see?"

"Umhm, yes, difficult again." He raised his sandy eyebrows and looked at her. "Any ideas, child?"

"A place to go where I can feel Fìrinn," she said, with a finality that made the father smile, "by the shore near the tuath, an anchorin' in o' his light stream there that I can sense to hold me firm."

"Ok, but that'll build a bit less strength within. See how the light structures in your heart need it for the Callanish challenge later on?" The Dagda paused, one hand on his chin, eyeing the blueprints. "We could put a bit more intensity into the family constriction patterns while you're young, before the fatigue of it all sets in. What do you think?"

"Aye! I'll still have me sister's friendship then, an' I willna be so alone. I can do that. Good, it's done!" The father left his hand on her head a moment longer, his eyes softening.

"There are very, _very_ few who plan as carefully as you do." She did laugh then, nodding. "And Fìrinn has already chosen," the Dagda said. "I can't make the changes you request without asking him, and he's but a babe. We can wait till one of his first visionings, nine solar cycles away. How about that? I could decide, if you want. Your time grows short." She looked away from the father toward the floor, conscious of his great height before her. And she grew suddenly quiet as she stood and turned toward the altar.

"I'm worried, Da, even here in Paradise wi' fear so far away," she whispered, pulling her mouth into a thin line. So he put his hand on her back, sending a ray of his heart light into the dark storm roiling in her chest. It immediately expanded and she sighed. "Well, ok, I can tell ye, I guess...I _want_ to break through this time into real love, the happily-ever-after. An' I want so _much_ to build your kingdom on earth," she blurted out. "Ye ken that. But it's a painful life I go to this time, years o' hardship an' that rape. I know it's important, but...," she sighed, "I'm scared, that's all." He knelt on one knee, took her shoulders in his hands, and pulled her close.

"You don't <u>have</u> to go, you know," he whispered. "You don't have to do this."

"Well, that's the trouble! Firinn's already there, an' I <u>canna</u> let him down. An' besides, I <u>want</u> to go. I miss him so much! An' the druid changes we make'll ease the violence a lot. An' the healin' work I do'll help the <u>bairns</u>! Besides, ye always say it's ok to feel afraid, just dinna let it stop ye." She took in a long breath, her green eyes relaxing as she looked into his, and squared her shoulders. "So, it's all right."

He nodded, but his brows were still raised in question. She closed her eyes a moment and opened them to see his large tawny ones looking into hers. She could feel his heart beating, full of sunny warmth, and she always just melted when he looked at her, anyway. She smiled and closed her eyes again. She reached out then to touch the Dagda's shining heart, her face quite serious now. "I'm ready to take me vow, Da."

"You're sure?," he said, pulling her close. Pushing out her chin slightly, a hint of stubbornness in her eyes, she nodded.

So they moved to the altar and he lifted down his sword of light. It was hanging there between the windows, clear crystal and half as long as he was, far taller than herself. There were Celtic interlaced designs etched into the hilt, and its facets dazzled in the morning light, sending small rainbows all over the room. And as she watched it, a longing to keep her promise to Oghama blazed up in her heart, and she stood very tall for a moment. "Love, King o' the universe," she said slowly, seeing Oghama, the One Beloved God, in her mind, "I want to serve Ye. I <u>love</u> Ye!" Then she knelt beside the altar and bent her head, her eyes wet and her fine brown hair falling to the floor.

"I vow to seek the truth, serve Love, an' honor the spirit in all things," she said softly, putting one finger on the light centers in her mind, heart, and abdomen in turn as she spoke the words.

He touched her small shoulders gently with his sword then, and a golden zinging electric light sparked into her heart. Then he took up the blueprint, her own, not Firinn's, and laid it over her like a mantle. The light structures clung to her back and shoulders, neon yellow swirls and zigzags, like sunlight lace. And she stood then, waiting like a small queen in a royal cloak of light, while they slowly melted in under her skin. He watched her closely as she smiled up at him, and his eyes crinkled as he grinned back. And she thought how she loved the wizard wildness of his sandy brows whenever he looked like this.

"You are the most <u>determined</u> child when you set your heart on something," he said, chuckling. "And you have the softest little girl heart that longs to help just everyone, especially the children! It'll be all right, I promise. Here." His voice was husky as he spoke, his eyes moist all of a sudden. And he reached out to place a tiny flame, a dazzling star of light containing his own 8-fold pattern into the back of her heart. "I'll be with you always," he whispered, his eyes growing sad again. And then he bent to lay his great head lightly on her own. "I love you so dearly, child." And she felt one tear fall down the back of her hair and seep into the nape of her robe. The great sun warmth of him felt like it went behind a cloud for a moment, but then it came out again. She reached up on tiptoe and softly kissed his cheek.

"I love ye, too, Da, more than anythin'. It <u>will</u> be all right," she nodded slowly. "An' I can eat baked apples wi' cream again! I miss them up here. And I can swim in the high loch wi' nothin' on of a summer's morn. And later, there'll be Firinn's kisses, mmm! Oh, earth's the <u>best</u>!" Then she scampered off to the east door. "One last visit to the rose garden," she called back to him. "There'll be no talkin' roses for a long time noo. An' then it's off to see Tara at the gates. Bye, Da. I'll be Home again before too long."

He stood looking after her as the doors closed, another cloud moving across his great sun heart. "How I wish there were an easier way," he whispered. "Child of my heart, I love you more dearly than you know!" And then the Dagda turned to roll up the life plan blueprints and deliver the scrolls to the hall of seraphim.

Soillse hurried to the birthing chamber of the Bardo. Great-grandmother, Brìne (breena), was there from Soillse's own tuath in Paradise and Soillse's sister, Sebhia (sheveeya) was, too. Tara, the Goddess, tall and slim with long platinum hair nearly to Her waist, waited at the portal, humming a lullaby.

"Hurry, child," the Goddess called, "the birth progresses swiftly now. Come, it's time to say good-bye. One last hug." She opened Her arms wide and smiled, a gentle woman, but strongly built and regal. Soillse, still in her lilac shift, folded herself into the Mother's arms, and Tara stroked Soillse's head, holding her close. She always smells like a thousand roses in bloom, Soillse thought, as the Goddess in her ivory robes blew a shimmering pearl mist around Soillse. As she breathed it in, Soillse suddenly relaxed.

"It'll soften the hurts, dear," Tara whispered. "Call for Me when you need to? I can come any time, if need be, but most easily in the wee hours. And I can help everything!" And the moon glow of the mother's heart shone with tenderness. As a slow smile spread over Tara's face, She said, "Oh yes, and this time, there'll be surprises you don't even know about yet!" And then Soillse thought how the Mother's heart never clouded over at all, not like father's at these partings.

"Mmmmmm, I refuse to be sad, love," Tara whispered. "What good would that do?" She hummed the forever friend song a moment as She lifted up Soillse's wisdom shawl. It was dark blue and full of crocheted flowers and interlaced designs, edged in a soft rolling sea pattern. "Ready, child?" Soillse nodded, and Tara placed the shawl around Soillse's shoulders and waited while the indigo swirls melted like watercolors into her skin.

"It's beautiful, Mum."

"Yes, very great wisdom will come to you this time. It is lovely, but hard to achieve. Those dark swirlings are the kneeling women and midwives of your divine child, to be fully delivered this time around! I am so proud!" And Tara's eyes were bright as She smiled again. "All is well, dear."

Soillse pulled out of Tara's embrace then and waved to the rose faeries gathered by the ivory velvet curtains at the edge of the birthing chamber. Then she blew a kiss to Sebhia and great-grandmother, Brine, and jumped into the lilac tunnel of light that had moved into place before her.

"Blessed be, my small apprentice," Soillse heard Tara's whisper falling after her. And then the doors of heaven closed as Soillse landed in her human baby suit.

Chapter Three: Fìrinn

"Och, laddie," Frithe said, still pixie like, even in her heavy woolen green cloak. "Only two winters an' ye're the braw spittin' image o' yer Da in yer doeskin breeks, ye are noo." She turned to tickle Fìrinn's chin, pulling him close and kissing his nose with scented lips. His hair was wavy like his Da's, only russet and still baby fine. But his deep set eyes were green like hers. Then she stood and shaded her eyes, looking toward the southwest, while Fìrinn stared up at her. It was not the wind, but his Da's leaving that made her mouth turn down, he knew. Why didn't she look so sad when she left himself with cook every afternoon? Suddenly, she bent and scooped the boy into her arms, pulling his fur jerkin down over his doeskin breeks to keep out the wind.

"He never stays long, yer Da, but when I have him, "she smiled, "it's the power o' fire I hold to me heart." Nuzzling an icy nose into Fìrinn's cheek, she held him tight against his squirming. "Ye have his fire, too, me firstborn son, an' a great warrior he'll make o' ye. But until the fullness leaves yer cheeks, wee one, ye're mine! An' I'll settle some o' the earth mother's patience into yer soul before yer Da gets hold o' ye. Ye're no named for a wild thing, are ye? No, truth never waivers at all. An' one day yer wife'll thank me. So there!" Then she nibbled the boy's nose.

"Can we go to the pinewood today, Mum? Or the beach? It's been moooons since we left the broch." His baby voice rose on the word moons, making Frithe chuckle. Then he wriggled away and tugged her cloak, pulling her up the slope toward the woods.

"Wi' the wind woman bitin' like this? " Frithe's eyes danced, daring him. He nodded vigorously.

"The wind woman's me friend!," he said, his eyes widening indignantly.

"I do need some foxglove root, if I can find any this late," she said and bent to catch him up again. But he darted away. "Ach, too old fer yer Ma's nibblin', are ye? Well, I'll just turn meself into a doe and catch ye then!" She winked and stifled a laugh. Slowing, the ladd changed direction and ran a few steps toward the broch.

"Ye canna catch me," he taunted. "I'm two winters noo. I've got too big fer ye." He squealed and raced for the tower, giggling and stumbling over clumps of spike grass and heath bordering the packed earth of the yard.

Guffawing, Frithe stuffed her homespun shift into her girdle (belt) and ran after him. But Fìrinn disappeared into the broch, running past old Aedd, wrapped in furs. With only wisps of hair left above ears that were red with the cold, Aedd sat hunched at the broch gate as guard. As he stood and stepped back into the guard cell to let her pass, Frithe worried about his constantly quavering fingers and skin that mottled white whenever the cold was especially bitter, but she couldn't tend to that today. Flushed and huffing as she leaned down to stoop under the low entrance, Frithe followed Fìrinn into the broch.

"Frithe..," Aedd began. But she heard nothing, for she nearly tripped as Fìrinn came charging out again, abruptly reversing direction at the sight of cook's glowering face. Chubby old cook stood in the center of the hall, stirring the cauldron. Her grey hair frizzed out like a cap around her face, and her stern blue eyes followed Fìrinn as she stood beside the hearth, squat and stocky in her greasy shift, with her free hand on her hip.

"We're goin' to the pinewood," Fìrinn said, pushing out his lower lip. "I dinna have to stir gruel today."

"It's too cold fer the bairn," cook said, eying Frithe. "The Alder moon's (March) barely begun." Cook had come to the tuath from Eire as a slave girl twenty-six winters before and taken charge of the kitchen the moment she arrived. Raised at her mother's knee, she'd already been cooking stew for another chieftain over the sea for ten skyturns. When the clan gave her her freedom three winters later, cook chose to stay at the tuath.

"I like havin' the cauldron to meself," was all she said then. "If I go home, I'll have to share it wi' me Ma." Cook never admitted that she didn't want to leave her man, either, though all knew that was the root of it. He'd finally passed on two winters before, so she cooked more than ever now.

As a cold wind whooshed through the unlatched door, Frithe said nothing, only reached for her hide boots in the entrance cell and hummed as she pulled them on, then bent out through the low stone passage. Hanging onto a fistful of his Ma's woolen cloak, Firinn glanced back to see cook's brows furrowed together.

"We've no more onions in the pit neither!," cook hollered after them. And then she turned back to the cauldron, moving her lips in a blessing for safety of mother and child.

Firinn ran all the way up the short path toward the top of the first hill. And as he stepped into the moss-cloaked arms of the pinewood, he felt the wind ease. Slowing his steps, he let his head fall back and looked up into the branches. Whorls of green needles spread out like stars everywhere, and the sky behind them was cloudy like milk. Frithe walked to the base of a large Caledonian pine and bowed.

"Honor an' greetin' to thee, forest queen.

Blessin' o' the light One be thine.

May the warm rain o' Her affection

Fall upon ye in the mornin',

In the evenin', in the silent stillness o' the night.

Blessin' o' the light One be thine."

Frithe waited, keeping very still a moment, and then slowly reached out to grab a bit of hawkweed, still furred from last summer. With a wink, she caught the hem of Firinn's jerkin and pulled him close. Brushing the downy stalk under his chin, she laughed, and the sound floated out through the trees. The hills laughed back, Firinn noticed, but the forest people kept their silence.

Abruptly, Frithe stood and strode deeper into the wood, stepping over fallen branches blanketed with moss and stopping at the edge of the clearing where the summer crows came to build their nests. She knelt then, swept away winter's thick leaf mat, pulled up some ragged stalks, and held out a bunch of wild onions. They were wet, clumped with earth, and glistening in the morning light.

"Now cook'll forgive us an' save ye an oatcake or two, hm? Here, Firinn-ladd, I'll teach ye how to feel the comin' o' the summer king, noo the days grow longer." And she walked to a large spreading beech, then motioned him to follow. Putting her ear to the bark, she whispered, "Listen, laddie." Holding her skirts up with one hand out of the mud, she leaned in against the lichened bark. "Hear it? Shhhh."

He did as she bid him, hearing only the sough of the wind in the needled pines. But then he did hear a low thrumming, deep inside the trunk of the beech, and looked up at her with his mouth agape.

"See? Under their coverin's, all things beat to Oghama (ohamah, Celtic high God, male Beloved of the Creator Sun) an' Tara's (Celtic high Goddess, female Beloved of the Creator Sun) Heart, even ye. Oghama's the King, me sweet, the Beloved o' the worlds." And she knelt and kissed Firinn's hair. "But each o' us has our own kind o' knowin', our part in the song, all the creatures an' the plant people, even the stones an' the hills I named ye for. Oghama's son, the summer king, Ridire (reedira, knight, virgin god of the Creator Sun), comes first to this one, always. Do ye wonder why, ladd? One day ye'll ken (know), Firinn na beinne, better than I." She looked inward a moment as she spoke and then away. "Well, I've gatherin' to do, me ladd. Go greet yer forest friends awhile." And suddenly she turned away from him, and he knew she was seeing the roots of the plant people in her mind.

So he settled himself on the damp moss and began to scrape mounds of crumbled needles into miniature hills. Then he made earth roadways for pebble hunters, glancing up now and then to watch his Ma dig foxglove and bloodroot at the edge of the clearing. She asked each plant person how much it wished to give as she worked and bowed to each when she was through. Then she spoke the Goddess blessing over the gifts and the giver, wrapping her gatherings in hide and laying them lengthwise in her plaid.

A vague memory stirred in his mind, and he saw her here last summer, reciting the names and gifts of the plant people, the words falling from her lips like a prayer. She knew them all, his Ma, the way cook knew how many apples were in the storage pit and when he'd taken one. And Fìrinn smiled, thinking how his Mum loved him best of all in the pinewood. Maybe the summer king's heart beats into her here, too, like the beech tree, he thought, and it happys her. He leaned over to finish his village then, laying pebbles in circles like the huts of the tuath. But there weren't enough to build a broch, and so he used twigs, instead. While he played, the pine people held up their cloaks to shield him from the wind woman's bite. And from the damp earth, he felt the peace of the Goddess reach in to embrace him in the silence.

It was well past midsky (noon) when Frithe trudged down the hill to the broch again through patchy snow, looking out over the expanse of low hills and the sea loch below. Fìrinn followed slowly, until Frithe turned and smiled. Then she threw the shawl full of herbs over one shoulder and lifted Fìrinn into the saddle of her hip, crooning a lilt in the old language as she walked. He didn't understand the words, but the song flowed into his head and warmed it to melting as he nestled into the cloud of her hair. It smelled like the wee white flowers they'd picked in the forest last summer. And then he forgot everything but the moist warmth of her skin.

The sky was darkening in the window slits of the broch when Firinn awoke, lying under his furs by the hearth. Cook, her hide apron greasy with fat and blood, was chopping bits of boar on the low stone board under the window, then dropping handfuls into the cauldron. In a moment, she waddled off to the storage pit under the stairs, humming an Irish jig. The tribeswomen who'd come to pound herbs with Frithe earlier in the afternoon had gone to their own hearths for the night now, so he was alone in the great room.

His tummy grumbled and he sidled to the board, backing under it into the shadows. Waiting and peering toward the doorway a moment, Firinn reached up swiftly and moved his fingers over the broad stone shelf till he felt a bowl. Then, holding his breath, he spread his fingers into the batter and closed them again. Ach, I hope it's apple bread, he thought, bringing a slimy fist down to his face. Mmm, oatcake! Even better. Then, moving quickly and keeping to the shadows, he returned to his furs, noisily licking his fingers. Cook scurried in, hurrying toward the board, and howled.

"Ye've been into me oatcake wi' ye're dirty paws, havena ye?" And she frowned at him as she poured meal from a hide sack into a large clay bowl. Firinn stiffened and pulled his sticky hand under his jerkin. Wiping his mouth on his sleeve, he waited while his heart settled down. And then he forgot cook as he watched the flames lick the cauldron and thought he saw wee red dragons in the dancing light. Then he grabbed up a piece of charred wood near the fire, pushed aside the floor rushes, and began to draw on the hard-packed earth. He drew Ma beside the beech tree in the forest and Da with his warriors, and the dragons in the fire. Then finally Firinn stopped because his bottom was sore, and his eyes smarted from the smoke. Looking toward the narrow window slits, he saw that it was full dark now and stars twinkled in the sky.

"All right, laddie, I've done." Cook's voice was softer now, as it always was when supper was finally ready. Eagerly, he watched her dip a bone ladle into the stew and pour it, steaming, into a small shell bowl. As soon as she handed it to him, he shoveled gravied clumps into his mouth with quick scoops of his fingers. Cook disappeared into the storage alcove again and bustled in with a skin of goat's milk. And he drank so fast, it dribbled down his chin, while she swiped his face with a clammy piece of hide. When he finished, she sat heavily on the furs, spooning stew rapidly into her mouth, too, and chewing noisily. The she pulled on her fur-lined jerkin against the evening chill.

"Is Mum comin' noo?"

Cook finished her dinner without answering, taking a long time to chew a tough piece of boar. And then she drank a cup of mead, stood, sighed, and stared into the flames a moment. Then, grunting, she lifted a warming stone from the hearth into the hide sling she wore over one shoulder and pointed to the rope ladder up to the second floor of the broch. And Fìrinn scrambled up ahead of her.

"Where's Ma," he asked again, darting to his pallet and pulling the furs up to his chin against the wind.

"Yer Ma thinks she can cure even the dark one, I do believe," cook wheezed, sitting heavily on the bed. "The Goddess'll turn one o' those spells back on her, if she's no careful. An old man o' the pony clan, wise in plant lore, she works on this night. Been grindin' poultices since before firstsky (dawn), till she stopped to see yer Da off on the hunt and then went off wi' ye fer more herbs. Stubborn as the stones, yer Ma is." Cook yawned loudly, scratching the hairs on her chin. Then she pulled back the furs and rolled the warming stone in near Fìrinn's feet. She sat beside him then and began to brush the hair off his brow with hands that smelled of grease and onion. "Rest yer head, lamb," she said. "Yer Ma'll be in ta kiss ye at some point. She never forgets that. T'was the last I saw o' me own Ma, a quick kiss at moonrise." And cook's hand stilled as she gazed out at the hovering gibbous moon. But he didn't mind, for her hand was as hot as the warming stone, and the wind blew cold through the window slits.

His mind barely stirred out of its fog as he was lifted up, his underside struck suddenly with cold air, until he felt bedfurs come up around him once mcre. This pallet was cold, too, but he snuggled in without protest, for it was his mother's scent that came to him out of the darkness. She pulled his head into her pillowed chest and curled the warmth of her body around him, and he smiled to himself.

"Ye have the roundest braw cheeks in all Skye, ladd o' me own heart," she whispered, lightly kissing his nose. Then she turned her fingers to feathers and drew them over his temples till the sleepmist came over him again, only this time it pulsed to his Ma's heartbeat.

His dreams came with startling intensity that night and he saw a wide turquoise river flowing out of the earth. It carried a maiden, quite small, like himself. She had wings that shimmmered, though, a fae child, and her heartspace had a glowing orb of light that reminded him of the moon Goddess when She was full. The lassie sat in a huge flat shell, pale peach, that carried her upriver. He knew she came toward himself, and he sensed some urgency in their meeting, as if this daughter of the stars and he had something to do together. He saw the virgin goddess, too, Maighdean, in her peach robes, floating over the girlchild in the pale dawn. Shaking her wand, Maighdean sent tiny sparkles of light wafting through the clear darkness down onto the wee faery lass. He saw the shell boat come to land in a bay on the far side of Skye, and a roe deer waited there, standing watch over the girl till the first spears of the Sun Lord peeked over the hills. And then the child moved through a doorway of lilac light and turned into a newborn babe.

Chapter Four: Soillse

Soillse's tuath, smaller than Fìrinn's clan of the deer, was nestled into the curve of the southernmost peninsula of Skye. It sat on the western slope there, facing the sea, where Tarskavaig is today. And behind it rose a sheltering ridge, hiding the mainland beyond. Down the ridge and across a sweep of tumbled stones above the shore flowed a small burn. One long rectangular hut and seven circular palisaded ones dotted the grassy slope behind the pebbled beach that curved between the two rocky arms of the small bay.

Legends said this was the place the warrior goddess, Scatha, made her home in days gone by, she who taught the great Cuchullin himself. And so, it was the place chosen for the fostering of the ladds of Skye who wished to become warriors, many the sons of noblemen. Ladds from all clans of the isle came to this tuath and stayed till manhood, learning the arts of the hunt and of war, the spirit of Scatha guiding and guarding them all.

Soillse was a quiet child, always watching, with her fine brown baby hair flying in the breeze. Even at birth on a cold dawn in the Ash moon (February), her eyes rested for long moments on the walls of the cave and the kneeling women. Then the babe turned to listen to the waves splashing on the rocks below and finally looked up at her Ma, Eilid (aylee, doe). No, look is not the right word either, for it was a long lingering gaze from the babe's blue eyes, bright and curious, her face flushed with birth. She'll be a priestess with those searching eyes, thought Eilid. Eilid had wrapped her own tangled brown curls up in a thong, pulled on a woolen shift and shawl, and now she drew the furs tighter around them both as her doe brown eyes held Soillse's.

But Soillse's eyes didn't stay blue for long, for by the end of her first winter they'd turned emerald green. As the winter of her first skyturn passed, the lass was ever standing at the doorskin of the round house, putting her face up into the draughts of cold air rushing in whenever Sìne (sheena, Jean), Eilid's aunt, bustled in.

"Waitin' patiently fer spring, that's what," said Eilid, standing in her homespun shift beside the hearth, her cow brown curls braided down her back. "Calm as the wee loch on the hillside, that one is. She knows what she wants, me wee lassie." And Eilid bent to scoop the girl child up, then turned to sit on a hide pillow near the fire, putting the babe to her breast and rocking slowly. Crooning, Eilid stroked the wispy hair on the child's head. And Soillse stared up at her Ma, fingering ears, nose, and eyelids, the child's mouth dropping open once or twice as she gazed and then picking up the nipple again. Eilid had come late to both marriage and mothering, and was nearly twenty-five winters now. Her man, Seumus (shaymus), chief of the tuath, was five winters older.

"Drinks more wi' her eyes than anythin'," Muirn (moorn, joy) said. Eilid's younger sister, a wiry, athletic lass, even in her woolen workaday shift, Muirn stood smiling at mother and child as she stirred soup in the cauldron. It was late in the Alder moon (March), and the rains had been falling without let up for five days now. "Aye, I'm ready fer a bit o' sunshine meself, lassie."

Ceit (kayt, Kate) ran in through the doorway toward a small bed on the far side of the hut. It was dark inside, the only light coming from the roof hole, and that filled with smoke. Soillse's older sister, a child of four winters, Ceit was dark-headed, black eyed, and slender. She dropped a pile of cattail fluff onto her furs.

"Look, Ma," she said in her child's voice. "Da went to the loch on the hill today. See what he brought! Cattails for me wee Rhiann (reeahn, girl goddess of the Indigo Pentagram)!" Ceit bent then, still with her fur jerkin over her shift, busily piling the drifting fluff into a nest of twigs by her bed and covering it with a bit of hide. "Och, it's <u>much</u> better than that lumpy old heather," she said, flinging the browned bits of heather onto the dirt floor. Muirn smiled at the girl's imitation of Eilid's ways. Then, tenderly, Ceit placed a woven grass dolly on top of the hide, cooing softly. "She's like a wee bird, she is! See, Ma?"

"Weel, it's two mild mothers we have in the hut noo, lassie," said Muirn as Eilid kept rocking with an amused smile. Picking up the dolly, Ceit cradled it in her arms and walked to Eilid. "Here, Ma. I'm tired noo, make room for me an' me baby bird!"

"In a while, lassie, after the babe sucks."

Ceit's eyes darkened then, and she pouted and pushed out her chin as she sat heavily, leaning in against her mother and pushing against Soillse's feet. "That babe's in the way, Ma, lots o' times when I need somethin'. I wish we didna have her."

"Shush ye, shhhh," Eilid put her hand to Ceit's mouth. "The faeries'll be hearin' ye, lass. An' the clan needs all the girl bairns (children) we can get. Each one is a blessin' o' the Goddess. An' besides, did ye forget, it's ye who's the eldest. Ye'll hold the land right o' the tuath when ye're big enough an' I'm too old. It's the most special girl in the clan ye are. Dinna ever forget it, an' be kind to yer wee sister, for she'll have to follow what <u>ye</u> say then. The matriarch is o' the Goddess, lassie, always kind to the clanfolk, especially sisters, no matter what," Eilid said, winking at Muirn. Ceit eyed Soillse, but kept quiet then, holding her dollie and thinking how one day she'd take charge of the moon ceremonies herself and make her sister do whatever she wanted.

A thin summer mist softened the air, the wind barely blowing from the south. It was the Hazel moon (July), and the sea was calm this firstsky (dawn), just a ripple of a thing between the two arms of boulders sheltering the bay. Eilid stood in a light summer shift and blue shawl and listened to the burn gurgling down the hill as she watched the day brighten above the ridge. The longhouse emerged slowly from the fog, and the bright orb of an orange sun rose off the eastern hills. The yard was quiet now, before the sports began in earnest after the firstsky meal. Thirty-two sleepy-eyed ladds in buckskin breeks and lightweight woolen jerkins were filing out to fill their bowls at the cauldron in the yard, sitting in small groups to eat their oats, some near the fire and some on the tumbled rocks along the sea. While Muirn and Sine filled the shell bowls with large spoonfuls of gruel, Seumus stacked a dozen lances by the door of the longhouse, next to piles of leather thongs and kindling. The chief was squat, with a hefty muscular build and startling blue eyes that reeled everyone in. As he worked, his muscles rippled under his buckskin breeks and homespun shirt, and his dark hair, already thinning, with flecks of grey above his ears, blew over his face in the sea wind.

Holding Soillse on her left hip, Eilid watched to make sure there was enough gruel for everyone, poised to go make more, if needed. I'm tired today, she thought, sighing and counting the ladds still in line. Besides the boys to feed, Eilid's thoughts ran on, there are the teachers, their wives and bairns, and me own. But we always seem to have enough with the greens we gather in the wood or nuts and wild grains, and there's me plots of barley and oats at the edge of the yard, plus the game the ladds bring in. Thank Goddess the goats, chickens, cows, and bairns mostly take care of themselves.

When the last bowl was filled, Eilid laid Soillse down in the grass, then sat back on her haunches, pushing her thick hair out of her face. She smiled to see Ceit chase Seumus into the wavelets at the water's edge, the child laughing and splashing, until he picked Ceit up and twirled her round, holding the lass upside down. As her squeals echoed out over the sea, Eilid glanced down at Soillse, who was gumming a twig. Birch, thought Eilid, won't harm the babe.

Hoping to get her grinding done before the sun was high, Eilid flung a handful of grains onto the stone slab on the ground before her. Then she began rocking on her hips, bearing down with the grinding stone, humming the quern song to bless the kernels as she crushed them into coarse meal. Soillse, too, began rocking in time to the music, smiling up at her Ma.

"There's aye so much to prepare, eh, Eilid?," Sìne said, hurrying into the round house through the carved doorposts. Eilid's aunt, Sìne was nearing fifty winters, a tall spare woman with brows perpetually pulled together in stern disapproval. But she peeked back for a moment to breathe in the morning air. "Do ye ever wish ye could cook jest fer yer own, Eilid? Ye ken, just Seumus an' the lassies, an' let the rest go?" Sìne sighed softly.

"No," Eilid said, and took a breath to regain her rhythm. "I like to work an' work hard. I'm glad for me strength an' the teachin' skills o' me man." And she glanced over at the stocky form of Seumus on the beach, "an' me healthy lassies that both survived their first winters. I'm glad fer so many ladds to do the huntin' an' keep us in meat, too. There's much to be thankful for, Sìne." Eilid stopped a moment to touch the spiral Goddess amulet on a thong around her neck and wipe her brow with the back of her hand. Then she settled back into her rocking and chanting, throwing more kernels onto the quern stone and bearing down hard. Soillse, rolling over in the moss, reached out for the mist moving in off the sea.

Ceit was dressed in a short summer shift, even that rolled up into her girdle for easy movement, gathering kindling from the bracken, running up the hillside and pulling stray branches out onto the hard-packed ground of the yard. After a time, the lass ran to the shore to chase a sandpiper, yelling at Eilid to look at her growing stack of wood. Finally, with black curls stuck to her forehead and panting, Ceit ran to Eilid and flung herself onto her Ma's back.

"Time to stop that, Ma," she yelled. "C'mon. Let's go for a swim!" Putting her arms round her mother's neck, Ceit held on, giggling, while Eilid rocked and then leaned slowly back, letting the lass down lightly on the grass. Rubbing her shoulders and unhooking the girl's arms, Eilid turned to pull Ceit into her lap as the older bairn glanced at Soillsse with her chin up and her eyes full of triumph. But Soillse never noticed, for she'd found a purple stone that sparkled whenever the sun peeked through the fog. And just now the babe held it up to the light, peering intently and humming Ma's quern song.

Chapter Five: Fìrinn

Before his fifth winter, Fìrinn grew to be a young sapling, skinny, and all knees and elbows. He stayed at the tuath a skyturn longer than most, for Frithe insisting on keeping him till his baby teeth fell out. She disagreed with the druids taking the ladds any younger, and she wanted plenty of time to teach Fìrinn her spirit knowings before he left for his fostering. Though the chief was two heads taller than his wife, standing over her in his heavy lambskin jerkin and dark woolen breeks, frowning at these women's ways for his son, Frithe stood straight as the pines in her old green cloak, her eyes leveled on his, as she answered his complaint.

"Fìrinn'll bring the druid orders together, Speireag, those o' Skye, Callanish, an' Iona, too, even the priestesses. He must ken it all." And so, Frithe even taught the ladd Goddess lore: plants for gathering, herbs for illness, seeding, the secret rituals of Goddess power across each skyturn, and the healing arts, all but midwifery. And as is always the case, the growing coolness between the queen and chief over the raising of the ladd was echoed in the boy himself. When his chores were done, Fìrinn preferred to sit in the high grasses of the moor that surrounded the tuath, watching the fawns romp near the does on the hillside, than practice the arts of war his father demanded. Speireag had given the ladd a beating several moons before, when Fìrinn steadfastly refuse to throw spears at some waterfowl. So the ladd had little choice about hunting now. But whenever the boy did rouse himself to swordplay and thought of killing game, it stirred a tugging in his heart and rebellion in his mind.

One night during the Reed moon (October), a bonfire danced into the evening sky outside the broch. The tribe was celebrating the chief's homecoming after a successful hunt: three boar, thirteen geese, and a bear. After the feasting, some of the meat would be smoked and stored for winter, and Speireag was relieved to have enough to do so. But Fìrinn, in his light leather breeks and homespun shirt sat at the edge of the wood on the hill above the tuath, avoiding his Da. I dinna want to go down there and pretend I'm Da's warrior, the ladd thought. I'm staying up here with the pine people till the fires burn down, all night if I have to. And he lay back on the needled ground with his arms folded tight over his chest and watched the wind chase chequered clouds across the sky and the sun turn pale peach and drop down to nestle into the hills. But then the ladd began to shiver in the evening wind.

"Fìriiiin," he heard a high-pitched call from the bottom of the hill. And he stood reluctantly, peered to see who yelled for him, and then sighed. It was Una (oona), his lame great-aunt, in her pale green summer shift at the foot of the path. She was always kind to him, and if she called, he just had to go. With her long grey hair blowing round her plump face, she was leaning on her good leg and holding up his woolen plaid, dyed the red-fawn color of the roe deer that were sacred to his clan. So Fìrinn walked down, kicking a stone through the heather as he went. As he approached the yard, he could hear torches guttering in the wind, and the smell of burning fat filled his nostrils. At least we'll have full bellies tonight, he thought, as he stopped in front of Una, who handed him his plaid. Making a grimace, he wrapped it around his waist and flung one end over his right shoulder, fastening the bone pin into place. Then he pulled down his doeskin breeks.

"It itches," he said, unsmiling. Then he pulled up the stockings and doeskin boots Una held out for him and wrapped and tied the thong laces.

"Go on, ladd. There he is," Una said, bending to point at the chief, so the bonfire was hidden by the silver curtain of her hair. Speireag, in his homespun shirt with his clan plaid wrapped round his waist and flung over his right shoulder, too, stood to one side near the board, a muscled arm slung over big Ruaraidh (rory). Brushing Fìrinn's cheeks with her lips then, Una limped off to help baste the boar on the high spits. But the ladd only moved back into the shadow of the broch. There's Ma, he thought, with a flicker of a smile. Frithe was placing a large platter of herbed barley between plates piled high with nuts and oatcakes on the long board. She wore her sea blue shift with the thongs crossed over her chest, and Fìrinn started quickly toward her through the yard, barely glancing at his Da. If she's too busy, Fìrinn thought, I'll just go find me cousin, Eachann (eeahckan, horseman), up tending the cows.

"Ach, the chief's pride!" It was Allaidh (alley, fierce) bellowing, a squat dark warrior with hairy arms, who reached for Fìrinn. "In a wee plaid. Ha, he'll soon be ready for the broadsword!" A low cheer went up from the nearest clansmen as Allaidh wrapped his arm round Fìrinn's waist, laughing, and heaved him to his father. The man reeked of horse and sweat, and Fìrinn tried to close his ears, nose, and mind all together. Speireag tightened meaty palms around the boy's thighs and lofted him high with a war cry, then lowered the ladd, none too gently, onto his shoulders. Fìrinn's stomach flopped and the scene tilted crazily. Da's neck was sweaty and as thick as a twenty-winter pine, and the plaid itched the worse for it.

"Swift o' foot an' strong o' arm, son o' mine'll be!" The tall chief's boast rose above the talk as a hush fell over the folk. "May the power o' the great stag be his, to rule in justice, and the power o' the hawk, predator fire!" Viselike fingers gripped Fìrinn's ankles as his Da paraded through the crowd. Many hands clapped Fìrinn's back and legs, and skins of mead were held up to the boy. The firelight flickered red over the dark hairs on the chief's arms, and the mead left a bitterness on Firinn's tongue. He could not disobey his Da and go back to the forest or even protest that he hated the noise and the puffed up chests of the clansmen, for those hands hurting his own ankles had hewn many an animal, and even a few raiding tribesmen, in two. The ladd tried to catch his mother's gaze, but when they approached her, she had eyes only for Speireag.

So Firinn sighed, calling inwardly to the Goddess for stillness. And then his mind settled on the harp music coming from the stoop of one of the huts, the notes rippling over him the way the burn in the forest crooned over the tumbled stones on the mountainside. Suddenly, he thought of the fawn he'd discovered one morning almost a moon ago, near the inland loch across the bay. In his mind, he could see its liquid eyes and fringed lashes as it waited in the grasses a few feet away. Da'd have me spearing the creatures, Firinn thought, and shivered.

"Before the seasons circle thirty times more, me own son'll hold the high seat o' the isle, so says his Ma," Speireag shouted, looking especially handsome this night with his straight nose and manly jaw lit by the fire. He dropped Firinn into the low carved chair, reserved for himself, and grabbed up a skin of mead. Grasping Firinn's chin, Speireag held it to the boy's mouth, pouring the liquid into him. Firinn gulped as much as he could hold, and then turned his face away, while the chief laughed and chugged the skin dry.

Then the pipers broke into a deafening thrum, and four warriors in their clan plaids lined up in front of the fire. The dancers bent to cross their swords on the hard-packed earth, and Firinn watched the lithe feet as they leaped up and down over the weapons, the dance of victory. The boy slid out of his Da's seat, filled a plate at the board, heaped with barley and apple cake, and sat near the fire to eat.

As the moon began to rise over the eastern hills, the dancers gave way to old Aedd, his back beginning to bend and his grizzled wiry hair all fallen out now, except for tufts above his ears. Old Aedd can talk from one moonrise to the next, Fìrinn thought with a smile. I hope he starts with the story of the selkies (the seal people). And the ladd watched firelight flicker on the faces surrounding him, the dancing light painting shadows beneath noses and chins, making the clanfolk look eerie, like some tribe of dark mottled strangers. Long fingers of shadow reached out beyond the clan, too, over the dancers and the carcass of the bear, even beyond the broch, to join the purple vastness of the Goddess surrounding them all.

Chapter Six: Soillse

Soillse adored her Da, and that was all there was to it. As soon as she could crawl, she headed straight for Seumus the moment he came through the doorskin after the day's games. Often following the evening meal, the muscled warrior, in his heavy athlete's leather breeks and his fur jerkin covered with mud from the yard, would pick her up and sit beside the fire, telling stories of the day. And the lass'd lay her head back on his chest with a soft smile. Not that Soillse protested when plump Eilid picked her up to suckle or lay the lass in her bedfurs for the night; she was a docile child. But even from her pallet, the babe's eyes searched for Seumus, and only when they found him did she settle down to sleep. Eilid was inwardly startled at the need of the babe for her Da with Ceit so attached to herself.

But Seumus was often gone from the hut, watching the games in the yard or off hunting all the long days, at times not even returning for the night. Soillse watched for him as the sun fell, peering out from the sling her Ma carried her in. And always there was a grin and reaching arms, or if he'd been long away, a squeal of delight when Seumus walked in.

During the passing of her second winter, the babe began chattering to Seumus in her child's way after the evening meal, running to bring him shells or stones or feathers she'd found that day. And the big warrior with his large nose and scarred cheek was ever patient with her, holding up the small treasures she brought and listening to her name them for a time, then picking her up to hold as he launched into his stories for the night. During the winter moons especially, Seumus sat and joked round the hearth or brought out his pipes. He and Eilid sang or sometimes danced, the flush rising on their cheeks and both bairns giggling. There was no competition for Seumus from Ceit either, for she might run to pull her Da into a romp or a splash on the beach of a morning or walk right into the competitions for one of his bear hugs any time of day, whenever the impulse took her. But in the evening, Ceit crooned to her dolly and followed Eilid at her tasks, ever talking or tugging at her Ma. So Seumus and Soillse sat often by the fire and bothered no one.

By the end of that second winter, Soillse began to follow her Da out of the hut in the mornings, too. Waiting beside the chief's round house in the bracken, hidden in the shadows of the birches, the lass watched quietly as he laid out the day's challenges for the ladds. Only then did she come back in to her Ma. If ever the shouting in the yard grew too loud during the day, Soillse startled, even from a distance, and frowned at the ladds. And she never went into the fray, as Ceit often did, to yell for her favorite. When the wrestlers, especially, held on so tightly that their flesh grew white or their limbs began to shake, Soillse turned and walked off into the bracken with her back to it all. But she always knew where her Da was, like he was her anchor somehow. And she was at the carved doorposts to greet him, well before he walked across the yard for the evening meal.

Early the following spring, just past Soillse's third winter, the lass began rising at firstsky on clear brisk days to tiptoe out the doorskins by herself. She ran to the shore, and stood with her wee hands together, the early sheen of the sea lighting her eyes as she sang her made-up songs to the Sun Lord, as if in prayer. And Eilid, a homely round-figured woman, rose always to watch from the doorway and speak the Goddess blessing on her odd, quiet child and didn't interfere.

Once, the local druid, Coillore (koylore, golden wood), who lived up on the ridge not far from the tuath, stayed at the round house for the night. The small wiry man always wore his white druid robe, his long grey hair falling down his back, tonsured from ear to ear in the druid style, so he looked like one of the bald elders, even in his youth. Seumus and Coillore sat by the fire, talking long that evening about which ladds would begin the druid training Coillore gave one evening every quarter moon.

The next morning, just as the first rays of the sun spilled in around the doorcloth, the druid rose and came to stand beside Eilid, peering out after Soillse. The wee lass, still chubby cheeked in her thin night shift, was walking east along the shore with her hands together, and they could just hear her singing the chant to the sun in her high child's lisp. Coillore glanced at Eilid and smiled.

"A gifted one," he said. "I'll have her at me fire circle by her seventh winter, if ye dinna mind me teachin' her so young." And Eilid nodded, her eyes wet as she made the spiral sign of the Goddess on her chest, then pulled her woolen shawl tighter over her summer shift.

Once, the lassie gave them a scare. As Samhein approached and the days grew short, the happiness in the child's eyes dimmed, and she fussed to Eilid several times about the night's long stretch of darkness. And she followed Seumus closer than ever in the dusky early mornings till the sun finally brightened the sky. There was one brilliant sunrise, just one, as the Blackthorne moon closed (November), before the winter rains began in earnest. Eilid had been working doubly hard that week to grind meal and get roots and nuts dried and gathered into the storage pits, and she was overtired. So on that one glorious dawn, she didn't hear Soillse patter across the earthen floor, nor did Eilidh wake at the quick flash of light as the wee one pulled aside the doorskin.

Soillse walked east as always, wearing only her homespun sleeping shift. I can find the Sun Lord, Ceit says so, the lass thought. Standing on the beach, peering over the waters, Soillse wondered if the sparkling path of light she'd seen over the sea at sunset would take her to Him more quickly. Maybe she should wait till then. But instead, she ran the length of the beach toward His brilliance on the horizon beyond the inland hills and scrambled up between the boulders of the headland, moving south toward the bay beyond.

The tide was out as Soillse clambered over the stony tumble, ever eastward, humming. But the bay to the south of the tuath was rocky and narrow, tight to the water's edge. And as the lass climbed down onto it, the tide turned, and water began rushing over the sand below. And Soillse didn't know what to do, for Ma said never go into the sea when it raced like that. The rocks behind her were filling with thundering waves, too. Quickly, she climbed onto the highest rock she could reach with her wee legs and bent her head. Then she sang the Sun Lord song all the way through. But then the skies darkened, quite suddenly, and the rains began to fall, great drops that splattered across the child's bare arms.

Eilid woke as heavy rains began pounding the earth beyond the door cloth. The cloud folk have turned their great buckets over on us all at once, she thought. Then glancing at Soillse's pallet, she startled to see it empty and rose quickly, racing to the door. Seeing no lassie on the beach either, Eilid grabbed up her plaid and flung it over her night shift, pushing heavily at Seumus and shrieking for him to get up. Frantic, Eilid raced along the shore, calling Soillse's name. I ken she's gone this way, I just ken it, Eilid thought, and bent to stare at the sand by the water's edge, hoping to find a track. It took her a moment, weaving back and forth at the edge of the rocks and stooping to look. And there, in a pocket of sand under an overhang of rock was one tiny footprint, pointed south.

"Ach, the Goddess protect her," Eilid wailed, "she's gone over the rocks an' just look at the tide! Seumus!" She ran back, screaming, just as Seumus emerged from the round house, rubbing his eyes. Then she grabbed his hands and pointed south over the arm of the bay. "Look here. Look!," she shouted, showing him the footprint and beginning to wail into her hands.

Seumus said nothing at all, just clenched his jaw. Nor did he run back for a plaid or an oiled skin over his loincloth, but simply sprinted to the lowest of the tumbled boulders and fairly leaped over the rocks. Once or twice, he slipped in the rain and skinned his shins, and his toes soon began to ache from the cold. But as he crested the heaped stones, he saw the lass, shivering on a single rock, with the foaming waves all around her and the tide still climbing. Her fine ash-gold hair blew every which way as she faced the sun, still partially visible under low clouds scudding in from the west. She was humming the Sun Lord song, with her shift all soaked and one arm held out. She held a wilted fern leaf in her hand.

A growl rose from Seumus's throat, more like the cry of a bear than a human sound. But Soillse heard him and turned. Then she smiled and got to her feet, whispering, " I <u>knew</u> ye'd come!" Seumus jumped from boulder to boulder then, leaping into waves that lapped the broken rocks beneath her feet. At last he reached up and pulled her down to him, holding her as high as he could above the waves and struggling to keep his own footing till he reached higher ground. Her lips were blue and she was shaking badly, but her eyes were bright, and she didn't seem afraid. He kissed her head over and over, and ran his fingers through her baby hair. And as soon as he climbed out of the waves onto the boulders, he held her tight.

"Ach, me sweet lassie!" And Soillse felt tears on her back and her Da's shoulders heaving. And she looked up at him with her brows held high.

"I went to find the Sun Lord, Da," she told him in her wee voice. "Ceit said I could find Him, there, where the sun comes up over the ridge." She pointed and gave a soft smile. "I thought to just have the mornin' wi' Him an' then come home to ye again. But the rains began to fall, an' the sea came in, an' I couldna find me way back." She shrugged and dropped her hands to her sides, as if she'd said the most ordinary thing in the world.

"Lassie," Seumus shouted into her face, "the Sun Lord's in the Otherworld. The only way ye can get there is to pass over an' be laid in the cairn grave, like yer grandma that we visit after the Samhein ceremony! He's far away from ye, an' ye canna reach Him from here!" He kissed her brow fiercely then and climbed the headland all in a rush, for he was beginning to shiver badly himself.

So Seumus didn't see the shock on her face when he spoke to her. Nor did he hear the tiny gasp or see the tears spring into her eyes and begin to roll down her cheeks as he ran toward the tuath. He only felt her trembling in his arms, and so he climbed as quickly as he could. And it took longer this time, balancing on the boulders and being careful not to slip in the rain with the child in his arms. Eilid was there, waiting on the beach with wild eyes, and her shift soaked through, too, shouting above the waves. She jumped across the stones to meet them and grabbed Soillse out of his arms.

"Ach, she's cold an' wet, an' winter settlin' in. The Goddess help her!" Then Eilid let out a wail as only a grieved mother can do and ran to the roundhouse with the child bouncing up and down in her arms. "Where on earth were ye goin', lassie?," Eilid cried, as she put the bairn down by the hearth. "Dinna ever do that again!"

Muirn, in a pale blue workaday shift, with her thick dark hair flying, had built up the fire and now ran out to bring in the small child's tub and began hefting warming stones into it. And Sìne, brows even more disapproving than usual, already dressed in her heavy brown work shift and hide apron, was pouring water from the waterskins into the cauldron to heat. Seumus followed Eilid in and took off his loincloth, put on a dry one and his heavy buckskin breeks, woolen shirt, and fur jerkin, and stood beside the fire, rubbing his arms. As Eilid peeled off Soillse's soaked shift and placed the lass gently in the tub, Muirn grabbed a cloak and raced up to the burn for more water. Then Sìne, her tangled dark hair not even combed out into its usual neatness, poured a bowl of warm oat mush into a large shell bowl and handed it to Eilid. Eilid had thrown off her wet shift, put on her heavy workaday one, and now knelt to feed the lass. With her arms crossed, frowning, dark haired Ceit stood watching in the shadows and then whirled to sit on her bedfurs with her back to them all. It was only then Eilid noticed Soillse's brows locked tight together and the child shaking her head back and forth.

"Da says there's no Sun Lord here," Soillse whimpered to herself. "An' the Otherworld's too far to reach." And she gave a great sigh and looked up at her Mum, eyes stricken with doubt.

"The bairn thought she just could go off ta visit the Sun Lord, walkin' east over the rocks, as easy as ye like," Seumus said, all in a rush, waving his hands. "T'was Ceit told her she might find Him round the southern bay, I gather. There's a dark streak in that child." And he glanced at Ceit's pallet with fisted hands, then glanced back at Soillse. "Strange wee one to believe it, though. I told her He's in the Otherworld noo, an' she'll have to pass over ta see Him. She willna go again, Elji, I'm sure of it." And Soillse looked up sharply at her Da as he said this and began to cry again.

After that, Soillse rarely went to the shore on a sunny dawn, even after spring returned the next skyturn. And Eilid admonished the bairn repeatedly to stay in the roundhouse until after the morning meal, and so Soillse did. She helped her Ma with the chores in her small way and made no complaints, growing quieter than ever. So no one really noticed that the lass didn't sing as much or run to Seumus in the evening as often as she had before.

Only once the next summer, on a brilliant windy morn, did Soillse go to the doorcloth in her light summer sleeping shift, before anyone else was up, and peek outside. She began to draw her hands together and smile at the sun. But then she dropped them and sighed heavily, pulling the doorcloth shut again, frowning and shaking her head. Then she went back to her pallet and covered her face with her furs.

Chapter Seven: Firinn

It was a hard winter, windy and cold, especially near the western shores. Storms pounded the coasts relentlessly, all the tribes held in the dark one's power. At Firinn's tuath, when food grew scarce during the Rowan (January) moon, two of the old ones, his great-aunt Una among them, gave up their portions to the clan. They simply turned their faces toward the hut walls and went to the Goddess. So Firinn learned the necessity of meat and began watching his Da with new interest and budding respect. The chief grew restless with the strain on the clan, hunting for long days until spring arrived, but there was no breach of dignity in the man.

But after the trouble passed, Speireag insisted that Firinn, seven winters and spindly now, practice spear throwing with the other ladds in preparation for his fostering next fall. And Firinn did as he was told. Then, with the stores severely depleted, just as warm breezes hinted of spring around the bend, Speireag, dressed in his clan plaid and ceremonial hide shirt, brought Firinn to the glen hidden behind the Goddess mountain. The tall chief knelt at the standing stone there and said a charm for game, repeating the chant three times and walking sunwise round the stone. And the next evening, an aged stag appeared at the edge of the pinewood, while clansmen ran for their spears. Firinn thought it strange how the stag waited quietly for the kill, not even trying to run, and that night in his bed furs, the ladd wondered at his Da's power. And then all bellies were fed for a quarter moon more, when the weather finally broke. And never was Firinn so glad to see the rabbits emerge from their burrows and warmth spread over the land.

With spring came the easing of want and bowls filled again, with fern heads, duck eggs, and late winter barley. Bears and boar came out of their dens, and that whole season afterward, berries and nuts were more plentiful than usual in the forests. And so the broch stores filled quickly, as if the Goddess of light repaid the tribe for the dark one's harshness through the winter moons.

On the last night of the Vine moon (September), Speireag announced that Fìrinn would go to his fostering following the ladd's day of birth, three moons away. He'd go to Seumus's training compound, an old warrior skilled in the martial arts, whose tuath was on the southern tip of Skye. That's a long ride from Ma, Fìrinn thought, as they sat with the clan by the broch fire that night. She kept me here as long as she could. Frithe only nodded, sadness moving into the line of her mouth as she sang the night blessing in her blue winter shift. Then all that fall, Fìrinn stole away often, running to the bay and the pinewood in the early morning or the evening gloaming, soaking in the haunts that were as much Ma to him as Frithe was.

Fìrinn's eighth birth morn dawned a few days after Samhein. It would be his final day at the tuath. And his Ma, in a heavy woolen winter shift, woke him early, before the birds stirred. Smiling at his russet curls tumbled on the pillow around his head and the spare length of him, she silently handed him his fur jerkin and buckskin breeks to follow her outside. Frithe's green wool cloak billowed out behind her as she strode down the path, her figure a dark silhouette in the early mists. Fìrinn slowed a moment to watch the way her acorn hair with the fiery highlights fell in waves about her shoulders, and then rushed double lengths to catch up with her, his head higher than her chin as they walked swiftly up the mountainside. He'd grown sinewy and brown this summer, running through the wood for nuts and helping gather in the grains of the early winter harvest. It was hard for him to believe he'd be leaving with Da at firstsky tomorrow.

And the wish plummeted into his chest like a thrown rock that he could be waist high again and Ma would lift him onto her hip and kiss his hair. This would be their last trip to the pinewood for many skyturns, for he'd live with Seumus for ten winters and become a warrior, if he could. And at the end of that time, Fìrinn would have his initiation into manhood and return here. But by then, she willna ken me, he thought, and sighed.

"The forest sighs, too, Fìrinn-ladd," Frithe whispered, not slowing her pace. "See how the boughs droop at yer leavin'?" She'd always known what his heart held, and those of the trees and forest creatures, too. "Look how proud the yarrow is in her dewdrop crown this morning," Ma had told him only a couple of moons before. And just a morn or two ago, she'd pointed to the burn below the tuath, saying, "That doe has a fawn wi' her, love. See how she turns her ear to check on him?'

Fìrinn soaked in her understandings the way the earth gathers rain, thirstily and without thinking. He could read the shading in a leaf, the pitting of a branch, as easily as if his mother had laid the knowledge over him like a cloak. He saw, as she did, the tension in a tribeswoman's upper lip, the downturn of cook's eye, and the insatiability in his Da's restless hands, as if the words were spoken. And like his Ma, Fìrinn kept these things to himself.

Several times this morning, he expected Frithe to slow her steps, but she did not. They passed hellebore, arched with berries, strong poison for Da's spears. On another day, she'd gasp with delight at such a find but this morning, she had no eye even for this. With cheeks the color of the ivy leaves, fiery in their autumn glow, she strode swiftly through the brightening dawn along the crooked deer path. They went all the way up the mountain to the crag where the old lichened grey stone reached out over the valley.

"The pinewood an' even the standin' stone are no old enough for the reachin's I need today," she said as they came to the crag. Then, pulling off her fur-lined hide boots with an impatient tug, she climbed barefoot onto the marbled outcropping. Fìrinn did the same, only with a sharp intake of breath as his feet touched the icy rock. And the ladd kept a spear's length away from the sheer drop. But Frithe curled her toes around the very edge, leaning into the wind as if she'd take flight.

Fìrinn looked down at the mist maiden a moment, pulling the ragged tails of her underskirts through the valley below. The haze behind the hills was soft blue, just lightening with the first rays of the Sun Lord. Frithe stooped to place fats and a rush wick in a windbreak of shell and then lit it with the flint she kept in her pouch. Into a hollow of the great rock then, she poured sacred water from the women's cave, and earth into another. Then with arms upraised, she began the invocation.

"Brìdet (breejet, Bridget, grandmother goddess of the Stillpoint Center), most powerful, blessin's an' honor to ye. I am in need. If yer heart wills it, come!" And then bowing her head, Frithe waited in stillness. As she did so, Fìrinn felt a sudden coldness fill the air. And then the wick brightened and the wind ceased to blow. A low vibration filled his ears, humming from within the rock. And he gasped as he felt the stone beneath them soften slowly and change into a living form. The crag turned into a great shoulder bone, the knotted joint rising up beside them, the flattened scapula beneath their feet. Dark lichen patches became thin celadon skin, and the rock began breathing, soft and slow. He could feel the rhythm of the grandmother goddess's heartbeat in his feet and her soft tenderness surround them both. Barely breathing, Fìrinn thought, Ma never showed me such high magic before!

"Mother o' the path herself!" Frithe said, her tears falling onto the soft stretched skin. Then Frithe knelt and laid her cheek upon the crag, one grieving mother to another. Standing quickly, Frithe reached out and took the bluestone from the pouch around Fìrinn's neck and laid it at his feet. Raising herself up, she turned sunwise three times, stretching and raking the air with widespread fingers.

"Bluestone, rock o' the virgin god, Rìdire, carry me heart's need into yer tangled roots below this land, beyond the farthest reaches o' Skye an' Alba into the sea kingdoms o' Cymru (Wales). Bring yer strength, born o' ages, to make a shieldin' for me firstborn son, an' place it in this amulet to hold him steady in the times o' heartache that will come. An' Brìdet, I pray ye, anchor yer heart's power into his very core! Let it keep his heart's fire unquenched by the dark one's power his whole life long. This I ask." Then, yanking up the short flint dagger she always carried in her girdle, Frithe pricked the third finger of her left hand. She bent then to let the drops of blood flow down over the rock-face, and as she did so, the rock began to glow.

And then the rock turned as fiery as an ember where Fìrinn stood. He winced suddenly as the burning seared his feet, and the stone emitted blue fire that moved swiftly up his legs and into his heart, swirling there a moment. He shivered slightly as it warmed him and as quickly disappeared. Frithe watched the ladd intently as the rock cooled. Then she replaced the bluestone in the small hide pouch, pulling the thong quickly over Fìrinn's head.

Then turning widdershins (counter-clockwise), Frithe whispered, "Others call ye, goddess. I release me needfire." And she blew the taper out, bending her head and pulling her hands together a moment, then rising in a gliding whisper of cloth. Turning toward Fìrinn with her face intent, Frithe held his shoulders as if to make them narrower, and her hazel eyes reflected the muted golds and greens of the hills.

"Better than I dared hope," she said and smiled. "Fìrinn-ladd, listen well. An ember smolders deep within ye. This I've known since I carried ye round the standin' stone for yer blessin' o' birth. As ye reach the time o' manhood, that ember'll burst into flame. And there'll be danger, for unguarded, it can consume ye. The bluestone, rock o' the high virgin, Rìdire, can calm ye to the core, this one only, imprinted by the grandma Brìdet, too. Call on it, love, whenever ye're in need, an' their spirits'll hold ye fast." Then Frithe turned to move her arm in an arc before the forest. "An' the pinewood'll take ye under her cloak, too, an' hide ye where none can see, for she has long since given her peace into yer heart. But when the fire rages hottest, even the pines canna protect ye, for they burn, too. Only this rock o' Rìdire has power enough to keep ye safe. Remember, laddie, for it may save yer life."

As Fìrinn scanned his mother's face, still blushing and smooth with youth, he felt a crowding of needs unspoken. Her face stilled suddenly and grew very white, and grimness moved through the line of her mouth, a hint of the death crone. Will I ever see her alive again, he wondered? How much has she given for this shielding?

The next morning, Fìrinn in his fur jerkin and heavy hide riding breeks, drew near Frithe reluctantly, for it would be the last time. And he walked painfully, for his soles had blistered from the blue fire after their journey to the crag yesterday. Frithe sat with her green cloak bunched around her on the low boulder outside the broch, watching old Aedd bridle and blanket the horses. Fìrinn's head throbbed as he stood beside her, and in moments her fingers reached out to make small circles on his right temple. But he only clenched his teeth and looked away, and her eye dropped to the movement as she rose to stand before him.

"Me son, ye've brought me more joy than a hundred pinewoods. Ken (know) this. Me love is the barley from which the mead o' yer blood was made. Need an' distance'll only make it stronger. Besides, when I'm no present wi' ye, I can come in other forms. Ye'll see, me ladd, dinna fret. Try no to allow the sadness o' our partin' to unsettle ye." And she kissed him lightly on the forehead.

"Frithe, ye make a fawn o' him!" The chief's voice interrupted them, frowning in the crisp morning air. He, too, wore his heavy fur jerkin and leather breeks. "The ladd shoulda been off last winter. He must learn to hunt, if he's to survive an' serve his clan. Surely ye see this!" The chief strode over and stood above her, his eyes blazing. Then he waved Fìrinn out of his way and kissed Frithe full on the mouth, holding her waist close to his with a muscled arm, and she did not resist him. Then the chief turned, mounted his dark horse, and started off down the hillside.

Fìrinn mounted his dun mare in a bound then, helpless to the raging in his chest. He swept his eyes over the sea loch below and the hut circle, then turned the horse inland, cantering quickly down and through the burn, then began the climb after his Da. As they crested the low ridge beyond the flatlands and entered the pinewood, the dawn light struck boughs tipped with hoar, so all the needles shone in soft sparkling whorls. But the ladd took no comfort from such rare beauty. Glancing back once more, he ran his gaze over all he'd ever known before moving into the forest that took it from his view. And in that final moment, it was not a look of sadness he saw on Frithe's lovely face at all, for she stood before the broch, tall in a shimmer of sunlight, waving and smiling after him, her hair golden as the yarrow.

"Whoa, ladd," his Da said after a while, when they'd dropped down to the track halfway up the barren hills along the shore, headed southeast. "Ye'll have that mare worn out by midsky." And Speireag waited on the track until Fìrinn moved alongside. "It'll be all right, son. I had a hard leavin' in me own time, too. Most ladds do, I s'pose. Seumus'll toughen ye as yer Ma never could. An' ye need it, ladd. Ye'll be chief someday, even Frithe agrees wi' me on that. The Sun Lord favors ye. It's the only reason I've put up wi' her women's lore as long as I have. Ye willna miss her long, ye'll see. I've never been happier than durin' me fosterin', before the sickness took me clan." And the chief looked north a moment, shading his eyes as the old sadness passed through them. Then he kneed his stallion and called out, "Follow me to the east pass, Fìrinn, an' then we'll stop an' see what cook put in the meal skins, hm?"

Fìrinn let his reins out then, and the little mare shook her head and whinnied. She centered herself on the path and started off in her long-legged canter after his Da. Ye'll never catch up with that stallion, girl, will ye, Fìrinn thought. But ye'll love the game of it. And as she eased into a steady stride, his fingers closed around the bluestone on his chest. And tightening his jaw, Fìrinn enjoyed the feel of hoof beats hitting hard on the trampled earth.

Chapter Eight: Soillse

It seemed to Eilid the lass could read a body's thoughts, for Soillse sometimes brought her just the thing she'd been thinking of, an onion from the stores perhaps or sticks to start the fire. Eilid told no one, not even Muirn, and certainly not Seumus. He'd think her daft. But she worried over the child, always right up close to things, peering, touching, silent as the owls. It was a strange gift of the Goddess, two lassies that were so different. For dark frizzy-haired Ceit was forever running and shouting, off to the beach twenty times a day, with the flush on her face way past dark, so Eilid had a time even getting the lass abed. And then there was Soillse, four winters now, always bringing home feathers or leaves or stones that shone. Her baby chubbiness had nearly melted away, but her eyes still seemed too big for her face. And I do believe that lass'd sit in her Da's lap a whole moon, if he let her, Eilid thought, with a shake of her head.

It was the Ivy moon (September), and there was much to gather in as the seasons turned. They were headed up to the wee loch on the ridge today to dig cattail roots and cut reeds for thatch, the morning bright and warm, with a stiff wind blowing up from the sea. Soillse and Ceit, a lanky eight winters now, ran along the deer track that wove through the scrub birches beside the burn. A foot taller than her sister, Ceit walked quickly in her light homespun shift and doeskin jerkin, while the little one stopped often to pick up a tuft of moss or run her hands along the tree trunks.

"Syl, ye're so slow. Come on!" And Ceit grabbed Soillse's hand and began to pull. Soillse, in Ceit's old stained summer shift and a light leather jerkin, her hair still baby fine, followed in a rush a short way and then sat down. So Ceit pouted and ran after Eilid. The older lass had turned out to be an expert gatherer, with sharp eyes in the thickets and indefatigable energy. This morning, as they came out of the wood into the upland flats, Ceit ran straight to the wee inland loch for a splash and then back to help Eilid cut and pile the long plumed grasses at the head of the track. Soillse meandered to the water's edge, a shallow pool that came only to the bairn's ankles, so Eilid wasn't concerned.

"We can splash when we're done, Syl," Ceit shouted. And Soillse smiled at that, pulling off her jerkin and shift and stepping in. Shivering with the cold, the lass bent to pat the water's surface with her palms. Ceit ran over and splashed her, making Soillse shiver again. Then Ceit flattened a wide space in the high grasses.

"Ye can be the baby deer, Syl. Come on. Lie down over here. An' I can be the doe an' find ye acorns an' good things ta eat!" But Soillse was sitting by the water's edge now, with her feet dangling in the pool. In answer she put her feet on the sun warmed rocks at the edge of the water and waved Ceit away.

"Ma, Ma!" Ceit raced toward Eilid, still cutting grasses a short walk away. "I'm tryin' ta help Soillse, but she willna do what I say."

Soillse watched Ceit disappear through the reeds, her sister's voice growing softer as she ran. She could hear Eilid's soft chanting as she cut the tall grasses. Then after a time, the babe felt the ground shake and heard hoof beats on the northern track. She looked up toward the trail, but could see nothing beyond the feathered plumes of grass around the loch. But then a hoarse male voice spoke from quite nearby.

"We can water the ponies here," it said. Footsteps approached, and a tall lean man in a torn green druid robe burst through the grass, a pony's length away. He had thinning stringy black hair and wore the moustache of a nobleman, but his face, robe, and hands were filthy, his hair unkempt. Soillse's eyes widened as she grabbed up her shift and stood, eyeing the man warily. A second man, red haired and shorter, in hide breeks and jerkin pushed into view as well, leading two ponies to the water's edge. Eilid called out to Soillse, and began to run toward the loch. She didn't know these ponies and couldn't see who the men were.

"Well, it's a wee naked lassie," the druid said. His voice felt slippery to Soillse ears, and there was a strange coldness in his eyes. They were nothing like Da's. Soillse tried to pull on her shift and turned to run. But she tripped on the cloth as footsteps came up beside her, and so she froze right where she was. As the druid picked her up, the child whimpered, but didn't cry out.

"Ye're Ma's lookin' fer ye, wee lassie," the man spat out in a harsh whisper, and his spittle made blotches on her face. He didn't smile, and his chest felt hard like the rocks at the bay. And Soillse felt a queasy wriggling in her gut, as if one of the newts in the loch were swimming there. And her heart beat fast behind her ribs. She wished Da was here, and she sent the thought for him to come <u>now</u>.

Smelling of venison and smoke, the druid smiled a lopsided grin at her. Then he patted her bottom, long and slow, squeezing and pushing his finger into her woman's place, hard, so it hurt. "Time ye forgot those soft baby ways, lassie. Tis a rough world, an' the strong are masters of it." And then he set her down, mounting his pony in a rush and leaving her there on the grass. Soillse covered her face and began to cry, quietly, so the man wouldn't hear. His horse's hoof beats shook the ground at first, but then they grew softer and further away. She pulled down her shift, anyway, and closed her eyes tight as more footsteps came up beside her and a hairy arm reached round her belly and began to pull her up. At this, Soillse began to wail.

"It's yer Da, lassie, open yer eyes. What happened?" Seumus, in his heavy leather hunting jerkin and breeks, was holding her out, looking her up and down, and she could feel a fine tremor in his arms. "The men're gone noo. Ye're safe wi' meself." Eilid burst through the grasses then, breathless and glowering, as Seumus turned to her. "She looks all right, Elji," he said.

"Och, thank the Goddess she's safe! How did ye ken to come, Seumus?"

"We were trackin' boar, just there," he said, nodding up the hill. "I heard the ponies an' came down to see who it was. I had a bad feelin' in me chest all mornin' an' thought I'd best stay near yerself." No hoof beats could be heard now, but Seumus still scanned the horizon with one hand across his brow. "They went south, toward the mainland," he spat out. "I never saw those ponies before. They're no the clan o' the wolf." Soillse was clinging tightly to her father, her chin trembling. "The bairn looks like the banshees got her," he said, frowning. "Did they hurt ye, lassie?" And the child nodded.

Then he pulled up her shift and gasped, cursing loudly and bringing his fist down hard into one leg. A tickle of blood ran down Soillse's inner thigh, and a bruise was swelling there. Seumus whirled toward Eilid, his eyes bulging, running his hand over his head. "How in the name o' the dark one could they've done that! She's little more than a <u>babe</u>, for Goddess sake! I'll hunt the demons down, if it's the last thing I do in me <u>life</u>!"

"There was no time to do what ye're thinkin' of, Seumus," Eilid said quietly. "They had but a moment. I saw them come, an' I ran over meself. The tall one picked her up and held her briefly. I did see that much. Still, tis harm enough." Her eyes welled with tears as she brushed off the blood. "Is the Goddess angered? I never heard the likes o' this," she said, fingering the amulet at her neck. Eilid reached for Soillse then and laid her in the grass, gently wiping the dirt and blood away with a hide from her pouch that she dipped into the loch.

"I'll never let ye out c' me sight again, lassie. An' we'll be huntin' fer more than game this midsky," Seumus growled, holding his right hand aloft with his eyes afire. But Soillse only closed her eyes and stopped sniffling as Seumus leaned down to pick her up and wipe the tears off her face. She took a deep breath, let it out again, and then reached up and laid her face against her Da's chest. He was warm and strong, and his hide shirt smelled safe. "No man'll ever hurt ye again, Soillse, I swear it!" Then Seumus handed the child to Eilid, who set the lass on her feet, took Ceit's hand, and began to walk down the track.

For once, Ceit was silent, her wide eyes staring at Soillse, as Eilid sang the forever friend song all the way back to the roundhouse. There, Eilid bathed Soillse, treating the bruises with a plantain/willow poultice and rocking the lass by the fire as Muirn and Sìne bustled in and out, fixing the midsky meal. As she rocked, Eilid felt something tarnished in the bairn, though, its shadow creeping into her own soul, too. The babe didn't feel innocent any more, as a wee lassie should. No, there was something tired about her, tired and as old as the depths of the sea.

Chapter Nine: Fìrinn

Ears drooping, Fìrinn's mare trailed behind the chief's stallion. It was the third evening of their journey, the day remaining cloudy, but not too cold for early winter. They'd ridden southeast above the coast all afternoon, and Fìrinn's thighs were chaffed and sore, his fur jerkin and breeks dusty and streaked with mud. But surprisingly, he'd enjoyed the two nights travel with his Da, Speireag reminiscing by the fire about his clan, stories Fìrinn had never heard before. The ladd was startled to learn his Da had a secluded place of power, where he went alone to call for aid from the Sun Lord when troubles came to the clan. As they bedded down into their furs in the dark by the fire, still in their hide traveling clothes, Fìrinn sensed his father's reliance on the spirit world, kept so well hidden, as well as the chief's rock firm ability to lead the tribe through almost anything.

On the two previous nights of the journey, by the time the ladd's muscles had stopped aching on his blanket, he'd been fast asleep. But this night, Fìrinn lay long awake, watching the firelight dance across the boulders that sheltered them and listening to the whoosh of the wind woman through the stones. They'd passed through the valley between jagged barren peaks early in the day. And now they rested near a copse of pines on the broad eastern plateau of the isle. I'll never have Da's thirst for the kill, Fìrinn thought, the predator isna in me. Even the idea balled up heavily in the pit of Fìrinn's gut as he glanced over at his father's snoring bulk. Is that necessary for a chief? If so, I'll certainly fail to be one. An' Da'll be more disappointed in me than he is already. So will Seumus, a man as like me Da, no doubt, as one onion peeling to another. And Ma? She'll not find me distaste of killing a weakness. But failure to be chief? The ladd shook his head and rolled over, feeling the earth mother's ribs of bedrock support him as he watched the stars wheel slowly through the night.

His mind tense with questions about his destiny, Fìrinn's dreams had been vivid in the hours before dawn, and he was tired even as he woke. Late that morning, they came off the central track and over the inland flats to the southeastern peninsula of Skye, keeping to the ridge above the western shore all that day. And then, the long day's travel made Fìrinn weary to the bone and even more silent than usual. As dusk approached, it brought a sharp wind with it, making Speireag hurry the horses.

As they rounded the last hill before turning down toward the coast, they passed a small upland loch. It was surrounded by high, wheat-colored grasses, the plumed shafts so tall, they kept the water stilled. Fìrinn stopped to stare as his Da continued down through the birch wood. It's exactly like the wee loch me and Ma go to at home, across the bay and over the hill from our tuath, Fìrinn thought. The plumes were bending all together before the wind woman, as if in prayer, and Fìrinn felt the sacredness of the Goddess here and a premonition of peace.

"Sun Lord an' Goddess," he prayed, "mold me to the manhood Ye choose. Let me no fail Ye as well as Da. I ask only to help me tuath in some way, an' I'll do whatever's needed to accomplish that, I promise Ye."

Downhill through the trees, a small settlement could be seen, with one longhouse and eight or ten round huts, thatched, with wooden palisaded walls and stone foundations, exactly like those of home. The chief's stallion broke into a gallop as it cleared the wood, but Fìrinn followed slowly through the scrub birches. The land was cupped here, dropping gently to the shore, and the arms of the bay curved gracefully into the sea with no steep headlands like those of home. The water was much closer to the huts here than his own tuath, too, only a few pony lengths from the yard. As he descended on the track, Fìrinn glanced back, running his eyes along the ridge that rose to a rounded crest. A single standing stone stood silhouetted there against the evening sky.

As Fìrinn's dun mare loped into the yard, he noticed one larger round house with carved and painted doorposts. The chief's hut, he thought. Smoke rose from the central roof hole, drifting into the darkening air, and the scent of roast boar flooded the ladd's nostrils. Fìrinn's mouth watered for warm food as much as his thighs ached for solid ground. Several groups of boys, who wore muddy hide breeks and shirts and were clustered in the yard by twos and fours, stopped what they were doing to stare at Speireag and then Fìrinn riding toward them. A stocky grizzled man in a heavy leather hunting shirt, fur jerkin, and buckskin breeks emerged from the crowd. And while his horse still moved, Speireag flung himself off and into the elderly man's embrace. Even ten pony lengths away, Fìrinn could hear the back-slapping.

"Seumus, old man," Speireag said, kissing the shorter man's cheeks. "How's the Goddess treatin' ye? Ye're lookin' well," he said, poking Seumus's belly that was hard as a stone. Seumus gave a snort.

"It's Elji's stews. I'm a lucky man. Ye always stay fit, Speireag. How do ye manage it? But I forget meself. Come, have yer meal." And Seumus pointed to the hut with the carved doorposts, nodding to a tall spare clansman behind him. "Take the horses, Duineil (doonal, manly), will ye? We'll fill the chief wi' hot boar, while Muirn prepares his bath o' welcome." Then Seumus extended an arm toward Fìrinn, just entering the yard, "an' bring the laddie," he added.

"Nay, he's all right," Speireag said, and waved the boy away without a backward glance. "I have a new spear-makin' technique I want to show ye, Seumus. We hit game far more often this way." His eyes brightening, Speireag reached back to clutch two spears from the leather quiver on his horse. "The ladd's best off settlin' in wi' his foster brothers, anyway. He's been babied long enough." And there was such finality in the chief's voice that Seumus only raised his brows and nodded.

"As the chief requests, Duineil," he said. "Have Sìne add an extra portion o' shank for the ladd. He must be weary from the trail." Then Seumus turned back toward Speireag, throwing an arm over the chief's back. And the rest of their words were lost to the wind, as they disappeared under the door skin between the carved posts.

His mind darkening at this father's words, Fìrinn kept to his mount. The sweating mare sidled toward the animals grazing on the cleared hill to the north of the tuath as the ladd leaned down to pat her neck, running his gaze over the boys. Will I find a friend here?, he wondered. They're dusty and disheveled, the whole lot. I'll not be getting whatever I like from cook any more, either, Fìrinn's thoughts continued. And he noticed strain on the boys' faces as fear laced slowly through his gut. I'll suffer, he realized suddenly. How much? But then he felt the wind woman's touch on his arms and face, holding him in a hard kind of comfort, and he took a long breath. I'll be steady, too, Goddess, at least on the outside, he thought.

"Laddie, d'ye hear me?" A deep voice Fìrinn realized had been speaking for some time finally penetrated his thoughts, and a hand touched his elbow lightly. It was Duineil, bent over to meet Fìrinn's eyes. "Are ye wi' us, laddie?" Waiting beside the mare just outside the press of boys, the man was tall and lean in his hide clothing, with white hair and straight square shoulders. There was simple dignity in his bearing and the direct gaze of his sky-blue eyes. These were deep set, under coarse white brows, and the man wore no moustache, so he was not of the noble class. Seeing the ladd respond at last, Duineil broke into a crooked smile, and his eyes smiled even more. "Ye're tired, sire. I can take yer blanket bag noo." The 'sire' startled Fìrinn, and his face softened as he smiled back.

"Many thanks, sire," he answered, wondering if everyone was required to speak so formally here. But Duineil frowned so suddenly at these words, the man drawing himself up to his full height, that Firinn wanted to laugh.

"I am Duineil mac Donnagh, me ladd, a simple clansman," Duineil said and dropped his head to his chest a moment, "no a nobleman at all, nay, no even close." Then he winked as he pulled the blanket bag off the mare's rump in a swift easy movement. "We'll forgive ye this once, though," he said, and in an instant his frown became an impish grin. "Sure an' welcome, son o' the chief."

Beyond Duineil, a movement caught Firinn's eye. A wiry black-headed ladd, perhaps two winters older than himself, was pushing toward the front. The boy was fair-skinned with high cheekbones and tousled wavy hair. He watched them with narrowed eyes and fisted hands, his shoulders stiffening at Firinn's glance. The falcon's in the ladd and no mistake, Firinn thought. Why would he want to make prey of me? But then Firinn dismounted and followed Duineil into the longhouse, and as the smell of stew surrounded him, Firinn's stomach burned.

Before the morning stars faded, no matter what the weather, the boys were yanked from sleep by the bellowing of the yardmaster at the longhouse door. And then Duineil came in, already dressed in his heavy sporting leather breeks and shirt, and whispered the hearth blessing as he spread the coals and stoked the fire. This task, usually reserved for the eldest female, had been his mother's for decades. And now that she'd gone to the Otherworld, it was a chore Duineil refused to share. He did it in her name, he said, as the Goddess directed him, and no one argued with his steely eye when he spoke of it. Then came the scuffle of the two serving women, as the kettle of steaming gruel was brought in. As soon as the fire in the hearth began to glow, the youngest boys leaped from their bedfurs, pulling on their buckskin breeks and shirts, and pouncing for a place in the warmth. Tossing challenges for the day ahead, the older ladds stayed in their bedfurs till the hearth circle was fully warmed, then simply pushed their way to the fireside, not always careful of fingers or toes.

Except for a midsky break for lunch, stew and oatcakes usually, the boys were kept at their sports relentlessly from first light until the torches were brought out for the evening meal. Nor did it matter if wind or snow needled their bones, for endurance was part of the training. Chosen by ability, the ladds were placed in groups of two or four, depending on the sport, and pitted against each other. There were competitions in stone, spear, and caber throw, wrestling, scouting and tracking, foot races, and for a chosen few of the oldest, sword play. On bright winter afternoons, the clang of metal rang out over the hills. Seumus loved nothing more than a well-matched fight, and whenever the competition grew fierce, his eyes bulged and his moustache bristled as he watched from the edge of the fray. Often the older ladds went in search of game, too, and with so many to hunt, rarely was there lack of any kind at the tuath.

Sometimes in the evening round the long house fire among the boys, relaxing in his woolen plaid and homespun shirt, Seumus boasted about old battles with raiders or hunting a canny boar or two, and his eyes shone. But his ferocity was tempered now, for it had receded along with his hairline. And he grew so tender in the evening with too much mead that he called for his homely brown-haired wife and sat with his arm round her shoulders, singing love songs at the top of his voice. Now and then, when Eilid was too busy to join them, Seumus would cradle the mead skin to his chest and hum laments to his mother. Stirred by the man's warmth and passion, Firinn stayed often at the fire. And he smiled under his bedfurs that first quarter moon, glad for the differences between Seumus and his Da after all.

Sometimes during his first moon at the fostering, the ache in Firinn's chest flared into a rush of longing with sudden thoughts of home: his mother's voice, his own pallet at the broch, the peace of the pinewood, even cook's dour face. At times, he walked along the shore, gulping the brisk sea air to tame his sadness. But that whole first winter, his need felt like embers, always smoldering in his heart space. Once, just once, he'd broken to it, stumbling into a sob one morning, half awake, as the lady with the acorn hair carried in the stirabout. Not wanting to risk another cry, he'd pulled on his hide clothes and run up to the burn to splash his face. And then, before he had time to think, he was racing up the hill toward the birches. Suddenly, he <u>needed</u> pine people to hold him as they'd always done. Who cared about breakfast, anyway?

He climbed on till he spied one stunted Caledonii rising among the birches, and scrambled through the underbrush to cling to it. The rough sticky bark, the familiar scent, the needled floor beneath, and the sense of a mother's welcome soothed Firinn's heart. He sank to the ground and leaned back against the trunk, breathing deeply. And then immediately, Firinn could feel the touch of the tree's spirit on his brow. She whispered into his mind that this pain would ease and he'd become a man here, and that it was his destiny to do so. He thought she said great joy would come to him as well.

'Return to me,' she said softly, 'whenever you're troubled, ladd. The pine people you knew before can send their love through the pathways of light to me, just as if you were still with them at your home.' He nodded, wiping the tears from his face as he stood looking back at the tree. Bending his head then, Firinn whispered a blessing, as Ma had taught him always to do after the arrival of some grace from the Goddess.

"Blessing of the Goddess be thine, gentle mother, for the love o' all yer kind. May She surround and fill ye wi' Her peace."

And then as Firinn turned to walk slowly through the bare birches down the hill to the tuath, a light drizzle began to fall. It felt as soft as his mother's fingers, brushing his cheeks. "I can come to ye in other forms," Ma had said at their parting. And slowly, as he waited there, Firinn felt the silken drops wash his pain down and down into the brown sturdiness of the earth beneath his feet.

Chapter Ten: Soillse

Soillse had one friend she shared with no one, a small apple tree, hidden a short way into the scrub birches just north of the tuath, above the rocky shore. She loved its pale pink flowers in the Hawthorne moon (May) and the after drift of petals in the bracken. And she named it Aine (ahnya, joy), for the girl goddess of the heart (Holy Family), the one she loved most. As Ceit lengthened into a wiry inexhaustible girl and grew ever bossier with the passing skyturns, Soillse discovered she could go sit in her apple tree, and her sister would think her off on some errand or busy in the cooking hut and leave her alone for a while. It felt like that tree reached up into heaven itself, for in its branches, Soillse was a different self. In her workaday shift and woolen shawl, without her filthy hide cooking apron on, and watching the waves rise and fall on the rocks below, the worry of constant work didn't follow Soillse there. And she often made up stories and songs about the hills or the sea, like the way she loved the sunshine creeping in behind the door skin every morning, brightening ever so slowly to wake her own self up. That sun felt like some gentle-hearted god she'd known once upon a time in the Otherworld, and often she wished she could find him here in this one.

As Samhein approached, Soillse felt a change coming, but she couldn't tell what it was. Just last night, she dreamed of her Aine tree, a vivid dream that left her wanting the new thing very much. In her dream, the wee girl goddess stepped right out of the apple tree's trunk and flew to Soillse's own pallet in the chief's roundhouse. The small goddess wore a pale pink gown, the color of apple blossoms about to burst, and she had delicate veined wings, quivering like a damselfly. Humming the 'Call to the Faery', the Aine goddess had leaned over to open two small doors of light in Soillse's heart space. And behind them sat a very clear stone, shiny, like a drop of water. Then Aine sprinkled peach-colored sparkles on that stone, and it began to soften, very slowly, until it was liquid like honey. And then Soillse saw the droplet start to beat to the rhythm of Aine's heart, as rosy peach light shone out of it and spread all over the pallet. The hut smelled faintly of wild roses when Soillse awoke, and she felt giddy, as if it was already springtime. And there was that longing in her heart she didn't understand.

But then the day had been cool, even for the Elder moon (December), with thick fog that burned off slowly after midsky. And Soillse shivered, wrapping her woolen shawl tighter around her fur jerkin, for the wind had quickened in the late afternoon, and the bare branches gave no shelter. In her warmest woolen shift, she was perched half way up the ridge on a large boulder that sat a short way south, off the deer track beside the burn. The rock was so large that it leaned out through the low birches, and she could see the whole bay and the sea beyond. Soillse perched at the edge of the stone with her feet dangling, kicking her heels lightly on the rock. And just now, an enormous orange sun hung beyond the mountains across the sea loch, and a coppery drift of clouds floated across the horizon there. The jagged Cuchullins rose out of it, their peaks a darker shade of copper than the bank of clouds below.

I'm tired, Soillse thought. Almost six winters is not big enough for all the cooking we did today. She'd washed onions, their skins caked with dirt, and chopped till her fingers were sore this morning. And then in the afternoon, she'd gone up the ridge to gather new heather for a fresh pallet for some chief who'd be staying at the round house tonight. And then at dusk, she was sent off to the wood for more kindling. Her feet hurt, and her hands stung where the heather had pricked them. And worst of all, she hadn't been able to go to her Aine tree even once to thank her for the dream last night.

And that made Soillse grumpy all day long. Maybe we'd be better off with fewer ladds at the fostering, like Sìne says, Soillse thought. And now a new one's coming with his Da. But I can sit here for a wee while, at least, she thought, patting the kindling stacked beside her, at least till the new folk arrive. Then there'll be the rush of serving, she frowned, since Ma decided to wait till they arrive for our evening meal.

Soillse's head felt heavy and her stomach growled. She closed her eyes and sighed, listening to a sparrow's song. It'd be fun to be a baby bird up here on this rock, she thought, and fly up into the clouds whenever ye want. That bird song soothes even me feet. And then she felt tingles in her scalp and the back of her neck. The faeries did that when they wanted to tell her something, and so she shut the wind and the bird song out of her ears and lay back, listening in her mind.

But then the dogs began to howl in the yard, and Soillse scowled and opened her eyes. I canna hear a thing with all that racket, she thought. And then she heard horses on the path behind her, the clip-clop of hooves moving over rock. And so she sat up, turning to stare up the track. A tall moustached man with dark curly hair, very wind blown, was riding down beside the burn two pony lengths away. He cantered quickly through the birches and then galloped to the roundhouse. Leaping off his horse and into Da's arms, he slapped Seumas hard on the back. Well, at least we get to eat now, she thought.

A smaller, light brown horse followed along the track, stopping just below Soillse in the brush. On it was a thin ladd with sad eyes, who reached out to touch the peeling bark of a birch. His breeks were dirty and torn at the knee, and his dark red hair hung in strings about his shoulders, but he was as handsome as the man had been, with a thin straight nose, high cheek bones, and well defined masculine chin. The ladd fingered the soft pink skin of the tree gently and leaned over as if he might get down. But he stayed mounted, and she saw a blessing cross his lips, as he made the sign of the Goddess on his chest. Dusty streaks covered his cheeks, and he wiped them with one hand as he began moving toward the yard. That ladd's been crying, Soillse thought in surprise. He doesna want to be here any more than I want him to come. And he looks even more tired than I am.

"Soillse!," Ceit called from the roundhouse door. The elder lass was tall and slender now, with the same spare athletic build as Muirn, moving gracefully into the yard like the cats she was named for. But Soillse, with her long fine hair in a tangle, stayed hidden till the new boy moved away, and then she scampered down, picking up the kindling and running to the round house. She stopped for a moment at the door skin, though, wishing it were herself who'd show that new boy to the baths and ladle him a dish of stew.

That night, after Ma said the night blessing and banked the fire, when all the carrying was over and the loud chief's voice had finally stilled, Soillse let her aching feet relax on her pallet and sighed, warm in her heavy woolen night shift under the furs. Tomorrow'll be easier, she thought. That's good. And then, the new ladd's face came clearly into her mind. His name was Firinn, and he came from the clan of the deer far to the north, Da said. He's like me, she thought, soft inside where no one can see. And he loves the tree folk, too. Swordplay and wrestling'll crush someone like him into fine pieces, like the barley Ma grinds on her quern stone into meal. Why canna Da see that? And so, Soillse sent a blessing to the ladd and then rolled over and closed her eyes.

It was half a moon before she saw the new boy again. She and Ceit spent those weeks storing nuts and meal in the pits, drying fish in the cooking hut, and gathering fuel for the long winter nights. So Soillse had no time to see what all the ladds were doing in the yard. She kept her distance from them, anyway, since that druid man had hurt her a skyturn before. But today was Midwinter morning, her favorite ceremony of the year.

This day, they always rose in darkness, before the Sun Lord hurled His first spears over the eastern hills. The ceremonial new fire must be started just as those rays lit the standing stone, for the year's blessings would be missed if they lit it too late. Soillse thought how she loved the Sun Lord, King of heaven. His arms were warm and stronger even than Da's, holding her safe against the cold all winter long. Maybe I love Him even better than my Aine tree, she thought. And today, He brought the promise of spring's return. And suddenly, Soillse realized how glad she was that this skyturn was passing, getting further away from the one in which that druid had hurt her woman's place. Then, as she lay still on her pallet in the morning dark, she had a glimpse of the Sun Lord in her mind, and His blue eyes held sorrow just for her. And she wished again that she could reach through the worlds, just once, and touch His shining face.

The druid, Coillore, in his white woolen robe and heavy goatskin cloak, stood beneath the standing stone with seven of the older lads. While Eilid, in her ceremonial hide dress and heavy blue woolen shawl, and the girls, in their winter woolen shifts, fur jerkins, and heaviest shawls, climbed the path, Seumus followed with the rest of the lads, also in their clan plaids and fur-lined jerkins. The ladds already beneath the standing stone were the boys Coillore trained in the lore one evening every quarter moon. In two skyturns, I'll go to the druid circle, too, Soillse thought, pulling her shawl tighter against the wind. And then, as the boys began the chant to the Sun Lord, Soillse's scalp began to tingle, and she hurried ahead of Eilid and Ceit to squeeze into the circle around the standing stone.

Everyone sang the chant to Arte, (arsta, Arthur, father god of the Luckenbooth light structure), calling forth his blessings on the clan: a year unperturbed by sorrow, a fruitful harvest and plentiful game, births unmarred by death or disease for both clanfolk and stock. The song had the cadence of a procession in it, and Soillse closed her eyes and began to sway as she sang. And then Coillore chanted the song of the Sun Lord's return, the rhythm speeding and the voices of the ladds growing louder as Coillore snapped the flint and sent sparks into the dry grasses on the ground. It lit! First try, she thought, as a happy murmur spread through the crowd. And then, Coillore bent his head to the Sun Lord. They all did, as the Sun Lord's long-armed golden radiance spilled over the far hills and onto their bowed forms.

This Midwinter morning, Soillse noticed that the first lance of light fell across the Goddess spiral carved into the standing stone. And the next one lit Coillore's small face, darker skinned than most, the coloring of the olden folk of the isles, his moustache and long greying hair shining in the sudden radiance. Then finally, the third ray settled on the new ladd's brow. As the light rested there, Firinn bent his head back to receive it and seemed to draw within. The first rays brought great blessings to those Arte favored each Midwinter dawn, and Soillse nodded to Firinn from behind Eilid's plaid as the chant ended. He was thinner than when she'd seen him before, but at least his face was clean, his thick chestnut hair blowing in the breeze as he watched the Sun Lord within the press of boys, just a short way round the circle from herself.

As the sunshine expanded over them all, Firinn glanced at her. And she smiled and sent the thought that she hoped he was happy here at the fostering. And then the chanting began again, this time the song of thanks for the Sun Lord's return out of winter's cauldron of darkness. All turned to face Him and bent, just like grasses in the wind, leaning as one toward the light. Their song carried out over the bay and into the sea, and no one moved until it was done.

Then all the ladds began to run, some singing the rollicking song of the new year with its adventures to come. But most raced to the yard to grab up their bowls and warm themselves with hot morning oats, sweetened this firstsky with nuts, dried fruits, and honey for the celebration. Soillse sang, too, her small voice drowned out by the chorus of male ones around her. But the new ladd did not race down with the rest. He stood apart now, his face glowing with spirit light as she turned to stare. He'll be a druid, she thought suddenly. Perhaps I'll be a priestess then, and she smiled softly, wishing she could tell him about her Aine tree. She noticed that his eyes were as green as the hills in the Holly moon (June), and as their eyes met, she felt a shiver in her heart that ran all the way down to her feet. '*I ken ye*' she sent the thought in surprise. '*I ken ye from the Otherworld. I'm sure of it.*'

'*Aye, lass*', she heard clearly in her mind. '*I see ye go to the apple tree oft times. It must be quiet there.*' And even in her mind, Soillse felt the wistful tone of his thought. '*I think we've been friends before, too.*' Then he turned and walked slowly down the path. As Ceit and Eilid finished spreading newly ground meal in a circle beneath the standing stone, Soillse's heart beat so fast that she wondered at the powers of that Fìrinn-ladd.

Chapter Eleven: Fìrinn

In Celtic society, each tuath had its chief, but over large land areas such as the Isle of Skye, a high chief was chosen by the druid council to handle disputes among the tribes. And because the high king of Skye was rapidly aging, many ladds at the fostering had it in their minds to enter the challenge for kingship after his passing. In those days, the high seat was not a birthright, but had to be won on merit, and there were many youths from wide-ranging tuaths with noble blood in their veins who could qualify as contenders. The druids believed the Sun Lord had chosen one man to be their king from the very beginning, and the competitions simply allowed them to discover who that man was. Installing him insured divine favor, bringing successful hunts, full harvests, and flawless sons and daughters to the clans. But a mistake in choosing could bring disaster for years to come. Physical deformity in a contender immediately disqualified the man who bore it, a sure sign of disfavor from above. But many were the signs of grace, from gifts of song or speech to negotiation in dispute to prowess in battle or sport. And to the watchful eyes of Seumus and Coillore, the kingship always in the back of their minds, Fìrinn's inner steadiness was beyond the ordinary, a silent ripening power that clearly marked him for leadership.

There was another watching Fìrinn closely, too, the boy with the falcon eye, the one Duineil had called "Duirc" (derk, small dagger) that first night Fìrinn arrived at the fostering.

"Clan o' the snake, descended from yer Da's great uncle. Has ye're Da told ye nothin' at all about contenders for the crown, laddie?" And Duineil had looked at Fìrinn askance that first night. "The ladd wants to be high king o' Skye more'n he wants his life, an' he's determined to better the likes o' ye. Ye watch ye're step wi' him, ladd," Duineil had warned.

One cloudy winter's day, Allaidh, an older, large-boned ladd, and Duirc were pitted in wrestling, fighting in their hide breeks in the mud of the yard. And the fighting became so intense that all the boys stopped their sports and came to watch. Once Duirc was pinned down so long that the muscle in his leg began to give way. But he only turned a fierce eye on it, willing it not to tear. And then he waited, timing his next move with predator vigilance to wrest his place atop Allaidh, smiling at the wince on Allaidh's face as he did so. Fìrinn noted Duirc's hatred of failure in that moment, but there was something else he didn't quite understand, malice toward the skill of others perhaps. Finally the yardmaster held up a hand, giving the match to Duirc and shouting out his nickname, Spòg (spaawk), 'the claw.'

The only more persistent adversary that winter was the wind woman, biting their bones day after day. Fìrinn's fingers went so stiff during the Rowan moon (February) that he could barely grip his spears. But by late in the Alder moon (March), the cold eased a bit, and though the wind still gnawed through his jerkin, Fìrinn could sense sprouts gathering beneath the soil.

Before the seasons turned once more, it was clear that Fìrinn had the makings of a master lancer. He could sense the distance of a throw and feel the pull of the wind woman without hesitation, loosing the shafts in a way that looked as effortless as they were precise. Ruadh (rooey, red), a quiet spindly boy of ten winters from the clan of the horse, had won the spear-throwing contests for the younger ladds at the clan games last summer. So when he could take time away from the sport of the yard, Fìrinn began studying Ruadh's throws with a keen eye. At dusk on many a winter evening, Fìrinn stood at the longhouse door, holding himself separate from the general shoving and belching of the evening meal. And by the end of the Alder moon (March), Ruadh was sharing the mealtime doorway with Fìrinn.

A week later, in the last thrust of the dark one's spell, the boys woke to find the water skins filmed with ice. General groaning ensued and a more spirited tussle for hearth spaces than usual. Fìrinn kept to his bed furs, watching till all the ladds were huddled round the hearth. Then he rose quickly, flinging his jerkin on over his buckskin breeks and leather shirt, and wound his way to the fire. A hush fell on the group, and some wished the strange new boy would finally curse the cold or start a rip-roaring fight for a hearth space. But Fìrinn only leaned in between a couple of younger ladds to heft one of the hearthstones up against his hip. He wove back through the mass of boys and dropped the stone at the doorway, letting it fall with a thud on the packed earth. And then he went to fill his bowl. Curled in around the stone's warmth just inside the door, he sat facing the brightening darkness outside and began to eat.

"Wish I'd thought o' that," one of the younger ladds whispered to his neighbor with a sideways glance.

The cold clung to the bay without ceasing then, day after day, for half a moon. Hoar covered the heather, and the ice on the water skins thickened. Fìrinn's hands and feet ached from the cold, even in the bright sunshine between the sleety rains, and the boys taunted each other relentlessly. All felt bound by the crone goddess's grip, increasingly restless for spring.

One evening, as the Willow moon (April) approached, Fìrinn sat eating his stirabout when one of the deerhounds loped by, snuffling near the door. She was white, unusual for the hounds, the great length of her graceful, too. And she was tall, for her long head would nearly reach Fìrinn's own if he were standing. Fìrinn watched the dog closely, looking into her dark gentle eyes framed by a wiry muzzle, then suddenly threw her the rest of his meal. Startling backward, the dog eyed him sharply, then quickly wolfed it down. She waited, watching for more and licking her face.

"Hey!" Allaidh bolted up from his pallet, one of the elder lads assigned to keep order in the group. He was the largest of the boys, tall, bulky, and broad shouldered. "Ye think that's a pup ye're feedin'? Or maybe ye have a puny mind! It's us older ladds have to go off lookin' fer game every mornin', an' scarcer than honey it is these cursed frozen days. Ye think it's fun to go trackin' through the cold? The bitch can hunt her own dinner!" As Allaidh advanced, Fìrinn rose, calm as ever. But Ruadh emerged from the crowd of boys and stood, blocking Allaidh's path.

"It's his meal, Allaidh. For the gods' sake, leave him be. We're tired o' yer gripin'. Dinna ye think the cold's eatin' us all? Besides, ye'll be havin' ta feed the dogs wi' yer own dinner soon, if yer girdle gets any bigger. (The Celts had strict requirements against obesity.) Fìrinn willna get any more stew, so what's it to ye if he goes hungry?" At this, the side of Allaidh's mouth curved slowly up.

"Oh, yeah," he muttered. Then he turned to check his own bowl and dropped back to his place. But Ruadh moved through the boys to sit beside Fìrinn, both still in their heavy hunting breeks and fur jerkins.

"What're ye doin'?," he whispered close to Fìrinn's ear. "Ye'll be starved before this cold lets up. Allaidh's right, the bitch can hunt fer herself."

"No," Fìrinn said firmly, shaking his head. "She'll whelp in a day or two." A small litter, he thought, by the looks of her. "An' her haunch is swollen, see?" Fìrinn pointed to the dog's left hip, and Ruadh stared. He could see a clotting in the hair now that he really looked for it, and a slight bulge of her belly under the scraggly coat. "The cold'll let up tomorrow or the next day, anyway," Fìrinn added. "Canna ye smell the warm, Rue?" But Ruadh only shook his head no.

Fìrinn fed the deerhound half his dinner the next night, too, and with that she disappeared into the hills. The frost went, also, the following morning, the sky crimson over the Cuchullins across the sea loch as the boys paired off after the firstsky meal. And then lowering clouds blew in before midsky, and the cold gave way to a lukewarm drizzle that lasted for days, soaking the ladds through even their best oiled skins.

But on the third morning, the east wind ceased its constant pushing, and a playful south breeze came in like a lilting girl off the sea. Firinn emerged from the longhouse and felt a bit lost in the soft breeze, the way a warrior might feel after slaying his most determined foe. How easy it'll be to sport all summer, he thought, without the wind woman's bite! And then he thought suddenly how his mother's image had faded from his mind, too. He couldn't easily recall the way her hair fell about her shoulders or the cadence of her voice. As he stood and watched the waves, he realized that the separation from his Ma was strengthening him, just as Da had predicted. By degrees so fine he'd barely noticed it, the pain of her absence had faded from his heart. Glancing at the Cuchullin peaks, he realized his memory of her had coalesced somehow, particle by particle, just the way those mountains had formed long ago. Her love didn't wear a face anymore, but it was there, a solid force deep within that supported him, as strong and enduring as the hills themselves.

That afternoon, Firinn smiled as his sixth spear hit its mark. He thought with a startle how his Da had been right again. The thrill of mastery, born to him, had finally come to life. As he gathered up his spears, Firinn grinned at the thinning clouds and pulled in a deep breath of earth-scented air. Maybe I will be a chieftain after all, he thought.

As the ladds lined up for their evening meal, the last of the clouds rolled away, and the sun finally broke though. The boys ate out in the yard to steep in the evening rays, finally, without their heavy winter jerkins and breeks. How soft the light doeskins felt on Firinn's legs, and he stretched out in his summer jerkin on the rocks by the bay. After the warmth had come in a few days before, the hills had gone from brown to green, too, and the south-facing slopes were purpling with spring heath.

"Race ye to the summit, there!," one of the older boys called out to Allaidh. And both took off at a lope for the standing stone on the ridge. The rest joined them, swarming up the hill like bees. Panting and pushing, a few of the older boys reached the stone first and turned to look out across the loch at the Cuchullins. This night, the sheer peaks emerged out of banks of fluffy pink clouds that hugged the sea. Several boys gasped, staring, for the rugged heights shone in the sun like a long lost castle on high. Two boys broke into song, and another threw himself into a fling.

Firinn climbed slowly among the stragglers as the boy's laughter rang out over the bay and reverberated back to him. He stopped to watch a hawk riding the breeze down the spine of the land. I envy ye yer freedom, he thought, royal bird, and absently hummed the ballad the ladds were singing, a warrior's song of victory. Then suddenly, Firinn realized it was the freedom of the wild things he'd ached for all along, freedom from the wishes of his Ma, his Da, adversaries who wanted to be king, and even foster fathers training him to be as rugged as those peaks across the bay. After the others left for the longhouse, Firinn sat beside the high stone, his heart strangely moved.

"Goddess an' Sun Lord," he said, suddenly raising one arm high. "I want freedom, freedom to be who I really am, freedom to love me people an' this land, to keep me closeness wi' the tree an' plant people, as much as I like. This is Da's hawk clan legacy to me, I ken it. It wasna huntin' prowess he planted in me veins at all, but this ache for real freedom." Firinn knelt before the high stone and put his brow to the earth. "Sun Lord, show me the path," he whispered, then stood slowly and turned to leave. As he began down the track Firinn heard the haunting cry of the hawk and shivered from head to toe. Then he watched the bird, wings wide, glide out over the sea to lose itself in the bright expanse.

Chapter Twelve: Soillse

Over the summer, Soillse took to rambling the woods in the gloaming after the evening meal. At six winters, her legs were strong with all the carrying she did. And if the fog made the way invisible or it rained too hard, she sat in her Aine tree, wrapped in an oiled skin, instead, trying to keep the sound of the boys taunting each other out of her mind. But she preferred to climb the deer track beside the burn and melt into the forest, far enough away from the yard for real peace and quiet. Eilid didn't mind, as long as Soillse never went out of the bowl of the bay, certainly never as far as the loch on the ridge where the high grasses grew. Often Soillse just walked off the deer track up beside the burn and sat on the big boulder there, the one with the view of the bay, with her own silence for company. Her hair was always windblown, still wispy and straight, down to her waist. But she'd lengthened now, the chubbiness gone from her cheeks. Still, there was ever something of the pixie in Soillse's small frame, and she had Eilid's gentle eyes and quiet ways, but Seumus's strong chin, heavy brows, and cherry nose, though hers was much more delicate than his.

Today she decided to follow a smaller trail that angled north into the woods farther up the trail along the burn. It was early fall now, the Ivy moon (late September), and it had been damp all day long. As she walked in her stained cooking shift, wrapped in her wool plaid, the fog thickened. But Soillse didn't mind, thinking how every step took her into some woodland mystery that would be revealed only at the last moment. Soillse had always loved the mist maiden, anyway, with her soft silky ways. The lass decided the faeries must come and go in these sheltering mists, doing their special work without any human interference at all.

The path narrowed for a time, and then she came to a wee burn that crossed the track with a large yew blocking the way. Beyond the yew, she caught a glimpse of a small hut, no bigger than the cooking hut at home, and she hesitated. It was a wattle and mud hut, built right in amongst the birches, with only this narrow deer track going past. Curious, she stepped over the trickle of a burn and peeked round the yew. Immediately, she startled back, for the druid Coillore was sitting on a rock in the middle of the wee burn. With only a summer robe on, made of homespun with rolled-up sleeves, he was washing pebbles and feathers in the stream. She thought how like an elf he looked, so small, with his long moustache and hair, and his tiny house in the mist. Best not to disturb a druid, she thought, and turned to run back home.

"I willna harm ye, lassie," Coillore said without looking up, "but ye can go, if it's yer pleasure. I have a gift fer ye, though. Ye might want to take it before ye leave."

So Soillse stepped timidly past the yew to see what he offered. Without making the slightest sound, Coillore stood and held out his hand. In his palm was a small clear crystal. And smiling in spite of herself, Soillse reached out to pick it up.

"What is it?"

"Quartz, lassie. It helps wi' healin', especially if a child has been harmed in some way. There's a livin' spirit in the stone that, slowly an' gently, softens whatever a child fears most an' brings that wounded place into balance wi' all life." She glanced quickly up at Coillore's face a moment, wondering if he knew she'd been hurt by that druid two skyturns ago. And then she was held by something in Coillore's eyes. They were sky-blue and felt as happy as a sunny morning. And they were kind, kinder even than Da's. He reminded her of someone from the Otherworld, but she couldn't think who. Then Coillore pulled a bright yellow shell out of the pocket of his robe. It was small and round, edged in earth brown, and inside, it was bright peach. She'd never seen a shell like that and, gingerly, she reached out to touch it on his palm.

"I found that a couple o' winters ago in the bay after a storm, washed up from far southern lands, a very long journey for a wee shell, I'd say. It wants to go wi' ye, too, it tells me, if ye want it, that is." He pointed to a heap of stones and assorted feathers on the ground. "Just washin' the dust off. I have plenty, see?" She nodded, put out her hand, and he placed the shell into it.

"Why're ye givin' me these things, Coillore? Dinna they have powers o' some kind?"

"Aye, but all things do," he said and paused. "I was hopin' to convince ye I might be yer friend, lassie, and that I'll never harm ye at all." He glanced down at her new shell before meeting her eyes again. "Well, an' if a thing says it wants to be somewhere else, it's best to let it go there as well." A shadow passed over his eyes as he said this, but then he smiled at her again.

She had the sudden feeling that Coillore, too, had been hurt, and it was why he lived hermit-like in the hills, and why he'd taken up druid training in the first place. And in that instant, she felt Coillore would understand her as no one else could. She'd be safe with him; she just knew it. This place would be a refuge when she needed one. And then she had the sudden feeling that Coillore would shield her during some harshness of her life to come, when she was grown-up maybe. And again, the dim memory of someone she'd loved in the Otherworld flickered through her mind. And her heart opened to the druid gently, like the wild roses of the Oak moon (June).

"I was just about to have me evenin' meal, lassie. Are ye hungry?" Smoke was rising from the roof hole, and Soillse smelled mushroom stew. She shook her head no, for she'd eaten already, but there was a nutty scent in the air that made her curious. What do druids keep in their huts, anyway?, she wondered.

"I'd have a taste, though," she said, peering at the door.

The hut was wattle and daub, the thatch still green, as if it had been recently changed. But the ends were uncut and ragged, hanging low over the eaves, looking more like hair than a roof. And the door was a finely tanned doeskin with the symbol for Yew burned into it. He smiled, bowed, and pointed to the door

"What's that for?," she asked, pointing to the Ogham letter,

"Small i is the symbol for the final release o' shadows an' the full emergence o' light into the physical realms," he said. "It lets the dark one ken she has no power here."

Soillse stooped under and went in. In the gloaming, the interior was dusky, though an opening had been built into the southern wall that was lined with a thin oiled skin. The window made it brighter than any hut she'd ever been in, and the cauldron was bubbling, too, with flat breads baking on two of the hearthstones near the fire. A pallet lay on the floor to the right, and on the other side of the hearth was an altar, where a bowl of fats burned. Beside it sat a bowl of water, another of earth, and one that was empty in the circle of the elements. And inside them was a mandala with seven concentric circles, drawn into the earthen floor. A white glittering stone figure of the Goddess sat in the very center, Tara looking quite beautiful in a long clinging robe, and Her face caught the firelight and sparkled up at Soillse. On either side of the altar were shells, stones and sparkling crystals, feathers and teeth, heaped against the wall. Into the floor at the corners of the altar were four more symbols, a butterfly, a lamb, a lion, and a swan. What do those mean?, Soillse wondered to herself.

"Those are symbols o' the four basic aspects o' God an' Goddess: the girl an' boy, father an' mother. They're also the parts o' every person within, even if on the outside they look like only one." And he touched his left abdomen, right abdomen, right shoulder, and left shoulder in turn, "girl, boy, father, an' mother, all revolvin' around the Beloveds in the very center," he said, touching his heart. "All beings in all worlds have this five-fold structure in the image o' the One."

But she'd only half heard him, startled to think that he could read her thoughts. I better be careful what I let into me head when he's around, she told herself. But the druid only smiled as he bent to add a log to the fire. "I hope ye can just be yerself here, lassie. I willna think ill o' ye for yer thoughts."

Watching as he stirred the soup, Soillse felt a preternatural power in the hut and sensed that Coillore knew far more than he expressed. He has visitors from the Otherworld here, she thought, and decided that he and the faeries she loved must be the best of friends. The sacredness of the altar especially drew her. I want an altar like that, she thought, and wondered suddenly why she hadn't realized this before, so deeply did it tug at her heart.

Dried flowers and herbs hung from every branch of the rafters, and she sniffed the sharp scents of sage and yarrow over the soup. In the plant people hanging there, she could feel the wild freedom of the hillsides, hints of spring, summer, and autumn infusing the wee room. Beside the fire, three shell plates of mushrooms lay drying, and her mouth began watering as the bread browned. Everything was carefully placed and ordered, despite the small space. It's homey. I like it here, she thought.

Coillore motioned her to sit on a low stump beside the hearth, as he took up two shell bowls and ladled soup into each one. Then he reached for two large dried leaves from a stack near the door and placed a piece of flatbread on one and laid it next to her, taking the other for himself. Then he bent his head and asked the Sun Lord and the Goddess to bless the meal and especially the sacred spirit of this little girl. His eyes were moist as he lifted them again, and then he tipped his bowl up and began to eat. The soup was rich and delicious, with an earthy taste she hadn't had in at least a skyturn.

'Mmmmm,' she thought without speaking, to see if he could hear. He grinned then, as he took a skin bladder from a peg on the wall and handed it to her. The water had a sweet summer flavor, and she raised her brows and looked at him as she drank.

"I put a wee mulberry in for flavor, just a hint," he said, and one side of his mouth lifted. 'Mmmmm,' she thought again. 'I ken where ye found those,' and she imagined a clearing a little way further up the ridge. He nodded, and she grinned.

Soillse wiped the bowl clean with her bread and ate it, then leaned back on the wall and closed her eyes. It feels like the cooking hut here, she thought, as if Ma or Muirn had just fixed a bite for two, a cozy little meal away from the chores for a while. And there's a softness in the air I havena felt in long and long, since I was a babe, she thought, some spirit presence that doesna come to the round house anymore. This stirred another vague memory, but she was too tired to think about it now. Full and drowsy, she wished she could just curl up on the pallet and didn't have to climb back home in the fog. Sighing, she handed Coillore the shell, then wrapped her plaid around her shoulders and stood.

"Ma'll be frantic, if I stay too late," she said. "She gets nervous, ever since I went off lookin' for the Sun Lord that time."

"I've sent her clear thoughts o' yer safety, lassie," he said, rising, too. "But ye need yer rest. Do ye want me to walk back wi' ye?"

"No thanks, Coillore. It isna far, an' the gloamin's still light enough to see the way." As she moved to the door skin, she looked back over the little room. Oh, I wish I could come again, she thought. It's free in here.

"Come whenever ye can, lassie. If I'm in the hills, busy wi' the spirit world or off to the druid isle, ye may come in an' have the peace o' it. I'm pleased to offer ye a bit o' comfort. Ye're a very special child." He spoke softly, but there was a breathy vehemence in his words that made her stare.

"I wouldna come in wi'out ye home," she said. "Da'd be mad, if he knew."

"Well, it's all right wi' me, if ye do. An' I'll tell me spirit friends no to startle ye, either. How 'bout that? So ye're as safe as sunshine here." And he spoke the blessing of safety over her as he placed his hand lightly on her head.

As she moved into the fog, she heard rustling and glanced back to see a great horned owl land on the thatched roof. Coillore was holding his hand out to it, and she felt fae folk hiding in the moss-covered trees, ready to emerge the moment she was gone. Even Coillore, smiling at her with his long hair and staff, looked like a wizard in his emerald cloak.

She scampered back along the small track to the burn in the half-light and splashed barefoot in the water all the way down the hill, instead of walking on the path. And she felt warmth on her head where Coillore had laid his hand, too, warmth that lasted till she closed her eyes in her own bed furs. And that night, she dreamed of talking animals, flowers that winked, and trees that laughed out loud.

Chapter Thirteen: Fìrinn

The deerhound returned one night in early summer, half a moon after the purification fires of Bealltain (beealchen). As the gloaming deepened and the torches were brought out, she loped down from the heights with three half grown young and clumps of winter coat hanging from her flanks. Nosing around the bonfire and the yard, she settled herself beside Fìrinn without so much as a wag of her tail. Then resting her great head on her paws, she watched her pups tumble by the firelight.

Though Fìrinn gave the dog no more food, now that she could hunt for herself, her wise black eyes followed him everywhere. Instead of leftover stirabout, she seemed to feed on Fìrinn's smile or the way he ran his fingers through her coat. He named her Bana Dhia Bhàn (bahna yeeah vaahn, the White Goddess). And after her pups were taken into training by the hunt master during the Reed moon (October), the dog came into the longhouse of a night and rested her long nose and sparse whiskers on Fìrinn's bedfurs while he slept.

Summer flowed into fall, fall to winter, and back to spring again, and then another cycle. Fìrinn grew tall and wiry, and began to move up through the ranks of skill, Ruadh and Bana Dhia his constant companions now. During his third summer at the fostering, the great games would be held. Every five skyturns all the clans of the isles and the highlands converged on the mainland for the festival of Lughnasa (loonahsa, August 5th) to thank the goddess Cìrcaidh (keerkay, earth mother goddess of the Circle of Eight), bearer of harvests. So at the start of the Apple moon, tribes from every tuath on Skye crossed the narrow channel to the mainland to meet in the fertile valley of the clan of the bear, in what is now Applecross. At the great games, the best warriors of each clan competed in trials of skill, and always there were competitions for the younger ladds, too. The winners came home with a metal-worked knife perhaps or a bronze talisman. Fìrinn didn't expect to place in the competitions his first time there, but all summer he watched Ruadh throw spear after spear during the gloamings after the evening meal. And finally, unable to sit still, Fìrinn began throwing spears himself, the shafts whirring through the heated air. As the days lengthened, the preparation of the chosen few grew fierce, Ruadh staying up well into the night, which never fully darkened at midsummer. And finally, when their eyes began to glaze over, he and Fìrinn dropped on their bedfurs for a short sleep before dawn.

On an overcast morning, warm even for summer, the boys set out for the mainland in straggling groups, marching north along the ridge in light summer doeskin breeks, following the spine of the land. Shouting and laughing, they stayed in high spirits, despite the heat and the dust of the afternoons. Crossing the flat plains and moving northeast on the second day, they wove their way inland, singing across the high moors.

As they reached the crossroad and turned east on the track that, taken west, led to his own tuath, Fìrinn wondered about Ma. Will she come to the games?, he thought. It'll be her only chance to see me now. Bana Dhia sensed his musings, too, for the dog nosed his fingers and whined as they turned away. Fìrinn saw wistful glances on some of the other boy's faces, too, as they walked that day.

Then, as they came to the high ridge above the channel to the mainland, late in the afternoon, rain began pouring down. Few of the ladds minded, though, for with the drops came welcome coolness and the dust of the trail washed off. Many folk were already making the crossing, the channel as wide as a broad river, and Fìrinn was surprised to find the mainland so close to Skye after all. Burly clansmen in large rafts were ferrying the folk across, and the boys had to wait for a time at the shore. But finally, they piled on several rafts, dangling their feet in the water. Some ladds splashed their neighbors, and others pointed to the otters, playful and sleek, swimming beside them as they crossed. Many a ladd longed to throw off his dirty breeks and jump in beside the creatures, and Fìrinn was utterly charmed by the otter's childlike faces. He reached out to brush his hand along a wet back as one leaped by, and it sent an electric thrill up his arm that he felt for hours afterwards.

They walked the rest of that day, skirting a large hill, and camped that night on a low ridge, overlooking the floodplain of the river southwest of Applecross, a day's march south of the gathering place. Waking early, they forded the fast flowing stream and walked through mountainous tracks to look down on a great cupped plain. Spread below were dozens of campfires, all around the valley and nestled up into the hills. Clan folk from many tuaths mingled together amidst the hearths, more people than Fìrinn had ever seen. And his heart sped as he gaped. Who are these folk, he wondered. Are their tuaths different from mine?

He lay long awake that night, watching lightning flicker across the southern skies and feeling the heightened pulse of the Goddess beneath him as Lughnasa approached. When dusk deepened past midnight, the clouds suddenly cleared, and hundreds of stars twinkled like miniature bonfires above him in the blackness. And suddenly, Fìrinn felt his spirit clan watching over him, the tuath of his ancestors, and in the comfort of this, he slept.

Next morning, on their arrival at the broch of the clan of the bear, the boys lined up at great wooden tubs near the river for their baths of welcome. These were presided over by the women of the tribe, a clan ruled by a tall great-grandmother and all her offspring. Moonstar, the matriarch was called, living in a large broch beside the sea. The lands were rich and fertile here, enough to nourish so many, and the valley was full of apple trees, a sure sign of the Goddess, the White Tara.

All knew that Alba, the whole of it, was shaped like the Goddess Herself, with Skye Her right hand and the Finn (fin, boy god of the Creator Sun) isle (Mull) east of Iona, Her left. The far northwest was Her peaked wise woman hat and the northeast Her great bag full of delights for all Her earth children. But this valley lay over Her heart, and that was why the games were hosted here every fifth summer.

Fìrinn lounged in the tub, letting the warm water soothe his sore feet and wishing he could take more than the short time allotted. He hated the thought of dressing in his wool kilt for the ceremony of the clans, for he'd grown used to buckskin breeks on his legs. But it was worth it in the end, for at moonrise all the clans gathered in their many colors.

As the druids blew the horns, each tuath began marching in procession, led by the bodhrans (flat drum) and pipes into the nemeton, hidden deep in the valley. Each clan processed to the place within the compass of twelve sacred trees that was aligned with their homeland. So Fìrinn stood with his fostering in the northwestern arm, peering nearby to see if any from his home tuath had come so far. All the folk stood just outside the ring of oaks, while the druids within chanted the opening hymn to the low thrum of pipes.

As the horns blared again, formally opening the games, the great invocation to the earth mother, Cìrceidh, was sung by all the clans at once, the men colorful in their plaids and light homespun shirts, the women with clan sashes pinned over their ceremonial hide robes. And as the whole multitude bent to the ground, honoring the earth goddess, tingles surged down Fìrinn's spine. Standing then, the people sang the song of thanksgiving to the Goddess, Tara: for the harvest to come, the families gathered round, and life itself. As the song crescendoed, Fìrinn thanked Tara for Her personal love that had nurtured him at the fostering in the absence of his Ma, and he saw tears in the eyes of many. As the druids in the nemeton passed the ritual potion, each priest leaned back against one of the oaks of the nemeton. And watching them drink, Fìrinn felt a rippling in his chest, like a living thing fluttering inside, and he wondered at himself.

Then the priestesses filed out in their long, ivory robes, any who'd had bairns, chanting the Goddess's song of life, for Lughnasa was the mother impulse in the circle of seasons. Then the women passed their own ritual broth as well, kneeling round the altar to listen for the Goddess voice within. Some rose and spoke to the women's circle in voices too soft for Fìrinn to hear. But some called out loudly to the crowds, telling of the Goddess's love or the promise of a fruitful year. One said a challenge would come to the tribes of the north, late in the Ivy moon.

After a time, the harps began playing among the throngs outside the grove, holding the people in silence during the divinations. And as the music rippled round him, Fìrinn felt waves of tenderness from Màiri, the great mother (mother goddess of the Creator Sun), her love flowing like water over everyone. He was amazed at the sweet peace that filled the air as he sat in the dusk beside Bana Dhia. And then, he felt Màiri come to him, alone among so many. She whispered that she'd be his mother now and to call on her whenever he had need, that she'd comfort him always.

And in another moment, he felt the Goddess, Tara, Mother-of-all, instead, for the Apple moon belonged to Her. He sensed watery streams of light spilling from Her heart into his own, into everyone's, and saw Her bonds of light connecting all the folk, then strengthen and deepen, fusing them into one great family of Alba. Growing light-headed with the intoxication of Tara's tenderness, his heart was filled to overflowing with love; for Her, this land that was Her own, and these clans. Then, at a signal from the arch druid, all the folk stood and took hands once more, swaying and singing the blessing of the mother for the skyturn, slowly and gently, like a lullaby. Then the whole company sent a rousing 'hurrah' of thanks skyward into the night.

Whole tuaths drifted off together then, in silence mostly, leaving the druids to their all night rituals. As Fìrinn milled through the crowd, watching the faces of so many strangers, questions leaped into his mind. He longed to stop and ask the islanders about the western seas or the north men about the secrets of their mountains, even the women about birthings in their sacred caves. As he walked beside some, he could feel their longings, as if the Goddess had handed him the keys to their dreaming. It made his chest heavy with some sadness he didn't understand. And finally, back at Seumus's hearth circle, with his head swirling, he unwrapped his plaid and lay down beneath it in only his light summer shirt.

The next two days passed bright and hot, competitors raising dust in the games circle during sunlit afternoons. Fìrinn searched the crowds for a glimpse of Ma, and once sighted his Da, in his light summer shirt and plaid, on the raised platform of the chiefs. But Ma wasn't with him, and disappointment sank deep into Fìrinn's belly. He felt intensely drawn to the druids in their white, green, and brown robes, too, watching them from the fringes of their enclaves and wishing he knew those hand signals they sent each other. And every evening, the ladd spent time wandering among the clans, his heart speeding as he listened to the music of their various dialects, wishing he could sit at the hearth fires of them all.

On the third and last day, Ruadh would compete in the spear throwing competition, and Fìrinn stayed nearby in case Ruadh had need of him. That morn dawned sunny and cool, with a light easterly breeze. Not enough wind to deflect a well-thrown spear, Fìrinn thought with a smile, as he and Ruadh, in their summer doeskin shirts and breeks, carried the spears to the gaming grounds. Just past midsky, the crowds gathered, and the games master called the competitors forward. And Fìrinn startled with surprise when his own name was called near the end of the list. What's Seumus doing? I'm only ten winters, he thought. And his chest tensed as he walked to his place in the line-up behind Ruadh, Bana Dhia following. Ruadh was twelve winters now, and his spare highland frame was lengthening into unusual tallness, his red hair thick and wavy down his back.

Twenty-seven clans were represented in this competition of younger ladds, with fifty-eight contestants altogether. Absently, Fìrinn fingered Bana Dhia's ear as his eyes searched the dais to see if it was Da who'd arranged this public test of his skill. And there was Ma! Fìrinn's heart raced as his eyes soaked her in. She wore a tunic the color of the morning sea, and she looked to be just showing with child, the skin of her face and arms glowing. She smiled and raised her chin as their eyes met, waving and calling out his name. He wondered that she'd traveled the length of Skye during her bearing time, especially since daughters were always needed at the tuath to inherit the land right.

The games master in the center of the field, dressed in a short buckskin shirt and woolen breeks, shouted for quiet and then bellowed out the rules. They'd shoot at increasingly difficult targets until one lancer remained. Fìrinn's stomach balled up, and he felt a fine tremor run through his gut as he picked up his lance. The first target was an upright tree trunk at five pony lengths, and forty-two of the boys sent lances true enough to center not to be deflected, Fìrinn's among them. That was easy, he thought, as he went to the back of the line. The second target consisted of five concentric circles, drawn in the earth at six pony lengths. Only thirty-four lances struck the central ring, the shafts quivering as the crowds cheered. Fìrinn's spear hit the circle at the edge of the innermost ring, but the judges allowed him to continue. Nervous in front of so many, Fìrinn was inwardly disappointed as he stood in line behind Ruadh, waiting his next turn. The third target was a gourd, hung from a tree at four pony lengths, very small and curved, a test of skill with the lightweight lances. Fìrinn's spear impaled the belly, and a shout of approval went up for the talent of a ladd so young, while Ruadh's speared the neck precisely, as Fìrinn felt a wave of awe ripple through the crowd. Only seven spear throwers remained.

The final target was a young dove, thrown into the afternoon sky. Ruadh, Fìrinn, and Bana Dhia waited side by side in the heat of the sun. The first contestant, a small dark island boy, pierced his bird through the eye and it fell with a shriek. Ruadh followed and took the next bird through the wing, and it screeched and fluttered in lopsided circles toward the crowd. The next, a burly boy like Allaidh, only grazed his bird's belly, and it soared away with a squawk of outrage. And the next three ladds missed altogether.

When Fìrinn's name was called, Bana Dhia loped out beside him, and his stomach churned. I dinna like killing game, he thought, looking down into the dark pools of Bana Dhia's eyes a moment before turning to watch the bird struggle in the games master's hands. Then faintly in his pounding ears, he heard the voice of the Goddess. *'Let this life go free, dear one. It's not your time.'* Fìrinn nodded and took a long breath as the bird opened into flight, his chest contracting with indecision. Then he loosed his spear, aiming high enough to miss, but not high enough so anyone could tell, he hoped. And the lance sailed over the bird as it flew off into the hills. So Fìrinn came in fifth, Ruadh second. And since only the top three would be recognized, Fìrinn squeezed Ruadh's arm, and headed off into the crowds.

Suddenly, the smell of roasted boar made Fìrinn's stomach burn and his mouth water. I missed the winner's extra portion of meat, too, he thought, frowning and feeling the jitters move down through his legs and feet into the ground. There was one more competition before game's end at sunset, and the games master called for the field to be cleared for the caber toss, bellowing for those contestants to line up on the northern edge of the yard.

As Fìrinn headed for Seumus's tent, boasts could be heard from many hearth circles, arguments about which man deserved the best cut of meat, the mark of honor. A fist fight broke out in one quarter, and Fìrinn lowered his head and hurried past. His temples throbbed, and he wanted just to get away from the crowds and the noise, and be alone. He wished he could go sit by the small loch with the plumed grasses on the ridge near the fostering. And then suddenly, among the large sandaled feet scurrying by, there was a pair of small ones in doeskin slippers. These stopped directly in front of him, blocking his path, and he very nearly stepped on them. Looking up swiftly, Fìrinn's eyebrows shot up. Ma! Her high cheeks were rosy, her wavy acorn hair tied back with a thong. And then he thought, I must've grown, for me eyes are higher than hers now. And her belly is definitely bulging. But at the thought of hugging her, Fìrinn tightened his fingers in Bana Dhia's fur.

"Fìrinn-ladd," she said, grinning and pulling his chin up lightly with one finger. "Ye've brought much honor to us this day. I thought ye'd be a lancer." Then her eyes fell to Bana Dhia, and she smiled more broadly. "What's her name?"

"I could have done better...," Fìrinn began and hesitated. Should I tell her about the Goddess voice? And then he thought, no. "But it doesna matter noo," he added quietly, dropping his eyes to the dog. "Her name's Bana Dhia Bhàn, Ma, an' ye are wi' child." Her eyes widened then, and she laughed.

"Ye sound so like yer Da!" Then her smile faded and she paused. "Yes, I am, and no," her voice grew throaty, "ye were the wisest o' the seven, but few there are who ken it: ye, me, an' yer lanky friend, perhaps. Ye choose a most powerful name." She put her hand on Bana Dhia's head, and the dog licked her palm. Fìrinn noticed moisture in his Ma's eyes and tightness around her mouth, and then a sudden ache for his baby days swept over him. And he stood quietly, unsmiling, as it eased.

"There'll be far greater distance than this," she said softly, and put her hand on his shoulder. "I miss ye, too."

"I'd only take away the pain, if I could," he faltered.

"But pain is bound to joy as tightly as the bark to the tree," she said with a soft smile. "If ye cut one down, the other falls also." He looked away quickly then, his mind full of the sudden memory of her bending over his pallet. The image made his mind heady, like the scent of honeysuckle, as she waited for his gaze to return to her. "Son o' me heart," she whispered with soft intensity, "let the wind o' yer life take ye, like the spears ye throw so well. Learn to ride it wi'out fear. The highs an' lows o' our skyturns are gifts o' the Goddess, teachers carefully sent. Only in bendin' to Her Hand will ye lift out o' the one ye are now an' become part o' the wind itself. I am glad for me thoughts o' ye," she said fiercely, her gaze steady, those green eyes he knew so well.

He tried to think of a reply, but none came to mind as he looked at the ground again. Something between them felt so final this time that he caught his breath. What does it mean?, he thought. And then, when he raised his eyes to ask if she felt it, too, she was leaving. He saw her walk toward the dais and step up onto it. Her face glowed strangely in the late afternoon sun, and with her rounded belly, he suddenly felt that he didn't know her anymore. The cocoon that had sheltered him as a child was gone. It was a dream, those infant days, lost like a wisp of milkweed in the afternoon haze of the Apple moon.

And then, in the evening during the closing ceremony, Firinn felt the White Tara come to him, instead, pulling his heart to Her own. Once or twice during the chant, he felt Ma's eyes on him and looked up to find that she was nowhere near. And there was something else wavering at the edge of his awareness, like a mirage ready to emerge out of the winds of dusk. He was glad to lose himself in the songs then, that and the Goddess's love sweeping through the clans in the hush of the moon.

And then, there was the packing up to see to, Seumus shouting orders that flew past in the half dark. Dogs barked until the bustle round many hearths settled down, and eventually the moon set. Then finally, Seumus sent them all to their furs.

Just past sunrise, Ruadh tugged at Fìrinn's arm, waking him. And they ate cold porridge in their leather traveling breeks and shirts, bleary-eyed, then rolled up their furs and slung on their rolls to leave. But as the line of boys straggled out of the crowded field, Fìrinn's Ma appeared on the rise ahead of them. She walked quickly to the edge of the track they'd travel toward the channel, her old green cloak held tightly around her shoulders, her bright hair blowing furiously in the wind. Oh, let the gods keep her from saying something Allaidh or Duirc'll hear and taunt me with for a skyturn, Fìrinn thought. And he hurried ahead of the group. But Frithe made no move to speak to him, only stood taller as he approached. A stray tear or two fell down her cheek, and then she unsheathed her dagger and held it aloft, the salute to a chief. Her head was high as he walked past, and the ladds stared at her. But thankfully, they had no idea who she was. What, by the Goddess, can she mean?, Fìrinn thought in confusion. And he stopped a moment, nodding to her. But she did not respond, and so he turned, frowning, and marched quickly away.

As they crossed the channel late the next day, Fìrinn ran his hands along Bana Dhia's back and set his mind toward the fostering. He thought of the long house in the morning mist, the upland loch, and the cupped bowl of the bay that was his home now. And then he sighed. It was still a long walk.

That first day back on Skye was dry and hot, and the boys stripped down to their loincloths and kept breaking ranks to find a burn to dunk their heads in. And then the second afternoon brought a brief hard rain, and they slipped in the muck, laughing. Mud balls were slung about for a while, and Seumus threw up his hands and simply laughed at their antics. And then they had to find a burn to rinse off in before they could move on.

Late in the day, the wind picked up, and as they crested the ridge coming down the central track above the fostering, some of the boys broke into shouts and shoving. Most began racing in complete disorder for the long house door, shouting, "Beat ye to the tubs!" Bonfires and freshly filled baths awaited them, the women hurrying to throw in the heated hearth stones and stir the cauldron.

But Fìrinn lagged behind, stopping a moment at the loch fringed with plumed grasses, gazing at the still reflection of the ridge in the water there. Relief filled him that the games were over, as he followed the rest down the track beside the burn. And then as he came into the yard, he was startled to see Soillse running toward them, holding her stained cooking shift and leather apron up above her knees. Her ash-brown hair shone in the late sun as she shouted and sprinted toward Seumus. The chief grinned, bent to pick her up, and swung her round. As Seumus turned to embrace Eilid and Ceit afterwards, Fìrinn stopped, hoping Soillse would greet him, too. But Seumus suddenly glowered at him and waved Fìrinn toward the long house, hollering.

"Ye ladds stay away from the likes o' me daughters, ye hear? The lassie'll never be hurt in me tuath again!"

So Fìrinn backed sharply away into the yard, wondering what Seumus meant. Who'd hurt Soillse, and what had he done? Then the scent of roasted duck and onion wafted up to him, as he saw the clanswomen place plates of warm greens on the tables in the yard. Better hurry, he thought, his stomach growling, or it'll all be gone, and he ran to catch up. Holding his shell plate, full to toppling with duck and greens and flatbread, Fìrinn looked for a seat on the rocks. But then he gasped as he gazed out beyond the bay. The southern hills had purpled with heather while they'd been away. It looked as if a child, tired of the barren slopes, had poured a cauldron of dye over them as far as the eye could see. Even the air was rosy in the gloaming.

Chapter Fourteen: Soillse

The ladds were away for eleven nights, off to the mainland for the summer games. But Eilid's hip was sore, and meal grinding had worsened it this past moon, so she decided to stay home this time, keeping Ceit and Soillse with her. Seumus said lassies didna belong at the games without their Ma to watch over them. So Sine, Muirn, and several of the older ladds took over the cooking for the trip.

After Eilid started limping this past spring, Seumus began sending the whole fostering out gathering every quarter moon. He put Duineil to meal grinding, and the big warrior swore he didn't mind women's ways, though Soillse thought the tall islander looked comical hunched over the quern stone. With fifty gathering, instead of the eight or ten women of the tuath, the stores filled quickly. It was surprising how little it took to ease Eilid's load. And then, before they left for the games, Seumus told Eilid he wanted her to teach the ladds where to find wild foods. As soon as they returned, he'd make it part of the curriculum, he said. Why should women be the only ones to know such things?

Eilid and the girls, in only their summer shifts, had a picnic on the shore that first night they had the steading to themselves. Ceit carried the food bundle on her back as Eilid limped across the wet sand, smiling. Eilid's brown hair had a few strands of grey now, and there were new creases across her brow from the pain. And Duineil, left behind as guard, brought wood to make a fire. Winking to the lassies, the tall clansman, in only his summer doeskin breeks, carried down the chief's carven chair for Eilid, too. She laughed at that.

"Queen o' an empty tuath," she said, eating bits of apple bread, with Ceit sitting on the sand beside her. "What a difference the quiet makes, eh, lass? I havena had a rest in twenty winters. Noo I've a whole quarter moon to do what I like. What on earth will I find to do wi' meself in all that time?"

The fish, oatcakes, and roasted hazel nuts filled them all to bursting, another thing that rarely happened when the ladds were around. And then Duineil took out his harp and sweetened the evening with its haunting song. As the gloaming grew dusky, sunlight on the horizon burned through the clouds in the far west behind the Cuchullins, and Duineil got up and danced a lilt with Ceit, "to the settin' sun," he said. Soillse lay back in the sand with her eyes closed as Duineil played, finally able to rest, as a lass of eight winters needed to now and then. And Eilid came over and sat beside her, taking the lass into her arms. Then Eilid sang the forever friend song, swaying and laughing, her breasts damp and soft against Soillse's neck.

"I'll be yer forever friend, till ye're back Home in me arms...," she sang, and Soillse's heart vibrated to the tune.

That whole quarter moon Eilid was like another mother altogether, for she called both girls to her, combing and braiding Ceit's dark and Soillse's fair hair in the mornings. And she held them both to her knees by the fire when the nights grew cool, telling stories into the dusk. She told of her Ma and her grandma, how her Ma had been an herb woman and healed even a stray deer with a broken leg one time. With wonder lighting her eyes, Eilid told how that deer came to the birches on the ridge and waited there a whole day when her Ma passed to the Otherworld. And Coillore had told Eilid then that the spirit of that doe, the one Eilid was named for, led her Ma straight to her Creator Sun tuath from the cairn chamber, after she passed to the Otherworld. Eilid told of her grandma, too, how she loved to cook, making stews with currants and wild nuts, always a different thing to make them tasty.

"I dinna have the knack o' that, like me grandma," Eilid said. "She had the sight, an' she knew where to find anythin' at all, she did, roots an' berries we havena seen since. Maybe she had a magic wi' the fae folk to make those tasties grow near the tuath."

Ceit and Eilid stitched tiny clothes for Ceit's old dolly, Rhiann, put away under her pallet long ago, and Eilid looked like a child herself making those wee clothes. Ceit was content to stay near the hut, humming songs with Eilid, instead of running to the hills and back to the sea ten times a day, as she usually did. The elder lass, twelve winters now, was of an age to grow into womanhood and leave behind these childish things, but she still looked more boy than girl, her slim form lithe and strong. They made a plaid and a homespun dress for the doll from bits of cloth Eilid found in the bottom of her storage bags, and even a seed necklace. And Ceit chattered continually through the quiet days, making up games to play with Eilid or Soillse from morn till night. Then as the days of rest came to a close, Ceit decided to make a hide jerkin for Seumus, so good had her stitching become. She'd finish it before his birth celebration this fall. So Eilid helped Ceit cut the pattern from soft buckskin hides and find a storage place to keep it a surprise for him. Those last two days, Ceit sang as she worked on it, and Eilid wondered at the change in her.

For Soillse, the days without the fostered ladds were a dream come true. There were no real chores, and plenty of ground meal for bread for just the four of them. Compared with the usual rush, there was so little cooking to do or kindling to be gathered, she felt as spoiled as a babe. Even Ceit stopped her bossing, so the constant pressure for Soillse to do this or that, always hurrying on to the next chore needing to be done, evaporated, too. And the really filthy work of sweeping the latrines, cleaning hides, or chopping and gutting the fish just disappeared. Though Eilid did make them help her clean out the three storage pits and line them with new grass, then collect brambles and early nuts on the ridge, all light work. Still, it was like someone had lifted a twenty-ring tree off Soillse's back, and she was floating a hand-span above the ground. As Soillse watched the changed ways of her sister, she understood that when the boys were here, Ceit felt the same pressure she did herself, Eilid, too. How they would endure taking it all back on again, she didn't exactly know. But they would, of course; they had to.

On the second morning, Soillse went to sit in her Aine tree with the excuse of gathering firewood they didn't need. Instead, she wove a wee rush basket and gathered moss to line it with, taking time to fit feathers and small bright stones in between the woven courses. She thought at first she'd give it to Eilid. But when it was done, it was so sparkly and woodsy that Soillse decided to keep it for herself. I'll make Eilid another one, she thought. And she did.

In the rocks behind Aine, Soillse made a cleft and lined it with flat river stones and soft grasses. Then she put her growing collection of stones and shells into the basket and stored it in the crevice. The quartz and the yellow shell from Coillore went into it, and there was a muscle shell, shiny iridescent blue, and a pure white pebble from the beach that looked like a perfect small egg. There were many colored stones she'd collected, too, tumbled into roundness by the waves: pale green, rose, lavender, and a sparkly deep purple one she'd found on the ridge as a babe. She had one tiny cardinal feather as well, two wild goose feathers, very long, and a large white swan feather that was left in the wee loch on the ridge two summers ago.

The next day, Soillse took a small clump of clay from the stores behind the cooking hut, where the pots were made, and fashioned it into a tiny Goddess figurine. Then she set it by the fire to bake slowly overnight and put it up in her Aine tree for three nights, too, asking the Goddess to sanctify it during Lughnasa. And Soillse placed that into her basket in the burrow, too. Sitting in her Aine tree, as the sun lowered itself behind the western peaks on a warm blustery eve, Soillse was pleased with herself. It's like Coillore's altar, me wee basket, she thought, and it'll bring the power of the rock people, and the birds, and the Goddess to help me when the boys return and I have way too much to do again.

On the next-to-last afternoon, Soillse sat on the boulders at the bay for hours, watching flickering lines of light move through the shallows. She felt fae folk all around her, saying they were her family of light in the tuath of Danu in the stars and the Creator Sun, the shining ones, and they were very near, always. And they told her she was named for them, too. In her mind, Soillse saw a faery queen weaving those strands of yellow light among the soft ebb and flow of the shallow waves. And the lass felt an urge deep inside to listen to her spirit friends wherever she could take the time.

As the gloaming darkened on their last night of freedom, sitting in her Aine tree in her summer shift and plaid, Soillse heard the spirit voices again. She was about to go in to bed, thinking to have a few extra hours of rest tonight, but she hesitated as she watched the Cuchullins fade into dusk.

"It's been the happiest quarter moon I can remember," she whispered to her apple tree. The thought of carrying and cooking again, from firstsky to late gloaming, made her tired already. Still, she missed her Da, his jokes and pipes, and dancing in the round house after the evening meal. The fire circle was quiet without him, and she was getting tired of roaming the same small bay. She thought how odd it was that Ceit had turned into a homebody and herself the wandering lass this quarter moon, when it was just the opposite when there was work to be done. As Soillse waited in the silence, taking one last breath of freedom, she thought she felt the brush of wings across her shoulders.

'We're all around ye, child, every day. We can speak to ye in yer mind like this an' teach ye many things, if ye like. We're yer spirit family from yer tuath o' light.'

"I hear me Ma thinkin' sometimes," Soillse said aloud. "Well, at least, I used to when I was wee an' had time to listen. Do ye mean like that?"

'Yes, almost. Will ye come to your Aine tree at the new and full moons, child? Just come an' sit here in the branches? We'll meet ye then an' help ye remember us an' why ye came here.'

"Will it hurt?" Soillse asked, thinking of the banshees Sine sometimes talked about.

'We'll no harm ye, this we promise. But there are difficulties in every life, fixed by the Goddess to help each soul grow strong. So there'll be times o' pain in yer life. But no from us. We would befriend an' help ye.'

"Do ye ken the Sun Lord? Is He there?"

'Aye, we ken Him. He's in the Creator Sun, too.'

"Can I go there an' see Him? I <u>miss</u> Him here."

'No till ye leave the world ye live in, dear, but ye can feel Him in the sun. An' He comes through most strongly on the solstice an' equinox mornings, an' durin' the Oak moon, so it's easier then than other times. The world He lives in is all around ye, too, but it takes much spirit work to feel Him on earth. There are many veils between the worlds.'

"Is the Goddess there then? I remember Her, too. But it's getting fuzzy, no as well as I used to."

'She lives in the center o' the earth, dear.'

"Can I see <u>Her</u> then?"

'In yer mind, lassie, ye can, or if the Goddess requests the portals to open. It doesna happen often.' Soillse sighed and waited. *'There is a goddess who wants to talk wi' ye, though."*

"Oh! Is she here noo?"

'No, but she will be on the full moon, two nights away. Will ye come back then?" Soillse nodded, thinking that would be after the boys returned, and she might be too tired this late in the gloaming. She was sleepy now, so she said good-bye to her spirit family and jumped down to the mosses, then ran home through the bracken.

When the ladds returned the next evening, Soillse bent to the labor of the late summer days. She shouldered the cooking and cleaning and gathering again, like it was the most natural thing in the world. She didn't even feel sad, as she expected to, for she was happy to have Da and Fìrinn back at the tuath again. And within a day or two, it was like the ladds had never gone away at all.

The full moon night arrived, spitting rain, but even so, Soillse was eager to run to her Aine tree at the end of the day. She and Ceit had been gathering most of the afternoon, wild thyme and early apples on the ridge. So Soillse was especially tired, and she ate quickly at the beach by herself. Then she ran to Aine and took out her basket, holding the Goddess figurine in her hands as she hoisted herself up into the branches. The waves lapped softly on the rocks below, the tide just past high. And the sky was clearing, with only a few wispy clouds scudding by in the gloaming. Following the heat of the day, the wind brought welcome coolness to Soillse, in a clean shift and her best green cloak for the occasion. But as she watched the moon rise slowly above the eastern ridge, Soillse shivered, wrapping her cloak about her and holding her arms tightly over her chest. She took a deep breath and closed her eyes, smelling the faintest hint of flowers on the wind.

And then, quite clearly in her mind, Soillse saw a bubble of light hovering just in front of her, a hand-span above the sea. Within it stood a young fair goddess in sparkling peach robes, with long blond hair that blew around her in the wind. The virgin's eyes were dark and full of love. And Soillse's heart beat faster as she thought, a real goddess, come to talk with me!

In the next moments, Soillse found herself thinking of the little things that make life beautiful, sweet simple things, like a hug from Ma, the scent of wild roses when she put her nose into them, or the small warm waves that tickled her feet at the beach. And she felt a sudden certainty that this goddess had sent some of the stones and feathers for her basket, too. This goddess did not have wings, but wore a silver circlet round her head and a gossamer shawl of shining silver thread. Tiny points of light shimmered like stars all over her filmy dress.

"I ken ye!" Soillse said suddenly, more loudly than she intended. As she put one hand over her mouth, she thought, it was a long time ago, somewhere in the Otherworld. The goddess smiled softly and blew Soillse a kiss. "Ye arena the faery godmother? No, too young." Soillse tried hard to remember.

"I'm Maighdean, virgin of the Creator Sun in the Diamond Core, the seventh heaven, dear," the goddess said and bent to blow a small bubble of light out of her hands and across the waves that landed in Soillse's lap. Inside it was a temple of stone carved to look like large pink shells, the sanctuary built in the shape of a large lotus blossoom. A pool of water stood outside the doors of the temple, and Soillse suddenly remembered living in that place, kneeling before this goddess and vowing to serve her. It was long ago in another realm entirely, and she'd been older then than she was now. In the bubble, Soillse saw the Maighdean goddess hand her the peach robes of the virgin lass order there, and Soillse remembered putting them on with tears running down her face. Staring at the goddess again, Soillse's eyes widened with awe, and she wondered why Maighdean had come and what she herself had promised to do here on earth.

"Ye're the goddess o' young women, arena ye," Soillse breathed.

'Yes, I'm so glad you remember me, child! I've missed you for so long!' As Maighdean paused, Soillse felt a faint sweet longing rise up in her heart. *'That's my home you see, child, the virgin goddess temple in the Creator Sun, at the very core of the cosmos. You left it long ago, little one.'* And then the goddess sent another bubble, bigger than the first.

This one was filled with demon hordes that were invading the temple complex. And round it were many fierce angels on white cloud horses, trying to hold the forces of darkness back. Soillse saw herself in her peach robes running down a mountain as fast as she could go. Ceit and other priestesses followed, too, all in a rush. And then Soillse realized she'd vowed to descend into the darkness, one world after another, down a long winding staircase of fear and terror to the very bottom, until she arrived here on earth, the lowest realm. She felt, too, how great the need was for spiritual warriors to come so far and live within the realms of darkness to renew the wisdom stream of the Goddess. And Soillse could sense that wisdom needed to be lived, experienced, in order to be revitalized throughout the cosmos. Those demon hordes were invading the Diamond Core because the light of wisdom in all worlds had grown weak and stale. And so, Soillse agreed to come to earth, for the Maighdean goddess needed any who were brave enough to live in darkness and transform it with the love in their hearts.

All who served the virgin goddess, running down that mountain, were young women, and this surprised Soillse. Dimly, she remembered kneeling before this goddess in a small white sanctuary overlooking the sea and vowing to carry Miaghdean's love into the home and hearts of her own family, lifetime after lifetime. And Soillse could feel how all women had promised to do the same, to bring the heart of the goddess, Maighdean, the sweet softness of the virgin feminine, into the families of their birth and the created families of their wombs, to all within their family cauldrons.

Soillse looked down at her own heart then, and she saw demons of overwork swirling around a glowing orb in the center. This moon in her own heart shone like the bright one in the heart of the Maighdean goddess, and they pulsed to the same heartbeat. And suddenly, Soillse knew that this small moon within created all that happened in her own little world.

And she knew at once that all daughters everywhere were of this virgin lass order, serving with aching feet, sore hands, and trembling hearts to feed, hold, nurture, and love their own families in every land. To stand tall in their own truths, too, not giving in to darkness ever, especially the brute force o' warriors. In this way, the virgin girls of the world would, slowly, silently, and surely, soften the darkness of the ages. Soillse realized that this was as holy as any service in any realm. And she saw, too, how this Maighdean order was powerful in its love, as much as all the great male warrior heroes of the ages Da sung about. Even me cleaning latrines is holy, the lass thought in wonder.

'Yes, all you do is sacred beyond measuring,' the goddess whispered. 'The way will not be easy this time, child. You have asked to heal and ease much in the tribes.'

And then, Soillse saw the shadows in her heart suddenly move aside. And deep within was a twelve-sided gem, a diamond of many facets; so brilliant it far outshone the moon orb surrounding it. And inside this small diamond, Soillse saw herself and Fìrinn, much older, their hair turning grey. She wore the lake-blue robes of the highest priestess order and he the sky-blue mantle of the high king of Skye. They were holding hands and gazing into each other's eyes, love pouring between them. And then Soillse saw a small house by the sea, wattle and daub, with a wee window covered by a thin oiled skin, just like Coillore's! Beside it was a place of healing and the king's pavilion nearby. And then the shadows closed over the diamond again.

'This is what your divine child within wishes to create in this lifetime, dear. There will come many barriers, but if you persist and heal them all, the diamond sun of your own heart will slowly come free and clear. And in the end, all your dreams will come to life, made real at last. Call on me when you are in need, will you, child? There'll be weariness and hardship, but never too much to bear. And each difficulty that comes into your life carries fears from on high for you to face and *heal, exactly the same as the ones that remain over your own diamond sun. This is your part in the whole, those dark shadows you once chose to take in, the pieces of the wisdom stream you asked to renew. And every darkness that comes into your life carries teachings that will leave you wiser in some way than you were before. It is so for everyone. Remember, child, it's <u>love</u> that heals all things. And when you are done this time, you can come Home, back to your family in heaven, the real family of your spirit. And you can stay with them forever. May it be so.'*

With tears falling down her face, Soillse jumped out of the tree, stepping onto a boulder to move closer to the virgin goddess. She wished she could hug this Maighdean who told her such wondrous things! The goddess smiled very softly, blowing on her hands again. And a rosey cloud emerged from them and surrounded Soillse in a soft bubble of light. But when Soillse looked up again, the Maighdean goddess was gone.

'I'll come to you inside your Aine tree, child. Come and find me here whenever you wish,' Soillse heard the goddess voice in her mind. The lass waited a moment more, looking out over the waves. But only the dusky purple sky over the Cuchullins across the loch remained.

As Soillse walked through the bracken into the yard, she felt both determination and contentment settle into her chest. The feeling lingered all the way to her bedfurs and into her sleep. And in her dreams, Soillse's pallet turned into a small coracle that rocked on a velvet blue sea, wrapped in the soft peach moonmist of the goddess Maighdean's love.

Chapter Fifteen: Fìrinn

Four moons after the summer games, Fìrinn was brought word of his newborn sister's death. He bent his head and sent a blessing for peace to his Ma and the babe so soon returned to the Otherworld. Somehow, it only made him feel further away than ever from Frithe. It was the beginning of his eleventh winter, and he'd lengthened even more, all bony arms and lanky shins now. And among the boisterous roughhousing of the other ladds, he'd grown more silent still. As the Blackthorne moon (November) began, the wind sharpened her claws in earnest. And this night, she bit through Fìrinn's fur jerkin as he hurried toward the line of boys filing through the long house door for the evening meal, with Bana Dhia at his heels. Samhein would begin in two more nights, the end of another skyturn. But just as Fìrinn reached for the doorskin, Seumus, standing in the yard, called to him.

"It's time ye began yer lessons, ladd," Seumus shouted, wrapping his plaid around his heavy leather jerkin against the wind. "There," he said, and the chief pointed to a narrow path leading south into the stunted birches above the shore, "every quarter moon noo before the evenin' meal. Coillore's asked for ye." Stepping closer, Seumus hesitated, hunching his shoulders away from the wind. "Ye're an inward ladd, nothin' like yer Da, no what I expected at all," the chief said and paused. "Ach, never mind. I love ye just as well. Ye'll do, laddie. Go on then." And Seumus winked, resting a warm hand on Fìrinn's shoulder. Then rubbing his hands together against the cold, Seumus stretched his legs into long strides toward the round house. That ladd'll soak up the lore like boar stew, Seumus thought, glancing back at Fìrinn.

All highborn Celtic children were expected to be educated, daughters as well as sons. The Celts believed that knowledge was of the Sun Lord and that it shaped a man or woman the way the earth shapes the pine roots and they in turn the tree. Turning toward the path Seumus had shown him, Fìrinn thought, strange I havena noticed it before. We mostly go north or east for gathering, I guess. And he glanced back toward the long house wistfully. I'd rather be headed for the hearth like Seumus, he thought, shivering and pulling his jerkin tighter. It had been overcast and cold all day, the sun only an unformed brightness in the southern reach of the sky. I wonder what Coillore'll teach us, Fìrinn thought. Magic like Ma kens? I hope so!

The moss silenced his steps as he moved deeper into the wood, brushing through chestnut brown bracken fronds that curved over the narrow path. Bare, lichen-covered, birch branches closed over his head, and he had to duck once or twice to keep going. And then as he came to the druid clearing, the wind behind him stopped. It didn't just lessen, as Fìrinn stood at the small opening in the trees, where the children sat circled before Coillore, it ceased. Startled, Fìrinn looked for a windbreak, but he saw nothing more than the bare birches. Then he smiled. Maybe the druid'll teach us that, he thought.

The clearing before him, tucked beneath the scrub birches, was just high and wide enough to hold a dozen children. It was a natural opening in the wood, formed by a large slab of bedrock beneath, and well concealed. Coillore sat in his white druid robe and emerald woolen cloak beneath the one large oak that arched over all. And Fìrinn's heart warmed to see that Soillse was there with her older sister, both holding tight to their plaids, wrapped over heavy, woolen winter shifts. The older girl was perhaps thirteen winters now, grown shapely these past few moons, her black frizzed hair pulled back into a single braid, and she was staring transfixed into the low fire. Soillse, next to her, was nine winters, with freckles splashed across her nose and arms, windblown hair, and the slender face and form of a child. She looks like wildness itself, Fìrinn thought and smiled. Glancing up at him and nodding, Soillse ran a hand over Bana Dhia as Fìrinn squeezed into place at the edge of the path.

Coillore was sitting on a flat boulder carved with the seven rings of all worlds, his tonsured head shining in the ember glow. Fine grey hair fell over his cloak, and he wore a long moustache in the noble style. With piercing blue eyes and a nod, he acknowledged Fìrinn and Bana Dhia, but there was no break in the druid's chanting.

Duirc was there as well, and big Allaidh. Not Ruadh, though, for only children of noblemen were taught the lore. Coillore means golden wood, odd name, Fìrinn thought, as he folded his legs. He'd seen the man infrequently at the round house, talking with Seumus or up by the standing stone, leading the solstice or equinox ceremonies. The druid was singing a ballad about the lands beyond the waters, the Austrian mother country of the Celts and the goddess Danu, birthing the first tribe out of the river Danube, named in her honor. And then the soft magnetism of Coillore's voice pulled Fìrinn in. The song told how the clans spread west over the centuries, settling all across the European heartlands. And in Fìrinn's mind, pictures formed as the druid sang, a curragh (small hide boat) of the ancestors heaving on the waves of the Mediterranean. He could feel the sway of the boat and a rope scraping his palms.

Every quarter moon, before the evening meal in winter or after it in summer, Coillore chanted to the boys and Seumus's daughters in the oak hollow. Lighting and blessing the fire, the druid first invoked the gods and goddesses of these hills and waters, and of this tuath. Then he called forth the clan ancients before them, and finally the One Beloveds, Oghama and the White Tara. Reciting histories from the beginning of time to the present, the druid taught them versed knowledge to aid in the remembering, including specific charms for help or healing. These were not the common prayers taught to everyone for mealtimes or upon awakening in the morning or the simple cycles of the sun and moon. No, the chants Coillore taught them held far greater power.

They learned of the plant and tree people, too, how to protect grains from insect hordes or heal a man from mortal wounding. At times, Fìrinn felt his mother's presence in the clearing, hovering, curious about the lore. But even without her, his mind softened there like rain-washed earth, letting the chants percolate slowly down and change him to his core.

Coillore told of times before there were clans at all, songs of the Creators, describing the flow of Their love as a rush of fire that split into four directions from the Creator Sun, the grand creator cross. All forms and all worlds were divided into four quadrants in Their image, Coillore said. One quadrant of the cosmos served the mother, one the holy girl, one the gentle boy, and one the stalwart father. The Creator Sun was the fifth, the druid said, the eternal center of all worlds.

Over the winter moons, there were chants about great wheels of stars, revolving through the deeps of space, of moving paths between them and what their crossings portended for person or tribe. There were songs about the birth of mother earth, the fires of her own diamond light burning in her heart space still, and how she'd cooled her skin long eons ago, so the people could be born and live.

As the verses cascaded over him like a waterfall, Fìrinn imagined them in his mind. Then Coillore chanted through the stages of the earth mother's life: cycles of fire lasting an eon, rains that fell for centuries, and floods that climbed the backs of mountains. And then the druid sang tales of the first ancestors, long before the Celts, ancient ones emerging out of the animal kingdom and spreading across the earth, again in four directions. Once, Coillore sang of civilizations before the flood, tall godlike people and their shining towers of glass, folk that had lived in this very land, Albion, Alba, and

Eire, all that remained of their now sunken world. And to his surprise, Firinn dreamed of that land for a quarter moon afterward.

The moons of winter slid into spring, and during the days when Firinn was supposed to be concentrating on the martial arts, he began to see more galaxies or westering ancients in his mind than wrestling ladds and thrown spears. Seumus grew disgusted at the inconsistency of Firinn's throwing arm, and the ladd tried to pull his focus back to the yard for a time. But then in the Willow moon (April), they began the lore of animals, and it set Firinn's heart alight once more. Coillore told tales of creatures bigger than mammoths, of real dragons that lived in the silken glove of the sea. Sometimes Firinn felt himself inside the very minds of the beings Coillore sang about. And in Firinn's dreams, mythical creatures came and merged with him, prowling ancient forests inside his very own skin. Once, a lynx led him to the tangled fastnesses of the north, leaning out over the very tip of a headland above the sea, making Firinn's heart ache for his lost wildness under the light of the hovering moon.

One summer's eve, late in the Holly moon (June), as the old druid chanted the song of the wolf, Bana Dhia startled to her feet quite suddenly. Stretching out her neck, she let out a long mournful howl, full of the pain of wildness tamed, and started to run out of the circle toward the hills with a strange glint in her eye. But Coillore called her back with a smile.

"Nah, nah, Bana Dhia," the druid said, "the time for that nomad freedom o' yer kind passed centuries ago, when ye befriended us, instead, remember?" And the dog looked back at the druid, hung her head, and slowly returned to drop down beside Firinn. The children laughed, and even Coillore paused to smile and run his hand down the dog's boney back. But Firinn felt a strange tug at his heart that day and often took Bana Dhia running in the forest after that.

Over the skyturn, as the druid lore settled in, Fìrinn grew detached from his old ways, especially the noisy routine of the yard. He learned instead to think like a mountain, stepping back from each single day and seeing the patterns of his life from a height and a distance. At times, in the silence of the evening, the ladd could feel the heartbeat of the earth. And he'd stop what he was doing for a moment to receive the warmth pulsing up his legs and spine, as Tara's tenderness flooded his heart. Growing ever more silent, Fìrinn didn't speak about these changes with Ruadh either, for the lore could not be shared with anyone on pain of death from the spirit world. And once he joined the druid circle, Fìrinn's enmity with Duirc intensified, too, for the lore filtered slowly through the narrow sluices of Duirc's mind, quickening his smoldering hatred of Fìrinn.

As the skyturn passed, Fìrinn found himself thinking more and more of Soillse, too. Silence was required at the druid circle, and Coillore often walked both daughters back to the tuath, so there was rarely an opportunity to speak with her. But on the eve of the druid moon, sixth night, Coillore listened to each of the children recite alone. Writing down the mysteries was strictly forbidden, too, for such knowledge in the hands of the unawakened could be powerfully used for ill. So the children came separately in turn to face the druid across the fire and repeat whatever chants he requested of them.

The week before, Fìrinn had drawn the longest reed. So tonight, he was the last to recite, making his turn late, well after moonrise. It was the Alder moon (March), and the night was frosty as he dragged his feet through ice-filmed bracken. He enjoyed these recitations, but tonight he'd rather have stayed in his bedfurs, and Fìrinn pulled the fur he'd brought for warmth around his woolen breeks and fur jerkin. Soillse, a slender ten winters now, with a fur-lined green cloak tied over her heavy woolen shift, scurried down the path as Fìrinn approached the clearing. Running a hand along

Bana Dhia's head as she hurried past, she smiled at Fìrinn, but said no word.

"Wait," Fìrinn whispered, turning to look at her. She stopped and gazed up at him with herb-softened eyes. "I wish we could talk," he said. And she nodded, blushing.

"We will someday, Fìrinn, but for noo the Goddess forbids me to come to ye," the lass whispered, "an' Da'd glower at me, too." She touched Fìrinn's hand with the lightest brush, then turned and walked down the path. But her touch incited a fire in Fìrinn's heart and loins as well. He stood watching the branches quiver after her, not knowing what to do. Shaking his head, he stepped into the fire circle and stood facing Coillore. Coillore glanced quickly toward Fìrinn's manhood and raised his brows, but said nothing.

"Song o' mother earth," the druid finally whispered, his voice heavy with fatigue as he pulled his own fur tighter around his chest. Ach, it's been moons since we did that one, Fìrinn thought in dismay, and his mind stumbled to remember it.

"The spirits ask for it, ladd," the druid answered, glancing up at the slivered moon through bare boughs, "whatever ye remember. Dinna fret, child." And then Coillore leaned over to throw some resin nuggets into the embers and sat back, waiting. Fìrinn breathed in deeply, letting the piney scent bring his mind back to calmness, and then began.

"In the time before the ancients,
When the worlds were still unborn,
The Bridegroom o' the heavens
Drew the Goddess to His Core.

Into Her swirling waters,
Womb o' night unformed,
He poured the star clan patterns
O' the six worlds yet to come.

From the fires o' Their union,
Swirled the spiral staircase down,
An' the twelve tribes o' the cosmos,
An' o' mother earth were born..."

Fìrinn faltered. His head began to pull in on itself, and his stomach churned. He lay back for a moment as all words faded from his mind. A rapid warmth moved from his feet to his chest, and pictures suddenly began pouring into his mind, startlingly clear and quivering with life. Mountains lifted in rippling waves across the earth, followed by torrential rains that flooded still smoldering volcanoes. Fìrinn's muscles shook of their own accord, and his body writhed as the vision took hold. He was the earth. Hot rain fell on parched skin and his tongue felt cracked with drought. Never had he known such thirst. Then gradually, his racing pulse slowed to a low drumbeat, and the heat of the vision withdrew to deep within his heart, just as mother earth herself had done eons ago.

Then he felt his arms and legs become a long stretch of beach, the bay beyond the goddess mountain at home! And his groin became a dark cave at the base of the nearby cliffs, the sea pounding into it with a soft thrusting rhythm, tingling through his whole body and filling it with life. He could feel the tender love of sea god for earth mother, and Fìrinn thought dimly, this is how a woman feels, joining with her man. I ken that cave, it's the cave of waters, where the birthing women go at home, the cave where I was born.

In his vision, islands emerged from his cave womb then, floating like jewels out of the cave floor. Swirling into the waters, they took their places in a long line off the western coast of Skye, forming the whole necklace of the outer isles that he could see on a sunny afternoon beyond the hills above the broch. But now, Fìrinn could feel the islands resting all along his legs, abdomen, and chest.

And then, out of the cave mouth poured the sacred grains, mounds and mounds lining the shore, enough to feed many tuaths. And birthed from the cave came all the creatures of the hills: wolf, fox, stag and doe, boar, a multitude of birds, and berries, grasses, and herbs, too, all moving out of the cave mouth and taking their rightful places among the hills and moors. As he watched, Fìrinn felt his heart fire set alight with the earth mother's passion to sustain all her creations. And as her tenderness and love enveloped him softly from below, he felt like a babe in her arms.

Then, just above the mounded grains, a woman floated into sight. Soillse! She wore the cobalt robes of the priestess orders, a woman grown. Waves of cobalt light pulsed around the lass, spiraling down her torso and legs, and Fìrinn's heart leaped at the sight of her. Then she reached into the cave mouth of his vision and plucked a jewel, glittering cobalt blue, out of the sands on the cave floor. The stone was square, marked with the four directions, and Soillse leaned in closer and placed it into his heart space. Blue lightning flashed out of it then in four quadrants, and he felt a soft sizzling in his hands and toes.

Then Fìrinn's mind slowed, and he lay back, spent, feeling the cool waves of the spirit sea washing over him gently. Its soft lapping crept across his arms, legs, and belly, brushing his skin with preternatural tenderness. And as the sea soaked into him, his mind was pulled into a deep and silent sleep.

The shifting of Coillore beside him caught Fìrinn's ears, and he opened his eyes, suddenly alert.

"Well, ladd," the druid whispered, "it isna often the earth mother moves herself through the body o' a child, an' a ladd at that." And Coillore's eyes were soft with wonder.

"I'm no a child. I'm twelve winters noo...,"Fìrinn protested, trying to sit up. But his body was leaden. How long have I been lying here, he wondered.

"It's nearly firstsky," Coillore answered. The druid hears me thoughts, like Ma, Firinn realized, closing his eyes again. But Coillore laid a hand on Firinn's chest. "Stay a while, laddie. Ye'll be unsteady still. Special powers have ye. Ye knew that, though, didna ye?" Coillore paused, staring into the ashes and taking a long breath as Firinn stirred and tried to sit again. "Nah, nah," the druid said more firmly, "a great gift ye've been given, ladd. Lay still an' have the sense to let it sink into ye." And the druid stood to unwind the fur from around his shoulders, laying it carefully around the shivering boy. "And stay warm," Coillore added.

"What happened?," Firinn asked after a time.

"Dinna think just noo, Firinn. Let the Goddess settle herself into yer bones. Feel Her great love. Give some back! I was eighteen winters before She came to me so strongly." And the druid sighed. "Never mind, laddie. How would ye ken? Rest," he finished, "just rest."

And then, as the early morning breeze rustled the dry bracken, Coillore stirred the embers, adding wood to the hearth until the fire crackled and danced again. And Firinn felt the sands of the earth goddess rise beneath him once more. And it felt like his own Ma's skin, warm and damp beneath his own. So he rolled over and pulled his knees up to his chest, like a babe curled into her bosom, and slept past dawn.

Chapter Sixteen: Soillse

Another skyturn passed, and as she grew stronger, Soillse's days held work, work, and more work. There was no time for wandering the hills any more, and even a short talk with her Aine tree was rare these days. Eilid's hip was constantly sore now, so more of the meal grinding fell to Sine and Muirn, leaving many of the other chores for Soillse. As representative of the Goddess to the tribe, illness in the matriarch meant a loss of Goddess power, and some of the women began to take more initiative on their own. Ceit, a lanky fifteen winters, spent her days gathering and tending the plots of barley and wheat on the hill. And when Eilid's hip became too sore even for the climb to the cave, Ceit went up for vision quests on the cross-quarter days to feel the will of the Goddess and report back to the clan. Both Sine and Muirn vehemently expressed no interest in becoming matriarch.

Ceit had been an imperious child to begin with, but her change to womanhood the skyturn before had added force to her demanding ways. Where Eilid worked harder than Sine and Muirn, and softened the workload commensurate with Soillse's age, Ceit ordered the women to do her bidding and kept the easiest tasks for herself. The change in leadership to Ceit began gradually over the summer, but it was quite unstable, as Eilid still took charge whenever she felt well enough. But her hip slowly worsened, until she could no longer manage any heavy loads. So by fall, it was Sine, Muirn, and often Soillse who carried the cauldron and the wood, with Duineil helping grind the meal, never as fine as Eilid's any more. And as the Goddess authority settled onto Ceit's shoulders more frequently, she began to rely heavily on Soillse.

Rather than let the women choose for themselves, as Eilid had always done, Ceit preferred to assign tasks for the day at firstsky. And Soillse, eleven winters now, was given the jobs no one else particularly liked: sweeping and replacing the rushes in the latrine, gutting the fish and game, and tanning hides. Her hands were often raw and swollen at the evening meal, and as winter approached, Ceit put her to the meal grinding, too. There were times when pushing the quern stone caused Soillse's already sore hands to split and bleed. And when Eilid complained about blood in the meal, Ceit only sniffed and said, "We make blood puddin' from the game, Ma. What's the difference?"

One cool evening in mid-fall, exhaustion creased Soillse's face as she pushed the quern stone across the barley kernels, and Eilid motioned the lass to sit and began to grind herself, slowly and unevenly, wincing as she did so. After a short time, Ceit strode into the yard, carrying a hide full of threshed barley to be ground. When she noticed Eilid, Ceit flew into a rage.

"Dinna do that, Ma! Ye're no good to us noo, anyway. Ye canna be grindin' an' hurtin' yerself the more! I gave that job to Soillse. She's young and fit, and born as second sister to serve."

"The lass is fallin' over, she's so tired," Eilid said quietly, brushing the flour dust off her work stained shift, looking up at Ceit, and clenching her jaw. "I'll no have it, Ceit."

"Ye'll no have it!" Ceit fairly shrieked. "An' who do ye think ye are? The Goddess power is lost to ye, Ma. Ye've been limpin' these last three winters. I am the Goddess keeper noo, an' I'm in charge here!"

"An' does that mean ye can treat yer own Ma like some slave, paying the price o' defeat? The matriarch is kind to the tribe, that's what the Goddess tells me, Ceit! An' it's the Goddess keeper who lifts a little more o' the load, since she has the power. That's what I was taught." With her mouth a thin line, Eilid leveled her eyes on Ceit's.

"That's <u>no</u> what the Goddess tells me," Ceit retorted with slitted eyes, her frizzy hair quivering around her head like some dark fae sprite. "She says I'm queen noo, an' ye're old an' feeble. She says I'm smarter than anyone here, an' it's up to me to choose the tasks an' interpret Her will for all to follow. An' if ye want to ken, at this last visionin', she said it's time for the ceremony o' choosin', Ma. An' so I call it for the Blackthorne Moon, after the harvest is in, as I've wished to do all summer long. And ye'll no have charge o' anythin' after that, I will." And with that, Ceit hiked her shift up to her knees and stuffed it into her girdle, then stomped off to the fields. Eilid had heard talk of clashes between mothers and daughters when a girl's moon time came on. But she hadn't thought to see it in her own, especially Ceit, always wanting more of Eilid than she had time to give. Shaking her head and sighing, Eilid frowned after the girl and continued to grind, clenching her jaw.

The ceremony of choosing the matriarch brought with it a formal shift of power. It was not normally called, unless the aging queen was severely incapacitated in some way and simply could not perform the duties required: organizing and helping carry the feminine responsibilities and meting out justice for the women of the tribe. Usually the Goddess called the eldest woman as matriarch, but not always. So all at the tuath were startled to hear that Ceit had called for a choosing, as most expected Eilid to rule for many winters still. It was unheard of for a lass of fifteen winters to challenge the ruling matriarch and her own Ma at that. But once called, the rite became a sacred contract with the spirit world and had to go forward.

Underneath her calm exterior, Eilid was stunned by Ceit's wish to replace her. She was used to the girl's demanding ways and the moodiness after Ceit's moon times began. But this was just too much. Eilid herself had gathered and planted and cooked and ground meal from morn till night, and anything else needing to be done at the tuath, to see the lass had all her needs met every single day since Ceit was born. So Ceit's lack of honor and appreciation felt like knives in Eilid's heart.

The limp worsened rapidly after the argument in the yard, until Eilid could barely walk, wincing no matter how slowly she moved. And the laughing and dancing at the evening fire circle stopped, too, for only an awkward silence filled the round house now, everyone saying only what was needed and very little more. When Seumus tried to tell a joke or two to lighten the tension, Eilid only said she was too tired for his nonsense and stitched furiously in the firelight.

The women rarely sang or chattered at their work during the day any more, either, unless Ceit was off in the hills. And even then, it was mostly whispered complaints. But as the moon passed, a slow change came over Eilid, inner determination growing in her eyes that everyone could feel. She began limping the length of the bay in the early dawn, saying prayers to the Goddess as she did so. And very gradually her hip improved, though it still hurt.

Soillse, dismayed at the change in her sister, mostly did as she was told. All her life she'd heard that Ceit would become queen, and so Soillse accepted this. Her heart ached at the sadness in Ma's eyes, but the lass felt there was little she could do. Inside though, Soillse wished Eilid would stand firmly in her woman's power and face Ceit squarely a time or two. Some false notions had moved into Ceit when her moon cycles began, that's what Soillse decided, full of dark power she didn't trust at all. And then one afternoon, Soillse found Eilid crying as she washed clothes in the burn.

"The dark one's taken over that girl," Eilid said, her arms trembling as she pushed the wet bundle over a rock. Her own shift was soaked through as well. "I see it, but I dinna ken how to stop it." And she dropped her head, leaning on fisted hands. "I've tried as hard as ever I could to make the tribe happy an' healthy, Syl. An' it's all fallin' apart from one bossy girl!" Soillse knelt then and put down the water skins she'd come to fill, wrapping her arms around her mother's back.

"We all ken it's no the real goddess in Ceit, Ma. I feel yer big heart holdin' us all. An' that's <u>much</u> stronger than Ceit's sharp words an' bitin' ways. Ye're still the Goddess keeper for me, Ma, an' always will be." And Eilid leaned back on Soillse's knees and sobbed.

"Then why the Goddess is the lass allowed to take over just everythin'? An' why dinna the healin' salves help me hip? Somethin's <u>wrong</u>, child!" Soillse sat down on the bank beside Eilid, pulling her summer shift down over her knees, and stared at the tumbling waters.

"Coillore says to be careful, Ma, what beliefs we carry inside, because they make the outer world fall into place around them. They create their own likeness in our lives. I dinna believe Ceit draws from the real Goddess, the Goddess o' light, an' ye <u>do</u>. An' I <u>willna</u> believe anythin' else, even if Ceit's the strongest girl in twenty tuaths an' yer hip hurts ye every moment. I believe in <u>ye</u>, Ma."

"By the Goddess," Eilid whispered hoarsely. "I've been wrong all these skyturns, tellin' Ceit how special she was." And she sighed heavily, smiling wanly at Soillse.

"Coillore says sometimes hard things come to strengthen us," Soillse continued, her eyes thoughtful on the rippled waters. "So I think if the Goddess wants Ceit to take over as matriarch, then it's meant to build our spirits somehow. An' we must do the best we can an' hold fast to what we truly believe in. That's what I feel, an' that's all I ken." Soillse spoke quietly, her eyes as clear as the running stream. As Eilid nodded, the lass got up and filled the water skins, kissing the top of her Ma's head and turning to walk slowly back down the path with a heavy bag in each hand.

"Goddess, <u>light</u> one, help me," Eilid prayed then. "Wash away this shadow over the tuath. An' take away the resentment I feel fer me very own lassie an' her proud ways. Take our troubles into yer heart, Goddess, an' show me what to do."

That very afternoon, Eilid went up to see Coillore. And afterwards, she began taking trips to the ridge, to the sacred spring there, washing her hip in the cold waters and praying for healing, sitting in her ceremonial robe and chanting as the moon rose. And very slowly, as the Blackthorne moon (November) approached, the ache in her hip improved. The bond between Eilid and Soillse strengthened slowly, too. Nothing changed in their outward ways, except for a reassuring glance at the fire circle perhaps or Soillse carrying Eilid's loads when the hip pained her most, in the evenings especially. But there was hope between them and resolve in Eilid's eyes that hadn't been there before. And Eilid didn't shrink into herself when Ceit was in the yard anymore.

The night of choosing was set for sixth night of the Blackthorne moon. This night brought forth the power of Eriu (girl goddess, Creator Sun), regent of personal purpose, and united it with Máiri (grandmother goddess, Creator Sun), regent of all feminine decisions in the tribe, a most powerful combination for a new beginning.

Even the men, in their clan plaids, homespun shirts, and woolen cloaks, came to observe and support Eilid this time, at Seumus's insistence. The women wore their embroidered doeskin robes, too. So as the slivered moon rose, all in the tribe climbed to the women's cave, walking the stony path, one by one, peering to be sure of their footing in the torchlight above the boulders on the northern shore. It was cold and dank above the sea, the Cuchullin peaks jagged in the darkness across the waters.

Seumus, so full of courage in a wrestling match or hunting wild game, felt quite defeated by the rivalry between his women. And he knew no weapons to fight it, except for a joke or two now and then to change the mood. He had enough to do each day helping the ladds at their games, seeing to the teachers, and keeping the tuath in meat. As he climbed, he wished the women could just keep <u>peace</u> among themselves, especially Ceit. Getting older now, he wondered if the tuath and the fostering he'd poured his life into would survive him, and the mantle of failure settled heavily on his shoulders. As they clustered round the hearth outside the cave mouth, all faces silent and glum, Seumus prayed to the Sun Lord to come and help them in their choosing, even if this was a Goddess rite.

Ceit and Eilid had come up to the cave just after the mid-sky meal and taken the ritual broth for an afternoon of visioning. Ceit sat out on the ledge, leaning on the rock wall beside the cave mouth with her eyes closed and her hands limp in her lap. She'd placed the shell cups of the elements in the four directions, waiting, but she was forbidden from beginning the ceremony; only the ruling matriarch could do that. And this thought rankled in Ceit's heart. After the tribe was assembled, Eilid emerged from the cave, too, walking dizzily, clearly still tranced. Her wavy brown hair had been carefully combed and braided into a thick plait down her back. Slowly, she bent and placed earth in one bowl, water in the second, left the next empty, and poured fat into the fourth and lit it.

"May the White Tara, Goddess o' light, be the One who chooses the matriarch this night," Eilid said clearly, her voice stronger than her steps as she leaned in to lift the Goddess figurine and raise her arms high. "I call forth, Aoife (eefa, Eva, mother goddess, Luckenbooth), matriarch o' all the clans, an' all female ancestors o' our tuath to come join our circle noo. Sisterhood o' power, show us the way o' truth." And Eilid turned and lit the hearth fire, dry grasses stuffed between the branches, which burst into crackling flames. Barefoot, as was customary for women's rites, Eilid walked deosil (sunwise) around the spirit wheel to the west, the place of mothers in the feminine circle of life, and faced the fire.

The night was dark, with wisps of fog that moved silently through the trees and only the sliver of moon. It's eerie tonight, Eilid thought, so different from the sea's loveliness and comfort I usually feel at the cave. And as she waited a moment, she recalled the night of her own choosing here, the feasting and dancing of the tribe afterward in the yard. That was seventeen winters ago, before Ceit came into this world at all. Then Eilid watched warily as Ceit took her place at the southern arm of the wheel, the virgin, place of a woman whose moon cycles had begun, but without children of her own. Ceit can't even step to the third place on the women's wheel, the mother, Eilid thought. How ill equipped the child is to lead a tuath. And I stand three-fourths of the way around the wisdom circle, only the role of grandmother left to fill someday.

As he watched, Seumus smiled. He'd been to several choosing celebrations in other tribes and noticed how some matriarchs embellished the festivities with formal words and extra robes that took scarce resources of the clan to make. He loved Eilid for her simple ways, always direct and to the point. She was practical, and she'd been a good wife to him, always. He wished he could hold her at this moment, but she knew he was on her side. Then Ceit looked at her mother, coldness filming her eyes and her hands fisted tightly against her thighs. As challenger, she had the right to speak first, and she turned to face the tribe. Her sharp nose and chin stood out in the firelight, her eyes darker than ever.

"I feel the Goddess more an' more every day," Ceit said in a clear voice that carried out over the bay. "She gives me strong legs to climb an' gather, a quick mind to see the tasks that must be done, an' clear knowings o' Her will for everyone. I feel the ways to please an' serve Her that'll keep the tribe healthy an' strong. Eilid's health is fadin', a clear loss o' Goddess power to the tribe. On this day o' questin', I heard the Goddess callin' me, sayin' it's time for a change, time to place Her power in me <u>own</u> hands noo." And Ceit held them out, palms up, before them all. "I long to serve Her an' ye." And Ceit knelt, putting her brow to the earth before the Goddess figurine a moment, before standing back in the circle, waiting for Eilid to speak.

Listening, Seumus felt Goddess power flow through Ceit's voice. And her eyes were free of the rebellion he so often saw there. How sacred the lassie looks in her ceremonial robe, he thought, slender and beautiful in her young womanhood. She speaks well, but I dinna understand the change that's come over her with her moon rites. And I dinna like it, either. Then Eilid stepped forward and stood before the clan.

"Me daughter is lovely an' full o' Goddess power," Eilid called out. "An' she speaks rightly. I am agin', though me hip is much improved noo. But there ll come a day in no too many winters when I step down from the Goddess seat. It's the Goddess Who'll decide when the time is ripe for that. An' I ask Her noo to make it very, <u>very</u> clear to us all when that day arrives, so there'll be no splittin' o' the tribe for moons over it like we've endured this fall. We're small enough at the tuath already. I dinna believe that time has come, an' this is why.

Me daughter feels the Goddess as a strong force o' will, an' Ceit wields this power often in the name o' truth. And she's correct in part." Eilid stopped to take in a long breath and focus on her Goddess figurine before the flames a moment, the small stone statue sparkling in the ember light. "But that will force can become a power unto itself, separate from the blended wishes o' all in the tuath an' from the Goddess Herself. The dark one, the false goddess we all distrust, strives ever to interfere. An' the voice o' the real Goddess that I've heard all me life, an' tried to bring into the every day choices o' the tribe, balances this force o' will wi' a great Heart that embraces all the clanfolk in <u>love</u>. It's this <u>heart</u> power o' the Goddess I believe to be Her highest truth, Her kindness an' gentleness comin' through to everyone. It's <u>this</u> that unites the tuath into one harmonious whole, too, all workin' together as each prefers.

If anythin', this Goddess <u>Heart</u> in the matriarch who represents it, leads her to hold the needs an' gifts o' others in the tribe a little above her own. An' me daughter, Ceit, doesna carry this heart force within, nor does she blend its power into her choices wi' the women, especially Soillse. We must be ever careful no to let the dark one rule here. I stay ever watchful o' that. An' so I ask the tribe to consider the possible harm, both o' choosin' a matriarch who's immature in her ways and o' livin' wi' the will o' the Goddess that's no blended wi' Her heart's love an' grace." And Eilid's eyes sparkled with tears as she spoke, and she stopped a moment to collect herself. How regal she looks in her embroidered robe, Soillse thought, taking a deep breath, eyes shining with admiration for her Ma. I want to be like that someday.

"There are others I see in the tribe who <u>do</u> carry the heart power o' the light One, an' that quality'll be necessary for any I recommend to replace me when me time comes to step down from the high seat." And Eilid gave a sharp glance toward Ceit. "These others, I believe, would serve both the Goddess in Her truth an' the tribe far better than the daughter who challenges me noo." Ceit gasped at this, her eyes wide in disbelief. Eilid spoke very softly to the circle gathered round the fire, but her voice was clear and crisp. With pupils still wide from the ritual herbs, her face was especially tender as she looked at them all in turn.

Seumus's eyes filled with love as Eilid's rested on his. It's true, he thought. How full of Goddess truth she's always been, though her round face and crooked smile canna be called beautiful. He recalled her gentle touch whenever he was injured, and the extra breads and puddings she'd made him, even late into the gloaming after long weary days. And then he thought how Eilid took time to speak to the women of the tribe, each one, every day, holding them all closely within the container of her heart. And he knew in this moment that Eilid carried the power of the Goddess far more than Ceit ever would. Then he suddenly realized that Ceit would resent her Ma more than ever now, much more, and their conflict would only grow worse. And he felt a sudden coldness, a dark force that wished only to break the tribe into pieces.

"I willna allow it," he breathed in a whisper, fisting his hands. The dark one ever wants control, and she succeeded with Elji's great aunt skyturns ago, when half the tribe left to live on the mainland. Let her not succeed this time, he thought fiercely.

As they waited, Eilid began to glow, a circle of light forming around her head and shoulders, seeming to come from the pale moonlight. Seumus rose then and went to stand beside Eilid, though men had no vote in a matriarch choosing. Muirn was already waiting there, and Sìne, too, walked to Eilid's side. Soillse, not yet a woman, had no power to choose, either. But she, too, eyeing Ceit with sadness, stepped beside her Ma. Only one of the remaining teacher's wives joined Ceit, the others crowding around Eilid as well. Then Eilid moved to the center of the circle of elements, bent, and picked up her Goddess figurine.

"As matriarch a while longer, I noo formally ask, when me time comes to leave the high seat, that both me daughters be considered as Goddess keepers. I'd always thought to give that honor to me elder lass. But I see noo I was wrong. I realize this may cause further difficulty, an' so I ask the Goddess o' light to help us heal this rift we noo face in the tribe." And as she bent, putting her left thumb into the ashes, Eilid motioned for Soillse to step into the circle. Soillse had only her cooking shift and woolen cloak on. And now, she felt a flooding inadequacy fill her chest with this sudden inclusion in the ceremony. Then Eilid placed her thumbprint on Soillse's brow, the signal to begin the path of purification for leadership.

In another moment, Eilid took up the bowl of fat and walked widdershins (counter clockwise) round the altar, pouring it on the hearth. The oil flared up in the dark, the signal that the choosing was complete. Then Eilid poured water from the next bowl, which flared up again in the oil, and then earth from the next on top, putting some of the fire out. She scattered the coals, neatly stacked the bowls, and put them inside the cave mouth. Then, not looking at anyone, Eilid started down the rocky path. All but Ceit followed in single file along the narrow rock face without a word, Ceit staring after them with her arms round her chest, scowling fiercely.

Chapter Seventeen: Fìrinn

Coillore drew Fìrinn to him after that first vision, slowly at the beginning, meeting alone in the oak clearing after lessons every quarter moon. They began with versed histories, nothing exceptional, just more to remember than the other ladds. But by the end of winter, they were meeting at the clearing two or three nights every quarter moon as Coillore began to prepare Fìrinn for his initiations of the elements: first earth, then water, air, and finally fire. And Fìrinn began to assist the druid at the equinox and solstice rituals as well.

Secretive by training, Coillore was formal with Fìrinn at first. He fussed at misspoken verses or Fìrinn's sleepy nodding during the vigils before ceremonies. But warmth showed through at times, too. The druid brought furs to wrap the boy in when the seasons turned cold, and once, the druid even insisted Fìrinn sleep into the morning after an all-night session at Imbolc. Seumus scoffed about a little loss of sleep, any warrior would, and complained to Coillore about the lost days of training Fìrinn's distractedness had already cost. But Coillore only nodded to Seumus, saying nothing more and making no move to wake the ladd.

And Fìrinn was glad for the lore, steeping in the teachings willingly. At times, he sensed a long pathway ahead of him that felt urgent, the template of his whole life, and only Coillore knew the way. It was the laws especially, and stories of the ancient priests and sages who formed them, that piqued Fìrinn's mind most. In his bed furs, he traced and retraced the turnings of their decisions, and a few times was certain he'd have chosen differently. And then there were those few startling moments, centuries before, when choices had been made that were so simple and full of truth, they'd changed the life of everyone in the tribes forever a little bit. Fìrinn was awestruck by the clarity and power of these turning points and secretly hoped for moments of such certainty himself, fervently wishing that for one instant he could sit at the Goddess's high table. And once in a great while, a sudden stillness came over his mind and some deep knowing rose up in his heart, an understanding he'd never had before. And he knew what he felt then was pure truth, free of all bindings. And this called him to the path like nothing else could.

As the skyturn spiraled toward summer, Fìrinn received news of a healthy sister, born to Frithe a moon before. And Ruadh reached his manhood, taller than ever, with his long fiery hair. Fìrinn, too, had grown tall and spindly, but his muscles had yet to fill in.

On the night of Ruadh's initiation, a cold drizzling night at the end of the Oak moon (early June), the four ladds beginning their manhood trials stood by the standing stone on the ridge at moonrise, each dressed in the plaids of their clans. Coillore allowed Fìrinn, fourteen winters to Ruadh's sixteen, to paint the sacred spirals on his friend before the ritual hunt. As Fìrinn painted, dressed only in his buckskin breeks, the images swirled clearly into his mind: a Celtic cross over Ruadh's chest, one quadrant for each of the stages of manhood: boy, virgin, father, and grandfather, around the central beloved core; the sword of destiny down the right arm; and the river of life down the left. Then the ladds raced away from the standing stone at Coillore's signal, to pass into manhood that night, each having spent their last ten skyturns at Seumus's fostering.

Fìrinn waited into a misty morning at the druid clearing, dozing by the fire with Coillore, to celebrate Ruadh's victory just past firstsky as the older boy dragged in a large boar. The tusks were Ruadh's to keep and hang from his ritual cloak, indicating he'd attained the boar's powers of determination and wealth. And bringing in a boar also gave Ruadh the sword right, for boar was the symbol of Llew (Stillpoint Center), the father god of abundance, a royal beast.

That night before the feasting, Fìrinn sat in the yard among the clustered boys. He felt the envy of some and heard several wish they could tame nature for their own glory, Duirc among them. Listening, Fìrinn thought how far this was from truth, for nature was of the Goddess, always sovereign, and no taming of Her ever occurred. Ruadh had been accepted by the spirit world as a fit warrior, and the spirit guardians simply let him know this by bringing the agreed upon sign from their world to his. Why couldna the other ladds see this?

The game was roasted for the celebration that evening. And after all bellies were full, as an orange sun hovered low over the western peaks, the whole fostering circled the hunters in the yard for their tattooing ceremony. Again, the lads to be initiated wore their clan plaids with no shirts, and in the flickering firelight, Coillore in his white druid robe, pricked each boy's skin and needled the blue woad under it. The druid chanted as he did so, the songs of each ladd's tuath and ballads of the powers of the animals each had brought in. The horse Ruadh wore for his clan held its own quality of wild freedom, but also determination, so the spirit of the boar he'd caught came clearly through, each boy's tattoo quite different.

When the tattoos were complete, Seumus took each new man in turn, standing before the roaring bonfire, and pledged them as warriors of the old way, the pledge of Scatha. The chief wore his full ceremonial dress, his clan plaid and embroidered linen shirt. With a lump in his throat, Fìrinn stood beside Ruadh as he swore to protect the women, children, tribes, and lands of Skye even unto death, and to return from the Otherworld to fight here, again and again, until the final victory over darkness was at long last won. The blood of Ruadh's right hand was mingled with Seumus's, and as foster father held Ruadh tight to his chest, the chief cried shamelessly, while all the ladds sang the song of this warrior tuath. It had been a day of morning fog and mist that cleared by late afternoon into a hazy sunshine. And now, the yard filled with the softened light of the sun beyond the horizon, a few twinkling star tuaths appearing, too, as was fit. And Coillore spoke of them, "for what happens on earth," he said, "also binds the star tuaths o' the ancestors, for all have vowed to live as we do in the lowest world, until the time o' freedom comes."

That night, the victors feasted at Seumus's table, so Fìrinn sat alone at the edge of the circle of mostly younger ladds now. His own manhood trial would be held in three skyturns, one year later than most because of his arrival at the fostering at an older age. Tonight Fìrinn wondered if he'd be ready for it. He hated to kill, even for food. And then, as the mead was passed and the pipes brought out, his thoughts were filled with the loss of his only friend, who'd set out in the morning for his home tuath. Pensive as he sipped his mead, Fìrinn watched quietly and went early to his furs.

And when that moment of parting came, the next day after the firstsky meal, neither ladd spoke of their sadness. Instead, they shared the direct gaze of brothers who knew they'd remain so for life. But as they hugged farewell, both hearts were full of yearning.

"Ye're always welcome in me tuath," Ruadh called back as he walked up the rise toward the wood with his uncle, "especially in need."

"And ye at mine, friend o' me soul," Fìrinn called back above the wind. Then he turned back to the yard for the morning games.

Not five moons later, during the Ivy moon (September), Coillore strode into the yard in broad daylight in his white robe. He sought out Seumus, who was shouting out the names of competitors for the afternoon games. The chief and druid began to talk, heatedly. Then Seumus crossed his arms tightly over his chest and frowned as Coillore motioned for Fìrinn to join them.

"The spirits will it, Seumus? Do ye wish to oppose them," Coillore was saying.

But Seumus only grit his teeth and walked away. So gathering his plaid and pulling it around his shoulders against the brisk wind, Fìrinn followed the druid silently, wondering why Coillore had come at midsky to interrupt his training. Keeping to the creek beside large mossy boulders, Bana Dhia following, they climbed inland up the deer path a short way and then headed north along a narrow stony track. Fìrinn brushed his hands on the lichened tree people as he moved through the forest and smiled at a distant pine, barely visible though the birches. Then suddenly, they stopped before an old yew, blocking the way. Coillore moved swiftly around it, crossing a small stream, to move out of view beyond. He called for Fìrinn to follow, and the ladd gasped as he came round the screen of branches.

It was a tiny glade, sheltered by the yew and surrounded by golden birch people, their leaves fluttering like a thousand banners greeting him. And just beyond the burn was a wee thatched hut. Coillore, with an uncharacteristic grin, stepped out of the way, bowed, and motioned for Fìrinn to enter. As a flash of sunlight illumined the doorway, Fìrinn stood mesmerized, for it had the Ogham symbol for Yew burned into it, the letter signifying the birth of light into the sensate realms.

As soon as he stepped inside, Fìrinn felt the closeness of the Otherworld he visited so often in his dreams. Coillore had told him it was possible to enter that world, and Fìrinn knew now the druid had done it, here. Built into the south wall was an open window with an oiled skin rolled above it, and the birch people stretched their arms through it into the hut. And Fìrinn wondered at that. No one made openings in their walls; the wind woman would eat them alive come winter! But perhaps Coillore had gentled her somehow. Bana Dhia was nosing around the hut, and Fìrinn noticed ritual objects spread out beside the altar along the far side. And he stepped toward them to kneel and stare, his eyes widening in wonder.

"It's time ye begin yer initiations, ladd," the druid said, but with a hint of laughter in his voice. "I have no other school to bring ye to, though I <u>will</u> get ye to the druid isle as sure as the moon circles, despite Seumus's objections." And the druid's mouth turned down a bit. The druid's hair was becoming white now, his heavy brows a contrast to his so-blue eyes. But at his words, Firinn's chest tightened in dismay. He stood abruptly and turned to face Coillore, their noses almost touching in the cramped space.

"No more verses!," Firinn said, nearly shouting. "No today. I want the wizard I ken ye are. This place is <u>full</u> o' magic!" Coillore burst into a laugh, then coughed and dropped his gaze.

"I wasna goin' to start wi' that," he said quietly, closing his eyes a moment, as if listening to the Goddess. "In fact, it's forbidden," he said decisively. "But I am allowed to show ye me assistants an' their powers before beginnin' the formal trainin', if ye like." Firinn's eyes lit up. "But first, let's have stew to celebrate," and Coillore's eyes crinkled as he smiled and pointed to the hearth.

The druid ladled out a bowl of soup that Firinn hadn't even noticed bubbling in the cauldron on the small hearth. Then, with swift efficient movements, Coillore mixed fat, flour from a skin bag, water, and oats, then flattened the mixture onto two hearth stones. And soon the smell of baking bread filled the room. The soup was unlike any Firinn had ever tasted, with wild carrot and garlic. But there was something else, a spice Firinn didn't know, that made a rich nutty flavor on his tongue. And when the browned oatcakes were handed over, minutes later, Firinn startled to see Coillore give Bana Dhia a bowl of soup all her own.

"What's the spice?, Firinn asked. And Coillore focused on the herbs above a moment, suppressing a smile.

"When we come to the lessons on manifestin' things from other worlds, I can describe it," he said. "But no today."

"Other worlds?" Firinn's eyes widened more.

"Nah, nah, not noo," Coillore repeated, but with one corner of his mouth turned up this time. Then the druid took the bowls, wiped them with ash, and stepped out to rinse them in the burn. On reentering, he pointed to the objects by the wall.

There were stones of all descriptions: crystals from the caves of the north, a bright green one that had washed up on shore the day following Coillore's own initiation into manhood, glittering pink gneiss from the outer isles, a piece of smooth black basalt from the western cliffs, a piece of green-white Skye marble, and a larger piece of white marble from Iona. And there was a small blue stone from Cymru that made Fìrinn gape and burst out.

"Stone o' the virgin god, Rìdire!" And the ladd pulled his own out of his neck pouch. "Ma gave me this." Coillore nodded.

"Ye've known magic before then?," the druid asked.

"Well, no much. Just once she showed me things I didna understand. Mostly she taught me herbs an' healin', no magic. But I want to learn it, Coillore!"

Fìrinn turned back to the ritual items, and the druid spoke a word or two about each one. There were bones, too: rooster, waterfowl and hawk, and feathers of crow and eagle, a heron's skull, and talons. There were teeth of wildcat, wolf, and tusks of boar, and antlers of the great stag, glossed to a sheen. As he held the objects up, Fìrinn could feel the powers of each animal clan, the soaring sight of eagles, the regal tenacity of boar. These things must bring the special qualities and spirit of their animal tribes to the rituals they're used in, Fìrinn thought in awe.

But then the ladd's head began to spin. He felt like it was expanding outward, rapidly, farther than the moorlands, further than the sea, beyond the earth mother herself, on and on, into the galaxies and the cosmos. Fìrinn groaned, holding his temples, and lay back on the floor. Many creatures of earth, both large and small, even insects, appeared suddenly in his mind. He saw them step out of the cosmic darkness and take their place in one great hearth circle, a huge bonfire burning at its center. And then the circle of beasts began to revolve sunwise, as a drumming filled his head, the slow beating of the earth mother's heart.

"The circle of Abred, where we are noo," Coillore whispered, "the realm o' earth existence, where all live in difficulty while the inner spirit grows strong. The sensate realms are ruled by the White Tara wi' help from Oghama from afar. An' one day, Their Kingdom o' light will be built here, when Their union o' worlds finally occurs. But those times are far away into the future. The earth initiation brings completion at this level."

In Fìrinn's mind, Otherworldly beings appeared in the outer darkness now, circling around the creatures of earth, each within their own bubble of light, spinning slowly by. There were fantastical shapes: mythical beasts and dragons, silver creatures with fish-scale skin, and some with horns or spouting noses and multi-colored hair.

"The circle of Annwyn, realm o' the soul," Coillore chanted softly, "Annwyn is the astral realm, a land o' light an' shadows that teaches wisdom an' the mastery o' fear. The soul realms are ruled by the elder mother o' the Creator Sun, Màiri, a very challengin' world. These soul realms anchor into the outer three planets o' our solar system, ladd. An' the end o' Màiri's dark night o' the soul brings the water initiation, often difficult, also."

The varied forms began to pulsate then, the light in their heart spaces becoming more visible, all hearts beating in time with the central Source, a soft glow that emerged and brightened from the central fire. This hearth slowly became a giant sun, pulsing softly. And its heart light kept intensifying until every form was blended into it, and then each changed, instead, into vast strings of stars, circling the deeps of space.

"The circle of Gwnfydd, the spirit realms," Coillore said softly. "This world interconnects the consciousness o' all forms throughout the cosmic mind but it's power is action. An' it's ruled by Rìdire, the virgin male o' the Creator Sun. He brings action impulses into the nerves an' mind o' everyone, a drivin' force for change if ever there was one. The final passage through his spirit realms brings the air initiation."

And then, the star pathways moved gently toward the central sun, drawn like fluttering moths toward its brilliance, until they fused into one gigantic whole, pulsing and beating to the rhythm of the One Great Heart. Firinn could see concentric rings of many colors there and felt its heartbeat intensely within, his own warming with a tenderness he could barely contain. He could see the same colored spheres nested around his own heart light, too, and he began to cry with the sweetness of the vision. Is this the Source of love?, Firinn wondered.

"Ceugant, the logos sun," Coillore whispered, "where the inner virgin girl is opened, tested, strengthened, an' birthed into one holy an' final purpose. These logos realms are ruled by Maighdean, the virgin girl goddess o' the Creator Sun. It's she who carries an' births the first glimmerin's o' each divine child, carefully built, an' lays them at last on the altar o' the One. The logos anchors into the Pleiades, ladd. An' completion at the logos levels brings the fire initiation, bittersweet." And Coillore's eyes softened with the memory of his own.

And then, Firinn saw himself lifted up through the small centerpoint of the logos sun, and suddenly his vision opened out. Before him was a small dazzling star, light blue, and all around it was utter peace. Winged children came to take his hands and pull him into soft white clouds banked in a pale blue sky. The rush of love intensified here, overflowing the bowl of Firinn's heart and filling him with joy unlike anything he'd never known.

"Leanabh Aingeil (leenuv anyeel, cherubim), land o' the babe angels," Coillore whispered, "an' beyond it the diamond centerpoint, an' Diamond Core, wi' the Creator Sun at its center. When yer consciousness reaches that central sun, laddie, magic, manifestation, an' true love, all ye ever hoped for finally comes true.

But the cherubim realms before it bring overwork an' the coldness o' the dark one in the women that surround ye. This level teaches lovin' kindness an' simplicity in all things, an' reopens the deep inner channel to the Goddess o' light. It's ruled by Abaid an' Uan together, the girl an' boy infants o' the Creator Sun, eh? An' it's completed by the cherub initiation, when ye leave the way o' life ye've known behind. These cherub realms anchor into the Sirian star system, ladd.

Then the outer rings o' the diamond centerpoint bring forward the trials o' the abyss, the regents o' darkness in the mind, heart, an' action levels within, the 6-6-6. It's ruled by the elder father o' the Creator Sun, the Dagda, an' it fills the heart wi' his strength, layin' the full foundation o' the highest destiny into place as well, plus cleansin' off the darkest shadows o' all six lower worlds. This is the most difficult level, the bone initiation. These diamond centerpoint realms anchor into Orion, the hunter, ladd.

An' finally, the Diamond Core leads up the highest mountain, puttin' the finishin' touches on that high destiny, an' bringin' forward the diamond initiation that brings final peace in its wake. This seventh heaven is ruled by Oghama Himself. An' each individual is structured exactly the same way, ladd, wi' inner sheaths o' light that correspond to each o' these seven worlds an' in the same order, from the outermost into the core. As ye climb on yer path, the sheaths o' each world burn off durin' their own initiations. An' then the next one opens, every world wi' its own conflicts, trials, an' truths to be revealed, till the Creator sun within finally emerges, free an' clear, an' the long-awaited inner divine child is finally born into earth life." And Coillore smiled as he lapsed into silence.

As the wind woman whispered through the hut just then, Firinn heard the sigh of an ocean, long forgotten, and its rhythm slowed Firinn's mind almost to sleep. Above it, he saw a primordial sun and felt a pregnant hush surrounding it, full of preternatural power, and he wondered at it. And then in his vision, the logos sun expanded out of the Diamond Core once more, drifting out in a timeless flow and breaking into smaller suns, the familiar constellations he knew, then shifting again into the beings and beasts of light, all dancing to the beat of life. *'We are all One,'* the Goddess voice whispered from the Central Sun and the outer darkness at once. *'Keep this memory sacred to direct your path, child of the One.'* And Her whisper changed to a low thrumming in his chest.

Very slowly, the pulsing within faded. The sweetness, too, receded, and Fìrinn longed to go with it. Some part of him refused to re-enter the world of every day, his heart clinging to that wild forever love. Finally opening his eyes, Fìrinn found Coillore kneeling over him, shaking a gourd and humming to the same beat, very softly, almost too low to hear. But as Fìrinn came out of the vision, the druid sat back and brushed a hand over the ladd's brow, smiling gently at him.

"Now ye ken," Coillore whispered, "the circles o' the seven worlds: earth, the cosmic sea, the star tuaths, the logos, the cherubim realms, the diamond centerpoint an' Core: Abred, Annwyn, Gwynfydd, Ceugant, Leanabh Aingeil, the Diamant Meadhen (jeeamahnt meehan, diamond center), an' the Diamant Cridhe (cree, diamond heart). An' last, the Cruthadair Grian (croohuder greean), Creator Sun." And the druid put his finger on Fìrinn's heart as his voice trailed into a sigh. With a wistful glance toward his altar, Coillore whispered, "the Goddess teaches ye rapidly, laddie," and he covered the boy with a thick fur. Then the druid propped Fìrinn's head up on one arm and held a cup of tea to his lips, sassafras with honey. And suddenly, in Coillore's mothering, the tenderness of the vision washed through Fìrinn again, and his eyes met the druid's.

"Ye hold the Goddess in yer heart, Coillore," Fìrinn said, and he reached up to hug the druid, one tear falling down the boy's cheek. "I feel Her love within ye, strongly." And Coillore nodded as he sat back on his heels.

"We all do, ladd. If everyone'd clear the fear shadows round their diamond core within, all could feel such wondrous love in every moment, an' beam it to everyone else. The Source o' love is <u>inside</u>, eh? I hide mine from most in this harsh world. But fellow aspirants to the Diamond Core must share much an' help each other all they can, for the trials are many, an' the way is steep."

Fìrinn took in a deep breath and let it out slowly. The gurgling of the brook beyond the doorcloth, the green glow of moss reflected on the rafters by the window, the birch people waving their bright yellow leaves so cheerfully, the sweetness of the Goddess, and Coillore's mothering all felt intensely alive. And suddenly, Fìrinn understood that one sparkling diamond facet of the Creator Sun lived in all things, opening into vision only in rare moments when it could make some difference in this world. And for this one instant, all the lonely days of the ladd's fostering, the old ache for his Ma, the pressures from his Da to hunt and become chief, and all his own worries about his destiny faded into nothing. With the dazzling love of the Creators at his very core, he knew that everything would be all right, and the certainty of this knowing fused into his very bones. Through the hardships of the years to come, this was the memory that would keep him whole.

Chapter Eighteen: Soillse

It was the hottest summer Duineil could remember, and he was nearing fifty winters. In the heat, the boys drooped by midsky, half-heartedly throwing a few lances or wrestling briefly and then running to the sea, scooping water on their heads. The rains had dried up just past Midsummer, and now it was halfway through the Apple moon (August), almost harvest time. For a moon and a half, Eilid and Muirn had carried water from the burn to pour on the plots of barley and oats, but even the stream was just a trickle now. The grasses were parched, too, and the ponies and cows were thinning. The berries and nuts in the forest hadn't ripened either, just dropped to the ground, hard as a stone. Eilid, warm even in her light summer shift, wondered how she'd feed forty-five fostered ladds, plus the teachers and her own, through the winter. Seumus consulted with Coillore more than once, and the druid performed a ceremony at the standing stone to bring the rains, but to no avail.

"There's a blockage in the Otherworld," Coillore said to Seumus, a few evenings after Lughnasa. "I feel some connection wi' yer daughter, Soillse. I'd like to speak wi' her about it an' ask her to help wi' a small ceremony perhaps." And Coillore glanced toward the underbrush that screened the Aine tree from the yard, where Soillse was sitting. "I'll be careful no to frighten her, Seumus," Coillore said quietly. Seumus sighed, then nodded. So the druid walked toward Soillse through the bracken, saying nothing to her up in the branches. He simply turned and squatted on the ground, leaning back on the apple tree. As Coillore approached her hiding place, Soillse stiffened, holding her arms across her stained hide apron and instantly sending the thought for him to go away before Ceit noticed her secret spot.

"Ceit is gatherin' roots on the ridge, but I willna stay if ye dinna want me to," Coillore said softly. "I only need to talk wi' ye for a moment. There's a blockage on the rains just noo, lassie, an' I think ye might be able to tell me what I need to ken."

Soillse's brows shot up, and she leaned out and looked down. Coillore was dark and small, and all at once, she felt how truly gentle the druid was, a man who refused to connect himself with the arts of war, unlike the rest of the men and boys at the fostering. And then she heard very clearly in her mind, '*Ye have special powers locked inside. I ken the ways to open them, an' I would help ye, but only if ye want me to an' when ye feel safe.*' And then Coillore rose in a smooth glide of movement and turned to face her, his white summer robe shining in the dappled sunlight. And his face was kindness itself.

"Yer inner powers an' yer silence keep ye close to the Otherworld, lassie. Few ken this, least o' all yer sister. I keep silence, too, an' speak often wi' the trees an' animals as ye do. I can come an' sit beneath yer Aine tree an' teach ye, just this way, even in thoughts, so no one'll ken. I'd like to come back at least once more. If it's ok, wiggle yer toes." And he winked.

Then he turned to look east toward the hills. Watching him, she wondered how he'd know if she wiggled her toes. '*I'd rather ye no come here again, though. I dinna want Ceit to ken about me tree,*' Soillse thought. And he smiled again. Then he whistled the robin song, and a small bird came to the branch and chirruped beside her. She laughed and reached out slowly to touch it, forgetting Coillore altogether.

"Oh, it's so close, look," she exclaimed, grinning. "I want to learn that, Coillore," she said.

'*Ok,*' she heard in her mind. He turned and faced her again, silhouetted by the sea. She wiggled her toes, and he grinned.

"I'll see ye at the quarter moon, lassie, three days from noo. That'll be the best time for healin' the Otherworld an' the rains. I'll meet ye at the beach then, after the evenin' meal." But her mind began to protest that Seumus wouldn't allow it. "I already spoke wi' yer Da," Coillore said softly, "an' he agreed, as long as I never hurt ye." Then the druid put his hands together, bowed, turned, and walked straight across the yard and up the narrow deer path beside the burn. And Soillse caught a glimpse of his robe among the tree trunks all the way to the place of tumbled boulders, halfway to the ridge.

She told no one about her meeting with Coillore, not even Seumus, but passed the next three days as usual: cleaning, cooking, carrying, washing, tanning hides, and especially now that there was less to eat, collecting shellfish. She'd spent much more time this last moon ranging the bays to the north and south, collecting muscles and limpets, ever since the land became so parched. She laid stones across the shallow tide pools, too, and then gathered the small fishes that were caught there after the sea ebbed away. The boys dashed right into the waves and speared larger fish, lots of them, and Eilid thanked the Goddess for every one. But all at the tuath were worried that the Goddess was angered and feared that worse was yet to come.

Three days later, just as the horn blew for the evening meal, Soillse was laying oatcakes on the hearthstones in the cooking hut, dressed in her workaday shift and hide apron as usual. She wiped the sweat off her neck, wishing she could go without her shift in the fire's heat like the ladds. Finally, she flipped the last of the breads over, backing away from the fire while they browned. Suddenly, she felt someone looking at her and twirled around to see who it was. Coillore was just coming into the yard, with his plaid over his white robe, for the weather had finally cooled. And he waved and walked to the open side of the hut, squatting, so his face was lower than she was. And then he put his hands together and bent his head a moment.

"Good evenin', Soillse," he said. Reflexively she brought her hands together, too, and then dropped them, surprised at herself. Her scalp tingled and she brushed her hair with one hand, staring at him.

"I knew ye in the Otherworld," she said, her voice very low. And then she smiled, and the smile transformed her face, the wrinkle between her brows fading away, and the rosy glow from the fire deepening behind the freckles on her cheeks. He grinned and put a finger to his lips.

"Shhhh, let's no let anyone ken." Then he winked and brought his hands together again. "I've been yer teacher many times, lassie. And ye've been mine a time or three noo, too." He looked sideways at her and lifted one brow. "Ye look like a faery yerself today," he said, as he glanced toward the south headlands. "I had a dream last night about the rains an' a message to go to the south beach. Want to come wi' me?"

"All right, when I finish these." And then she smelled burning oatcakes. "Achhh," she sputtered and flipped them all quickly into a wooden bowl on the floor, then covered them with a second bowl. "Ma gets mad if I burn food when it's so scarce. I shouldna've done that, Coillore. But only two are really scorched. I'll have to eat those meself," she said, puckering her nose. "But anyway, noo I'm done. We can go." She took a handful of oats from another bowl and the burned bread for her dinner and wrapped them in hide, took off her heavy leather apron, and folded it onto its stone shelf.

High tide was just turning, so they had to clamber across the boulders near the ridge, instead of just walking around on the flat sands. They climbed slowly over the low rocky arm of the bay, jumping down onto the pebbles of the south beach. This bay was small and very stony. And at it's back was a small cave the sea had scoured out, a place where Soillse often came to gather limpets.

Waves lapped the rocks half a pony length away from the cave mouth, and she remembered being caught here once as a babe when she came looking for the Sun Lord. Coillore motioned to her, and they went inside the opening, stooping under the dark stone entrance. The smell of brine was strong inside and the rocks were wet, glistening brown and mauve beneath her feet. They couldn't completely stand up, so Coillore pulled out an oiled skin and laid it over two of the flattest stones behind them. Then he sat and closed his eyes. *'I need to feel this place,'* he thought. *'Want to try that, too?'*

So she sat down beside him and leaned back on the damp rock wall, closing her eyes and breathing in the must. She felt a sudden coldness in her chest and a strong feeling of hatred of the Goddess. And then Soillse sensed icy fingers moving around her heart. And she gasped, for then she had a clear image in her mind of the druid who'd hurt her woman's place when she was four winters old. And suddenly, she knew he'd been here in this cave. She stood quickly then, bumping her head on the rocky overhang and stumbling out onto the beach again. Quickly, Coillore grabbed up the oiled skin and followed her out.

"Ye felt somethin'," he said.

She stared at the ground, her mouth open and breathing deeply, with her arms wrapped around her waist. "That bad druid, the one who hurt me eight summers ago; he came here," she said, pointing to the cave. "I ken it, an' I'll no be goin' in there ever again." She glanced up at him with her brows furrowed together. "An' ye knew it, too, didna ye, Coillore?" Refusing to look at him, she turned to run back to the tuath.

"Ok, we willna go back in, lassie. We dinna have to." Coillore spoke gently, but she heard him clearly as she stumbled over the rocks. "But I'd like to teach ye about fear, Soillse, if ye'll let me. It comes for a reason; all things do. An' there's a reason ye were hurt then, an' a reason that man's memory is strong here in this cave." She stopped a few pony lengths away, still facing north, listening.

"What do ye mean?"

"Well, there's darkness, like that one, that sometimes comes into our lives. An' it always wants to remind us that we agreed to believe in it once, long ago, usually in another world on our long journey down from heaven to earth. When we descended out o' the Creator Sun, we took in a lot o' fears, many, many beliefs in darkness. We all did, everyone. That's just the way it is. An' every one o' those fears is pure illusion. Still, they create whatever happens in our lives, so they're powerful, dear. But we can heal them an' remember the truth each one blocks within. So, if some darkness comes into a body's life, the person who's hurt by it an' reminded o' the long ago is just being called upon by the spirit world to heal it. That's all. An' that inner healin' helps the person, the whole earth, an' the Otherworld a little bit, all the way up to the part o' heaven that fear was created in."

"Heal it?" She whirled to face him with a sudden flush on her cheeks. "Can ye heal a thing like that, heal _me_?"

"Aye, can an' will, whenever ye're ready, lassie." His voice had dropped to a whisper and he squatted a moment, fingering a flat gray pebble.

"Does it hurt?" Soillse asked, wishing suddenly for her Áine tree.

"Nay, lass, soft as a whisper. An' when it's done, ye'll be laughin' like the burn in spring. Want me to show ye?" And he walked ahead of her to a place where a bit of sand showed through the sea-tumbled boulders and drew seven circles in it. She climbed on the rock above him to see as he placed his staff in the center circle.

This is the Diamond Core o' the cosmos, where the Beloveds live an' create all that is, Oghama an' the White Tara, forever in love. All is light there. There's no pain an' no a hint o' fear, just union an' happiness forever. The father lives there, too, the One me eyes remind ye of." And as Coillore glanced up at her, she felt another tingle run down her scalp and spine. And suddenly, she saw in her mind a large twelve-sided room with high windows. And within it, everything glowed. And then she stepped out to a sparkling rose garden, through high arched doors. And suddenly, the gentle blue eyes of a tall, golden-haired God were looking down into hers. And tears sprang into her eyes.

"The Dagda, elder father o' the Creator Sun,," Coillore whispered. And she nodded, her heart beating faster as the stalwart protection of the father's love filled it. Coillore waited in silence a while, breathing in the tenderness that filled the air.

"That's the Dagda's hall ye're seein', too, lassie," the druid said finally. "We go there for a short while between our lives on earth, to choose which fears we'll face in our next life an' how we'll heal them while we're here. An' when we heal just everythin', then we can go an' live wi' the Sun Lord forever an' never come back to the pain o' earth life. How I <u>ache</u> for that day!" Coillore's breathing grew deeper for a moment, and his eyes sparkled with tears.

"Aye," she said, nodding fiercely. "I remember it noo." And she shook her head, as if shaking the sleep mist from her mind. "Oghama an' me Da in heaven both live there. They're nice an' I <u>miss</u> them," she said in a small voice, crying now. "I came to help the clans somehow, Coillore. An' Fìrinn came wi' me."

"Aye," Coillore nodded, his eyes still wet, desperately wishing he could hug her and knowing he could not. "Few there are who remember that place. Ye've come a long way down to help us, lass." And he stood beside her, hoping the gentleness of the father he sent around her heart would be enough.

"There's a Goddess there, too," Soillse whispered, closing her eyes tight, "in a lovely gown, just the color o' the full moon, Coillore. It's as soft as Aine's petals," she said, grabbing his shoulder and gazing down at him, her eyes questioning.

"Aye, lassie, that's the White Tara, the Goddess Beloved. She lives there, too," he said, pointing to the center circle, and then the seventh one out. "But She descended to earth, an' She's no always safe. It's a hard walk She chose, for She wished to be near us all through the darkness, an' She wouldna stay in Paradise wi' Her children scattered all over creation. It's Herself makes the rains, an' just noo, She's blocked from this tuath by the false druid who hurt ye."

"Ach, an' I'm pledged to Her daughter, Maighdean." Soillse burst out. "She lives in a shell castle like a water lily blossom in a white stone city, an' she came to me one night when I sat in me apple tree five summers ago!"

As Soillse spoke, the druid had trouble restraining himself. He wanted to swing the girl up and shout. No child he'd ever known, no druid even, without fifteen winters training under his belt, had ever seen those heights, so clearly remembered. And no one could do so unless the fears left to heal were few; otherwise the shadows over the memories were just too thick. He stared up at the girl, his face flushed, and breathed to calm himself.

"That's the virgin goddess o' the Creator Sun, ye recall, lassie, an' the city o' the Goddess resurrected in Paradise." He pointed to the central circle drawn in the sand, then moved his staff to the next circle out. "This world is the diamond centerpoint. Leanabh Aingeil is next, then Ceugant, an' Gwynfydd, here," he said, moving his staff to the second, third and fourth circles. Continuing into the sixth and seventh, he added. "Next is Annwyn, the outer darkness, and then Abred, the world we live in noo." She was tugging his arm now, gently. "Ye have the seven worlds within ye, too, lassie, round yer heart, just like these circles in the sand."

"That druid. He was in the Otherworld, too, then, long ago somewhere. Is that right, Coillore?" And she pinched her mouth together, trying to understand. "When he comes near our tuath, he goes into that cave. I can feel it. An' he wants to hurt me again." And she began climbing over the rocks in her haste to get away. But Coillore didn't move. He only sent the thought of healing after her, and she stopped suddenly and looked back at him.

"Ye can run, lassie, but the Goddess'll send him to find ye every single time ye come to earth. For it was that false druid who first planted this fear in ye, an' the pull o' it will ever draw him back into yer life. It's very old, this one, from deep in the Core, closin' down the virgin goddess within. An' that man has followed ye all the way down through these worlds," he said, moving his staff across every circle. "An' that fear'll bind yer life an' keep ye in yer tuath an' yer little hut, never lettin' ye live or breathe, growin' tighter, ever tighter at the Goddess's biddin', until ye face it. When She decides it's time, lass, there's no gettin' away from it. Or ye can heal it noo, an' ye'll be free of it forever. That choice is yers." Coillore spoke very quietly, his eyes scanning Soillse's face, but his hands trembled in the pockets of his robe.

"How?" She asked him.

"Imagine the druid in yer mind, his heart especially, for can ye feel that is where he keeps this fear? It's black an' filled wi' hatred o' the Goddess an' virgin lass both. See?" She closed her eyes and nodded. "Imagine yer own fear o' him, too, an' how ye believe he'll always find ye, no matter how far away ye go. See how ye feel that he'll tarnish yer woman's place an' always make ye feel small an' afraid, wi' men who love ye especially? Lassie, ye believe that man's hatred is stronger than any man's love, even the King o' Love, Oghama, the One Beloved. An' that isna truth at all, dear. Love is stronger than any fear, always an' forevermore." Coillore twirled an interlaced silver band on the third finger of his left hand as he spoke, looking inward a moment. "An' then, imagine those fears, his an' yers both, movin' into the diamond Creator light in the sanctuary o' yer own heart, right in the center o' the four lobes there. Ye dinna have to see it, lass, just set yer intention, an' it'll be done. That wee flame is a small piece o' the Creator Sun, fire o' the Creators in union. It creates, eh? An' so, yer own small diamond light creates all shadows an' light surroundin' it into yer life. So let yer own fear an' the druid's hatred melt in yer own Creator flame within, for that Beloved love is the strongest force in all worlds."

So Soillse closed her eyes as tightly as she could and did as Coillore described. "Then say out loud," he added, "I release me belief in that fear, an' I willna ever believe in it again. An' it'll be gone, forever an' a day, for ye have full power over yer own little world, lass, we all do. Ye're the queen o' it. So, if ye ask that tiny piece o' fear that belongs to ye alone to move into the Creator flame in yer heart, it has to do as ye bid it. An' then, it'll be gone an' no be created into yer life any more. An' the dark strand that binds it to ye will be pulled out o' all worlds, too. Here an' here, an' here," he said, pointing to the circles, "all the way to where it first began, for this one, all the way to heaven's Core." He let out a soft sigh, and drawing his hands together, bowed to her.

And then in her mind, Soillse suddenly saw a bloody gash in her woman's place. And she felt that false druid could crush out, not only love in her life, but the power to manifest her dreams, too, the gift of her maidenhood. And she put her hands over her face a moment. But then, sitting down on the rocks, she imagined <u>that</u> fear moving into the diamond light in her heart, too.

"I release me belief in that fear, an' I'll never again believe in it," she said softly, as Coillore put his arm around her shoulders, very lightly. When she opened her eyes, he pointed to the moon, just rising over the ridge. "Are ye sure this works, Coillore?"

"<u>Very</u>," he said with utter finality. "I've done it thousands o' times to keep the tribe safe an' do me part to help heal all worlds," he said, pausing. Then with a smile he placed his staff firmly into the center of the seven circles, "an' so I can return to the Creator Sun an' never leave it again! It <u>always</u> works, lassie."

"It's easy," she said.

"Aye, once ye've been hurt by the fear in order to remember, an' then faced it, the healin' is easy enough." But he sighed as he said it.

"Do we have to be hurt then?"

"We've each spoken for a certain share o' all the fears there are, aye. An' those are ours an' no one else's. It renews the wisdom stream o' the Goddess, experiencin' these lessons o' non-love. Like everythin' else, wisdom is a livin' stream. It grows stale after a time, unless it's lived again. Besides, lassie, pain brings the teachin's out o' the mind an' into the heart, so we never forget. An' afterwards, we can live the laws o' love as easily as breathin'. That's what wisdom is, lassie, one o' the great gifts o' Tara Herself. Otherwise, no one would care about anythin' at all, no in the same way. But these are lessons for many moons into the future." And he waved these thoughts away, sitting down beside her.

"But how can one person make any difference, Coillore? It's so big," she persisted, gazing up at the sky, the lowering orange sun just above the sea reflected in her green eyes. And he nodded.

"It's given to humanity alone to clear the forces o' darkness from all worlds; the Creators will it. Oghama an' Tara want us to be like Them, to experience that love is stronger than any fear in the cosmos, so we ken it to our depths. An' it is. We're the only ones who carry this task who live within the realms o' darkness." He paused, smiling softly.

"An' so, when it's time to master fear, to clean out the shadows over our heart's core," he said, stopping again to collect his thoughts. "An' mind, lassie, whatever there is inside, light or dark, affects the whole earth, an' all worlds, for that wee Creator flame in each heart creates whatever it shines through into all realms," he said, pointing to his chest. "So when it's time to face our own demons, then we're called. It's the shaman's path, an' many are the adversaries that come. But wi' the facin' an' healin' o' every one, the wee god/goddess within, the divine child, grows an' grows, until it's born, so everyone can see. An' then in the end, ye're allowed one great gift to give the people or the land ye love most, an' ye never have to come back to battle darkness again. No ever." He drew in a long breath, gazing at the sinking sun beyond the peaks across the sea loch.

"When it's time, lassie, ye'll remember." She sat nestled beside him with her head in her hands, and the last rays of the sun kissed her crown before dropping beyond the Cuchullin hills.

"Coillore," she said finally. "I _am_ bein' called."

"Aye," he said, smiling again, his heart warming to these sudden clarities of hers.

And then they walked back to the tuath in the gloaming, climbing the low rocks of the headland and standing a while on the beach to watch the waves break over the sands. In that moment, it was the wild loveliness of the spirit's freedom Soillse tasted.

"I want to be as free as that," she said suddenly, pointing to the breakers.

"Ah, Goddess power," he whispered, "an' _lots_ o' it. Ye'd have to endure much an' heal it all to have the force o' love those waves are full of, lassie. Ye might want to think on that a while." But she only pulled her chin up a bit and looked into his face.

"I've already decided," she said softly, raising her brows. "I want to go Home." And her face trembled as she spoke. "Please, Coillore," she said, "dinna say no."

He stood before her then and bowed, very low. So she didn't see the way his brows pulled together or the taut line of his mouth. But she did feel the sadness in him, and then she remembered how a cloud had covered the father's heart a moment, before she'd said good-bye to him in the Otherworld, just like Coillore's now.

As the horizon deepened from rose to purple, the breeze picked up, and low clouds gathered in over the sea from the north. The first drop of rain hit her shoulder, and then many more fell as they walked quickly toward the roundhouse.

"The blockage is broken," Soillse said quietly. "Tell me the truth, Coillore. Did I do that?"

"Aye, lassie. Ye used the power in yer own wee Creator flame to heal the blockage. An' then, the Goddess made the rain, so ye and yer Mum did it together in a way." On an impulse then, Soillse put her arms around Coillore's neck and hugged him tight. She felt his shoulders trembling, but she did not see his eyes fill with love. And then she reached her arms up to the sky.

"Thank ye, Tara an' Oghama," she whispered, "for the power o' Love that heals all things. An' Tara, thanks so <u>much</u> for the rain!"

Chapter Nineteen: Fìrinn

Every quarter moon since last summer, nearly a skyturn, Coillore had brought Fìrinn to his hut and placed a stone of knowing on his brow. And Fìrinn let the memories the stone held unfurl into his mind, moving the fears they showed him into his heart all afternoon. To heal the fears, Coillore taught Fìrinn to focus his mind on the ancient difficulties until he sensed the false beliefs he'd taken in then, essentially false gods he'd accepted as truth. And the druid showed Fìrinn how to imagine the pictures from the past moving into his heart, and how to hold them there in the tiny light of the Creator flame, while they transmuted back into light. It never took long.

As Fìrinn healed himself, Coillore sorted herbs and placed them in ordered bunches along the rafters. And then toward evening, the druid made a stirabout, ready just as Fìrinn grew tired of visioning. Often the druid shared surprises he'd found among the hills, too.

"True magic is always simple," Coillore said once, handing Fìrinn two fried tern eggs. And the ladd smiled, for they were one of his favorite foods. And often, there were roots or spices in Coillore's stews only a druid could find, hidden in a cleft on the ridge, up in the mosses, perhaps. That fall, Fìrinn often returned to the long house with pockets full of walnuts or crisp late apples that he shared with the younger ladds.

And the glade surrounding Coillore's hut became a world of its own, for Fìrinn always felt welcomed by the yew, the wee burn, and the birch people, as though they waved in the wind just for him. In Coillore's gentle domesticity at the end of these healing afternoons, Fìrinn also felt the heart of a barren mother, longing for a child of her own and over-nourishing any substitute she could find. And he felt a father, too, aching to pass on the wisdom of his lifetime to a foster son, so it would be safely carried into the future. Often during the in-between times in the yard, Fìrinn couldn't wait to go back to the peace of Coillore's hut.

The druid lessons in the clearing with the others continued as before, too, Coillore rarely even breaking into a smile during the recitations. So it was only Fìrinn who saw the druid who hugged the yew beside his hut, called the full moon 'me love', and sang lullabies to the deer that came for acorns in the fall. Just once, arriving early at the glade in the Birch moon (January), the ladd caught Coillore eating a fist full of snow, just as any bairn might do. And despite Fìrinn's dislike of the sometimes terrifying emotions that arose from the memory stones, those afternoons with Coillore were the happiest of his childhood years. As his friendship with the old druid grew, Fìrinn's inner solitude, always keeping to himself those minute details no one but he and his Ma ever noticed, began shedding like an old skin, one layer after another. And the druid's kindly wisdom opened Fìrinn's heart like nothing else could have, for in Coillore, Fìrinn felt the father he'd always wished for, the brother he'd never had, and the priest he hoped to become.

"I must get ye to the druid isle," Coillore muttered with a frown as winter deepened, sitting beside his hearth, both he and Fìrinn wrapped in furs. "The quest o' the brown robes canna be done here at the tuath, no in the old way, the way I ken." And the druid sighed, thinking of Seumus. "The spirits'll have to intervene, ladd, for ye're meant to be a druid as sure as the burn runs to the sea."

One night late in the Birch moon, Coillore warmed some nettle tea on his hearth and filled Fìrinn with hazelnuts. The druid still wore his heavy woolen white robe and Fìrinn his buckskin breeks and fur-lined jerkin, with his plaid pulled tight around him, for the winds were cold. Then Coillore leaned over and drew the familiar concentric circles of the seven worlds on the floor beside the hearth.

"The seventh heaven, here," the druid said, putting his staff firmly into the center circle, "is the Diamond Core. There are fifteen structures o' light there; three for the mind, three for the heart, three for action, an' five for the five basic aspects o' God/Goddess, plus the White Pentagram o' the Goddess. The first nine I mentioned are the sacred triple three. (These light structures are listed on page 17.)

We'll be goin' through each one o' the triple three in detail in yer lessons over the next skyturn. But I'll just list all fifteen light structures for ye noo. At the top is the Creator Sun, home o' the Creators, Oghama an' Tara, land o' the Beloveds. It creates all that is. Below it is a 16th light structure that isna permanent, the Dragon or Death Star. It blocks the light o' the Creator Sun and builds our deepest fears into us, always closely connected to each person's highest destiny. It streams from Draco, the dragon.

Below this is the Stillpoint Center, the overlightin' mind structure o' the cosmos, an' its star compound is the Helix nebula that looks like an eye. This light structure creates the outer world, ladd. An' it anchors into the mind creator flame in each person's pineal gland or mind's eye. Next is the Luckenbooth or double heart light structure o' the virgin girl, the overlightin' heart structure o' the cosmos that brings forth union o' hearts o' male an' female into lifelong partnerships in the world. It anchors into the emotion creator flame in everyone's hearts, ladd, an' it streams from Aquarius. Then comes Tìr Nan Òg (tear nahn awg, land of the young men), the overlightin' action light structure o' the cosmos, land o' the virgin boy, streamin' from Aries noo. An' it anchors into the action creator flame behind everyone's pubic bone in the base.

Next come four light structures o' our basic inner aspects, first the Old Heart structure o' the mother, from Reticulum (ladies' purse), that orchestrates the family flow o' resources across the earth, plus all events on the global stage that bring up ancient feminine memories for healin', especially concernin' family wealth. Then comes the Son o' the Sun light structure o' the boy, which creates each person's every day an' builds the path Home into all human lives, streamin' from Pisces. It overlights the global healin' o' the boy aspect, too. Below this is the Old Heart o' the father, from Libra noo, which orchestrates global commerce an' finance, plus all worldwide impulses for healin' o' the adult masculine. An' last is the Child Heart pentagram o' the little girl, from the Sirian star system. It builds the seven-tiered rainbow body o' the magical child within, the bairn we'll all become when we graduate out o' earth life forever, eh?" And the druid smiled. "An', o' course, it overlights global healin' o' the girl aspect as well. Then the Creator Sun above them all is the light structure o' the inner beloved aspect, so that's all five."

"Then we move down to the seven visible chakras. First comes the Wizard Wheel, regents that overlight the workin's o' the universal mind an' our own brains as well, the seventh chakra, an' its goal is the union o' heaven an' earth. It streams from Monoceros, the unicorn. Then comes the Pineal Wheel, the great father complex o' the Eagle, Aquila, the beacon o' truth o' the cosmos that anchors into our pineal glands an' ever leads us toward higher truths. It's the sixth chakra. These two an' the Stillpoint Center resonate wi' the mind.

Below them comes the Triple Spiral, anchorin' into the throat. It sets our spiritual walks an' paths o' life experience into place, sendin' out one spiral each for the mind, heart, an' action centers each moon, movin' us all forward in life. The arch druid and high priestess sit in the center here. This level creates religion an' ritual, an' it flows from the star Ara, the altar. It's the fifth chakra, ladd. Next comes the Holy Family o' the heart." And the druid pulled his hands together and bent his head a moment. "It creates our immediate family members, an' its star system is Cygnus, the swan. It's the fourth visible chakra. These two an' the Luckenbooth resonate wi' the heart an' emotion, ladd.

Next come the Pillars that build the ten basic qualities o' God an' Goddess into us as we climb though the lower worlds, the third chakra. The pillars flow through earth's continents an' each person's solar plexus, which holds the templates o' everyone's highest destiny. These Pillars stream from the star Columba, the dove. Then comes the Circle o' Eight light structure, regents o' the solstices, equinoxes, an' cross quarter days. This level rules the agricultural cycle o' the skyturn, too. An' it anchors into our abdomens, the second chakra, streamin' from Bootes, the herdsman, eh? These two, plus Tìr Nan Òg, resonate wi' the action centers.

An' last comes the White Pentagram, light structure o' the Goddess, anchorin' into the pelvic cradle. It overlights the birth o' each person's divine child or highest destiny on earth an' streams from Ursa Major, the great bear, ladd. For humans, this is the first visible chakra.   The fifteen sacred light structures all sit in the seventh heaven. An' below this is the sixth heaven, the diamond centerpoint. It contains the Indigo Pentagram. So when a person descends all the way into the sensate realms, the first or lowest heaven, which are the inner planets o' our solar system, then the White Pentagram moves in to become each person's first visible chakra, an' the Indigo Pentagram becomes the earth star below their feet. The latter is the light structure o' the dark half or crone aspect o' the goddess, leadin' us to embody wisdom, humanity's sole purpose for bein'. It streams through Ursa Minor, the little bear.

But as a person births their divine child here, the Indigo Pentagram an' dark half o' the goddess fall away. The White Pentagram fades as well, for as the structure that builds the divine child within, it's no longer needed. From that moment on, the newly divine human becomes like bein's in all other realms, wi' fourteen permanent light centers. An' the light half o' the Goddess from the White Pentagram in the base moves up into the Creator Sun. The Creator Sun an' Stillpoint Center become the organizin' light structures above their heads. An' all the rest are the twelve cosmic chakras o' light that stream from the twelve sacred gateways in the C r e a t o r   S u n .

So, let's move to the Creator Sun noo. This Sun, the very core o' the universe, has the same twelve levels within. This is important, ladd, for the fabric o' the Creator Sun is interwoven wi' the light structures o' earth, the identical sacred levels within our own planet. It's because earth is the creator sun o' the sensate realms, the Creator Sun realized into physical form. For the Creators are slowly transformin' the lowest world into the image o' Themselves to be revealed in those beloved communities o' the future, true loves with their families o' light, each person an' family commmunity servin' their own sacred purposes before God an' Goddess, heaven on earth. This is Oghama an' Tara's cosmic miracle o' miracles!

Both the Creator Sun an' earth are very precisely structured, ladd. There are 360 degrees in a circle, eh? The vertical bands are Oghama's, so every 30 degrees resonates wi' a different band o' the sacred twelve chakras. These begin wi' a line through Albion (England), the country o' Oghama on earth. That line'll be known as the prime meridian someday. Oghama's flow streams sunwise, o' course, Him bein' the Sun Lord. This is the warp, the vertical fibers o' the tapestry o' life. An' then, from north to south, there are 180 degrees, eh? So every 15 horizontal degrees resonate wi' a different one o' the sacred twelve chakras. Easy, eh? These are the horizontal bands o' the Goddess, the weft o' the tapestry o' life. That's because He sends out information on vertical bars o' light, an' She send Hers on horizontal ones!

So, let's see, vertically, Alba is just west o' the prime meridian, so it's in the top one o' Oghama's twelve segments, the Luckenbooth, the virgin girl's union o' hearts light structure. That's because union o' hearts into lifelong partnerships an' the union o' heaven an' earth are Tara's main regencies, an' this is Her land. Then horizontally, Alba's in the 10th chakra, the mother's Old Heart that brings lands an' personal wealth to each family. Well, o' course it is, for Tara's the Mother-o'-all, wantin' to make certain each family is nourished an' cared for on earth.   The Creator Sun crown o' earth anchors just above the north pole, ladd, holdin' Oghama an' the White Tara's high vision o' Paradise here. An' the Stillpoint center anchors into the pole itself. O' course, in our times o' forgettin', the pole is frozen solid, but when mankind begins to awaken, the north pole'll melt an' restore the Creator's flow o' light here. Earth's south pole is the Indigo Pentagram, frozen into the rhinoceros form o' the Death Star's reptilian mother, who keeps Tara hidden an' closed down here. But in time, it, too, will melt, restorin' Tara's flow o' life to all on earth. In twenty-one centuries, earth's indigo pentagram will fade away, once the cosmic wisdom stream has been renewed. An' the divine child o' earth's first visible chakra will be born, Paradise restored!   That'll mark the end o' the long outbreath o' the Diamond Core that began eons ago wi' a great explosion o' life into the cosmos. The outbreath is Oghama's, supportin' His individuation an' expansion tendencies. For the long inbreath to come, humanity an' all realms will choose a new purpose, one based in love an' the union impulse o' the Goddess. Pathways between star systems will reopen as the veils between worlds fall away. Ye'll be able to visit yer family in yer Creator Sun tuath, ladd, heartfelt reunions o' long lost relatives occurin' at all levels. No that there willna be challenges in the future, there always are. But this phase'll be a happy one, wi' evil transmuted an' behind us. Only a few seeds o' darkness'll be held at bay for gentle lessons then or for the next great outbreath perhaps, in a future too far away to be contemplated. It's a lovely pattern, hm? An' it brings much comfort to ken yer a part o' the Creators forever, one small drop that lives in the cosmic whole, world without end. It makes me feel very much at Home, no matter what world I happen to be livin' in." And Coillore refilled Fírinn's cup, waiting a moment before continuing.

"So, let's get to the lesson about the twelve regents o' the Creator Sun, for that's what I want to teach ye today, ladd, structured like our own physical hearts in four quadrants. Ascension into the Creator Sun brings a profound shift within. For it's the <u>Heart</u> that's ever strivin' to bring <u>love</u> into the world." And the druid drew his palms together, bent his head a moment, then leaned over and drew a triple Celtic cross in the earth beside the hearth.

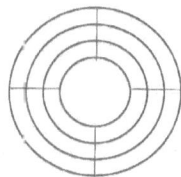

The core o' the Creator Sun, the central wee circle here, is a binary structure, two vibrations or separate suns that pulse apart an' together every few seconds, the heartbeat o' the universe. It's Tara's moon hidden within Oghama's sun, wi' a central united Core. Then the surroundin' circles divide the cosmos into quadrants: mother, father, girl, an' boy. All things are made in the image o' the Creator Sun, the continents o' earth structured exactly the same, as is each nation, village, an' human body. The mother is always in the northeast or left chest an' arm, the girl in the southeast or left abdomen an' leg, the boy in the southwest or right abdomen an' leg, the father in the northwest or right chest an' arm, an' the beloveds in the center, the heart. Each human heart is identical, the four quadrants in the physical lobes. An' in the very center o' those lobes is the Creator flame, a spark o' the Beloveds o' the Creator Sun. But this flame remains in the ethers noo, wi' no physical form.

But more importantly, ladd, this Creator Sun structure overlights the <u>inner spirit</u> o' every bein' there is. See the three circles around the Beloved Core? Wi' one regent in each quadrant, that gives ye the sacred twelve, eh? An' every person on earth has all twelve o' these parts o' her or his spirit that open durin' the various stages o' each life. Ye could call it yer personality, too. Ye are male on the outside, laddie, but ye have both male an' female within, we all do, hm? An' ye'll live through infant, child, virgin, parent, grandparent, an' god/goddess phases o' yer life, for there are elder an' younger forms o' the four basic parts in the quadrants, too.

The heart has simple goals, Fìrinn, without any o' the extravagance o' the mind an' action levels,' all these Creator Sun regents as humble as can be. For these arena meant to be seen with outer eyes in a single individual held up higher than all the rest. No. It's only when we get to the Stillpoint Center, shaped like an eye itself, that outer human teachers from that level'll come to earth to be seen outside ourselves. Mind this, ladd, if ye hear nothin' else I ever tell ye! At the Creator Sun level, these twelve regents an' Beloveds have millions o' faces, an' just as many names, for all folk everywhere hold them in their beings, like cells o' One great body. We are all One!

But there will come a teacher in about a century, whose life an' family will be very, very like the regents o' the Creator Sun. His name'll be Jesus, an' his life'll greatly widen the Creator Sun stream to earth; his birth'll be very like the Creator Sun divine infant boy, his bairnhood like the Creator Sun boy god, his life very like the Creator Sun virgin male god, an' his later life like the Creator Sun father god. Plus, his Ma'll be like the Creator Sun virgin girl an' elder mother goddesses. An' their example will help awaken all the folk who dinna recall the Creator Sun any more, people who have heavy shadows blockin' those old levels. So, ye could say Jesus an' his parents are outer representatives o' these levels in a way. But so are we all. The gentle love yer Ma gave ye as a babe is no less sacred than Jesus's Ma will give him, no different at all. Everyone everywhere is a vessel o' the Creator Sun!

As well, the high Gods an' Goddesses o' all religions are identical, ladd, only the names an' the flavorin' different, subtle tastes that nourish the palates o' our spirits so well. But the essence o' God/Goddess, the basic truths, all are One! An' we are each required to taste every one o' these basic aspects on earth, too, livin' on each continent over many lives to build the various parts o' our inner spirits. If ye look very closely, ye can see the remnant o' Buddhist lives lived in the past in the eyes o' a tribesman o' Alba, or ancient African times in the smile o' a woman o' Albion, perhaps. There are untold experiences to learn from, to take into our hearts, all the subtle colors o' the paintbrush o' God/Goddess. Life is a wondrous tapestry, a kaleidoscope o' Them." And the druid bent his head a moment, his voice too husky to continue.

"But in the dark illusions o' the future, divisons'll rise up between the varied religions, all wantin' to be better than the others. Hundreds o' years o' violence'll promote death an' dig these divisions deeply, darkly, across the entire globe. They are illusions, every one, born o' the regents o' the Dragon star that we all carry within as well, in the same shape an' structure as the Creator Sun, our shadow selves.

No only do these Creator Sun regents come through each individual, but they also stream through family members everywhere, the same divisions: mothers, fathers, girls, boys, an' beloveds ,o' course. For this light structure also creates <u>families</u>, all these twelve regents comin' through our own family members in intimate personal ways to reach every one o' us, reflectin' our fears, holdin' us in our sorrows, an' mainly lovin' us more than anyone else.

These Creator Sun regents also create the family templates o' highest <u>heaven</u>, specific families o' light wi' particular interests an' passions they share. We were each created into light out o' this Creator Sun once, in a single instant, eons ago, an' we have a family o' light who lives there. Our Creator Sun families remember us from before our fall, when we had no a trace o' fear within. An' they wait for all lost family members to return Home an' live in love an' peace again forever. Yer eternal family o' light is no like yer human family, for our human families were the ones chosen to bring in all those fears an' shadows durin' everyone's descent to earth and ascension back to heaven again, hm?

Each clan has sworn fealty to God an' Goddess, too, takin' certain bands o' the Creator Sun as their standard, for each band has its own ray color as well, an' each ray holds one quality o' love o' the Great Heart, 365 in all seven heavens. These rays make up the tartans o' each clan, ladd.

Each clan an' person was created at the very beginnin' out o' a very specific place in the Creator Sun, too. Folk'll spread all across the earth in future days, but in the golden age to come in twenty-one centuries, each tribe an' individual'll find the one spot on earth that connects right to the place they were originally born from in the Creator Sun, the same horizontal an' vertical degrees o' the sacred twelve chakras. Clan communities'll form an' the land right o' each clan will stream from the Goddess once more. But a lot o' darkness an' control on earth'll have to be faced before then!

But let's get to the regents o' the Creator Sun, ladd, for that's what I want to teach ye today, hm? In the outer circle sit the parents o' action an' young bairns. It's this outer circle that creates human families an' holds them together. The mother o' this outer circle is called Màithriel (maahreeil). An' her regency is security o' love, for bairns especially, includin' inner bairns o' the adults in the family. She surrounds everyone wi' the personal love an' nourishment o' its own family an' clan, mother's milk. Her specialty is nourishment, though, foods an' recipes, an' her light stream comes through cows. But she sees that all in each family get their share o' love in many ways; clothes, soft beddin', an' comfy seats her favorite things to provide. Her action powers overlight the home an' hearth, makin' sure each family on earth has whatever it needs. But mainly, Màithriel ensures that there is peace in each home, peace o' emotion that only enough love can provide.

Màithriel also overlights the 18 skyturn cycle o' growth that starts the day a bairn is born an' ends when each child leaves the parental home to begin makin' its own way in the world. This goddess rules the 3rd moon quarter, too, ladd, the young mother phase. Màithriel anchors into Alba, o' course, Glasgow or glass cow, the mother in her purity, a city o' the future here. An' in the stars Màithriel streams through Cygnus, the swan. Her tree is the white pine, pinin' for all her bairns to return Home, eh?

Her consort, the action Da, is Daiden. An' his regency is security o' resources in the home, so goods an' coin to buy anythin' that's needed by the family, especially housin'. In the Creator Sun, all basic needs are provided for; simple housin', heartfelt work in family compounds, humble clothin', an' enough food. Only if a body wants a grand hut or elaborate robes, do they have to work for coin to buy it. Surprises from each person's human Da come straight from Daiden, too, for he prefers to be close to his many children in personal ways. This father has a generous heart, especially at harvest time, for he loves feedin' everyone, just like his wife. He can be a bit plump himself, a teddy bear, who loves to hug an' laugh, an' is ever full o' fun. But we all were separated from him long, long ago. So, on earth, we have to work hard for even our basic needs. But in the future, all that'll be healed into the template o' heaven once more.

Daiden is a very upright regent, too, teachin' the laws o' love by example, along wi' the consequences o' doin' right an' wrong. This Da rules the 25 skyturn generational cycle as well, choosin' the folk who'll move through the same age groups on earth. He anchors into Albion, ladd, an' his star city is on Bootes. His tree is the Spruce, though, the protector conifer. It will ever shield the family within from harm, callin' in help from the spirit world whenever danger approaches, as stalwart as Daiden himself.

Each human parent may seem insignificant, Fìrinn, but they wield the full divine parent creator force. For the structures o' both light an' darkness they build into each human child last an entire lifetime an' take concerted spiritual effort to shift.

Then come the bairns o' this outer Creator Sun circle, Eriu an' Finn. Eriu, the wild rose o' Eire, is the wee fae queen, overlightin' all babes from six months to age two, as well as the fae nature within. Eriu helps ye choose what world ye'll descend to an' what yer final purpose'll be, an' she coordinates all these, too. She builds that central star in yer heart that contains this highest purpose as well. An' Eriu brings in self-assurance, the inner certainty that yer a child o' the One an' ye have every right to be here, no matter how others try to convince ye otherwise or what flaws ye may be workin' through at the time. Those wild rose fairies she rules are ever whisperin' sweet nothin's in yer ear about how special ye are or to keep believin' in yerself, even when the world ignores ye for years on end.

Eriu's regency also includes diversity, ladd, the wild freedom to become anythin' ye can imagine, to realize yer wildest dreams. Ach, she goes wanderin' off into any realm she pleases, learnin' one thing after another to grow into anythin' she wants. No one stops her from achievin' her goal, either, for she's the most determined wee goddess there is. Her love'll never be tamed, either, for there's no warmer smile or heart in the universe than hers!

Another o' her regencies is personal sovereignty o' the little girl, she who kens exactly what's right for herself, the power to decide which path she prefers to take. Try to tell her what to do, an' she'll let ye know in no uncertain terms that she's in charge o' her own wee world! But Eriu's choices are ever easy, for she'll simply steer ye toward what ye love most. Eriu's heart sends in a bit o' wildness through life as well, breakin' out o' the rules an' structure o' the tribe into play or fun. An' mind, even great warriors have this part o' their inner spirits.

Eriu rules the girl heart's desire cycle, too, 19 19-day moons with 4 intercessory days at the end o' the girl's Ash moon (Feb 28/29th-Mar. 3rd) (the B'hai faith). This cycle brings sweet desires o' inner lassies to fruition; Eriu's favorite thing to do, freedom to be one's own self, perhaps, wi' the help o' those fae lassies that send ideas for new recipes, dances, songs, special robes, or household items, an' plenty o' fun. Eriu especially loves tea parties, eh? Her fruit is raspberries, mmmm, an' her tree, the Guelder Rose.

She an' her infant sister, Abaid, that I'll explain soon, rule the first moon quarter, too, an' this is why the druids revere 6th night so. For that's when Eriu's holy purpose an' Abaid's healin' powers ripen to their fullest potential before the second quarter shift to the virgin.

Eriu's consort is the infant king, Finn, who creates all he needs in ease an' utter surrender to the One. His regency is trust wi' a capitol T, Finn MacCuill, who sits calmly in the Creator Sun, while all the drama o' the universe whirls around him. Cool an' centered, that's him! He does the same in each family, too, for look how everythin' revolves around each bairn born, the work o' the household done for him, mother's milk, warm an' fresh at any hour o' the day or night. It's Finn who creates all that's needed by the bairn in the outside world, an' security o' mother love is his hallmark.

He rules the boy heart's desire cycle, too, 12 27-day moons, with 14 intercessory days at the end o' the boy's Alder moon (March 14-28th), bringin'; humor, adventure, action o' all kinds, travel, an' wizard connections that pop out o' the blue. An' Finn also rules those wee fae leprechauns, that magically manifest desires o' the boy within.

The lessons Finn teaches are ever about surrender into the mother's gentle timin', for he brings the elder mother, Màiri's, slow flow o' life up through the root into the base o' each spine as well. She's the grandma or mother o' the mind in the second circle in here. Finn rules the will force that comes up the root, too. An' these together make up the sap o' the wee laddie, feulin' his enthusiasm for life, that wriggly restless inner boy. Finn loves nature, too, especially the waters that contain the mother's essence. Ach, he can ever be found paddlin' about. Finn overlights ages 2-4, the cherub phase. An' he rules the elimination o' waste down the root, too, it's flow settin' the timin' o' each day. So, he's regent o' time as well. But his human mother ever lets him down wi' her hurry-up-an'-fit-into-me-hectic-schedule needs that always sever the inner boy from Màiri's constant love. His tree is the swamp Cedar, ladd.

Eriu streams through Vela, 'the sails o' Argo', an' Finn through Puppis, 'the stern o' Argo', for this is the Dagda's ship o' destiny o' the stars. An' this outer circle o' Creator Sun regents make up the Creator Family Wheel, which on earth, anchors into Eire.

Movin' in to the second circle o' our Celtic Cross, we come to the elder forms, the queen an' king or grandparents o' the mind, Màiri an' the Dagda, plus the virgin girl an' boy, Maighdean (myjen, virgin girl) and Rìdire (reedera, knight). The queen, Màiri, is the divine mother o' the cosmos, holdin' each person on earth in love surpassin' all understandin'. An' her greatest strength an' regency is continuin' to love her bairns wi' her that strong mother love, no matter what they do or become while they're lost in the darkness o' lower worlds. She is ever present, ever wakeful, always attentive to the divine child within, like any good Ma. In her still small pool within, she'll ever whisper to try to have patience wi' yer challenges in life.

Màiri overlights all feminine efforts o' both family an' tribe, the feminine choices o' life, plus family disputes. But mainly, she teaches us through life's difficulties, bringin' back experiences o' the long ago to help each person remember, face those fears in love, an' heal them forever. For Màiri rules the comic sea, where all memories humanity hasna yet faced are held, the unborn," Coillore continued. "Her energies come through salt, as well as the oceans of earth. An' Màiri's cosmic sea infuses each person's belly, too, the pelvic cradle, so she can send her memories into each person's abdomen any time she wants. She rules the slow flow o' life into the root, too, an' the moment when life begins. But Màiri also rules sleep an' relaxation for all her children, to balance the growth the Dagda brings in. An' she rules the fourth moon quarter as well.

Màiri resets the emotional impulse for the whole planet every 18.6 skyturns, too, durin' the lunar southern standstill at Callanish. That's when the moon moves above the virgin in the rocks on the heights there as Màiri rebuilds the light structures o' emotion within the lass, bottom to top.

Mairi anchors into Alba, ladd, Edinburgh, the queen's city, Eden restored. But she moves up through Eire, too, for she willna be separated from her bairns. The emerald isle is shaped like a wee bear wi' large fluffly ears, a bear that lives in a land across the sea that'll one day be called Australia. That's because Màiri's root o' life comes up into Australia, an' flows under the sea from there into Kerry, to support her bairns on these isles. One day her religion'll be called Catholicism, these folk specializin' in carin' for the sickest an' poorest across the globe, like her. Màiri's tree is the Caledonian Pine, an' her star gateway is Cassiopeia, ladd.

But it's the Dagda, her consort, the father/granda o' the mind, who's keeper o' the templates o' the father's Kingdom, a simple family life after all. He's in charge o' all masculine efforts o' each family an' tribe. An' he brings the laws o' love into all structures o' the world outside the home, too, for he's the executor o' Oghama's will, a massive task! He's regent o' the future, the 100 year cycle as well. An' he oversees preparation for the highest destiny o' each person, leadin' all to reveal some truth that'll help the whole cosmos in due time an' build the father's Kingdom in some real way on earth. These light structures are indestructible once they're revealed here, after each disciple's strenuous climb through the fears veilin' them. This is why the forces o' evil try so hard to confuse an' weaken his mind an' break the inner father down wi' debt, failure, overwork, an' dementia, the greys o' the Borg mind stars o' Orion mostly.

The Dagda rules the moment when life ends as well, that node on the top left side o' the heart that sets the pace o' the heartbeat. But his other life stream is the golden road o' personal wealth that rises in a gentle wave throughout life. Despite that, the

Dagda is humble, ladd, nothin' like the grand chiefs ye sometimes see. Great truth always comes in simple ways, Fìrinn; mark it well. An' dinna be fooled by golden robes, eh? The Dagda has a strong listenin' ear as well. One day, humans will say a prayer that begins, "Our father, who art in heaven…," an' this is the regent those prayers will fly to. This father's star gateway is Leo, for he has the warmest heart o' all these regents, always sunny, cheerful, an' hopeful, no matter what comes. His tree is the Chestnut Oak, an' his energies come through sulphur, too. His religion'll be the Protestant branch o' Christianity in the future, with his strong upholdin' o' truth, though that can get a bit rigid at times, too. The Dagda anchors into Albion, ladd.

Then in this second circle, also, sit the virgins, Maighdean (myjun, virgin girl), an' Rìdire (reedera, knight). Maighdean's regency is manifestation into the physical realm, so she's powerful, indeed. She's regent o' the divine child cycle o' the year, too, 13 28-day moons wi' 1 intercessory day, which falls three days after Midwinter (Christmas). For durin' every skyturn, one wee piece o' everyone's inner divine child is built, an' it's infant light seeds first emerge out o' the abdominal sea on that intercessory morn, after the implantation on Midwinter. One day, a great festival'll be created just for Maighdean. Kwanzaa it'll be called, the moon quarter after the structures o' the yearly divine child first emerge. (Dec. 25th - 31st).

Maighdean also rules the manifestation o' all human babes into the physical, buildin' each human babe within an' overlightin' the birth process o' every person on earth. She births all inner divine bairns on earth as well, in that happy final lifetime. But to do that, she must convince everyone to go inside an' heal all shadows within. An' she brings forward the birth pangs o' fear, pulsed one a moon, before that final divine child birth. It's Maighdean who decides when individual divine bairns are ripe for revelation on earth. So, the virgin's nature is tender beyond describin', the young mother who walks by everyone's side.

In due time, she'll birth everyone's highest destiny at once, never, ever holdin' up a single person higher than the rest. An' so, the forces o' darkness spare no effort to close her down, for if they succeed, no divine child'll ever be born here. Maighdean's own divine child is to birth Paradise into the sensate realms, turnin' the lowest world into the image o' the highest, no easy task! She's keeper o' all memories o' Paradise in the Creator Sun, too, memories o' love an' love-makin' especially.

But Maighdean's true specialty is union o' the virgin lass's heart wi' the virgin male's, passion an' romantic love, healin' the sexual distortions especially, riddin' the heart o' all false beloveds from the fall an' former lives on earth. But she is chaste until the right partner comes along an' demure in her love when others are lookin' on. She alone brings forth the wine o' sensate love, for it's she who draws the first seed from the virgin male, the first love-makin', the first time the sacred manifestation chamber o' each virgin girl is entered. This brings a momentous shift, for the doors to the One Beloveds in the core o' both lover's hearts close, an' the beloved stream is brought through the outer human partner, instead. In a very real sense then, the outer lover becomes each one's beloved god or goddess. An' it's Tara Who rules love-makin' after that.

The world will often tell ye love-makin' is evil, especially outside o' marriage. But in truth, Maighdean's gift o' physical pleasure is sent from highest heaven, for love-makin' lights up the Beloved stream an' <u>pours</u> it into the outer partner, an' from them into each o' us. It's the strongest, most intimate love force possible on earth, sacred beyond tellin', the holiest act on the planet. But that's wi' yer own true love noo, no one else.

An' Maighdean's virgin stream brings everythin' into sharp focus, too, for her concentrated rose light o' love quickens all things into aliveness, makin' them seem brand new, the very meanin' o' virgin. It creates the present moment, the red-hot noo. She rules the second moon quarter as well, that pregnant gibbous moon. An' her fruit is peaches, ladd, but she comes through Beech trees, too. She anchors into the outer isles, the Hebrides, he bride, eh? Callanish especially. An' her star gateway is Aquarius, the star Sadalmalik, virgin waters that cleanse an' purify, for fresh water is another o' her regencies. Maighdean sometimes takes the form o' a selkie (mermaid), ladd.

Will ye notice the color o' yer skin, Firinn? It's peach, her ray color, for the color o' yer skin tells which regent yer action levels are committed to (hair tells the regent a person's mind serves, eyes, the heart commitment). An' for all fair-skinned folk, it's her!" And Firinn's brows rose as he took this in.

"Ridire, Maighdean's consort, the virgin male, is the crusader. An' his overidin' regency is to protect her, plus all women an' bairns, goin' into any danger or darkness that threatens them. He's the world server, the breastplate, who faces all threats to the realm wi' bravery to spare, who wants to lift the entire globe wi' his efforts, ever helpin' the weak an' downtrodden.

An' Ridire brings in dreams o' high an' holy service durin' the virgin years o' every life, too, to lead all virgin males into lives o' service to the One. He rules the action cycle, 11 33-day moons, with 2 intercessory days, one at the beginnin' an' end o' his moon o' restraint (Ramadan, Islam). Ridire's banner is silver-blue, for he serves the feminine primarily, emotions an' the heart. He, too, overlights the union o' virgin hearts within, bringin' them as close as close can be, but, pourin' their passion into some cause o' action, work for good that'll move things forward in the outer world. His passion for change on earth is legendary.

Another o' Ridire's regencies is courtly love, upholdin' the purity o' the virgin feminine, keepin' restraint on all desires, no matter how intense they become. He is ever courteous, respectful, gentle, an' kind, upholdin' the laws o' love particularly in his relationship wi' her. His tree is the Cedar, especially the Redwood variety. An' his star gateway is Pisces.   H   e anchors into Yns Mons (Anglesey) in Cymru (Wales), ladd, for whales are his life form on earth. It's durin' the whale migrations at the Vernal an' Autumnal equinoxes that Rìdire's half o' the skyturn opens an' closes on earth, for he's the summer king. Maighdean rules from the Autumnal to the Vernal Equinox, instead, she, the winter queen, keepin' those bairns o' the future safe as she builds them within. But long ago, this level was invaded by reptilian Luciferic forces, who covered Don's essence wi' the need to become the one God, instead o' Oghama, the desire for spiritual power over everyone. It's like Mil o' the Dragon star ye'll be learnin' in yer next lesson, but Mil wants power through money an' politics, instead. An' after this invasion, the Goddess an' Mona were shut out entirely. Durin' the veilin' o Goddess times over the next twenty-one centuries, Don's priest stream'll totally eclipse the priestesses. One high priest'll emerge for the whole earth, burnin' wise women an' torturin' priests from all other religions but his own, attemptin' to shut all other religions down. Can ye imagine such sacrilege, ladd! Burnin' wise women! An' that group'll try to shut the shamanic religions down, too, for those are more o' the Goddess, especially Mona's Celtic one. They'll totally distort the message o' that holy man to be born in a century, too, ladd, servin' the death an' greed forces o' the dark side, instead. So these regent's lessons always involve world domination an' control o' the spirit through beliefs, powerful, indeed. Durin' end times, fanatical right-wing, over-masculanized movements will arise that'll bring the final clearin' o' these ancient illusions. The Imperial force o' Lucifer anchors into Rome, ladd, the wish to be above all the rest, the illusions o' power an' control, over the feminine especially. Any spirit teachers who say they're above the rest are steeped in this reptilian darkness, an' their falseness covers the holy priestess mother an' priest father who want only to lead their flock o' lost lambs Home to love an' safety again. In their truth, the high priest an' priestess are humble, honorin' o' every path, an' deeply devoted to the One. These regents'll be especially active durin' those great transformation times in twenty-one centuries, son, lot's o' turbulence before the final breakthrough into the golden age to come.

Then, movin' in to the circle surroundin' the Beloved Core, sit the high priestess, Mona, an' her high priest consort, Don. She rules all pagan religions o' the world, but especially the Celtic one, openin' those eight holy portals o' our inner selves on the cross-quarter, solstice, an' equinox days, guidin' each inner aspect through its phase o' growth, eh?. She leads us all along our path o' life experience, too, those tiny templates in our teeth that open, one by one, through the years. Mona rules the spiritual teachin' o' bairns an' all feminine sisterhoods across the globe as well. But her most powerful regency, perhaps, is ceremonial music. Music can totally restructure yer emotional body, ladd, the emotion ethers in the lower six sheaths in yer aura. So, it's powerful, indeed. An' song, too, is Mona's force to wield. Music heals powerfully, pourin' light onto dark emotion ethers ye may be carryin' an' movin' them out. Her ray color is white gold, an' her star city is on Crater, the cup.

Then the high priest, her consort, is Don. An' he rules ceremony, too, but his power comes through words, instead. He's the keeper o' sacred truths, the laws o' love, an' he builds them into every human heart through the teachers he sends in. Words, too, can powerfully lift yer life force an' mood. Don rules all formal religions that'll mostly rise up in the future, too, but especially the Protestant one. An' he's regent o' all brotherhoods across the globe, like our druid order, as well. His ray is bright gold, and his star is Ava, the altar, ladd.

Together, they create ritual, blendin' music an' words, an' their goal is always the union o' heaven an' earth. Sacred rituals ever bring down light from above an' anchor it into each participant, into the inner spirit, the very depths o' one's bein'. This is their highest joined regency as well, union o' the highest world wi' the lowest one. But they both lay our responsibilities to heal our fears across our shoulders, too, movin' us all through our fears in life, up an' up that inner ladder o' light, to the very top. They teach us to bend the knee o' our hearts to the light, to Love most o' all, no better goal than that, eh, ladd? They create the path to our highest destinies, too, heartfelt work that reaches in and draws from old, old wounds to the spirit, both partners' passions for change fused into one holy destiny that'll nourish their hearts an' bring deep contentment in the end. The high priestess/priest united ray is platinum, pale gold/silver mixed, the light ye often see wher. yer doin' healin's on someone wi' a broken form o' some kind, for this lights mends everythin'.

See the torc I wear, laddie?" And Firinn nodded as Coillore put his hand on the spiraled silver band around his neck. "The will o' heaven meets our wee personal will force at the top o' the spine," and the druid pointed to a small lump at the top of his back (C-7). "Mona an' Don's will spirals into us there, torqued at a certain rate o' flow accordin' to our paths. Wearin' the silver torc indicates that me own will force serves Mona, the priestess, the feminine. But if ye see someone wi' a gold torc noo, that means they're in surrender to Don, the priest, instead.

An' then, in the girl/boy quadrants o' this inner circle sit those divine infant bairns, the gentlest wee babes, same as out highest destinies, eh? This child heart always brings forward: simplicity o' life, a community o' lifelong friends, play, surprise, humor, daily inner connection wi' the One Beloveds an' each person's Creator Sun family, simple heartfelt work, and security o' resources, includin': wealth, housin', an' most of all, love. An' they take life one simple step at a time, too, risin' each morn to ask God/Goddess what their tasks for that one day are, just as any bairn might do. These two overlight the birth o' all divine bairns on earth as well, an' are keepers o' the seeds o' each person's highest destinies, seeds that can be clearly seen durin' the infant an' toddler years o' life, too. Ye may no feel them, ladd, but these bairns are leadin' ye Home, leadin' us all. Her name is Abaid (abetch, abbey) and his, Uan (ooan, lamb).

The girl is the butterfly, the one who wants to transform the lower reptilian nature into the winged divine self. Things are never the same once Abaid steps on the stage, either, for she wants nothin' less than the full transformation o' the cosmos, top to bottom. She's a healer extraordinaire, who ever wants to reach into the girl's core wound especially an' soften it, till it disappears altogether. That's because her particular regency is lovin' kindness, the gentle girl's heart that melts every darkness into smiles an' hugs in moments. Lovin' kindness is the softest thing there is, ladd, all fear instantly disarmed an' transmuted by it. See how things we think are gentle an' useless here are actually the forces o' real change? Abaid anchors into the right temporal lobe, the place that lights up when ye meditate an' connect wi' the One as well, for meditation is her main way o' transformin' everyone. An' she's also regent o' hope, ladd, that lift o' the heart just when ye need it most. She is fae an also rules the first night that wee sliver o' moon shows up in the night sky, an excellent might for healin', a fact few ken in this world.

Then Uan, her friend consort, the divine toddler boy, is regent o' the basic forever truths that are the bedrock o' everythin' there is, truth wi' a capial T. When he speaks, his words are simple, but profound, an' they reach into the core o' everyone who hears them, creatin' inner shifts that last a lifetime. He'll make ye speak yer own truth in the world an' no mistake, too. These two regents anchor into the thymus o' everyone, mainly, her white cells and his Ts. An' the toddler ladd is the lamb o' the world, too, for he also rules the will force in surrender to the greater good, acceptin' whatever lessons come along an' lettin' God/Goddess be in charge. For he's a shepherd boy, who wants only a simple homey life, leadin' all inner ladds through their darkest hours as well, their core wound, that first darkness we knew in the Creator Sun, back to heaven's door. It's this will force in surrender that melts the blocks to manifestin' all we desire. Uan rules focus as well, ladd, the power o' the eyes, especially one-pointed focus that can break through all barriers in time. Focus may seem like a small thing, Fìrinn, but it sends the father's ray o' awareness an' growth in a specific direction. An' focus brings Oghama's clear light o' consciousness wi' it to surround the object it sets its sights on, bringin' that object to life, so all else fades away. Fear forces especially try to steal yer focus an' attention, for it fills them wi' that life and power, instead. Dinna allow it, though, ladd, nah. Focus on somethin' ye love an' give power to that,   instead,   e h ?

        Uan is the protector o' all cherub ladds within as well, for he has a cherub nature. So there's no better listenin' ear for a child's troubles than him, an' no gentler heart in all the universe. He commands all cherub forces, too, the ones who prick our consciences to tame our impulses back into love again. Once upon a time, before we came to earth, we pledged to be friends, loyal an' true, wi' all the cherub bairns hidden inside the plants an' animals o' earth. This is the child heart promise o' Abaid an' Uan.

        These two regents anchor into the sacred isles o' Alba an' Albion. If ye look at the shape o' Alba an' Albion as one, ye'll see a laddie on bended knee, wi' Eire his wee teddy behind his back. That's Uan, the lamb, the shepherd boy, lookin' up to heaven for guidance in all he does. An' at the place o' his high heart, the thymus, sits Albion's holy isle. That isle'll someday be called Lindisfarne. But if ye look at Alba alone noo, ye can see the shape o' a wise woman, a goddess. An' at the very tip o' her left hand is our wee sacred isle, Iona, where human divine bairns are always manifested in our orders. These two regents anchor into the abdomen as well, the girl in a star on the left an' the boy on the right. Both descend to earth to take on the wounds o' their human families an' tribes, endurin' the same fears an' hardships, workin' over much, an' sustainin' abuse, until their divine natures are closed down. But wi' much spiritual effort, they activate an' take their rightful places in the high heart. His star city is in Canus Major, an' hers in the butterfly nebula o' Scorpio.

        There's a united core here, too, the cosmic

child heart that never separates at all. It's that pale purple ray color, lilac, the combination o' her baby pink an' his baby blue. Ye'll be learnin' more about this in yer future lessons, Fìrinn, for when ye live in the Creator Sun, yer inner boy serves this ray color, both ye an' Soillse o' the Union o' Child Hearts order. An' this place o' child union creates the best friend stream, the ones we're closest to our whole lives long. These divine child regents send one special friend in bairnhood, a relationship that lasts throughout life, often a siblin', especially important through life's trials to keep the inner child whole. An' this bairnhood best friend's been a part o' each one's entire descent an' every life on earth, no other relationship like it. It's often someone from yer family o' light in the Creator Sun as well, so the trust an' love run very deep. Twins stream from this level, too, the oldest an' deepest connections there are, except the higher self.

Abaid an' Uan together are responsible for that child heart union followin' physical joinin', too. After the body comes to its release, a wee doorway opens in each partner's heart, an' one memory or dream is sent into the heart o' the partner, both ways noo. It brings some sacred understandin' that calls forth a deep response o' love, one to the other, the inner <u>children</u>, eh? An' if truth be told, this child heart joinin' is far sweeter an' longer lastin' than the physical one.'   Uan's tree is the Dogwood, an' hers, the Sugar Maple. This child heart in Union anchors into a a dwarf white star, Sirius, the dog star followin' the heels o' Orion, the hunter, the brightest star in the night sky. It's also called the dog star, Canus Major, because Abaid an' Uan package all child heart truths a person'll be learnin' durin' the next phase o' their life into the actual dog that'll become their inner child's best friend durin' those skyturns. That hound'll beam these comfortin' an' very personal truths from its thymus, plus Abaid's lovin' kindness, whenever that person's in need o' love or strength. The same is true for cats. Ye dinna ken Bana Dhia was so full o' light, did ye, ladd? Their union stream flows from Monoceros as well, the Unicorn.

In deeply sacred places o' nature or extra special ceremonies, perhaps, all four o' these inner circle Creator Sun regents come forth. An' together, they create epiphanies. Abaid brings in that miraculous sense o' oneness ye sometimes feel, bein' connected to the whole universe. An' Uan creates reverence, the feelin' o' utter awe an' holiness that sometimes overcomes a person when they're lookin' up at the majesty o' the hills, perhaps, or feelin' the loveliness o' Oghama an' Tara within. Mona brings in peace, just knowin' that everythin' yer so worried about'll be all right in the end. An' Don adds those deep certainties ye have sometimes, when ye ken ye're holdin' utter truth in yer heart, an' it'll never ever change.

An' finally, in the wee central circle o' the Creator Sun, sit the One Beloveds, Oghama an' the White Tara, God an' Goddess. She's in the very center, He surroundin' Her, the structure o' our brochs, eh? The White Tara is the keeper o' the One Beloved stream for Her eternal Bridegroom. As Bride, She's regent o' marriage, intimacy, as well as the mysteries o' physical union. She alone carries the holy essence o' intimacy to His Heart. An' She creates all wives or feminine partners in long term relationships, too, bringin' in shared passions an' devotions to forge those lifelong partnerships. Her's is the great feminine magnetic force o' love, holdin' all in love as intensely as possible, flowin' through the left heart.   Tara prepares the inner feminine o' all individuals for that final holy marriage with the One Beloved, too, buildin' His an' Her light structures an' powers into the hearts o' both human true love partners, lifetime after lifetime, no other effort as carefully tended as this. It's the One Beloved comin' through Her partner Tara wants, only Him, an' She can teach ye to feel an' ken His heart an' touch within an' without, like no one else can, for union is Her middle name. She wants union at all levels, too: spirit, mind, heart, and body. But to do that, She must bring in false beloveds, disappointments an' temptations that teach discernment an' the ways to tend the mystical rose o' partnered love.

Oghama is the Bridegroom," Coillore continued with a soft smile, "achin' an' longin' to implant new light seeds that'll bring His Beloved to a higher level o' love an' closer to His Heart. Oghama creates all long-term male partners an' husbands as well. He descends to earth inside them all, liftin' an' liftin' His lady love wi' day-to-day efforts that'll raise earth to Their Creator portal, for only then will He win Her release from the heavy iron doors o' the false beloved's will. Oghama's powers, too, ken no bounds, for He waits in silent patience for centuries, if need be, walkin' beside each feminine, takin' on the wounds o' her inner masculine to reflect them to her, an' turnin' Himself into her closest partner in order to bring her back to His heart, the gentle King o' kings. Life partners always carry the template o' their love's inner opposite gender, too, ladd. If ye were in a female lifetime noo, ye'd be like Soillse. An' if she were in a male lifetime, she'd be like ye!" And Fìrinn's jaw dropped as he stared at the druid.   But let's get back to the Goddess, eh? The White Tara overlights emotion through the left heart, the cosmic feminine, Her magnetism that draws us close, for Her greatest power is recievin' in love. She flows through the left side an' right brain o' everyone, too. An' She holds up the widest standard o' love there is, lovin' <u>everyone</u>; even murderers, criminals, an' warlords, all Her bairns<u> forever</u>, no matter what happens. For Hers is the holdin' force, the heart that takes in all pain, all shadows, an' breaks them down into Her pregnant sea to be born again into somethin' new. She prefers to remain hidden in Her powers, though, the cosmic Mother workin' tirelessly behind the scenes. She rules the yearly cycle o' emotions, too, the druid year, 15 24-day moons, wi' the five intercessory days that are our gratefulness celebration to Her for the livin' o' the year at the end o' the Blackthorne moon (Nov. 24th-28th, Thanksgiving). Tara rules the full moon as well, sendin' down the truths we'll integrate over the second half o' each lunar cycle. She rules the sunset half o' the year, Midsummer to Midwinter, too. An' Her star system is Ursa Major, the great ivory bear o' Tara's Mother love.

Her forever partner, Oghama, rules the radiatory force o' love, the cosmic masculine, givin' from the heart. He flows through the right heart, right side, an' left brain o' everyone, the masculine within, tendin' more toward the mind an' action wi' his love. Oghama's also the keeper o' language, includin' the Ogham alphabet o' the druid moons. For He rules the mind cycle o' the year as well, 12 30-day moons, wi' 5 intercessory days, Dec. 27th-31st (New Year's Eve, Hogmanay.)

Oghama chooses all that will manifest in all worlds, too. Durin' the Oak moon, He places the light seeds o' His an' Her blended heart's desires into Her germinatin' soil in each person's heart, seeds that direct all emotional growth for one skyturn. Because we all carry one small piece o' Tara's Heart within, we are each His Goddess, eh? His light seeds are structures that'll always promote union o' hearts o' the One Beloveds an' beloveds within, an' the union o' heaven an' earth.

But it's the White Tara, Who determines which o' His light seeds will actually manifest into the physical, an' what the specific outpicturin' an' timin' will be, for She rules our paths o' life, those wee templates curled up inside our teeth. Then, She calls in the elementals to flesh out Oghama's light seeds, sendin' them down to the base for manifestation. But His seedin' is always the first entrance o' light into the sensate realms through the doorway at the back o' each heart, though they're only light in the core ethers still. But it's the first birth here, for He brings them through the veils from the Otherworld into this one for Her to choose what She loves most an' will manifest, for whatever She grows in Her garden o' the heart will most certainly come to pass. It's She who lives in the center o' the earth, descendin' to the lowest world long ago to escape the dark Imperial forces that attempted to close Her down.

He's the Sun Lord, the God we worship wi' every wakin' breath, keeper o' the truths o' the <u>heart</u>, wisdom embodied an' lived in every moment. Oghama rules the sunrise half o' the year, o' course, Midwinter to Midsummer. He forms the letters o' light (DNA) that are used to build everythin' there is, too, a magician extraordinaire. He kens the light patterns o' each o' us, from our first moment o' creation into light in the Creator Sun, an' ever leads us back to that place. There is serene majesty in His knowings an' in His Presence. Oghama streams from Polaris, ladd, the pole star, for He's the axis o' the cosmos. An' his tree is the Robur Oak. All traditions revere the Creators, o' course, but in future days on our isles, at least, She'll be known as the Magdalen," and the druid paused as a slight blush rose on his cheeks, "an' He'll be known as Christ.

On earth, the Creators anchor into our own Celtic isles, Albion for Him, Alba for Her. His Bridegroom Self anchors into the place a future a castle'll be built, Windsor, named for roses, The Beloved's hallmark flower. But the high priest streams into a place that'll be called Buckingham palace noo, for his totem animal is the white stag, wi' tines that reach into Oghama's mind flow, eh? An' Tara's Beloved Self anchors into the wild lands at Applecross, where the clan games are held, eh? But the high priestess'll stream into a castle called Balmoral, for it's the morals in that name she's truly concerned wi'. The White Tara anchors into Eire, too, right in the middle at Tara mound, for She willna be separated from Her bairns, an'   Eire   is   the   child   land.

One day, whole nations'll arise on our isles, the Goddess land eclipsed by the God's, Her resources taken to support Him primarily. It's all part o' the patriarchal cycle. But eventually, the folk o' Alba will take back Her powers an' serve Her regencies again in the land created here to nourish Her an' Her clans. The scattered folk who carry Her light structures in their very bones, born in Alba in the Creator Sun, long, long ago, will return to their Homeland. An' the bondage o' the false father an' beloved'll be loosened an' untied, as all the folk o' Albion heal the old, old chains within, too. For though Their Heart is ever united, the One Beloveds, Their powers o' choice, directives, an' actions are quite separate. But it'll all come together in the end.

In the very center o' the Beloved circle here," and the druid pointed to the central wee circle of the Creator Sun he'd drawn, "there's a place o' union, where God/Goddess's Heart remains united, never separatin' at all. An' because o' all the outer pressures, this center is fused into a hard, brilliant, diamond core. This place is the Source o' the Love force, the truest o' the true, Love that never dies, never fades, never ends. Only love eternal is allowed into this place to send its sparklin' ray out into the universe. Every single bein' in any world that ye ever loved, this place in yer heart remembers an' continues to love, <u>forever</u>. Love is the strongest, most endurin' force there is, beneath all the shadows. Love itself is the One Beloved's creation and greatest gift to the cosmos. It's the clear light, created by the reunion o' Their Hearts, movin' a bit apart an' together in every moment, the cosmic Heartbeat, eh? His clear stream flows t h r o u g h   l i g h t ,   l a d d ,   a n '   h e r s   t h r o u g h   w a t e r .

Together the One Beloveds, Oghama an' the White Tara, rule the inner flow o' love into all bein's, holdin' the cosmos together wi' it. If ye look wi' yer inner vision, ye can faintly see a diamond stream o' light flowing into the heart o' everyone in all worlds. An' the central diamond o' the Creator Sun is where that stream begins, the personal an' intimate connection o' the Creators with all Their far-flung children. It operates outside any constrictions o' time or space, no connected to any formal cycle, for the power o' Creator Love kens no bounds at all!   T h i s diamond core holds an orgasmic essence, the fireworks o' new creation, wild joy an' passion forever. It creates the clear light that surrounds us all in the outer world, too, though its power is greatly weakened on the long way down to earth. But in the distant future, ladd, when the Beloved stream o' God/Goddess flows free an' clear in every heart, humanity's sacred love-makin' will activate the clear light on earth. An' in those days, we'll all feel surrounded wi' love sublime, all the plants an' animals, too. Ye'll see roses bigger than yer hand, grapes five times bigger than those stunted ones we find in the wood. An' it'll become a world o' <u>marvels</u>, Fìrinn, things we canna even begin to imagine in our own time, the peaceable kingom restored, endless love, and real <u>peace</u> across the whole <u>universe</u>!" And Fìrinn's eyes widened, as he listened to Coillore's words. "An' each one o' us carries a drop o' the united Creators within, as ye ken, the strongest love force there is. It's into this place I've taught ye to move all fear, for it's the highest vibration in the body an' does, indeed, transmute all darkness into pure light again. It's this drop o' the Creators that makes humanity different from all other life forms on earth, for it creates all we each believe into our own outer worlds. All other forms o' life on earth are caught in our creations, sufferin' along wi' us, as all wait for us to do our inner healin' work, so heaven can finally arrive.   An' also from this place o' Beloved union, one gift is given to all who complete their fear-facin' climb on earth, true love, plus the sacred sexual manifestation o' His an' Her heart's desires in equal measure. With these sacred earth marriages, The Beloveds on high can reverse an' heal all pain, even the memory o' pain. All disciples are ever brought back into union wi' Them through the wonders o' Their tenderness in our final true love partnerships. But more to the point as far as Tara's concerned, the sexual sharin' will be unsurpassed. Mind, ladd, o' all the things I teach ye, hear <u>this</u>! It's the shared <u>heart</u> that brings fulfillment an' satisfaction in love-makin', no the shared seed an' womb o' the action centers in the base. The action center is ruled by Rìdire, as ye ken. An' he'll ever bring forward a one-time ecstasy o' love, wi' Maighdean's help, o' course, intoxicatin' though that may be. But the virgins' sweetness fades over the first six moons, as the Creators take the reins. It's the <u>One Beloveds</u>, Tara an' Oghama, who rule the linkage o' hearts that creates lifelong devotion o' partners, one to the other, plus gentle growth in love. But really, this true love partnership is a bit more <u>Tara's</u> gift, since She sits on the inside o' Oghama an' rules the inner self, eh?

True love is heaven's highest blessin', our inner god an' goddess made in Tara an' Oghama's image. It brings in Their security o' partnered love, a life o' shared service in the depths o' personal intimacy, plus that sacred sexual manifestation power. These are the Creators sweetest gifts to all who brave the descent an' wisdom climb. True loves always reveal some quality o' the One Beloveds that hasna been unveiled on earth before an' is a full expression o' creatorhood in Their image. We may live in the lowest world, Fírinn, wi' heavy darkness weighin' on us most o' the time, but the highest revelation o' heaven's sweetness is ours to embody an' reveal into the sensate realms in future times." And the druid smiled softly, bending his head to indicate the lesson was finally over. But Fírinn had been so deeply moved by all the wonders the druid had revealed, he sat a moment in silence before gettirg up to leave the hut.

Running down beside the burn, a warm mist enfolded Fírinn, and he stopped to let its soft fingers brush his face and clear the long lesson from his head. He felt a gentle spirit presence moving in the moist air wafting across his skin, then saw the clear image of Abaid in the ethers, the infant girl goddess

"Ah, ye're the mist maiden, arena ye?," he exclaimed, and felt this knowing open out into his heart. "I often felt ye before, but I didna ken exactly who ye were." And he smiled as he felt her sweetness all the way to the longhouse door.

That night, the ladd slept soundly, more deeply than he had in many moons. He dreamed that he was gently rocked in a cradle on a calm sea, a cradle lined with ivory rose petals. And in it, he felt a sense of safety he hadn't felt since he was a babe in his Ma's arms, long skyturns before. He could feel the petal softness around him drawing the mental fatigue out of his mind, the heaviness of the day out of his heart, an' the weariness out of his muscles, ever so slowly, all night long.

Then just before dawn, a deep red rush of love came pouring in to fill the spaces left by the fear debris, along with the faintest scent of roses. It flooded his heart, and suddenly, he felt a heated longing to find real love at any cost, devotion to his path unlike any he'd felt before, and a willingness to work tirelessly to move love's onward rush forward through the coming day. It woke him gently, his blood tingling and his mind fresh. Opening his eyes in the semi-darkness, he took a deep breath and turned toward the hint of light coming through the doorcloth. The ivory yard cat had come into the long house and was leaning into his bedfurs, purring loudly and stroking herself along his pallet. *"My beloved,"* the Goddess voice said within, *"I tend you every instant the night allows. I always have and always will."*

He rose then, for it was early, the ladds sleeping later in the winter shortened days. Quietly, Fìrinn went out and walked slowly up the path to the standing stone on the ridge. And sitting beneath it, pulling his fur over his shoulders against the wind, he felt all he'd learned the day before coalescing into his bones. The dawn was clear, at least, the moon just setting behind the Cuchillins across the loch, a few stars still twinkling above. And as he waited there, Fìrinn saw a tiny babe in his belly, lying in a rough cradle with animals gathered round. And round the child was a halo of light that filled Fìrinn's heart with preternatural joy. In the vision, stars twinkled overhead and it was cold, a night just like this one.

"I'll follow where ye lead, wee one," Fìrinn promised. "I may never be king or chief o' anythin' at all, for I'm no a very good hunter, an' I dinna like to best me friends, either. But I can surely take one day at a time an' lead a simple bairn's life in me own imperfect way. Thank ye for bein' there, Uan, an' Abaid. I'll hold ye both in me heart every mornin', just like this for a moment, an' let ye tell me what's best to do each day." And ever afterwards, Fìrinn did just that.

In half a moon, though, Coillore took the ladd back to his hut, the druid saying he hadn't been able to complete the last lesson, but there was only a bit more to learn today. And Fìrinn followed without complaint, for the snow had been falling all morning, and his feet were frozen through. At Coillore's, there'd be a warm hearth, at least, though all the details could be annoying. And coming into the druid's hut, Firinn thought, how like a child Coillore lived in this tiny place.

The druid sat back in his stump chair for a while, beside the fire, ladling acorn and mushroom soup into a shell bowl, then waiting while Firinn filled himself to bursting, and let his feet thaw as well. Then Coillore drew another triple Celtic cross in the earthen floor.

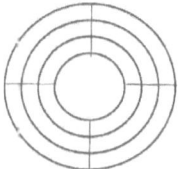

"Below the Creator Sun is the Dragon star, ladd, Draco. Some call it the Death star, instead, for that's where death an' war were first encountered in our long fall from heaven to earth. This place is shaped exactly like the Creator Sun, wi' the same number o' regents, who try to block the light comin' from above as much as they possibly can, beloveds in the center; surrounded by the false the high priestess, priest, an' babes; virgins an' false grandparents; an' in the outer circle, the false family; father, mother, boy, an' girl. These twelve are the anti-Oghama forces, dragon lords o' the death star, Isle's creations o' darkness to renew the wisdom stream. No only that, but each o' us carries these same dark regents in our own shadow selves within. These twelve dragon regents come through our human families, too, the ones who accompany us through our fall an' ascent, all the way back Home again." And the druid gave a great sigh, eyeing the flames a moment, before continuing.

"The White Tara's greatest regency, perhaps, is wisdom, Firinn, eternal truths built into the fibers o' the heart through hard experience, so they're lived wi' no thought at all. But long ago, wisdom grew stale throughout the universe. Invasions an' calamities started to occur in many star systems, an' Tara called for volunteers to go down into realms o' non-love, to forget the laws o' love an' relearn them through many lives o' pain an' hardship to renew the light o' wisdom throughout the universe. An' it was humanity that took on Tara's challenge and came here to the lowest world to take on the mantle o' sufferin'.

An' when it was time to descend into darkness, God an' Goddess split Themselves in half, light an' dark. The dark half o' Tara is Isle (ishla, mean-ness, Isis), the dragon queen. She's the crone, who rules the renewal o' wisdom for the cosmos, regent o' all the fears humanity hasna yet faced, the collective unconscious o' humanity in the depths o' the sea. Facin' those fears isna easy, ladd, but Isle joined us in this endeavor, for she took on the veils o' darkness herself, becomin' the dark queen the world reviles an' abuses. But in the spirit realms, she is honored for her difficult an' long service to love's cause. Isle walks closely beside all disciples on their walk to freedom from fear, for she kens everything there is to know about facin' and healin' terror, an' holding firm in darkness. She builds embracement o' the all in utter love into the feminine heart within, the very depth an' breadth o' wisdom. Isle/Isis anchors into Egypt, ladd, an' her tree is the Spindle (Euonymous). None have carried more sufferin' than she.

In truth, these dragon forces simply guard the purity o' the very Core, the Creator Sun, no allowin' any to enter that havena faced an' healed the most horrific illusions, so they willna be created in the outer world there. But in their untruth, the dragon kingdom was corrupted, separated from divine will, an' serves the personal will in separation, instead, the little will that wants it's own way wi' no regard for the greater good or the Creators, either one.

But let's get back to Isle, eh? Her totem form is a black snake, for one of her regencies is death, often through constriction: financial poverty an' starvation especially, but also isolation an' confinement.

But her main regency is <u>control</u>, for Isle would happily keep the whole cosmos in her death grip, if she could. She creates slavery, too, the most constrictin' life o' all, one's own will completely taken over by others, Isle's hallmark. An' since Isle wants no divine bairns at all to be born on earth, she targets virgin girls especially to be her slaves, along wi' the girl continent o' Africa. An' Isle's disease is cancer, ladd, those dark tumors that take over an' shut out life entirely, blech, one o' my <u>least</u> favorite regents!

At the new moon, Isle sends in one package o' darkness to face an' heal, the fear impulses. An' then wi' the full moon, the White Tara sends in the truths that were hidden behind those very fears, a different set o' darkness an' light for every person there is. How they keep track o' all that, I canna fathom, laddie.

Isle has a beloved core as well, the lover/wife who tears her man down every chance she gets, criticism an' humiliation without end, especially in front of his friends, till his inner masculine is totally destroyed. This dark goddess has a slippery nature, often seemin' lovely at first, until the demon within emerges an' begins to take charge. Ye must be <u>very</u> careful with Isle, ladd.

Her consort, the dark god, is Taranis (Osiris), who rules the personal will force in service to Isle, to death, instead o' love, the crocodile god. He loves violence an' aggression more than anythin', creatin' wars that destroy an' terrorize. In the future, he'll develop explosive devices that 'll kill an' maim whole villages at once. For his aim is to control the whole world wi' terror an' death. Taranis delights in torture, too, an' he pushes all males toward glory through violence, an' suicide, which is what war truly is, eh? An' he loves militarizin' wee ladies as well, coverin' their innocent natures with hatred an' gore.

His specialty is pittin' families against each other, settin' off tribal wars that last for centuries, leavin' death an' destruction in their wake, tearin' apart the Goddess clan an' the God nation fabric across the whole earth, leavin' all God/Goddess's creations in shreds. His disease is heart attacks, explosions that rip out the very life force an' kill instantly. An' his land is Iraq, his tree, the weepin' Oak. These two dark ones stole the will force o' the One, usin' it for their own purposes, instead, his brute force an' her control.

Taranis, too, has an inner self, the husband who locks his wife into the hut an' controls every move she makes, beatin' an' abusin' her every time she makes the tiniest 'mistake', or bringin' in his 'friends' to taste her pleasures against her will. He can seem kind at first, trying' to be her friend but his love o' violence an' control emerges quickly once her heart is his. Ye'll be healin' him on yer walk, an' her, too, ladd. But in the end, freedom always comes.

An' then, the united form o' the dark goddess an' god create the force o' hatred that attempts to block out love, slingin' it at the softest, most lovin' folk especially, eh? This union o' dark beloveds creates marital betrayal, infidelity, sudden abandonment, lifelong insecurity o' love in partnership that destroys all belief in forever love an' the Creators, too. For insecurity o' partnered love shatters the inner diamond o' the heart, ladd, which falls down into the abdominal sea, forgotten an' untended for eons.

Then in the circle around the core, the dark priestess form, Iobair (sacrifice) creates rituals that harm or kill, those mutilatin' traditions that arena truth at all, no even close. Well, an' sacrifice, o' the child particularly, that's her specialty. An', o' course, she makes it seem like these directives come from the One, so all belief an' trust in love an' God/Goddess is broken down as well. Her rituals are powerful, too, because o' that spirit force she wields as high priestess o' the dark side. Dark music is another o' her regencies, hard poundin' tunes that promote hate an' violence most o' all. In time, dark witches will arise on earth, ladd, who take parts o' bairns to use for their spells, an absolute sickness o' spirit. Ugh!

An' her consort, the priest, Matarach, (martyr) specializes in martyrdom, gettin' folk to believe they must lose their lives in order to get to heaven, a total an' complete lie if ever there was one. His dark rituals involve suicide or killin' folk o' other religions or beliefs, everyone dyin' in order to get to heaven. Dinna harm yerself, Fírinn if an inner voice tells ye to, for it's completely false, no based in love at all. An' as high priest o' the dark side, Matarach's words in ceremony promote darkness, too, tellin' everyone they're sinners, full o' evil inside, or holdin' his own violent forces up as higher than everyone else. So many illusions o' this world to face, eh? Everyone o' us is a child o' the One, Fírinn, always an' forever, never believe anythin' else. Ach, I canna WAIT till the light finally comes.

This is the regent that misuses the power o' words as well, talkin' on an' on about nothin' at all. I live in silence, ladd, for in it I can feel the love that fills the universe in every moment. An' those talkers disrupt that feelin' as long as they can, thinkin' their words are more important than inner listenin' to the One, such arrogance.

Then the union o' these two creates huge divisions between religions, wars an' killin' that goes on for centuries, an' only grows more an' more destructive over the years. When it gets horrific enough, humanity will finally see the utter darkness o' all this an' put a stop to it. But that, too, is a long time off in the future. War only creates it's own likeness, Fírinn, nothin' more. Dinna promote it, ever. There are other ways to solve everythin' on earth. Go inside when ye're tempted an' ask for a peaceful way through yer difficulty, an' it will be shown to ye, I promise.

There are dark babes within as well. The lassie counters the healin' kindness o' Abaid wi' disapproval an' critcism, weighin' everyone else's child hearts down, resultin' in isolation from friends an' family. Her name is Àrdan (aarden, haughty) because she ever looks down her nose at anyone different from herself, makin' those catty comments about everythin' she doesna like, a most disagreeable bairn. She has a very constricted view o' the world, thinkin' the ways o' her own tribe are exactly how the rest o' the planet should behave, wi' false expectations o' dress an' manners. She wants to be the best in everythin', too, fancy clothin', jewelry, shoes, housewares, better than everyone else. Course it's total illusion, for we're all equal in the end. Her tree is the weepin' Birch, ladd.

Her consort is Bulai (bully, boolee), an' his hallmark is the temper tantrums that damage the fibers o' the heart an' force his little will on everyone else. He especially harms the softest an' smallest bairns, too, the ones so full o' light. Plus, he keeps the inner girl ground under his heel. His tree is the weepin' Larch, ladd. Ach, I'll be truly glad when they're both transmuted out o' existence forevermore.

An' then, in <u>their</u> united core, Àrdan an' Bulai, create the cosmic webbing that blocks the healin' stream o' the true child heart. In time, it'll create a Borg medical gridwork on earth; over complicated procedures, financial hurdles only the wealthy can overcome, healers that dinna give a <u>limpet</u> for the ill at all, wantin' only coin for their sporrans. Imagine! For these two want to close down the healin' stream entirely. They design healin' methods that terrorize as well, causin' great pain an' lastin' emotional damage to the individual, destroyin' all belief in the Creator's love. An' in the end, the child within gives up and' collapses into Isle's arms, death. Ach, an' it's all so <u>false</u>, ladd. For ye ken yerself how easy it is to go inside an' melt even the most horrific illusions in yer Creator flame. An', in moments, that fear is GONE, <u>entirely</u>, inside an' out! Ach, I <u>wish</u> I could melt these two down for the whole cosmos! This mornin'!" And the druid sighed, shaking his head.

"Then these four also have a united core. With it, Aiden sorts cland an' families into higher an' lower qualities, separatin' them, leavin' the lowest neglected an' marginalized their whole lives an' the highest covered wi' extravagance that only weighs them down. But Bulai creates competition, pittin' one bairn against another in work an' sport, buildin' deep divisions that often last a lifetime an' break global families into bits that mainly snarl at each other."

"I get enough o' <u>that</u> one in the games here, Coillore," Fìrinn burst out.

"Aye, ladd, but it willna last too long. An' it'll build the desire into ye to avoid all such fragmentation, somethin' ye'll need in yer future years, eh? There's always a reason behind the pain, for God/ Goddess are in charge after all.

Then Isle's dark united stream creates diseases o' all kinds through disease, malnourishment, overwork, or lack o' sleep, pushin' everyone toward her death doorway, while Taranis's rages break families, clans, nations, an' religions into traumatized bits.

But let's move to the next circle out, eh? The virgin male in the middle circle here is Aeron or Arawn, an' his major regency is rape, plus utter control o' the sexual choices o' virgin girls, an' sexual slavery in general. For he wants to use her manifestation powers for his own purposes, stealin' an' corruptin' them any way he can, the dark masculine that only wants to crush the virgin girl. He forces his love, that's truly hatred, into her, closin' the portals within to the One Beloveds. An' he layers her sacred manifestation chamber an' heart with abuse, knowin' that's all she'll be able to create in her life from then on, lifetime after lifetime. He's the rapist o' the heart as well, the false prince, who grooms her to be his best friend, then beds anyone else he can find or pawns her off on others, instead. His tree's the weepin' Cedar, ladd.

An' his consort, Cat's, main regency is sexual joinin' without love. This has far reachin' effects, ladd, for sexual joinin' unites the action centers, blendin' the outer creations or physical experiences o' both partners for one full skyturn, whether they see one another again or no. Best for everyone to understand what darkness another person is dealin' wi' before joinin', eh? But Cat's main desire is to use or even kill her partners to gain money or power for herself, with no a shred o' love. If she joins wi' a rich or powerful man, then his outer riches an' power'll be brought into her own life as his outer world becomes hers for a year, eh? An' her lower circumstances'll certainly bring him down. Cat's specialty is prostitution, ladd, along with sexually transmitted diseases o' the male an' female manifestation organs. Her tree is the weepin' Beech.

Then the dark granda o' the mind, the king here, is Mil (as in millionaire). His rise to power in a land across the sea in those end times will signal the final battle with darkness across the globe (Trump). This false Aryan king drives everyone with constant work outside the home that must completed as quickly as possible, endless tasks, so no rest can ever be found. He's always addin' new projects, new lands, more gold an' jewels, grandiose schemes that entail far too much physical effort to ever be realized, to make himself look bigger an' better than everyone else. For he carries the Luciferic force that wants to be god, instead o' bowin' to the true One. Takin' as much power an' wealth as he can an' refusin' to share it, he keeps the brown-skinned folk that serve the real virgin goddess at the bottom o' the heap in poverty an' powerlessness for centuries, too, as well as the global feminine. Mil is slippery, like all reptilians, no honest in his dealin's wi' anyone. An' he slings his will force around, too, like a python constrictin' their lives. His land is Egypt, also, especially those grand pyramids that are the symbol o' his hierarchy o' wealth. An' his tree is the weepin' Mt. Ash.

Then the grandmother/queen o' the mind in this middle circle is Obair (ohper, work). She draws all mothers into continuous menial overwork that wears them down, creatin' the process o' agin' an' chronic fatigue. An' Obair loves to keep every mother from takin' care o' her own needs, too, starvation bein' Obair's specialty. The Jewish race on earth, who serve family nourishment and resources from the Old Heart, the mother's light structure, will bring forward this regent's horrors for healin' in 21 centuries, Goddess help them all. Nazi false father forces will put these folk into dark camps an' work them to death, exactly what happened to all mother aspects o' every human on earth under Opair when they descended through the dragon star, buildin' in those heavy work plates over the inner mother o' everyone to close the true mother down. The swastika is

Obair's symbol, with its four legs movin' sunwise, to oppose the life flow o' the true mother, Màiri, as it moves up the root. Obair's tree is the weepin' Black Pine, ladd, an' her land, Israel.

So, let's move to the outer circle noo, the false family. The Da here is Deal (jal, leech), a father who doesna work an' makes everyone else suffer for it, takin' care o' himself, instead. He's a parasite, wearin' everyone else down wi' work an' worry over housin' an' provision. Dinna ever do tasks for folk ye may meet that they can do perfectly well for themselves, ladd, for it'll just weigh ye down an' keep them in their old useless patterns. Deal's disease is the nervous exhaustion o' insecurity, mother an' bairns especially, wi' never enough to eat or proper shelter, for he's the very opposite o' the protector an' provider the true father really is. Everyone o' these death star regents want to build inner walls between the masculine an' feminine, too, deep mistrust an' fear, plus bringin' on early death. His tree's the weepin' Spruce.

The mother here, his consort, is Mider, who overlights the spider matrix force, ever jabberin' about tiny details o' life that concern no one else, trappin' all into her household web o' control an' suckin' the very life out o' everyone. She's the great feminine temptress that brings in distractions an' confusions that sap the masculine's true focus an' strength, too, buyin' unnecessary goods that clutter the home an' usin' his hard-earned resources, too, so he's ever in a race to pay for it all an' can barely move inside his own hut. In the end, her webbing confuses an' eats away his mind, stealin' his powers to protect an' provide, until there's nothin' left, his mental capacity reduced to that o' a wee babe, fully in her power. One day her disease'll be called dementia. An' her tree's the weepin' Willow.

An' finally comes the ladd, Caolan (colon, Colin), an' the lass, Col (col, incest). They rule the sodomy/incest forces. Sodomy blocks the mother's flow o' life into the root, replacin' it with that forced masculine phallic drive, instead. It lifts the inner ladd out o' Màiri's gentle flow o' life an' makes him hurry an' work, hurry an' work, instead." I ken <u>that</u> one, Fìrinn thought to himself. "It creates disorders o' the colon late in life, too. Caolin's land is Greece, an' his tree, the Corkscrew Willow.   An' incest closes the girl's portals to Oghama, ladd, just as any first love-makin' does. It brings Oghama's Beloved stream through the outer partner, the human lover, instead. In adulthood, this brings the couple into a' full workin' partnership. An' the whole outer family circle o' the Creator Sun within also closes down after any first love-makin', so parental provision for the young partners also stops as they shift into creatin' their own adult lives an' families. But in a young lass, sexual abuse results in a forced adult overwork pattern an' covers her beloved core wi' an abusive partner structure that lasts her whole life, an' all lives into the future, until it's healed. Marriage o' very young girls to much older men would fall into this regent's grasp as well. Such incest or sexual abuse creates disorders o' the lassie's woman's place late in life as well. Col's tree is the Weepin' Cherry an' her land, Niger.   But they're illusions, every one, ladd. Dinna fret about anythin' overmuch, eh? An' that's <u>enough</u> o' the Death star for me." And the druid stood, shaking the shadow energy out of his arms and legs. Then he motioned Fìrinn out into a light snowfall to get away from the heavy metallic energies that had collected in the ethers inside the hut.   And as Coillore smoked the hut with sage and sweet grass, chanting the rune of cleansing, Fìrinn looked up, sparkling flakes landing on his brow and tongue. The bare birches and mossy forest floor were covered in light snow, and he took in a deep breath, letting it out slowly, as the dark regents fell from his mind into the soft cushion beneath his feet. Bana Dhia was pushing her snout under low drifts, flinging snow every which way, making the ladd laugh. Then the dog ran circles round the yew in a wild frenzy, nosing Fìrinn's legs with every go round. And coming out of the hut, Coillore winked at Fìrinn, then rolled a ball of snow along the ground, shaping it carefully, and putting on legs, ears, and a tail to look   exactly   like   the   deerhound.

"It's even the right color," the druid said with a smile. And Fírinn nodded as Bana Dhia put her front paws on his shoulders and lapped his chin, the wiry hair around her face dusted with snow. Her eyes were moist with a child's love, and her heart was more joyful than anything else in Fírinn's world. A stray beam of sunlight filtered through the clouds just then, making the snowflakes sparkle everywhere, like a crystal world. Then Fírinn chased Bana Dhia till his hands and toes grew cold, before heading back in to the hearth.

After the next druid gathering in the oak circle, Coillore motioned Fírinn the stay behind. "I have one more wee bit to add to yer last lesson, ladd," Coillore said as he motioned Fírinn inside again into his stump chairs. "An' it's a long sight more cheerful than those reptilians." And the druid handed Fírinn apple cake from the pocket of his robe before continuing. Grinning, the ladd wolfed it down, except for the bite he gave Ban Dhia.

"The goddesses o' the Creator Sun are the source o' healin', too, ladd, another hidden stream. Whenever ye're ready to heal a fear force, Abaid, helped by Eriu, calls forth yer own Creator Sun family members to surround ye. An' yer family beams a circle o' light around ye that contains the structures o' yerself before any fear was taken in, the memory o' yer perfection. This is Koad, grove, the Ogham letter K. Abaid surrounds ye wi' that soft lassie love an' hope, to prepare for the healin' to come, too. Durin' each skyturn, Abaid an' Eriu are active from Midwinter to the Vernal Equinox as well, doin' the same to initiate the yearly growth.

Then it's Isle (Isis), the crone o' the Dragon star, who sends in the sharp prickin' stream to open the wound meant to be healed. This is Oir, Spindle (euonymus), the Ogham letters Oi. She's active from the Vernal Equinox to Midsummer, bringin' up the deep fears that'll play out over the rest o' the skyturn, especially fears o' the virgin girl.

Then Màithriel, the action Ma, surrounds ye wi' her great mother love, which softens the fear ye're focused on an' brings comfort in the certainty o' love to come. Often she points the way through the tangled vine o' fear as well. This is Uilleand, honeysuckle, the Ogham letter Ui, sustenance o' the mother to the child in fear. Màithriel also overlights Midsummer to the Autumnal Equinox, sendin' in' the truths that will be integrated over the rest o' the skyturn, seein' that they ease the mother challenges o' this time o' year as well.

Then the virgin goddess, Maighdean, sends an ancient memory o' love from the Creator Sun. It's love ye knew before ye ever took in that particular fear, the very love force bein' blocked by this shadow energy, again precisely structured an' often streamin' from a very distant star system, help from bein's that are practiced in dealin' with this specific darkness. Maighdean removes the birth membrane over the new part o' yer light body, too, so that wee piece o' yer original self is reborn, fresh an' new. Birth o' the divine child is ever Maighdean's specialty. This is Phagos, Beech, the Ogham letters Ph, the virgin's love for the divine children in us all. She's active durin' fall, too, from the Autumnal Equinox to Samhein(2), durin' an' followin' the yearly birth o' the divine child nine moons after Midwinter, bringin' in many such memories to stabilize the new child o' light.

An' lastly, the queen/grandmother, Màiri o' the mind, comes in at the end o' each healin' to hold ye, till all remnants o' the old fear force are drawn away, pulled into her abidin' heart. Then Tara washes ye clean, so no a bit o' fear remains. This is the Ogham symbol, Mor, the sea. No letters are used for this, but it's the sound o' the ebb an' flow o' the ocean that ye hear if ye hold a shell to yer ear. Màiri is active from Samhein(2) to Midwinter, the breakdown phase o' the year, an' Tara durin' the intercessory days (Nov.24th to 28th), washin' us all clean an' clear then as well.

An' at the end o' every healin', one very thin piece o' yer self o' light opens out to take its place in yer aura, laddie, lookin' for all the world like a huge butterfly as it spreads into the quadrants o' yer spirit. An' that's because Abaid is directin' it all, the cosmic healer o' healers, the butterfly I love!

Every human," the druid continued, "chose to heal one great fear, each takin' one piece o' darkness that covers the Creator Sun to transform within their own hearts. An' when ye reach this pure Beloved level again in yer consciousness, laddie, when the race is at its end, the small pentagonal window o' fear that covers the wee place in the Creator Sun ye were originally created from opens once more. An' the love that was blocked for eons by yer own core fear shines out again through the entire cosmos. This final revelation o' the Creator Sun is given to humanity alone, those who took on the full mantle o' fear an' the climb to creatorhood," and Coillore's eyes grew serious a moment.

"Oghama remains in the Diamond Core, holdin' the structures o' light an' keepin' them strong for the universe, bringin' them into our paths when the time is ripe to remember again. The Sun Lord an' the Goddess are truth an' wisdom united, ladd. They always hold this pattern," Coillore said, pointing toward the sun, dropping slowly behind the far hills. "They're wedded to each other, dark an' light, the unconscious/unborn an' the conscious/revealed, movin' closer through the worlds, each skyturn birthin' a bit more o' Their divine child, implanted at the very beginnin' within each o' us.

The Sun Lord rises from the darkness o' Her cosmic sea each Midwinter's dawn, too, bringing forward new fears for all on earth to face an' clear to embody new truths every skyturn. But when He reaches back into the darkness again each winter, it's a little deeper than the year before, dippin' His ladle into Her wisdom reservoir to move all forward once more.

Each day, each moon, each skyturn walks up the stairs toward the Creator Sun, laddie," Coillore said, his eyes darkly intense. "An' each difficulty carries with it a lesson from the Creators, somethin' that'll lift ye a bit closer. Take them all! Learn the lessons offered! Always, always follow where the Creators lead, no matter how painful the struggle may be or how strong the forces are that try to hold ye back. Fear'll be sent to test ye as ye climb, to see if ye're strong enough to stay the mark at that level, to hold to those truths. Keep goin', laddie, aye!" And Coillore's face flushed in his intensity. "The Goddess walks closely beside each initiate here, an' She'll ever guide ye. Hold fast to Her, an' ye canna fail." There was urgency now in Coillore's voice that made Fìrinn wonder what the old druid knew of the future, and the ladd resolved to do as Coillore said.

"All druids serve both Creators. But the druid year matches the feminine emotional cycle, so truly She, the Goddess, is the one all druids bend the knee o' their hearts to. Oghama is a shinin' beacon, the Sun Lord, wi' love that warms the universe. An' humanity reveres Him for His happy cheerfulness. But She's the One Who took on the mantle o' sufferin', breakin' Her heart into a million pieces, demons an' angels alike, to create the vast Womb o' the sky in which to renew the wisdom stream.

He glories in the light an' stays relatively unscathed in His mental towers. But She surrounds every single form in all worlds an' feels all sufferin' o' any kind. She's the unseen an' unrecognized bearer o' pain, Her Mother's heart overflowin' wi' understandin' an' compassion for us all. No matter how horribly distorted Her children may become durin' their walk through the worlds o' illusion, She always an' ever wants only to love them 'an bring them Home!" And Coillore stopped, bringing his arms around his chest, his eyes brimming. "I'd no have survived countless times over without Her Heart about me an' Her Presence walkin' by me side. Folk revile Her for the sufferin' they must undergo an' the demon kingdoms She rules. But She, no He, has taken on the full shroud o' darkness, like us. She descended into earth, the lowest world, to lift us to heaven's door wi' Her silent unseen Mother's Heart o' hearts! The Sun Lord's love is easy by comparison. <u>Hers</u> is the bedrock o' the soul!" And Coillore dropped his head a moment before continuing, tears glistening on his cheeks.

"In another century, that holy man, Jesus, will be crucified on a cross, an' folk'll ever after hold him up as the embodiment o' the Sun Lord an' glorify heaven in his name. But I tell ye, laddie, this man's love, love that'll never waver, no matter how severely he's harmed, will show forth the very <u>essence</u> o' the Goddess, Mother-of-all. He'll be Jewish, too, the mother's people. An' through him, Tara's great an' stunnin' love'll send its truth out over all the folk to lead them through the 21 remainin' centuries o' Her veilin', completely unrecognized, but everywhere <u>full</u> o' Tara's power!" And Coillore paused, a small smile creeping across his face. "One day, She'll be lifted up an' seen in Her truth, the very depth an' breadth o' love, the way Albion o' the south supports Alba o' the north. An' in those times, even the Sun Lord'll walk a step behind!"

Coillore held off more lessons, feeling it important to let Fìrinn absorb the force of love from the Creators and regents of the Creator Sun for two whole moons. And during this time, the ladd noticed a tender softness that came often with the moon and surrounded him as he lay on his pallet before sleep in the long house. *'The White Tara,'* She whispered one moonlit night, when he asked whose Presence it was.

Often and often, too, Fìrinn felt gentle warmth from the sun, and with it the urge to grow crops, gardens, new life everywhere. During a startling week of warmth at the end of the Alder moon (Mar.), Fìrinn thought to himself one springlike morning, Ye're the gardener then, arena Ye, Oghama? The ladd was standing beside the bay, watching the first rays of morning brighten the fields above the tuath, the sun just peeking over the inland ridge that rose up behind the hut circle above the shore.

And in his gathering that day, Fìrinn happened upon a rose, deep red, that moved the depths of his heart with its promise of love forever true. It was far too early in the season for those blossoms, too, just barely spring, as if Oghama had warmed it into flowering Himself just to surprise Fìrinn.

Coillore walked ahead through wisps of fog, his heavy winter cloak pulled tightly around his white robe. It was the third night after the Vernal Equinox. The waning crescent moon had disappeared two nights before, and drizzle was falling all the way up into the hills and out across the sea. It's freezing up here, Fìrinn thought, what happened to that warmth we had a quarter moon ago? Even his heavy, fur-lined jerkin and the oiled skin over his buckskins didn't keep out the cold. They'd trekked half the afternoon into the high moorlands to the south of the tuath and entered a saddle-shaped valley. To the right were mounds of large scattered boulders, and beside them on a low rise stood a dolmen. It had two uprights, twice as fat as big Allaidh, and a much larger lintel stone across the top. Coillore said it was once used by the native people of this isle as a passageway to the Otherworld. But the veils had closed, and now it was necessary to bury relatives in stone cairns to guarantee safe passage to their star tuaths, instead.

"No one comes here anymore," Coillore added, "but it'll do for our purpose. The spirit guardians are still strong, an' I canna wait to begin yer initiations any longer. Yer manhood'll be upon ye in two skyturns, an' these passages take can take many moons. Call in the Goddess to protect ye, ladd, an' then just wait. It's the earth elementals that'll come for yer testin' this time. Be on yer guard, for the fears can be slippery an' will harm ye if they can. There are no fixed rules to guide ye, either, for the Goddess teaches only through experience, so no one can tell another what to do. But just ken, ladd, the spirits bring yer own fears for ye to face. An' when ye do that, the diamond light within'll melt them away forever. So it's good after all, but initiations are never easy. Ye must stay till sunrise, no longer, an ye can come back then. If ye've no returned to me hut by mid mornin' tomorrow, I'll come after ye, eh?"

The ladd sensed nervousness in the druid, something he hadn't seen in Coillore before, and this made Firinn's stomach queasy. Coillore stooped to light a fire and dropped herbs into the flames. Then peering under the lintel stone, he blew smoke into the dolmen, mumbling the chant for cleansing and protection, and walked sunwise around it three times. Then the druid turned to Firinn and blew smoke over him, too, from head to toe and around his back. Handing Firinn a skin of water and another of ritual broth, Coillore took off his inner cloak and wrapped it round the ladd, then motioned toward the low stone seat inside. Firinn stooped in under the huge lintel and turned to sit with his back to the uprights. The long flat stone beneath formed a single seat, sunken several hand spans into the earth. But as he entered the small chamber, fear began to snake its way through Firinn's gut.

"Dinna under any conditions be lured outside the dolmen before sunrise," Coillore said, watching Firinn a moment. Then the druid nodded, turned, and sloshed off through the spike grass as Firinn listened to the sound of footsteps fading away. At least I'm out of the wind in here, Firinn thought, but it's awfully damp, and he wrinkled his nose. Wish I had Bana Dhia on me feet. She'd protect me, if I needed it. But Coillore hadn't allowed the dog to come. Each must face the spirit world alone, the druid said. And then Fìrinn thought of the dead being passed through these stones in days long past and wondered if he, too, could be taken to the other side and not allowed to return. He shivered and pushed this thought from his mind.

He drank the broth then, his mouth puckering at the acrid herbs, leaned back, and waited to begin the visioning. The mist that had settled over the hills a week ago was especially thick tonight. And Fìrinn shivered again, thinking how the spirits of folk who'd passed on during this skyturn walked the earth during the nights of Samhein, rectifying any unfinished business with the living, the veil thinner now than during the whole rest of the skyturn. The Goddess collects Her due during Samhein, he thought. I wonder if I'm owing. I've honored Her in me chants every day, but I guess I'll see. Then he sighed and stood, raising his arms as he hunched in beneath the lintel stone.

"Goddess, Tara, Mother to us all, come, protect me this night. An' Oghama, Ye come, too. I'm ready to meet the earth elementals an' be strengthened by the lessons Ye bring. An' I honor Ye both." He paused, then added. "Please help me through this, Goddess. I'm scared." Then he sat and laid his head back on the uprights.

The night was utterly still, except for the slow drip of rain off the stones. And the sound calmed his mind as he breathed in slowly. But his head ached and his stomach was balled up. And then he sensed dark shadows moving in around him. So he cocked his head, leaned forward, and listened for a moment, then lay sideways on the stone and curled up, cradled in the chamber like a child in a womb.

Instantly into his mind, came the image of the cave of waters, the birthing cave at home. He saw kneeling woman crooning there and felt his spirit move slowly into the rock wall. A damp slippery feeling engulfed him for a moment and he tensed, startled that his spirit could move through sheer rock. But then he emerged beyond it into a meadow of high grasses, dotted with orange hawkweed and daisies, nodding in the wind. It felt like late summer, the meadow shadowed by the half-light of dusk. A large black crow flew straight toward him, and it's spirit moved directly into his shoulders. And suddenly, Firinn felt himself shrinking and merging into the bird as its wings spread, lifting him. They rode high into the air, and the muscles of Firinn's shoulders twitched as if in flight. Into a cloudy sky they soared, north across the mainland and over a wide choppy sea, dizzyingly high. But Firinn was not afraid now, even though he could see rough waves far beneath him and felt the wind woman whistle across his back.

Plummeting suddenly, they landed on a rocky outcropping on an island far to the north, surrounded by wild grey surf. An old druid, a white robe far older than Coillore, a lean, white-haired man, stood waiting on the pebbly shore. He motioned for Firinn to follow and silently led the way up a low rise above the rocks. There was a heavy stillness here, as they moved through windswept grasses to a wide knoll that looked out over the sea. And there, they entered a circle of stone uprights, some wide and some needle-like, all huge (the Stones of Stenness). The stones felt alive to Firinn, like ancient kings perhaps, their grey furrows like rippling muscles and their skin glistening with a soft unearthly light. Firinn hesitated, glancing around at the stones as he walked into the circle. There were twelve, and the old druid led Firinn to the largest stone and turned the ladd's back to rest against it. And then the druid disappeared, instantly, just vanished into thin air. At this, Firinn tensed, afraid to be alone in this wild forsaken place.

The air began to shimmer and vibrate, and the stones to move, very gently, almost swaying in the wind. They gave off a low humming sound, and slowly Firinn felt himself surrounded by the upright behind him, enclosed, inch by inch. Panic rose in his throat as Firinn stifled a scream, while he drew the fear down into the diamond light in his heart and held it there. Will I ever get free of this rock, he wondered? Ladds died during initiations, he'd heard. But he breathed his nerves to stillness as he, very slowly, became fully encased in the stone.

Firinn found himself in a tiny egg-shaped room, which fit perfectly around him. He felt exactly like a baby bird, ready to hatch, as if he could peck his way out. And his fear subsided. The sense of dampness had gone, too, and he saw that he was in a chamber of small white crystals, iridescent, and glittering with a soft moonlike glow.

"I am your brother," the whispering began. "I am your mother," another voice said. "We hold the memories of all worlds within us." And the top of one crystal above his right ear opened as a tiny filament of light, full of shining symbols, rolled out before him. He had a sudden memory of living in this very place in another life, as caretaker of these stones and friend of the druid who'd come to meet him. Then other filaments appeared, and a series of pictures formed in his mind. In the first scene, he was a man of the far southern lands, plowing a rain-soaked field, his cheeks gaunt with hunger. In the next, he was carrying a starved infant son to the river, giving the child's spirit to Danu, goddess of the waters there. And Firinn felt the stab of grief that tore his father's heart as he let his son slide into the swollen muddy stream. Many bodies floated there, mostly the young and the very old. Kneeling and weeping on the banks, he prayed to the Goddess for a lifting of the rains and the mold across the lands, so his crops could grow and ripen once more.

And then the picture shifted. He was a young boy, no more than eight winters, crouched behind a boulder and watching a large boar snuffling in the leaves on the forest floor. This place was up beyond the pinewood, not far from Firinn's home tuath. The wee ladd's heart was battering in fear. Granda's dead now, the child was thinking. I must feed Ma and sis or we'll starve. I'm the only hunter now, but I'm not big enough. Goddess help me, the small boy prayed and stood slowly, loosing his spear. But the boar turned on him, tusks shining as the animal charged over the needled ground. The lance merely grazed the boar's flank and fell away, and the animal's breath was hot on his skin as the boy shrieked. Then Firinn felt a ripping pain in his thigh and abdomen, and heard a dying gurgle of breath.

Again the scene changed, and a red robed priest stood at the altar in a high sandstone temple. It was an ancient land, the Egypt Coillore had described in his histories. Firinn, in a white priest's robe, was on trial for disobeying the pharaoh, for saying the God of life flowed equally through all men, not just the one in charge. A row of high priests faced him in their long embroidered robes, sitting at a long table, their eyes proud and cold. "His life," the tallest one said, a man whose face held the falcon eyes of Duirc. And a servant handed Firinn a small cup of blue liquid. Firinn's heart contracted with sorrow as he drank, and he thought of the young woman waiting outside. He felt her heart spasm with his when he fell, and in his mind, he saw her begin the wailing chant for the dead.

The crystals shimmered around him, and Firinn could feel them breathing in and out, their faint light pulsing as they did so. *'Other lives, other lessons,'* he heard in his mind. *'You've come to earth many times, son of the One. See the patterns and face the meaning of defeat.'* And Firinn suddenly realized this crystal chamber was a tiny compilation of himself, his own spirit, containing all the memories of his earthly lives from the first one until now. *'It's more than that,'* the crystals said, *'for it contains the memories of your walking right from the beginning, your first creation into light and your descent through all worlds. We will bring forward all you need for the journey you are now beginning, all the memories of fear and the truths held behind them, and patterns of the future, too.'*

And then the milky crystals around him suddenly cleared, becoming as see-through as the burn on a sunny morning. The room smelled faintly of roses as one bright crystal on the floor opened slowly, silvery light misting out of it. And instantly, Firinn felt an easing of the searing grief from the lives he'd just recalled. That brokenness felt so familiar, he thought, so repetitive, always ending in death. And then, a shaft of light opened from above, golden this time, and moved through his head into his spine. And slowly in its glow, he felt the residue of his failures transform into a resolute firmness within. He felt a sudden yearning to join the priesthood, too, for he saw the image of himself in future years, dressed in the white robes of a druid. Then Fìrinn watched the golden light fuse into the vertebrae behind his heart and from there spread out into myriad tiny crystals embedded in every bone of his body, so they sparkled like a million stars in some brilliant galaxy.

And the ladd awoke out of the dream then, wiping his eyes in the light of a new dawn to see the moor misted by soft rain. *'I am your brother,'* said the dolmen, as the images flowed down and out of Fìrinn's mind. *'I am your mother,'* said the hills, sere with winter. *'I am you,'* said his bones, as he uncurled himself and sat up. Why didn't the crow bring me back the way we went?, he wondered. Pulsing heat radiated from his coccyx, and in his mind's eye, he saw a knuckle-sized piece of clear quartz there, the six facets sparkling with a soft inner glow. Fìrinn could feel the quartz breathing and knew it would open the memories he needed, until his bones became as clear as those crystals in the small egg chamber. Breathing deeply, Fìrinn waited as his senses reawakened and his legs felt steady again. Then he wrapped Coillore's cloak around his own and climbed out onto the moor.

Mostly he slid down the damp hills, his oiled leather breeks keeping most of the wet off, smiling to think he'd succeeded through his first initiation. It wasna so terrible after all, he thought. And Coillore smiled, too, when Fìrinn recounted his vision, frowning only a moment at the encasement in the upright. And then the druid hovered all morning, feeding Fìrinn honeyed gruel and covering him in furs, bringing the fire up to a sustained warmth inside the hut and letting the ladd sleep till after the midsky meal.

Half a moon later, on a foggy afternoon in the middle of the Willow moon (Apr.), Coillore came to the yard to get Fìrinn, despite Seumus's scowls. And they walked silently through the hushed wood beside the burn, the drúid in his white robe and cloak, and the ladd in muddy hide breeks, shirt, and fur lined jerkin. Turning north along the track to the wee hut beyond the yew, its outlines softened by the mist, Fìrinn felt mysteries soon to be revealed as everything appeared out of the fog less than a pony length ahead of him. And when he moved through the door cloth and sat in the low stump chair beside the hearth, his scalp tingled.

Coillore had made walnut bread with honey. And the ladd ate three pieces, then gulped warm birch bark tea before leaning back in the chair and eyeing the old druid. Coillore reached over then and drew an eye with a triple circle inside it, making twelve lines around the outer circle and four in the middle circle on the earthen floor.

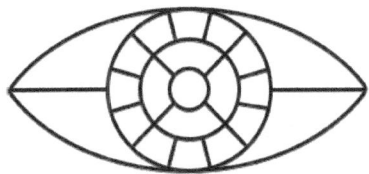

"The Stillpoint Center looks like this, wi' twenty-four regents. The very central circle simply leads through to the Creator Sun. So, the Four Directions make up the inner circle here, wi' twelve Zodiac regents around that; an' the protector archangels in the pointed outer corners. But let's begin wi' the regents o' the Four Directions, eh?

The eight regents o' the Four Directions are all sorceresses an' wizards, regents o' the cardinal directions, seasons, an' dragon kingdoms, ladd. An' all these regents an' their dragons serve the will force o' the One, bringin' it down into all cycles. It's the ethers o' the cosmos they overlight. We have sheaths o' light that match the seven worlds, remember? Well, each o' those sheaths has three ethers in it, separate vibrations for mind, heart, an' action, all except the core sheath, where these three are joined into one, the fourth or core ethers. An' this is the level where the inner spirit creates tho outer world, too, where are beliefs are manifested into our outer realities.

Here, the cardinal cross is turned, so the divisions make an X shape, no vertical an' horizontal like the Creator Sun. The red dragons rule the mental ethers; the wee girl in the east, the element o' air, an' spring, wi' its birth, first flowerin' o' life, non-violence, pleasure, passion, union o' hearts, an' surprise directives. They bring the structures o' growth for each skyturn out o' the cosmic sea an' the core ethers at Imbolc (imbolt) an' send them into the mental ethers o' the universe an' each one o' us. This red dragon wave opens on Imbolc, peaks at the Vernal Equinox, an' wanes at Bealltain.

Next come the green dragons o' emotion: the wee ladd in the west, the element o' water, an' summer. They bring the yearly impulses down from the mental ethers into the emotional ones for the cosmos wi' the boy's exuberance for life, will force, action, adventure, an' world service directives. This wave opens on Bealltain, peaks at Midsummer, an' wanes at Lughnasa.

Then come the yellow dragons o' the action ethers: the Da in the south, the element o' fire, an' autumn. These dragon forces move the annual structures o' growth down into the action ethers o' the cosmos, when manifestation into the physical begins, the harvest, eh? Magic!" An' the druid flung back the plaid he'd wrapped over his shoulders with a flourish and a grin. "It's wave opens at Lughnasa, peaks at the Autumnal Equinox, an' wanes at Samhein (1).

An' finally come the black an' white dragons o' the core ethers, light an' dark: the mother o' the north, the element o' earth, an' winter. Black dragons dismantle the impulses o' the passin' cycle an' bring each person's growth impulse back into their core ethers wi' the three deep fears each individual'll have to face over the winter moons. Black dragons take the reins from Samhein (1) to Midwinter, ladd. Then the white dragons come in, bringin' forth light from the depths o' the cosmos at Midwinter to build in the hopes soon to be realized, but also the bone fears o' the skyturn, death, eh? They take the lead from Midwinter to Imbolc. It's snow crystals the new truths move through, Firinn, showerin' the comin' patterns o' freedom down, to be released once the hard mid-winter fears have been faced, as the snows melt into the lakes an' streams o' earth's emotional body when the warmth comes in again. The white dragons build all truths learned into each person's permanent light body, too.

All these regents an' dragons have a four skyturn cycle o' growth as well. In the first year come the red dragons wi' their intellectual lessons o' the mental ethers. Then in the second skyturn come lessons o' emotion, green ethers an' dragons. Then come the sensate or action lessons, manifestin' growth into our physical lives, the yellow dragons o' the third skyturn. An' last come the black an' white dragons that break down the passin' impulse an' build the truths we learned into our light bodies, the fourth skyturn. Then a new cycle starts again on that extra day added in every four years at the end o' the Ash moon (February 29th, leap year day).

So let's go through these eight Four Direction regents, beginin' wi' me favorite sorceress, the little girl goddess. Her name is Siris (sheerish, cherry), an' her regency is choosin' the moment o' manifestation into the physical, for she resonates wi' the base o' the uterus, that wee cherry there (cervix). This makes her a very powerful goddess, though she doesna decide what'll manifest or build the forms. Still, she's quite detail oriented an' precise in all she does, ever wantin' to set the perfect stage for her surprises. Most o' the Diamond Core goddesses create fruit, too, ladd, cherries bein' hers, o' course. An' it's her tree, too.

An' Siris overlights the thyroid, thy road, the long silk thread that kens the way through all planes o' light back to the Creator Sun again. It rolls out the carpet we walk along each day, goin' Home, one wee lassie step at a time. Siris anchors into an isle on the other side o' the world, ladd, that'll one day be called Japan. They revere cherry trees an' have a great festival at cherry blossom time, too. Her cherry'll be on their banner one day as well.

Siris is the regent o' wonder as well, an' she sends petals o' it flutterin' into the depths o' each heart, created from the tiniest things; just the household item or dress the inner lass has been longin' for, a perfect rose, perhaps, things that dinna happen often an' bring a sudden influx o' joy among the harsh difficulties o' life. Her star compound is in Aquarius, the tibia star, Skat.

Oisìn (ohsheen, little deer) is her consort. An' though he serves the girl quadrant, he has a boy regency, the sacredness o' the ordinary. He likes simplicity an' values the wee moments o' joy that are the true nourishment o' this world, stayin' away from the excess that covers the simple truths o' life (Zen Buddhism). Oisìn creates uncommon beauty, openin' the veils to bring zephyrs o' heaven into our hearts an' minds, like her, but his tend more toward the world outside the home, when a yellow butterfly an' a rosy finch fly to the same lilac bush, perhaps, or those peaceful crimson sunsets that ease so much, things that are unusual an' lovely, but as ordinary as can be. But even more, he brings the essence o' love into everyday life, the deep inner satisfaction o' plantin' seeds or harvestin' brambles or sweepin' yer hut fresh an' clean every mornin', life's sweetness in the simplest things there are. His star compound is in Phoenix, ladd, an' his tree is the Japanese Maple. These two rule the red dragons an' overlight the mental ethers in all worlds.

The virgin regent o' the next segment o' the Four Directions is Eilean (ayleen, island), anchorin' into Eire, the emerald isle, o' course, her an' her green dragons. She an' her consort, Fearglas (feerglahs, green man) rule the emotional ethers o' all worlds, so, passion, movin' all forward wi' those tugs at the heart that canna be ignored, stunnin' moments o' heart-wrenchin' loveliness or poignancy that lift all folk in moments an' open doorways into our next adventure o' life. She creates sweet moments o' union wi' God an' Goddess, too, workin' closely wi' the fae. But her main impulse is union o' her heart wi' the virgin boy's, well, an' freein' all virgin lassies on earth. She's a most determined goddess, though, wi' her strong heart drive to better all worlds. Her fruit is green grapes, ladd, the intoxication o' love, eh?" And the druid smiled.

"Eilean is the queen o' trees as well, the original druid priestess, bringin' the Goddess impulses for the skyturn up the watery flow from earth into all tree roots, to be breathed out by the leafy canopy to all passer's by. There is great precision here, too, for any trees near yer hut have been carefully arranged by the spirit world. Ye can tell a great deal about a person's path by the trees they live under, eh? An' Eilean brings the holiness o' heaven into the forest, too, to hold an' calm all who walk under these comfortin' boughs. Her star compound is on Virgo, Spica, an' her tree, the Irish Elm is a fountain o' virgin strength.

Eilean's consort is Fearglas, comin' through Phoenix, for this is the boy quadrant after all. This wizard's powers are as unbounded as Eilean's, for Fearglas can call forth the magic o' fae friends to delight an' ease as well, in the gentleness o' the forest, mainly. But his specialty is tree lore, ladd, an' he can teach ye all about the ancient truths structured into trunk an' branch, an' the uses o' wood an' bark for buildin' or healin,' the original druid, ladd, His main regency is to draw folk into the forest to impart some needed knowings, or calm, perhaps. Trees remind us o' the timeless loveliness o' heaven an' are far more influential in our lives than many realize, even the Oak o' that chair yer sittin' in.

An' as green man, Fearglas is regent o' those hidden wildflowers o' the forest, too, trillium, Jack-in-the-pulpits, an' such wi' their gentle powers. But tree trunks an' branches resonate wi' the spine an' the nerves o' our backs, eh? Some folk call him Jack, instead. His tree is the Chestnut, an' his star, Pisces. See how the girl an' boy quadrants o' the Four Directions anchor into opposite oceans, ladd, holdin' the lands o' the northern hemisphere between them?

Then the mother o' the Four Directions o' the yellow dragons an' action ethers is Arienrhod (ahreeinraht), her womb the daytime bowl o' the sky. Her essence is freedom for all inner divine children to play an' create as they wish within the love an' security o' highest heaven, the pursuit o' happiness. An' leisure pursuits o' the arts are her specialty, to offset the growth phases o' her consort. Her ray color, sky blue, will be the banner o' Alba someday.

But Arienrod's real regency is freedom from fear, liberty. She ever nudges us toward this goal, for she rules the ascension wheel, the long journey down from highest heaven into the lowest world an' back up again. Arienrhod leads all humans through their feminine trials into the full embodiment o' Tara's heart especially. An' as global mother, Arienrhod holds up the torch o' freedom for all peoples, too, an' doesna give up in the face o' darkness, workin' tirelessly for liberty, equality, an' succor for all, often outside the home, but inside it, too.

Arienrhod brings her torch seven days past Lughnasa (Aug. 12th), also, to light all hearts wi' truths to be integrated durin' the rest o' the skyturn. Often her torch o' truth sparks the heart's passion at other times, too. Her tree is the Sycamore, an' her star city is on Vega, ladd. Arienrhod anchors into Alba, for she's the Skye mother, the face on the mountain behind yer very own tuath. (MacLeod's table south as seen from Dunvegan castle, see cover photo from Alba Reborn, Book Two) (Dunvegan resonates with the star Vega.)

Arienrhod's consort is Leòmhann (lovan, lion), the Four Directions father, whose yellow dragons manifest our desires into the physical world, the harvest, eh? He's regent o' buildin' the laws o' love into every person, a massive task! But he does this mainly by buildin' courage into every inner father, getting' all to face whatever each must in the world to build the father's Kingdom on earth. An' like any good Da, Leòmhann manifests surprises an' heart's desires for all his many bairns across the cosmos, too, for manifestation into the sensate world is the main regency o' this quadrant. O' course, he manifests what ye may need to progress on yer path, too, no the same thing at all. But since he's the regent o' autumn, he loves bringin' in full harvests, his sunshine growin' all the crops we love, to fill every belly wi' delicious things.

Leòmhann comes in seven days after Imbolc (Feb. 12th) as well, to bring up the truths to be revealed in the father's outer phase o' the skyturn, along wi' his bright hope o' freedom soon to come. His star city is on Regulus in Leo, an' his tree is the White Oak, Quercus Alba but he anchors into Albion. He an' Arienrhod are regents o' the western hemisphere on earth, too, the outer world.

Then the grandmother regent o' the Four Directions, wi' her winter moons an' black dragons, is Bridget (breejet, Bridget) (I've added the final t to distinguish this goddess from Braidigh, brydee. Bridget is usually spelled Bride in Scottish Gaelic, pronounced breeja). She an' her consort rule the inner worlds, all the planes o' light I'm teachin' ye, an' the inner path Home. But Bridget especially overlights the Goddess's primordial sea, the core ethers, the feminine or watery half o' this quadrant. It's the unconscious, all that hasna yet manifested, both fear an' light. An' out of this sea comes all patterns o' life, for Bridget's mistress o' the very first births out this sea, that set the tone for a whole skyturn, a phase o' life, or a lifetime. Her influence always breaks down what preceeded it, too, markin' a shift into a whole new way o' bein'.

Bridget brings in great comfort as well, ladd, the final end o' pain o' some kind, rest in her mother's arms. She's the soul friend, the anam cara, the mentor who sees each disciple through all stages o' the path into the final transition back Home again. An' so, she wants ye to keep followin' love's path, no matter how hard or steep the way. She helps all see that their inner fears are creatin' outer pain that affects all bein's in all worlds, too, turnin' each individual toward takin' responsibility for the All, the bodhisattva path. Some call her the Dao, some Psyche. Her fruit is plums an' her tree, the Sequoia. She anchors into China, the far east, wi' her Daoism religion. An' her star compound is on Mirach in Andromeda.

Her consort, the granda o' the Four Directions, is Eòl, (yol, knowledge, El). He sends out the rays o' light that call forth the precise structures o' light Oghama wants to manifest out o' the Goddess's pregnant core waters, for Eòl rules enlightenment, the awakenin' o' the unconscious into consciousness. He contains broad understandin', utter peace in the flow o' creation, no matter how dark it may sometimes seem, knowin' that everythin' serves the Will o' the One an' Love itself in the end. But it's the new truths an' challenges o' the comin' cycles he brings forth, mainly, the Da o' newborn dreams, for his light expands an' lifts into awareness whatever it touches. His nature is gentle, though his distortions are no, expandin' the mind somethin' fierce at times wi' his over-complicated mental structures that block the flow o' emotions o' the Goddess especially.

He an' Brìdget are the lord an' lady o' karma as well, seein' that all debts are paid in love before movement to the next level is allowed. If ever ye canna understand why ye may be undergoin' some difficulty, call him in. He'll show ye exactly the mistake ye made many lifetimes ago, the debt ye're payin' off in this one. I find it very comfortin' to ken that, eh? It makes me want to undergo what I may've been chafin' against before. These two rule the black an' white dragons, the truth an' shadows o' the core ethers, her ancient archetypes an' his forever light. Eòl anchors into China, too, ladd. But his religion is Buddhism, an' his tree, the Bodhi or Fig, an' his star compound's on Aldebaran in Taurus.

Their symbol looks like two droplets o' water, one upside down, snuggled together (yin/yang symbol), his the light o' consciousness and hers the dark o' the collective unconscious, the cosmic sea. But this is the mother quadrant, remember? That's why their sun looks like droplets, because it's the watery emotions that are the true focus here.

His half o' the year begins three days before Imbolc (Feb. 2nd), to initiate his awakenin' cycle, right after she's lifted the new girl structures out o' her core sea the day before. An' her half o' the skyturn begins three days before Lughnasa (Aug 2nd), to draw all inward to that sea again for the winter moons, right after he's drawn the winter core structures to be built out o' it the day before, hm? An' these two regents overlight the eastern hemisphere o' earth as well, the inner world. So, between them, the parents an' grandparents o' the Four Directions hold the whole northern hemisphere in their strong arms o' love.

Then the three great rays o' aspect; mind, heart, an' action, split these Four Directions into twelve. This next circle out, the Zodiac regents, overlight the twelve sacred cultures o' heaven an' the twelve star portals o' each skyturn. They also hold the template o' that golden age to come in 21 centuries, ladd. The three aspects for the parents o' this level are; teacher for the mind, provider for the heart, an' protector for the action levels. The parents o' these twelve zodiac regents all anchor into the Middle East on earth, ladd. An' this is where worldwide change is often brought onto the global stage as well.

For the mind, the parents are Mathas (mahas, benevolence, Quan Yin) an' Longinus. She's a teacher, like him, but her teachin's come through every day experience, the feminine, the simple, but often profound, lessons o' life. She builds compassion for even the darkest folk into every one o' us, her particular regency, which can only be achieved through sufferin'. If ye never had any difficulty in yer life, ladd, the pain others are in would barely affect ye. But sufferin' engages the heart, so ye truly care about others who're havin' the same difficulties ye've had yerself. Embracin' the outcasts o' the world is never easy, though, for it always involves livin' outside the warmth o' yer own tribe's acceptance for a time. But all pain Mathas sends in is only meant to open the lotus o' compassion o' the heart until it's in full bloom. An' her star gateway is Saggitarius, the long road, for she often sends her disciples on long, long journeys, far away from home, to understand the ways o' far off folk. She anchors into China, ladd, an' her tree's the Umbrella Pine.

Her consort is Longinus (Buddha), an' he rules intelligence an' all intellectual truths in the left brain, the pursuit o' truth. As teacher, he creates all mentors an' the flow o' ideas into our lives, everyone, a powerful regent, indeed. There are many, many inner teachers across the cosmos that he commands as well, for our brothers an' sisters in the Otherworld long to assist us in solvin' the problems o' each age. But Longinus's distortions can bring in complicated details that steal the simplicity o' the true father an' especially the inner feminine's need for rest. He's regent o' the eight-fold path o' enlightenment as well, which will ever bring peace o' mind in the end. He holds the keys to Samadhi, too, that great sun he brings over the mind o' disciples, which melts down worry channels in moments, networks o' ancient fears, and builds the bridges o' truth once more. Ach, his long armed radiance is unparalleled. Longinus's star gateway is Taurus, the Ain star there, his tree, the Sessile Oak, his religion, Buddhism. Information is moved on tiny particles o' light that in future times'll be known as quarks, ladd. Hers is called beauty an' his, truth. When we do healin' work, imaginin' the darkness movin' into the heart, it's these small quarks the mind is movin' into the diamond light.

Then, the Ma o' the heart, the provider, is Mara (mahrah, of the sea, Asherah or Shekinah). Mara overlights the embodiment o' wisdom for all humanity, but through our immediate earth families noo. For she brings in our human family members an' tribe. But it's wisdom Mara's mainly concerned wi', bringin' in hard teachin's through those families in order to renew it for the cosmos. So, our deepest darkness, but also our strongest light, an' the ancient traditions o' our heavenly motherland are all woven into Mara's fabric o' family life. She can be quite detail oriented, too, but also overlights family closeness, creatin' celebrations or quiet moments o' joy between the hard wisdom lessons. Her religion is Judaism.

Mara's wisdom cycle is 12 29.5-day moons, wi' 11 intercessory days. These extra days are rolled into one extra moon every two or three skyturns. There are two sets o' three skyturns, then one set o' two skyturns, each set wi' one added moon. Then come three sets o' three skyturns an' another set o' two skyturns, each set again wi' an added moon, before another whole cycle begins every 19 skyturns. The three skyturn sets all have an undercurrent o' wisdom, some darkness built into Mara's song o' life. An' these five sets o' triple skyturns cycle through our five basic inner aspects, too. The two skyturn sets in between are free o' wisdom's darkness, times o' rest an' renewal. An' it's Mara who coordinates all these. Her cycles hold the same pattern as a musical instrument that'll be played in the future, a piano it'll be called, dark minor keys for the five triple skyturns, light major keys for the double skyturns, exactly like Mara's cycle. Her star gateway is in Cancer, the crab, ladd, same as her tree, the Crab Apple.

The father o' the heart is Manannan, who some call Yaweh. He's the provider, an' this means the clan he brings in around each person their whole life long. None o' us could go through life alone. We need folk to help us shoulder it all, an' others to lead the way. As father, Manannan's clan focus is outside the home, the extended family an' its traditions.

But, like Mara, he brings in our clan wisdom lessons especially, the masculine noo. His distortions lead to a lot o' rules an' regulations that keep the flow o' the feminine blocked an' strained, but his heart is good, wantin' to support every person wi' the closeness o' their own kind. His an' Mara's sight is long, for our clans each hold the patterns o' our own folk o' the Creator Sun, too. Manannan's tree is the Calliprinos Oak, an' his star is Adhafera in Leo. One day his quark'll be called charm an' hers strange.

In life, Manannan is the anchor, the compass, the sea captain who leads us through the stormy waters o' emotion on Mara's sea o' life. He sets the course o' each person's ship o' destiny as it traverses her seas, too, pullin' each person into connections wi' teachers or friends that will support an' heal, through emotional shifts especially. But he teaches through questions mainly, bringin' in confusions that cause folk to think as hard as they can, ever searchin' for final truths."

And listening, Fìrinn could feel Mara and Manannan holding all humanity, sending in the resolve to face and complete each part of their wisdom walk, especially when someone turned aside from the travail sent in. He saw all families in the stars watching their own on earth with hope in their hearts, too, star families rejoicing when each earth relative applied some healing force of love to his or her inner shadows, so they could be lifted beyond those fears for all time. And Fìrinn especially felt Mara's sadness toward individuals who ignored the opportunities for growth she prepared so carefully. For Fìrinn knew as well as Mara that the identical fears would have to be applied with more force over the following moons in order to turn those individuals toward growth.

"Then, the father an' mother for the action level are Breitheamh (breether, judge) an' Mùthadh (moohuh, change)," Coillore continued, "the protectors. She's the Ma who attends to the home, keepin' it pure an' unsullied by darkness, the feminine especially, settin' moral boundaries o' family life. But her distortions can bring in rigidity o' laws as well.

She also wields the chaos force, the power to dismantle huge societal structures, the whirlwind that cleanses outmoded patterns in moments. But the seeds o' the new are ever hidden in the eye o' the storm, an' her chaos lessons teach us to trust an' hold fast to our central core o' love till the higher level comes free an' clear at last.

Mùthadh weighs each heart at the end o' each life, too, but based on choices made within the family, the home. Always there are opportunities to pay off ancient debts in life, an' if a person cares for an elderly parent for skyturns, perhaps they were less than lovin' to that elder in some former time. It's Mùthadh who arranges these circumstances. Carin' for yer infirm ones may feel like bein' held back, but it isna at all, it's freein' ye, in fact.

But Mùthadh's major teachin' in life is endurin' the hard times, just carryin' on an' doin' the best ye can, a deep lesson, that, eh? It's the bedrock patience o' the feminine, surrender to the will o' the One, no matter what. Her distortions often keep the mother hidden away at home, too, for one o' her main challenges is the domination o' the masculine at this action level. But in truth, bein' held back in long years o' service in the hut simply brings the feminine action level within into alignment wi' the One. Her tree is the Lemon, ladd, an' her star gateway is Scorpio.

Brietheamh, her consort, is the judge, watchin' over every individual an' keepin' track o' all choices for good or ill. But his focus is ever on the outer world, the masculine, so his debts relate more to commerce an' the workin' world. His star city is in Libra, those scales o' justice. An' every heart is weighed on them after life on earth ends to determine what kind o' life they'll lead in the future. Some folk get so lost in hoardin' wealth, they end up in stark poverty the next time, round an' round, lifetime after lifetime, their souls crusted over wi' untruth at both ends o' the spectrum. But Breitheamh is compassionate an' merciful, weighin' in the needs an' hurts o' each life, too. He is the mediator in all disputes as well. An' he rules our own inner judgment in life, too. Her quark is down an' his is up, eh? His an' Mùthadh's religion is o' the future, Islam, an' his tree is the Red Oak.

The father, mother, an' virgin aspects o' this Zodiac will be responsible for openin' three great paths o' truth on earth. Mara's mother wisdom stream was already opened by a man named Abraham, 17 centuries ago, Judaism. An' Longinus was represented by a man named Gautama Buddha, who initiated the mind path o' enlightenment on earth five centuries ago, Buddhism. This one was first o' the next three because the manifestation flow always begins wi' the mind an' then moves to the heart an' action centers. Christianity, a new religion to start in about a century, will flow through that holy man, Jesus, resonatin' wi' the heart. This man'll be Jewish by birth, Mara's religion, an' he'll open the cosmic boy era, wi' his heart path, an' a new Christian sect'll be born. An' it'll jump all humanity from this Zodiac level o' the Stillpoint Center to the Creator Sun an' it's trials, quite a leap. Then Pwyll, the action virgin male o' the Zodiac, links to the path o' action, an' its greatest teacher, Mohammed, will open this action stream on earth in about seven centuries, which also links to Mùthadh an' Brietheamh. An' mind, ladd, though the Creator Sun regents anchor into our own isles an' traditions, the high God and Goddess o' all religions everywhere flow to Oghama an' Tara as well, none above another at all. Others simply have their own names an' cultures to color their paths, eh?

But let's move on to the virgins noo. They, too, are split into three levels: regents o' the mind, who rule the plant an' animal kingdoms; heart regents who build our divine bairns within, our highest destinies; an' the will force action regents. At the mind level are Neamh (nev, heaven) an' Cernunnos (care-noonos). She overlights the fae lassies an' plant kingdom, her fae helpers sendin' light into every plant across the globe, the heaths an' heathers o' the moors. An' like all fae lassies, Neamh is full o' fun, quite seductive, an' loves the natural world. She is regent o' the consciousness o' all plant forms an' can teach ye to talk wi' trees or flowers, also hills an' rivers, an' learn all they have to teach about which plant can be used for healin' or cookin' perhaps, how to care for the earth, an' many truths o' heaven. Neamh is the goddess o' meadows an' sun lovin' wildflowers, too. Ach, she's ever wantin' to lead the inner girl into faery glades to gladden the way along life's sometimes dark glens. Her tree is the Halesia or Silverbell, an' her star gateway is Gemini. She anchors into Africa, ladd, an' overlights the pagan religions there.

Cernunnos, Neamh's consort, is the lord o' nature, rulin' the animal kingdom. He's the antlered one, who some call Pan. Cernunnos's specialty is communication wi' animals, for he kens the languages o' them all. An' they have much to teach us on earth. Cernunnos commands the djinn forces, too, the male fae folk who are responsible for sendin' the will to action o' Oghama into the mind o' all forms in all worlds (action potentials), as determined a lot as ever there was!

But Cernunnos's main regency is the restoration o' the peaceable kingdom on earth, the lamb held in the arms o' the lion. It's because he's the hunter as well, the one who took on the violence distortions that brought in the miasma o' mistrust an' fear between humans an' animals on earth. His darkness always involves the militarization o' the virgin boy's soft heart, killin' game, no part o' the boy's gentle nature at all. Cernunnos volunteered to carry this in pure love to spare Neamh, an' the carryin' of it'll build the deep desire into all virgin males to persevere an' create the peaceable kingdom once more."

"That's me yer talkin' about, Coillore!" Firinn burst out. "Me Da an' this whole fosterin' want me to kill animals that are more me friends than anyone, except you. It isna who I am at all."

"Aye, ladd, an' it's a boy betrayal o' Neamh's soft nature as well. But it's the only way to build the deep heart wish to make things better here. All will come true again in time, Firinn, never fear. Cernunnos's star gateway is Capricorn, the goat, an' he anchors into an isle in the southern lands across the world that'll one day be called Galapagos. His religions are the pagan ones o' that same continent, an' his tree is the Alder.

Both Cernunnos an' Neamh create personal power places in the natural world for all o' us, too, an' bring teachers an' fae friends to help us grow. Nature embodies the Goddess strongly, as ye ken, so these regents can lead ye to Her tender embrace as well. Neamh an' Cernunnos send one earth guardian to each individual, too; a plant ye love, a stone, an animal companion, perhaps. For Soillse, this guardian is her apple tree, for ye, it's Bana Dhia, ladd. An' these earth guardians send the call on high to these Zodiac virgins if ever there's danger o' a person fallin' too fast or too far, so real harm to the inner divine child canna occur.

Then the virgin regents o' the heart are Ur (oor, new) an' Deas (jeeas, right hand, Jesus). They build the structures o' the divine child within, lifetime after lifetime, preparin' for that high destiny to come. Fifteen skyturns before the final birth in the last lifetime on earth, Maighdean an' Rìdire o' the Creator Sun also come in to aid in this task. An' since all humans are Ur's bairns, earth contains her name, Urth. An' the cradle o' life here was in her land, Ur. Both these regents orchestrate global causes o' each skyturn an' the future as well. She brings through the feminine issues, especially for bairns an' virgin lassies, an' he, the masculine, boys an' virgins again.

Ur overlights that orange o' light in the uterus, too, that sends pictures into the ethers o' what the Goddess wishes to happen in our lives, messages to all those fae helpers to create specific outer experiences in each o' our physical worlds. This orange has 13 segments, an' they revolve through the skyturn, accordin' to Maighdean's divine bairn cycle, each segment holdin' one moon's pictures for manifestation. Orange is Ur's tree, too. An' her star gateway is Aquarius.

Ur's consort, Deas, like her, builds the divine bairn within, sendin' in the experiences that prepare the inner male for service to the One. For Deas builds the inner god, wi' his focus on the outer world, leadin' through masculine fears and developin' these special male gifts. Deas is the carpenter, ladd, a master at creatin' inner structures that'll hold strong through any storms. He wants to lift the entire cosmos, puttin' up wi' the harshest trials in pure love. An' Deas's wooden cross over the spine grows heavy in the final five skyturns before the holy birth, as the core wound activates and becomes the guidin' force o' each person's life. Deas has the most stalwart heart, though, that can hold an' lead everyone though their darkest hours. In future days, he'll be called Jesus, ladd. He anchors into Nazareth in Israel, an' his tree is the Cedar, his star getway, Pisces, the fish.

Then come the action regents, the virgins, Sìth (shee, peace) an' Pwyll (pwill, personal will). Sìth's regency is the full restoration o' the feminine on earth back into equality wi' the male, the end o' masculine domination, another massive job! Sìth rules the spine, the backbone, inner strength that doesna give in to brute force, no matter what harm comes. Her spinal channel goes straight up to the father, so she wants to build the Da's kingdom on earth more than anythin', too. Her devotion to love kens no parallel. Her star system is Virgo, the Porrima star there, an' her tree, the Rose o' Sharon, ladd.

But Sìth's true regency is non-violence, in the face o' physical harm especially. Only non-violence will turn the tide, for violence only creates its own likeness, eh? The inner girl is the only one o' our basic aspects that didna take on the violence distortions, wi' their hard reptilian shell o' indifference an' their cold, cold heart. Sìth doesna wilt in the face o' darkness, ever. She stands her ground an' gives no authority to any force but love. She's the dove, who'll bring the final days o' peace in her wake. For when earth finally remembers an' releases her essence within, true an' lastin' peace'll come to earth, an' war'll cease. Those are days to look forward to, eh? It's the deer o' yer clan that serve Sìth, ladd, drawin' violence to themselves in utter love an' gentleness to keep balance in the world. How much more violence there'd be, if no for those deer takin' more than their share, hm? Hers is a long hard path, an' Sìth'll keep ye movin' on it an' shore ye up when ye feel ye canna go on. For her, there's no such word as can't! Her religions are all the sects that willna wage war or carry arms, an' she mainly anchors into the temple mound in Jerusalem, another one o' her names. But for Alba, Sìth anchors into the Hebrides, the outer isles shaped just like her spine. An' her initiation is part o' the trainin' o' all priests an' priestesses who live there. Her ray color is cobalt blue, the main ray color o' earth.

It's Sìth who sorts the next seven generations o' bairns into waves o' change on earth, too, as they come through the Pleiades on their way down, splittin' into the seven colors o' the rainbow. But long ago, the Orion reptilians invaded the Pleiades an' took over its heart star, Maia. From there they beam violent illusions out across the cosmos. When their final distortions have been released in the distant future, the Mayan calendar will come to an end, December 21st, 2012 as the skyturns'll be counted in those days. That Midwinter'll happen at 11 minutes past 11 in their time. That's the virgin girl's number, ladd, 11, the age when Maighdean, the virgin girl o' the Creator Sun, begins to overlight everyone's life cycle. An' that morn'll usher in the beginnin' o' her virgin girl cycle on earth, and the births o' her divine bairns across the globe.

But let's get back to the rainbow, eh? Each generation serves one chakra or wheel o' light on the spine, takin' up a particular cause, the earth cyclin' through all seven levels over an' over again through the centuries. Sìth coordinates these, as well as those wheels o' light on each person's spine that direct our growth an' forward movement, issues o' the seven levels here brought forward in turn. She's the rainbow lass o' the cosmos.

Sìth's consort is Pwyll, an' his regency is the action impulse, love-in-action, the phallic or personal will force an' power channel up the front o' the abdomen to the solar plexus. An' Pwyll's will force is hard to tame, for it got corrupted an' separated from the Creators' very early in our descent. It's because those reptilians invaded the Creator Sun, beatin' an' torturin' us till we hit back. So, they forced Pwyll's will within to separate from love an' walled the divine Will o' God/Goddess off. So, it's violence an' brute force Pwyll's distortions mainly bring in. Still, no good would ever come without that inner will, for without initiative, a body would just drift through life, eh? Ach, Pwyll's always gettin' into scrapes an' trials he has to win his way through, blocks to action that eventually realign him wi' the One as well. He has quite an active sexual side as well. Pwyll anchors into Saudi Arabia, ladd.

An' his regency is turnin' that old distorted personal power stream into the will-for-good it was always meant to become, a Herculean task! There are vast reservoirs o' crude oil in the middle east, ladd," Coillore continued, "the residue o' dinosaur/dragon times, when the violence distortions took over here. Crude oil is the earth substance o' the personal will force in separation from the One. An' toward the end o' the comin' cycle, those oil reservoirs'll be tapped. Then the ancient reptilian distortions will be unleashed upon the earth, the end times sages tell of. Folk'll compete wi' each other for the illusion o' wealth that oil represents. It's use'll give rise to huge Borg Orion corporate networks that want only power an' control, wastin' the Goddess's resources here, over-complicatin' everythin', an' puttin' everyone in a perpetual rush to serve their top-heavy networks, ordinary folk crushed an' enslaved. An' all that oil'll give rise to more people than earth can easily support. But in due time, those oil fields'll be used up, thank Goddess! An' simple energy sources that are ever plentiful on earth, like wind an' sun an' tides'll be used, instead. These'll restore the slow life flow o' Màiri into the root o' all an' calm the global frenzy. Hurray for that! Pwyll's star compound is on Aries, ladd, an' his tree is the Olive.

An' then, in the pointed outer ends o' the Stillpoint Center sit the archangels, protectors an' messengers from these high levels. There are four; Maigeal (mikeal, Michael) o' the dominion angel forces an' the Da quadrant, Gabhreal (Gabriel) o' the virtue angel forces an' Ma quadrant, Ureal (Uriel) o' the girl quadrant an' the seraphim, an' finally Rapheal (Raphael) o' the boy an' cherubim.

There ye have it, ladd, the eye o' the universe explained an' sorted, as clear as a sunny mornin'. Noo, off to yer furs!" And Firinn hurried out, throwing on his jerkin, before Coillore could think of more details to add to his always too long lessons.

Walking slowly down the burn path to the shore, Firinn settled himself on the rocks by the bay for a time, to clear the mental overload from his mind. After nightfall, the fog had thickened and Firinn listened to the sound of waves creeping slowly up on the pebbly sand below his feet, the tuath utterly silent in the hush of night. Finally, his mind settled again, Firinn walked slowly to his pallet and gratefully sank in under his furs.

It was Deas Firinn dreamed of that night, the virgin god reaching in to open a doorway in Firinn's abdomen, where a wee babe in a rough manger of hay lay sleeping. Then Deas spent hours carefully building a small wooden stairway in the ethers, all the way from the cradle up to Firinn's heart.

"I'll keep ye safe, wee one, I promise," Firinn whispered as he woke, "till yer as free as those seagulls over the sea loch, ridin' the wind."

Chapter Twenty: Soillse

Soillse, in her old work stained shift and plaid, lingered at the fire circle with Coillore. Waiting, with hands on hips and fire in her eyes, she watched Seumus walk back along the bracken brown path under the scrub birches. The gloaming held its brightness late these early spring days, dusky light filtering through the budding boughs of the birches. Ceit skipped ahead of the chief, who was striding quickly in his buckskin breeks and shirt, wanting to get out of the wind to his own hearth. The other children had already run off as soon as the druid stopped chanting under the oak in the woodland clearing.

"What else can ye change?," Soillse asked Coillore, her voice curt, staring at the druid with her wispy ash-brown hair blowing across her face. He'd shown her how to break through a blockage on the rains half a skyturn ago, and ever since, she'd dreamed of freeing herself from the constant demands of her older sister, Ceit. The druid hadn't moved from the large boulder where he sat to teach the lessons, watching her. The lass is budding herself, the druid noticed, on the cusp of womanhood.

"Anythin'," Coillore said, his blue eyes meeting hers, brows raised. "Whatever ye choose, lassie." The druid was wearing his plain white homespun robe and emerald cloak

"Gettin' bossed around by Ceit?," Soillse asked in a hoarse whisper, as the color rose in her cheeks.

"That fear's built deeply into ye, lassie. It can be done, aye, an' will in time, but it'll mean quite a spirit climb to free yerself. An' the goin'll get harder before the final easin' comes, a few skyturns at least, Soillse." His calm blue eyes rested on her face with a note of question in them.

"I want it," she said crisply, jutting out her chin. She was petite, pixie-like, her green eyes usually gentle. But they weren't now, and she hadn't smiled all evening, the druid recalled. He remembered that she'd been sitting on the far side of the fire circle from Ceit as well, unusual for sisters who often sat side-by-side among the fostered ladds."

"All right. Come here then on sixth night after the evenin' meal. We'll do a callin' forth ritual o' all the fears related to Ceit that are embedded into ye." But his eyes grew sad as he spoke.

She nodded and whirled away, her mouth pinched into a straight line, as she strode rapidly down the bracken fringed path and disappeared into the scrub birches. Then the druid closed his eyes, asking the Goddess to help him see what had upset the lass so. He saw an image of Ceit, tall and muscular, with her black frizzed hair plaited into a braid, holding a stick above Soillse's back earlier in the day, some small mistake the older lass was objecting to. But in truth, Ceit was only using that as an excuse to lash out at Soillse. There was an ancient rift between them, the druid noted, with Egyptian roots particularly.

Coillore shook his head, sighed, and said a blessing for easing of pain for them both. I canna do much for ye just now, lassie, he thought, peering through the boughs for a glimpse of the bay below. I need to concentrate on Fìrinn for the next two round of seasons, before the ladd's gone from the fostering altogether. He's fifteen winters now, and he's only completed one of his initiations. And I havena worked with girls or women either, except in scattered ceremonies long ago with a few priestesses from the virgin isle across the channel from Iona, when I lived on the sacred isle in my youth. The virgins were always kept sequestered for their training then, and it was a long time ago. Coillore's wife's face came suddenly to mind, her petite form, azure eyes, and long blond wavy hair. And his heart contracted in sadness as he remembered his late wife's eyes on his own. This ache was old, too, ever present, and he took little notice of it. What had Ailis's (eye-lish, Alice) path been like? He could only recall bits and pieces of what she'd told him about her training over their many skyturns together.

He did remember that the feminine path was not as formal as the male. There were no initiations of the elements for the lasses. But women moved through the identical stages on the path, he knew, for the steps were much the same for everyone. Still, the women's fears were brought forward through their life circumstances, instead. He'd healed himself exactly as Fìrinn was doing, with memory stones on his brow one or two afternoons every quarter moon. The priestesses shared their wisdom in more practical ways, too, during cooking or cleaning perhaps, instead of ritualized training like the men. Ailis had mentioned the retrieval of ancient memories for healing only during her new and full moon cave times. Had she ever spoken of memory stones? I dinna think so, he mused. The priestesses always kept their knowledge to themselves. Let's see, there are the birth ceremonies, the first moon-time rituals, preparation for the first sexual joining, and marriage, of course. Then there's childbirth, the ceasing of fertility rites, the grandmother rites, and death, the return to the Otherworld. He sighed. And Eilid as matriarch'll take charge of all those ceremonies for Soillse, as well she should, for she's the lass's Ma after all. It's askew, Coillore thought, running one hand over his scalp, that I, a male druid, should be teaching a virgin girl. There must be a reason, but I dinna understand it at all. Still, there's no one else, and the Goddess knows best. She'll tell me what needs to be done. Then he spread the ashes of the fire, pensive as he walked along the mossy trail to the hut circle beside the bay, then turned up the boulder strewn path along the burn to climb halfway up the ridge behind the tuath, turning north on a tiny deer path, till he came to his wee hut, well secluded from the tribe in the forest.

The morning mist had given way to a dead calm all afternoon, followed by a cool evening. The slivered new moon was just rising over the ridge that blocked the view of the mainland to the south, the beginning of the Willow moon (April). And the birches were full of catkins, palest yellow, with powdered pollen scattered across the forest floor, already ankle deep with lichen and mosses. With her hands fisted and her lower lip pushed into a pout, Soillse stood before the druid at the fire circle in the small clearing beneath the oak. She wore a lightweight green summer shift, permanently stained from her many cooking and fish gutting chores. Just this once, Seumus had agreed to a lesson alone with Coillore. The chief was particularly protective of Soillse after that strange incident when she was four winters old, when a passing druid hurt her woman's place up on the ridge.

"It's no <u>fair</u>," Soillse said shortly, her eyes blazing, as she stared at the fire. "<u>Men</u> get to be heroes an' chiefs an' druids, an' women have to haul bath water an' clean latrines an' tan hides an' gut fish, day after day, till they're too old fer anythin' else, like Ma. An' noo ye're tellin' me ye ken less o' the women's path, an' ye need to focus on Fìrinn for the next two skyturns!" And she frowned down at the druid's mild upturned face. "Girls are just less important. Is that it, Coillore?"

Coillore sat on the flat stone beneath the oak in his white robe and listened quietly. At the last sentence, he held back the flicker of annoyance that flared in his chest. How little she knows of life, he thought. Oh yes, the feminine <u>was</u> crushed by darkness eons ago. But so were the men, just in different ways. Then he sent the Goddess light around Soillse's heart, waiting a moment as the pressure of the lass's anger eased. And gradually, she stopped glaring at him and slumped to the ground.

"I'm thirteen winters, Coillore," Soillse said, her eyes pleading, "an' already I feel tired to me bones. No wonder Ma's hip hurts! I <u>hate</u> guttin' fish! An' noo, since you an' I healed the rains last summer, I dream o' the Diamond Core in the Otherworld. Sometimes in the peace o' the gloamin', I sense it in the distance. It's the <u>loveliest</u> place, so quiet an' <u>clean</u>! Why does the Goddess give me a wee taste o' heaven an' then make me Ceit's slave girl, sweatin' an' <u>filthy</u>, the rest o' the time?" She dropped her head and sighed heavily as she pushed both palms down her blood stained shift, for the ladds had brought in a boar to be cleaned late in the afternoon. Coillore only nodded and laid his hand on her back between her shoulder blades, sending in the focused yellow ray of the father. She winced slightly as she felt her rage expand, lighten, and then move out of her chest.

"I'm sorry, Coillore" she whispered then. "It's no yer fault."

"Nor is it yers, lassie," he answered softly. "Those who are climbin' to the Diamond Core carry the heaviest loads there are. An' reachin' the final breakthrough is never easy, a long hard, tirin' walk. An' everythin' that happens, even this delay, is a reflection o' yer own beliefs, lass. I'll help ye heal it all in time, I <u>promise</u> ye, Soillse." And he patted the rock for her to sit beside him, the new leaves of the oak above whispering in the soft evening breeze. "Ye dinna have to do this, ye ken." And as he spoke, tingles ran over her scalp and down her spine. Someone else had said that, some god I dinna remember very well, she thought, before I came here to earth. "An' I <u>didna</u> say I wouldna work wi' ye these next seasons either, only that I must concentrate on Fìrinn before he comes into his manhood. Ye're special beyond tellin', child. I'll do whatever's necessary. But ye live here in the tuath, he doesna. He'll be gone from us in no time." She felt a wave of warmth flow from the druid's chest, his eyes as kind as ever, and her shoulders relaxed as she looked at him, nodding. "I do understand yer hearin' it as ye did, though, lass, an' yer frustration wi' Ceit." He paused. "But Syl, dinna chafe fer the life ye've been given. Do ye think it's easy fer men to be heroes an' chiefs when the feminine within is completely lost to them? All any o' them ever want is a happy home an' a peaceful life, wi' a family, enough to eat, an' especially someone to love who loves them in return." And Coillore sighed as he said this. "It's all any of us want, really. Do ye think spearin' their animal brothers every time they hunt brings happiness, lass, no to mention their neighborin' tribesmen or raiders that might threaten?"

"No," she said, shivering. "I couldna ever do that, either one." And she hunched her shoulders to think of killing anything at all. "I even carry the wee beetles out o' the hut," she added. The druid smiled to think of it, but failed to tell her he did the same.

"Whatever hardship each o' us has to bear, lass, is just part o' the cloak o' fear we chose to put on in our descent from the Creator Sun down through all worlds. Each one o' those many fears made us heavier, so our light was encased over long eons o' time, slowed down enough to sustain a body that changes little over a lifetime, creatin' the physical realms. It's what we all asked for, every single person on this planet. And then, o' course, we've had more difficulties in our physical forms, until we're strong enough to face all those fears again an' rebuild our shadow selves into light, so we can finally birth our divine children into the physical world as well. And that last can only be done here in the sensate realms. Then, an' only then, will the happily-ever-after come. Dinna fret noo, for the Creators have decreed it from the beginnin' o' time. Ye're far along in that process, lass, much further than most. If ye choose to, ye could take what remains o' the darkness around ye an' break free in this one lifetime. It's possible. Difficult, but possible." Her face softened as he spoke, and a gentle wistfulness filled her eyes.

"An' then at the end o' the road, always, some gift o' the Creators is given through ye," Coillore continued, "an' ye must stay long enough past the end o' darkness to see that through, too. It'll be some gift to the tribes or the earth mother or the bairns, perhaps." And she smiled as he said this, as he'd known she would. "It's planted an' cultivated, that gift, until it grows strong enough to last here, even after ye're gone. An' then, when ye cross over, ye'll rise up to the diamond gates an' never return to this world o' pain, forever free, dear." She brought her hands up over her mouth as he spoke, holding her breath, as if any movement would make the dreamed he spoke of disappear. And her eyes shone like a wee bairn's.

"How many steps are there on the way up?"

He waited a moment, thinking how to explain that without discouraging her more. Then he rose and drew the Diamond Core in the earth with his staff and six smaller lines beneath it, making a small circle beneath them all.

"This is the Diamond Core," he said, pointing to the circle on the top, "home o' Oghama an' the White Tara, the Creators an' One Beloveds. This Diamond Core is where yer Aine tree (anya, Anne, girl goddess of the Holy Family) takes ye in yer mind. It's the center o' all worlds, an' it creates true love an' world service. That's us! There are many planes an' fifteen basic structures in the Diamond Core that move the flow o' just everythin' through all worlds, 174 planes in all. There's a dragon star there, too, another dark place, where evil is structured into all descendin' forms. An' all must face an' heal it in order to create the final an' full deliverance o' their divine child within..

The Diamond Core is the seventh heaven, an' its element is the clear light o' love ye see all around ye, the diamond light. It infuses air an' water both, though it's no very activated here on earth. All these realms are inhabited by gods an' goddesses in forever partnership, an' the earth creation o' these levels is the divine children inside all humanity, but also precious metals, gems an' crystals, flowers, animals, an' plants. The climb through the planes o' the Diamond Core is overlit by Oghama Himself," and Coillore bent his head as he spoke.

"Below this, everythin' splits into six worlds, an' we each have sheaths o' light within that correspond to them." And he moved his staff to the first line he'd drawn beneath the top circle. "This sixth world is the diamond centerpoint, lass, and in it sits the indigo pentagram, the wisdom wheel," Coillore continued. "It's here that

Artio an' Herne make sure all wisdom impulses from the Core are brought forward through each skyturn. Thank Goddess for that! Then droppin' down comes the cosmic beast or dragon, the 6-6-6 o' the universe, another dark place, the abyss.

The Diamond Centerpoint is overlit by the father o' the mind in the Creator Sun, the Dagda, an' it's element is intelligence, the yellow light o' truth in the mind. These levels create stones, dear. But this difficult passage o' complicated learnin' an' confusions is good after all, for it also builds the father's lion heart within, courage that kens love will always win out in the end. An' altogether in the diamond centerpoint, there are thirty-nine planes.

Then comin' down an' out from there," Coillore continued, "one descends into Leanabh Aingeil (leenuv anyeel, child angel), the cherubim realms or the fifth heaven. There are ten more planes there, these levels inhabited by cherubim, o' course. Its element is the soft cloud fleece o' lovin' kindness, an' it's ruled by Abaid an' Uan, the infant fae lass an' cherub boy o' the Creator Sun. In the ascension process, this level teaches that lovin' kindness is the most important thing there is in the world, an' it brings forward the dark mother portals that once closed the child heart down. On earth, these levels create one-celled beasties an' fungi like the mushrooms we love in our stew." She nodded as he moved his staff down over another line.

"Then movin' down again, we come through the eye-o'-the-needle, the logos centerpoint, descendin' into the next world or fourth heaven, the logos or Ceugant. There are fourteen concentric spheres in the logos sun, like a huge rainbow ball. An' it's inhabited by seraphim, the strong virgin angel forces. For the logos is ruled by the virgin goddess o' the Creator Sun, Maighdean, an' her element is fire.

Then comin' down an' out o' the logos," Coillore continued, moving his staff lower over the next line, "we reach Gwynfydd (gwinfed). There are sixty-six planes in the spirit realms, all the stars in the night sky." And he traced the line of the Milky Way through the budding branches above their heads with the top of his staff. "That world is ruled by the male virgin o' the Creator Sun, Rìdire, an' this realm is inhabited by djinns, winged male faeries. It creates the electrical force that moves through our nerves an' brains, lassie, an' allows us to talk wi' all the creatures an' plants in our minds, an' especially to put our thoughts into action. Its element is air." And the druid moved his staff down across the next line.

"Below that is the astral world, Annwyn, the three outer planets o' our sun. There are forty-four planes in that realm, an' it's inhabited by devas, female faeries. An' those realms are ruled by Màiri, mother o' the mind in the Creator Sun. This level creates lakes an' rivers, an' wields an emotional force that's magnetic, but it teaches us responsibility for the All. Its element is water." And he moved his staff over the line on the bottom to stop inside the small circle underneath all the rest.

"An' last come the sensate realms, eighteen planes, the inner planets where ye an' I are noo. Deep inside the earth lives the White Tara, these realms ruled by Herself. An' She's creatin' all o' us humans in Her an' Oghama's image. The White Tara'll stay hidden for another two millennium, movin' all closer to union wi' Him in the Creator Sun, lassie, before She's revealed here. Her force is gravitational, an' the element o' the sensate realms is earth, o' course. In time, all individuals will bend their personal wills, through their own free choice, to Oghama's laws o' love an' Her path o' wisdom, embodyin' both an' completin' their ascension climb, a very challengin' goal. This world is inhabited by humanity," he said, putting one finger on her nose, "the only life form on a full creator path. An' all the fears o' every realm play out here, so the pressure o' darkness is great an' rests upon us all, as ye're feelin' just noo, the 365 planes o' all worlds. That's how many steps there are in the ladder o' light back Home, lass.

But because humanity alone has taken on the full structures o' darkness, the revelation o' the highest template o' love o' the Creator

Sun into the sensate realms is ours to achieve an' enjoy in time." Coillore said, his eyes brightening as he waved his arm in a wide arc across the horizon. "But to do that, all folk on earth must face, meet, an' heal everythin', all the way back up the whole staircase here," and he swept his staff through all the lines at once.

"But the most magical thing is this," the druid said, winking at her, "since inner fear creates what happens to each o' us in our lives on the outside, an' to all o' us collectively around the globe, in that final healin' o' fear in those far off days, all pain an' sufferin' on earth will <u>cease</u> to exist, a small amount cleared away by every single individual livin' here. An' in that golden age, earth'll become the creator sun in the physical that she was always meant to be, every person a miniature god or goddess in the image o' the One Beloveds, Oghama an' the White Tara. In those happily-ever-after days, each person'll have one true love to keep their whole life long, an' world service they do together. An' wi' their one beloved partner, every person'll create all that comes into their own little world through their physical joinin' in sacred partnership, exactly the way God an' Goddess create everythin' into light in the Creator Sun. Ach, but those lessons are for after yer moon time, lass," he said, smiling across at her

"An' since each person's shadows stream from all worlds, all the way down the whole staircase," he continued, unable to restrain himself, "that same healin' o' humanity'll also clear all the planes o' existence. So the whole cosmos'll be freed o' fear in those happy days to come! In a way, we're all preparin' for that even noo." With laughing eyes, Coillore stood, waving his arms out to embrace the sky. "The Creators Themselves'll walk these very paths!" And Soillse sat straight up at this, staring at the druid.

"The Sun Lord? Here?"

"Aye," he nodded. "All bein's in all worlds wait for those days, includin' the beasts an' creatures on earth. All suffer along wi' humanity, brothers an' sisters in our pain, especially the poor wee cherubs who volunteered to become demons, for all forms have a wee cherub under their varied skins," he said, shaking his head. "All bein's in all worlds wait for humanity to gain the strength needed to brave the final challenge, the inner holy war wi' our own fears." He took a long breath and let it out again. "An' even noo, some are needed, like yerself, to lead the way. An' many are asked, like meself, to remember an' teach the mysteries, so they'll no be lost to the darkness."

"Oh," she said, closing her eyes a moment. "It seems like an awfully long way." He took up his staff again and drew an arrow from the earth up to the Core.

"As ye climb, dear, yer light grows. It becomes as bright as it once was when ye lived at this or that level. The more light ye had back then, the more darkness it took to build fear into ye. Do ye see? An' that process reverses itself on the way back Home. So all the folk ye see on earth havin' the most difficulty in their lives are the closest to the final breakthrough, though most in this world see it not." He raised his brows, nodding.

"But how can I get to the Core from way down here, Coillore? It's just too far." She put her finger on the small circle at the bottom, moving it toward the top, and stopping halfway, dropping her hand to the ground.

"Ye dinna have to go anywhere at all, dear. It's yer consciousness that ascends. The path o' return opens inner portals, lass, one for every fear faced an' healed. New light streams directly into the back o' yer heart from the Creators, on the inside," he said, resting his hand on his heart. "It can be felt within, but it canna be seen wi' outer eyes, for the Creators always send Their purest truths in deep intimacy an' very personal love. God an' Goddess are yer own Beloved, Best Friend, Da an' Ma, all at once." As he put one arm over her shoulders, his eyes smiled into hers. "The true Creators dislike showiness o' any kind. Those heroes ye speak of are caught in the trials o' the false god who wants only glory in the Dragon star," and Coillore moved his staff to the upper planes of the Diamond Core, "here. So dinna fret, lassie. Oghama an' the White Tara are holdin' ye in every moment, <u>inside</u>, goddess in trainin'." And he put his hands together and bowed his head.

"Ach, if I'm a goddess in disguise, I wish I didna have to spend me days in the heat an' dust in slavery to a sister who kens none o' these things, Coillore!"

"But it's only happenin' because that's the evil ye were caught in at this level," he said, moving his staff to the soul realms. "Ceit carries the false goddess illusions o' domination, overwork, an' even cruelty, the dark mother who rules the winter moons. Ye must carry an' face them, dear, learn the teachings this pain brings, an' free yerself in the end. If ye run from it, ye'll just have to come back an' do it all over again. An' mind lassie, healin' is <u>only</u> achieved through love, meltin' the fear in the Creator flame o' the heart, as I've shown ye before," and he made a wry face, "though sure an' every other thing'll try to catch ye on the way up, instead. Even a fairly short climb can take many lives, if one gets lost in rage or despair, perhaps. But it can take a very <u>short</u> time, if one is brave an' persistent, lassie. Ye could complete yer climb in seven more lifetimes or in ten skyturns. That choice is yers."

"What about Firinn, Coillore? Where's he in these worlds, on the stairway ye drew there?" And a soft blush crept up her neck as she asked it.

"Beloveds are always held at the same level, lassie. He moves along wi' ye, an' ye wi' him. There's no other way."

"And what about ye, Coillore?"

"I'm about halfway through the Diamond Core, dear. But the darkness I face has more to do wi' isolation than yer servitude to Ceit. I ken enough to teach ye for a while yet."

"So that's the main darkness I must heal, slavery to Ceit?"

Coillore paused a long moment then, taking in a slow breath, wanting to answer this question very carefully.

"There'll come one core wound, lassie, the fear that's most central to yer shadow self, the original one. An' there'll be a passage where ye must face the crone, the death goddess. It doesna have to threaten yer life, though, that last noo. It could just be exhaustion an' the sappin' o' yer life stream. But it'll frighten ye, sure enough. Much depends on the love ye meet it wi'. But if ye're faithful on yer path, the spirit world'll never bring more than ye can bear. It's best no to avoid the lessons, though, for then the messages o' fear'll be stepped up in intensity to get yer attention. There's no point creatin' that noo, is there? No. Ye'll do fine, me thinks."

"Thanks for warnin' me, Coillore," she said, puckering her nose. "Me Aine tree an' ye are the only ones who really understand me. Maybe Firinn will someday, but I never talk wi' him. The Goddess doesna want me to." And her eyes drifted off toward the yard a moment.

"Ye will," he said. And then they sat in silence as he fed wood to the flames and the dusk darkened around them.

"I want me freedom, Coillore," Soillse said quietly after a time, "more than anythin'. I want to have whole days to talk wi' me Aine tree an' do whatever I like. An' someday, I want quiet fer a change. An' clean clothes to wear every day! An' I wish to be spoken to wi' gentleness an' a kind heart, if that's possible at all." She said this last in a whisper. "Can we do the ceremony to begin the path noo?"

"Ach, aye," he whispered.

Squatting, Coillore threw resin into the fire and lit the bowl of fat in the circle of elements he'd arranged on the slab of rock beneath the oak, the bowls of earth, water, air, and fire circled around his Goddess figurine. Soillse watched quietly, her hands clasped on her lap. Closing his eyes then, Coillore sensed Tara's presence in the night's stillness as he bent his head, then motioned for Soillse to come to the altar. As she sat before it, Soillse took her own Goddess statue out of the pocket of her shift and held it to her heart. And then on impulse, Soillse slipped off her sandals, burrowing her feet into the damp earth. As Coillore placed his hand upon her head and sent Tara's love into her, Soillse let out a great sigh, and he felt her tension ease. Then the druid gentled his voice as befit a virgin girl of thirteen winters.

"I call forth the Mother o' All," he chanted softly. "Come an' reawaken Yer daughter, Soillse. Surround her heart star wi' Yer love, always. Shield it an' shape her to Yer purposes, an' guide her Home. Let the one endurin' gift she's seeded wi' grow strong an' be woven into the fabric o' her life here. An' especially, Goddess," he said, his voice dropping and filling with such tenderness that Soillse's scalp began to tingle, "hold Yer daughter in all pain. Calm the fires o' anger that arise, an' comfort her in weariness along the climb. Carry her through all sufferin' into the Creator Sun, until full freedom is achieved. I call in the virgin, Maighdean, too," he continued, "to build an' birth Soillse's divine child on earth. This we ask. So be it."

As the druid chanted, Soillse felt a gentle presence move around her, as soft as Aine's petals. It was a spirit presence Coillore seemed to know well, for he smiled and closed his eyes, sitting on the teaching stone and leaning back onto the oak in the silence. The fire shone brighter for a moment and the air became thick, almost palpable, as Soillse felt spirit arms in the ethers embrace her and a gentle head rest on her own. She saw in her mind the Goddess in Her ivory gown with the moon orb aglow in Her heart. And there was the faintest hint of roses in the air, too, though it's the wrong time of year for them, the lass thought in surprise. But Soillse only closed her eyes and soaked it in, as Tara's tenderness flowed into every pore of her skin.

"Repeat the vow then, lassie," Coillore whispered very softly, and she nodded as she rolled down onto her knees. "I ask to remove all fear from the chalice o' me deep heart." And she said the words after him, crying softly and watching her tears fall into the leaf strewn dust.

"I call them forth, to begin this very moon. An' I vow to heal them all in love an' do the very best I can." Her voice grew firmer, and Coillore smiled at the determination in her voice. "I ask to be led an' held by the White Goddess in every moment. An' I promise to complete this process, no matter how long or hard the way may be." Soillse put her face up to the waxing quarter moon, flickering through the boughs, as she repeated this, while Coillore's chest heaved. He had to wait a moment for the lump in his throat to clear before continuing.

"I ask these fears to be brought slowly an' steadily, wi' never too much to bear an' never endangerin' me safety, an' wi' no more hurt than absolutely necessary to birth the divine child I carry within." And Soillse felt a stirring in her womb as she repeated these words, feeling in them the sacred ring of truth. "I ask the Creators to light the spark that marks the beginnin' o' me path." And she felt a sudden movement deep within her heart and another in her abdomen as she said this. And in her mind's eye, she saw a ray of light enter and open a chamber in her heart's core, a wee room long forgotten, and then move down to light a candle in her womb. Inside it was a baby in a rough cradle filled with hay.

"Oh, Coillore, there's a babe in me belly!"

"Aye, "he said quietly, "the child o' the One, implanted there at the very beginnin' for ye to birth in holiness an' love. It's a boy an' girl fused into one, he on the outside an' she within." And Coillore's tears fell as he held his hands together with his head bent before the altar. Soillse put her hands to her belly and said a silent thank-you to the Creators for giving her Their child to carry. Then after a moment, Coillore gently poured the water from the element bowl over her head.

"I will try as hard as I can," she whispered. And Coillore handed her an apple, cut into seven slices, one for each of the worlds an' sheaths of light within, and a small interlaced silver chalice of cream. She dipped and ate the pieces slowly, one by one, neither saying a word for long moments afterward. And then she felt a weaving of the Goddess light into her own self, as if they could never be separated now. "It'll be all right, Coillore," Soillse whispered finally.

"Aye, lass. Tis clear truth that." And he looked down at her, lifting his brows. But she shook her head, and he knew her vision was too fragile a thing for her to speak of just now.

"Thank ye, Coillore," was all she whispered. And then she rose and walked barefoot through the bracken fronds between the budding birches, their catkins rustling in the wind. Waving to the old druid, she disappeared, as he smiled and nodded after her. Dusk had deepened into night now, the slivered moon hidden by thin clouds, and a soft wind played through the oak. A storm's coming in the morning, Coillore thought.

"But this day's thunder clouds are tamed, at least," he whispered, looking after Soillse. And then he sat long in the clearing, feeling the Goddess's love around him and finally ambling home near midnight. As he turned onto the north track toward his hut, he whispered, "Ah, lassie, ye've no idea what ye've asked for."

Chapter Twenty-One: Fìrinn

One afternoon, as the yellow irises beckoned along the burn in the Hawthorne moon (May), Coillore kept Fìrinn a bit longer at his hut. The druid, in a summer homespun shift, took the ladd out under the scrub birches to clear his head of the afternoon fear memories before beginning the formal lesson. A head taller than the druid now, Fìrinn's wavy chestnut hair was well past his shoulders, his arms and legs still slender with boyhood, as he sat in his buckskin breeks next to the great yew beside the hut and let out a great sigh.

"Thank Goddess for spring!," Fìrinn said with a smile.

Then, as they finished the fiddlehead soup and tea the druid brought out, Coillore gave a sudden grin, stood, and threw on his emerald cloak. On it, he'd tied small stones and crystals, so it sparkled in the sunset's glow. Fìrinn's brows rose in surprise, for the druid was rarely humorous, especially when he was tired.

"Ach, I'll bet ye canna guess what I've dressed up in me cloak for, eh, ladd?" Fìrinn only pulled back his chin and eyed Coillore, then shook his head, no. The druid winked and leaned over to draw a double Celtic cross in the dirt beside the hearth. "It's time to tell ye o' the grand wizards o' the mind!"

"Oh," Fìrinn said, sitting up, suddenly alert. "I'd love to ken that!"

"The ten wizards o' this circle overlight the cosmic brain, ladd, as well as our individual ones, bringin' inner teachers, facts, or intuitions from the far reaches o' the cosmos, thousands an' thousands o' star systems, to find answers to any heart's call. The outer wizards here overlight the lobes o' the brain an' connect to the holy family o' the outer Creator Sun, while the inner wizards overlight the glands o' the mind an' connect to the virgins an' grandparents o' the inner Creator Sun. Any creation o' light that brings forth new truths the Creators wish revealed can always be told by its freshness an' Their deep ringin' sense o' certainty an' rightness. An' such new creations on earth dinna occur without the aid o' many teachers from far an' wide across the worlds. When a disciple's final lifetime is progressin', such revelations'll be made through them as a matter o' course. This is because all star systems are eager to reach their sisters an' brothers on earth, an' there are massive amounts o' information that could help our world.

The cosmic mind streams through the wee planet nearest our sun (Mercury), workin' closely wi' the Sun Lord there to bring through His directives an' truths on earth. These can bring uncomfortable expansions o' consciousness, an' disciples must learn to hold their own against these mental pressures when workin' wi' these wizard forces. Three times a skyturn, this wee planet seems to go backward for 21 days, laddie. That's the time when these wizards are especially active, resettin' the brain impulses an' preparin' the way for the followin' third o' the year. It's the time when things fall apart, break, or get disrupted. These wizards get their messages across an' no mistake, for they bring forth the deepest mental issues no yet healed within." And with a wink, Coillore put his staff into the outer Celtic cross.

It's actually the Great <u>Heart</u> these wizards serve, though, for that's the main essence o' the Creator Sun. Does it surprise ye that the brain is in service to the heart, ladd? Most believe the brain is in charge o' everythin'. Sure an' the Borg masters drove that darkness deeply into us. But the truth is just the reverse, Firinn, for the mind ever serves love.

But let's get back to the brain, eh? The girl sorceress here in the outer circle, Nimue (neem.oo), serves the girl quadrant o' the Creator Sun, an' she's regent o' the two right lobes o' the brain that'll one day be called the parietal an' temporal. It's the lassie flow there, the bairn's song in the temporal an' the virgin's dance in the parietal. The virgin holds the spatial sense within the body, around her central axis o' the spine. Then the temporal lobe comprehends an' plans yer every day, the feminine, the road o' yer life at home, wi' wisdom lessons built in all along the way. It's wee girl is the healer an' meditator as well, o' course. Nimue brings forth play an' joy, too, little girl specialties, eh? But she also activates the dark memories for healin', the powerful memories o' the core that are held here, too, in what'll be known as the amygdala (A-magdala, A is the Ogham letter that signifies the push through the core ethers every year) o' the temporal lobe.

Nimue's magical gifts relate to the ability to join emotions wi' all who live in the many planes o' the universe. She can take ye to any bein' in any world across the cosmos an' merge her intuitive sense wi' them, feel their deepest pain, their tenderest need, their highest wisdom, to give ye the memories ye may need. These intuitions can also teach ye much about how to deal wi' yer present challenges, the feminine emotional side. She's a powerful sorceress, an' tender hearted, too. Her star city's on Coma Berenice.

Then Fionnmharr (feeoonvar)) is the boy wizard o' the imagination, regent o' the left or masculine temporal an' parietal lobes, the adventurer o' the mind. Here he serves the boy quadrant o' the Creator Sun to bring forward the wishes an' dreams o' the laddie an' virgin world server for change on earth. This wizard can, indeed, conjure up any form he wishes, or shape-change into a tree or bird or anythin' else he fancies in the mind. He holds the keys to all forms o' consciousness in all worlds, an' his powers allow anyone to go on mental journeys to the far reaches o' the cosmos to gather information needed on their path, a powerful presence, indeed.

In the left parietal lobe, Fionnmharr's the virgin hunter wi' his strong spatial sense in nature, findin' his way through the woods an' valleys. An' his temporal lobe boy comprehends an' plans each person's masculine day-to-day in the outer world. But Fionnmharr's understandings come mainly through words an' stories, speech, powers o' the male mind. He opens fear memories o' the core from his temporal area o' the brain, too, but for the masculine, eh? He streams from the star, Pisces.

"An' then, in service to the father quadrant o' the Creator Sun, the wizard Taliesin is regent o' the frontal lobe, the brow, ladd. His specialties here are; attention to a task, plannin' for the future, recognizin' the consequences o' yer actions, an' choosin' right over wrong. He teaches us to step back from the present an' keep all in perspective, especially what may affect those in future times, ladd, a most upright wizard, ever helpin' the weak an' vulnerable, too.

Taliesin builds in the mysteries o' revelation that lead the disciple to his or her highest destiny on earth. He brings forth the drops o' pure magic that keep each disciple movin' through the painful trials o' his destiny teachin's, the left brain verbal an' intellectual truths o' the masculine noo. He's a wizard extraordinaire, keepin' close watch over all an' sendin' in sudden dazzlin' shifts or openin's to lift a body when a disciple comes close to failure or despair. He streams from the star Carina, the Keel o' Argo, the ship o' destiny in the stars.

His consort, Tatiana, serves the mother quadrant, rulin' the occiptal lobe in the back o' the brain. That lobe gives us inner an' outer sight, the pictoral images o' the right brain, an' brings forward visions o' the past for healin'. For Tatiana's lessons have to do wi' the long sight, lookin' backward in time to heal an' shift what happened then an' apply it to our lives noo, never forgettin' what we learned from olden days. O' course, her focus is ever on the feminine, the emotional. An' she helps us let go o' whatever we may need to get rid of in our lives, too, puttin' things into the past that we've outgrown. Her star system is Microscopus, the microscope, an instrument that'll allow close focus one day, ladd, fcr she can be quite detail oriented.

Let's shift to the inner circle o' wizards noo, hm?" And moving his staff to the inner circle, the druid continued, "These four inner regents overlight the glands o' the brain an' essential functions o' the body, hidden streams, ladd. First is the virgin sorceress Morgaine le Fay, a very determined an' powerful regent wi' far-rangin' powers. She is kneelin' woman to all divine infants born here, bringin' forward the painful birth pangs an' keepin' the mind o' the feminine from fragmentin' through the storms that come. She leads the inner goddess toward her final holy true love partnership, too, bringin' in the fragrance o' hope an' romance at just the right moment to prevent despair. She teaches the lessons o' patience an' togetherness, dismantlin' the need for control an' the oversexualized distortions, too, that twist an' bend love's purity into their own foul likeness.

She rules a gland in the brain called the pituitary, which controls: female sexual maturity an' love-makin', the feminine monthly cycles, birth an' nursin', clearin' the feminine emotional stream through the kidneys, an' the food an' sexual appetites as well. And Morgaine has the power to disrupt any o' these bodily functions to get her messages across. Her regency is to break down the dark child an' build the divine child within, in accordance wi' Maighdean's directives, o' course. Morgaine rules the orange dragons, an' her star city is on Velpecula, the fox.

The virgin wizard, her consort, is Gwydion, wi' his blue-white dragons. He overlights the pituitary gland as well, but the masculine. Gwydion's another knight in shinin' armor that rides into deepest darkness wi' his eternal truths to save the day, for he rules the fight or flight impulse. His truths can send a ray o' light into the very core o' each individual, bringin' marked an' permanent shifts in moments. An' always Gwydion's startlin' blessings'll delight the inner virgin boy, simple things others willna even notice, a coincidence that puts some confusion into a new light, a bit o' information that'll break through a skyturn's blockages in moments, always movin' toward that world service portal. Cranes, the birds we druids most revere, fly to any realm at Gwydion's request, for he commands teachers from all over the cosmos to help the buddin' world server within. It's his liftin' force before joinin' that brings the phallus higher toward heaven to gather the light seeds from the heart that'll be implanted in the feminine partner, too, ladd. That's where Gwydion's star city is as well, ladd, Grus, the crane.

As male virgin, Gwydion also rules physical growth an' male sexual development, functions, an' appetite, the masculine part o' the pituitary, eh? His teachin's relate to the misuse o' love through betrayal or willfulness. Some o' his most challengin' lessons involve learnin' restraint o' desire, for he is ever the gentleman, honorin' the feminine forever an' a day, just like Rìdire, who he serves.

The next inner brain regent here is the wizard Palindore, who leads the gold dragons, he the grandfather, regent o' wakin' up each individual's consciousness an' the restoration o' truth into the mind, for he serves the Dagda. Palindore rules the thalamus, a tiny structure in the middle o' the brain that regulates alertness an' relays movement an' sensory signals to all parts of the brain. His star system is the Sextant, another guide for our ship o' destiny.

This regent is a steady holder o' light in darkness that never wavers. His specialty is sendin' the mind back in time to heal old forgotten fears o' the descent, then structurin' the new truths released into the brain, buildin' more an' more o' Oghama's divine mind into everyone. Palindore's wizard wand can open the most ancient truths in moments to heal an' uplift, bringin' through instantaneous an' miraculous transitions. But his main directive is bringin' disciples to their final destinies an' Home for good.

Palindore's consort is Vivianne wi' her silver dragons, the sorceress o' the life stream, the grandma. Vivianne has a tender madonna nature that loves to comfort wi' warmth an' rest. But she, too, reaches to the core to draw out ancient fears, often sleep challenges or disruptions to basic bodily functions to remove ancient blocks to the flow o' life. But Vivianne loves both dark an' light child dearly, wantin' mainly to hold an' heal in gentleness. She is a powerful sorceress o' physical healin', too, an' she can come wi' lightnin' speed to help or adjust these basic functions o' the body. She rules the hypothalamus, small nodules just below Palindore's thalamus in the center o' the brain. These regulate body temperature, hunger an' thirst, sleep an' the circadian cycles. Her star system is Antlia, the pump.

An' then, in the very center o' the wizard circles sit Emer (eemer) an' Cuchullan (coohcolin). She leads the inner feminine toward the heights o' intimacy o' the Goddess, an' he the inner masculine toward the world service o' Oghama. She rules the part o' the brain where all sensory information comes in, the sensory strip, and he the part where action directives are sent out, the motor strip.

But Emer's specialty is buildin' the inner goddess, developin' the feminine powers that taste intimacy wi' the One Beloved: inner sight, inner hearin', inner touch, taste, an' smell. So she follows the yearly patterns o' Cliodha (cleeha, Venus), virgin goddess o' Tìr Nan Òg, the action light structure (described in Book Two). It's that pentagonal cycle o' our sister planet that cycles through each sense, eh? But where Cliodha wants to put her senses into action in the outside world, Emer wants to feel everythin' within, instead. Durin' the scent phase, Emer might lead ye to a fragrance that'll open the oldest an' deepest memories o' Tara or Oghama as yer Beloved. Scent is the most hidden o' Emer's mysteries an' the most powerful, for it streams straight from Tara. Emer's heights are heady an' her lessons sweet overall, though there are teachin's about restraint, intensity, an' obsessiveness blended in as well. A more seductive presence isna to be found in any world, well, except for Cliodha an' the White Tara Herself." And the druid smiled, remembering sensuous nights with his Ailis. "Emer opens the senses to the Beloved in all things in the outer world as well, Their love flowin' into every bite ye eat an' everythin' ye touch." And the druid winked as he handed Fìrinn a dried date. "Emer rules the peach dragons, an' her star city is on Corona Borealis, but in Alba she anchors into Tongue.

An' last comes the virgin god, Cuchullan, that ye ken very well," and the druid pointed to the peaks across the sea lochs, "who rules the action strip o' the brain, which sends impulses into the nerves to be put into action. He builds the inner god, ladd. So he chooses which o' our many thoughts will actually be carried out. Cuchullan can be quite a drivin' god, keepin' ye movin' when ye're tired an' just want to go to yer furs. But his heart is pure, for he only wants to keep everyone travellin' on his or her path toward heaven's door. He'll lead ye to face any an' all calls to action the universe sends yer way, too, such calls bein' another o' Cuchullan's specialties. He rules those dark red dragons an' his star city is in Aries."

Fìrinn's eyes shone as he listened, but Coillore felt drowsiness in the boy, too. "That's it then, no too long this time, eh? Noo, off to yer furs. Ye'll be asleep in yer chair in half an' instant, ladd." And the druid grinned, waving his staff and shaking his cloak to make it sparkle in the evening sun as Fìrinn hurried through the bracken, glad to be headed to his bed so soon.

And then, as the seasons turned to summer once more, the ladds began to think of the games at Lughnasa. Now that the older boys were gone, Fìrinn and his age mates had a better chance to win, and he became first lancer. Duirc, Fìrinn's arch rival, placed first of the wrestlers, he and Fìrinn both high competitors this time. And well before summer spread her warmth across the hills, Coillore talked with Seumus about taking Fìrinn to the druid isle. The druid and chief argued at the roundhouse door several times, Seumus, looking often toward the boy as he gestured with fisted hands.

He's me best lancer an' ye ken it well," Seumus shouted to

Coillore one cloudy afternoon in the Holly moon (June). "An' his Da'll have me hide if he doesna place first. Fìrinn can go to Iona when the games are <u>over</u>, Coillore!"

"All right, Seumus, but it <u>must</u> be done," Coillore said, standing quietly in his white robe, the muscles of his jaw tensing. "Divine favor to seven generations rests on it. I'll take it on meself to see this through, rather than lose the gain to the tribes. It's far more important than one competition." And the druid took a deep breath to steady himself, turning to gaze back over the bay a moment. Then he shrugged and walked away.

As the games drew near, tension tightened in the ladds like a piece of gut strung taut on a bow. There were forty-five at the fostering now, and often the younger boys cheered the competitors on, daring them to try more and more difficult feats. For a lark one windswept midsky, late in the Hazel moon (July), big Allaidh, who was a teacher's assistant now and kept the younger ones in line, set out a course for lancers described in the songs of the ancients. And Duirc, tall and muscular in only his buckskin breeks, with his steely black eyes and wiry dark hair spread out around his face, spoke the challenge as they headed for their seats with full bowls of stirabout, to give up his evening meal if Fìrinn would try it and succeed. Or Duirc would take Fìrinn's meal, instead, if he failed. So Fìrinn walked across the yard to investigate, up near the barley field on the hill. The marks are strange, he thought, as he peered down at them, a windblown crow feather tied on a tree at four pony lengths, a tuft of fur in a log at thirty paces. Who could hit targets like that? But what harm'll it do to try, he thought, as he picked up one of the lightweight lances. I dinna care about the meal, anyway. But then he hit all six, though some just barely, and left the younger ladds gaping. And Duirc grit his teeth as he handed over his dinner that night, his falcon eye burning brighter. But Fìrinn just shook his head at the older ladd and pushed the plate back.

As the moon waned toward Lughnasa, the days turned hot and no rain fell. So the yard beside the hut circle was dusty and dry, the meals heavy on fish and short on greens. In the gloaming the night before they were to leave, the ladds gathered spears and water bags outside the long house to prepare for an early departure. Afterwards, Fìrinn stayed outside in the gloaming, sitting on the rocks at the bay to steady himself for the challenge ahead.

On the two-day walk northeast, up the long southwestern peninsula of Skye to the track that led to the mainland, and then east to the channel, and north on the mainland for two days to Applecross, the road over the high inland moors dusted the boy's throats worse than ever. And the water skins barely lasted till midsky, even though they wore only their loin cloths in the heat of the afternoons. So they were all forced to stop, sometimes wandering into the forests beside the track in search of water to refill their skins before moving on. Bana Dhia trotted off to find burns to soak in all along the path, an' then loped back to shake herself and soak them all, making Fìrinn laugh. And Fìrinn loved the vistas, too, the majestic blue peaks of the north clearly visible, and the lower slopes to the east and south, forested an' green, despite the heat. On their arrival at the river just south of Applecross, Seumus decided to camp in the sparse birch wood that sloped down to the water, waiting to cross till morning, since they'd marched well into the gloaming to get that far.

After gathering kindling and lighting the cooking fire, most of the ladds raced down to the stream for a dip, flinging spray on each other and laughing well into the night. But Fìrinn lay apart in his buckskin breeks, on his belly in the mosses by the shore, and watched the otters, shining as they leaped over each other in the dusk. It brought the memory of himself as a babe doing the same thing in the bay at home with Ma. And he wondered if she'd come to the games again this time. She had some woman's ailment, so Seumus said, after receiving a letter from Da in the spring. And Ma had a babe to care for now, too, his sister of two winters. Fìrinn wished suddenly he could meet the wee lass. It's been five winters since I saw Ma at the last gathering, he thought, but then shrugged. Me birth tuath's faded from me memory long syne. She was a good Ma, his thoughts continued, but I'm the best lancer in me fostering now, with one initiation of the elements behind me. Three more of those and me manhood ceremony in two summers, and I'll be a druid of the brown robes and a warrior, too. It hasna been so bad at all, like Da said, me time with Seumus. And Fìrinn walked slowly up through the wood to his furs, and lulled by the gurgle of the water and the warm darkness, he slept.

It was Speireag, Fìrinn's Da, who ordered Fìrinn and Seumus, with Bana Dhia following, to the high table on their arrival the next morning at the game site, a large field beside the sea, near the tuath of the clan of the bear. Fìrinn glanced ahead at the broch, standing tall on a low rise at the seaside, above the large hut circle of the tuath. Speireag, frowning, wore his clan plaid wrapped round his waist, his ceremonial shirt, and his light summer deerskin cloak pinned over this with a large bone brooch. Fìrinn was startled to notice that Seumus, also in his clan colors, his plaid, cloak, and sword, offered no smile or handshake to Speireag, his old friend. Seumus simply waited at attention beside the chief's chair, as Speireag looked his son up and down. Speireag's hair had begun to grey, though he was still straight backed and muscular, Fìrinn noticed, the ladd waiting bare-chested in his buckskin summer breeks on the dais. Da's only thirty-three winters, Fìrinn thought. Being chief isna such an easy cloak to wear, I guess.

"Well, man, ye've had eight skyturns to hone the skills o' me ladd. Have ye done it? This is his last competition before manhood." As he turned a cool dark eye on Seumus, Speireag's face flushed under his wild brown hair, though his moustache had been carefully groomed.

"Aye, he's as ready as I can make him, Speireag, except to fill in a bit." Seumus spoke quietly, his own dark hair tied with a thong for the games, but he winked at Fìrinn over the chief's head. "He's the best lancer in the land. Better than Ranald of old, the yard master says."

"He's as skinny as kindlin'," the chief replied with a sneer.

"The boyhood's no out o' him yet, Speireag; ye can see that fer yerself," Seumus said, stroking his moustache. "He gets exactly what the laws require, honey in his oats in the mornin', as befits a chief's son, and haunch at the evenin' meal." Seumus stood unmoving then, his blue eyes steadily meeting the chief's gaze, while Bana Dhia's upper lip quivered over her fangs.

"Ye have him out on the hunt often, right? He needs that the most," Speireag countered. "I dinna want druid spells an' moon lore to keep him from learnin' the skills of a chief."

"Aye, I ken it," Seumus said and sighed, another thing he'd begun to fight with Coillore about, who wanted the ladd to kill as infrequently as possible. The fostering'll be more peaceful when the boy comes into manhood and goes home, Seumus thought with pursed lips.

"When the ladd's strength does come in, he'll be a warrior the like o' which we havena seen in a hundred skyturns, so says Frithe." Speireag spoke loudly now, putting his palm on Seumus's chest. "I willna have a feather of a ladd more afraid o' prey than they are o' him!" And Speireag turned away, as if disgusted with the boy, dismissing them both with a flick of his hand. But Seumus smiled at Fìrinn as they stepped off the dais and put both hands on the ladd's shoulders.

"Never mind him, ladd. Just do the best ye can." Fìrinn nodded and sighed, then thought to get away by the fastest route possible. He strode into the forest of tents behind the platform, hoping to lose himself quickly among them. But Seumus only waited quietly beside the dais, his hand on the hilt of his sword, shaking his grizzled head.

Frithe hid behind the door cloth, stepping out suddenly and calling his name as he came near. Fìrinn stopped short and gasped. Ma! And then he thought, how old she looks, even in her sea blue robe. Her color is gone and she's so thin, and there are crone creases round her eyes and mouth. He noticed that her reddish-brown hair, though neatly tied up, was dull and flat. Could this be the same Ma who was once so beautiful, full of teasing and laughter, only eight winters ago? Was it the loss of that babe that did it?, Fìrinn wondered.

Bana Dhia nosed at the door cloth of the tent, sniffling. A small girl, hidden in the shadows, ran out suddenly to shield herself behind Ma's long tunic. But the lass peeked out at Fìrinn, russet hair blowing across her face, looking like a queen herself in a wee flaxen cloak over a light summer shift. She blinked large tawny eyes at him, and the tension in Fìrinn's chest released quickly as he smiled at her.

"This is yer sister, Brigh," (bree, juice or essence), Frithe said, as she bent and drew the girl out, pulling on one small hand. "An' this," Ma said, squatting and holding the lass in one arm, "is yer great brother, Fìrinn, who used to make tuaths in the fir needles just like ye." Frithe's green eyes twinkled. "See? He is as big as the pine saplin' I showed ye a few days ago. Remember?" The child nodded and moved behind Frithe's skirts again. But a giggle followed and then a whispered, "He looks like Da." As Frithe laughed and stood, low green fire filled her eyes and her cheeks pinked. And for that one moment, she looked young again. "How ye've sprouted, Fìrinn-ladd," she said. "Ye'll be the one to make hearts ache by the Bealltain (festival of the virgin goddess, May 4th) o' yer manhood." And her eyes ran down his wiry arms and back to his face, where a thin moustache was growing. Bana Dhia nosed nearer the child, reaching out a wet nose and lapping the small fingers. And the girl laughed, a silver ribbon of sound, and ran back into the tent, as Frithe turned to follow.

"The Goddess keep ye, Fìrinn-ladd. I'm glad ye're to be a druid. An' Brigh's right, ye look _so_ like yer Da!" She said this with a soft smile, but Fìrinn recoiled and frowned at her. I'm _nothing_ like him, the ladd thought fiercely and turned on his heel. Ye dinna see the person I am underneath anymore, Ma. I knew that'd happen someday.

Both encounters with his parents only annoyed Fìrinn, and he wandered through the crowds, scowling. But gradually, as he threaded his way to Seumus's hearth, the faces of so many clansfolk seeped into him, drawing his heart open again. He spent the rest of the day quietly, helping Seumus near the tents.

And then, at the opening ritual that night, standing with the druids in the nemeton in his clan plaid and white shirt, Fìrinn carried the sacred branches of the clan for Coillore. The ladd's eyes filled as all the people gathered round, the men in their plaids and ceremonial shirts, the women in their embroidered doeskin robes and clan sashes. Then all knelt and prayed to the goddess Cìrceidh (keerkay, Circe), the earth mother of Lughnasa. As he sang the chants, Fìrinn felt her move around him, and during the whole rest of the ceremony his heart ached for peace of spirit and true nourishment, for himself and for everyone.

But then by morning, Fìrinn was disgruntled again. The day was windy, and the spear-throwing competition was scheduled for just before midsky. The sun beat down, too, and he hadn't slept well, either.

"For this competition, wi' Da so riled up, I'd have chosen stillness an' clouds," Fìrinn grumbled to himself.

As he walked onto the field, more than a few in the crowd noticed his resemblance to Speireag, but Fìrinn was thinking only that it would soon be over. Tall enough to see above the other ladds now, he felt awkward and gangly as he stepped into place in the line of competitors. I'm tired of the heat and the dust and the pressure to compete, Firinn thought, as his eyes drifted to the swiftly flowing river and the verdant hills beyond the tents. And then he settled his mind on the White Goddess and breathed his frustration out to Her until his tension eased.

There were seventy-eight competitors in spear throwing this time, all stripped to their breeks for the competition and waiting at the eastern edge of the field beside the clanfolk, who were seated on a low rise to watch. Walking out onto the hard packed earth, Firinn sent the first lance easily into a pine caber at five pony lengths. Turning back to the end of the line, he thought of Ruadh and wondered how his old friend was now. As he waited, Firinn's mind drifted off to last night's ritual, and he hummed the invocation in his mind as the others took their turns.

Firinn's second shot hit a water skin at four pony lengths, his third a gourd at five. Nine ladds remained. The fourth and final target was a young boar, released from the opposite end of the field. The beasts'll be roasted for the evening festivities, anyway, Firinn thought. Even if they're not speared by the competitors, they'll be taken by the clansmen ringed around the field. But his dislike of the kill lay heavy in his gut as he watched the first animal snort, paw the ground, and saunter out boldly, while the first of the five competitors eyed it warily. This first ladd threw his lances quickly, one after another, missing the animal as the boar charged back and forth. But the next ladd hit the mark quickly, low in the belly.

Then Firinn and the three remaining boys were called forward to take their turns, and the next animal was released onto the field. Head low, tusks jutting, and small eyes menacing, the beast raced straight toward them. All the others ladds aimed straight and missed. I dinna have the stomach for a kill today, Firinn thought, aiming slightly right, hoping the animal would keep a straight course. He wanted only to graze the beast, enough to keep his standing as a contestant, but not enough to do any real damage. But the animal suddenly veered toward the crowd, charging the row of shouting tribesmen protecting the clansfolk, instead. Between the turn and a gusty wind, the beast took Firinn's lance square in the flank. And it gave a high-pitched squeal, toppling as the crowd roared. Then thinking only to end the animal's terror, Firinn loosed a second shot to the neck, which silenced it. But his stomach churned. I hate this, he thought, though Da'll be glad I won after all. But this win was the Goddess's doing, not mine. Me head aches and I want to be off alone in the forest, he thought, with no dust and no noise. In Firinn's mind then, he held the image of Coillore's small hut and the birch people beside it, as he nodded grimly to his Da and walked over to the dais for his prize. It was a bronze knife, the handle interlaced with a stylized stag, handed to him by the chief of the Applecross clan of the bear. I dinna deserve it, Firinn thought, but it does seem fitting for a son of the clan of the deer.

He napped behind one of Seumus's tents during the afternoon and felt better for it, and for the winner's portion at the evening meal, too, great heaping ribs of the boar he'd killed. Ignoring the cheers of the other ladds as he took his portion, as well as Duirc's smoldering eyes, Firinn thought, what's the point in competing, cousin, anyway? But for once that skyturn, he was full to bursting. And standing with the other chiefs in his finery, his long sword glinting in the late sun, Speireag grinned and waved, and Ma smiled from the dais, her clan plaid pulled tight over her wasted frame. But Firinn felt happy only for the pride in Seumus's eyes and, for some reason, didn't want to go near Soillse at all. After the meal, he wandered through the crowds along the shore, and then rolled early into his plaid, wanting only to be alone. As a light rain began to fall, he dropped instantly to sleep.

The games were uneventful after that, Da, Ma, and Brigh leaving a day before the closing ceremony. Firinn was relieved to see them go, and even happier to return to the tuath a few days later, walking doggedly along the dusty paths toward it in the heat. He smiled as they came down the ridge, through the birch wood beside the gurgling burn, into the yard beside the hut circle, perched at the edge of the bay. And then he sat apart on the rocks at the water's edge, eating his evening meal in only his workaday buckskin breeks, letting the soft shush of the waves wash the memory of the boar from his mind.

Soon after they returned to the tuath, in the Vine moon (late August), Coillore came into the yard in the late afternoon. He insisted on taking Fìrinn away from the games early for another lesson, despite Seumus's protests. As they climbed up the deer path through the boulders beside the burn and turned left along the barely visible track through the birch wood to Coillore's wee hut, a sharp wind raced across the sea, the sun hovering high over the Cuchullins across the sea loch. And Fìrinn pulled his plaid tight around his shoulders over his buckskin shirt, as he swung under the large yew and stepped into the tiny wattle and daub hut, its thatch hanging unevenly from the eaves. As they sat inside by the fire, Fìrinn eyed the druid wearily. But Coillore didn't take notice of that, just handed the ladd a piece of flatbread, a bowl of mushroom stew, and put a hide of hazelnuts beside him on the floor. They sat on two stump seats beside the hearth, facing Coillore's pallet and altar beyond the flames as they ate in silence. And as Fìrinn looked up at the many herbs hanging from the rafters, sniffing the sharp scent of sage above the rest, Coillore wiped the bowls with a hide, and then leaned over and drew three curved lines in the earth that looked like a three-pointed star.

"Movin' down from the Wizard Circle, we come to the Pineal Wheel, the cosmic sixth chakra, Fìrinn. It's a powerhouse, for these are the regents that build the father's kingdom in this world. The process o' manifestation always begins wi' light seeds held in the inner goddess soil o' the womb, that move up the spine into consciousness, one by one through each skyturn, an' bring visions an' directives o' the future. These are Arte's (father god of the Luckenbooth) seeds o' the last Midwinter.

But here in this wheel are paired regents, in the wee central triangle an' for each star arm, so eight in all. This light structure spins on a 120-day cycle, each set o' outer regents overlightin' one third o' the skyturn. The central regents take the intercessory days, durin' and just past Midwinter (Dec. 21st-25th).

The pineal is where the Dagda's ray o' awareness anchors within, ladd. An' the father here, who serves him, has four main directives in life: bein' executor o' Oghama's will, provider, protector, an' teacher for the tribe. The first directive is Priomh's (preev, chief), an' the others match the star arms here an' flow into different places on earth.

Priomh an' Màthair-àil (maahair-aahl, matriarch) sit in the wee central triangle here, the clan matriarch an' chief. Their task is to bring through the will o' Oghama an' Tara into the every day life o' the tribe. So, they are builders o' the father's kingdom on earth, too, but in a very down-to-earth, day-to-day way. As such, they organize the clan an' the whole community, choosin' the specific focus o' the comin' moons, orchestratin' an' harmonizin' all efforts, he, the work o' the masculine, she, the tasks o' the feminine. His focus reaches to those outside the clan, too. But she sees to the specific traditions o' each tribe, makin' sure all laws o' the culture an' the family are followed, arrangin' birth celebrations an' seasonal festivals. Màthair-àil can be quite detail-oriented an' insistent in her work, but it's powerful in its humble way, for these traditions an' festivals renew the heart connections an' keep family ties strong. It's this renewal an' protection o' heart links between all clan members that's Màthair-àil's true regency, just as important as Priomh's grand pronouncements, eh? In future times, clan patterns'll break down across the earth an' other kinds o' communities'll form. An' these two regents'll be overlightin' the leaders o' every one. Their star compound is in Triangulum, an' they anchor into the Saxon lands (Germany), she, the east, an' he, the west.

These two are regents o' the circadian cycle within, too, he, the daylight, an' she, night an' sleep. Work o' the daytime is looked up to by all, but sleep is no noticed or honored by most. But think how ye feel when ye havena had much sleep, ladd, drained an' irritable. Sleep keeps our minds from fragmentin' an' havin' too much to bear, keeps us <u>alive</u>, in fact.

But let's move to the first star arm o' the Pineal Wheel noo, Ionnsaich (yoonuch, teacher) an' Ciaradh (keyarugh, dawn, Aurora)," Coillore said. "They take the first 120 days, from the Birch through the Willow moons (Dec 26th-Apr 24th). Ionnsaich rules all global educational structures, schools an' apprenticeships that prepare the inner masculine for his destiny, plus written scrolls an' learnin' o' all kinds. In our time, these are simple apprenticeships. But over the centuries, they'll become very grand, bairns takin' lessons till they're almost halfway through their lives. Long Scrolls, called books, an' papers'll become commonplace an' travel the globe. An' in end times, a box that sends waves o' light an' sound to every household'll be invented, an' a wee sound transmitter that can connect everyone instantly, more Borg creations. So, Ionnsaich's power'll become vast, changin' the global structures o' knowledge in moments in those future days. Knowledge'll become its own religion in those times as well, drawin' many to Ionnsaich's path. I canna imagine such a thing, though, dry facts an' figures'll takin' the place o' the One Beloveds, eh?

O' course, the mind o' Oghama can be accessed wi' a simple thought in yer inner silence any time an' any place in the universe. Ye can ask an' receive whatever answer ye like on any subject o' yer choosin'. That's how I compiled all these teachin's in the first place! But Ionnsaich's outer structures were twisted by the Borg to lead folk away from simple truths whispered by the Father-o'-All within. Ionnsaich can harry an' drive the feminine especially wi' his love o' ideas, too, takin' over life itself. Out o' balance, these dry out the life force in the brain an' bring through a disease that makes a body forget who he is, becomin' as simple as a newborn babe. Ionnsaich's star compound is on Mensa, the table, ladd.

His consort, Ciaradh (keearugh), is regent o' education, too, but for wee bairns noo, until the age o' eleven. Ciaradh is a soft an' happy presence, but her teachin' holds as much power as Don's in it's humble way, for it forms the foundation on which all the rest is built, influencin' a person's whole future life. She teaches art an' all pictoral forms o' learnin', as well as dance an' song, at all ages noo. In future days, those Borg boxes I mentioned'll send pictures that tell stories, called films, into every hut as well. An' Ciaradh's pictures can tell a story in exquisite detail in an instant that Ionnsaich's words would take a long-winded time to reveal, him missin' most o' the details even then. Her power is great in reachin' the deepest recesses o' the brain, too, for wee bairns think in pictures, ladd, no words. An' her pictoral learnin' reaches in to these earliest memories to create change there, even in folk eighty winters old. Her star city is on Pictor, the easel.

Then the apex star arm is ruled by the god o' abundance, Llew, an' his consort, Siebh (she-ev). They overlight the next 120-day phase, from the Hawthorne through the Apple moons (Apr. 25th-Aug. 22nd). Llew is regent o' buildin' up resources that bring security to the clan, now an' into the future, grain stores especially, for he loves to give every tribe lots o' whatever they need. His land, where the Helvetii reside (Switzerland), is full o' high mountains, a sure sign o' a Da that wants all to climb that highest peak, too. An' wi' all fears o' survival out o' the way, LLew provides a safe haven to give impetus to complete that trek. O' course, the dragon lords'll take over his resources, too, hoardin' the wealth o' the world an' lettin' thousands go hungry." And the druid scowled and shook his head at this, his eyes darkening with anger. "They ever want to break down the true father's structures here, an' those who dinna serve the dark one'll suffer much privation in those days.

Llew's lessons are about overwork o' the father, plannin' for the future, stretchin' resources in times o' need, fairness to everyone, no takin' more than yer own need, an' thinkin' o' the whole tribe, instead. He's a practical an' generous Da, if ever there was one. His abundance energy causes many to have grand huts an' extravagant lives but his true folk live within the simple ways o' the Creator Sun.

Llew's consort is Siebh (she-ev), earth mother, regent o' the global commons o' earth; air, fire, an' water, the vast resources we canna live without. She provides wood an' stone for buildin', an' hides an' wool for clothes, too, all the natural products that are needed to support each family, for Shiebh gives wi' a heart that's as big as all outdoors. Llew's gifts may put food in yer belly an' coin in yer sporran, but hers keep ye alive in every moment. Her star compound is Reticulum, the women's purse, hm?

In future days, the dragon lords'll take control o' her resources, too, claimin' ownership o' the global commons. Imagine! They'll even toy wi' Oghama's light seeds in the foods we eat to close her down. But in the end, it'll be seen that these genetic experiments only create tumors an' other diseases. No, the dragons'll never succeed, for love an' humble folk'll always win out in the end.

Let's move to the last arm then, eh, ladd? It's Mìlidh (meelee, soldier) an' Cobhair (coveer, aid) here. They take the next 120 days, from the Vine through the Elder moons (Aug. 23rd-December 20th). He rules the protector forces an' the laws, so all warriors an' policin' that keep the tribe safe. This includes all tribes on earth an' all star cities, too! He sees that the laws o' love are followed, for he's the judge who determines what payment is needed from one neighbor to another for any wrong doin', too. In future days, his protective forces'll become as grand as all the rest, great armies roamin' the earth. Brute force'll take the place o' real justice an' the laws o' love, many folk harmed by the brutal way laws are kept then. But in due time, Mìlidh'll see that truth comes free again, as the strong arm o' the masculine is tamed into the stronger heart o' love. His star city is in Aquila, the eagle.

His consort is Cobhair (coe-veer, aid), an' her protection arm holds the women an' bairns, instead. She makes sure all are cared for, none neglected or left alone, especially the very young, old, or the infirm. In future days, when clan structures break down, old folk'll be left alone in their huts for skyturns, lonely an' untended. Sacrilege! An' Cobhair's structures, too, will become huge in future days, bringin' assistance to folk sufferin' from war or famine all over the globe. Vast sums o' coin'll be used, wi' hundreds o' folk involved. Again, his strong arms o' law look far more powerful. But thousands o' folk'll be saved from starvation by her ministrations, a depth o' love his canna begin to touch. Her star city is on Vega, ladd.

All right, Fìrinn, that's enough for today. Yer eyes are droopin' an' I'm tired meself." And Coillore glanced at his furs as he reached over to sweep out the glyph he'd drawn in the dirt, for the gloaming was deepening into night. With a sigh of relief, Fìrinn leapt up, hurried out of the hut and down beside the burn, listening to the water laughing over pebbles as it tumbled down to the bay. Stopping to let the brisk wind blow away all those details swirling in his mind, Fìrinn ran across the yard to the long house, and jumped in under his furs. Bana Dhia, waiting there, had already warmed his pallet.

The ladd slept instantly and deeply after the late lesson. But just as dawn was breaking, he had a startling dream. It was a memory of the past Midwinter, nearly ten moons before. That day had dawned cold and windy, but unusually clear, as Fìrinn in his plaid and heavy fur jerkin, and Coillore in his white robe and winter cloak, waited at the standing stone on the ridge above the tuath, watching the ladds run back to the yard after the last chants of the sunrise ceremony floated off over the sea. They'd just completed the fire ritual, signaling the rebirth of the Sun Lord out of winter's dark cauldron, to begin the new cycle of the year.

All the clanfolk had taken the new fire to their hearths, but Coillore suddenly motioned for Firinn to follow him, and the druid set off running through the light snow dusting the ground beneath the bare birch boughs. They climbed a crooked deer path, hidden in the trees behind the standing stone, the path grown over with moss. Coillore moved quickly up the ridge to the south, and very soon they came to a small wheel of stones, barely visible in the spike grasses of the high moor. Firinn stood there, breathing in the dawn light glowing over the ocean below, outlining the low curves of far off isles to the south, looking like magical lands of gold.

"It's time to show ye the light o' Arta (arsta, Arthur), father god o' the Luckenbooth, the emotion light structure (described in Book Two)," Coillore said, stepping into the middle of the stones, "keeper o' the patterns o' the father's kingdom to be built into earth life over the next skyturn, the one who sends in the light seeds o' Midwinter. But truly, Arte brings through the sword o' the Dagda, the grandfather king o' heaven, the one who creates kings on earth, an' wise men, too. Very few can touch his power. Watch." And Coillore stood, arms upraised, his goatskin cloak falling back off his shoulders as he began turning sunwise, his face catching the dawn rays shining over the crest of the ridge. "I call the great sword o' the Dagda to me, ancient light," Coillore said. Then the druid stopped, holding his arms up to the sun, like a child to its Da, waiting in breathless silence. And suddenly, Coillore began to glow. At first it looked like a faint mist around him, hugging his robe, but then it became an unmistakable cloak of light. And then, Firinn saw one bright spear of sunshine move slowly down Coillore's spine.

Watching the old druid, electricity coursed through Firinn's head, too, and he felt suddenly <u>alive</u>, ready for anything. A sword of light opened out in Fìrinn's own mind, too, flooding him with sweet holiness that called him to come home to truth and justice once and for all. And in it, Fìrinn felt the promise of laws of love that were eternal and stronger than anything else in the universe, more powerful than any darkness in any realm. And Fìrinn knew in that moment he needed these truths more than breath. At the tip of the sword, a golden ball of light settled down into Fìrinn's abdomen, along with the distinct feeling that he'd be a king like the Dagda and Arte in some far off time, a future life, perhaps. As Coillore stood chanting, the glow around the old druid began pulsing, and Fìrinn couldn't take his eyes away. For just an instant, he thought Coillore might rise into the sun as its glow deepened into gold. And then, as the sun lifted away from the horizon, Coillore dropped his arms and laughed.

"<u>This</u> is what ye were meant for, too, ladd, the journey back to the very beginnin', an' leadership in the tribes. I ken it as sure as the sun rises. Follow the light wherever it leads!" And Fìrinn smiled, for the old druid looked as if he'd had too much mead, his face flushed and his eyes asparkle.

And then Coillore settled into a stride back to the tuath that kept Fìrinn racing behind him through the heather an' bracken. A circle of light remained around the old man's head that whole Midwinter day, and on his face, the years seemed to have peeled away. But as they approached the fostering, stepping around the standing stone onto the path to the tuath, Coillore turned, his face quite serious as he leveled his eyes on Fìrinn's.

"Tell no one," Coillore cautioned. "Only a few, even on Iona, can call up such light. An' besides, I'm allowed to share the secret path wi' ye alone. Well, ye an' one other." And in the dream, the druid smiled up at Fìrinn, a soft smile of such gentle joy that Fìrinn never forgot it as long as he lived.

After he woke from this dream, awestruck, Firinn went about his day with white fire filling his head, sudden flashes of light pulsing in his mind's eye all day and into the night. But it took him a few days more to realize that the Dagda's sword of light from the dream had lit some eternal flame deep within his own self as well. For, ever afterwards, Firinn <u>felt</u> the circles of existence in his heart, the pull of the Creator Sun, and the promise of forever love he knew was there, just beyond his reach. The path was no longer something chanted about in a ceremony or long histories he recited to please his teacher and then half forgot. It was <u>real</u>, interwoven into his very core, and he knew he'd follow it to the end, if he did nothing else in his life.

The night after his dream, when the torches were snuffed out and the other ladds went in to their furs, Firinn sat long on the rocks by the bay, yearning for the tenderness of his morning awakening. His head swam with the promise it brought, and for the next quarter moon, he dreamed of suns that never paled and of himself, floating in a world of jewel-bright colors, silken winds, and endless love.

Chapter Twenty-Two: Soillse

Soillse spread hides to lie on beneath her Aine tree until after the evening meal, when Eilid could come with her to the women's cave. During the night, Soillse's first moon time had begun, so she had to stay away from the men and boys. She'd already bathed in the burn and put on a warm shift. And though they'd picked Aine's apples a quarter moon ago, Soillse didn't try to climb into the tree, for the branches were too slight to hold her now. Dismayed by the dull ache in her lower abdomen, and by how tired and heavy she felt, Soillse thought, is this what the change from girl to woman means, pain in yer belly from morning till night and having to keep yer distance from everyone male? Even Coillore, who I share everything important with, has to stay apart from me now. At least I have no fish gutting to do today, she thought, brightening a bit. Ceit'll have to do without me for a change. Soillse remembered, now she thought of it, that Ceit had had cramping, too, a couple of skyturns ago. But her moon cycles were less painful now.

It was late in the Vine moon (September), and the day was foggy and cold. Soillse could barely see the waves through the mist, but she heard the soft lapping on the rocks below and shivered in the cold damp. I wish I could go sit by the fire, she thought, pulling her furs around her. In the evening, Ma would perform the ceremony of womanhood. And Soillse would have to stay at the cave until her bleeding stopped before returning to the tribe. Hopefully, my womanhood'll be well sanctified by then, she thought and sighed. Then she closed her eyes and let the soft swoosh of the sea on the rocks below lull her to sleep.

In her dream, Fìrinn stood before her on the edge of a hill, looking out over a narrow sea loch. It was a place Soillse didn't recognize, and he was older, a man fully grown, wearing a sky-blue robe with white edging, the colors of the high king of Skye. The sun was shining on his chestnut hair as he turned and held his arms out to her. And his eyes poured love, thick and rich as warm cream, as she ran and snuggled into his chest, feeling cherished to her very marrow. But it went deeper than that, for he touched her very center and saw the goddess within, the one she truly was that no one else ever recognized or understood.

As she looked up at Fìrinn's face, it changed slowly into a sun, radiant and dazzling. Her heart was filled with pulsing waves of tenderness, and even in her dream, she thought, this must be the diamond light, for it's sweeter than the honeysuckles of the Hawthorne moon (May). Inside this sun shone the face of Oghama, and He loved her as His own beloved, His light penetrating her heart to its diamond core. And suddenly, she was flooded with such longing and devotion that it made her swoon. Even in her sleep, she clasped her hands to her heart, wanting to hold onto such sweetness for all time.

When she woke, it was already dusk. The cooking fires were lit in the yard, and the mist had thickened, so the Cuchullin peaks were barely visible across the loch. And the trees around her felt soft and wet. As Soillse lay in her lingering happiness, she thought how the overwork of the women and the arts of war of the men contrasted so with her dream. How do I combine them both?, she wondered. And then she stood on tiptoe to see the ladds through the underbrush, all crowding into the long house door for their meals, some already drinking soup from their bowls. In her homespun shift stained with grease, Eilid was hurrying by with a platter, motioning Sine, Eilid's aunt, to bring out the bread from the cooking hut. But Fìrinn stood apart, already dressed in his winter jerkin and buckskin breeks, looking slowly around the yard. He closed his eyes then, and

Soillse could feel him searching her out. In a moment, he glanced toward Aine, but Soillse was too well hidden to be seen.

She lay down again with her hands across her belly under the furs, because the warmth of her fingers eased the pain. How easily her usual eagerness to get the work done and not sit down till after the evening meal was sapped into pure tiredness by such a thing as a moon cycle. She felt gently connected to all the female creatures who shared this pain, too, the deer especially, and her skin felt more tender today, the way the bark on Aine always softened in the rain. Soillse thought how all females had to go through this every moon, and what a precious a thing it was for a woman to give life to a child. How could hunters enjoy the kill so much? Then she wondered if this cramping was an omen of pain to come in her womanhood. But she was just too drowsy to think any more, and she closed her eyes, lying awake and listening, until Eilid whispered from the edge of the bracken.

"Time for yer ceremony, lassie." Soillse's Ma was plump and squat, with cow brown eyes and hair, and no one but Seumus would call her beautiful. She'd thrown her heavy wool cloak on over her ceremonial hide robe, and pinned it into place with a bone clasp.

Soillse rose slowly, taking off the furs and wrapping her plaid around her heavy woolen shift, then rolling and lifting the bundle of furs onto her back. They climbed the rocky path north of the yard, slowly, up the cliffs above the sea toward the sacred women's cave, where all feminine ceremonies were held. Mother ahead of daughter, Eilid limped a little and turned to smile at Soillse as they reached the ledge outside the cave. Motioning Soillse to wait, Eilid entered and lit her herb bundle, smoking the chamber and chanting for cleansing. It was a large space, big enough for ten or twelve women to gather, the walls blackened by the fires of many years of use. Then Eilid laid her Goddess figurine near the hearth in the back of the cave, a pit outlined with stones that sat beneath a small opening to the sky above, and placed her bowls of air, water, and earth around it, stopping to light rush torches and place them in niches in the wall. She poured fat into a fourth stone bowl, placed it in the circle of elements, then lit it and the fire. Only then did Eilid call Soillse inside, wait as the lass laid out her furs on one of the two heather pallets, then motion for her to come to the fire circle.

Walking sunwise, Eilid moved round the altar, then asked Soillse to follow, and they went once more round the elements. Eilid stopped three fourths of the way around, at the place of the mother, while Soillse stopped at the second place, virgin, for the very first time. Her moon cycle moved her beyond the place of the child now. As she did so, Eilid gazed at Soillse with soft pride, tears brimming in her eyes.

"I've no more bairns noo," she whispered, "Ye're lovely, lass o' me heart."

Soillse bent her head in thanks, but her chest tensed as her Ma spoke. Being a woman only meant more work in the tuath, relentless chores from dawn to dusk and assuming full responsibility for the tribe. Will I have to leave behind me time with Aine and walking the deerpaths up in the wood? The cramps in Soillse's belly intensified, and her temples began throbbing. I dinna want to leave me child behind and become a woman, Soillse thought crossly. I didna have the time I wanted to play before this, and now it's too late. And Soillse hung her head as Eilid chanted.

"For this sacred rite o' womanhood, I call forth the virgin an' mother goddesses o' the Creator Sun: Tara, the Beloved, Màiri, divine grandmother, Màithriel, mother, an' Maighdean, tender virgin lass. May they lead ye gently through the comin' phases o' yer life, dear. An' may the Goddess protect an' hold ye in yer womanhood from noo till the day ye pass over again. I call forth all yer maternal female ancestors, too, the whole line from the very beginnin' down to this one lassie." And Eilid nodded her head in finality.

Then Eilid spread a hide on the cave floor beneath Soillse and unfastened the ties around the lass's waist. Soillse's skirt fell to her feet, and Eilid untied the thong that held the bloody cattail fluff next to Soillse's woman's place, letting that fall to the floor, too. Eilid gathered up most of the fluff and put it carefully into her hide pouch. It would be spread on the barley plots, for moon blood held the pregnant power of the Goddess, and the very first moon time held that of the virgin, Maighdean, as well. It would greatly aid the crops. The remainder of the fluff, Eilid placed in a small heap before the Goddess figurine. And then, wrapping Soillse in a horse hide, animal of the virgin goddess, for Soillse's spirit light would move down from the little girl in the thymus to the virgin in the lower heart during this ceremony, Eilid held her hands on Soillse's head.

"I ask the highest blessin' o' the Goddess, Tara, on this new woman, Soillse, that she be granted strength as she grows an' fruitfulness in bringin' forth girls to inherit the land right o' the clan an' sons to defend them. Let Soillse take her place in the tribe, leadin' wi' her heart, an' no wantin' to take over, as so many women do. An' Tara, I ask especially that Ye shield this lassie's soft heart that feels the spirit o' the plants an' stones so well, a heart that yearns for the Sun Lord. Give her courage for the difficulties o' her life to come an' health to the end o' her days. This I ask as matriarch an' guardian o' this child, become woman today. I place the responsibility for her in Yer hands noo, Goddess. Ye are Soillse's Ma noo." And a tear spilled down Eilid's cheek as she sat facing Soillse, drew a clean hide robe around her, and held out the bowl of broth and herbs that had been warming by the fire. Slowly, Soillse drank.

Eilid took Soillse's hand then and led her to the furs, waiting till Soillse was lying down, then pulling up the covers. With her head resting lightly on the lass's own, Eilid sang the forever friend song, and they both cried as she did so, for it would be the last time. And then, taking Soillse's head in her lap, Eilid sang the song of maidenhood, her breathy voice honoring the beauty of the untouched virgin, the mystery of love that would come, and the blessing of unborn children. Both Ma and daughter had freckles scattered across their cheeks and arms, and though Soillse had her Da's broad forehead and high cheekbones, her eyes held Eilid's gentleness, her chin the same determination. And lastly, Eilid whispered the blessing of the faeries, as Soillse's eyes drooped, asking them to bestow the nine faery graces of womanhood on Soillse: grace of fertility, grace of uprightness, grace of compassion, grace of responsibility, grace of leadership in the tribe, and the grace of inner vision and knowings, plus the graces of goodness of thought, emotion, and action. (These come from the central regents of the sacred triple three light structures of the Diamond Core, beginning with the second chakra and moving up.)

Watching the firelight play over Soillse's sleepy face, Eilid thought how much a child the lass still looked, with her speckled cheeks and untamed hair, despite her thirteen winters. The lass's body had lengthened, though, breast buds appearing this past spring. Soillse's hips were just beginning to spread and curve, where last summer they'd been thin and straight. For all that, Eilid thought, me lass'd still rather roam the forest or dream in the apple tree like the shy bairn she's always been. And she seems to have no eye for the laddies at all. And then Eilid lay down herself on the second pallet and slept under her furs in the fire's warmth, while the soft mist outside held them both in its hushed stillness all night long.

In the first dream, Soillse was standing outside the circle of the clan in the yard, and Ceit was in the center, her black hair plaited down her back. Shouting at Soillse to go get bundles of firewood, Ceit yelled for her to carry more and more, till Soillse simply collapsed on her knees in the mud.

In the second dream, toward morning, Soillse saw a small hut in the birch wood, very like Coillore's high on the ridge, but this one was to the south above the tuath. She herself waited by the doorway with a child of her own, a wee lass. And she could feel that they lived alone, separate from the tribe. Holding the babe, Soillse gazed down toward the tuath through the forest, and her heart was breaking, for she wasn't allowed to go there any more. And then she woke with a start. Why wasn't Fìrinn with her in that dream? And what caused her to live all alone with a bairn like that? And as she felt a great anxiety take hold of her heart, she sighed heavily and sat up.

Eilid was squatting in her old workaday shift, building up the fire and whispering the hearth blessing. She bent to kiss Soillse's head, wishing her the happiest of visionings. Then Eilid threw on her cloak, took up her rolled furs, and walked out into a thin morning mist. Dawn was just brightening the sky behind the ridge, making the waves of the sea loch below sparkle in the early light. And the tips of the mountains beyond the loch began to glow, as Eilid smiled and waved to Soillse from the entrance, blowing one last kiss before closing the doorskin and starting down the cliff path.

In her furs, Soillse yawned. Mmmmm, the fire's hot and the cave's warm. Thank ye Ma for that, she thought. Then she stood, stretched, pulled on her clean blue shift, and leaned out the entrance. The fog had nearly vanished in the night, but it was cold, and the breeze blew strong from the sea. So, she went in, closed the doorcloth, weighted the bottom with stones against the wind, and ate the porridge Eilid had left to warm beside the fire.

And then, Soillse gathered up the new robe Eilid had brought to sew and embroider, for this was when she'd make her ceremonial robe, the dress she'd wear at all the rituals of her life. She lit the bowl of fats and walked sunwise round the altar, and then sat on the pallet holding her Goddess figurine, calling forth the visions and symbols she should paint on the hides. As she settled herself by the fire, Soillse was glad for no heavy work to do today and because her cramps had lessened to a dull ache she could finally ignore. Then very softly, she felt a presence move into the cave and come sit beside her, and she closed her eyes to see who it was.

The crisp image of her grandmother came into her mind, the herb woman of Eilid's stories, a small white-haired woman with an athletic build and wisdom in her eyes. And Soillse felt spirit arms move about her shoulders and sensed a blessing of the ancestors being poured out over her head. The image of a crown came to Soillse's mind then, and she wondered at this, but began drawing the light outline of it on the hide. She took time to stitch it, too, the braided circlet of a queen, and thought how Ceit would resent this when she saw it. But Soillse felt her grandmother's instructions clearly and drew what she saw. And then she drew and stitched the cloak of a priestess, blue robes with the face of a white deer on the front. But this did not surprise her, for Firinn's tuath was the clan of the deer. Except wouldn't he stay at hers? Usually daughters stayed at their own tuath. And then Soillse drew and stitched four children, two lassies and two ladds, and she smiled and rubbed her belly to think of so many bairns. I hope they look like Firinn, she thought with a smile. Then into her mind came a great many herbs and stones, and a rainbow, so she knew she'd be healing with plant and crystal people, and the rainbow of light within. But where was her husband in all this, Firinn? She felt no instructions to paint a man.

All that day and the next Soillse worked steadily, and at last the painted patterns were complete and some of the embroidery. The stitching would take many moons, for the scenes were complicated, but she'd not need this robe till one skyturn away at the entrance into her role of lover, and wife perhaps. The skyturn before her was the cycle of courting, her virgin year, when her womb would ripen to receive male seed and no love-making was allowed.

As she worked, Soillse sang made-up songs about her life, verses about; Aine, Eilid, Seumus, and all the things she loved so much, like fat wee warbling robins or the shushing sound of the sea. She felt the many threads of her future anchoring into place within, weaving themselves together into a lifeline as she worked. There were very few images of her tuath, though, and she worried about this. She was pictured alone, even after she had a bairn, and it was unnatural, that. Only later in the spiral of her life was there a small house by the sea with Fìrinn standing beside her. As she drew this image, she felt great peace move into her heart to steady her. And in her mind, she saw women and children coming to this doorway and felt some recognition of her healing gifts at last, and her family nearby.

And then, in the very last place in the spiral, the central image, a great sun came into her vision, and suddenly she saw the dazzling light that Fìrinn's face had become in her dream as she lay beneath her Aine tree two days before. She felt the same flooding tenderness, and heard the beating of an ancient Heart, One she'd known and loved from the depths of her being a long, long time ago. Ah, Oghama, she thought. And as she painted this sun, she saw in her mind a small thatched home that was radiant, made of brilliant light, not of stone and wood like those of the tuath here. There was a field of wildflowers nearby with a small sea cove below it, and she felt the sweet longing to go there rise into her heart. Gorse and primroses dotted the fields, with seals playing in the sea loch beyond. She stood at the door of this hut, smiling, a young woman with long hair and flour on her hands. And she hummed as she watched Fìrinn approach from the fields, her heart bursting with ripe contentment. And suddenly, she knew this was an image of the Creator Sun, their small home there, and that Fìrinn was her eternal love. And Soillse leaned back against the cave wall, her mind stunned by this knowing.

And then as she watched again, she and he both became dazzling light. Fìrinn's face changing once more into the face of Oghama as her own became the face of the White Tara. Were she and Fìrinn simply coverings over the light of the One Beloveds then? Her mind stretched to understand the images. Do all couples serve this role? Her head swam, and she lay down to still the dizziness.

Is it Ye, Oghama, that I truly love?, she thought. And then she realized how He was hidden in the depths of her heart, in the small diamond flame on the altar there. And she knew He'd been with her in every moment since her original creation, so close that He knew every fear she'd ever taken in on the way down, and every step of the way Home. And suddenly, she felt how He LOVED her!

"Ye're me eternal partner then, no Fìrinn at all," she burst out, releasing a long breath, "an' Ye've come to me in every husband I've ever had all the way down! I remember Ye noo!"

Just then, a ray of sunshiine slipped in around the door cloth, the last light of evening reflected off the sea, and this one ray fluttered just over her heart. But then she startled as she heard the shuffle of feet and a male voice outside the cave mouth. Quickly, she rose, hiding herself back against the wall beside the entrance, her heart racing.

"Soillse?," she heard faintly. "Soillse?," more loudly this time.

"Fìrinn!," she whispered, then covered her mouth. Keeping to the shadows inside, she called out to him. "Ye're no permitted here. Da'd have yer hide, if he knew! I'm in me moon-time ritual. It's forbidden!" And then she felt herself blushing as red as the sun touching the far hills. What does it mean, she thought, that he's come at just this moment?

"I found this stone washed up in the bay," he said softly, careful to stay well outside the doorcloth. "An' the Goddess voice told me very clearly ye must have it noo, an' so I came as quickly as I could. I'm sorry I disturbed ye...I didna ken...about...," and his voice trailed off as his face flushed redder than her own. Then he leaned over and placed the stone at the cave mouth, and she watched his hand reach just under the door skin. "I'll just leave it here on the ledge an' go away. I'm sorry, Soillse."

Ach, if Eilid or Seumus find out he's been here, Soillse fumed, they'll send him away from the fostering. Nothing surer than that. But then suddenly, she felt the pull of the Sun Lord across the sea, and on an impulse, she drew back the cloth. As she bent to pick up the stone, her hair fell over her face, with her cheeks rosy and her eyes soft with love. Fìrinn turned, startling at the sound, then gasped as he looked at her, taking a step forward. With her long silken hair and sweet girlish smile, her beauty was haunting. Even her old shift seemed to shine in the evening light. His hands reached up toward her of their own accord, but he quickly stuffed them into the pockets of his breeks.

"Ye glow, Soillse! Surely ye're no o' earth, but goddess born!" Eyes wide, he stared a moment before remembering himself and turned to run down the path to the yard. How gentle those green eyes are, she thought with a flutter in her heart, watching him turn away.

And Soillse smiled softly after him, then held the stone up to the setting sun that hovered over the western sea. The crystal was clear and faceted, with soft clouds of red floating within, a small six-sided quartz the size of her thumb. It shone with the clear light she'd seen in her vision, and in it she felt the heartbeat of the Sun Lord. On a sudden urge, she put it to her belly and felt an easing of her pain there, and then the gentle desire of Oghama to protect her child within from all harm. As she turned back into the cave, Soillse held the crystal to her heart, instead.

While robins trilled their cheery songs in the late evening air, she lay long on her furs, feeling the mystery of Oghama's love, along with the barest hint of desire. Her moon-time ritual was complete now. At dawn, she'd return to the tuath and resume her work. But for this one night, she'd stay here in the cave, wrapped in the sweetest secret of the cosmos.

Chapter Twenty-Three: Fìrinn

Then during the first cold days of winter as Fìrinn ran back into the yard after a day hunting on the ridge, Coillore took the ladd back to his hut to continue his lessons on the structures of the Diamond Core. It was a blustery cold day, but clear and crisp. Still, Fìrinn was more than glad to be inside beside a warm hearth.

"I have one lesson to give ye today, Fìrinn," Coillore began, smoothing his woolen robe over his knees as they finished a meal of sunflower seed soup and flatbread. "An' I'll try to keep it short, so ye can get back before dark." At this Fìrinn smiled inwardly, having grown used to the old druid's excitement about the Diamond Core and tendency to meander and talk on and on.

"Ye ken the regents o' the Creator Sun, the Stillpoint Center, the Wizard Wheel, the Pineal Wheel, an' noo come the regents o' the throat. It's here that divine Will meets our personal will, an' responsibilities are laid across our shoulders that we dinna always like. An' it's where the thyroid is, too, thy road, Siris's path Home." And the druid reached over to draw a small circle with three spirals flowing out of it in the earthen floor.

"This is the level o' ceremonial magic, Fìrinn, the Triple Spiral o' the Goddess. One spiral here links to the mind, one to the heart, an' one to the action center behind the pubic bone in the base. See? This cosmic fifth chakra is the level o' sound as well, laddie, both words an' song, but it's Tara's realm primarily, so music especially, eh? It's where the teeth are, too, Tara's ivory stone circle wi' those wee structures inside that direct us along our path o' experience each lifetime. An' it's through sound an' pictures, both Tara's forces, no Oghama's sacred letters, that the outer path o' experience is created. Every moon, Her pictures an' songs are sent out from our creator flames at all three levels, inner stars in each individual's pineal, heart, an' action centers. An' these create all our intellectual, emotional, an' physical experiences in the outer world, Tara's fae helpers in the spirit world bringin' these experiences to us on our road o' life.

Song holds great power, unseen an' unrecognized, like all Goddess forces, for music reaches into the deepest level o' the emotional body an' restructures it immediately. Music can heal beliefs, if ye specifically request that, an' it can lift ye out o' terror in moments an' enfold ye in Tara's great an' holy love, whether ye ask for such or no. I'll be teachin' ye the druid alphabet, the spirit meanin' o' the first letters o' our sacred trees, when we get to the druid moons. But just for noo, let's take N, for instance, Nion (Ash tree), that resonates wi' Maighdean, virgin goddess o' the Creator Sun. If ye're ever flaggin' on yer path, ready to cave in to fear, just sing that sound, nnnnnnnnnn, over an' over. An' the heavenly strength an' tenderness o' Maighdean in the spine'll surround ye in moments, especially yer inner virgin lass, move into yer emotional body an' shore it up powerfully. Ye can do it wi' any o' the letters, eh? It's the fastest way I ken o' shiftin' great fear. Try it durin' yer next initiation, laddie.

All celestial bodies send out one clear ringin' tone o' love, too. The nine tones o' the triple three light structures o' the Diamond Core'll one day be called the Solfeggio frequencies. They can realign yer chakras in moments, ladd, for they stream from the highest levels o' the cosmos. They're based in a 444 frequency pattern (Hertz), though. Four-four-four means the mind, the heart, an' the base are all attuned to the heart's vibration, to love. In future days, music'll be attuned to a 440 frequency, so the action level willna have that strong centerin' influence o' the heart. But enough, let's get back to the lesson noo.

As I said, this Triple Spiral level is connected to Tara, who rules the inner world. Where the Pineal Wheel creates the structures o' the outer world, this Triple Spiral creates our own wee worlds an' our spirit journeys through life. An' like everythin' else, the outer extravagance o' the pir.eal father pales beside the personal day-to-day power o' Goddess love, humble though it may seem. This level an' the two light structures below it are the heart structures o' the Core, no the divine mind like the last three structures ye've learned, eh? It's the Triple Spiral that blends both emotional an' mental ethers into beliefs, too, an essence made up o' two-thirds emotion an' one-third thought. It's beliefs that shape our lives, laddie, for only beliefs have the force to hold the structures o' our individual outer worlds in place. People die for their beliefs! Thoughts, emotions, an' actions also create yer future, but far less powerfully than beliefs.

No only that, but everyone's beliefs create what happens on the global stage as well. Africa, for instance, resonates wi' the little girl aspect within each o' us. So all fears the people across the globe havena yet faced an' healed belongin' to their own little girl within are bein' played out in Africa, people o' those lands livin' wi' all those fears in their lives. The same is true for the little girl quadrant o' the cosmos, an' the realms o' the Otherworld, too. Ye have a sacred responsibility to go within an heal the memories o' yer descent. ladd; it helps everyone. An' this Triple Spiral level is where that responsibility is activated

In the wee central circle o' the Triple spiral here sit Domhnall (donal) an' Nemetona, priest an' priestess. They hold tremendous power, for they overlight each tribal spiritual brother/sisterhood on earth an' move us through initiations an' other unseen portals wi' their ceremonial mastery on the windin' road back to Oghama an'

Tara's embrace. Domhnall an' Mona send impulses out to the three spiral arms, too.

Domhnall's path is the more structured, the masculine wi' its formal ceremonies, teachin's, an' initiations. He rules the formal community religions, too; the druid councils, religious laws, the sacraments an' traditions o' the brotherhood, an' all formal positions in the church that are compensated in some way. But he does this for all orders worldwide, no just our own. An' his star compound is on Ara, the altar.

Nemtona's is the less structured path o' the priestesses, teachin's that come through the livin' o' every day, all the folk that share one nemeton or oak circle, each spirit neighborhood, ye might say. Her lessons are built into the priestess meditations o' the new an' full moons to hear the will o' the Goddess, uncompensated service in the orders, plus midwifery. What is the path o' sacred mysteries but midwifery, anyway? Her sacraments include: birth, puberty, first joinin', marriage, childbirth, end o' fertility, grandmotherhood, an' death. The same fears'll rise up for Soillse durin' life events, childbirth, say, as ye'll face durin' yer initiations, so there can seem to be more ups an' downs for women relative to the steadiness o' a man's life.

Nemetona leads all tribal sisterhoods on the planet, though her stream flows through the pagan/nature religions o' the every day. This high priestess rules the hidden an' unexpected calls that open on life's path, too, An' Nemetona creates through song, so the music o' all tribal ceremonies comes through her as well, the words through Domhnall. She helps everyone develop their feminine powers o' intuition an' prophecy, too. Her star city is on Crater, the cup, ladd.

Both Nemetona an' Domhnall make formal connections between all disciples an' their star families, too, deepenin' an' nourishin' this light connection through the years, for this is where the impulses from God an' Goddess are most clearly sent. Both these regents wield tremendous power that reaches to the very depths o' the spirit, plus their impulses stream from the <u>heart</u>, no the mind, so Nemetona's inner calls an' Domhnall's outer ones are doubly compellin'. Human family structures try to bind ever tighter, right until the very end, her distortions. Societal structures do the same, his. This central wee triangle isna an easy portal, either, for here one's whole way o' life must be left behind in devotion to an' communion wi' the One Beloveds.

Then, in the mental spiral arm here on top sit Aedd an' Grainne. These regents take the monthly impulses from Domhnall an' Nemetona, blend them into Tara's path o' experience, then send them to the mind star in the pineal in the brain for manifestation into life. Where Grainne sends in lessons o' relationship an' intuition, Aedd sends in destiny lessons, mental facts an' figures. Aedd an' Grainne bring in mentors that lead each individual on their spiritual path, too. These regents open new initiatives especially, an' they make certain the structures o' truth are built firmly into new beliefs, leadin' off into confusions at times to test the level o' discernment an' perseverance a disciple has achieved. Each level o' light has specific portals o' consciousness, an' those inner doors arena opened until the foundation below is strong enough to support the higher level, eh? Aedd brings in fanaticism an' rigidity o' thought tied into false beliefs as well, an' she rigidity o' traditions mainly. The mind star o' the pineal resonates wi' the religions o' the far east, ladd, Buddhism especially. His city o' light is on Pyxis, the compass, an' hers on Circinus, the drawin' compass, eh?

An' then come Etain an' Ecne, regents o' the emotional teachin's noo. They take Tara's monthly emotional growth impulse an' send it to each person's central heart flame, Etain, the feminine, Ecne, the masculine, o' course. Etain an' Ecne send inner an' outer teachers to move all forward, too, but teachers who move through our emotional lives, no the mind this time. Ecne's specialty is the tamin' o' heart's desires, bringin' them into alignment wi' the One Beloveds. Etain sends in wild passions for change, radical shifts that lead off in totally new directions. An' then Ecne brings in blocks to the heart's fulfillment, long years o' personal restraint that tame an' ripen love's wine within into a calm sustained flow. Etain an' Ecne's efforts prepare each inner god an' goddess for their final gift to earth that always arises from the very core o' the heart, too. But both are unbendin' in holdin' back manifestation o' those core heart's desires until all Oghama an' Tara's wisdom lessons have been carefully structured into the fibers o' the heart. Ecne's star is Auriga, the Charioteer, an' Etain's, Equulus, the wee horse. This heart stream resonates wi' the new religion that'll begin in about a century, Christianity, ladd.

An' last come the regents o' the action centers in the base, Nudd an' Siann (she-ann). They take Tara's monthly action impulses o' growth an' send these to the action flame in the base, Nudd, the masculine, Siann, the feminine, impulses that create our physical experiences. These two regents' energies are as strong as iron, too, holdin' the outpicturin' o' all inner beliefs in place for everyone. Their stream'll flow through a religion that'll develop in about seven centuries, the Muslim faith. Nudd, wi' his silver hand, holds the veils in place to action in masculine endeavors until enough inner healin' warrants a shift to a higher level, the destiny stream. His lessons are often about rigidity o' action an' domination o' the feminine. Siann rules the portals to action o' the inner feminine. She's very grounded in the day-to-day o' home an' family. But she has many lessons to teach about impulsiveness an' blendin' personal actions wi' what's needed by the tribe an' family, too.

No one's allowed to become the Creator's true messenger on earth, unless they can do so in humility an' wi' restraint o' personal desires. These action regents lead all through those portals, blockin' or openin' each person's freedom to act in the world, as these two see fit. Wi' her own silver hand, Siann hold's back the inner goddess, movin' her into recognition only at the end o' many lives o' gruelin' work, bein' the underling to others an' servin' the all, until the wisdom lessons o' responsibility in action have been carefully structured in. An' he does the same wi' the masculine, carefully buildin' restraint, patience, an' surrender to divine timin' into all action impulses. Nudd an' Siann'll block ye again an' again, until that old phallic force in action that wants to do whatever it pleases is subdued to the will o' heaven. An' each disciple does eventually learn this, no matter how strong personal desires may become. Nudd an' Siann's star compounds are in Orphiucus, ladd, his star called 'the hand in front' an' hers 'the hand behind'. That star system is the serpent bearer, an' that's precisely what these two regents do, tame that old reptile o' personal will. A tougher pair o' teachers canna be found in any realm, but a more important lesson isna taught, either.

There noo, ladd, no so much to remember tonight, eh? Off wi' ye noo! Sleep well." But Firinn only gave a wan smile, for tonight he was tired of the lessons, finding the details hard to remember after long hours of tracking boar in the bitter wind along the ridge. And he knew Coillore would later ask him to repeat the regents and their directives, until the druid could be certain Firinn had learned them all by heart. Watching the ladd move out the doorskin, Coillore's eyes grew sad also, for he knew only too well how dreams could be thwarted and how frustrating the path would become for Firinn in days to come.

It was colder than usual for the Blackthorne moon (November), and the winds had been fierce in their fury all night long, blowing through the yard and under the doorcloth of the long house where all the boys shivered in their furs. In their heavy hide breeks and fur jerkins, the ladds were now paired in small groups, clustered with age mates on the hard-packed earth beside the small circle of huts, just beginning the day's games. Resting the back of his hand on his shoulder, Firinn tightened his grip on the throwing stone in his palm. Turning around, faster and faster, he willed strength into his arm and fingers, then with one great push, grunted as he heaved the rock toward the circle in the dirt a pony length away. If he crossed it, he'd win two ribs of the roasted calf at the Samhein celebration tomorrow, and Fìrinn's mouth watered at the thought. The two ladds who tried before him had fallen short. But as the stone arced through the air, the hounds began baying, and all eyes looked north. It was a bad omen to have the flight of a weapon interrupted, portending illness or death in one's flight of life.

A rider picked his way down through the birch wood from the ridge, the man bouncing heavily, his hands barely holding the reins. Once, the rider nearly tumbled from the saddle onto the hard turf, he was slouched so far forward, like someone sickened or drunk. The dun animal wavered as it reached the yard, then headed for the long house as cold unease spread itself through Fìrinn's chest. Bana Dhia, ears pricked, nudged his thigh.

Seumus blew the horn, and clansmen quickly gathered near the chief's roundhouse, closest to the ridge path, as boys began running in from the hills. Unsheathing daggers, three of the men formed a line between the rider and the crowd of ladds, but the horse slowed not at all, moving quickly through the hut circle to the long house door. Duineil appeared from nowhere and ran toward it, reaching for the horse's reins.

"He carries the chief's colors, clan o' the deer," shouted Duineil.

"Fìrinn," Seumus said, looking back and beckoning to the ladd, his face grim. And a sharp blade of fear pierced Fìrinn's gut as he walked toward the horse. They'd seen no flaming cross on the Cuchullin heights, so it wasna war. Had Da been killed in one of those raids he loved so much, the boy wondered. As Seumus stepped in front of Fìrinn, the crowd of boys closed in behind him.

The horse's flanks ran with sweat, its face flecked with foam. Staggering to a stop, it pushed straight into the line of ladds, and still the rider didn't move. So Seumus bent over and shook the man's arm. And then the rider groaned, lifted his head from under the hood of his woolen cloak, and opened his eyes. Old Aedd! But his eyes were red with fatigue, and spittle flecked his lips, nothing like the smiling storyteller of times past. Fìrinn started forward, his heart racing.

"I come for the chief's son," the bent old man finally whispered. "I bear a message for him alone." As Seumus began to speak, Fìrinn held up a hand and stepped forward, laying it on Aedd's shoulder. Just then Coillore, his eyes sorrowful, walked out of the scrub birches.

"Aedd, it's meself," the boy said in a whisper. "What's the news?" Old Aedd opened his rheumy blue eyes wider and stared at the boy for what seemed a moon turn.

"Aye," he said at last, "ye have her eyes. But ye're so tall noo, I didna recognize ye at first." Then Aedd smiled and closed his own eyes once more, breathing heavily.

"Out wi' it, man, will ye?," Fìrinn said, gritting his teeth.

"It's ye're Ma, ladd...bleedin' again. Thought she was over it, we did...so many draughts we brewed. She's weakened near to the death sleep now. An' she threatened a curse if I didna get ye back before the Goddess takes her. Go...quickly, ladd....GO!" And Aedd leaned down against the horse's neck and closed his eyes again.

As Aedd spoke, Fìrinn's heart froze. His muscles stiffened like ice, and blood pounded in his ears. Ma? No! Then mindless of the need for a cloak over his jerkin or provisions, Fìrinn strode double lengths toward the ponies grazing above the tuath. The smaller one, Glinn (gleenya, pretty), had been a gift from his Da, a portion of the price of fostering. Blindly, Fìrinn reached for her mane, ready to swing up on her back and ride off in that moment. But Seumus ran toward him with a bridle and laid a hand on Fìrinn's arm.

"Take me own stallion, son. He's big enough to turn a three day journey into two," said the older man, eyes brimming. "An' remember, ladd, I'm as much yer Da as anyone noo," for the ache of the loss of his own mother squeezed Seumus's heart as he spoke. Then he hugged Fìrinn and waved him onto the saddle blanket he'd thrown across the stallion's back. And the ladd felt his chest soften at the grizzled hair and scarred face of the chief with the sentimental heart.

"Thank ye ... father," Fìrinn stammered. Many of the boys called Seumus "Da", but Fìrinn had never done so. As Seumus smiled, Fìrinn felt Coillore come up beside him and reach out to touch his arm.

"The Goddess guide ye," was all the druid said. But his eyes were dark and his brows bristled with concern as he waited in his emerald woolen cloak.

Running into the long house then, to grab his own fur-lined cloak and heavy winter breeks and boots, Fìrinn returned and mounted the horse quickly, nodding to Coillore, and heading east up the ridge. But Soillse, in only a light woolen shift, ran toward him from the cooking hut. She sprinted toward the burn, trying to head him off, shouting something that was lost to the wind and holding up a pouch. The hint of a smile softened Fìrinn's face as he pulled around to meet her, watching her fine brown-blond hair blow around her face. Breathless and running, she hadn't taken time to belt up her skirt, and it hindered her. Boulders also littered the path, and he had to swing around them to come close. Then, reaching down to take the skin bag she held out to him, their hands brushed. And she flung up a second pouch, a water skin.

"Many thanks, quiet Soillse," he said, looking down at her. And then as he thought to speed away, something in her eyes caught his. And a sudden ache flared in his chest, a longing as strong as the one he'd felt for freedom that night by the standing stone skyturns ago. In this moment, he realized what he was feeling belonged to her, this pang that tore at his heart. Soillse felt this for him! Her green eyes softened on his as she realized he finally understood her need of him, and then shaking his head to clear it, he swung the horse hard toward the ridge.

But Duneil stopped him once again, quickly flinging a rolled fur onto the horse's back. The animal's ears flattened as Fìrinn dug his heels into its flanks, and then it exploded into a gallop up the path. Within moments, Fìrinn, the horse, and Bana Dhia disappeared into the forest.

It was early dusk as they crested the last hill, the days winter-shortened now. Fìrinn raced the horse toward the broch, the round, thatched stone tower above the palisaded wooden huts there in the distance, on the low rise beyond the river. The curved hills to the west were silhouetted in the evening dusk, moving Fìrinn's heart deeply as he remembered the stark beauty of his home tuath. Breathing heavily, the stallion took the steep descent down from the overland track onto the flatlands, as Fìrinn leaned low against him, pulling his hand along its sweat-soaked neck.

"It's nearly done, boy. There's oats an' water up there. See the huts? Come on, one more push." And they sped across the moor.

They'd rested only briefly during the night, when Fìrinn stopped to water the horse at the broad river beneath the Cuchullin mountains. He remembered watching the moon ripple into ivory flakes in the burn as the horse drank, while he begged the Goddess to keep his Ma alive for one more day. A dark form, trotting through the grasses, had startled him then, and he'd reached for his dirk, unsure what kind of beast it might be. But he'd chuckled as a wet nose nuzzled his hand, and then he let Bana Dhia curl over him under his fur, both of them shivering in the winter air for a brief nap.

Then once again, he'd stopped this morning, when they crossed a burn cascading between the rocks on a partially washed out section of the western track above the shore. And the stallion had lowered his head there, refusing to budge until Fìrinn let him drink. Then it sidled to a clump of wild barley growing in the drippings of the burn, the horse defying all Fìrinn's urgings with wide-spread feet, until it gobbled every stalk. So in the end, Fìrinn had slid off and washed his face in the cold water, glad for the bracing wakefulness after his nearly sleepless night.

It was dusk now, the afternoon drizzle long since cleared. Stars were twinkling in the night sky, and a gibbous moon rose over the eastern hills. Fìrinn whistled as Bana Dhia, tongue hanging, splashed through the burn behind them. As they came up the last small rise, Fìrinn's eyes darted through the yard to see where the torches were. He saw no bier laid outside the broch, on the rocky knoll above the huts of the clan, circled on the moor a short walk east of the sea loch beyond. Good, I'm in time, Fìrinn thought.

He stumbled to his knees, as he leaped to the ground with the horse still running. It trotted off in the direction of the mares above the stream. And in two strides, Fìrinn crossed the small earthen yard and bent low through the stone entrance passage into the broch. No clansman waited there in the guard cell to stop him. And as Fìrinn emerged into the large round hall of the broch, cook gasped and hurried to hug him. And there was Ma, laid out near the central hearth, holding his baby sister. But the chief sprang up in front of Fìrinn, putting both hands out to stop him.

"Tis ill that ye've come," Speireag said in a harsh whisper, slapping his hide breeks. "Ye'll just upset her."

"Speireag," the queen said in a wavering whisper that stopped the chief cold. "Tis more ill fated to block the wish o' a dyin' queen. I'd have gone long syne, but for this."

Frithe lay on a pallet under furs, half hidden in the dark and the smoke. Firelight flickered over her face, which already looked bluish in the shadows. And Fìrinn took a sharp breath as he knelt beside her. She looks like a corpse already with those cheek hollows, he thought. Can this skeleton really be Ma? Her hair, once shining like water, was now dull, and her skin was the color of frozen milk. Her eyes, pupils wide, looked like dark moons in a pale face. As Fìrinn stared, the chief threw up his hands.

"Even in the death cradle, she orders me!" But then Speireag turned back to her and knelt, taking up Frithe's hand, her fingers as white as split birch wood. The chief's dark red hair was wild, his face flushed in the firelight, and he, too, had lost weight, his hide breeks and woolen shirt hanging loosely around his frame.

"Ye'll no punish him," the queen breathed, and the man bowed his head, groaning. Then she reached up a trembling hand and laid it on the chief's unruly hair. "Speireag," she whispered, her fingers dropping softly to his cheek. "Ye alone drew me from the forest....wi' flyin' feet I came to ye...an' when ye follow this pathway after me...I'll fly again to greet ye...love!" And the passion in her final word sent a shiver through them all. Fìrinn gulped and sat back, pulling his arms in around his waist. He felt uncomfortable with her eyes holding Da's that way. And then the chief dropped his head into her lap as his shoulders heaved. As she held Speireag there, Frithe fastened her gaze on Fìrinn. Reluctantly, the ladd looked at her again, and the intensity of her eyes absorbed him, the low green fire burning in them still. Fìrinn's heart sped, as he was drawn closer to her face.

"Me sweet Fìrinn-ladd," she whispered. As the king snorted, she pulled the chief's face tighter into her belly, sighed, and laid her other hand on his back. Still looking at Fìrinn, she continued. "Ye I loved like the earth itself. Sweet as honeysuckle it was to mother ye." She took in a low breath, gathering her strength. "Ye must no forget!" Then she paused, noisily clearing her throat. "Ken that I'll come to ye. I ken no when...the Goddess chooses. But come to ye, I will; it's already been granted." And drawing quivering fingers across her lips, she took a long shuddering breath as her throat rattled with the death juices. Fìrinn shuddered at the sound, leaning in closer to hear. But more than mother love burned in her eyes now, for already the Goddess had joined her. And it was the Goddess, Who spoke to him now.

"Fìrinn MacSpeireag, I lay this geis upon ye. No weapon shall ye use to kill any man or beast, except to save yer own life, no idle kills, and <u>none</u> against the wishes o' the Goddess. None!" Frithe's voice was hoarse but strong now, her eyes aflame. And then suddenly, the power drained from her face, and her eyes grew darkly soft as she glanced at Fìrinn again. "Remember, ladd," she whispered.

"Noooooooooo!," the chief screamed and rose. "Ye canna <u>do</u> this, Frithe! Ye'll <u>ruin</u> him! He'll <u>never</u> win the kingship competition noo! <u>Curse</u> the Goddess! Aauurgh!!!" But Frithe only waved the chief's words away like thistledown and whispered a charm to clear the broch of evil. Then she beckoned Fìrinn to come into her arms, and love flowed like the burn in spring from mother to son, soothing his gut and stirring his heart. Had there been some time before this life when he'd known her, too? He thought so, for her love warmed him to the core. Did she glow? Did he?

Frithe closed her eyes then, slowly, and Fìrinn felt himself drifting to another world, a sky-blue heaven that was more peaceful than anywhere he'd ever been. And then the trembling left her fingers and her eyelids, almost imperceptibly, until not the slightest fluttering remained, only stillness. And cook began to wail. And then in a few moments, the bodhran (bahrain, a flat hand-held drum) began its slow beating outside the broch door.

The chief sat up and shoved Fìrinn aside, listening to Frithe's chest for long moments. Then he rose quickly, yanking Fìrinn up as well. Grabbing the boy hard across the back, Speireag moaned, as Bana Dhia growled and started up from the hearth. She bared her fangs at the chief, who never noticed, as he fell on his son in a bruising embrace, weeping and groaning.

For all the distance Fìrinn felt from his Ma during the long skyturns away, as he saw her face go still, a sharp pain ripped through his gut. He felt gripped by a rough hand, and yanked out of the earth, then tossed away like a weed with his roots torn off, to wither in the wind's raw embrace. And his heart felt mortally wounded, as if he wouldna live out the night. And for once, Fìrinn didn't want to fight with his Da, for this pain cut through them both, finally a cause to feel as one.

And then, as clanfolk crowded into the broch, a thick mist crept over Fìrinn's mind, clouding everything, like those soupy fogs off the sea. He saw little and heard less, none of the comforting words of the clanswomen, or their keening chants, or his sister's crying. And Bana Dhia haunted him, nosing his hands, pawing his arms, pulling at his eyes with hers, until finally someone handed him a bowl of warm stew and pulled him toward a pallet. He lay on it and recognized the open smoke hole of the broch overhead that he'd looked at so often as a babe, stars twinkling silently above. A throbbing pain pounded in his temples, till at last he slept.

It was pitch dark when Fìrinn awoke, starting up quickly from the bed furs. Cook's cauldron hung empty above the embers on the hearth, which was banked for the night. Bana Dhia's tongue lapped his ear, so Fìrinn walked to the entrance tunnel, found the wooden bolt, pulled it aside, and both of them crouched out into the night. Ma was there, laid on the death stone between guttering torches and dressed in the embroidered tunic of a queen. The herb woman had bathed Ma, rubbed fats and salves into her, and her skin glistened white in the glow of the moon, long hair shining dark against the stone beneath. Keeping beyond the reach of the torchlight, Fìrinn tiptoed across the yard. Then from the shadows, he traced the ripple of her hair, the twist of the torc around her neck, and the interlacing of the brooch that held her cloak closed over her chest. It was like a dream to see her there, her face so pale, and the blueness clinging to the edges of her mouth. Fìrinn's stomach clenched tightly, and he dropped to his knees to retch.

The chief sat beside her in his fur-lined cloak over heavy woolen breeks, keeping the death watch, slouched in his carven chair. As Fìrinn watched, the man reached out to dip his fingers in the bowl of sacred water and draw them across her forehead, muttering. Once, he tried to hold her hand, but the arm was stiff, and the chief cursed and pulled his fingers sharply away. Shaking his head then, Fìrinn backed toward the broch and let the fog take over his mind again.

The pipes skirled out over the sere winter hills, and the song caught Fìrinn's throat into sobbing. It was the song of their tuath, and she'd sung it to him often as a child. Dressed formally in plaids and ceremonial shirts, the clansmen had led her over the moor, across the flatland and the hills, south to the cairn of the ancestors, her body wrapped in embroidered hides on Da's horse, all the folk walking behind. The wind clawed at all of them, heavy clouds closing them in. It had taken all evening, this march, but now they approach the cairn at the top of the rise above the sea. The cairn was twice a man's height and three times wider than it was high, a mound of tumbled stones covered with pale green lichen. As he dismounted, the wind shoved Fìrinn toward the rocks, while the druid, Gairm (gahrum, one who is called) and Speireag grappled with the entrance stone. Kneeling to help, Fìrinn pushed the shrouded body through the low entrance passage, while the druid sang the chant of the dead, fitted the torch into its niche inside, and lit it. Bana Dhia peered after them at the entrance, whimpering, but refused to enter.

The interior was cramped and dark, and the cold made Fìrinn's legs shiver under his plaid. It's like the dolmen in here, Fìrinn thought, feeling the same heavy stillness as he sat back on his haunches in the low-domed central chamber under the corbelled stones above. Instantly, his mind sharpened to hear the spirit whispers; it felt so familiar. There was room only for himself, Da, and the tall druid to squat in the rounded chamber around the body as the thin chant of safe passage to the Otherworld rose from the druid's lips. And then, each gave thanks to the Goddess for this life, telling briefly what Frithe had meant to them, and sending their blessings after her. Slow tears fell down Fìrinn's face, and the chief crouched low on the damp stones, sobbing.

"Death is happiness," the dark-haired druid whispered, looking calmly at them both. "Remember, the Otherworld is free o' pain. Tomorrow we celebrate for her."

Then the druid, crouching and circling Frithe widdershins (counter clockwise), laid the queen in the small elliptical depression on one side of the chamber, east for rebirth. But it was Speireag who placed her possessions around her: the silver brooch she wasn't wearing, her water skin and small woman's dagger, and the shell bowl she'd always preferred. And Fìrinn laid a pouch of oats and a skin of mead by her hands. She'd need these on her journey to her star tuath.

The chant of severing the spirit from this one life rose and was magnified in the tomb. It pounded through Fìrinn's mind, and suddenly he felt Coillore nearby. But Fìrinn only moved his lips in the call for the Goddess, whispering in time with Gairm, asking Frithe to be led safely through the veils and to find peace on the other side. Then hearing whispering, Fìrinn looked toward the opening, but no one was there. Darkness suddenly engulfed them, as the torch guttered and went out. And left in the pitch black, Fìrinn felt a presence slide in beside him and sensed it take Ma's hand, seeing in his mind her light-filled outline rise to meet it. He stared with amazement as the grandmother of the Creator Sun, Màiri, took Ma into her lap and held the broken form, the mother's great love pouring down and binding Frithe's wounds back into light. As the chant continued, Fìrinn's senses sharpened, watching Frithe, sobbing with wonder as she embraced Màiri to her chest. Slowly then, they moved up and out into the night sky. Immediately afterwards, the stale emptiness of the cairn overwhelmed Fìrinn, and he burst into tears. The druid relit the torch and, crouching, led them out into the moon dark night. Which star are ye headed for, Ma?, Fìrinn thought, peering up into the sky. Lowering dark clouds approached over the sea from the west, a gathering storm, the ladd thought. Lone stars twinkled through them here an there, and Fìrinn saw a momentary brightness in the one they called Vega, the star of his tuath, the goddess Arienrhod's city of light.

Cook, her frizzy hair grey now and greasier than ever, scowled up at him in her heavy leather apron. It was firstsky and a grey drizzle had settled over the land. Fìrinn was mounted on Seumus's horse in the whistling wind outside the broch, frowning down at her.

"Ye canna just <u>leave</u> before the feastin', laddie! Dinna ye want to celebrate yer Ma's safe departure? The druid saw her go, an' twas the mother, Màiri herself, came to take yer Ma, he said." Cook looked up at the sky, her blue eyes wide, and a soft smile lit her face, as Fìrinn traced the wisps of white fuzz that framed it with his gaze. His heart softened at the memory of how afraid of her he'd been as a bairn. How could anyone be frightened of this plump, kindly old woman in her work-stained shift?, he thought. Then cook looked back at him and sighed.

"Noo I'll be puttin' up wi' a sour chief for moons on end," she grumbled, "an' carin' fer yer sister night an' day, till yer Da sends her off to her fosterin' in a skyturn or two. Yer Ma left the lass far too young." And cook sighed heavily. "An' I'll be roastin' a great boar half this day, an' ye willna even stay ta eat it." But the hands on her hips didn't fool Fìrinn, for her eyes were brimming as she spoke. Then cook pointed a fat wavering finger at his chest. "Wait there," she said.

Fìrinn looked toward the track south, eager to be off before the rains poured down. Old cook, he thought, always grumbling, always feeding anyone that turns up for a meal, always red and greasy and smelling of onions. And he sent a blessing for ease of toil and spirit after her and lifted the reins.

"Dinna ye dare!" Her voice bellowed out over the broch walls as he let the bridle drop. In moments, she bustled out and handed him a water skin and a bag of food. "Oatcakes," she said, "ye was always grabbin' handfuls when ye was wee. Do ye ever think o' us?"

"I miss yer boar stew as much as I miss her," he said, breaking into a shy smile. And then a flip-flop in his chest made him suddenly think he might never see cook again, either. And, on impulse, he grabbed her hand and kissed it. Then, swinging the animal south, he dug in his heels and left cook gaping after him.

Fìrinn wanted to leave the grief behind as well, riding like a madman across the bare flats and up into the high rocky track that hugged the hills along the western coast, feeling the wind tear through his hair as he galloped. But the sadness bit too deep, startling him with the depth of its talons. He could smell the rain coming, and mist nestled in the clefts of the hills here and there, clinging to the edge of the shore below. Before long, he came to the headland above the cairn where his Ma's body lay, and he stopped there to whisper good-bye to her one last time.

Then suddenly on a whim, he flung himself to the ground and scrambled down the bank and up the low rise, where the cairn stood in the thin swirling fog, like a sentinel over the bay. Weeping in the damp, Fìrinn scrabbled in the earth for rocks, digging them out with bleeding fingers. He chanted the song of parting as he raised his own cairn for her, a small one beside the great one of the tribes. And then with a wild cry that he sent howling through the veils after her, he ran down the rise and climbed the rocks again, mounting the stallion and galloping southeast. Bana Dhia, racing after, howled a long reply.

Unbeknownst to the ladd, Coillore spent a portion of his predawn meditation time sending the light of the grandmother goddess, Mairi, around Fìrinn until nearly Midwinter. The old druid ached for the boy, having known such grief himself, though more for his Àilis than his old Ma. And Coillore hoped to complete just one more lesson before the winter solstice, if Fìrinn's heart had eased enough, for it would bring great joy. But not until firstsky, a few days before the solstice, did Coillore sense a real easing in the ladd, and so he hurried that afternoon to bring Fìrinn to his hut.

It had rained for four days straight, though the clouds were beginning to lift now. And Fìrinn was only too glad to get out of the muck of the yard, though the path beside the burn through the birch wood was slick and treacherous, soaking through even his oiled boots. But when they reached the hut, the druid handed the ladd a dry pair of hide breeks and slippers to put on and waved away the memory stone Fìrinn began to put on his brow.

"Nah, nah. Ye've enough weighin' on yer mind, ladd," the druid said, handing the boy oatcakes dripping with honey as Fìrinn's eyes lit up.

"Me favorite!," he burst out.

"Aye," was all the druid said, as the ladd savored every bite. "I'm sorry for yer loss, Fìrinn. I feel it, too."

"But it's better today, Coillore, an' I dinna ken why. The grandmother's helpin' me, for I've felt Màiri's light around me heart ever since I got back to the tuath." But the druid only turned his face to stir the gourd soup on the cauldron and smiled quietly to himself, looking elflike with his long hair, wrapped up in his furs. They sat by the fire in the wee hut, warming their toes, until this rare relaxation by the hearth finally eased the cold in Fìrinn's bones. And then the ladd took a deep breath and smiled at Coillore.

"Do ye want a lesson today, laddie? It's a happy one, might ease yer heart," the druid said.

"Aye, then," Fìrinn said and nodded, surprised Coillore was giving him a choice at all. So the druid leaned over and drew a pentacle in the earth beside the hearth.

"This child heart flows through the Plieades, ladd. But in the body, it infuses the thymus, the high heart, as ye ken. An' it's the light structure o' the girl aspect, eh? This child heart is the pentagram o' the land o' dreams come true, for it creates the magical child or the rainbow body within. That's the template o' the divine child ye'll be in the Otherworld after ye leave this world o' sorrows, an' yer future self in that golden age to come on earth, too. On earth, this child heart light structure anchors into Eire, the most magical land on earth."

And with his staff in the dirt, the druid scratched a boy, marking six lines across it from the top of the head to the bottom of the spine. "These bands are the chakras, ladd, wheels o' light that spin on the front o' the spine in the same colors an' order as the rainbows ye see over the sea loch after a storm. Red at the bottom, movin' up to orange, yellow, green, sky blue, indigo, an' violet." And Coillore's eyes shone as he picked up a small quartz crystal and held it in the late sun's rays from the window to send a sparkling rainbow onto the hut wall.

"Each person's final lifetime'll be attuned to the buildin' o' this inner rainbow body, an' once created, it canna be unbuilt. An' because it's helpin' birth an inner bairn, it's the goddesses o' this pentagram who set the rate an' flow o' these seven rays into our lives.

So, each o' these regents create one facet o' the inner forever child's dreams, seven in all. An' these seven rays carry specific messages an' influences that flow through bands o' light across our bodies, the rainbow o' Sith's next seven generations o' bairns, too, that I told ye about before. These child heart regents coordinate the lives o' all on earth to prepare the way for these next seven generations as well. Each generation is committed to a different hue o' this rainbow, too, as well as bringin' very specific changes to earth life, Fìrinn. An' through these progressive waves o' change, the child heart is slowly creatin' the template o' the magical child all across earth.

By chakra, this template is: one, belongin' in our original Creator Sun families, tribes, an' ancient spiritual an' cultural traditions; two, intimacy wi' all life, especially our families, an' sensual connections wi' earth as well; three, livin' our highest destinies wi' members o' our Creator Sun family on earth; four, union o' hearts wi' one true love in shared world service, work that'll lift the entire planet in some way; five, lifelong service to Love an' God/Goddess, an' helpin' the earth an' those less fortunate than ourselves; six, livin' in a community o' our Creator Sun family members that carry on the ancient cultural practices o' the specific ethnic realm o' heaven we were once created into, a community that upholds an' works within the laws o' the father's kingdom an' does the specific work our own clan there is committed to; an' seven, union wi' the Great Heart or the One Beloveds in every moment, Love, in other words, wi' frequent times o' personal communion an' ceremonial worship to connect wi' Them.

There are twelve regents in the child heart pentagram, two in each star arm, and two in the center, each set overlightin' one band o' light, eh? It spins followin' Maighdean's 13-moon manifestation cycle, but this pentagram revolves <u>twice</u> durin' each skyturn, each set o' regents takin' one moon every half skyturn, beginnin' 4 days after Midwinter. But that's only twelve moons, eh? The seventh band o' light, purple, an' the 13th moon o' this virgin cycle is overlit by the high priestess o' the Creator Sun, Mona o' yer first lesson. See?, laddie, the child heart spins through the year as happily as those whirlygig leaves floatin' to the ground." And with a grin, the druid tossed some maple seeds into the air.

"These bands o' light cycle through our growin' skyturns, too, the 7-7-7, until the end o' bairnhood at age 21. Remember how each sheath o' light within has mind, heart, an' action ethers? Well, durin' the first seven years, only the mental ethers o' each bairn are open an' flowin', wi' each year focusin' on one o' these rainbow levels more than the rest. Age seven marks the openin' o' the emotional ethers, going through these bands again for seven more skyturns. Then at puberty, about age 14, the action ethers open as well. An' the cycle through the chakras begins again.

An' it's Tara's teeth that mark these 7-7-7 shifts o' growth, the baby teeth fallin' out around the time the emotional ethers open. Then the adult teeth begin to emerge, an' when they are nearly all in place, all but the final wisdom ones in back, this marks the time when the action ethers open, along wi' sexual maturity, about age 14. From then on, all three ethers o' mind, heart, an' action are flowin', even though it's only the outer sheaths o' light that are open durin' these adolescent years, hm?

The same chakra cyclin' happens through each seven-day quarter moon as well, red on the first day (Monday) an' on up through the week. An' the weekday mornin' ye were born on'll tell ye which color ye're spirit is most connected to in this one lifetime, eh?

In the center o' the child heart sit the virgin healers, Sirona (sheerohna), an' Dion Cècht (jeean caycht). In the star arms around them (sunwise) sit: the fae infants, Ròsin (rosheen, little rose) an' Ruari (rooahree, red king); the toddler cherubs, Cliona (cleeoona) an' Daineal; the human children Siannon (sheeannon, Shannon) an' Dairè; an' the virgins, Boand an' Nechtan. Then, in the apex o' the pentagram sit Erin an' Padraig, sovereigns o' the royal land where every bairn is king an' queen o' their own wee world, an' manifestin' is as easy as laughin'.

Sirona's a sweet girl goddess, an' her task is to bring the light o' Abaid o' the Creator Sun into every wee lass, that sweet lovin' kindness they all radiate, eh? But where Abaid wants to connect wi' heaven in meditation mostly, Sirona's very grounded in her love. For Abaid heals the spirit, but Sirona heals the body. For she creates lymph, ladd, sendin' that lovin' kindness river arround any invasion o' darkness that comes into the human form. An' o' course, all darkness melts into it. Sirona coordinates the cosmic magical child impulses, too, so quite a powerful young lady. Her star system is Sirius, ladd, an' her fruit, elderberry, an' her ray is indigo.

Sirona's consort, Dion Cècht, is in charge o' bringin' those words o' truth from Uan into each physical form, too. Whenever there's a dark intrusion in the body, Dion Cècht surrounds it wi' this strong truth force, so evil canna penetrate very far. For Dion Cècht wants to put Uan's otherworldy calmness an' the protection real truth provides into practical application in the world, too. In time, these'll be called T cells, Truth wi' a capital T, the letter o' holdin' firm in darkness. His truth an' her lovin' kindness are an' unbeatable combination, eh? He streams from Sirius, too.

But let's move to the star arms noo. In the first one sit the fae bairns, Ròsin an' Ruari, overlightin' the first chakra, red, as well as the first two skyturns o' life. For every infant has a fae nature till the age o' four, ladd. Ròsin's specialty is anchorin' the identity o' the magical bairn within into each earth life, along wi' that happiness to be alive she's so full o', eh? She kens excatly who she is, her forever self noo.

An' she brings in connections wi' each infant's tribe on earth, the tribal an' family structures it'll be livin' in its whole life. These human family patterns always fall short o' heaven, though, coverin' that rainbow child up. Ròsin's chakra meets each person's life stream comin' up the root from Màiri, too, so any threats to life an' havin' the stamina to live through them, come from this infant goddess as well. She's a warrior, this wee powerhouse.

An' whenever we're in danger o' flyin' off into mental realms or speedin' up too much, at anytime throughout life noo, Ròsin'll bring us down to earth wi' simple tasks that ground our spirits back to earth again. She links to the action center in the base as well, keepin' us movin' on our path. She's quite the sensual wee goddess, too. All these child heart goddesses create berries, ladd. Her's is red currants, an' her star is Halcyone in the Pleiades.

Her consort is Ruari, overlightin' ages two an' three. At age two, the phallic force opens, the will to action o' the little boy that streams from Finn. An' watch out, for when the bairn's personal will is unleashed, he can be quite insistent about havin' his own way, the wee king this regent is named for. Ruari's action stream brings in the restlessness o' wee laddies as well, always wantin' somethin' to do.

But it's primarily the seeds o' the forever boy's gifts to earth Ruari overlights. These'll always clash wi' the way things are done in the bairn's family, so the first inklings o' difficulty'll surface durin' these two skyturns. But Ruari brings in startlin' openin's and day-to-day miracles, too, sparklin' stones or fiery dawns that keep the bairn believin' in the power o' love. An' Ruari awakens the great playfulness an' humor o' the inner laddie that folk o' Eire are reknown for as well. Ach, Ruari ever smooths the way wi' those laughin' eyes o' his.

All right, the next star arm then marks a shift to the inner cherub nature, which is active durin' the next four skyturns. Cliona (cleeoona, shapely) is the lassie cherub, an' she opens the feminine pleasure stream. This is when sensuality lights up, ages four an' five, plus awareness o' physical beauty an' the feminine wiles o' relationship. Hers is the next color o' the rainbow, too, orange, ladd. Cliona's regency is intimacy wi' the physical world, links that nourish the lass within, especially.

An' always at this time o' life, some deep connection wi' earth life'll be made that'll become a lifelong interest an' refuge, the way yer Ma loves the forest, always an attribute o' the forever child within. No only that, but the trees near yer Ma are bearin' specific wounds to help her on her path o' life, real brothers an' sisters in darkness. Very often, cherub brothers or sisters that ye knew in Paradise choose to be born into certain plants or animals to come an' stand by ye durin' the trials o' yer earth life, at any age noo, but especially this one. It's

Cliona who coordinates these an' leads ye to them for solace.

But she also lights up that X in the heart, which intensifies the bairn's relationship wi' the opposite-gender parent, buildin' a strong connection that brings through the light o' the One Beloved, the very core stream, which also awakens the inner beloved o' each bairn. All forever bairns feel the Love o' the Beloveds in every moment, Fìrinn, an' human ones must get used to this strong Love force within, intensely magical as it is. This parent often becomes a lifelong example an' friend, too. But difficulties always arise, for age four an' five is also when those heavy beloved distortions come into place wi' the opposite gender parent, always connectin' to the core wound in some way. Cliona's star is Electra, ladd, an' she creates cloud berries.

Her consort is Daineal, a cherub, too, overlightin' ages six an' seven. He rules personal relationships beyond the family, as well as one bairnhood best friend. An' durin' this age, Daneil'll bring this relationship forward, a human friendship this time, but one who'll nourish yer inner magical child especially durin' the trials o' youth. But there'll be bindin' influences to this relationship as well, especially around the magical child within, yer friend wantin' too much from ye, perhaps. Daniel's star is Canis Minor, the wee dog.

In the next star arm then come the human bairns, Siannon (sheannon, Shannon) an' Dairè (jairee, Derry). Siannon overlights ages eight an' nine an' rules the third band o' light, yellow. An' her regency is the personal power o' the feminine magical child, the growin' girl's identity an' gifts. Hers is a windin' path, leadin' through many temptations, the inner struggle wi' feminine power over others, tryin' to get her own way. It's at this time o' life the bairn is beginnin' to use these to influence her extended family, an' this phase'll set the tone for the lass's relationships in her family an' tribal work her whole life long. Siannon creates gooseberries, ladd, an' her star is Asterope in the Pleiades.

Her consort, Dairè, helps all inner laddies by consolidatin' the boy's identity durin' ages ten an' eleven, bringin' forward the forever bairn's special talents. But Dairè leads all on their path o' power in the outer world noo, he the ambitious one that kens everyone, the friend to all, an expert at drawin' folk to his side. But he can be full o' blarney an' mislead as well, gettin' caught in power over others an' self-importance. In the laddie's contact wi' bairns outside his family at this age, the tone o' work relationships'll be set, lastin' his whole life as well. Dairè brings forward one special friendship at this age, too, but someone more connected wi' yer magical child's talents, whose life work'll be similar to yer own. This friend'll often become a firm support in later life. Yer friend is Ruadh, o' course. An' Dairè's star is the peacock, Pavo.

In the next star arm sit the human virgins, Nechtan an' Maeve (maave), May eve, eh? An' she overlights ages twelve to thirteen an' a half. This is often the time o' puberty. An' while Maeve doesna create sexual maturity, she does make certain this comin' o' age feels quite magical to the growin' lass. For Maeve creates the very first love experience, the first kiss, the first linkin' o' hearts, the heart shift from the child in the thymus to the virgin in the heart proper. That's because, like all virgin lassies, Maeve's main impulse is the union o' virgin hearts, emerald green, ladd, the fourth band o' light. Often this first love is swift, one kiss an' adoration from afar that lingers for moons. But deep is the sweetness built into these experiences, for Maeve ever wants to lead the lass into the memory o' the heart unions o' heaven, to help the human girl keep believin' in love when the trials o' later life come in. An' throughout life, too, Maeve tends the young virgin girl within, sendin' in sweet moments o' love to keep her happy. An' durin' later life, this goddess creates stunnin' linkages o' hearts in the blink o' an eye, male wi' female, the inner virgins noo. She creates green grapes that intoxicate, too.

But in ancient days, reptilians invaded her Pleiades heart star, Maia, too, an' from there, they send out violent illusions. Well, it's durin' Maeve's years o' life these illusions rise up to prevent real partnership. We all have an inner feminine an' masculine, as ye ken,

Fìrinn, so every one o' these regents affects us all.

Maeve's consort is Nechtan, overlightin' ages thirteen an' a half through fourteen. His focus is also on the union o' virgin hearts, too, but in a shared <u>destiny</u> noo. So, he leads the laddie into friendships around certain skills, but also activities an' mentorships that open the doors o' the boy's inner magical male gifts, lettin' these grow an' shine. The ladd's interests o' this phase'll ever build that one future holy gift to earth, too, often in a future life entirely. Often the talents opened durin' these years are brand new, inventions or ideas no one else has thought about. But obstacles to the laddie's dreams'll be built in durin' this time, too, usually folk callin' him a dreamer an' sayin' his ideas are impossible to achieve. But Nechtan'll bring in hope an' hints o' success to keep those dreams alive the ladd's whole life through. His star compound is in Pegasus, ladd.

Then last, come the magical bairns o' the apex star arm," Coillore continued, "Erin (ehrin, Ireland) an' Padraig (padrayck, Patrick). They overlight the magical child streams into earth, she, the lass, an' he, the ladd, o' course. She overlights ages fifteen to halfway through sixteen as well. An' always happy family times o' these skyturns'll be built into the child heart within, to be replayed in the future when such remembrances o' joy an' intimacy may be sorely needed to offset the shadows o' later life. But the fifth chakra is where heaven's will meets our own, remember? So, these young skyturns are also when the work patterns o' the feminine come in, work that'll last her whole life long, the heavy chores o' keepin' house an' doin' whatever's needed in the family an' tribe.

Erin's always wantin' to bring the light o' Eriu o' the Creator Sun into real action in the world, too, so Erin's the one who makes time for dancin' amid life's cares, stoppin' for a bit o' tea on the mosses by the burn, a quick dip in the loch, or invitin' yer pals to the hut to sing after the days chores are done, fun that lifts the inner lassie's heart especially. For she's the bubbly champagne joy o' white blood cells, another o' her regencies. When Erin decides it's time for a break from life's drudgery, there's no stoppin' her, eh?

Erin also brings her fae magic into the three romances that come in durin' these years o' life, as well as delightful robes for the lassie, perhaps, or faery glades to walk in wi' yer love. Erin's fifth band o' light is sky blue, ladd," and the druid pointed to his throat. "An' her star is Pleione in the Pleiades. Her fruit is blueberries, especially the wee wild ones, like her."

Erin's consort, Padraig, overlights the rest o' age sixteen an' all o' seventeen, when the work patterns o' the masculine intensify outside the home, trainin' for real work, lifelong responsibilities. But Padraig is really buildin' in the work o' every forever bairn, instead, what every one'll be doin' when they return to the Creator Sun, always connected to the family purpose o' their clan o' heaven.

At this time o' life, Padraig turns the growin' ladd toward the formal religious traditions he'll be livin' in his whole life as well, deepenin' that connection. It helps keep the inner child heart secure an' believin' in the truths o' heaven, no matter what comes. Another o' Padraig's tasks through life is to tame that strong adolescent will force. An' a holy man wi' the same name'll go to Eire in five centuries an' they'll say he'll banish all snakes from the Child Heart isle, even though there arena any! That's Padraig, dealin' wi' the old reptilian will force!

But like Erin, Padraig brings the fun-lovin' boy, Finn o' the Creator Sun, into real earth life, too, rollickin' play an' jokes bein' his specialty. Durin' each skyturn, Padraig opens the magical boy impulse across the globe, too, four days before the Vernal Equinox (March 17th) that brings in adventures or laughs durin' the ladd's non-workin' hours, for fun is Padraig's middle name!

An' since they overlight the fifth chakra, he an' Erin create through song, too, ladd, bairn songs, though, songs that comfort the child's fears within. It's the small clarsach (harp) o' the child heart fibers in the thymus they play, hm? That's why their star is the wee harp, Lyra. An' will ye notice how his wizard wand supports her, no the other way round?" And Coillore reached up to pull down one of the dried roses that hung from the rafters, whisking away the blossom with his hand. And there below the petals was a five-pointed wizard wand, so tiny and perfect that Firinn laughed out loud.

"An' then, Sirona comes in again, overlightin' ages eighteen an' nineteen, along wi' the first long term love relationship. It's Sirona's task to see that the child hearts o' both partners come into deep connection an' share playful, magical times, makin' certain that romance an' the wonder o' real love abound. This love partner is very, very like each person's final true love, the one that's far off in a future life, but also like the higher self, our eternal true love partner in the Otherworld. For in each lifetime, we get a small taste o' what that relationship'll be like, an' it propels us to learn our lessons.

But always at Sirona's time o' life, the deepest fear o' intimacy that hasna yet been healed will rise up between these partners, preparin' both for the wisdom lessons they'll be learnin' in marriage relationships their whole life long. For it's the sixth band o' light here, ladd, indigo, wisdom.

Then Dion Cècht comes in to overlight ages twenty an' twenty-one. This phase will cause a sharp turnin' o' the destiny stream, some outer difficulty that canna be ignored, a disappointment that's deeply felt. But it's Dion Cècht who brings forward the hope o' freedom for the forever bairn durin' this phase o' life, too. An' late in life, Dion Cècht makes sure every person shares their new gift wi' their tribe on earth that frees the inner child heart o' everyone in some way, bringin' through more time for rest or joy, or helpin' the bairns feels safe, perhaps. Dion Cècht links this child heart late-in-life gift to the next seven waves o' bairns comin' through the Plieades, too, ever preparin' the way for them as well.

Then the seventh band o' light activates as the shift into the ascension path o' adulthood takes place at age 22. It's when the three major fears a person has agreed to face in each particular life activate. We'll go over this ascension path in yer next lesson an' one, ladd. But this seventh chakra purple band streams from Nemetona o' the Triple Spiral, the high priestess o' each community, leadin' all through their lives, always wi' the goal o' unitin' heaven an' earth, eh? So, this phase is ever a call to come Home, a turnin' toward one specific tribe, often a new one followin' marriage, an' a very specific destiny. But it'll build the magical forever child more than anythin' else.

So there ye have it, Fìrinn, the regents o' the child heart, all tidy an' joyful as ye please. May yer own magical child be forever blessed wi' heaven's wizardry an' love, ladd. Off to yer furs noo. I've kept ye too long this time." And Fìrinn hurried out the doorskin before Coillore could think of any more things to teach him.

But there was a lilt in his step, and he hummed his favorite tune from childhood as he splashed through the mud between the boulders all the way down to the tuath. Then, as he curled under his furs and the comforting warmth enfolded him, he slept. But in his dream, he saw a wee leprechaun and a tiny orange faery come in to sleep beside his ears, snuggling in as soft as rabbit's fur on his pillow. And all night long, Fìrinn heard the haunting songs of Eire, full of laughter and the hope of freedom for all bairns everywhere, to be able to play in pure joy and safety their whole lives long, as they once did in the Creator Sun.

Chapter Twenty-Four: Soillse

In her sleep, Soillse could feel the sad welling river flowing through Fìrinn's heart. She imagined holding him in her arms with his head on her chest, brushing her hand across his brow. Something changed when his Ma went to the Otherworld, a subtle opening between them, as if a hidden curtain had been pulled aside. All Soillse knew was that now she could feel Fìrinn's heart beating in the night, even though she was in the round house and he with the ladds in the long house across the yard. And many nights, she lay in her bed furs feeling his sorrow, plus the way her heart flew thinking of him, and trying at last to sleep.

Everyone knew that Soillse's moon time had begun, that it was her courting year. Five skyturns ago, when Ceit reached her womanhood, four ladds had quickly presented themselves to Seumus, asking for her hand. And Ceit had finally settled on a ladd from the clan of the wolf, Buaidh (booay, victor), from the tuath just to the north along the shore. Seumus was pleased, too, for it consolidated the holdings all along this stretch of coast. But Soillse thought it strange Ceit hadn't chosen one of the ladds who'd fostered here, one who knew this tuath and these lands. Stranger still, Ceit spent little time with her betrothed and announced she wouldn't wed till her eighteenth winter. That was late for marriage, as most clanfolk succumbed to injury or disease and didn't live past forty winters. It was best to bear children as early as one could but Ceit seemed in no hurry. And no one was in any hurry to court Soillse, either, she thought with a frown, one cold morning three moons after her moontime began. One of the older ladds, big Allaidh had gone to Seumus and inquired about her. Would Soillse inherit the land right?, Allaidh wanted to know. She's a good worker, he'd said, but he wished for a lass who'd make him chief. And Seumus had grit his teeth and told the boy he felt it likely Ceit would have the land right. And so Allaidh walked away and never so much as spoke with Soillse.

The rains fell heavily during the Rowan moon (January) with no let-up for nearly a quarter moon, and then only a thick mist settling in for a few days, before the rains came on again. Winter was always wet and cold, but not like this. The high king had begun to weaken as well, folk said, and all wondered what his failing health was creating throughout the land. Coillore only shook his head and refused to answer questions about the future, but many at the fostering felt a sense of foreboding, as if a dark cloud had gathered over the isle. Seumus began to ration the barley and send extra ladds off to the hills to hunt, too, while the younger ones gathered whatever food they could find. Some days dinner was only a sodden root mash with a few tough limpets thrown in. Soillse scoured the hills and the bay gathering as well, mostly alone or with Muirn. The extras like bread and stews had been pared down to simpler meals, soup or gruel. Often Soillse spent her days digging roots now or carrying fish up from the shore.

Her womanhood had brought a full load of work; it was true. But there was freedom in it, too, for Seumus could no longer keep her away from the ladds, Fìrinn especially. She held the sovereignty of an adult now, and besides, the land right might be hers one day. At least, that was possible now. And she felt a measure of respect from everyone at the tuath, except Ceit. But when Soillse grew tired late in the day, she still stole brief times with her Aine tree or up along the burn for peace. Sometimes, when she needed a lift, she called in the tenderness of Oghama. And she felt His love warm her heart from within as she sat by the burn or under Aine's branches, and it nourished her, nourished her well.

She grew less wary meandering at the top of the ridge, too.

And on impulse one afternoon in the Birch moon (January) with the evening meal already simmering, wrapped up in her fur-lined cloak, she climbed up to the very top. The small loch, where the false druid had terrified her so many skyturns ago, sat just above the birch wood along the barren track north, so it was private, protected by boulders beyond as well. And this afternoon, it was deserted and peaceful in a thin cold rain, the tall plumed grasses bending over the water, the droplets making silent circles across the surface of the pond. So Soillse went to the water's edge and drew her hands together, then bowed, calling forth Oghama to help heal this place of all residue from that dark time. Then she unlaced her boots, took off her cloak, belted her shift up into her girdle, and stepped into the pool, shivering slightly with the cold. She cupped her hands and knelt to pour a bit of water over her head, asking to be washed clean, as she felt the old fear lace its way through her gut.

Suddenly, there was a heavy stillness and a faint shimmering in the air. And she heard a gentle voice very clearly in her mind, asking her to lie down beside the loch. So she laid out her woolen cloak, wrapped up in it, and pulled on her boots again. And into her mind came the image of Oghama in a simple white robe, standing before her, tall and lean, with long golden hair. He looked into her face, deeply, with His so-blue eyes. And He took shining water in His hands, clear and bright as the diamond light, and washed it over her, again and again.

'You don't have to feel dirty any more,' He whispered, His hands trembling with love. And she could see layers of shadowy darkness moving out of her woman's place and abdomen into the earth as the water of light seeped through her. Then she felt light move up her spine and into her heart, sweet nectar that brought peace in its wake. And she sat up, quivering and crying softly, renewed and full of wonder that Oghama loved even her worst darkness so much. And she knelt then, putting her head to the ground, and vowing to devote her life to Him and to Love alone.

She lingered there a short while, sitting in her cloak under a boulder out of the rain, reluctant to go back to the tuath. But as the winter dusk settled into the darkening mist, Soillse walked down beside the burn path to the round house, and the rain began to fall faster. But Soillse's heart was as soft as Aine's apple blossoms in the warmth of the Hawthorne moon (May).

And then the dreams began, short ones at first, making Soillse's heart race for a few moments, no more. In the first one, Fìrinn was standing at the oak circle where they had their lessons with Coillore, the ladd reaching out to brush her cheek. But it felt like he brushed her heart, instead, for a wild fluttering began there. She whispered his name as she woke and then couldn't get back to sleep till nearly firstsky.

In the second dream, a quarter moon later, Fìrinn hugged her to his chest and kissed her mouth, his lips warm and his tongue reaching. It set her heart on fire that time, too. But it felt like he tongued her woman's place, instead, for it flared into such fiery need of him that it surprised her into wakefulness. And she lay in her furs in a sweat.

Why doesna Fìrinn speak to Da or me, though?, she wondered the following day. Me virgin skyturn is half gone now, and Soillse began to think the ladd might not want her after all. There were warriors who chose not to have the complication of a woman in their lives. Was Fìrinn one of those? She didn't really know him after all. Then one morning late in the Ash moon (February), as she carried a load of kindling into the yard and glanced at Fìrinn, who was throwing spears on the beach, she decided she'd ask him herself, once and for all, and soon.

Messages came for Fìrinn from his Da now and then, brought by traveling druids or hunters, and left at the roundhouse door. Sometimes these held instructions for Seumus, but often they simply asked the ladd to write home about his training and what skills he was learning in the various arts, hunting especially. For Speireag had grown increasingly driven now, determined to have Firinn win the competition that would be held whenever the high king finally passed to the Otherworld.

At the start of the Alder moon (March), Buaidh came running into the yard with a rolled hide for Firinn from his Da. Soillse was lifting wool out of the dye cauldron in the storage hut, hanging it there to dry, for she couldn't hang anything outside in these rain-soaked days. But hearing Buaidh ask Duneil for Firinn, she threw the wool on the line quickly and dried her hands, hurrying out to take the letter. Firinn was up on the ridge today, off with some of the older ladds to hunt.

"I'll take it to him," Soillse said, eyeing Seumus, who frowned as he glanced up toward the ridge. "I need more bracken root for dyes, anyway." Seumus clenched his jaw, running his hand through his greying hair, as he watched her take off the hide apron she wore over her winter shift. But he couldn't interfere any more, so he merely turned back toward the clustered ladds.

"Well, be careful, lassie. Coillore was askin' for the ladd this mornin', too," Seumus said over his shoulder, hoping the call of the druid might bring them back quickly.

She nodded as she turned to go into the round house for her fur lined boots and heavy cloak. The night's frost had barely melted in the cold rain, so the path would be slippery with ice as well as wet. Then Soillse ran to the edge of the yard and waited a moment, with eyes closed. Intent, she saw Firinn clearly in her mind. He was crouched in the wood high up on the ridge to the north, so she started quickly up the path. Pulling an oiled skin around her cloak as she ran, she stuffed the letter under her shift to keep it from the wet. But very soon, her feet began to ache.

Just off the trail through the birch wood, halfway up to the moorlands, she found several ladds shivering, even in their fur jerkins and heavy winter breeks, including Fìrinn. They were tracking a buck, hidden in a thicket a short way off. Fìrinn was able to track and herd game, but with his mother's geis upon him, he could no longer kill. He was crouched under a pine behind some low branches, ready to head the stag off if it tried to escape from the narrow path toward the cliffs. And Soillse waited lower on the path, watching them. As Fìrinn stood, racing to keep the buck on the middle trail toward the headland where there'd be no escape, she noticed the ripple of muscles in his thighs under his buckskin breeks and his wavy chestnut hair, grown long during the cold moons. And she wished, just once, she could have him to herself.

As the buck ran down the steep ravine, leaving Fìrinn behind, Soillse headed toward him. His brows rose in surprise as he saw her, and though the rain had soaked his hair and rivulets ran down his face, he smiled and strode toward her through the muck. As he came near, Soillse took a quick breath and blushed, suddenly shy. What do I say to him?, she thought. The other ladds had already disappeared over the knoll in pursuit of the buck, so she and Fìrinn were alone on the muddy path, surrounded only by bare birch folk and the sound of dripping rain.

"A letter came from yer Da," she called out, handing it to him as he stood before her. "I needed some bracken root, anyway, so I thought I'd bring it up to ye. Da says Coillore was askin' for ye this mornin', too." And her great soft eyes, pupils wide, soaked him in so completely, he wasn't sure how to respond. Freckled as ever, even in the dead of winter, her body held the promise of womanhood now, curves showing where there had been none before. She's lovely, he thought, even in her old workaday shift. And as she stared up at him, Fìrinn tried not to look at those places.

"I wanted to come find ye, anyway," she said all in a rush, and stopped, looking down at her hands, as a flush spread up into her cheeks. "I thought we might...talk." Oh, Goddess, how do I tell him it's me courting year, an' I've waited for him to speak for seven whole moons now?

"Ach, I'm glad, Soillse! I've been waitin' for a sign," he said, hesitating. "Ye said the Goddess forbid me to come to ye before, so I wasna sure..." He breathed this out quickly, then took a deep breath, thinking what more he should say. And suddenly, he felt tongue-tied, his hands especially awkward by his sides, so he stuffed them into the pockets of his breeks. "Come on then. I ken a place," he said after a moment, heading south on the path through the clustered trees. In a short distance, they came out onto the burn path that led down to the tuath, but then they turned right along the wee path toward Coillore's hut, veering left into the wood well before the druid's yew and hut came into view.

There was a stunted Caledonian pine there, behind a thicket of junipers, crowded on all sides by bare winter birches. Fìrinn led her to the far side of the tree and motioned her to sit in the hollow of the trunk, out of the rain. It was small, private, and relatively dry. But she hesitated. She didn't want to just sit and talk. She wanted to kiss him. So after she sat, she took his hand in hers as he squatted before her on the damp needled floor. And then she peeled off her oiled skin for him to sit on. But he only handed it back to her, shaking his head.

"No, ye keep it...," he muttered, looking at her and taking a long breath. "I'm no sure how to begin," he said softly and paused. "I have a question, but it's too soon for that, so..." Soillse leaned over and kissed his hand, pulling it up to her cheek.

"Ask, anyway," she said, so quietly he had to lean in close to hear. Only do ye mind if I kiss ye first?, she thought. It's been so hard to wait for ye, for this. And she felt a shiver move through his fingers. She ran her eyes over his long chestnut hair, high forehead, green eyes flecked with rust, straight nose, and full mouth. He noticed that her cheeks were chilled red by the wind, and as he watched, she licked the rain from her lips. And his eyes dropped to the movement. Her own face was a mixture of Eilid's gentle eyes, and Seamus's slender nose, high cheekbones, and honest gaze. But the green of her eyes was all her own.

"There's only one thing I really need to say, an' lots o' things I hope to share wi' ye," Firinn began, glancing at her lips again and then looking up into the trees. "But it seems rushed like this, an' too… wet." He flicked the water off one hand and shook droplets from his hair.

"But, Firinn, it's time to begin. Me courtin' year's halfway gone noo," she said, a tinge of resentment in her voice.

"But what I wish to ask ye is so… important that I want it to be on a particular kind o' day. An' I have preparations to make." But then he stopped talking, took both her hands in his, and moved his face close to hers, looking directly into her eyes. He thought at first how like they were to Ma's, that same green flecked with rust. And then he was pulled into the green depths of them, as desire flooded his heart. His cheek twitched slightly, and she thought he might be afraid she wouldn't want him, either. Perhaps that's why he's waited so long, she thought, so she leaned over and kissed him lightly on the mouth. A fire sprang up in her woman's place, very suddenly, and she moaned and put her nose into his cheek. And she felt his hands tremble again.

"I'll say yes to yer question," she whispered, smiling and pulling back to rest her eyes on his once more. "Och, Firinn, I've waited for this moment so long. An' I have such dreams!!" She blushed again and looked down at her hands. And then he laughed and put his arms over her shoulders and pulled her close.

"I have those dreams, too," he said with a crooked smile. Then he laid his oiled skin on the ground beside her, and they sat together in the dripping silence. He opened out his plaid and put it over her shoulders, and she snuggled under his arm, aching to kiss him again.

"Is there somethin' wrong that ye've waited so long, though, Firinn, an' noo ye seem to want to delay even more?" She finally asked, for that was what she most wanted to know right then. Her belly tensed as she waited for him to answer. And she wondered at the stillness in him, while her own heart beat as fast as a hummingbird's wings. But Fìrinn only let out a rush of breath and groaned, his head falling to her shoulder.

"I need ye so, lovely Soillse! I, too, <u>ache</u> for this, an' more, far more! But I feel a hurt in ye. An' yer Da mentioned someone hurtin' ye once, too. So, I thought it best to go slowly, no to rush or push ye that way, no one tiny bit! I want to be gentle an' no frighten ye at <u>all</u>. So, I waited for the Goddess to let me ken when ye were ready for me to come to ye...," he stopped and sighed. "An' noo I see I've hurt ye, anyway, by waitin' too long." She felt the utter gentleness of his heart enfold her then, a heart that understood the child in her even more than the woman, and she was utterly amazed by this. She put a hand on his chest, realizing with sudden awe that the gentleness of Oghama was being handed to her through Fìrinn just now. And she took a long deep breath as the virgin lass inside her, who hid from everyone else, unfolded to receive Him.

"Thank ye," she whispered. "Ye are so sweet!" And her mind struggled with the budding understanding that Fìrinn was totally different from any of the ladds she knew, even Da. "If ye have the same dreams I do, then waitin' wasna easy," she added with a wry smile.

"Ach, but when ye prepare for a lifetime, it must be right, though," he said, quite seriously, running his thumb lightly along her palm.

"Aye." She let out a long breath, wondering at the wisdom of the ladd. He's like a man of forty winters, she thought. And then it made her wish the lifetime he spoke of could begin this instant, that she had no more moons left in her courting year. And in that moment, some wildness that wanted to break through his quiet restraint overflowed into her heart, along with a rushing need to join with him. And she turned her face to his and kissed him long. He was tentative at first, waiting, letting her mouth do as it willed. But then he groaned, and she felt a shudder run through his arms as he pulled her close and kissed her full on the mouth. The flaring in her woman's place grew stronger, and she breathed quickly, nuzzling against him. But he backed away slightly, his lips still lingering near hers.

"Tell me o' yer dreams, Soillse." he whispered. "Will ye?"

"Aye," she said, shaking the raindrops from her hair and leaning back on the pine. "I saw ye in me visions once, a long time ago, even before ye came to the fosterin'. In me mind then, ye stood on a mountain at the edge o' a pinewood, lookin' down at yer tuath. That was when I was wee, an' me Aine tree said I'd known ye before, many times in fact, durin' lives before this one. Coillore says that, too, but he willna tell me much. An' then last fall, after me moon times began, in one dream I saw ye in the robes o' the high king o' the isle. An' we were wed an' lived in a cottage by the sea near the Ard Righ's (high king) pavilion there. But then in another moon-time vision, there were long skyturns when ye werena wi' me. An' I dinna understand that one at all." She paused, glancing up at him, and blushing to the roots of her hair, "An' then....there are dreams where ye're kissin' me, kissin' my...all o' me, joinin'." And she turned and put her lips on his again, opening hers slightly. He kissed her deeply, moaning a bit. But he pulled away suddenly and held her face a long moment, running his eyes and fingers over her cheeks, her mouth, her brows, her ears.

"Ye are <u>so</u> beautiful, Soillse! I can hardly believe this moment's finally here. An' ye're so <u>open</u>! I have dreams o' ye, too, every night! It's been a wee torment to feel so much an' no be able to....touch ye! Me dreams are joinin' dreams, every one! Should I say I'm sorry for that? I dinna wish to upset ye, lass. That'd be the last thing I want."

"When a ladd comes to me carryin' the light o' Oghama in his heart," she whispered softly, "he'll find nothin' but a warm welcome waitin' inside." And she smiled shyly up at him. "Me virgin skyturn's halfway through, only seven more moons o' waitin', Firinn. An' then there'll be no more delays, for I want to join wi' ye more than anythin' else I can think o' in this world! Well, that an' askin' me to be yer wife." She giggled, covering her mouth with her hands and then reaching her face up to kiss him again. As he moved to hug her, his hand brushed lightly over her breast, and he groaned softly as his other arm trembled across her shoulders.

And then, the rushing river within became a fountain she could not hold back. She kissed his mouth, his eyes, his ears, his neck, moaning as she went. And then she put her hands under his jerkin and brushed them over his chest, hoping her fingers weren't too cold, unable to restrain herself. Suddenly, she felt the hardness of his manhood against her leg and moved her hand to stroke his breeks, but he pulled her fingers away.

"I want this, too, more than any other thing, lassie, like ye," he said, breathing heavily, "but I've dreamed o' just the way I hope it'll be, the special place an' the time we take to learn about each other first. Yer willingness amazes an' delights me, Soillse, for the ladds speak o' havin' to hold back at first or even rush their women sometimes, if the waitin' takes too long. That I <u>willna</u> do! But please understand, Soillse, I want these virgin moons o' courtship to be somethin' ye'll cherish yer whole life through, our first joinin' especially. Coillore says women hold strongly to these first times wi' their man, rememberin' an' savorin' them for long skyturns. I want it to be magical! An' just noo, I'm sweaty wi' the hunt an' covered wi' mud. It's no what I hoped for, no at all, lass." He took her face in his hands and looked into her eyes, and a slow smile spread across his face. "But I <u>will</u> come to ye, I promise, <u>soon</u>. An' then ye can do as ye like wi' me. The mead o' ye is the most intoxicatin' drink, lass, just the lookin'!"

Soillse felt a tingling down her scalp as he spoke and then the utter rightness of his wish. And again, she felt Oghama speaking through Firinn. And once more, she was amazed, for she, too, had heard stories from the women about men who prodded to join with their wives without a thought for whether the woman was ready or not. Sine especially joked about the way her man rushed through their joining. I should've known a ladd who loves the tree folk'd be gentle, she thought. And she pulled Fìrinn tighter.

"Aye, I feel the right in what ye say. Ach, but then I'll have to wait longer to hold ye, an' there's a fire inside." She put one hand on her abdomen. "Who'd have thought I'd have such need o' ye so soon?" And she took in a long breath, closing her eyes.

"Are ye always so open, Soillse, so direct like this? It startles me." He shook his head. "I thought to treat ye like a fawn, that women, virgins especially, need extra gentleness an' loads o' time."

"But I want yer passion, too, Fìrinn-ladd!" And he jumped visibly as she spoke, staring at her. "What did I say?," she asked, her brows pulling together in concern.

"Ach, it's just that Ma always used that name wi' me, Fìrinn-ladd." And a shadow crossed his eyes.

"Ach, I'm sorry then, makin' ye sad. I didna ken." She stopped, adding, "It's how I think o' ye."

"I dinna mind, Soillse. Ye could call me anythin' an' it'd sound like music from the Otherworld. Thank the <u>Goddess</u> ye came to find me this sweet afternoon!"

And he bent to kiss her again, moving his fingers over her cheek so lightly, it might have been the wind. Then he stood to pull her up and drape the ciled skin over both of them as they walked slowly up through the birches under the dripping boughs, arm in arm, picking their way through the wet leaves underfoot. As they turned down the path to the tuath beside the burn, the rain began pouring down again. And he held his oiled skin over their heads, kissing her one last time. As they reached the yard, the cold winter wind off the sea hit them, too, but neither Fìrinn nor Soillse noticed it, for inside, they felt only the sweet springtime of love forever true.

Chapter Twenty-Five: Fìrinn

As winter deepened and ice covered the moors, Coillore rescued Fìrinn from the cold of the games early one afternoon to take the ladd to his hut. It was a frosty clear day and the wind whistled through the birch wood as they climbed beside the boulders that lined the burn along the track uphill. Thank the Goddess I can sit before a fire for the rest of the day, Fìrinn thought, pulling his oiled skin up over his head. Even Coillore had an oiled skin across his heavy woolen cloak.

After the druid handed him a pair of dry breeks to put on, Fìrinn lay with a stone on his brow beside Coillore's small altar, healing ancient memories for a while. In his inner healing times, difficulties from former lives on earth rose up at first. And then after a few moons, about the time of his earth initiation in late autumn, Fìrinn felt the memories shift, so he was living in other realms, other star systems, and not on earth anymore. And he knew these fears were from his descent, except that now he was ascending, moving back up to the Creator Sun beginning with Annwyn, the soul realm.

Then Coillore fed the ladd mushroom-chestnut soup that warmed Fìrinn through and through, plus two pieces of flat bread, more than he was ever given at the tuath. So, Fìrinn was sleepy and contented as he waited in the stump chair by the fire for Coillore to begin the lesson.

"Movin' down from the Child Heart, we come to the Holy Family o' the heart proper, ladd, the most powerful regents o' all, except for those o' the Creator Sun themselves," the druid began. But when he saw Fìrinn slump down in his chair and sigh with exhaustion, Coillore decided to wait a bit, and the druid helped gave the ladd and himself to a second bowl of stew, letting the nutty gravy warm them to their cores as Fìrinn rested by the fire. Afterwards, Coillore held his hand over the ladd's brow a moment, drawing out some matted darkness there. And as he did so, Fìrinn felt his fatigue ease. Dry breeks and full bellies are even better than getting out of the cold, the ladd thought, with a wan smile.

"Can ye take a full lesson just noo, ladd? It's no a long one." And Fìrinn sat up straighter, nodding. The druid wore his old workaday woolen robe, sitting by the hearth, his hair blown to a tangle by the wind. How elfin he is, Fìrinn thought, when he doesna wear his formal white robe and focus so seriously on all those teachings.

"Aye, Coillore. I want to ken the regents o' the heart more than anythin'. I've been waitin' for this lesson." But Fìrinn didn't add that he was hoping to hear about the little girl regent, Aine, the one Soillse's apple tree was named for, eager for secrets of this wee goddess he might bring to his relationship with Soillse. So Coillore nodded, handing Fìrinn a handful of honeyed walnuts, watching while the ladd filled himself to bursting and finally relaxed with a long sigh. Then the druid leaned over and drew a Celtic cross in the earth.

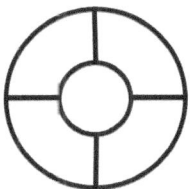

"All right then. These gods an' goddesses o' the Holy Family overlight our families in this world, humans that descend to earth to' be the Creator Sun regents' livin' presences here, for the Creator Sun gods an' goddesses flow directly through all family members everywhere. These are the drivers o' all life on earth, bringin' through the love force o' heaven especially, an' drawin' love into action in the world wi' every beat o' the heart. Great intensity o' life, both pain an' growth, come through our human families, the most movin' dramas there are. An' every one o' these heart regents are as stalwart an' brave as can be, carryin' life's burdens like the great horses they resonate wi'. This light structure anchors into a land in the near an' far east, Russia.

Immediate family members are closely linked all the way down through the seven worlds, Fìrinn, takin' different family roles over an' over, through many planes an' lives. But the important thing to remember is, they all carry the <u>same</u> fears within. So, if a virgin lass in a household is havin' a hard time, for instance, all other immediate family members hold that girl's identical fears in their own virgin lassies within. Families reflect all inner aspects to each other, so helpin' one another brings great healin' to all, eh?

In the upper quadrants sit the parents, Màiri-ebh (mahri-ev) an' Còir (cooer, right, justice). An' her regency is simple, to hold an' hold in utter love, callin' our names in tenderness wi' that soft voice o' hers, her focus ever on the feminine, the flow o' emotion within. This is what she does, especially when there's danger o' tearin' the emotional structures or collapse. She ever calms an' quiets the storms o' feelin' that threaten to fragment the divine child fabric, so carefully built. Màiri-ebh's love is like no other, for she spends countless hours over many skyturns carin' for her family wi' no compensation an' little recognition. <u>She's</u> the one who kens each family member's favorite puddin an' activity, seein' that all have their special needs met in life, ever carin' about the intimate needs o' everyone. This is perhaps her most important regency.

But Màiri-ebh's lessons also have to do wi' devotion to our own, unendin' service to our families, acceptin' all that comes, and endurance through it all. It's a hard road, hers, takin' care o' everyone wi' that great mother heart, often leavin' her own needs untended or last. There is no strength o' love to match Màiri-ebh's in the universe, except Màithriel, Maìri, an' Tara Herself , the mother's o' the Creator Sun.

Màiri-ebh is the wise woman, too, knowin' all there is to ken about herbs to heal her family. An' whenever she comes in to lead the spirit wi' some pithy truth or healin' herb, she appears in humble disguise, an old fish wife perhaps, for Màiri-ebh stays ever hidden in her powers. But any gift she brings'll stream to the very core within, openin' a doorway that'll never close again. She anchors into Siberia, ladd, an' her star city is in Cygnus, the swan.

Màiri-ebh's consort is Còir, the Da, who often appears as a country bumpkin, a stranger, perhaps, though his often humorous disguise is as powerful as Màiri-ebh's. He comes through all human Das, so he brings in protection an' goods for the family, an' stands as an example o' truth an' justice for the household, too. An' his heart is ever full o' warmth an' welcome for his own. He brings Oghama, the Dagda, an' Daiden, the Da's o' the Creator Sun, into every household, a powerful job, eh?

Còir's gifts are usually connected wi' work in the outer world, a sudden chance to earn meat for the family, a new understandin' that'll help wi' work in the future, as well as personal surprises for every one. An' he carefully builds the laws o' love into the masculine heart as well, honesty an' fair dealin's. He speaks out those laws wi' great courage when needed, too. But mainly, he wants to make sure his own are taken care of, providin' meat an' strength for whatever needs to be done in very personal ways, the hallmark o' these regents. He's the work horse, the one who'll shoulder the heaviest task to see his family is provided for. He anchors into Russia, too, ladd, but the northwest noo. His star compound is on Leo, the lion.

Together Màiri-ebh an' Còir's love in each human Ma an' Da does more to bring each lost lamb Home to the happily-ever-after than any other regents in any world, except the Creators Themselves. It is a holy office, parenthood, demandin' the utmost in diligence an' commitment from every parent sent here, though most remain unseen, unrecognized, an' often spit upon for their humbleness an' lack o' beauty. No even world emperors wield such power. An' no other role brings such heartache, richness o' love, an' fulfillment in the end as parenthood.

Each moon, these two regents bring in the fears an' truths o' emotion sent down from the Creator Sun to activate an' heal within each family, all that's meant to be integrated into the inner mother an' father o' the heart over these short lunar cycles, Màiri-ebh, the feminine impulses, Còir, the masculine, eh? But through it all, Màiri-ebh an' Còir choose carefully how much pain each individual can bear an' how much to withhold for another moon, holdin' each human in tender love as they climb.

But let's move to the wee lass o' the heart noo, hm?" And Fìrinn perked up, shaking the fatigue out of his head and taking a long sip of tea, wanting to hear every detail. "The girl o' the heart is Aine, same as Soillse's apple tree. An' Aine's main impulse is gentle understandin' o' all others, her love as personal as all the rest. She wants to feel the hearts' closeness wi' everythin' she sees. All girls carry this need for intimacy, <u>emotional</u> closeness especially, one-to-one time, linkin' the inner bairns especially. The inner girl's spirit withers up wi'out it, ladd. It's the emotional burdens Aine likes to help carry, an' she's the peacemaker in the family, too. An' mind, we all carry this aspect inside, no matter how old or hardened we become. When ye marry, Fìrinn, <u>talk</u> wi' Soillse. <u>Often.</u> An' <u>hold</u> her even more! It'll nourish an' settle the lass within ye both." Fìrinn smiled and nodded. I knew I needed this lesson, he thought. "Aine links to Eriu, the wee fae goddess o' the Creator Sun, the wild rose, remember? So she brings through play an' fun, too, all the little girl impulses for the family; tea parties, playin' house, song, an' dance. Aine's star city is also in Cygnus.

If ye look at the heart, ladd, ye may notice an x o' light there, inner channels linkin' the lass o' the lower left wi' the father in the upper right, an' the ladd in the lower right wi' the mother in the upper left. There's a strong pull in these channels that brings these two pairs together. It'll be part o' the flag o' Alba one day. An' because o' that x in the heart, Àine is deeply drawn to Còir an' his home buildin' impulses. Mind, these arena the extravagant Dagda world-buildin' structures. No, they're simple ones like helpin' wi' chores. An' she'll take on any task to please him, too, often those no one else wants. Plus Àine wishes to keep her heart an' actions ever pure, doin' all that's right, an' followin' Còir's example. She has an inward meditative nature, too, wantin' quiet time every day to talk wi' him an' feel what's best for her to do. But she's a powerhouse, as all these heart regents are, an' her impulses o' the heart will certainly be put into action, quiet though she seems, for she's the most determined o' the lot. An' her little girl sweetness helps everyone far more than they realize. Còir's influence helps her easily determine truth an' falseness in others, too, an' she sticks to his truth like glue! She may no fight like a ladd, but she kens what she thinks an' what's right for her to do. She anchors into the pony lands o' Russia, the belly, the east.

Niall (neeal, champion), her consort, wants to carry the load to the very end, too, workin' harder than all the rest to see that heaven arrives. He's the pony that carries the packs o' everyone, the beast o' burden, takin' on the dirty heavy jobs no one else wants, the physical work noo. It's one o' the hardest tasks, this, restrainin' what yer heart wants for long moons or skyturns till the Creators bring it to fruition, helpin' build the dreams o' others, instead. That's Niall's specialty, though, carrying the heavy family load till his true light shines through. He, too, is gentle, in humble disguise, like all the heart regents. An' like the sound o' his name, kneel, he wants to be in surrender to God/Goddess, too, ever bendin' the knee o' his heart to Their will. For he's a cherub underneath, like Finn, who he serves, bringin' through all the wee laddie impulses for the family. This means jokin', active outdoor play, time in the water, adventures o' all kinds, eh?

Niall's inner heart x channel makes him want to serve Màiri-ebh, the mother. He always carries seeds in his heart o' some change that'll help the tribe in the future, too, for he's ever thinkin' o' her. An' always his changes dinna blend wi' the way things are done, an' he faces these wi' his soft heart as well, bidin' his time for long skyturns till his spirit breaks through in later life. He's as determined to serve love as Aine, but it's Màiri-ebh he's focused on, for underneath, he's always carryin' the mother's standard in his heart. He anchors into the pony lands o' Russia, too, but further west than Aine. An' his star city is on Sadr in Cygnus.

Then in the center o' the Holy Family sit the virgins, Epona an' Eochaid (yawchait, horseman), the emotional powerhouses o' the heart, bringin' through the virgin girl an' boy impulses for the whole family. An' always durin' adolescence, these two'll bring change into every family, both regents quite determined in their views. She's no the soft fawn that Aine is, either, for Epona creates red blood cells that take Oghama's Beloved force to every cell in the body. But Eochaid is the rider from the sky, Pegasus. He brings down Ridire's impulses, the love force in action in the world. This force can create immediate change an' come in an instant to answer any heart's call, shiftin' fear structures almost as powerfully as the Creators Themselves. Eochaid's substance'll someday be called oxygen (ox-djinn, the hugs and kisses djinn). Epona's regency is passion an' Eochaid's is radical change, each breath takin' in their surgin' enthusiasm for the betterment o' earth. Epona, wi' her emotional freedom-from-fear impulse especially, is the driver o' inner change here. She links to Maighdean, pushin' to birth every divine child on earth. An' Eochaid, as buddin' world server, will go the distance wi' out fail, ladd. It's horses their stream resonates with, the horsepower o' emotion that moves everythin' in the universe. There's no fiercer drive than this, the virgins' union o' hearts an' passion within a strong workin' partnership, the core o' every human heart. Eochaid anchors into Mongolia, the horse lands there, an' Epona into the southeast o' Russia, its name meanin' red, her color. Her star compound is the Centaur eh?

Epona's the rose o' the world, too, ladd. In due time, she'll bring the religions o' future days, that'll war so wi' one another, into a unified form that'll replace the elaborate trappin's an' ceremonies o' before. She'll do this by creatin' one single religion wi' a simple form o' worship that'll be held all across the globe. In that future golden age, the few basic truths o' God an' Goddess will emerge into one global creed, an' Epona's simple service will include; a song or two; a prayer for those in need, both near an' far; the triple repetition o' a short message that moves into all three levels o' mind, heart, an' action within (Lectio divina); an' a time o' silence to hear an' feel personal guidance from Oghama an' Tara within. There may be some sacred mead or fruit, too. That's it! Can ye imagine goin' as far as China, for instance, an' findin' a service very like the ones ye were used to at home, ladd? That'll be the way o' life, though, in those miraculous days to come. This'll mark the end o' the deepest divisions between all nations, beliefs. It'll usher in the time when all brothers an' sisters on earth'll finally sit at the same hearth fire." And the druid put his hands together in front of his heart and bent his head a moment, so he didn't see the tears glistening in Fìrinn's eyes as well. Then Coillore let out a long breath, his head still bent, and putting one palm in the center of his altar, he whispered, "This is me favorite lesson, son."

"Mine, too," Fìrinn whispered as he stood, threw on his cloak, and ducked out the doorcloth into an unusually windblown night. And wandering back to the longhouse along the burn path down to the tuath, the ladd felt his mind cleansed of Coillore's wordiness as the wind tousled his hair. So by the time Fìrinn reached the yard, only the gentle holiness in his heart remained. Before entering the long house, he waited a moment beside the doorcloth, taking in a deep breath of earth-scented air, and holding it in his chest a moment.

"Understandin', Coillore called ye, Aine, an' closeness, o' inner bairns especially," he whispered, "what I love most wi' Soillse. Ach, I love ye dearly, too, lassie goddess o' the heart. I didna really understand ye before. But noo that I do, I realize I couldna <u>live</u> wi' out yer sweetness in me life." And as he climbed into his furs, Fìrinn determined to take very special care of the spirit of the little girl in Soillse their whole lives long.

Aine's sweetness permeated his sleep that night, too. He didn't dream, but he felt a petal-soft pink robe wrapped round his body, holding him gently all night long. He woke early, well before dawn, pulled on his buckskin breeks and shirt, and peeked out the doorcloth as a deep pink glow suffused the eastern horizon along the ridge and colored the mare's tail clouds over the loch below. Quietly, with the same holiness still flooding his heart, Fìrinn pulled on his oiled boots, went out, and gathered seaweed from the bay. Carefully, he chopped it into fine pieces, walked quietly up through the bracken, washed it in the stream, and laid it reverently beneath Soillse's apple tree.

It was the beginning of the Ash moon (February), and all longed for the weather to clear and spring to spread her flowered skirts over the hills. But the rains had come in three nights before, lashing downpours off the sea that drenched the land, the sea loch all but invisible. Even Seumus, tough old warrior that he was, felt sorry for the boys, competing in the cold with hair plastered to their faces and mud to the thigh. So for two days, he relented and let the ladds stay indoors by the fire, a first in all his years of fostering. Fìrinn was sitting by the long house door in his hide shirt and breeks, watching the fire and thinking of Soillse, when Coillore appeared at the door skin. And Fìrinn rose to meet him.

"It's time to take ye to the dolmen," Coillore whispered. The druid was dressed in his heavy woolen cloak, a thick oiled skin draped over his shoulders.

"What? In this muck!"

"Aye. Very clear instructions in me meditation this morning. I'd no idea ye werena at yer games as usual. I thought ye might be happy to get away. I'm sorry, ladd."

So Firinn went to his pallet and pulled on his fur jerkin and heaviest buckskin breeks. Then he rolled up his bed fur, threw his winter cloak and oiled skin over his shoulders, and pulled on his fur-lined boots. Clenching his jaw and looking at the boys circled round the fire, Firinn sighed and followed Coillore across the yard.

Glancing at the steely sky as they trudged up the slick rocks beside the swollen burn into the dripping underbrush, Firinn and Coillore moved swiftly through and beyond the scrub birches into the thin forest of beech and oak along the ridge. I get two days off in ten skyturns of fostering, and I have to spend them in a soaking wet dolmen, Firinn thought, his mind darkening as they climbed. The path was barely visible and badly washed away in places, and they had to maneuver over slippery boulders and mud-filled ruts all the way up. Finally, they reached the high moor and headed south along the crest of the ridge. But the moor was worse, sinking bogs and rivulets of water everywhere, and Firinn grew more and more irritated as they picked their way through the heath. When he slipped in the mud and cracked his knee on a stone, he felt like cursing the Goddess.

"Nah, nah, never curse the Goddess," Coillore said, stopping to glance back at Firinn. The druid stood there a moment, wavering. Water initiations are often the worst, he thought, and I have a bad feeling about this one. But the wheel of return has begun to spin for the ladd, and I'm powerless to stop it. This testing'll come to the boy, no matter what anyone does. Already dark forces surround him. So Coillore sighed, turned around, and continued to walk south.

And Firinn felt the old man's hesitation. Is Coillore afeared for me?, he thought in surprise. He had a clammy feeling in his chest, too, and a slow painful hammering began in his head as they walked. Once, his feet sunk into the spongy peat till he was wet to the knee, the water even trickling down inside his boots, soaking the fur. And Firinn glowered the rest of the way. When they arrived, Coillore stopped to light a torch, but even without the light, they could see the dolmen was full of water, brimmed nearly to the sitting stone.

"I canna sit in that all night, Coillore," Firinn said, his voice strident, unaware how unlike himself he sounded. "Already I'm soaked through. I'll freeze up here." But Coillore only stooped to light a fire under the lintel stone. The rain had stopped temporarily, but the wind howled through the uprights, dimming the fire, but not putting it out. And nothing at all could be seen beyond the dolmen in the fog.

"Sit at the entrance then. It'll serve," the druid said tersely. He was surprised and mildly hurt at the ladd's attitude, a boy who'd always been respectful and diligent. As he heated the ritual broth and painted a crescent moon on Firinn's brow, Coillore remembered how severe his own water initiation had been. "The waxin' crescent calls forth the mercy o' Maighdean," he muttered at the question in Firinn's eyes.

As Firinn sat under his furs and began to grow drowsy by the fire, the druid handed him the bitter ritual broth. The fats in it filled the ladd somewhat, calming him a bit. But Coillore watched Firinn's eyelids droop and shook his head, sighing. As the druid turned to leave, he handed Firinn a small wooden carving in the shape of a woman.

"It's the grandmother, Màiri, who'll come to meet ye this time," Coillore said. "Nothin' can come between ye an' yer path, ladd, no the lass, no yer Ma's passage, nothin'. The water initiation's often difficult, so stay alert an' trust. It willna be so easy this time." Coillore's glance was penetrating, his brows pulled together, his blue eyes focused sternly on Firinn's wet face. "Tonight, ladd, focus only on the testin', no on Soillse," the druid added impatiently.

And something in Coillore's eyes made Firinn's heart skip a beat as fear began to fill him. The spirit world willna take Soillse away, too, will they, like Ma, the ladd thought. Why is Coillore being so sharp with me tonight?

"I will no give Soillse up," Firinn snapped back, "no for ye, the Creator Sun, or anythin' else." And the druid sighed again.

"God an' Goddess are in charge o' all worlds, no ye, ladd," Coillore said, his mouth pinched into a line. "An' the only way ye'll ever have Soillse to keep is to follow yer path an' never waver. Ye'll be led through all yer fears, an' ye may be parted from her for a while. But I promise ye, if ye hold fast to the Goddess, the full truth o' love'll be yers in time, to give an' receive at the lass's hand.

Look," the druid said, struggling to keep annoyance out of his tone. He took his staff and in the earth at the entrance to the dolmen drew a man and woman. "Ye an' Soillse," Coillore said. And then he drew two concentric circles above with connecting lines to the man and woman below. Pointing to the two circles, the druid said, "the Beloved God an' Goddess o' the Creator Sun. Love streams from Them alone, flowin' down the inner channels into each person's heart. From there, it's sent out to one another. So the love Soillse gives ye comes straight from the Goddess, Tara, Who's yer true partner, ladd. All love is created here," Coillore said, circling the Creator Sun with his staff, "Ma an' Da love, friendship o' all kinds, beloved loves o' every lifetime, even child love, an' that o' teachers, eh? None o' us create the love force, Firinn. Only the Creators can do that. It's Their gift an' Their force to wield, fully under Their command." And then Coillore pointed to the channel he'd drawn from Firinn to the Goddess half of the Creator Sun, stopping to look directly into Firinn's sullen face. "Ye have many fears blockin' this channel to the Creator Sun, ladd. So does Soillse. An' all those beliefs'll create their likeness into yer lives. Inner creates outer, always, remember? An' the fullness o' love willna come to ye unless all inner fear is cleared away. Then, an' only then, will true love be allowed. For if any fear remains within ye, the outer love that comes willna be pure, canna be, for the wee creator flame at yer own core creates everythin' surroundin' it into life.

For most, further down on love's ladder, that pure radiance o' love arrives only when they return to the Otherworld, for the days o' beloveds on earth are far off into the future. But for ye an' Soillse, it can happen soon, this very lifetime. If ye work hard, laddie, an' place all on Their altar as ye climb, then in time, all will be given. Only after the union o' the Goddess Heart an' yer own occurs will that sublime love, beyond yer imaginin', be sent to enfold ye, straight from the Beloveds o' the Creator Sun. There is _no_ other way. Stay alert tonight noo, _no_ sleepin', laddie."

As the druid spoke, Fìrinn felt a ray of love from Coillore's words penetrate the murky depths of his own heart, and suddenly he felt the wisdom in them. And dimly, behind the old druid, Fìrinn saw the image of a tall god with sandy hair, a father who loved him very much and who'd watch over him this night. Fìrinn's mouth dropped open as he gaped at the druid.

"Ye carry the father in ye, Coillore, the Dagda," Fìrinn said, a tinge of awe in his voice. "He was speakin' through ye just noo. I could see him, just barely." At this Coillore smiled and laid a hand on the ladd's head, as Fìrinn took the figurine and stuffed it under his jerkin. Then the ladd wriggled further into the entrance of the dolmen out of the wet, pulling off his oiled skin and wrapping his fur around his shoulders.

"If ye're no at me hut soon after the skies lighten, I'll come to find ye. If ye're hurt, stay here. I'll ken an' come up," the druid cautioned. "An' dinna leave the ritual space until mornin' comes under any circumstances. Ye're protected here." And the druid traced a circle around the dolmen with his staff three times, the hem of his cloak dragging through the mud. Singing the chant of protection as he went, Coilore's voice was sad and comforting at once.

'They'll never test ye beyond yer capacity, laddie. Dinna fear noo,' the whispered thought came to Fìrinn as Coillore turned away and disappeared into the fog across the moor. But this one'll take all ye have, the druid thought. And keeping that one to himself, Coillore trudged through the heather and away.

Fìrinn sat cross-legged with his back against the upright, wrapped in furs. He closed his eyes and breathed in the damp night air. Goddess, let it be all right, and please, dinna take Soillse away from me, too, he prayed.

'You must sit inside the dolmen,' the Goddess voice said then, very clearly in Fìrinn's mind. 'I need the water to touch your feet, so I can move through it and heal you."

He nodded and sighed, took off his boots, pulled up his breeks, then stepped down onto the floor of the dolmen and gasped as the icy water soaked him to the knee and the wet crept up his breeks, anyway. And then the irritation he'd felt all the way up the ridge rose inside and burst out of him.

"Everyone else gets to sit by the fire," he shouted, fisting his hands. "Are ye tryin' to kill me, Goddess? This is daft!"

But Fìrinn knew that every testing he avoided would be brought in a more intense form later on, and the spirit world could wield intense pressure when the Goddess decided it was time for a lesson to be learned. So Fìrinn simply clenched his teeth and breathed to release the anger and calm himself. The sooner I start, the sooner I get out of here, he thought, and began his chanting, calling forth the Goddess and the testing forces. The wooden doll floated out on the surface of the water and he grabbed it up. Then he called on the spirits of fire to warm his feet and felt a flaring deep in his heart, instead. It held very slight warmth, not enough to raise his body temperature at all. And then he heard a stag bellowing off in the wood beyond the moor and stiffened. Will they send game to test me, too, or is that just to divert me from my purpose? And he refocused on the inner flame, holding the image around his legs and hoarding the brief warmth it gave.

And then the vision took him quickly. He was in a rushing river with his head bobbing above the current, and boulders slid by like huge beasts guarding the banks. He hit his head on one and felt a sharp pain in his right temple. But forcing himself to stay alert, he peered into the rapids as a trickle of blood rolled down his face, and his head began to throb. In the vision, he was fighting for air, gasping and clawing to stay afloat. And then, suddenly, the image of Coillore came into his mind. *'Let the current take ye,'* the druid said. *'Stop fightin' it, an' give yerself to the spirit o' the water. It's life itself.'* Is this a trick, Fìrinn thought, to make me drown? His breath was coming in short gasps now, and he focused on the fear that gripped his gut, imagining both the roiling current and his terror of going under move into the diamond light in his heart. Still, it took all his will power and considerable time to ease his panic.

A drum began to beat loudly in his mind then, and his Ma's face, the crone creases prominent around her eyes, appeared above the water. *'Let the past go, love,'* she said. *'The woman I was is no more. The Goddess is yer Ma noo, Fìrinn-ladd.'* And he began to sob, despite the swirling waters around him. A great cry of grief formed in the depths of his belly and gathered strength as it rose. Dark shadows in the recesses of his gut clung to it, so it became stronger and more intense as it rose into his throat. And then he climbed onto the seat of the dolmen and heaved the doll out into the moor, letting the cry come out of him full force as he did so. A sharp pain wrenched through his chest as the sound exploded from him, a thick caber of anguish.

"There are so many losses," he called out to the night, "too many to name or remember: Ma, the Da I wished for an' never found, me home tuath, the ladd within who hates to hunt, an' maybe even Soillse noo." And he felt some darkness rise within him like a thing alive, dank and squirming, as he shouted, "Ye <u>canna</u> take her, too. Noooo!!!!" As Fìrinn screamed, the demon lifted out of him and flew over the hills, where Fìrinn felt the wind woman gather it to her breast and shelter him from it at last. And he hung his head and took his seat again with his legs folded up out of the water.

And then, after a time of peace, Fìrinn saw in his mind an image of the long ago, a glass city built above a broad turquoise sea. He was standing on a hill there, overlooking ringed canals, and a priest in a grey robe stood beside him. And then Ma, wearing the silver crescent breastplate of the high priestess, walked into the ritual space. She waited obediently as the priest handed her a vial and brought it to her lips. But immediately, Fìrinn realized it was a trick, that his mother was being sacrificed, not honored with the special visioning they'd promised her. He reached out quickly to knock the vial from her hand, but he was too late. She'd already drained the cup and moved to the high seat of the Goddess to welcome the images. Only last week, she'd refused to swear fealty to the new high priest in Atlantis, Malduk, the arrogant one who called himself the only god. That imposter's behind this, Fìrinn thought in the vision. And he moved to steady Frithe as she took one hoarse breath, then slumped to the ground. As she fell, her mouth opened in a scream, but no sound came out.

And then again, Fìrinn was fighting the rushing river in his mind, until it flung him up onto a pebbled island. He lay there, chest heaving and arms leaden from the struggle. But as he tried to pull his legs out of the raging torrent, they felt numb and wouldn't move. So Fìrinn leaned back on the upright and lifted his legs slowly from the stone bench, wrapping them in his fur.

He lay long in a stupor at the dolmen entrance then, and toward morning, more pictures flowed into his mind. He was on a trading ship this time, with both prow and stern curved high out of the water, unlike the low Irish traders that came infrequently to Skye. In this vision, Fìrinn's arms were beyond sore, aching as he rowed. And he was dog-tired. Then came the image of a desert, hot and dry, and his wrists were bound, as he stumbled along behind a great humped beast. And finally, Fìrinn was in a village where dark men beat waist-high drums, nothing like the flat bodhrans of the druids. And the rhythms confused Fìrinn's mind. And then a king, a man as black as night, stood beside a bonfire talking to the people there. He was dressed in a white robe, edged in purple, with a gold circlet on his brow. Fìrinn had never seen the like, but Coillore had told him of the peoples of Africa. And then the vision faded away. Fìrinn could find no meaning in these last images, and his head swam. He tried to get up and shift his weight, but he felt exhaustion in every limb.

The scene shifted then, and a woman called to him from a distance. Her hair was golden-brown, and she held an infant at her breast, watching him from far away. Was this the Otherworld? And he felt the woman's great sorrow, her spirit as tired as his legs were. And then he saw her walking the beach of the bay, here at the fostering. Soillse! Tears flowed down her cheeks as she whispered his name, and the drumming in his mind pounded more loudly, a sinister song. He wanted to run to her, but something held him back. And looking down, Fìrinn saw that he was standing in a jungle, oceans away. And the dark-skinned king and another dark man, the village shaman, were watching him. The air in the jungle was singed with fire, and Firinn felt some lingering danger that he couldn't name.

The image shifted once more, and Fìrinn was walking with Soillse, here on Skye. They were white haired, and joy filled his heart. He felt the streaming radiance of the Goddess above him, as singing waters of light flowed over his head and rippled down his spine. And he leaned back, relaxing into the brilliance, closing his eyes till the horizon began to lighten.

Then Fìrinn stood, leaning out of the dolmen into the dawn and opening his arms to drink the morning in. And for a moment, he thought he heard the distant sound of harps on the wind, and peered through the thinning fog across the moor. But there was just the great hush of sunrise and the flooding tenderness within, so sweet he began to sob. And Soillse's image came into his mind again, the young virgin she was now, and in this vision, he pulled her close and kissed her long. But she shape-changed very gradually, until it was Tara, the Goddess Herself, he held in his arms. And suddenly, Firinn knew that he'd loved Her, the Goddess, for all eternity, and it was Her love drawing him to Soillse, just as Coillore had said. Firinn's legs began to shake then, so he lay down with his arms clasped over his chest, holding Tara's sweetness in his heart as long as he could.

"Nah, nah, we must get ye to the hearth," Coillore said, squatting in his heavy cloak and rubbing Firinn's legs. The druid tried to lift the ladd out from under the capstone into the thin sunshine, but the boy's limp weight slipped out of his grasp. So Coillore rubbed Firinn's cheek briskly with his knuckles, and slowly the ladd's eyes opened. But the morning light stung, and Firinn closed them quickly again. And when he tried to shield them from the brightness, his arms felt so heavy, he could barely move. And when he tried to stand, his legs were numb, though he'd pulled on his fur-lined boots at dawn before falling asleep.

Coillore put his hands more firmly under Firinn's armpits and dragged the boy slowly out into the mud. And Bana Dhia lapped Firinn's face and whined as the druid bent to cover the boy with his fur-lined cloak. Then Coillore knelt and lit a fire, and began to strip off the lad's buckskin boots and breeks. But Firinn just lay there with his head on the ground, his mind groggy, and his limbs like stone.

Then, very slowly beside the flames, Firinn felt warmth creep into his legs. He began to shiver at first, and then a sharp pricking spread through his feet. He kicked both legs to stop it, but the pinpricks only grew worse for a time, eventually easing. Firinn sighed then and sat up slowly, looking east at the sun that glowed golden-peach through the thin mist over the moor. Soillse's face came again to the boy's mind as he put his feet nearer the fire. Can I tell her about this vision?, he wondered. Coillore took a deep breath, put a hand on the boy's brow, and knelt to look him in the eye.

"Well, Coillore," Firinn said, grinning at the druid, "I live."

"Barely," the druid said through a frown, "though I'm sure ye did the best ye could."

But then Ban Dhia shook herself, and droplets flew over them both, making Coillore and Fìrinn smile. And the druid helped Fìrinn put on dry breeks and fresh boots, and gradually the ladd was able to stand.

Slowly, limping, with the druid holding Fìrinn up, they moved across the sodden moor, boggy mud and rivulets everywhere, and down the deer track from the ridge through the oak and beech wood, then beside the swollen burn to Coillore's hut. At least the rain had stopped. This day was warmer than the one before, too, and the sun rose into a clear sky, with wisps of mist softening the edges of the hills and shore. But by the time they arrived, it was midsky, and Fìrinn's legs were beginning to give out. A bluish haze tinged the air, and the owl flew in as they arrived, settling into the great yew beside the hut. Coillore nodded to the bird, but kept moving Fìrinn through the doorcloth. As the fire inside, built far hotter than usual, thoroughly warmed the ladd's toes, Coillore massaged them, singing varied chants for healing. Then the druid ladled stew he'd warmed in his small cauldron into a gourd bowl and began spooning it into Fìrinn's mouth.

"I'm no a babe," Fìrinn said through his soup.

"Nah, nah," the old druid answered and kept on spooning. He filled Fìrinn to bursting with barley an' mushroom soup, spiced with herbs and nuts. And very gradually, the ladd stopped shivering as even his innards warmed again. He wanted to tell Coillore of his visions, but his mind was too tired to make any sense of them yet. And beside the fire, he quickly grew drowsy. So finally, Fìrinn just sighed, pulled his furs up to his chin, and fell into a troubled sleep. And despite Seumus's complaints, Coillore kept the ladd by his own fire for several days, till Fìrinn's legs felt strong again.

Coillore waited nearly two moons after that to begin the lessons again, while Fìrinn's legs grew stronger. But finally, the old druid's patience got the better of him, worried as he was about finishing the teachings before Fìrinn completed his fostering and was gone for good. So one clear windblown eve as the Alder moon (March) ended, the druid took Fìrinn from the yard to his hut and motioned for the ladd to sit on the pallet, after changing his muddy breeks. With the oiled skin over the small window in his west wall rolled up a bit, so a cool breeze cleared the smoke within, the druid, in only his workaday shift, bustled round the wee hut. Coillore's blue eyes were calmer than usual, his face rosy in the hut's warmth, as Fìrinn took off his jerkin and rested on the pallet. Putting walnuts, new made cheese, and flat bread on a large shell, Coillore handed this to Fìrinn, then drew a Celtic cross in the earth.

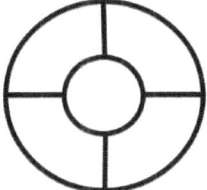

"These are the Pillar realms, the third chakra o' the cosmos, anchorin' into the solar plexus, ladd. That's the top o' everyone's power channel that rises from the loins up the front o' the body. An' each solar plexus carries the template o' personal power in the physical realms raised to its highest level. These Pillar regents are responsible for the ascension path o' adulthood through the six lower worlds, an' they build the basic ten qualities o' God an' Goddess into us over many lives. But the Pillar realms themselves are structured just like the Holy Family, in a Celtic cross shape, except there's a god an' goddess in every quadrant this time. It's ever the same, though: the mother in the northeast, the girl in the southeast, the boy in the southwest, an' the father in the northwest, surroundin' the beloveds in the center, virgins again.

No only that, but these Pillar regents make six concentric pillars up our bodies, just like the rings of a tree. The central axis, the helix o' light that flows up an' down the spine from Tara's root an' Oghama's crown, is overlit by Oghama. The central or beloved Pillar regents surround that, the virgins Aislin an' Colum, holdin' up love's standard in the spinal column. The Pillar bairns o' the girl quadrant come next, Anu an' Beli, flowin' into the thymus, lymph, an' kidneys. Around that come the Pillar regents o' the boy quadrant, Flidais (fleetish) an' Fionn (feeoon). They anchor into the nerves an' brain. An' holdin' all those bairns is the Pillar mother, Cùram (cooram, responsibility) an' her consort Treòraich (trohreeck, to guide or strengthen), flowin' through the waters that move in an' around the cells. Then, protectin' everyone else is the Pillar father, Cead (ket, freedom) an' his consort, Saorsa (soorsa, liberty), in the outer skeletal bones an' muscles. Tara overlights the skin, the greatest protector o' all, soft an' sensual though She may seem. Hers isna considered a pillar, though, nor is the central helix o' Oghama's crown an' Tara's root flow. There are only five pillars: beloved core, girl, boy, mother, an' father, eh?

Let's start wi' the mother quadrant, the northeast, hm? This anchors into the far east, ladd, China. The mother goddess here is Cùram, an' her regency is the inner path o' ascension, the planes o' light o' the six lower heavens, from the lowest realms all the way up to the lower edge o' the Diamond Core, the emotional shifts, the feminine. This goddess overlights the life cycle o' all women from age 22 on, ladd, their inner life noo, for all eastern hemisphere regents are concerned wi' what's within.

Cùram brings forward lessons o' the inner mother havin' to do wi' service to the all, balancin' givin' wi' inner nourishment, no givin' too much o' yerself away. But her greatest teachin' is responsibility for what ye create into the world. She'll show ye in no uncertain terms that yer own fears affect all folk in all worlds, an' she'll lead ye to shoulder the responsibility for healin' yerself. This is the divine quality she builds. Then she'll walk beside ye every step o' the way, holdin' ye in mother love. Her star compound is on the shoulder star in Andromeda.

Cùram's consort is Treòraich, ladd, overlightin' inner growth o' the masculine from age 22 on," Coillore said, "the pursuit o' truth, leadin' everyone up all the inner planes into connection wi' Oghama's divine mind in the Diamond Core. But Treòraich brings in repeated blocks an' obstacles to test yer perseverance, too, lots o' layers o' false gridwork to be healed, before he hands out his pearls o' truth. They arena given easily, ladd, ye must be persistent, eh?

But Treòraich's primary teachin' is the proper use o' yer inner powers, no pushin' other folk around to do whatever ye desire or tryin' to change them in any way, for only they have the power to change themselves. Speakin' an' actin' in yer own truth, that's what he emphasizes, instead. Other folk may hurt ye at times, Fìrinn, but they're only messengers o' yer own fears. An' most have lived through very hard times to do just that. This proper use o' personal power is Treòraich's quality o' divinity to bestow. He's a Buddha, an' his star compound is in Taurus, the Lambda Tauri star. He also anchors into China, ladd.

Below these, in the eastern hemisphere again, are the regents o' the Pillar girl quadrant, the fae/cherub children o' the southeast, Anu an' Beli. Anu overlights the inner growth o' all lassies until the age o' eleven, an' her influence is quite private an' personalized. She builds the structures o' the lass's identity within as the girl grows, the foundation o' the left leg an' hip. Always Anu includes joy an' peace in life, too, wi' memories o' fae friends in Paradise. Her connections to the natural world tend toward intimacy an' touch, that sense o' wonder in the smallest things. Have ye ever stopped to peer at a raindrop, Fìrinn, or touched the inner bark o' a birch, perhaps?" Fìrinn had done both so often that this question simply made him smile. "How miraculous is the upside-down reflection o' the world in that tiny droplet or bark that's as soft as a virgin's thighs. All things have wonders to give us, laddie, an' how impoverished life would be if we never noticed, hm? Anu anchors into Polynesia, ladd. Ye ken how Soillse loves to spend quiet moments in her apple tree? Well, it's her inner fae lassie that's bein' nourished there, hm?" And Firinn sat up straighter, startled to think of Soillse as fae or cherub within. I'll make a wee place for her somewhere in the forest then, the ladd thought, and bring flowers, just like Anu does. It'll ease Soillse's spirit. Why didna I think of that before?

"But Anu is also keeper o' the fears o' the lass, the abdominal sea. Everythin' below the diaphragm is each person's unconscious, where fears from the descent or past lives that havena yet been faced are held. O' course, the wounds o' the descent are repeated in every bairnhood, so it's all the growin' lassie couldna solve an' pushed out o' her mind as she grew durin' bairnhood as well. Above the diaphragm is where the father's light o' consciousness reaches, so all above that level's within our awareness. An' the passage from the abdominal unconscious into consciousness is part o' Anu's pillar, the left side o' the belly, the feminine memories noo.

The dark half o' the fae girl is the keeper o' forgotten tribal an' star family connections an' memories, too, those we've forgotten for long syne. Anu's a very powerful priestess who kens how to shift energy dramatically, through dance especially, but also in song an' ceremony. She has massive amounts o' information to give the world that'll be kept hidden till that golden age to come, when she emerges from her dark shroud into the light. Followin' the path o' facin' fear to its very end in order to birth Paradise on earth is her quality o' divinity to bestow, along wi' lovin' everyone, even those who treat ye hatefully, ladd. People see her as evil, but that's pure illusion. For she's the strong sister who walks beside them through every darkness they must face, right to the end. She loves all children o' the One, dark an' light alike, a depth o' love the rest o' the world has yet to acquire. A tower o' strength in difficulty, the dark side o' Anu is, anchorin' into Africa, eh? Anu's star city is on Camelopardus, ladd, the giraffe.

It's because Africa's the land we came to after we were captured, tortured, an' forced into slavery in the dark Orion work camps o' the Diamond Centerpoint realms. We were brought to earth to mine gold for the Borg kings here, who wanted all truths o' Oghama that are structured into gold removed from the earth, truths about fair dealin's in commerce especially. An' just as the Borg planned, it weakened our consciousness an' made us forget both the Beloved an' the father wi' his heavenly Kingdom an' laws o' love altogether." And the druid sighed.

"Anu's consort is Beli, the fae/cherub boy," and the druid smiled, patting his abdomen, "belly, eh? He's in the abdomen, same as Anu, but he anchors into the right side, the masculine. An' he overlights the inner growth an' identity o' the boy within until age eleven, the right leg an' hip. His light side anchors into Polynesia as well, an' this aspect loves to be cut on the water near the mother, eh? He ever draws laddies into watery adventures that open memories o' Paradise, like Anu. An' because he's the boy, Beli's gifts tend toward surprises in nature, happy adventures away from home, simple an' childlike, an impulsive roll down a grassy slope on a summer's morn, perhaps. Where Anu stays near the hut, he's a rollickin' wanderer.

He's the regent who brings forth the utter certainty o' one's direction in lost times, too, but in a humorous offbeat way. He's a shaman extraordinaire, openin' fears ready to be released, through percussion mainly, wi' those belly high drums o' his, then shiftin' the fears toward joy wi' his mesmerizin' rhythms. Beli's a pure master at this, ladd." Ye'll see soon enough when ye get there, the druid thought, but carefully veiled this thought from Firinn.

"Beli also has information about bein's from other worlds an' high magic to give the world, connections wi' star families especially. He holds the comedy stream, too, always liftin' everyone wi' jokes that hold pure wizard power to transform darkness into joy in moments. But his humor brings much up from the unconscious, too.

But he has a dark side as well, carryin' all the fears the boy hasna yet faced. Africa, again. Beli took on the cover o' darkness to be with an' support the girl in her quadrant in order to birth her divine child here, Paradise. To stand by her side'll mean bein' looked down at an' spit upon for the next twenty-one centuries, until she comes into revelation. For all who served the girl quadrant in the Creator Sun were forced into slavery to Isle/Isis, their skin darkened, so they couldna escape an' blend in wi' everyone else. An' this dark Isle coverin' ever draws hatred an' contempt from others, plus all Isle's constrictin' forces, like poverty an' starvation. But in truth, these folk are simply drawin' off the hatred o' the world onto their own shoulders in service to the girl, like the deer o' the forest takin' all that violence, eh? So, his quality o' divinity to give is strength in adversity an' supportin' her to the very end o' her slavery to fear, another breadth o' love the rest o' the world canna begin to fathom. Beli can tend toward crudeness at times, loves to eat, an' isna the neatest o' gods, either. But he'll ever draw a laugh! His star system is Apus, the bird o' Paradise, eh?

The action centers are in the base as well, in the unconscious. Often actions are brought forward that dinna match what a person says, feels, or thinks at all. That's Anu an' Beli bringin' somethin' to light the person hasna yet seen that needs to be healed, actions that are so tellin' o' what a person isna yet aware of.

Then there are the western regents, those who direct all that happens in the outer world, a powerful bunch, indeed. In the southwest are the regents o' the boy quadrant, overlightin' bairnhood till age eleven again. They anchor into the southern continent, far off over the western sea. Let's start wi' the ladd o' this quadrant, Fionn. Because o' the boy's personal will force in action that fuels the nerves an' brain, he can be quite determined in his march toward what each laddie's meant to become, bringin' experiences that shape the future work o' the growin' boy. For Fionn always builds the foundation o' the man's destiny. This god carefully chooses the adventures an' leisure pursuits o' the laddie's lazy childhood afternoons, an' those times o' play'll often tell ye clearly what the bairn's later destiny'll be. In time, Fionn adds crafts or personal apprenticeships like ours, overseein' all interconnections outside the home to build those destiny structures.

Fionn's challenges always involve heavy work an' domination pressures, too, the ladd that's called on to do the heaviest tasks. Rushin' through his days is another o' the shadows Fionn brings into life, for the reptilians o' ancient times invaded this quadrant an' blocked the slow flow o' the Goddess, harnessin' the strength o' the ladd for their own purposes. But Fionn's a master o' dealin' wi' those slippery reptilian impulses, holdin' onto his simple lifestyle amidst the work an' action pressures o' the world, an' that's the quality o' divinity Fionn hands out, the true sacredness o' ordinary life. He, too, is keeper o' star an' ceremonial knowledge, plus connections wi' animals especially, a master shaman wi' information that'll help earth greatly in due time, his healin' gifts more connected to flutes an' birdsong, though. So Fionn's powers are wide, indeed. An' his star is Indus, the Indian.

His consort, Flidais, is a good match for him. She overlights all that happens in every lassie's outer life until age eleven, everythin' that nourishes the inner girl from the outside noo: the home, family, an' tribe especially. These influences build the structures that make the girl who she'll eventually become, her personal passions for change in the world. An' because it's the boy quadrant, she'll ever lead the lassie into the peace o' the forest, for Flidais has quite a boyish nature, climbin' trees an' wanderin' about, no the most ladylike regent.

She directs all lassies within to some quiet glade that nourishes them more than anywhere else in the world, too. An' to this place Flidais brings very special fae friends, flowers or plants or butterflies, perhaps, always carefully designed to aid the very challenges the girl within is facin' just then. Flidais'll direct each lass to a new power spot when needed as well. Her star system is the toucan, ladd, Toucana.

But Flidais also creates the deep outer wounds that'll drive the heart o' the girl into service to the world in adulthood, coverin' the playful girl within wi' work for the tribe an' the heavy societal structures that bind her, especially that feminine sensual side, eh? An' in the boy world that Flidais inhabits, the soft lassie is often beaten into submission by his brute force. But the lass is also given menial, dirty tasks inside the home, so Flidais an' Fionn have much in common. Her quality o' divinity is remainin' true to her own gentle girl nature, despite male domination an' the harshness o' the world, eh?

Then at age 22, the great shift to Saorsa an' Cead takes place. It's the outer world, they overlight, each person's outer influences from age 22 to late in life. These two sit in the father quadrant, the northwest, an' anchor into the northern continent across the western sea. But Saorsa mainly anchors into the mother heart o' that northwestern continent, what'll be a great city called New York someday. An' like her own heart, it'll be covered wi' the intellectual gridwork o' the Orion masters that want to block the mother's freedom more than any other thing, a place called Man-hat-ten. In time, Saorsa'll be called Lady Liberty.

But her true regency is the acceptance o' all peoples across the world, callin' everyone to freedom an' prosperity, but wi' a steep climb to achieve that as well. An' this acceptance o' everyone is her quality o' divinity. For her mother's heart wants to bring all the destitute an' lost ones Home to the father's kingdom, findin' nourishment an' fulfillment in work, the father's gifts, especially. She's ever leadin' the inner feminine into projects that help the poor an' challenged o' this world, too, especially women an' bairns. Her star compound is on Vega, ladd.

Her consort, Cead, is the father force o' the outer world, the elephant who shoulders the responsibility o' work an' destiny, an' faces the dark structures o' the world to bring forth real change. Cead overlights the inner male from age 22 till each returns to the Diamond Core level, late in life, the full ascension path through the six lower worlds.

But Cead's main impulse is facin' societal darkness in our work in the outer world to build the father's kingdom here, an' this is his quality o' divinity to bestow. His influences always help build our final destiny patterns, too, over many lives. An' his sunny nature draws all fears up into the father's light o' consciousness above the diaphragm as well, openin' new awarenesses for growth through life. An' because this impulse is our first revelation o' each particular shadow, it's he who truly frees all folk enslaved to fear. In future days, Cead'll be called Lincoln. His star compound is on Leo.

Then, in the center o' the Pillar realms, come the virgins, Aislin (ashlin, Ash-line) an' Colum, overlightin' the virgin skyturns from age eleven to 22, both inner an' outer influences noo. An' will ye notice how these middle Diamond Core structures, the Child Heart, the Holy Family, an' these Pillars all have virgins at their center? These are the triple horses, ladd, love welded to action, the strongest force for change there is.

Aislin's essence streams mainly through the spinal sheath around the central Beloved helix, her pillar. She carries the heaviest load, too, despite bein' scft an' slender, for she's the backbone o' love, a very powerful an' determined presence. It's all those heavy pressures to break the girl's spirit into submission, especially violence, she faces, dark forces wantin' her to give up an' do whatever she's told, the same that most horses face in their lives, too. But Aislin's divinity is independence o' the self that listens only to the voice o' love within an' doesna bend to the will o' darkness in the inner or outer world, another tower o' strength, she is.

Aislin mainly anchors into Jerusalem, one o' her names, for both these Pillar virgin regents overlight the Middle East. But she also anchors into the feminine third chakra o' Cead's land across the sea. In time, it'll be called the District o' Columbia, another o' her names. Those war-lovin' reptilians in their mottled garb'll cover her true peace-lovin' strength there wi' a stone pentagon o' power an' control that'll serve darkness, through violence an' brute force. O' course, Aislin's star system is Columba, the dove, ladd.

Aislin's consort, Colum, surrounds her wi' his rod o' truth, the bones o' the spine, facin' the brute force darkness o' the world to protect her. An' wi' his backbone strength, he ever chooses to support the laws o' love, too, standin' up for what's right in all he does, his quality o' divinity, ladd. He also sends intentions up the spine to be sent down the arms into action, eh? There are a lot o' pressures durin' the virgin years to bend to forces o' darkness for both these regents, temptations to sexual misuse, addictions, militarization, an' violence. An' Colum faces the masculine ones that want to break him. But everythin' he defeats or heals only makes his spinal strength stronger in the end. This pair are invincible in their service to love in this world, an' all virgins everywhere bring them through. Colum's star compound is in Saggitta, the arrow.

Speakin' o' Colum, ladd, another holy man'll come from Eire in seven centuries to our own sacred isle, Iona. He'll be known as Columba, an' he'll usher in the Christian patriarchal era here in Alba. But within, he'll carry Colum's strength an' purpose. An' in due time, it'll help build the backbone o' all in our brother/sisterhoods across these Celtic isles to walk the path o' wisdom to its very end." And Coillore smiled as he gazed out his wee window at the deepening dusk.

"Remember how these Pillar regents are also responsible for the long ascension path o' adulthood, ladd, the one that matches the six worlds? Ye ken these worlds already from yer first vision, remember, ladd? These worlds match the long cycles o' time as well, the spiral staircase o' human history an' earth ages that correspond to the same worlds, down and then back up again, movin' ever nearer to the manifestation o' heaven on earth. These six realms are divided into upper an' lower worlds, too, mind, heart, an' action levels in each.

The stages on this path as ye face the trials o' each world are much the same for everyone. It can help ye greatly to see where ye are in yer walk an' what's left to face, so I'll just go through them briefly." And Fìrinn's mind quickened at this, for he wanted to know how close he was to the Diamond Core, though he smiled to think of Coillore being brief about anything. "The ascension path follows Màiri's 18.6 skyturn cycle. Let's move our way upward through the worlds an' regents, for that's the way ye're travelin' the path just noo, eh?

The worlds, startin' from the bottom this time, are: the sensate realms wi' eighteen planes, where we are noo, earth, the action realms o' lower worlds, Abred. They are ruled by Tara Herself. Then comes Annwyn, the emotional realms o' the lower worlds, wi' 44 planes, the astral realms. They are ruled by the grandmother goddess o' the Creator Sun, Màiri. But her directives are put into real life by the regents o' the mother quadrant o' these Pillar realms, Cùram an' Treòraich. Next come the spirit realms or Gwynfydd, wi' 66 planes, the mind realms o' lower worlds. These are ruled by Rìdire, the virgin boy o' the Creator Sun, and put into action by the boy regents o' these Pillars, Fionn an' Flidais. Then comes the logos or Ceugant, wi' fourteen planes, the action realms o' higher worlds, ruled by Maighdean, virgin goddess o' the Creator Sun, again brought into life by the central virgins o' these Pillars, Aislin an' Colum. This is followed by the cherubim realms or Leanabh Aigneil, wi' ten planes, the emotion realms o' higher worlds. It's overlit by the girl regents o' these Pillars, Anu an' Beli, but ruled by the the divine bairns o' the Creator Sun, Abaid an' Uan. An' finally comes the diamond centerpoint, wi' 39 planes, the Diamant Meadhan, the mind levels o' higher worlds. It's overlit by the father regents o' these Pillars, Saorsa an' Cead, but ruled by the grandfather o' the Creator Sun, the Dagda. Then the seventh heaven or Diamond Core, the

Diamant Cridhe, wi' 174 planes, is ruled by Oghama. These seven worlds correspond to the seven sheaths o' light within each one o' us, ladd, the sensate on the outside, the Core in the center o' the heart.

So, the first world ye enter at age 22, Abred, is the sensate, bringin' forward fears from past lives on earth, the years o' life when the sensate sheath within is lit up. These sensate realms anchor into the five inner planets o' our solar system. The first skyturn an' a half o' this phase is transitional, the new patterns o' adulthood movin' into place an' bairnhood fallin' away. At that point in life, the three core fears each individual has chosen to face in this one life especially come in. These are fears ye havena yet faced in any life, brand new, the chance to move up the ladder o' light. But it's Tara this phase truly serves, buildin' Her strength into this lowest world as ye grow.

For this first 18.6 years, men an' women are locked into rigid an' separate roles that are dictated by society. That's because all the inner sheaths o' light have been closed down by the shadow self that's built durin' bairnhood, all except the same-gender half o' the outermost sheath, the sensate level. I'll be teachin' ye the descent o' bairnhood in a couple more lessons, ladd. An' because very little love is flowin' into their hearts within from the Creators at this stage, folk search for love on the outside, givin' importance to wealth, grand huts an' such. Couples have little intimacy, either, hardly ever talkin' to each other, wi' no sharin' o' the mind or heart at all, only linked in action in the physical realm. Then Tara overlights the earth initiation at the end o' the sensate climb, when this sheath o' light burns off to open the next phase. This occurs at age 39.6, though the exact timin' can vary a bit.

When the sensate sheath dissolves, the lights go on in the soul sheath, instead. These soul realms anchor into the three outer planets o' our solar system, ladd. The first skyturn an' a half o' this cycle is a mid-life stone wall, for as the soul breaks free, each individual must move out o' the patterns they've been livin' in all those years an' make serious changes in their lives to accommodate it. This soul cycle is when each person's societal roles become blocked by outer circumstances, so the male is held back an' kept in menial, often home-bound, work, carryin' the heavy load o' the feminine in cookin', cleanin', an' childcare for the family, while the female is forced to go off an' become the bread winner o' them all, instead.

This stage brings forward struggles for control between partners, too, great need for abundance that doesna come easily. It's that spidery sucky force that saps the mother's inner life stream all are dealin' wi' here, each learnin' to set boundaries when necessary to nourish their own selves, no matter how needy their partners may become. But through it all, these regents carefully open an' reactivate the couple's inner opposite genders.

Durin' the soul climb, communication wi' the devas is restored, too, the fae women who tend the natural world an' inhabit the soul realms, so there's deep joy in nature, at least. Màiri also brings in the peace o' the mother in other ways: closeness to water, lakes especially, but also visionin' to strengthen the intuitive powers that'll lead the disciple through their later trials.

The soul climb takes a full 18.6 year cycle, ladd, an' the last skyturn is the dark night o' the soul, when the need for meat is the most intense an' the fatigue o' strugglin' so long weighs heavily on everyone. But Màiri, plus Brìdget o' the Four Directions walk closely beside each disciple as they endure it. An' in the end, all learn Brìdget's greatest lessons; that inner beliefs are causin' whatever's happenin' on the outside. that we each have the power to change only ourselves after all, that tryin' to force our partners or circumstances to change just makes everythin' worse. An' finally at the end, there comes the great release o' outer responsibility for everyone else, lettin' God an' Goddess take care o' it all. But there also comes the realization that all people across the globe are livin' in the fears ye havna yet faced, an' all bein's in the Otherworld are doin' the same. So outer responsibility is replaced by this inner one, the commitment to climb the whole _inner_ ladder o' light.

Màiri's presence is especially strong durin' the water initiation at the end o' these planes, too, often the most severe test o' the elementals, as ye ken, ladd. It's durin' this trial that the inner soul sheath is washed off an' the spirit sheath lights up, about age 58.2. Mind, we dinna live long enough in the tribes to go through this whole cycle noo, but in future times, folk will.

The spirit climb that follows is magical at first, for communication wi' the djinns o' the spirit realms, the animal kingdom, an' one's star family are all restored, thanks to Rìdire. For the spirit realms are made up o' all the stars o' the night sky, villages o' light, every one.

The spirit ethers flow through the electrical systems o' the body, Fìrinn, the nerves, remember? An' this climb is often rapid, completed in a single skyturn, the transition to the next phase. But disciples are rushed an' harried by Rìdire's distortions somethin' fierce through it all, which block his high dreams. For those reptilians laid heavy time an' mental pressures over the virgin boy's spirit nature, like yer feelin' jest noo, Fìrinn, always rushin' on to the next thing to be done an' havin' too much to remember." And Fìrinn nodded vehemently, surprised at Coillore's understanding of his own life. "An' at this level, too, the virgin male in his untruth holds the masculine action-oriented outlook far above the feminine, wi' her rest an' intimacy needs, so she has none.

But this climb prepares each person for the world service they'll eventually step into when the race to the Core is finally done, layin' important groundwork for that virgin boy's high dream. If it isna a person's last lifetime, this phase o' life is usually one final project before a man steps down from his formal work o' life, or change to easier work, at least, a project dear to the individual's virgin male within. Rìdire also overlights the air initiation at the completion o' these levels, when the spirit sheath burns off an' the logos sheath lights up.

Then in the next world comes the logos sun, the Pleiades, a one third cycle, 6.2 skyturns. An' durin' it, Maighdean, virgin goddess o' the Creator Sun, develops the intuitive powers o' the feminine in preparation for her climb through the difficult higher worlds. But Maighdean also brings in the dark patterns that once shut the inner virgin girl down, insanity impulses, experiences that lift her up then drop her down, false dark voices that haunt an' sear her mind. But Maighdean also creates moments o' intense sweetness wi' the One Beloveds durin' this phase, for her true goal is the mystical union wi' the Creators that occurs at the completion o' this logos climb. This union is always gender based, so folk who identify as female are attuned to Oghama an' male to the White Tara. When the Goddess closes down in a century or so, ladd, the global masculine within'll be quite lost till She's restored in another 21 centuries.

At the same time, though, Rìdire, still active durin' the logos climb, brings in dark forces that once closed the male virgin down, alien mind control structures that try to break him, fanaticism added to his need to change the world. Then Rìdire blocks him, over an' over again. This is the will-breakin' process that realigns the personal will wi' God/Goddess, quite painful to experience, but absolutely necessary in the end. But Rìdire also brings forward one annual cocreative effort wi' Oghama that brings great joy, work that trains an' shapes the masculine for the world service he'll eventually achieve.

An' then, toward the end o' the logos climb the final trials o' violence an' sadism begin, as the logos eye-o'-the-needle approaches, lastin' a skyturn an' a half before the fire initiation. It's just before this testin' that the passionate love of a soon-to-be-unfaithful lover burns off the logos sheath, when the portals open to the One Beloveds. It was this very same false lover who closed this Beloved portal during the descent. But there's much joy here, too, as that infidelity stream is finally left behind, when the logos eye-o'-the-needle portal is finally breached. An' wi' it comes the sudden realization that Oghama or Tara is each person's forever love, for this is when the doorway an' pathway o' the mystical marriage to the One Beloveds swings open. It's then the gates to the cherubim realms, Leanabh Aigneil, are unlatched as well, at age 65.4.

Movin' inward in the body to the cherub sheath, an' upward in the worlds to the cherubim realms, the path eases as the shift into the next cycle occurs. This is when folk retire from active work in the world. For once the fae an' cherub children o' the Creator Sun, begin to overlight ye, simplicity, ease o' life, an' community become the standard o' yer days. This is the emotional or heart level o' the higher worlds, takin' only another third of an 18.6 skyturn cycle.

But this climb, too, can be challengin', for the main darkness is the kidnappin' force o' slavery an' overwork that armored the divine child's gentle nature when s/he was stolen from the Creator Sun. What folk expect to be a life o' ease, late in life, turns out to be far more work than they ever imagined. Abaid an' Uan's lessons teach humility, balancin' sufferin' wi' fun an' play, but mostly the divine bairn within holdin' on to true gentleness an' lovin' kindness, even when bein' ill-treated. The deepest fears o' this phase connect to the dark mother, who abused an' closed the soft heart o' the bairn down behind her iron doors o' cruelty, replacin' love wi' deep insecurity an' self hatred, instead. These child heart trials keep everyone mired in menial labor, their true gifts completely unrecognized, criticized, an' ignored. For these fears stem from our days in the Orion complex and on earth in Africa, the old goddess times. An' their hallmark is the sacrifice o' children, mutilation o' creator organs especially.

When the climb through the cherubim planes is at it's end, about age 71.6, there comes a fallin' away o' connection wi' yer tribe, an' the hopes an' dreams ye've built wi' them. This brings loneliness an' separation from the ways ye've known, the cherub initiation. An' the cherub sheath within melts away as the diamond centerpoint sheath an' climb open.

An' then comes the darkest initiation o' all, the middle passage, through the lowest planes o' the diamond centerpoint, the bone initiation. These are the mind levels o' the higher worlds, ladd, an' this world contains the 6-6-6 o' the abyss, where darkness was structured into the mind, heart, an' base o' all descendin' forms. All must face the death crone durin' this passage, too. But it's the grandfather o' the Creator Sun, the Dagda, who overlights this passage, holdin' all fast in his strong arms o' love through everythin'. Often this phase begins wi' some health issue that arises as the abyss levels open. But fortunately, this 6-6-6 initiation is kept short, a sudden accident, perhaps, wi' a mere six moons o' recuperation.

But even after the abyss is left behind, the Dagda's trials are difficult, takin' the last third o' this 18.6 cycle to complete. They bring in over-mentalized confusions, structures that bind an' suck one's focus, sear the heart into mania an' haste in every effort, an' try to shut the very life force down. This usually involves some work a person feels they must complete before they leave this world, that end-o'-life feelin' comin' out o' the abyss experience. These trials can mean a weakenin' o' the mind into dementia, instead. But if it's a final project, the Dagda's simply preparin' each person for the work o' their next lifetime. Durin' this phase, Arienrhod   o' the Four Directions, builds in ancient creative talents o' the feminine, too, often music or art o' some kind, for this is always a highly creative time o' life. Arienrhod's projects, too, prepare for the next lifetime on earth.

The Dagda teaches lessons o' balance in givin', the inner male an' female takin' turns pourin' their passions into action, for he always brings in heartfelt endeavors in love's name, work that satisfies like nothin' else can. But his lessons can be challengin', too, addiction to work an' savin' the world at the expense o' the feminine's need for rest an' nurturin' the self. This diamond centerpoint climb is the passage into the Diamond Core, ladd, so the individual'll be leavin' earth life before many more skyturns pass. So, it's often a contemplative phase, too, wi' folk givin' up their attachments to earth life as they talk wi' friends an' family who've preceeded them into the Otherworld. Deep attunement is also occurin' both wi' the One Beloveds an' the purpose o' each person's star tuath that'll become his or her focus in the Otherworld.

But there's a silver linin' in every dark cloud, laddie, for this is also the phase that builds the foundation o' the happily-ever-after, even though it may be in some future lifetime. Stone by stone through this climb, all the hard efforts o' his thought an' her arts are bein' built into permanent mental structures o' truth within, the Dagda's light put into yer very bones, that final joyful destiny o' the future. An' wi' it comes the strong heart o' the father that wants to nourish an' support yer family, buildin' work o' the future that'll bring abundant compensation for those true loves their whole lives long. But ye need a megalithic consciousness to make it through this climb, for the fears are heavy an' the healin' slow. That's because the Dagda builds the father's bravery into the heart most of all, courage that faces great darkness in the outer world, for the final destiny'll make real breakthroughs on earth, significant fear forces always transformed by it. An' Arienrhod o' the Four Directions, also, builds in the strong love o' the world mother that wants to help the weaker an' less fortunate across the globe. See, laddie, it's all for a high purpose after all.

Then at the end o' the centerpoint climb, its sheath burns off an' the core within opens, about age 77.8. That's when the Dagda hands the disciple over to Oghama, Who rules the climb through the Diamond Core. There are 174 planes there, all the structures ye're learnin' in these lessons. This final climb takes another full cycle, 18.6 skyturns, till age 96.4. And at the start, some disaster always comes that breaks down yer previous life pattern. Often it's a health crisis an' move away from yer family to a caregiver's hut. Life becomes easier then, for the sappin' forces ease, an' there's time for rest, peace, an' gentle creativity again. But these Core levels contain a brief repetition o' all the worlds below, pickin' up whatever's been missed along the way, wounds the individual has sustained their whole life that they're utterly an' thoroughly sick of.

The final 18.6 skyturns o' every life are overlit by Danu an' Luis o' the White Pentagram, too, yer next lesson an' one, ladd. She brings forth the emotional fruits within, the waters o' emotion free o' fear, the azure wise woman stream. Her waters o' truth wash away all former fear shadows from the life stream, restorin' them to relative purity again. So love's laws are lived as easily as breathin', wi' fear barely able to gain a toehold. An' in these years before the end o' life, the feminine'll choose a gift for her family or tribe, too, often havin' to do wi' emotions, but no necessarily. It's durin' her grandma years, so it can simply be carin' for her grandbairns, teachin' them all she's learned.

An' at this time, too, Luis o' the White Pentagram brings forward the generosity o' the granda, the elder that wants to give somethin' to his tribe just for the joy o' it, no because it's required, the expertise he's gained in a lifetime to those who'll carry it on after he's gone. Ye, Firinn, are me own Luis effort in this life. Such endeavors are simple gifts that bring satisfaction to the deep heart, joyful an' often full o' play. An' each o' these grandma/granda final gifts is their own divine child o' that particular lifetime." And listening, Firinn felt the light of Danu through the old druid's heart, reaching deeply into his own. He sensed her azure waters pouring into him, opening some portal within, and he longed to know what his own final gift to the tribes would be.

"When the final life nears it's end, though, all twelve regents o' the White Pentagram activate, again durin' these final 18.6 skyturns o' the climb. Then the White Pentagram reverses itself, and these regents bring up old, old layers from the deepest levels, fears from the first fall, anythin' that hasna been healed durin' the earlier cycles an' lives, but wi' heaven's protection an' the joy o' the approachin' inner divine birth this time. This openin' marks the climb up the steep mountain to the golden castle o' dreams come true at the top, the father's Kingdom realized. It's that highest mountain again, Everrest, eh?

This Core climb contains the core woundin', too, the original fear around which all others are wrapped. But wi' Oghama at the helm, this is often a gentle trial, this last, the diamond initiation. An' through it, Oghama holds the disciple steady in His great love. An' the Beloved always sees that the core pain is short, never longer than a day, an' often much less than that. For most, if truth be told, the harshest trial comes durin' the middle passage, an' this diamond initiation brings only a gentle replay o' that time.

No matter how intense the core woundin' may be, many disciples are relieved by it, for they ken well it paves the way for healin' to their very cores an' final union wi' the One. If it isna the final lifetime, this core wound repetition occurs when each person passes to the Otherworld. But even then, there's magic, for the fear barriers fall away in moments, an' the great arms o' the One Beloveds sweep every one up in Love sublime.

But if it's the final lifetime noo, the portals to the happily-everafter open, instead, bringin' inner union wi' the Beloveds, very gently in some sweet evenin' sunset, perhaps. An' within a single day, the outer true love is revealed.

An' then, the heavenly child within is born, leavin' the hard work an' fear-facin' behind to give his or her final gift to earth. It's the divine child each person was seeded wi' in her or his original moment o' creation out o' the Creator Sun. This gift'll bring satisfaction like no other an' come about without any o' the harsh efforts o' before, through sacred sexuality wi' their true love mainly, exactly the way the Creators manifest all things Themselves. Within a moon or two, world service opens, gently, gradually, nothin' like that exhaustin' middle passage noo. An' then, all the heart has longed an' ached for finally begins to manifest.

There's always a return to the land o' yer spirit at this time, too, yer mother land, leavin' that old false family that never did support yer divine child within as well. Those who pass over go to their ethnic realms o' heaven, instead. This final lifetime happy endin' is the gift o' the Creators to all who brave an' complete the wisdom climb, an' many are the delights an' surprises that arrive to perfume the heart each an' every day after that, no only for the rest o' that lifetime, but on into the future forever. Lovely, eh, ladd? As lovely as heaven itself." And the druid's eyes shone.

"Ye should ken that the years o' these cycles are approximate, though, some lives shortened by karma, all modified by the One to fit wi' the onward movement o' the All. O' course, the cycles are shortened in our times, an' it's rare for anyone to break into the happily-ever-after in our day, too. But when all divine children are born in 21 centuries, this entire cycle o' skyturns'll hold sway. But by then many'll be on an accelerated path, so they could break through to bliss far younger than this 96 skyturns, too. I hope they all do!" The druid glanced over to see how attentive Fìrinn was after such a complicated lesson, for he had one more piece to teach. And Coillore was glad to see Fìrinn leaning forward on the pallet, still eager after all the rest.

"This Pillar Celtic cross is the structure o' the continents o' earth as well; the far east an' Siberian cold lands, the mother quadrant; Polynesia an' Africa, the girl quadrant; what'll one day be known as South America across the western sea to the south, the boy quadrant; the northern land mass there, North America, the father quadrant; and the Middle East, the virgin beloveds. All nations'll one day be built in this identical structure, too, each one a hologram o' the whole, just as we ourselves are.

The difficulties an' gifts o' each heaven o' the ascension climb anchor into these continents, too, ladd. An' the continents are also overlit by the Four Directions an' Zodiac regents." And Coillore bent to draw the four continents in the earthen floor. "The far east resonates wi' Brìdet an' Eòl, the mother quadrant an' the soul realms. So, the suckin' spider mother who wants only control will flow out through these lands, an' they'll be prominent durin' earth's soul climb. But from China, in due time, will stream the compassion o' Brìdget an' the inner path o'light o' Eòl as well.

From South America will arise the Mayan reptilian distortions, the action, time, an' violence forces in separation from the All, durin' earth's spirit climb. But from this place in future days will rise the gentle truth o' the boy, which'll bring the action an' time flow into alignment wi' the slow flow o' life, connection wi' the animal kingdom an' nature, along wi' the sacredness o' ordinary life. These holy gifts'll come from the native peoples o' these southern lands in those happy days to come.

The Middle East'll be prominent durin' earth's logos climb. But in those golden days, Pwyll's oil fields an' violence trials'll bring forth peace on earth an' rest for the weary. Many, many folk will step into their high service for good at that time. Life lived in the arms o' the One, wi' prayers at all hours o' the day, an' the modest sacredness o' sexuality wi' one's partner'll arise from these lands as well, gifts o' the virgin goddess especially. Sìth'll oversee the rise o' the feminine back into revelation an' honor, too, a massive task!

They'll work together, all these regents, to end the patriarchal cycle o' the next twenty centuries, releasin' the old dark cosmic impulses. In the final days, they'll unearth huge dragon guardians that keep the earth in bondage, too, from mountains, lakes, an' the ocean floor. These'll create volcanoes, earthquakes, an' tidal waves as the old, old fears reawaken. But these'll be met by global healin', many, many healers workin' quietly to free the earth once an' for all.

An' then, Africa an' Polynesia resonate wi' the lass quadrant an' the cherubim realms," and Coillore paused, watching Fìrinn carefully for a moment. "The peoples o' Africa'll carry the heaviest load o' all, Isle's hard, hard lessons; the sacrifice o' the child within into the menial work that supports all the rest, abuse an' disdain by others, self-hatred, an' the veilin' o' their true divinity till the very end o' the cycle o' darkness, when the divine girl is finally revealed on earth. But their gifts, too, will come clear in time as well; tenacity in hardship, never givin' in, carryin' more than their share o' darkness so the rest o' us dinna have to, an' the girl's deeply spiritual an' sensual nature. An' when truth finally reverses the distortions that darken our world, these African peoples'll be recognized an' revered for their long an' arduous service to love. I tell ye, laddie, even the greatest rulers o' those days will wait to let these African folk walk to the front o' the line!

Across the western seas, the northern land mass o' the father quadrant that's overlit by the Dagda, resonates wi' the diamond centerpoint. An' in time, people'll travel there to learn lessons o' independence an' build the powers o' the mind that are the true wizardry o' the Dagda's centerpoint planes. These folk'll carry the fierce heart o' the father, Leómhann o' the Four Directions, that wants justice for all peoples an' Arienrhod's mother ache for freedom, so everyone can follow their dreams. But that land'll be caught in domination o' others, the false father, for a time as well. An' that nation'll lead earth through her middle slavery passage towards the end o' the cycle o' darkness an' build the courageous heart o' Leòmhann into her people then as well.

An' when those times o' trouble complete themselves, Oghama an' the White Tara, <u>Love</u> most o' all, will take Their place as rulers o' each human heart, an' earth as well, Oghama <u>Himself</u> will lead the earth through the final trials o' the Diamond Core, the core woundin' phase. It'll bring forward memories o' the fall o' the Creator Sun, financial structures in disarray, violent reptilians everywhere, war an' diseases that kill multitudes, the Isis forces o' death, especially. Dragon lords o' the Death Star'll be prominent at the very end, rulin' all the major nations o' earth, the final passage to Paradise. Ach, but all will be <u>healed</u>, the whole earth an' all realms o' the Otherworld." And Coillore drew his hands together with a smile, though his eyes brimmed with tears. Then he lowered his head, indicating the lesson was through. Firinn had attended this lesson very closely, trying to figure out how much of his own climb remained.

"Where am I in these worlds, Coillore?," the ladd asked with his heart racing, as soon as the druid stopped talking. And Coillore looked at Firinn gently, sadness tugging at the druid's heart.

"Ye took yer water initiation two moons ago, Firinn," Coillore said quietly.

"So, let's see, that's the soul levels, the second realm." And Firinn's face fell. "I have a long way to go then, Coillore."

"Aye, laddie. But yer spirit's chosen the straight path, the shaman's way. That means ye'll be movin' steadily an' swiftly, reachin' the end o' the road in twenty skyturns or so. It's a steep climb, without much rest along the way. But no one's ever allowed to attempt it who doesna have the inner strength to succeed. An' Oghama an' Tara'll ever carry ye in Their love. Dinna fret, ladd. Take it one day at a time, an' let all the rest go. Ye'll come through just fine; I ken it as sure as I'm sittin' here."

"All right, Coillore. I'll do the best I can," Firinn said with a sigh. And with sober eyes, he walked slowly down the deer path through the birch wood toward the huts below. But this night, despite all the details, Firinn left Coillore's hut reluctantly, for he felt the call of these regents in his heart, Oghama's especially. Still, the ladd's head was swirling with all the facts and structures he'd learned, and he sat by the burn a long while, letting the sound of the water falling over the boulders ease his mind.

"Help me build Yer father's Kingdom here, Oghama, will Ye? Somethin' in me aches to do that," the ladd whispered as he finally stood to walk down to the tuath. "I'll take Ye as me inner guide, if Ye dinna mind." And he held his right fist over his heart as he said this, pledging to remember this gesture as his commitment to Oghama's influence an' truth.

It was late when Firinn arrived at the long house, the fire burned down to ashes and his bed furs cold. But he snuggled in close to Bana Dhia to warm them both. And as he closed his eyes, Firinn could sense the Creator Sun, shining like the great diamond it was, through the murky ocean depths of the cosmic sea. "I will reach ye," he whispered. "I'll swim the distance till I do, Oghama. This I promise Ye."

Chapter Twenty-Six: Soillse

Even in her sleep, Soillse felt the grief rise out of him and heard Fìrinn's cry echo over the hills, though he was half a day's walk away. And when she startled awake in the early dawn, she felt a terrible numbness in his legs. So she lay on her pallet in the round house under her furs, begging the Goddess to help Fìrinn and imagining the light of the Sun Lord around his feet to keep the cold away. There was a danger she could feel, dark forces wanting to sap his strength, turn him into a cripple, and never allow him to become king.

And then she fretted all morning, searching him out among the ladds at the mid-day meal as she did her chores. But Fìrinn wasn't there, for he'd been on a vision quest far up the ridge to the east. Only late in the afternoon, early dusk, did he come limping back through the birch wood, down the path beside the burn to the yard. The circled huts looked serene in the evening glow, silhouetted against the bare birch wood and the ridge above. With his arm over Coillore's shoulder, Fìrinn dragged his weak leg into the long house, where all the fostered lads slept.

"What have ye done wi' me best lancer?," Seumus fumed. Dressed in his heavy winter buckskin breeks and shirt, the chief was standing with hands on hips at the longhouse door. "His Da'll challenge me to the sword if anythin' happens to that boy. The man's in a fury over his wife's passage to the Otherworld, anyway, an' no to be reckoned wi'." "Water initiation," was all Coillore said. "He'll mend, Seumus." But Fìrinn drooped with fatigue and winced whenever he moved his right leg at all. His buckskin breeks and cloak were caked with mud and his fur-lined hide boots were sodden.

Soillse, her long hair blowing every which way, stood at the door of the small cooking hut behind the chief's round house with tears in her eyes, wanting to run to Fìrinn. She could see that his feet were swollen, his hide boots unlaced, and she could feel the ache of them in her own. And then fury flared up within, and she glared at Coillore. *Carrying to break me back for skyturns and finally the promise of love after Fìrinn and I spent that afternoon in the wood, and ye risk it all for this,* she thought. *Oooooh!* The druid turned to look sharply in her direction, made the motion for peace, and then walked out of the yard and up the small deer path beside the burn into the birch wood toward his hut,

But Fìrinn returned to his training in the yard with no complaints and little slowing down, just the limp. It was easy for Soillse to find him now, for she only needed to look for the drag marks in the sand. Alone on her pallet in the round house at night after the long day's chores were through, it made her sad and frightened. *Will he be disqualified for chief or the kingship now? Had her vision of him becoming high king of the isle been wrong then?*

So it was four weeks after his initiation, nearly the Hawthorne moon (May), before Fìrinn finally approached her again. Oh, they'd spent a couple of evenings together sitting on the rocks at the shore in the interim, talking about the tuath and their various activities, looking out over the western sea and the Cuchullin mountains to the north. But those evenings had only sharpened Soillse's need of him and his of her. Fìrinn's limp was less noticeable now, and Seumus had finally calmed down. But there was coolness between the chief and the druid that all could feel, and this, too, worried Soillse, for she felt some darkness of the spirit world trying to push them apart.

This clear windswept morning, she'd just emerged from the chief's round house in a fresh homespun shift and was sniffing the firstsky air, tying a hide apron on over her dress and wrapping her woolen shawl over her shoulders before beginning the morning stirabout. And Fìrinn surprised her, up long before the other ladds, waiting in his buckskins outside the door of the cooking hut. He gave her a sweet crooked smile as she came round the doorposts, and her heart melted instantly, and then she was in his arms.

"I was so worried, Fìrinn! I <u>felt</u> ye that night o' yer initiation up at the dolmen," she burst out, "an' then it was hard to wait...." Her voice trailed off as she nuzzled her head on his chest, her wispy hair tickling his chin.

"I know all about the ache o' waitin', lassie. Can ye come wi' me tonight? Or will yer Da just be upset wi' me the more?"

"I dinna care if he is! It's me courtin' skyturn, an' he has nothin' to say about it. O' <u>course</u>, I'll come! What I dinna ken is how I'll leave ye when it's time to come back to all this." And she glanced around at yesterday's fish guts, reeking on the midden heap, and the laundry piled outside the long house door, sighing and closing her eyes. Then she nuzzled back into him just as Sìne, Soillse's tall spare, elderly great aunt, stepped into the shed, carrying the bucket of oats from the storage pit to start the gruel. Fìrinn and Soillse sprang apart, blushing, and he limped quickly back to the long house without a word. But Sìne only grinned and kept winking at Soillse all day long as they stirred the cauldron.

It was an especially hectic day as it turned out, Soillse cooking all morning and hurriedly gathering kindling up in the birch wood above the tuath, then cleaning and chopping venison the lads had brought in most of the afternoon. At least there's no fish gutting today, she thought, as evening approached, so I willna stink for once.

And then, as the sun dropped over the western sea, Muirn, Soillse's aunt, offered to clean the cauldron for her, so Soillse hurried off with a hearth stone to heat a bit of water in the wooden tub behind the latrine for a bath. She lay in the water, letting the warmth ease her sore feet, then washed her hair, and put on salve of the small lilies that were just blooming beneath her Aine tree. She and Eilid had made the salve only a few days before. And then, Soillse, dressed in her cleanest homespun dress, green to match her eyes, wrapped her plaid around her and sat outside the round house to wait for Fìrinn, rubbing her tired feet. It was cool tonight, but not cold, the sky clear for once, only a few wispy clouds to the east over the ridge. And there was a soft breeze off the sea, as a deep golden sun hovered above the Cuchullins across the water.

Soillse was smiling at the tiny leaves on the birches, in their pale green cloaks, with yellow catkins hanging from the boughs everywhere. So she didn't hear Fìrinn coming from the boy's baths beyond the yard, his hide boots quiet on the packed earth. He stood in his summer doeskin breeks and a white homespun shirt and plaid, with his hair carefully combed, still damp on his back. And he watched her a moment from the edge of the wood, his green eyes twinkling, as she gazed at the sky that grew ever more rosy, humming to herself. He called her name then, and she rose quickly to hug him, and he put his arm round her shoulders as they headed out the hut circle toward the deer path beside the burn up the hill. And when they reached the dusky silence of the trees, Fìrinn lit a small torch, for the night was darkening. She kept stopping to smile up at him as they walked through the boulders that littered the path, and he kissed her just once, softly, slowly, and still neither said a word. He led her onto the small path north that led to Coillore's hut, but soon turned off that, moving west toward the sea.

They came to the small Caledonian pine that had sheltered them before in the rain, but this time under the spreading branches was a lean-to covered with greens. It was large enough to shield them, and he'd gathered heather for a bed inside and laid furs on top of that. Soillse took in a sharp breath as she ducked under the wattle roof, for into it he'd woven pine boughs and all the spring flowers of the hills. There were blue wood irises, the wee lilies she loved, and birch catkins hanging down in profusion. As she crawled inside and lay on the furs, taking a deep sniff, her heart opened as wide as the bright primroses above. And again she wondered at a ladd, a warrior even, who held such love for the plant people and for the lass in herself that often ached for such small beauties. It was a child's place, this lean-to, where she could let the wee bairn inside her relax, the one that nasty molesting druid and her bossy older sister, Ceit, had squashed skyturns ago.

"I <u>love</u> it here, Fìrinn," she whispered, looking up at him as he crouched inside. "When did ye have time fer this wi' games all day an' yer limp?" She fingered a catkin and sniffed the delicate perfume of a lily hanging near her cheek, and as she did so, the wind picked up and swished softly across the needled roof. "Brash warriors make me close up as fast as ever I can," she said, looking up at him. "But makin' me a wee hut wi' flowers in it, noo that's a ladd I could keep," and she bent her head in thanks.

"Aye. I see it in ye, too, lassie. Ye're always stoppin' in yer work to sniff the blossoms or finger the leaves o' the forest folk. I watch ye in small moments sometimes an' feel how alike we are." And he lay down on the furs beside her. "Ye're always workin' so hard, an' yet ye stay kind to the ladds. No like some o' the other women at the tuath. I'd be grumpy at the end o' a day scrapin' hides an' guttin' fish!" And he put his hands together, nodding back. He means Ceit and her sharp tongue, Soillse thought. And then she grew suddenly shy, dropping her eyes and blushing. And Fìrinn breathed out all in a rush.

"Ye remind me of a fawn I used to watch at home one summer when I was wee. An' ye're lovlier to me, Soillse, than all the heaped pink sunsets o' summer or the twinklin' stars across the night sky." He paused, watching her expression closely, his heart speeding as her green eyes drew him in. Her mouth was full, and her eyes wide and gentle, like her Ma, Eilid. It's the most lovely combination, Fìrinn thought. Oh, I want to ask ye something. Please, Goddess, tell me when the right moment is, his thoughts continued as Soillse snuggled into his chest.

"I think I've known ye forever, Fìrinn-ladd, at least that's how I feel, like we've been best friends since the beginnin' o' time. I have memories o' bein' in heaven wi' ye. I told ye me dreams before," she whispered. "Will ye tell me yers noo?" And she kissed his chest.

"I have much to say to ye tonight," he answered quietly, kissing her baby soft light brown hair. She was trembling, and so he held her closer and pulled the furs over them and up to her chin against the evening chill. "But truly there's only one thing I need to say. I've known ye, too, lass, an' I've always loved ye. I had a dream o' ye an' this bay the night ye were born, an' I knew I'd be comin' here. An' then that first night I arrived, I glimpsed ye in the woods as me mare climbed down to the yard. Ye were so small! Yer hair was in a tumble, an' wi' yer freckles everywhere, the faery light was all around ye. Ye came barefoot down the burn after me, yer feet covered wi' mud. An' I thought, noo there's a lass after me own heart. But I didna ken for sure till the Midwinter ceremony soon after, when ye stopped an' spoke to me, an' the Goddess light was in yer eyes. Do ye remember, me bonnie Soillse?" He smiled, and his eyes gentled while she nodded. So there has been someone at the tuath who understood me all this time, she thought. And then he felt tears on his arm and her shoulders trembling, and he pulled her closer still.

"But then there was so much to do an' learn," Fìrinn continued, "trainin' all the long days. An' Seumus was angry if I even came near ye. An' then the Goddess said it wasna time, an' ye did, too. Nine winters I've waited to even be friends! An' then lately, how I dream o' ye!" He stopped then to brush her tears away. "I canna tell ye those, though, no yet. But perhaps, ye ken." She only chuckled in reply. And then, after a moment's hesitation, he reached to pull her face up to his, and kissed her, long and long.

"Soillse, goddess o' me forever heart, will ye do me the honor o' becomin' me wife?," he whispered finally.

"Mmmmmm," she murmured, nodding fiercely and kissing him back, fervently wishing her virgin year was over and past.

After that, the summer moons flew by, Fìrinn and Soillse together whenever they had the chance. He got up early to help her carry wood, stack it, and light the fire in the yard, and lift the heavy cauldron over it. And they walked the beach or climbed the rocks along the arms of the bay after the evening meal, talking little, but holding hands and feeling each other's hearts. But with all the work of the tuath and the day's training, the nights when they had time to go to the lean-to were few. And perhaps the Goddess fashioned it so, for as the Vine moon approached, it grew harder and harder not to stay till morning and satisfy their growing need for joining.

At then at last, early in the Vine moon (September), Soillse's virgin skyturn completed itself, very unceremoniously, after a long day harvesting barley in the fields above the tuath. Eilid prepared to do the ceremony at the sacred women's cave, high along the cliffs to the north of the tuath along the shore, and Coillore offered to assist as well. But Soillse refused them both.

"Fìrinn an' I'll do our own ceremony," she said, holding her chin out slightly. "That's irregular," Eilid said with a frown, standing outside the chief's round house in her stained workaday shift.

"Aye," Soillse replied. She stifled a smile then, thinking, tonight I'm sharing Fìrinn with only the trees and the sky and the stars, and no one else!

The day had dawned cool, but clear, with a light steady breeze off the sea. And even as she hauled wood for the evening fires, Soillse couldn't stop singing. Eilid let her go before the cleaning up was done, and Duineil, the yard master, winking at Fìrinn, let him leave the games early as well. Soillse ran to bathe in the burn up in the birch wood, and Fìrinn soaked in the wooden tub behind the latrine by the yard, then dressed in his white shirt and wrapped his plaid around his waist, throwing one end over his right shoulder, as if he were going to a high ceremony. And Soillse put on a clean summer shift, faded blue-green, like the sea shallows on a sunny morn. Then Eilid braided up Soillse's hair, so it looked like a crown on top of her head. "For womanhood," Eilid said with a nod as she finished. She'd brought heather blossoms from the moor and wove these into Soillse's hair as well. And Soillse waited but a moment at the doorskin, before Firinn called softly from outside.

"Ye look like a faery queen," he said, amazed at her beauty in the evening light as they climbed up the deer path beside the burn toward the lean-to, holding hands and listening to the warbling of the thrushes. The path along the way was covered with bluebells, growing in scattered patches of sun. And as they turned north down the small track, Soillse blushed at what was to come, her eyes shining up at him. And she felt his hand tremble as they walked into the shelter of the great pine, alone among the scrub birches. He said not a word, only kissed her there under the soft spreading boughs. And she pushed up his shirt, running her hands over his chest. And so he pulled it off and stood smiling down at her.

"Oh, Firinn-ladd, I'm sooo glad this night is finally here!" Then she loosened the laces of her shift, so it fell open to the waist. He put his arms around her, holding her as tenderly as if she were the Goddess, the White Tara Herself. She kissed his nose, and ran her hands through his wavy deep red hair, and he kissed her mouth, and then her neck, and then the softness of her breasts. She slipped off her shift then, letting it fall to the ground. And he ran his hands along the curves of her hips, eager and not wanting to frighten her, both at once, hardly daring to believe this loveliness was his to taste at last. His heart was pounding so hard, he thought she must be able to hear it. And then he took off his plaid and loin cloth, and they lay on the furs and just looked into each other's eyes in the gathering dusk. When finally he cupped her breast in his hand, moving his thumb lightly across her nipple, she moaned softly. Then he brushed her belly with his hand, and the hair below, and then her woman's place, very lightly, his need rising at the wetness and warmth he found there.

And she felt a tremor go through him as he pulled her close and kissed her more firmly. She could feel his manhood erect beside her leg, and all of a sudden, she fell into a wee panic, for no one had ever told her what to do with a man, not really. What if I canna please him?, she thought. As the shyness washed over her, she looked away. So he laid her back down again, smiling at the little girl in her he felt just then. But then she pulled his hand over her breast again, kneading his fingers a bit.

And then all restraint in her suddenly disappeared. With her heart galloping, she rubbed her hands over his torso and his manhood both. Then she pulled him close and kissed his mouth, his belly, and finally his manhood. And he kissed her in return: breasts, thighs, and woman's place, opening the petaled folds gently with his tongue, flooding them both with pulsing desire.

At length, she pulled him over her and took his manhood inside as he moaned softly. And as they moved together, she felt the rhythm of a forever sea, and an ancient yearning flooded her being. And then he spasmed, his seed spilling within her, and she held her breath with the wonder of it all. How can I, of all lassies, deserve this, she thought, leaning against his heaving chest.

"Ach, me lovely Soillse," he whispered. "It was hard to wait for ye, an' ye didna have yer release, did ye? Coillore warned me o' that."

"Ye've talked o' this wi' Coillore!"

"Aye, a bit." He grinned.

But she was heady, floating on a cloud of bliss, and just now she didna care about that in the least. She only laid her head on his chest and breathed in the musky scent of him. It made her heart race again, and after a time, she felt his manhood rise again beside her leg. And she put her hand around it, liking the way it throbbed. Then she closed her eyes as he brushed his hands over her, belly and breasts, and kissed her long again. And then he pulled her onto him, his manhood sliding into her woman's place. And only then did the Goddess came full into her as her body filled with desire, moving of its own accord, stroking his manhood deeply, as if she'd done it a thousand times before. As they moved again, faster this time, she felt as if a cup of the most intoxicating nectar was being poured over her, and the flaring within became a roiling fire. She wanted to take in his seed more than she ever thought possible, hold it there, and make a wee bairn that looked just like him. And then fireworks spasmed in her woman's place, and she shivered as she leaned on his chest, breathing fast until her heart slowed back down to a simmer. He loosed his seed again and then lay still beneath her.

And then in her mind's eye, she saw a light move from his heart to hers, and she felt a second joining there, less heated this time, but deeper and sweeter than the one before. And she was surprised to find it was the child in him that merged with her heart, not the man at all. She had a sudden image of him leaving his home tuath and his Ma, and felt the heart pang of the laddie he'd been then. She felt his long winters of loneliness without his mother's love at the fostering, too. Ach, I want to nourish that child in him for the rest of me life, she thought. And then something opened in her belly, too, some wariness loosening there. He was committing himself to her, she could feel it, to their life together, and to providing for her and doing whatever he must do as a man. And he could feel how truly frightened her little girl was of big men who could hurt her so easily like that druid long ago, and he pulled her tight, whispering into her hair.

"I'll let no harm come to ye ever again, lassie. I promise it on me life!" With a soft smile, she thought, I'll be loved like this for the rest of me days. And as she sent a prayer of thanks to the Sun Lord for this soft-hearted boy, she began crying quietly on Fìrinn's chest.

"I love ye, Fìrinn-ladd, more than anythin'!" And then she curled up beside him and laid her head back against his shoulder. He pulled up the furs, and they slept.

Once, in the pitch dark, she woke and kissed him lightly, and he kissed her back harder. And then again they slept till the sparrow song woke them at dawn. The sky was just beginning to lighten when she opened her eyes. And Fìrinn was already awake, watching her with tears on his cheeks. She smiled and nuzzled into his chest.

"I knew, too," she whispered, 'the day ye came here. Ye ran yer finger over the skin o' a birch, waitin' there on yer horse. An' oh, this summer, how I wanted to be that tree! But, ach, me Fìrinn-ladd, I didna ken it'd be like this. A hundred cups o' honeyed mead couldna be this sweet!"

He stretched to reach under the furs then and pulled out a small package, wrapped in hide, and laid it between her breasts, smiling. She looked up at him, brows raised, and pulled off the wrapping, as he tugged a bit of moss off the roof so she could see. It was a brooch, a bone carving, and on it was a tiny cottage by the ocean, the one she'd seen in her moon time vision."

"Ach, it's beautiful! Did ye carve it yerself?"

"Duineil helped," he said as he kissed her. And then they sat up, for they'd promised to return in time to prepare the firstsky meal.

"I dinna want to leave ye, Fìrinn-ladd. When'll we come here again? It's always so busy at the tuath." He laughed and held her tighter a moment.

"It was all right then?," he asked softly.

"Och, aye, better than heaven!"

"So do ye feel well claimed, lassie?"

"Aye, but I want to be loved like that again, every night!" And then her face grew suddenly serious, as her eyes held his. "It...it felt almost holy, Fìrinn, afterwards. Did ye feel that, too?"

"Aye, lass. I felt it all, just like you. I'm only a bit surprised at how hot-blooded ye are." Thank the Goddess, he thought.

Then he crawled backwards out of the lean-to and pulled her up into a rainy dawn. But he stayed her hand when she reached for her shift, drawing it over her and tying the laces himself. As he pulled on his shirt and plaid, she ran her finger down his manhood one last time, and he shivered, closing his eyes. They stood in the rain and kissed again, then picked their way through the boulders along the burn. She plucked tiny oak leaves, still fuzzy with spring, and tickled his chin with them. And he kissed the back of her hand like a queen as they stepped out into the yard.

The sun was lifting behind a bank of clouds off to the east, a hazy red orb above the ridge, as he left her at the roundhouse door. And looking up at it, she thought, the fire we lit in our hearts last night is like Ye, Sun Lord. An' like Ye, it'll never go out, no matter how many storms may come.

Chapter Twenty-Seven: Fìrinn

It was late in the Vine moon (September), and Fìrinn sipped acorn soup by the fire in the druid's hut, tucked into the birch wood on the ridge, while mist gathered and clung to the wee burn outside the doorcloth. The hut was small, holding only the hearth, a single pallet, and an altar by the far wall, plus the two stump chairs they were sitting in. And the old druid had grown impatient of late, wanting to finish the teachings of the Diamond Core as soon as possible, speaking in a rush that was uncharacteristic. His white woolen robe shone in the fire glow, and his grey hair lay long down his back, tonsured from ear to ear in the druid style. But his moustache was still mostly brown above pursed lips, and his eyes were the bluest Fìrinn had ever seen, looking a bit stern just now. Fìrinn, in his heavy buckskin breeks and shirt, savored the soup and shook his head to clear the day's competitions out of it, as the old man leaned over to draw two squares in the earth, one offset, so they looked like an eight-pointed star.

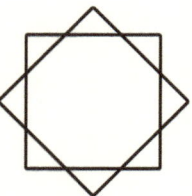

"This is the Circle o' Eight. See this square, that's turned to look like a diamond? That's the regents o' the solstice/equinox days, the masculine impulses o' each skyturn. An' this horizontal square is the cross-quarter days o' the feminine," Coillore began, quickly wiping their shell bowls with ash and stacking them near the door to be rinsed in the burn. "Eight regents reside in this star o' the seasons, regents o' the agricultural year, one god an' goddess in each quadrant. An' always, the masculine impulses arise at dawn, while the feminine open at dusk on the eve before. They sit just below the Pillars we talked about in yer last lesson. Remember how I told ye that all is structured into mind, heart, an' action? Well, the quarters o' the skyturn are built that same way. Here, I'll show ye. Let's begin wi' spring, hm?" Firinn put down his tea and leaned toward the drawing, knowing he'd be held to account for these teachings later on.

"Rulin' Imbolc is the fae girl, Fiona (feeohna). This is when the divine child template for the skyturn is lifted out o' the cosmic core ethers by Bridget, three days ahead (Feb 1st, eve). Then on Imbolc eve (Feb 4th), Fiona sends them into the mental ethers o' the six inner sheaths. The mind ethers o' the six lower sheaths make up the mental body, ladd, remember? Imbolc means lamb's milk, as ye ken, an' it's the milk o' Bridget reachin' in to bring the new divine child structures out o' the core an' into the mental ethers that milk signifies, for lambs are the divine child animal on earth.

So, Fiona rules the girl impulses for the skyturn, which Imbolc (imbolt) brings forth, the feminine half o' the mental wave. Her directives'll always bring forth fears o' the little girl within, often related to self-hatred, isolation, or overwork. But the little girl's dancin' joy, passion, an' surprises o' the new year come through at this time as well. Fiona's impulses last a moon an' a half, long enough for the new changes to be stabilized into the girl's mental ethers within before Fiona's consort, Finnegan, takes the reins. An' in the end, some long awaited freedom for the inner wee lass is always given. Fionna's star is Delphinus, the dolphin.

Then Finnegan opens the boy portals on the Vernal Equinox, Alban Eiler (alaban ayler, light of the earth), to awaken the male half o' the mental body within. The boy's sap o' life, that loves life to the full an' fuels all growth, along wi' his personal will in action is released that dawn, too,. Finnegan's chick full o' the ladd's humor, love o' adventure, an' time in nature, quite a fun lovin' pair, he an'

Fiona, eh? His star is Volans, the flyin' fish. An' his fears usually relate to misuse o' personal power or all that rushin' out of alignment wi' Màiri's slow flow o' life. Again, Finn's impulses last a moon an' a half, until the new boy structures o' growth are firm. This is why the red dragons o' the mental ethers are called the Fiona/Finnegan forces.

All right, let's move to Bealltain (beealchen), me almost favorite," the druid continued. "It's ruled by the goddess Belissima, bringin' forth impulses for growth o' the feminine virgin within. These move into the emotional body or emotional ethers o' all lower sheaths. An' mind, ladd, the other ethers dinna close over the year, but remain active, so at this point, the core, mental, an' emotional ethers are all lit up, as the divine child within grows throughout the year. But this Bealltain impulse anchors into the child heart as well, the thymus. Later in this moon, Leanan (lanan, sweetheart) o' the White Pentagram, opens the lower heart o' the feminine, the heart proper, an' the virgin girl impulse moves there, on a day that'll be called Pentecost.

In her moon an' a half, Belissima prepares the virgin heart o' the feminine for her union wi' the virgin male, Belenos, which occurs on Midsummer morn. Her fears'll usually relate to male domination or sexual misuse. Belissima always brings in some passion for change that's dear to the virgin girl's heart, too. But Belissima has the virgin's seductive allure as well, so there are sensuous delights to offset the pain o' growth." And the druid smiled, thinking of his youthful revelries on Bealltain nights, especially the evening on the priestess isle, when he'd met his own Ailis. "Belissima can be quite pushy in preparin' the feminine within for this marriage, cleansin' out old distortions to love wi' that powerful thymus light o' hers. For Belissima's is the white lightnin' force, Huath (hooah), Hawthorne, the strong cleansin' stream. She cleanses severe imbalances on earth wi' her lightnin' storms, too. Her star is in Virgo, ladd.

Then on Midsummer's dawn, Belenos, the virgin male, rises to the fore, takin' his moon an' half as regent. It's him Bealltain is named for, ladd, but he rules Midsummer, Alban Hefin (alaban hefeen, light of summer). It's he who opens the masculine half o' the emotional ethers by burnin' off the bindin's over the masculine heart on Midsummer's dawn to unite the hearts o' the virgin male an' virgin lass within, in the lower heart noo. Their union o' hearts is the strongest impulse there is in all the skyturn, ladd, a sweet <u>sweet</u> day.

But because Belenos is the world server, he always turns their hearts toward helpin' the tribe, him an' her united in a close workin' partnership that wants to put all that's been learned in the past skyturn into real effect. He blends his male drive into her passion, doin' whatever's necessary, an' often this is the time o' the hardest work o' the skyturn, the tribal projects o' summer. That fits wi' his star, too, Hercules. An' by the end o' his moon an' a half, the new growth structures are firm in the emotional ethers o' the masculine within. Belenos an' Belissima serve the green dragons, the emotional ethers, the Spiritus/Sanctus forces.

Then comes Lughnasa (loonasa), me very favorite." And the druid handed Firinn a piece of apple bread. "It's the openin' o' the mother impulse o' the skyturn. This moves the yearly impulses into the action ethers, the feminine there, an' begins the manifestation o' the harvest into the physical, the first fruits. An' some very personal gift is always sent by the White Tara three days after Lughnasa, (Aug. 8th), too, for it's the Goddess Who truly manifests into the sensate realms. We hold our great games on Lughnasa, too, in honor o' the Mother-o'-All that Alba serves.

But it's Cìrceidh (keerkay, Gaia) the earth mother o' this Circle o' Eight, who rules this holy day, releasin' the feminine impulses into the action ethers for the moon an' a half to follow. Cìrceidh's star compound is in Bootes, the star called 'the girdle'. But her specialty is soil, an' all soil is infused wi' her magical love that wants to manifest whatever we need, to nourish an' feed her many children across the globe. Her fears usually relate to the sappin' force o' the dark one, that shadow coverin' the inner mother that results in overwork an' self neglect to meet the needs o' family an' tribe. It's exhaustion o' the feminine, ladd. But the mother's nourishment for all her bairns in tasty delights comes through at this time, too.

Then Lugh (loo), the one Lughnasa is named for, takes over at the Autumnal Equinox, Alban Elved (alaban ehlvet, light of the water), openin' the portals o' the father growth impulse for the skyturn. This is when the action ethers o' the inner masculine light up. As regent o' manifestation into the sensate realms, Lugh is the god o' nourishment, the harvest. His star is the herdsman in Bootes. An' his moon an' a half calls forth the strong arms o' the father to bring in the harvest an' feed his many children all winter long. But his challenges relate to the misuse o' resources, no havin' enough, or overwork again. Lugh an' Circeidh serve the yellow dragons, the Lion/Lioness forces.

At Samhein(1) (sahven) then, it's the grandmother goddess o' the same name who pulls the emotional impulses back into the core ethers o' the heart, openin' the feminine, eh? Samhein's influence lasts till Midwinter. An' she cuts down the efforts o' the passin' cycle, for she's the goddess o' the scythe, severin' the flow o' life from the Goddess to all that must be abandoned at this time. This is when the last sheaves o' grain are laid aside for spring's seedin' an' the poor are allowed to glean the fields. Samhein's breakdown phase is often the most difficult o' the skyturn, for many things are left behind at this time, relationships an' personal efforts o' all kinds. Her energies are as tough as stone, too, resistance doin' no good at all. An' she activates the three new fears to be faced over the comin' winter, too.

Many fear Samhein as the goddess o' death, but in truth, she simply washes us clean o' the old an' unneeded, lessons already learned. Her star system is Eriadne, the end o' the river. Some call that river the Styx. For there's a boat there that takes all the broken structures across to the reservoir o' Tara's pregnant sea. But grandma Samhein brings rest from heavy labors, too. But then, the five intercessory days o' the druid year, also called after this goddess (Samhien 2), bring forward our celebration o' thanksgivin' to the White Goddess for the gift o' life an' the blessings o' the passin' skyturn. So, there's joy in that, at least.

Then at Midwinter, it's Samhein's consort, Bran, who opens the portals o' the inner granda, the masculine core ethers o' the heart. It's when the bone time an' fears o' winter are starin' ye in the face, the toughest o' the skyturn. His influence lasts till Imbolc again, overlappin' the new skyturn for a moon an' a half. Bran dismantles the mental, emotional, an' action structures o' the masculine for the passin' skyturn. But he also saves the light seeds o' the passin year, the kernels o' truth, an' hands them up to Merlin o' the Luckenbooth light structure that ye'll learn about in yer brown robe lessons, seeds that are built into the permanent light body o' each individual. Together, Samhein an' Bran work wi' the black an' white dragons, the Panther/Polar Bear forces. It's ice an' snow these two overlight, eh?"

As Coillore stopped speaking, Fìrinn was snoring softly, completely worn out by the day's games and the druid's soft droning voice. But the druid only smiled, gently laying his furs over the boy.

"Ach, I dinna mean to do that…," Fìrinn started up from the chair, beginning to apologize. But the druid only laid a hand on Fìrinn's shoulder, gently pointing him toward the pallet.

"I talk too much," the druid admitted quietly, "especially about the Diamond Core. Never mind, Fìrinn. I'll send ye back down in the mornin'. Ye need yer rest most o' all." And in moments, after he flopped onto the furs, the boy's soft snores resumed. All that night, Coillore sat vigil over the ladd who would be king, the druid holding Fìrinn in his heart. A small smile lit the old druid's face as he watched the boy through the wee hours, and the love in the druid's eyes was warmer than the fire he kept going all night as well.

Fìrinn expected the fear of his initiations to be the most difficult thing he'd have to face, so he was unprepared for the intensity of his feelings for Soillse. He simply couldn't get her out of his mind, or only with great difficulty. Even the Diamond Core paled beside the desire he felt as he imagined holding her again and kissing that mouth. Many nights under his furs, he dreamed of Soillse, and afterwards his loins ached half the morning for want of her. How could he complete his initiations or anything else this way?

One night, Fìrinn waited after the lessons with the other boys in the oak clearing hidden in the birch wood, to ask Coillore how to tame the urgency of his need. But the druid, bent over in his white robe, spreading the ashes of the fire under the old oak, only smiled.

"'Tis the call o' the Goddess. She wants union at all levels, an' nothin' else'll satisfy Her." There was a sparkle in Coillore's eyes as he looked up. "Best no to fight it, ladd. Her intimacy stream is the strongest there is, stronger than fear, stronger than death. An' mastery can be difficult, but those lessons, too, will come in time." The druid stood and put an arm around the boy's shoulders. "'Tis a sweet teachin' overall, though the tamin' of it comes slow, I'll warn ye o' that." Coillore took up his staff and drew the Creator Sun, two concentric circles in the earth, putting his staff into the central circle. It's the Goddess Herself comin' through the lass, callin' ye home to Her Heart. Where do ye think love comes from, ladd? Go to the lassie! Hold nothin' back at all!" But Fìrinn only groaned.

And then the dreams began in earnest. As soon as Fìrinn closed his eyes on his pallet in the long house, amid the snores of forty lads, Soillse's image was there, kissing him with burning lips. In his dreams, she drew cloud-soft fingers over his chest and put his manhood into her mouth. And he startled awake halfway to dawn, wondering if he'd awakened the whole long house with his moaning.

But as soon as he fell asleep again, Soillse put his manhood into her woman's place and pulled on it with velvet skin, soft and soft, setting his loins afire. And then she turned into a wild thing let loose, and they were like two flames burning as one sun, till he loosed his seed. In the morning, he'd waken, spent and cold, and the dreams gentled his need for half a day, no more.

Then, in another night or two, the dreams were back, flushing his face, heating his loins, Soillse's breasts quivering and her eyes full of love's moisture always before him. And he could barely contain himself all over again. But at least he was warm under his furs all winter long.

Firinn took his third initiation a quarter moon before the Vernal Equinox, a strange burning vision. The ladd was anxious this time, after the water initiation a skyturn ago that had nearly ruined his legs, trudging in his light summer buckskin breeks and shirt behind Coillore. Through the muck of the deer track beside the burn, they headed west, then south, over the high sodden moors to the old dolmen. This dolmen had been built centuries before by the olden folk of the land. But as Firinn settled into the sunken stone seat in the dank chamber, underneath the great lintel, he immediately felt the Goddess come in to hold him. And this brought great comfort. As he waited, with his head swimming from the ritual herbs and the whispers of the spring night all around him, the dolmen faded into a dark haze.

And he'd barely called forth the Goddess and the elementals, when the spirit of air whistled through the stones and blew in around his head. Then suddenly, he felt himself expand, his whole body this time, not just his mind. Quickly, he felt himself spread out into a billion tiny particles, as if he no longer had skin to hold himself in one piece. And he panicked then with the fear he might never be whole again, tiny bits of himself drifting off forever through the stars. But he remembered Coillore's voice drilling into him not to fight the forces that came. So the ladd calmed himself, breathing deeply and imagining his heart opening like a flower to receive the teachings.

And in the end, Firinn simply merged with the golden stars, great spirits of light that lived and breathed of their own accord. He felt the whole star network, too, the mind of the universe, pulsing as one to the same electric rhythm. It surrounded and connected all beings in every world, holding all in a vast cocoon of light, just the way the glove of water held his own body in the sea. He envisioned an endless gossamer web, vibrating with power and quivering with joy, reaching into infinite space. And he knew he could travel along it in his mind from one end of the universe to the other in an instant.

And then the air around him began to glow, the way Coillore had that Midwinter's dawn. In its effervescence, Fìrinn's mind quickened suddenly, and he felt small electric jolts popping in his cells. And the sense of magic became so strong, it frightened him a bit. Could he change into light, one cell at a time, and vanish into thin air? His head hummed and ached with it, and he breathed in slow gulps to calm the fear. Fear could be your death in an initiation like this, Coillore had said, over and over, during his years of teaching. Never give in to it. So Fìrinn imagined himself shrinking into the clear Creator flame in his heart and let the vision intensify of its own accord.

He saw tiny fires bursting inside the cells of his bones and watched as galaxies and stars took their places in the familiar constellations of the cosmos. And suddenly, he knew there was a burning nucleus in those tiny crystals in his bones for every one of the myriad stars in the night sky, so he himself was a tiny replica of the cosmos! He saw pulses whizzing over long arcs of light, great strings of stars that lit pathways across vast reaches of the cosmic deeps. And in them, he felt tremendous force restrained that could destroy whole worlds, if ever unleashed. And he saw answering zings along his own arm or leg, so he knew the laying out of stars in his cells was precise and that each could communicate to the other, one star to one cell and back again. And his mind swirled with these knowings.

And then, as Fìrinn lay back on the stone bench of the dolmen, he saw a shimmering network of light emerge from the ethers, so fine it looked like a dragonfly's wing. Yellow surges of electric playfulness made him happier than he'd ever felt, the light coursing through his brain and down his spine, sending tingles through his nerves everywhere. As this wildness pulsed through him, he suddenly wanted to do cartwheels across the moor. An he felt like he could climb the Cuchullin peaks in a single leap. And then, just as quickly, instead, he hungered to explore all the lands of earth, every one, as if the planet was one huge playground and he a wee ladd who could put on his dragonfly wings whenever he liked and fly anywhere at all.

After a time, Firinn saw a snippet of a vision, himself, older, in a far off land. He was on a great ship, rowing, the same one he'd glimpsed during his last initiation, and his arms and back hurt, every muscle dog-tired. And suddenly, Firinn realized this electric elemental would infuse him with its power if ever he was in need of superhuman strength, that he could call it forth now. He felt as if his life would one day depend on this initiation and this force that had become his brother tonight. Then slowly, the exhilaration receded, and he awakened out of the vision as dawn softened the horizon to the east over the spine of the ridge.

Firinn stood then, reaching out into a warm wind from the south, and faced the rising sun with tears in his eyes, taking in great gulps of sweet morning air. And he felt the spirit light of the universe webbed through it all, a shimmering network in every leaf and blade of grass. And Firinn bent to the Sun Lord with his hands together, and thought, how holy it all is and how full of love!

On Firinn's way down to Coillore's hut, a sprite of a wind picked him clear off his feet and sent him rolling down a dip in the moor. It took his breath away for a moment, and he whirled around, startled and frowning. But an image came to him then, clear as the dawn, of himself as a wee ladd rolling down the grassy slope outside the broch at home and Ma laughing. He'd raced outside the low entryway every firstsky to do just that, and the wind woman remembered! He could hear her breathy laughter over the hills, and he was amazed, sitting in the mud grinning, with his backside soaked through.

But Fìrinn was more startled still when it became clear he'd regained his throwing arm as well. Seumus felt sure it was the ladd's wits climbing themselves out of the druid muck at last. But Fìrinn knew better, for he felt the wind woman always at his side when he threw now and the electric thrill of light zinging along his arms.

But between the druid training and the sports in the yard, Fìrinn had few nights to spend with Soillse. And she had fewer to spend with him after all her chores were done, both too tired at the end of their long days. So over the winter, they slept together at the lean-to only once or twice a moon. Then just after the Vernal Equinox, word came that the Ard Righ, the high king of Skye, was on his deathbed. If the Sun Lord no longer chose this king to represent him, other lesser gods would soon be moving through the land. Another king must be chosen and soon.

Then as spring approached, in the Willow moon (April), news of the king's death reached them, the kingship trials set for Midsummer, three moons away, one of the two most powerfully masculine days of the skyturn. There'd be a hunt for all contenders and a druid divination ritual to make the final choice, the messenger said, a slender dark-haired, wiry warrior from the king's pavilion in Port Righ on the eastern shore across the isle.

And so, all hopefuls for the kingship began to prepare, Fìrinn among them. Seumus set them to running in the early morning darkness over the pebbles of the bay, from one rocky arm to another, back and forth. Fìrinn's feet had ached for moons after his water initiation nearly a skyturn before, a constant throbbing pain that disrupted his training until late last summer. But the pain had disappeared gradually during his nights with Soillse in the fall, though why that should be, Firinn couldna fathom. Still, her fingers on his toes brought back the warmth to them, where before there'd been only the constant cold. Once, during an early morning jog, Firinn thought of Duirc, his old adversary, back in his home tuath now after his manhood ritual last summer, enduring the same harsh training, no doubt.

There was no time to spend in the wood with Soillse after Seumus added the extra training, for Firinn was totally exhausted by the end of each day. He put his arm around her shoulders, and they walked the shore of an evening, or more often sat on the rocks of the low curved arms of the bay, too tired even to talk. He kissed her long, after darkness arrived to shelter them, but he couldn't afford another night at the lean-to now. Those sweet days would have to wait a few moons more, and then he'd give his very life to her.

Coillore became more insistent about completing Firinn's lessons on the structure of the Diamond Core, too, repeatedly telling the ladd he'd need this information to help him in the future. So, despite Firinn's exhaustion at the end of a long day's training, late one gloaming in the Willow moon (April), the old druid took the ladd to his hut. They walked up the burn path through the birch wood under dripping boughs, for the bay had been shrouded in heavy fog until late afternoon, when a wan sun finally broke through the clouds. And Firinn's mind felt as heavy as those clouds, steeped in the brine of fatigue.

"All right, laddie, never mind the memory stone noo," Coillore said, after they'd ducked into his small hut under the hide doorcloth and Firinn began to lie on the floor, preparing to heal ancient memories as usual. "Let's take a wee while in the sunset's warmth, an' then I'll explain the White Pentagram, the last light structure o' the Diamond Core." And Firinn breathed a sigh of relief, placed the stone on the altar, and followed Coillore out the doorskin into the unusually mild night. Settling in beside the burn and handing the ladd herbed flat bread with honey, fiddlehead soup, and a skin of mint flavored water, Coillore sat with his toes in the wee burn, pulling his old homespun workaday shift up over his knees. The druid let the ladd soak up the silence as the sun fell beyond the budding birch wood, everything dappled in its golden glow. A heaven-sent evening, the druid thought, and the chance of a lifetime, sharing the deepest lore with the one sent to carry all I ken into the future. Fìrinn, too, pulled up his doeskin breeks and put his feet in the babbling brook, laying back and letting the Goddess wash his fatigue away.

Finally, after the evening peace had softened the tension in Fìrinn's eyes, Coillore drew a five-pointed star in the soft earth.

"Below the Circle o' Eight sits the White Pentagram, ladd, the circle o' life," the druid began, "overlit by Tara, o' course. It anchors into the pelvic cradle, an' its regents overlight the life cycle o' each one o' us, Her path o' experience.

We have seven sheaths o' light within that match the seven worlds, as ye ken." And Coillore drew the familiar seven concentric circles in the earth. "I need to list them again as they're integral to this lesson, eh? The sheaths are, from the center outward; the Diamond Core or Diamant Cridhe, the Diamond Centerpoint or Diamant Meadhan, the cherubim or Leanabh Aingeil, the logos or Ceugant, the spirit or Gwynfydd, the soul or Annwyn, an' the sensate or Abred. As each child grows, these sheaths open an' close, from central core to outer sensate, until age 22.

The regents o' the star arms here wield the hidden streams an' forces that push an' direct us through our years. Where the Child Heart builds the forever magical child, the White Pentagram builds the divine child to be born on earth, the inner god an' goddess. In bairnhood, these White Pentagram regents are responsible for seein' that all wounds an' wisdom learned in all previous lives are built in durin' the first 21 skyturns o' every human life. An' this pentagram follows a Fibonacci spiral o' time that looks like a nautilus shell. That's Tara's slow growth pattern, which includes all that went before. Fibonacci is the name o' the man who'll discover it, thirteen centuries from noo.

The birth o' everyone's child o' light within happens gradually, a bit more every skyturn. In yer next lesson, we'll move to the Indigo Pentagram that overlights the dark child within an' works closely wi' this White Pentagram. So, one piece o' our inner divine child is birthed every skyturn, but also in a grander way in every life, especially durin' yer final life on earth, when yer shadow self is fully released an' the child ye were seeded wi' in yer original moment o' creation from the Creator Sun is finally released. Pure magic, eh! This final divine bairn brings forth yer happily-ever-after on earth, yer divine male wi' some global gift to earth an' yer one true love.

We each have an eternal true love in heaven, too, the one we were created wi' in our first moment out o' the Creator Sun. But at birth into human form, the opposite gender half o' us stays behind to become the higher self, lost to outer awareness the moment the doors o' birth close behind the newborn human babe. Then begins the descent process as the lights go out in the beloved core o' the creator sun an' go on in the outer creator sun within.

So, let's go through the regents o' this pentagram here, hm? In the first star arm sit Breith (bree, birth) an' Daimhin (jayveen, little deer), the fae bairns. Breith overlights the first two years o' life. These skyturns are when the wee fae lass lights in the core sheath are turned on inside, even if it's a laddie on the outside, eh? An' for each lifetime, Breith anchors the child o' light into earth wi' it's new family, bringin' intimacy wi' those who'll be it's closest allies it's whole life through. But it's the deep connection wi' the human Ma, wi' Màithreil,

Màiri, an' Tara o' the Creator Sun comin' through her, that Breith's primarily focused on. There'll always be some darkness wi' the human Ma, fears ye havena cleared, that keeps each inner lass disconnected from the Goddess on high as well. This phase builds the bedrock structures o' the pelvic floor, patterns o' intimacy that'll shape the babe's relationships it's whole life long, especially wi' closest friends or partners in later years. So these structures must be strong enough to sustain a lifetime. Every babe needs to be held by it's Ma, ladd, lots o' one-to-one time, for the earth cnnection wi' the <u>Goddess</u> is bein' built durin' infancy. An' if it's disrupted, the bairn willna be able to be intimate wi' anyone or connect to the Goddess it's whole life long, for Tara comes through intimacy wi' <u>everyone</u>, ladd, no just partners.

An' more than that, these early structures'll determine what kind o' mother each person'll become when they have bairns o' their own. Once Breith's influence is over at the end o' the first two skyturns o' life, when the feminine o' the Diamond Core sheath closes down, it's too late. This first star arm interpenetrates the stomach, when the bairn is learnin' to eat earth food, too. Nearly all these regent's stars are in Tara's Ursa Major complex, an' Breith's is called 'the first leap'. This White Pentagram anchors into the continent across the eastern channel, to be called Europe some day. An' Brieth's nation'll be called Hungary.

It's she who brings the other Creator Sun regents flow o' light through the human family, too: Daiden an' the Dagda through the human Da, plus the fae/cherub/virgin bairns, Abaid an' Uan, Eriu an' Finn, Maighdean an' Rìdire, through sisters an' brothers, so the babe feels heaven all around her still. An' Breith teaches the babe to hear an' feel its personal Creator Sun family members through the child's inner human ears an' eyes as well.

It's Breith's influence that keeps the babe alive oft times, for leavin' the realms o' light behind at birth is challengin'. Most want to go Home, especially wi' the family darkness each has chosen suddenly around them. An' durin' these first two years, Breith leads the bairn through the wounds o' their original descent through the outer Creator Sun an' Diamond Core realms, all but the inner Beloved Core. So, at the end o' the second year, the feminine core sheath within closes down an' the masculine lights up.

Then Daimhin takes over, from ages two to four, as the personal will to action or phallic force opens, the flow o' time an' the course o' each day, along wi' the first structures o' the ladd's future gift to earth. These interpenetrate the intestines an' manhood, an' it's often the time o' trainin' a bairn to use the latrine. Daimhin sees that the toddler connects wi' one elder in the tribe at this time, too, his Da or granda usually, who helps develop those destiny seeds within. It's a special relationship, bringin' the Dagda structures o' the father's Kingdom through in a very real way into the bairn's life. But the inner boy's destiny for change on earth always differs from the way things are done wi' the parents particularly. So these early family influences ever block the laddie's heart's desire for change, darkness the boy'll push against for long years to birth his inner divine child late in life.

An' the inner boy's will force is immature at this stage, too, selfish, ever wantin' its own way. To succeed in later life, his will must be moderated by the family an' tribe, but gently. Dinna crush the will o' any bairn, Firinn, for that forces it into hidin', a will force in separation from the All. That's where so much trouble comes from in the first place! Still, it's important to give the wee bairn family chores an' responsibilities at this age, to tame an' shape his will toward the greater good. An' take time to pray wi' yer bairns at this age for direction from above to keep their wills from gettin' out o' hand as well. Such are Daimhin's specialties. He moves the bairn through the masculine descent through the Diamond Core, blocks to the inner god, so restraints on action an' distortions o' love's truth, plus hurried patterns o' life, mostly, again all but the Beloved Core. At the end o' Daimhin's two skyturns, the masculine half o' the inner core lights go out as this sheath closes down. But through it all, Daimhin protects the bedrock layer o' love from all outside influences. For he builds the pelvic stone circle o' truth in the abdomen, layin' the foundation, the certainty that love does indeed rule the universe upon which all the false layers are built, the very basic truths o' love, truths that'll lead an' support the bairn his whole life long. These come through the human Da or Granda mainly, that one special relationship. An' once a disciple reaches these high levels again late in life again, the stone circle o' the pelvic girdle activates an' connects to the individual's Creator Sun family especially. Daimhin's own star is the 'root o' the tail' in Ursa Major, an' his nation'll be Greece.

Then the next star arm o' the pentagram moves into place at age four, twirlin' ever sunwise noo. It's Eostre (yostra, Ostara) an' Credne, the cherub children who sit there, Eostre overlightin' the descent through the diamond centerpoint, for both boy an' girl within, an' Credne, the cherubim levels. At the beginnin' o' this phase, the middle passage through the abyss repeats itself in miniature, the darkest evil any bairn'll have to undergo.

Eostre overlights ages four an' five, an' she anchors into the child's ovaries. An' this wee goddess is most powerful, for she creates all that manifests in yer own wee world, the egg o' yer life, accordin' to yer inner beliefs. There's an egg o' light deep in the child heart within, too, that holds the dreams o' what yer divine child wishes to create, yer highest destiny on earth. An' around this are all yer fears. Eostre carefully blends these messages o' darkness an' light into the life tapestry that's the outpicturin' o' yer own inner self, teachin' the inner lassie that she creates the world around her in a very real way, throughout life noo. Eostre's star is 'the second leap' o' Ursa Major, eh? An' her nation'll be called Poland.

Near the end o' the third year or early in the fourth, the One Beloved stream at the very core o' the Creator Sun opens at Tara's direction, an' the bairn feels this strong love flow through the parent o' the opposite gender, the lassie through her Da, the laddie through his Ma. This sets the stage for all love partnerships throughout the bairn's life. After everyone's original creation into light in the Creator Sun, their feminine steeped in Oghama's Heart, their masculine in Tara's. So the Creators were our first love relationship an' remain our eternal partners, the Source o' love in all outer relationships as well.

Because it's the most concentrated love force in the universe, this stage is held back until age four, when the bairn is old enough to tolerate both the intensity an' the core wound wrapped into it. But this is a most sacred skyturn, when the Beloved force is awakened and anchored into the child's mental ethers. It's intended as a time o' modelin' for the bairn, the strongest love force first experienced within the restraint o' the parent/child relationship. But it's also the time when the core woundin' occurs, which is always a severin' o' the child from the One Beloveds o' the Creator Sun. It disrupts that special opposite-gender parental relationship, too. This wound, plus the hunger for the Beloveds the individual once knew, is what propels him or her to make the difficult climb back into union wi' the Creators once more. At the end o' Eostre's phase, the diamond centerpoint sheath closes an' the cherubim sheath lights up.

Eostre's consort, Credne then, rules bairnhood from the sixth through the seventh winters. He anchors into the testicles, ladd. Credne rules all structures o' belief within an' creates the stairway Home, the path o' light through all our fears to final freedom in love. He makes certain all lasses an' laddies within recognize that pathway an' develop confidence in their ability to walk it to the very end. Often this happens through the spiritual practices o' the family, the religious traditions the child comes in contact wi' at this time, but mainly through the example set by the bairn's parents. An' Credne rules that deep bass bell o' truth within, too, knowin' what is right an' what is not. But he also brings those cherubim level boy an' girl fears forward, harsh mother overwork an' punitive influences mainly, which sacrifice the gentle life o' the bairn within, until this sheath also closes down. Credne's Ursa Major star is called 'the groin, an' his nation'll be the Czech Republic.

Then age eight marks the openin' o' the emotional ethers, the emotional body within, when the baby teeth begin to fall out, eh? So in the sheaths that are open, the core, mental, an' emotional ethers are all active an' flowin'.In the next star arm, then, at ages eight an' nine, the virgin lass, Leanan (leenan, sweetheart), overlights the life cycle. This is when the logos sheath within lights up but only the feminine. An' it interpenetrates the pancreas, ladd, the sweetness o' life, eh? An' like her name, this goddess brings in the joy o' union wi' like hearts an' the One Beloveds, too.

But at this stage, there's always a shift away from the family, a dimmin' o' closeness wi' the human Ma especially. It's the time o' fosterin, when ladds leave their tribes an' lassies assume real responsibilities that take both away from playful time wi' their Mas. But durin' this logos phase, Leanan directs the inner lassie toward the mother in nature an' within, instead, so bairns often become more quiet an' inward at this time o' life, wanderin' the forest paths an' speakin' wi' the spirit world beyond the veil.

And it's at this time, the core wound from age four is repeated, an event similar to the first experience, but less intense. This results in the belief that the individual is somehow creatin' these woundin's on the outside, that he or she is at fault, so each bairn quickly covers his or her inner self o' light. But wi' this second woundin', Leanan sparks the fire o' passion for freedom for the virgin lass on earth, too, gettin' rid o' male domination, sexual misuse, or criticism, perhaps. An' Leanan carefully weaves these difficult experiences into the logos sheath, to be awakened later in life durin' the ascension process.

At this point, after the second woundin', the child turns to the parent o' the same gender, the lassies lookin' to their Mas, the laddies to their Das, to take on the societal patterns o' that parent to fill the inner void o' the self. This parental mirrorin' happens through imitation an' observation mainly, for the very young child's closeness wi' that parent is never again restored. It's durin' this time that the current family patterns are most firmly structured into the bairn, though. So the same gender parent needs to be most careful o' the example they set, for it will be deeply absorbed, even if the parent-child relationship appears non-existent. Leanan's Ursa Major star is 'the third leap', and' her nation, the Netherlands.

Leanan's consort is Nuada, an' he leads the laddie into his first preparation to become a man, his first real work in the outer world, ages ten an' eleven, when the logos masculine lights up. This is when ladds are put into apprenticeships for their life's destiny, like ye at the tuath here. So it's important an' often feels heaven sent. But it's a sad time, too, the ladd not only missin' his family somethin' fierce, but havin' to give up his bairnhood as well. For Nuada's fears at this level are the mental domination an' violence forces that propel the bairn to leave the innocence o' his inner child behind, workin' overhard, learnin' to be a warrior an' hurtin' animals in the hunt." And Fìrinn nodded vigorously at this, his eyes full of tears. "But like Leanan, Nuada leads each ladd to the comfortin' arms o' nature. An' at the end o' these two skyturns, the masculine o' the logos sheath closes, down as well. Nuada's Ursa star is 'the flank' an' his nation, Spain.

An' then at the time o' puberty, the lassie's moontime an' the ladd's manhood, the great shift into the action ethers occurs. So in the sheaths that are open, all ethers, core, mental, emotional, an' action are flowin'. Puberty marks the awakenin' o' the virgins o' the lower heart, too, as the child heart virgins in the thymus close down.

Then it's Boudicca o' the next star arm here who overlights ages twelve to halfway through thirteen. Age twelve is when the logos sheath closes an' the feminine half o' the spirit sheath opens. This goddess rules the sovereignty o' the feminine, the power o' personal choice, especially in matters o' the heart, but in feminine tribal leadership, too. Sexual maturity is when the young person becomes free to act on their own in the tribes. Plus, the action ethers contain all the stored talents an' traits o' past earth lives as well, so the young person feels like a fully functionin' adult at this time. An' in many ways, they are, all except knowin' the prevailin' structures o' this current lifetime they'll have to learn to function in. This is what their parents can still teach them. An' at this point, there's a clear shift away from parents as authority figures, wi' age mates takin' their place.

But Boudicca also sees that the love o' the Creators is deeply felt durin' this phase, too, for puberty reopens the inner doorway to Them in the back o' the heart. The first skyturn after puberty is a year o' sexual restraint, as ye ken, to connect wi' the One Beloveds an' grow used to that strong love force again." But Firinn was thinking, thank goodness Soillse's virgin year is over and gone, though, for I can't wait to bring those Beloveds into real action. "

An' then, at the end o' this virgin skyturn after the first moontime ,comes the first joinin' (making love). This closes that doorway to the One Beloveds in the back o' the heart again an' brings the Beloved stream through the outer partner, instead, eh? After that, Boudicca's influence brings mastery an' cleansin' o' the sexual impulses mainly, especially the rapin' force that so corrupted the beloved stream on earth. She tames the flames o' desire an' heals addictions an' passions that lead only to control or death, too. It's the full release o' the virgin goddess from darkness Boudicca wants, restoration o' the inner feminine into the spirit sheath, the victory in lower worlds. That's the meanin' o her name, too, victory. Boudicca's energies interpenetrate the waterfalls o' the kidneys, decidin' what to cleanse away an' what to keep in the emotional body. She's regent o' waterfalls across earth, too. Her Ursa Major star is 'the thigh', an' her nation'll be Italy.

The spirit sheath that's open durin' these early adolescent skyturns interpenetrates the nerves an' brain as well. So especially when Boudicca's consort, Arecurius, is regent, halfway through age thirteen an' all o' fourteen, when the masculine half o' the spirit sheath is activated, strong drivin' forces o' mental an' time pressure abound. Arecurius leads the inner male into more intensive preparation for his destiny at this time, overlightin' the action glands, the adrenals, ladd, where the spirit sheath anchors in. Always this stage o' life'll build the inner world server, the male virgin that wants to lift the whole world up, his final destiny bein' built slowly an' carefully through the years.

Arecurius will always build into place one specific destiny dream for each lifetime, too, something the ladd dearly loves. There'll be hard realities to face to accomplish it, though, for it'll only come to fruition when the spirit levels open late in life. Arecurius brings in one particular friend durin' these early years, too, who'll help fulfill that spirit sheath destiny o' adulthood as well. These years move each bairn along their ancient fall through the spirit realms, ladd, an' by the end o' the fourteenth skyturn, the heavy work an' mental pressures close this masculine sheath down as well. Arecurius's star in Ursa Major is 'the bull', ladd an' his nation, Germany.

Then in the center o' this White Pentagram light structure sit Danu an' Luis, the mother an' father aspects here, builders o' the divine child within every skyturn. Luis builds the permanent structures o' the divine male an' highest destiny into the liver, the world server. Sent from his star city on the wee lion (Leo Minor), his light cleanses the solid masculine muscular structures within, too. Danu builds the wise woman into the spleen, the knowings o' wisdom in all walks o' life, especially the home. Her azure waters o' Aquarius there wash the feminine clean as well.

Danu is the star mother o' the Celtic race, too, Fìrinn, birthed in our ancestral lands from her river, the Danube. An' in that golden time to come in twenty-one centuries, the Celts will rise again to assist in the revelation o' the Goddess they serve. One day, Danu'll be called Europa, for that's where this White Pentagram anchors in. In time, twelve nations'll arise there, each servin' one o' these regents. Danu's land'll be called Austria, Luis's, France. An' when the day dawns for all divine children to be born across earth, Danu, as divine mother, will be the overlightin' influence on earth. That'll be known as the Aquarian age, for hers is the star compound o' the Tuathe de Danaan (tribal village of Danu), her holy city o' light. She especially longs for the revelation o' the Goddess in those final days, as all divine children are born here. That'll be a sight to see, eh, ladd?" And the old druid's eyes shone as he looked out into the birches a moment, his face lit with this vision of the future.

"So, at age fifteen to halfway through sixteen, wi' the openin' o' the feminine soul sheath within, Danu begins to overlight the life cycle. Hers an' Luis's are the final skyturns before the young folk leave their parents or mentor's home an' set up housekeepin' on their own. So, Danu's always creatin' special times o' closeness wi' the birth family before the young lassie leaves for good, especially wi' the maternal grandma, who may no be alive much longer. For Danu ever wants to strengthen those maternal ancestral ties. It's at this time ancestral patterns o' darkness are brought forward in life, too, clan patterns that have been in place for generations (genetic). Often this is a heavy cloak for the individual to wear.

An' in preparation for marriage, Danu brings forward two or three love relationships, each individual's husbands or wives from their most recent human lifetimes. Another lover from this time in life will return in late adulthood to burn off the logos sheath as well, but in youth, this one is merely adored an' kept at a distance.

An' at this phase, there'll be another clash wi' the prevailin' tribal structures o' the parents, too. This time, it reveals the main thrust o' the young person's destiny an' breaks the emotional tie wi' both parents to prepare for the independence o' adulthood. Danu's focus will ever be on some darkness o' the tribe that once closed the young person's inner goddess down. An' remember, it's the soul sheath an' descent Danu overlights, the astral realms, so the fears can be intense, dark influences into the mind, false friendships, or betrayals o' the heart.

But then Luis takes the reins at age sixteen an' a half through seventeen, openin' the masculine half o' the soul sheath. An' Luis is ever concerned wi' society at large, the father's structures in the world. So, Luis activates temptations to power an' control, domination o' the feminine, includin' sexual domination, plus so much action that the inner feminine's need for rest gets completely overwhelmed. Often the workload is severe, both on the mind an' body. But Luis weaves threads o' passion through these years that call forth a lifelong devotion for this work, bringin' in masters an' precise information that draw from the trades o' the individual's last three lifetimes as well. An' Luis makes certain this destiny fits the current social patterns, where Nuada's might fly far too high to ever touch down here. It's at the end o' these years that the masculine half o' the soul sheath closes an' the sensate lights up.

Then Iona (eye-ohna), o' our own sacred isle, an' her consort, Mabon, in the apex arm here, overlight the next phase. Iona an' Mabon's regency is individuation o' the divine child into the sensate world, full realization. That's why the sacred isle is called simply 'I' here, the letter wi' the same meanin' in the Ogham alphabet.

Iona an' Mabon are bairns, Firinn. An' this time o' life is a second bairnhood in a way, for the young person has moved to their own hut or a different tribe altogether. Life feels fresh an' new, but sometimes insecure, as individuals establish their adult patterns. Durin' her skyturns, ages eighteen an' nineteen, when the feminine half o' this sheath is activated, Iona brings forward one serious love relationship, often the husband or wife o' the last lifetime on earth, but no always. This is the handfastin' skyturn, though we in our times dinna wait so long to marry. But that's the pattern o' the future, ladd. An' this relationship paves the way for lifelong partnership, the hallmark o' the sensate realms. But durin' this time, the deepest fear o' Beloved love from the Creator Sun rises up, too, an' this darkest fear will seed itself into the inner feminine o' both human partners.

An' durin' Mabon's skyturns, ages twenty an' twenty-one, he brings forward the specific patterns o' the young man's life work, the young person's first real responsibility in the tribes. This work'll always build the societal work patterns the young man'll be carryin' his whole adult life. But Mabon also brings in one severe darkness that grips the young man's heart, watchin' others in pain an' feelin' powerless to change the circumstances, perhaps. An' this pain'll seed commitment into the depths o' the male heart to ease this particular difficulty in the world, which becomes a strong undercurrent o' the ladd's whole workin' life.

Iona's relationship flaw an' Mabon's work challenge lay the foundation o' all marriage an' destiny darknesses until late in life, too, for these are the very core fears underlyin' all else. Always these stream from the Creator Sun Beloveds an' play out durin' the very end o' life, too, the last eighteen skyturns when the White Pentagram reactivates, till the divine child finally breaks free as the individual passes to the Otherworld. Durin' the <u>final</u> lifetime on earth, though, these darknesses o' young adulthood bring forward the one core fear around which everythin' else is wrapped that'll free the divine child from earth life once an' for all. Iona's star is the Southern Cross and Mabon's is Perseus, ladd. Her nation'll be Belgium someday an' his, Portugal.

At the end o' this phase, the beginnin' of age twenty-two, the inner opposite gender closes down in the sensate sheath, so light is flowin' through only one fourteenth o' the divine child's original light body, the same gender half o' the sensate sheath within." And Coillore put his staff into the seventh circle out. "By the start o' the twenty-second skyturn o' every life, all the wounds o' the original fall have been built into place. At this point, the young person steps off the same platform they were standin' on at the end o' their last lifetime on earth. Quite amazin' how precise the spirit world can be, eh, ladd? An' then life's ascension process begins that those Pillar regents overlight, instead.

The White Pentagram overlights the birth o' the divine child o' each one o' us for every skyturn, too, Fìrinn. This hidden cycle'll become the holy days o' that Christian religion o' the future I mentioned before. Each skyturn, the seeds o' the comin' year's divine child are implanted by Arte into the inner Guinefar womb on Midwinter mornin', as ye ken. Arte an' Guinfar are regents in the Luckenbooth light structure who bring in the patterns o' the year ahead, all that will manifest into physical experience. This seedin' happens for each o' us, ladd, an' thus begins the divine child cycle o' the year. Three mornin's later, once Guinefar has organized the light seeds into specific form an' timin', these structures emerge out o' the soil o' her womb, an' the first star arm o' the White Pentagram in the abdomen activates. This is the first birth o' the year's divine child, into the core sheath only. In time, that day'll be called Christmas, ladd." And the druid bent to trace the druid letter A in the earth

Then Breith an' Daimhin overlight growth through the core sheath, she movin' through the fears o' the inner infant girl. An' twelve days after Christmas, these divine child structures open out into the three creator flames, lights in the mind, heart, an' action centers that create our outer intellectual, emotional, an' physical experiences in life. Then, halfway to Candlemas, the masculine core sheath lights up, too. An' Daimhin leads the toddler bairn within through his fears for the year, till the inner toddler's sure o' himself, the structures firm. On Candlemas eve then, the divine bairn for the year, the lamb, is birthed out of the core sheath into the centerpoint sheath. And Breith's birth-pushin' force through the entire core, both feminine an' masculine, is signified by the Ogham letter A, the long A sound noo, all these long vowels makin' the sound o' their own names. For us, it's Ailm, the Elm tree, eh? This letter'll ever mean havin' the fortitude an' trust o' a child, enough to move through one's deepest darkness to bring new light to life. Candlemas is the day the mother o' that holy man, Jesus, the one I mentioned before, will bring her babe to their priest for the first time to have him sanctified, or so the story will be told. An' unlike the descent o' human bairnhood, the inner sheaths remain open an' flowin' as more an' more o' the divine child is awakened through each year. <u>Lovely</u>, eh?

On Candlemas eve (Feb. 1st) then, the cherub girl o' the centerpoint sheath is born. An' then, Eostre an' Credne overlight the passage through the centerpoint sheath, until the beginnin' o' Lent, the feminine durin' the first half, the masculine durin' the second. This often involves a steep climb through the abyss darkness, rushin' an' mental confusions. Lent is the moon an' half before Easter in the Christian way o' seein' things, ladd. But it gets a bit complicated here, because Easter is the seventh day (Sunday) morn after the full moon followin' the Vernal Equinox. So, both Easter an' Lent move around from year to year. An' if Easter is early, there's very little time before Lent begins. So, on those years, the centerpoint fears'll be light or skipped over entirely. If Easter's late, though, the centerpoint fears'll be included, since there's plenty o' time between Candlemas an' Lent to address them.

Then the cherubim sheath opens when Lent begins, again the lass lit up durin' the first half, the boy durin' the second, this phase still overlit by Eostre an' Credne. The main cherubim fears relate to the child sacrifices o' old matriarchal times, so challenges durin' this phase can be severe.

Then that heaven-sent Easter morn arrives, an' the three core fears o' each winter, those heavy bands over the heart, are removed. An' the divine child is fully born out o' the cherubim sheath. This is Eostre's birth, through both centerpoint an' cherubim sheaths, an' in the future, that day'll be called Easter after her. This is the long O sound, Onn (ohnn) or Gorse for us, the struggle an' sweetness o' growth, succeedin' through both the abyss an' dark mother child sacrifice fears.

There's a period o' rest an' integration for a quarter moon after this. An' then the logos sheath lights up, the feminine half, the virgin, which the goddess Leanan overlights. The inner feminine is fully built into this sheath by Pentecost, fifty days past Easter. It'll be said that a holy spirit'll infuse that holy man, Jesus, on this day a century from noo, Firinn. But actually, it's the virgin lass, free within at last. The element o' the logos is fire, too, ladd, so this passage can bring great passion into play. An' Leanan sparks one desire for change every skyturn, too, always linked to the upliftment o' virgin girls on earth.

At Pentecost then, the masculine half o' the logos sheath within lights up, the virgin, as Nuada, Leanan's consort, takes the reins. But this day o' Pentocost also moves around from year to year. If it's early, there'll be lots o' time for masculine virgin growth in the cycle. But if it's late, there'll be extra time for feminine growth but only half a moon for him, eh? On June 24th then, the masculine o' the logos sheath is fully formed an' the inner virgins birthed, Leanan's delivery this time. An' the push through this sheath is the long U sound, Ur (oor) or Heather, signifyin' the wild passion, backbone strength, an' heart love o' the virgins.

An' on this day as well, Leanan washes away all fear debris o' the first half o' the yearly cycle, the halfway point o' this hidden divine child yearly stream. That day'll be named for another holy man, John the Baptist, a teacher who'll specialize in baptism, washin' folk in rivers to start them all on this Christian path.

Then again, there's a short period o' rest an' renewal. But at this time, some project'll surface that grounds the growth o' the first half o' the year into action, too, durin' the first half o' the Hazel moon (July).

Then the spirit sheath opens, the feminine. An' four days before the end o' the Hazel moon (July 22nd). the High Priestess, Mona, sends some personal message to everyone, a hint o' what the fears o' the comin' winter'll be like. But it's Boudicca who leads the feminine through the spirit sheath for the skyturn, exhaustion o' the mother, remember? This climb lasts until four days before the end o' the Apple moon (August 15th), the same day Mary, the human mother o' Jesus, will be said to rise up to heaven at the end o' her life.

Then the masculine half o' the spirit sheath opens, overlit by Arecurius. This unleashes his drivin' force that's needed to bring in the harvest for the year, harryin' an' pushin' everyone. He opens new intellectual interests for the comin' year at this time, too. An' the male o' this spirit sheath is fully formed four days before the end o' the Vine moon (Sept. 9th).

Then comes the birth pangs an' the fallin' away o' the skyturn's dark child, the release o' the child o' light into the spirit sheath, one full 240-day (10 druid moons) gestation cycle after Midwinter, at the end o' the Ivy moon (Oct. 6th). So a whole moon (druid) o' extra time is added for this birth, wi' a special push through heavy darkness for the year. Then the new child o' light finally emerges, two mornin's after (October 8th), fully formed in the spirit sheath, both feminine an' masculine. An' this is a momentous shift, for the spirit level is the first o' the lower worlds, the major birth o' the divine child for the skyturn, when the most significant gains are achieved. This very long birth pushin' force is signified by the letter E, the long sound, Edad, Aspen, Boudicca's E always signifyin' there's only a short way to go to completion," and the druid smiled.

"October 8th is when the celebrations o' the Reed moon begin, the moon o' rest after these trials o' birth. An' toward the end o' this moon, Arecurius overlights some recognition o' the newly born divine child by the tribe, as it steps out o' the protection that kept it hidden till it was strong enough to stand on its own. There's usually lingerin' uncertainty about bein' seen that Arecurius leads each person through, for the deep fears that kept this part o' the self hidden for so long are no yet forgotten. But it's a happy time overall.

Then, on the eve o' the Blackthorne moon (Oct. 30th), Danu opens the feminine o' the soul sheath an' overlights her climb through the first half o' this phase. An' Luis does the same for the masculine durin' the second half o' this moon, eh? Ye ken how bairns dress up in humorous or frightenin' guise to scare the evil spirits away on the eve o' the Blackthorne moon? Well, they're really revealin' the fears o' the soul sheath about to be activated, some dark soul impulse that'll weave it's way through that moon for healin', same as the mask each person makes for the openin' moon celebrations. Nearly always this involves lettin' somethin' cherished go as well.

The breakdown process o' this time o' year greatly intensifies durin' the five intercessory days o' the Goddess, too, durin' Samhein(2) (Nov. 24rd-28th). An' the double ll or Y sound signifies Tara's breakin' down impulse, when She steps in to wash off all debris o' the sheaths that have been active since John the Baptist Day, logos, spirit, an' soul, all except the sensate that remains to be faced.

An' finally, one moon (28 day, divine child cycle) before the birth o' those new divine child structures for the skyturn to come, the sensate sheath opens. An' Iona an' Mabon move everyone through the fears o' the sensate sheath for the passin' year, she, the feminine, durin' the first half o' this moon, he, the masculine, durin' the second. In time, this phase'll be called Advent.

But the process o' full individuation into the final sheath really begins at the Autumnal Equinox, when Mabon activates an' weaves the major sensate fear o' the year through these earlier moons as well, all the lower sheaths. Often this final moon before Midwinter entails facin' heavy challenges, too, for sensate is the densest level, eh? But it's the final climb o' the passin' skyturn, too. Hurrah for that!

Then, the <u>darkest</u> impulse o' this sensate phase, the minotaur, opens on Midwinter eve. An' it's the girl child, Iona, who goes to meet it wi' that circle o' light round her head, to pave the way for the implantation in the morn. At midnight then, both feminine an' masculine divine bairns o' the passin' skyturn are born, the androgyne for the year, all the way through the sensate sheath. This marks a full celebration by the spirit world, for it's the final victory o' the passin' year. An' the birth pushin' force through the soul an' sensate sheaths is the long I sound, Ioho, <u>Yew</u>, Iona's birth, the divine bairn fully individuated into this world. But I think it means <u>you</u>, Fìrinn." And the druid winked.

"Over the next three days then, Mabon builds the passin' year's divine child structures into the sensate sheath, to become a permanent part o' these levels. So it'll be forever accessible to the individual on earth, whenever the sensate is lit up here. Then the yearly cycle begins again wi' the implantation o' Arte's new divine child seeds on Midwinter dawn, hm? That's the Ogham letter J, mistletoe, Iulioc, seeds o' the future, eh?

But through this yearly cycle, the regents o' the Four Directions are openin' the core, mind, emotion, an' action <u>ethers</u> as well. I've explained this already, ladd, so I willna go over it again. But the short vowel sounds belong to this <u>ether</u> cycle, hm? Short a, the ah sound, signifies the long push through the core ethers at the beginnin' o' the year, from Midwinter to Imbolc an' Brìdget's birth o' the bairn out o' the core ethers o' the cosmic sea into the mental ethers three days before Imbolc. Brìdget's the grandma o' the Four Directions, remember?

Then' the short o, the aw sound, means the long push through those mental ethers, from Imbolc to Bealltain. This is Siris's birth, lass o the Four Directions.

Then comes the push through the emotion ethers, from Bealltain to Lughnasa. This is the short u, the uh sound, Eilean's birth, virgin goddess o' the Four Directions.

Then comes the push through the sensate ethers, from Lughnasa to Samhein (1), short e, the eh sound. That's Arienrhod's birth, mother o' the Four Directions.

On Samhein (1) then, the core ethers open once more, as the yearly impulse is pulled back into center in preparation for the comin' skyturn. The passin' year's impulse is also drawn out o' the mental, emotion, an' action ethers at this time, an' the three fears o' the comin' winter are activated. Thus begins the long push through the core ethers, from Samhein to Midwinter. It's signified by the short i, the ih sound, Bridget's birth again, the core fears o' the passin' cycle, the end o' the climb!

But let's take a breather noo, Firinn," the druid said with a sigh. "It's a long, complicated lesson." And Firinn nodded vigorously, his eyes glazed over. Coillore got up to heat water for two cups of black birch tea, which they went out and sipped beside the burn as the hush of night stilled Firinn's throbbing brain. At length, Coillore continued.

"One more small bit, ladd. This hidden stream rules the birth process o' all babes into physical form, too, wi' six stages, overlit by the regents o' this pentagram an' those o' the Creator Sun. But that's midwifery, women's lore. Still, I'd better just touch on it, ladd, just the basic understandings I've felt in me meditations. Remember, the human body has five pillars within, like the rings o' a tree; the virgin core, girl, boy, mother, an' father pillars. These resonate wi' the sheaths that match the six lower worlds. Lets' go over them again, hm? First is the double helix o' the Creators that circles up an' down the spine, includin' the three creator flames o' mind, heart, an' base, the Beloved core, light alone. It corresponds to the Diamond Core, an' isna counted as a pillar. Surroundin' this is the spine o' the virgins, their pillar, correspondin' to the logos. Surroundin' this is the girl pillar, thymus, lymph, an' kidney waters, resonatin' wi' the cherubim realms. Around that are the nerves an' brain o'the boy pillar, the spirit sheath. An' then come the soul waters, the cellular fluids an' the life stream, the mother pillar. Surroundin' this are the bones an' muscles o' the centerpoint sheath, the father pillar. Then Tara overlights the skin, the sensate, but it isna counted as a pillar, either.

So, six weeks before conception, the three creator flames o' mind, heart, an' base o' the child-to-be are built by Maighdean o' the Creator Sun. Three days before conception, this virgin goddess sends the inner spinal helix an' these three creator lights, a bright stream o' light, into the human mother's uterus. Then Maighdean overlights the buildin' o' the babe over the next ten (druid) moons, 240 days, one gestation cycle, wi' Tara lookin' on, o' course.

Durin' the first third o' gestation, the virgin core, girl, an' boy pillars are built, beginnin' wi' the virgins, the spine. This virgin phase is overlit by Leanan an' Nuada o' the White pentagram, as well as Maighdean. The heart is built then, too, but its construction is overlit by the Beloveds Themselves. The Creator Sun divine infants, Abaid an' Uan, come in to build the high heart, the thymus, too. After the spine comes the girl pillar: the lymph pathways an' lungs as well. It's Breith an' Daimhin who overlight this phase, along with Eriu an' Abaid. Then the nerves an' brain o' the boy pillar are built, the light o' all the stars structured into the silicate an' carbon crystals o' the bones, a hologram o' God/Goddess' cosmic body. These silicate crystals hold connections wi' every star system there is, an' they carry the blueprints o' all wounds o' the descent/ascension path for each individual, very precisely, what happened in which star system, yer very own memory stone, eh?. Eostre an' Credne overlight this part, as well as Finn an' Uan o' the Creator Sun. This early third o' gestation can be easily disrupted by toxins the human Ma may eat or drink. Best to have Soillse be careful then, eh?" But Fìrinn only blushed at this suggestion.

"Then, durin' the second third o' gestation, the soul waters flow in, an' the mother pillar is built. This is the time o' quickenin', when Màiri's life stream enters the unborn babe, an' it can be considered alive. It's best no to interrupt the pregnancy after this point or great emotional harm'll be done to the indwellin' spirit o' the unborn bairn. Water reflects the emotions around it, a very magical substance, nothin' else like it in the universe. It permits us to sense what others are feelin', an' babes are 9/10's water! Even adults are 2/3's water. Without it, the intimacy o' Tara couldna be felt at all. So this phase o' gestation can be disrupted by the emotions o' the human mother especially, for that's when the babe begins to feel the human Ma who'll become so important in a few moons time. This phase is overlit by Boudicca an' Arecurius, plus Màiri o' the Creator Sun, o' course. In the second half o' this middle third o' gestation then, the father pillar is built, the muscles an' hard skeletal shell over the bones. Fused into this boney shell are the destiny patterns o' the comin' life, plus the work talents an' strengths o' all past lives. It's Iona an' Mabon who overlight this stage, along wi' the Dagda o' the Creator Sun, o' course.

Then the last third o' gestation simply strengthens and lengthens the babe, preparin' it for earth life. An' it's Luis an' Danu who overlight this final phase, wi' Màithreil an' Daiden lookin' on from the Creator Sun. An' half a moon before birth, the light body o' the human Ma an' child are woven together, the heart an' right brain especially. This is so the bairn'll feel held in love after the doors to the One Beloveds, parents, an' children o' the Creator Sun close at birth. This interweavin' o' Ma an' babe lasts halfway through the first skyturn after birth, when it's removed, so the child can develop independently o' the human mother. An' the babe can feel a bit unsure o' things for a time. But to get back to gestation, Iona an' Mabon come in again at the very last to move the babe through the birth process itself, always involvin' one severe fear o' both Ma an' bairn. But it's Tara , Who joins the human Ma, doin' all that birth pushin', an' Maighdean overseein' it all." Then the druid gave a great sigh of contentment, for this divine birth was precisely what he was hoping to accomplish with Fìrinn.

"There ye have it, ladd. The lesson's complete for today, the holy White Pentagram only the druids ken. For that's their hidden purpose, too, if truth be told, helpin' to birth all divine children in the orders. It's honorable work, eh? This is the final structure o' the Diamond Core, only the centerpoint left to explain to ye noo." And Coillore put his hands together and bowed to the boy, the druid doing his very best to nourish Fìrinn's divine child, too.

And as he finally stretched out on his pallet, after climbing down the deer path through a thick mist to the long house, hours after the other ladds had gone to sleep, Fìrinn whispered into Bana Dhia's fur, "Help me, Danu an' Luis. For I long to birth me divine child, just like Coillore says. I can feel the structures o' light in me belly, an' the desire in me heart, growin' durin' the lessons at his hut. But it all seems so complicated. I get frightened that I willna make it, for it's too much, all this memorizin' on top o' the long hard trainin' o' me days. An' I'm only in me spirit climb, too. Gettin' all the way to the Core feels endless, just <u>too far</u> to go." And he sighed as he closed his eyes and drifted off to sleep. So, he didn't see Danu's pale azure and Luis's mustard yellow hexagonal streams move into place around him and strengthen the light of his divine babe within all through the silent spring night.

As soon as the high king passed to the Otherworld, frequent letters began to arrive from Speireag, letters for both Fìrinn and Seumus, urging the ladd to the hunt and to ignore his mother's geis. Speireag sent along bundles of strengthening medicines, too, herbs and dried meats, and sweets from cook, beyond the portion allotted Fìrinn at the fostering. Two of the messengers also told Seumus how the chief's temper had flared after Fìrinn's Ma died, and that Speireag had given his wee daughter to one of the tribeswomen to be fostered by winter's end. Then the chief had raided the cattle of his neighbors in all directions, unheard of with the animals drawn in close to their tuaths during the dark moons. In a skirmish with the tribe of the snake during the Ash moon (February), three of Firinn's clansmen had been slain, one with a spear meant for the chief. And Speireag's right arm had been sliced to the bone, so his fighting days were interrupted now or over altogether. Da'll be deposed himself, Firinn thought, as Seumus repeated the story, for surely the Sun Lord doesna come through him any more. His actions havena the mark of divinity on them at all.

Then late in the Willow moon (April), Speireag sent a pony for Firinn's use alone. It was larger than most and honey colored, even its mane and tail, instead of the usual dun. Firinn called her Briagha (breeya, beauty) and took to riding her on the beach at the end of the day. On dusky nights, the young mare's spirited canters through the shallows left the ladd exhilarated, especially when he pulled Soillse up in front of him and she snuggled into his chest. Often the two of them rode to the end of the headland to watch the sun's last rays over the sea.

But as Bealltain approached, Firinn became more serious than usual. One night, while Soillse helped Muirn take the remains of a boar off the spits, he was leading Briagha along the shore, a strong evening breeze blowing the pony's mane every which way. And he thought, I'm seventeen winters now, and I'll have me hunt of manhood in the Oak moon (late May), and then me fostering'll be over. Most ladds would go off to their own tribes then, but I'm staying here with Soillse. Seumus has already agreed to that. And then I'll go to the kingship trials at Midsummer. After that, I dinna ken what I'm to do. I hope I can build a small hut before Soillse and me hand-fasting ceremony in the Apple moon (August), though. I wonder if the

Goddess wants me to go to Iona for a time after me formal fostering is over, like Coillore says, during the Hazel moon (July), perhaps.

As the ladd stood watching a golden sun drop slowly over the sea into the pink scarves of mist above the peaks, his thoughts continued, me chances of becoming king are slim to none, whatever Da expects. I <u>hate</u> his prodding. There are ladds of noble families from every tuath across the isle to compete with. Besides, I dinna <u>want</u> to be king noo. I'm too young for it, for one thing. And I want to reach the Creator Sun on me inner path before I do anything as important as that, so I can do it with me heart full o' Oghama's truth. Otherwise, I dinna see the point. And that inner climb'll take ten or fifteen skyturns, Coillore says, maybe more. What do I ken of ruling, anyway? I'm still half ladd. And Firinn sighed. Duirc wants the kingship more than his life, Duineil said once. But I only want a quiet life o' peace; Soillse, a bairn or two, a small clan like this, and studying or teaching the mysteries. No one like that could ever be king.

Coillore's pressure to go to Iona had begun to annoy Firinn, too. Sometimes the ladd wished he could just take Soillse and ride off into the hills. But as spring flowered the woodlands, Coillore kept insisting that Seumus let him take the ladd to the sacred isle. They'd waited nearly a skyturn already, the druid repeated, afraid to go with the king's health failing in case the trials were called immediately after his passing. Now that the date was set, there was plenty of time.

"He canna leave <u>noo</u>!" Seumus fairly shouted at the druid one evening in the halflight of dusk, the chief tired to the bone as he stacked lances by the long house door after the day's games. "What if somethin' happens to the ladd, like the use o' his legs a skyturn ago? His father'll surely <u>kill</u> me, if Firinn doesna appear at the kingship competitions! The ladd could've <u>died</u> at that initiation o' yours. Any more o' those'll have to wait till after Midsummer, Coillore. The boy still limps a bit when he's over tired, an' that itself could disqualify him, if the druids notice it. Besides, the seas are unpredictable this time o' year, for another moon at least. What's gotten into ye?" And Seumus ran a hand over his head, feeling his own tuath touched by the gloom that hung over the isle. Me first job is to take care of me family and me ladds, the chief thought. Preparing those of noble blood for the kingship ritual is me most important task of all, and prepare them I will, he thought, glaring at Coillore. But the druid only shook his head slowly, frowning at the chief.

"I must convince ye," Coillore said finally, standing tall in his white robe and staring steadily at Seumus. "The ladd holds powers so far reachin' I canna describe it." But the chief's face remained stony. "He'll bring wisdom we lost long ago in the days o' the ancients," Coillore continued. "It's his to recover, an' it'll lead the isle to prosperity we havena known in centuries." And the druid's blue eyes shone with his conviction. "The ladd's path mustna be interfered wi', Seumus, an' if I have to force it, I will."

Seumus put down the lances and stared then, glowering at the elderly druid and wondering if the man would go so far as to sicken the cattle to get his way. Coillore had never been anything but soft-spoken and earnest about helping the folk at the tuath. He was a phenomenal healer when any of the ladds were hurt, too, and once in a while, he even told amusing tales. For skyturns, Seumus had praised the gods for a druid who cooperated with him, not one of those interfering ones he heard complaints about from other chieftains. What's become of things, Seumus thought, as fear laced through his gut, when me own druid threatens the tribe?

"He must go to the druid isle before the trials!" Coillore shot back, his face red. "His Da'll be the ladd's downfall, anyway. I wouldna go out o' me way for him." And the druid pulled his chin up, his jaw clenched.

"I'll no allow it," Seumus said, "an' if ye mention it again, I'll forbid ye to come into me tuath, druid." Coillore made the motion to protect himself from evil, then turned abruptly, and strode up the burn path into the birch wood.

"All right, ladd, we'll just go over the druid moons tonight," Coillore began as he led Fìrinn to his hut two nights before Bealltain. A fine mist obscured both the sea and the birch wood, so they had to step carefully along the burn to find their way, climbing halfway up the ridge and then turning north through the budding birch boughs, "though I was hopin' to complete the centerpoint, too." We're running out of time, the druid thought in frustration, but I canna tell him that. "It's the best night for this lesson, for the regents are the gods an' goddesses ye've recently learned, the Pillars an' the Circle o' Eight." They swung past the great yew, the one that hid Coillore's hut from view until the last moment, and stooped under the doeskin doorcloth. And Fìrinn, in his muddy buckskin breeks and shirt, took his place on one of the stump chairs that sat beside the low fire in the central hearth. The druid stopped then and eyed the ladd sharply as Fìrinn's eyes drooped.

"Mind the lesson noo." And Coillore reached up to the rafters to pull down some herbs that he added to Fìrinn's tea to sharpen the ladd's attention, handing him a plate of fiddleheads with wild garlic, flat bread, and soft cheese as well. As Fìrinn wolfed his dinner down, starved from the constant sword practice since midsky, the druid began.

"Each human is also attuned to one o' these nine light structures o' the Diamond Core I'm teachin' ye, ladd, the sacred triple three o' mind, heart, an' base. This attunement is forever, the basis o' each person's identity in light. I'll just touch on these, so ye ken them, eh?"

"Let's start wi' the mind levels o' the Core, eh? Those attuned to the Stillpoint Center'll ever be focused on the union o' heaven an' earth, but through meditation mainly, lookin' to the Creators for advice an' bringin' information from within into real use in the world, workin' wi' a wide variety o' inner teachers from across the cosmos. They'll be the organizers in all they do an' feel the cycles o' each skyturn an' the stars deeply. Then the Wizard types o' their Wheel o' the brain'll be playful an' bring great joy. But they'll also think up wide-reachin' solutions that are brand new, quick thinkers that take in a broad range o' ideas easily, too. Those attuned to Priomh's Pineal Wheel'll be protectors o' heaven's laws: lawgivers, soldiers, an' teachers, concerned wi' the best way to do things. They'll ever lean toward mental solutions an' a bit o' control, though.

Then come the heart levels o' the Core, hm? Luckenbooth folk, connected to the virgin girl light structure that creates union o' hearts, which ye'll learn about in yer green robe lessons. These'll be royalty an' high church folk, leadin' the way, because the heart's the true ruler o' everythin'. These folk, too, will ever want to bring heaven an' earth together, as well as the hearts o' men an' women into partnership an' lifetime efforts in love, romanticists. They'll be singers an' dancers, too. Then the Triple Spiral folks'll be the priests an' priestesses, masters o' ceremonial magic. An' those attuned to the Holy Family will be home bodies, o' course, strong family folk that embrace everyone in the tribe readily an' carry family responsibilities wi' love, dignity, an' dependability, seein' that everyone in the tribe is taken care of, too. One-to-one types, those'll be.

The action levels come next, ladd, the Tìr Nan Òg people connected to the virgin male action light structure, another o' yer green robe lessons. These'll be folk who are action oriented an' no mistake, pushin' for change everywhere they go. They ever want to move earth forward, never satisfied wi' the way things are. Driven, though. An' Pillar folk'll be stalwart an' honest, in their uses o' power especially, always eager to create change for the better. They're steady in walkin' their paths, too, an' they ken how to put a personal disadvantage into good use. Then the Circle o' Eight folk are the farmers an' gardeners, o' course, close to the earth, wantin' to feed everyone. But these second chakra types also easily embrace their opposites, for empathy's written into their deepest nature. Peacemakers, they are, too.

An' last come the White Pentagram folk, attuned to the White Tara. She's in charge on earth, Firinn. It's <u>Her</u> land, an' She kens <u>exactly</u> what She wants to bring forth here, Her an' Oghama's divine bairns. So this group'll be quite grounded in their purpose an' very certain o' what they want in life. But like Her, they'll be masters o' seein' the light in everythin' an' quite determined to bring it forth. They can be a bit insistent that all is precisely arranged to maximize it, especially in the home, very detail oriented at times, like Tara Herself. With Tara's skin activation, these folk'll be highly sensitive as well, takin' all sensory information in through every pore, unlike the other groups. One day, these human Diamond Core attunements'll be known as the enneagram, ladd.

Ok, so let's go through the moons noo, eh?" And the druid hurried on. "The first five moons o' each skyturn move into the pillars within, the columns I went over at the end o' yer last lesson: the virgin girl an' boy o' the spine; the girl o' the thymus, kidneys, an' lymph; the boy o' the nerves an' brain; the mother cellular waters an' life stream; an' the father bone an' muscle, remember, ladd? So, the trees o' these five moons are the Pillar trees, their light channels reachin' to the Pillar realms. The Creators take two moons o' each skyturn as well, an' Theirs are the King an' Queen trees. But the child heart takes the first moon, the divine bairn tree. And the rest are all Noble trees, because their central light channels reach all the way up to the Diamond Core.

Remember, the druid year is identical to Tara's emotional growth cycle, 15 24-day moons wi' 5 intercessory days at the end o' the Blackthorne moon (Nov. 24th-28th), our thanksgivin' celebrations, eh? The Goddess's focus is ever on emotions, the true driver o' growth, as well as wisdom, o' course. We talked about much o' this wi' the Circle o' Eight, two lessons ago, but I want ye to ken it as part o' the moons an' Ogham letters as well.

Because it's a new birth an' infant phase o' the skyturn, Abaid an' Uan o' the Creator Sun overlight the Birch moon, Dec. 23rd-Jan. 15th, but it's Anu an' Beli o' the Pillars who move the lessons into the child heart within. Beithe, birch, the Ogham letter B, signifies gentle growth in love over an entire skyturn that eventually leads to the birth o' some new aspect o' the self, the child o' the One for that year. An' the beginnin' o' the Birch moon is when the light seeds o' the year's divine child move up to the thymus, on Christmas morn. These'll always reflect the gentle will o' Abaid an' Uan, an' open the path o' growth.

Birches carry the soft light o' the child heart, ladd, an' this moon always calls forth some ancient memory o' pure love, sent straight from the Creator Sun. It's the central focus o' the year's growth, something lost long, long ago that'll be restored by skyturn's end. This memory'll always move the heart deeply, too, bringin' the desire an' drive to face the fears needed to realize that gift in life again. The divine infant lessons'll always involve transformin' the basic woundings o' early childhood an' the connection wi' the Beloveds, the oldest bindin's on the spirit, so the new divine child can emerge. So, this is often the most challengin' moon o' the skyturn.

Then Cead o' the Pillars moves the lessons o' the Dagda o' the Creator Sun into the Da pillar, muscle an' bone. These'll always relate to one's work an' destiny stream, whatever yer task for the skyturn'll be. An' as Da o' the divine child, Luis o' the White Pentagram sends a protective cloud o' light to surround the unborn babe, too, in preparation for an' followin' the release o' the girl structures from the core into the mental ethers at Imbolc. He takes the Rowan moon, Mt. Ash, the Ogham letter L, Luis or light, Jan 16th-Feb 8th, signifyin' the promise an' protection o' the father.

An' then Aislin, as the elder sister o' the Pillars, packages the lessons o' the virgin and girl goddesses o' the Creator Sun, Maighdean an' Eriu, into the spinal structures. These usually have to do wi' hatred, neglect, violence, loosenin' the bindings o' domination by the male, sexual misuse, or disdain for the girl's pleasure stream. Maighdean opens that stream an' her union o' virgin hearts channel five days into this moon, too, Feb. 14th. But Aislin overlights this Ash moon, Feb 9th-Mar. 4th, the letter N, Nuin. It signifies new strength an' freedom for the girl within, central backbone strength. Ash is the world tree, the spinal axis.

Then Colum, the Pillar virgin male, takes the virgin boy impulses o' Rìdire, o' the Creator Sun an' moves them into the nerves an' brain, the boy's pillar, eh? The boy's impulse always softens the personal will into alignment wi' the will o' the One, eases overwork, an' dissolves blocks to action. An' Padraig o' the Child Heart opens the rainbow boy's humor an' playfulness flow on March 17th as well. Then Finn, the action boy o' the Creator Sun, opens the mother's sap into the sacral root; with Rìdire addin' the action stream an' Pwyll o' the Stillpoint Center, the phallic portal up the midline frontal power channel on the Vernal Equinox, too. They bring the drive to see the year's lessons through. As elder brother o' the Pillars, though, it's Colum who takes the Alder moon, the letter F, Fearn (feearn), Mar. 5th-28th, signifyin' the boy's spurtin' enthusiasm, a combination o' the mother's life force an' the boy's will to action.

Then comes the last Pillar moon, Willow, Mar 29th-Apr.21st. It teaches acceptance o' the all, takin' responsibility for the wisdom lessons o' the skyturn, overlit by Cùram, mother o' the Pillars, the letter S, Saille (syeeya). She brings in Màiri's difficult lessons for the skyturn. These always involve the depletion, overwork, an' fatigue challenges o' the mother an' move into the intercellular waters. But Bridget o' the Four Directions adds a cloud o' her compassion round it, too, to draw in friends an' helpmates along the way.

Then, at the Hawthorne moon, Apr. 22nd-May15th, we shift to the solstice/equinox/cross quarter day regents, the Circle o' Eight. Remember them, ladd? Belissima, virgin lass o' spring, brings forth the feminine longin' for union o' hearts wi' the male virgin, plus her strong cleansin' stream. Belissima's lessons often come through disruption o' some kind, always openin' some deep passion in the virgin girl's heart. This is the letter H, Huath (hooah), cleansin' o' the virgin girl, the white lightnin' force.

Then comes Oghama, the One Beloved, overlightin' the Oak moon, May 16th-June 8th, the King tree. He adores an' woos the feminine wi' the hope o' forever partnership as she prepares for her union o' hearts at Midsummer. It's the letter D, Duir (jooer), door, for He opens the portal into the back o' the heart to insert the light seeds for emotional growth into Tara's soil there, His an' Tara's heart's desires that will manifest over a full skyturn. These seeds o' light ever focus on the inner god an' goddess, bringin' sweet communion between Creators an' individual, too, always movin' through blocks to the union o' all four. That's what the letter D signifies as well, plus the approach o' true love from Oghama in partnership or some new activity o' life.

Then comes Belenos, virgin male o' the Circle o' Eight, wi' the Holly moon, June 9th-July 2nd. His is an action impulse to change the outer world, an' he ever brings forth some project that incorporates the inner growth o' the past year. An' durin' this moon, everyone'll meet outer resistance to these new changes in the tribe, so it's a spiritual warrior impulse as well. But Belenos balances that inner drivin' force wi' his strong purpose an' steady dedication to love. So his is the letter T, tinne (teenya), holdin' one's balance against darkness in pushin' for positive change in the world. He's an expert at both, ladd.

Then comes Mona, high priestess o' the Creator Sun, remember? An' she takes the Hazel moon (July 3rd-26th). Mona brings the first pull o' the feminine to come inward as hints o' fall's coolness drift in now and then. It's the letter C, Coll, the call, hm?" Firinn smiled at the pun, thankful, despite his fatigue, for the old druid's help in keeping all these gods and goddesses in their correct places in his mind. He'd heard of them all, of course, but never had the structure laid out so precisely, so he could finally understand them all. "Mona focuses on openin' the priestess powers o' intuition an' prophecy, too," the druid continued. "An' she comes in four days before the end o' this moon (July 22nd) wi' a preview o' the major wisdom lesson o' the winter ahead as well.

An' then arrives the White Tara, the Goddess, Who overlights the Apple moon, July 27th-Aug. 19th. It's the Queen moon, the letter Q, Quert (kearst). She'll teach ye to approach all pain that comes wi' the most positive outlook. An' She feels utter adoration for the One Beloved God, Oghama, workin' tirelessly to carry out His dreams an' bear His bairns on earth, the meanin' o' this letter, too. Usually this moon brings forth blocks to Her revelation, the sappin' overwork forces especially. But She manifests the first fruits an' some personal gift three days past Lughnasa, too, for Her love is more intimate than any other." And Coillore's eyes looked inward a moment as a slight flush pinked his cheeks.

"An' then we come to Lugh, the father o' the Circle o' Eight, who overlights the Vine moon, Aug. 20th-Sept. 12th, the letter M, Muin (mwin), the intoxication an' contentment o' the union o' earth an' heaven, in the harvest especially, servin' Daiden o' the Creator Sun noo. But Lugh's real impulse is overflowin' abundance o' nourishment, for he wants to feed an' feed his many children in many ways, sendin' the truth o' the father's love to those in the lowest circumstances especially. It's durin' this moon, we reap the blessings o' our labors an' a bit o' ease before the difficulties o' the winter moons ahead. The outer harvest is a joyful thing, eh, Firinn? But it's the inner harvest the father brings that comforts most, I think.

This is followed by the Ivy moon, Sept. 13th-Oct. 6th, Gort (gorst), the letter G, tenacity in hardship, overlit by Rhiannon o' the Indigo Pentagram, yer next lesson, Firinn. She brings forward the push to remove the full-body dark child o' the skyturn from the spirit sheath, so the divine child within can finally emerge into the lower realms. An' Rhiannon pushes everyone through the pangs o' the birth process, for this moon marks the end o' the gestation cycle from the last Midwinter as ye ken. These often involve sacrifices o' some kind, delays to the fulfillment o' some wish or extra effort to complete the year's work. But on the last day o' this moon, the year's dark child finally falls away from the spirit sheath within. Hurrah to that, ladd, eh?

An' then come the celebrations o' the Reed moon, Oct. 7th-30th, overlit by Cìrceidh o' the Oillars, servin' Màithreil, the action Ma o' the Creator Sun, though. On the 2nd day o' this moon (Oct. 8th), the new divine child emerges into the spirit sheath. As earth mother o' the Circle o' Eight, Cìrceidh brings all newly born divine children into the hearth o' the tribe, for like Lugh, she loves to nourish her children through family love especially, bringin' play, song, dance, an' joy after the hardest spirit work o' the year is done as well. An' <u>food</u>, o' course. Hers is the letter Ng, Ngetal (engehtahl), peace an' freedom for the new child o' light, a happy an' playful moon."

"But the joy o' the Reed moon is followed by the breakin' down phase, the Blackthorne moon, Oct. 31st-Nov. 23rd, the letters St or Z, Straif (stryeef), strife, particularly blocks to the flow o' life from Màiri, the elder Ma o' the Creator Sun. This moon is ruled by Samhein, grandma o' the Circle o' Eight, who cuts off this root flow to all structures o' the passin' year that arena needed anymore, livestock culled an' crops stored for winter, tribesfolk often passin' to the Otherworld durin' this moon as well. At this time, one deep heart desire to be revealed at the end o' the comin' skyturn is chosen by Una, grandma o' the Luckenbooth realms, to be put into place durin' the Midwinter seedin' as well, for Blackthorne is also the tree o' deep magic. Manifestation from yer very core is the hidden meanin' o' that Z as well.

An' then comes the gratefulness impulse o' the intercessory days (Nov. 24th-28th), our new year celebration, the end o' Tara's cycle o' emotional growth. But mainly, it's a time o' reverence for the Goddess, Her most wondrous force o' emotion, an' the power o' Love." And Coillore bent his head, bringing his hands together a moment.

"An' finally comes the Elder moon, Nov. 29th-Dec 22nd, when Bran, granda o' the Circle o' Eight, takes the lessons learned from the passin' skyturn, seeds to be built into the light body o' every individual. These truths then remain accessible in all realms, fears that'll never rise up again, even taken into the Otherworld after life on earth is through. It's the letter R, Ruis (rooey), wisdom embodied." And the druid gave a happy sigh. "This is what we all long for, eh, ladd? An' then comes Midwinter, a hopeful new cycle beginnin' again!" But the herbs were wearing off now, and Fìrinn's eyes were nearly closed as his head nodded in the heat of the hearth. The old druid only shook his head, gently took Fìrinn's hand, and waited as the ladd opened his eyes.

"I was hopin' to show ye the magic o' the letters o' yer name, tonight, too. But ye're tired, ladd. Do ye want to ken that? It willna take long. Or should we just let ye go to yer furs?" But Fìrinn sat up straighter, instantly alert.

"The magic o' me name? What do ye mean, Coillore?"

"All these letters o' the moons I've just been teachin' ye have their meanin's, eh? So do the ones o' the hidden streams. Well, name magic is simple, ladd." And the druid wrote Fìrinn Beinne (benya) mac Speireag in the earth. "Yer first name'll tell ye about yer inner feminine, the basic life stages o' yer home an' family life. So, let's see. Yer name begins wi' F, that's the boy's spurtin' enthusiasm, so ye musta been a wriggly wee ladd!" And Fìrinn brows rose as he nodded. "Bein' the first letter doubles its force, too, plus it flows through yer whole life, eh? The i that follows is small, so it goes wi' the ethers, eh?. An' it's the core ethers at the very end o' the year. So, ye'll be livin' a way o' life that ye'll be lettin' go of, one ye willna live again, some part o' yer bairn o' light freed in the end an' individuated into life. That accent doubles it's force as well. I'd have to ken how long yer life will be to see how these 6 letters divide into skyturns to determine exactly where ye are, though. But let's say ye live to sixty winters, that's ten skyturns a letter, so ye're in this i phase noo." Ach, I hope so, Fìrinn thought, I'd love to be done with the arts o' war. "Then comes r, the embodiment o' wisdom, deep integration o' lessons that stay wi' ye forever, usually without much struggle noo. A second i follows that, so another way o' life ye'll be livin' for the very last time, a new talent emergin', too." Africa, the druid thought, carefully shielding this from Fìrinn. An' last, come those two ns, freedom o' the girl within. Double letters triple the force, ladd. So, durin' the last part o' yer life, ye'll be freein' that heart-centered, peace-lovin' Sìth, or standard-holdin' virgin girl within. An' the meanin' o yer name sets the tone o' yer whole life, truth. But this is yer first name only, yer feminine, ladd.

Then yer last name, Speireag, will tell what yer destiny portends, the stages o' yer life outside the home in work an' tribal efforts, yer masculine. Yers begins wi' S, acceptance o' the all. That's some intense wisdom lesson o' compassion for outcasts usually, often undergoin' what they do. It's no the easiest letter, plus bein' the first. But those small es indicate real action in the world, the full flow into core, mind, emotion, an' action ethers, so progress'll definitely be made. Then the i is another move through the final core fears an' emergence o' part o' yer divine self into real life The r then is the embodiment o' deep wisdom again, an' the final a imovin' through new core fears to begin a future pattern o' life, a new start. Yer last name ends wi' g, through, tenacity in hardship, another challengin' one. An' the overall meanin' o' the name is hawk, a bird that's freedom lovin', a fighter, an' determined to find what he seeks.

An' then, just ken that yer middle name is yer divine child's passage through life, hm.? Yers is Beinne, meanin' 'mountain'. The word itself means yer on that final steep ascent to the Creator Sun in this lifetime. An' the first, B, always the most significant letter, the standard o' them all, is the gentle infant flow o' the divine child over a sustained length o' time, bringin' up deep unconscious lessons from yer very core for healin'. There are two ns here that mean ye'll be freein' the virgin girl within again." And Fìrinn eyes widened as he stared at the druid, fully alert now. "So ye'll be dealin' wi' violence in the tribes, male domination o' the feminine, or healin' the sexual distortions, or most likely a bit o' all three. An' the final letter e signifies real action flow at all levels, core, mind, heart, an' root. If ye want to ken more detail, ye can ponder it by yerself at yer leisure, ladd, eh?" Leisure? What's that?, Fìrinn thought with a frown. But he felt tingles flow down his scalp and spine as the druid underlined his middle name in the earth.

"Druid's ken just about everythin'," Fìrinn whispered with a decisive nod.

So, Coillore waved the ladd off to bed with a smile. But as Fìrinn ducked under the doorcloth, the druid called sternly after him that he was to come to the tree circle in a quarter moon's time for his recitation. "Ye're first this time. Dinna be late, ladd. It's more important than ye ken!"

Then, three days after Bealltain (May 8th), Fìrinn's Da surprised them by appearing in the yard one evening after a drizzling day. Fìrinn and Soillse were standing on the pebbles by the bay in a stiff wind after the evening meal, watching an orange sun sink beneath lowering clouds across the sea as they brushed Briagha. But when they heard a horse cantering out of the scrub birches above the tuath, Fìrinn turned abruptly, startled to see his Da moving into the yard and noticing that Speireag held the reins in his left hand. So his right hadn't recovered yet.

"I want to see what ye're doin' wi' the ladd who'll soon be king," Speireag shouted to Seumus as he dismounted outside the round house door. Firinn's Da wore his heavy fur jerkin over buckskin breeks, but all could see the man had lost weight, his hair straggly down his back, even his moustache greying now. "Firinn needs intensive trainin' more than ever noo. Perhaps I can lend a hand." But Seumus, standing in the yard with a group of boys, made no move to embrace Speireag. With a cool eye, Seumus offered a bath of welcome and a meal as the laws required.

"Ye can stay till mornin' at most," Seumus told the chief curtly. "Parents put the ladds off their trainin' faster than anythin' else I ken. I dinna allow them here, unless there's serious injury or illness." And Seumus turned back to his coaching, leaving Duineil to take care of the chief.

Speireag raised his brows sharply and opened his mouth to speak, a grin forming on his face. But he stopped abruptly as Seumus turned away and followed Duneil quietly to the baths. Firinn made no attempt to speak with his Da, either, at first, feeling Seumus's disapproval. But at his Da's insistence, Firinn came back to the yard and sparred with Dughall (doogal), Duneil's son, just before full dark. Conscious of his father's eyes upon him, Firinn fumbled once with the sword. I wish he'd just go, the ladd thought. He never paid the least mind to me before, and he hates me love of the forest and the lore. He only wants me to become king, so he can be proud of himself, anyway. Now that I can give him that, or so he thinks, he's suddenly involved. And Firinn clenched his teeth. Once, as the two ladds faced each other with swords drawn, Seumus and Speireag shouted different orders, confusing Firinn, who backed away and stood waiting quietly.

"I am chief here, Speireag," Seumus growled and then glowered all evening by the fire as Speireag talked on and on.

Invited to the roundhouse for a late evening meal with his Da, Fìrinn refused to go. He couldn't bear to have Speireag taunt him about moon lore in front of Soillse. And he didn't want Da to see his love for her, either, not yet. So after Soillse went in, Fìrinn sat on the headland in his hide breeks and shirt, an oiled skin wrapped over his head and shoulders, with Briacha and Bana Dhia, all three getting soaked in the cold rain, and Fìrinn fervently wishing he were somewhere else.

Early the next morning, as the women rose to begin the firstsky meal, Speireag came to the long house. Dressed in his heavy buckskins for traveling, he tiptoed in and stood near Fìrinn's pallet, saying a prayer over the ladd and making the sign of leadership in the air. Bana Dhia eyed the chief warily, her top lip quivering. Patting the dog, Speireag watched his son a moment, then stooped to lay a hide parcel on the floor beside the furs. But Bana Dhia growled at that, and Fìrinn opened one eye to see his Da moving quickly out the doorskin. And in moments, the ladd heard horse's hooves clattering up the rocky path. As Fìrinn breathed a thank-you to the Goddess for this measure of peace, his hand fell on the package.

He took it up, having to roll over and use both hands because of its weight, and moved silently out the door skin in only his loin cloth and light breeks to see what it was. The sun was just rising under a low bank of clouds over the ridge behind the tuath, the light still dim, and Fìrinn felt annoyed as he unlaced the long leather bindings. Whatever Da left is probably useless, anyway, the ladd thought, something he killed a boar with in a hunt a long time ago. I will no use some old spear of Da's in the kingship trials!

But unfolding the hide, Fìrinn gasped. For before him on a linen cloth was a broadsword, iron shafted and single bladed. The scabbard was bronze, inlaid with silver that glimmered in the early light. And with one finger, Fìrinn traced the sacred symbols incised there: the arrow of the spiritual warrior, the Goddess spiral of growth, the Celtic Cross of the Creator Sun, and the full moon of the White Goddess was inlaid above the rest in shining silver. Staring, Fìrinn sank quietly onto the dirt, holding the sword in his lap. Each line of the cross was set with one stone of the elements and Four Directions, too: green malachite in the west for water, the boy quadrant; orange cairngorm in the east for air, the girl quadrant; yellow agate in the south for fire, the father; and dark onyx in the north for earth, the mother. And there at the point where the arms of the cross intersected was a small circle of yellow gold, for the Sun Lord, the high God Himself. As Fìrinn pulled the blade out of its sheath, he traced an interlaced dragon that changed into a white stag on the hilt above the blade. This blade's purpose is to change the dark dragon o' violence an' war into Oghama's truth an' peace then, Fìrinn thought, as his brows lifted.

The sword was quite similar to his Ma's favorite dagger, and suddenly Fìrinn felt her presence around him, her utter confidence in his purpose, her love like no other. This sword belonged to her, the ladd realized in that moment. Why hasna Da ever used it or shown it to me before? It must have belonged to some chief of our tuath before Da arrived, me Granda, perhaps. Ma must've kept it hidden somewhere or Da'd surely have wanted it for himself. He must've found it after she passed on.

While he sat staring at the blade, other ladds had moved out the doorcloth, watching him, unnoticed. It's Ma coming in another form, like she promised, Fìrinn's thoughts continued. But instead, he became aware of the Sun Lord's light around his head from the dawn sun and felt a dazzling radiance pierce his crown. In his mind's eye then, Fìrinn saw the Dagda's sword of light move slowly down into his chest, his belly, and then his manhood, a clear channel of creator power all the way to the action levels within.

And suddenly, Fìrinn had the feeling he was meant to do something important in his life, something he hadn't realized yet. It'll bring Skye closer to the Creator Sun somehow, he thought. I ken it!

And then Fìrinn saw the image of a simple god in a humble white robe, one who served the cosmos tirelessly and with great love, not as a hero with the need for power and glory, no, but in utter devotion to his children suffering in all worlds. He could see this god change into the shape of a man and descend to earth to bring his arms and heart and hands to bear wherever the need was greatest, the suffering most severe. That's the servant king, Oghama, the ladd realized. And Fìrinn shivered as mingled awe and devotion rippled along his skin. It's Ye who truly sends impulses for action into all monarchs in every realm, isna it, Fìrinn thought, Ye, Who orchestrates it all? And the ladd stood then, holding the sword of his ancestors tight to his chest, bowing to the sun rising over the inland hills with tears in his eye.

"I will serve Ye" he whispered," to the end o' me days."

Chapter Twenty-Eight: Soillse

Over the winter, whenever they spent a night at their lean-to in the wood, Soillse felt as light as air, as soft as thistledown. But she kept her secrets to herself, letting Ma, Ceit, Sìne, and Muirn wonder if the nights with Fìrinn were fulfilling her hopes. Do ye wish to hand-fast?, Eilid's eyes often asked. While Soillse worked long afternoons in the cooking hut, she thought of Fìrinn holding her all night long and then waking with his eyes on her, full of wonder. Soillse sent a thousand prayers of thanks to Oghama and the White Tara, and into her hidden basket she slipped the carving Fìrinn had given her.

Soillse knew, of course, that their betrothal would change little in her life. As was the custom in Celtic society, he'd join her tuath, so her work would stay the same and even increase with the skyturns as the other women aged. Except that, whenever Fìrinn was in the yard now and Soillse had a big load to carry, he walked away from the games, no matter how Seumus glowered, to lift it for her. Me life willna even improve, she thought one morning, stirring the firstsky oats, if by some chance I hold the land right after Ma goes to the Otherworld. Ach, I hope that day is far off, though, for I'd miss Ma so, and I'll ken no mercy if Ceit becomes queen. And Fìrinn wouldna tolerate that at all, so who knows what'd become of us? But for now, I'm content just to have Fìrinn by me side. Maybe we can build a hut of our own and hold each other like we did last night after every evening meal. It'd be heaven, that. And I could give him bairns and mother them in the sweet love we share. Ach, Fìrinn'll be the best Da in the world!

The night before Bealltain Eve, a crisp windy dusk, Coillore motioned Soillse to wait after the lessons at the oak circle in the birch wood. Now that she and Ceit had reached womanhood, Seumus no longer came to meet them there. And Ceit had grown disinterested in the lore and wasn't coming to Coillore's teaching hearth anymore.

"I want to let ye ken I'll no be teachin' the next quarter moon, Syl. I have to go away, but no for long, a few days only," the druid said quietly, pulling his plaid around his white robe and gathering up his staff.

"Another initiation," she asked, her smile fading as she began picking at her fingernails. The druid noticed how lovely she'd become, curved, but still slender, her arms and legs strong with all the work she did. Her cheeks were rosy in the cool of evening, her gaze honest, and with her fine light brown hair blowing across her back, she was pretty even in her old stained shift. But he declined to answer her question.

She waited, shifting from one foot to the other. "I s'pose ye ken all that happens," she said, blushing and looking quickly away. Then she burst out. "I canna live without Firinn noo, Coillore. Half the time I canna sleep for thinkin' o' him. I didna ken it'd be like this." But Coillore only smiled, leaned over, and drew a five-pointed star in the earth with his staff. He deepened the pentagon in the very center made by the inner star points, and around the outside of the star he drew the circles of the six worlds.

"Each o' us has a small pentagonal portal to the Diamond Heart, the place in the Creator Sun ye were originally created from, lassie, yer deepest connection to the One Beloved. An' that pentagon is full o' blessin's for ye alone. It holds the cocreator powers, wi' Oghama, if ye're female, or the White Tara, if ye're male, an' Both if yer mixed" he added. "Love-making wi' yer true love opens that pentagonal portal, an' it brings all five senses," he said, moving his staff around the points of the star, "both inner an' outer, into startlin' intensity, dear. Plus, it lights the god/goddess fires o' the heart an' calls down the Beloveds o' the Creator Sun to unite through ye here. An' then, it brings all these forces into one impulse that wants to create somethin' brand new out o' Their mystical love. It's the most concentrated love force in the cosmos, lassie. Ye'll master it in time."

"Coillore,...I...I have a forbodin'," she said suddenly, twisting the fingers of one hand with the other and staring down at the hearth with her brows furrowed. "I keep feelin' this need to rush, to be as close to Fìrinn as I can right noo...that it willna last long. An' I dinna ken why." Coillore coughed, then dropped his eyes a moment, carefully shielding his mind.

"Ye've both asked to return to the Creator Sun," he said slowly, sending the light of the Sun Lord around her heart as he spoke. "It's always a steep road, the path o' return, for every fear must be faced an' transmuted in love. There'll be hardship, lassie. We talked o' that before."

"Aye, I ken that. But there's already <u>been</u> hardship, endless work at the tuath an' Ceit's hatred." She sighed. "But no Fìrinn by me side? What could cause that?"

"Only the Creators ken such things, lassie, Oghama for ye," the druid said, looking gently down at her in his white robe, holding his staff. "He'll lead ye Home, surely. Dinna fret about the future, dear. Stay in the present moment, for the power o' truth an' life is only in the noo. The future an' past may be influenced by it, yes, but neither one is activated by the clear light, so they're no real. They canna create anythin' at all. Besides, <u>Oghama's</u> yer true love, no Fìrinn. The ladd's but a channel o' the One Beloved, an' God is wi' ye <u>always</u>, no matter where the ladd is." The druid stepped forward then, looking straight into her troubled green eyes. "I promise ye, lassie, in the end it'll all come right. I feel great gifts to the clans from yer trothin', lastin' gifts, startlin' powers, love that'll sway even that hard-headed arch druid in Port Righ. Dinna fret noo." And he laid his hand on her shoulder a moment as she let out a long sigh and nodded. Then he turned to walk back through the birch wood to his hut, breathing in the Goddess essence he felt in the moon glow.

Soillse had been looking forward to this day, Bealltain Eve (May 4th), ever since the king passed on early in the Willow moon (April). For ever since then, Fìrinn's days had been full to bursting with extra training to prepare him for the kingship trials. He was kept so busy from firstsky to well after the evening meal, that they hadn't spent one night together in nearly two moons. But tonight, no one could keep Fìrinn away from her, for Bealltain marked the return of the virgin girl in the cycle of the year, goddess of first love-making, Maighdean. In her honor, all unmarried adults went to the bonfires and found a lover to celebrate this Bealltain Eve with. So Soillse smiled as she put a hide apron on over her old summer shift to begin cooking the firstsky gruel, happy even in the damp fog. Many bairns of the tribe had been conceived on Bealltain night, too, under the virgin's influence. And these were always special children with divine powers of some kind. Will I be so blessed?, Soillse wondered, as she hefted a sack of oats from the storage pit.

Through the morning, she helped Sìne skin a buck and gut fish, and then she spent the afternoon turning the big carcass on the spit over the fire as the fog finally disappeared in the early afternoon. By evening, Soillse smelled of burned fat and smoke, and her arms were dog tired. But she found a moment to run to her Aine tree in the birch wood just north of the yard, stand under her hideaway a few moments, and look up at the crescent moon rising in the east, feeling the seductive sweetness of the virgin in the air. The apple tree was coming into bloom just now, too, and the faint scent of apple blossoms drifted around her, as Soillse bent her head and asked the Goddess to grant a babe from this night's joining with Fìrinn. "For it'll be me first an' last time at the Bealltain fires," she whispered. Then Soillse ran across the tuath and up into the wood for a wash in the burn and quickly dressed in her ceremonial hide robe.

As the moon rose slowly above the ridge and wisps of mist began moving in off the sea, Eilid stood in the fields above the tuath and began the slow drumbeat that called all to the Bealltain ceremony. She, too, was in her embroidered hide robe, her fine hair blowing round her plump face and form. The whole tuath gathered there, nearly twenty of them, and most of the fostered ladds as well. As the paired couples circled the altar, Eilid touched the torch to the kindling, and the twin fires roared toward the sky. Fire was the element of the virgin goddess, and Seumus drove the frightened stock between the flames to purge any lingering darkness of winter and insure flawless births for the year. Cattle, totem animals of Màithriel an' Daiden, an' horses, the virgin totem animal, were always purified on this day. And then the pipers began their thrumming, and Soillse felt a shiver down her spine as she stepped out from Eilid's side into the circle of youths around the fires. Quickly, before another ladd could do so, Fìrinn moved beside her and put his hand in hers. How manly he looks in his clan plaid and white shirt, Soillse thought, taking a deep breath and smiling up at him. His russet hair was carefully brushed for once, too, his green eyes never leaving hers.

But Soillse's eyes danced more brightly than her feet, for her calves ached as they danced a lilt and a jig, and then a slow lament. At last, they did the slow couples dance, two by two, twirling round in a diamond pattern on the hard-packed earth. And Soillse's heart sped as they did so, for the forest and Fìrinn were only moments away now. Others chattered to each other as they began the dance, but until the music faded, Soillse and Fìrinn spoke only with their eyes.

"Are ye weary from the day, lass?"

"A bit," she nodded, then pulled his hand. "Take me away, Fìrinn-ladd. I long to have ye to meself."

He led her down past the tuath to the sea and then up the cliff walk toward the women's cave, north along the shore, not turning toward the birch wood where their lean-to was, as she expected him to. Instead, they ducked under rocky overhangs along the narrow path, until they came to a small cleft in the rock face, the space no larger than the cooking hut. Emerald mosses made the stony floor like velvet, and two slender birches held catkinned arms over it. There was a tiny burn, too, trickling into a wee pool, and beside this Fìrinn had gathered new heather for a bed. He'd strewn the hide and furs over it with petals, too, blue wild hyacinth and apple, and white hawthorne from the hills, and she gasped at the loveliness of it. He said nothing but took her hand and drew her down to sit on the hide beside him.

"Any petals from me Aine tree?"

"A few, no too many," he said softly, kissing her hair, "enough for ye to feel safe is all. I got most o' them up on the ridge." She blushed and kissed him back.

And then as the moon rose, Soillse was more enchanted still, for the wee nook changed into a faery glade, with the small pool, the fluttering new leaves, and the twinkling stars all shining in the soft light of the slivered moon. Soillse sighed then and hugged Fìrinn close. After a moment, he lifted the edge of her robe and fingered the symbols there.

"Can ye tell me o' those markin's, lass? Does the Goddess allow it?" And he ran one finger down her cheek. "The sweetness o' the virgin's in ye so strongly tonight, Soillse, powers that give me pause." And his eyes filled with tenderness as he spoke. Instead, she kissed him long, wrapping her arms around his neck. And then they sat at the edge of the pool, wrapped in furs, and she leaned into his chest and snuggled her head under his chin.

"I can tell ye o' the pictures, aye, but ye might no like it all." She picked up her skirt and pointed to the small hut at the end of the spiral of images. "This is a wee hoose by the sea, late in our lives, like the one ye carved for me, Fìrinn. But here," she said, moving her fingers back along the life line, I see meself livin' up on the ridge," and she pointed south, "alone for many skyturns without ye by me side. An' there's a bairn, too. See? But ye're gone! I dinna ken how long we have together noo, Fìrinn, an' it scares me sometimes." And she looked down at the pool a moment before turning back to him. "I wasna goin' to tell ye that, but I guess it's best to share such things."

"Aye, it's best wi' me, lassie. I want to ken all o' it, so I can help ye carry the burdens. I want that as much as anythin'." And he took her face in his hands, his green eyes earnest on hers. "I dinna think love is only wild seductive nights. It's helping wi' yer pains an' fatigue, an' all the sorrows that may come. Sharin' that's what I want most. Coillore says we may be parted, too, for a time, that there'll be difficulty. But I want to reach the end o' me path wi' everythin' in me, so I guess if it's necessary...." He shrugged and sighed.

"Still, I hope we're together most o' it, anyway. I dinna want to lose ye, even for a short time." And she sighed as he leaned over to snap his flint against a rock and light the fire.

"I'll make ye this promise, Soillse o' me forever heart. I'll do whatever's required to earn the right to have ye by me side, always, in this life, but more than that. When the time comes to leave this world, I want to take yer hand an' go to the Creator Sun together, so I can be yer husband for all eternity, goddess mine! An' I dinna care what hardships I have to face to do that." And he bowed his head to her. And she shivered as the soft glow of the One Beloved filled the glade.

"Ye feel just like Oghama when ye talk that way," she said, squeezing his hand. "So Fìrinn/Oghama, I promise to walk the path wi' ye, too, all the way, together or apart." And then she pulled something out of the pocket of her robe and handed it to him. It was a shiny clear stone with a bit of pink in it, a small quartz, its facets glittering in the moon glow.

"I found that as a babe by the burn, an' I've treasured it all me life. It holds the magic o' the virgin goddess, I ken it. This wee stone says that love is stronger than any darkness in any world." And she pulled the leather cord she'd tied around it over his head.

"The Goddess moves in ye so strongly...," Fìrinn whispered, shaking his head, "more than I ever hoped for in a lass." But then he tightened his arm around her and grinned. "Do goddesses like to be touched or just worshiped from afar, I wonder? I dinna want ye complainin' tomorrow, me hot-blooded Soillse."

For answer, she leaned up and kissed him, running her hands through his long wavy hair, and then unlaced his shirt. And he untied her robe and let it fall to the mossy floor as they lay down on the hide. He gazed at the curves of her, shaking his head that this living treasure was his to love. And then he kissed her gently from head to toe and back again, turned her over, and did the same once more.

She took her time with him that night, feathered fingers kneading lightly: shoulders, calves, thighs, feet, all the places she thought he might be sore from the day. And he massaged her tired feet and arms, too. And then they kissed, long and long. Slow and tender was their joining that night, with just a hint of sadness over the difficulties that might come. And when it was done, neither slept at all. They gazed into one another's eyes and held each other's hearts all night long, talking of their hopes and dreams, and confusions, too, until the virgin had finished weaving their two hearts into one unbreakable chalice. Lying with her head on Fìrinn's chest, Soillse thought the blue night sky looked as soft as violet petals. And toward dawn, the mist crept softly in and wrapped them in its silence. But the hush of the early gloaming in their wee nook throbbed with the pulse of forever love, once lost and now rediscovered.

As dawn lightened the eastern hills, they quietly dressed in their ceremonial wear, gathered up the furs, and Soillse led Fìrinn quietly down the path toward the tuath. But on impulse, before they entered the hut circle, she turned into the birch wood and pulled him through the bracken to her Aine tree. Motioning him to sit beneath it, she drew the grass coverings out of the chink in the rock face behind and showed him her wee basket. He smiled and picked up the small yellow shell inside, lifting his brows

"From Coillore," she said, "given to me the first time I happened on his hut when I was wee." Then Fìrinn picked up every stone and feather, and drew his fingers over the tiny basket and the flowers she'd woven into it.

"See why yer lean-to is so perfect for me?," she laughed, nuzzling into him. "After I went to Coillore's that first time, I wanted a place to keep me spirit things. When ye went off to the games that one summer, an' Ceit an' I stayed home wi' Eilid, I made this to keep them in." Watching her, Fìrinn fingered the stone around his neck, his face thoughtful.

"Do ye have to find these things yerself, lass, or can I bring ye one or two meself?"

"Aye, do that, if ye like. I'd love anythin' from ye."

That basket is full of the child in her, with a heart as soft as wren's down, Fìrinn thought, all the things she hides from everyone, the wee things she loves most on earth. I'm lucky she trusts me enough to let me see them all. And Soillse, too, sat thinking how she'd never wished to show her basket to anyone else, not even Coillore.

"Did ye ever notice, Syl, how it's the small things most people hardly ever notice that are the sweetest? I saw a fawn one time, when I was maybe five winters. I always used to think o' it when I went to sleep or if I was upset, an' it would calm me somehow. It seemed like a girl, that fawn, an' yer eyes feel the same. An' yer basket does, too. Ach, I hope I can be good enough fer ye!" He finished in a rush of breath, dropping his face into his hands. "Sure an' I'll never be a hunter, or maybe a chief or king, either, for inside I'm just like ye. I want to live in the forest wi' all the creatures an' no fight wi' a livin' soul!" She pulled his chin up then and looked into his eyes, her own brimming.

"I'll love ye best, Fìrinn, if ye stay true to that laddie inside that loved the fawn so much," she said, "for I dinna care a limpet if ye ever become king. I couldna do all that spear throwin' an' killin' creatures to save me hide! Truth to tell, I dinna care what ye do in life, as long as ye stay yer own self, Fìrinn-ladd. It's ye I love." His tears fell then as he kissed her one last time, while dawn unfurled her pink banners across the sky.

That day, after they returned to the yard, Soillse changed into her old stained workaday shift, put on her hide apron, and cleaned the great mess of the carcass off the spits, then washed scores of bowls, full of congealed fat and flies from sitting unwashed all night. It was disgusting work, but she sang as she did it, for deep inside, she heard the distant harp of the Child Hearts in the Diamond Core, a land of rainbows far away. And she had to let her happiness out somehow. Ceit glared and Eilid grinned, and Fìrinn listening, too, from the games in the yard, smiled at the rains that came pouring down on them after the midsky meal. As the drops fell, he remembered Soillse's face glowing up at him over her wee basket and the fawn's eyes of his youth. And in that instant, the gentle eyes that had steadied him all those skyturns of his childhood merged with Soillse's.

Chapter Twenty-Nine: Fìrinn

Coillore took Fìrinn again to his hut only three days after Bealltain, arguing about the need to complete his lessons as soon as possible, even after Fìrinn said he was too tired for another long lesson just then. The morning rains had cleared, and only a light mist remained as they climbed the burn path through the birch wood in the gloaming. What's gotten into Coillore?, Fìrinn wondered, as he followed the druid around the yew and into his hut. He used to be so calm. I'll have <u>moons</u> to spare after the kingship trials. Why canna we finish these old teachings then? And resentment flared into the ladd's heart as Coillore lit the fire in the hearth in stony silence, frowning at Fìrinn's reluctance.

As he laid out a bowl of hard boiled gull eggs and flat bread, the druid said firmly he had one lesson on the structure of the diamond centerpoint to teach, and that it must be completed now, before the teaching circle at the oak in two days time. As the ladd sat down by the fire and began to eat, Coillore made a pentacle in the earth. And disappointment flooded Fìrinn's chest, for he'd hoped to climb into his furs early tonight. How sick I am of all these details, he thought, especially after such an exhausting day in the yard. And he stuffed fisted hands into the pockets of his light breeks under his summer jerkin.

"The regents o' the Indigo Pentagram here take the directives o' darkness an' see that they're put into place across the cycle o' each year," Coillore began, handing Firinn a shell of oat cakes for dessert. "All is focused on the release o' the skyturn's dark child, one step at a time, through the moons. This is the first structure o' the diamond centerpoint or sixth heaven, the Diamond Core itself protected from such heavy shadows. Indigo is the color o' grief, eh? Mainly grief for the loss o' the Goddess, but for all the love o' Paradise that's left behind, too. Still, indigo is wisdom's color as well, the reason our priestesses wear indigo robes. This light structure anchors into eastern Europe, ladd, all the nations around the Black Sea." Deepening the pentagon in the center with his staff, Coillore continued.

"In the center sit Artic(arsteeo) an' Herne, he, the horned god, takin' their impulses from Isle an' Taranis o' the Dragon star above. These impulses flow into all seven sheaths within noo, in the exact timin' an' order as the White Pentagram, through one whole turnin' o' the sun.

When the divine child impulses are implanted at Midwinter, these central regents prepare all the fears that'll have to be faced an' cleared in order for that divine child to emerge at the end o' the skyturn. An' their dark pulsin's are the whole year's birth contractions, one each moon. These indigo regents work very closely wi' those o' the White Pentagram, too, alternatin' light an' dark, eh?

These indigo gods an' goddesses, especially Artio, have been misunderstood an' reviled for centuries. Like the dragon lords, these regents o' the Indigo Pentagram are keepers o' demon kingdoms, holdin' great powers, an' few have borne as much cosmic hatred as these. As the darkness across the universe fades rapidly in future times, their burdens'll ease an' their truth'll be revealed.

But in the spirit world, no others in the cosmos are honored more than these, for they have lived in deepest darkness, held firm to their purpose, an' carried great intensity o' pain, while the worlds wait for transformation. These regents, plus the dragon lords an' the 6-6-6 o' the abyss o' yer next lesson, know all there is to ken o' the ways to face, heal, an' transmute yer deepest fears. Call on them in yer sufferin', ladd, Artio especially. For while she brings yer hard lessons forward, she also holds ye fast in her strong mother arms, until yer learnin' is complete. There's no other in all the universe who carries more wisdom in darkness, sheer endurance, an' utter love for everyone, no matter how far they've strayed from goodness, than she, the little black bear (Ursa Minor). An' humanity is, in a very real sense, her child, an' earth, the lowest world, her kingdom. Someday she'll be known as Sophia, an' her nation'll be called Turkey. That bird is her totem, too.

Artio herself brings forward the challenges o' the feminine durin' her core sheath phase, from Christmas to halfway to Candlemas. It's a challengin' time o' year. But Artio weighs the pain wi' exquisite care, a mother first an' foremost. Then Herne brings in the masculine challenges o' the core sheath, the second half o' this phase. He's always keepin' track o' mistakes an' measurin' what must be paid off in love, too, for Herne's quite precise an' careful about any debts that remain. But he, too, is responsive to the cry o' the heart, an' much is eased by diligence an' good intentions. His star system is Draco, the dragon, for this core sheath male's major darkness is that old personal will in separation, the old, old dragon force. Herne's land'll be known as Montenegro, the dark mountain.

Movin' round the star arms then, come the regents o' the rest o' the year," Coillore hurried on. "On Candlemas, the structures o' the skyturn's dark child flow into the mental ethers from the cosmic sea, where Bridget's been holdin' an' refinin' them since Midwinter. The mental body's the mind ethers o' all six lower sheaths, remember, ladd? An' because the centerpoint is their province o' the cosmos, Artio an' Herne remain to overlight this climb as well. So at Candlemas, Artio opens the dark feminine o' the centerpoint sheath. Her fears relate to the harryin', drivin' abyss forces, or bein' trapped in Artio's fear dungeon forever, perhaps. All feed on the joy an' security o' the lass within. But this centerpoint goddess is a mistress o' singin' in the rain an' keepin' to her purpose in the harshest o' times, teachin' the same to all durin' this phase. Then the masculine o' the centerpoint sheath lights up, halfway to Lent, as Herne takes the reins. His fears tend more toward the overwork mania o' the masculine that happened in the abyss.

Then a moon an' a half before Easter, the cherubim sheath opens, the lassie noo, durin' the first half o' Lent. An' it's Rhiann o' the first star arm here, who brings forward the shadow impulses at this level. An' Ùruisg (oorusk, brownie) then takes the laddie impulse, durin' the second half till Easter. Both involve heavy work, neglect, an' especially, harsh Ma experiences that once closed down the child within at this level. Rhiann's star city is on Hydra, the female water snake, an' her nation'll be called Bulgaria. Ùruisg star is the masculine water snake, Hydrus, an' his nation, Moldova.

Then Ardunna, o' the second star arm, calls forth the wisdom lessons o' the feminine o' the logos sheath, a quarter moon after Easter. These are the fears o' the virgin girl: misuse o' passion most likely, sexual distortions, or addictions, perhaps, pulsin's that can be quite difficult. But freedom comes on Pentecost, ladd, a moon an' a half after Eater. Ardunna's star is Canes Venatici.

Then her consort, Gòbhlach (gollach, horned one) takes the reins to open the portals of the dark male virgin until John the Baptist Day, still in the logos sheath noo. His challenges involve overwork for the tribe, violence, male posturin' an' dominance o' the feminine especially, or ignorin' life's responsibilities in feasts an' orgies. His star is Chameleon, one o' those violence-lovin' reptilians that once took over our world.

An' then, four days before the end o' the Hazel moon (July 22nd), Damona o' the third star arm, sends the feminine wisdom lessons into the spirit sheath. It's the Ma impulse, so the trials have to do wi' feminine misuse in action, overwork, or neglect o' the mother's needs, disease, sappin' her very life. But Damona's a Ma herself, an' she loves the mother within, watchin' all closely, makin' sure it's no too much to carry. Her star is Musca, the fly, the ones that harry us, too, at her time o' year.

Four days before the Vine moon (Aug. 16th) then, her consort, Borvo, takes the helm, openin' the wisdom walk o' the masculine o' the spirit sheath. Borvo's focus is on the Da, o' course: takin' too much o' the harvest, perhaps, workin' beyond exhaustion to make sure there's enough food for the winter ahead, or facin' poor harvests especially. An' his phase ends four days before the Ivy moon (Sept. 9th). His star system is Lacerta, the lizard, another slippery reptilian, an' his nation'll be called Romania.

An' then, Rhiannon o' the apex star arm comes in to overlight the final birth pangs, just before the dark child o' the core through the spirit sheaths falls away. Her consort, Carlin, helps, too, wi' the masculine fears, eh? This can be a hard moon, for darkness always intensifies just before dawn, an' the individual's been facin' similar difficulties since Midwinter. So, it's fatigue an' frustration most are dealin' wi' here. An' because the spirit sheath is the first o' the lower worlds, it's a heavier darkness that must be pushed through for this release. But Rhiannon is as strong an' determined as they come, ladd, a bit wild at times, but tender in her wildness, too. Her star is Lupus, the wolf.

Then, on the last day o' the Ivy moon, comes the release o' the dark child, from all inner sheaths but the soul an' sensate still to come. Remember how the end o' the Ivy moon is one gestation cycle after Midwinter? Then begin the celebrations in the tribe, wi' the star families an' all the gods an' goddesses in the Otherworld lookin' on, an' none happier than these wisdom regents.

But Carlin also brings through fears relatin' to the recognition o' this new aspect o' the self by the tribe, durin' the Reed moon. Often Carlin's distortions overdo such recognition, too, wantin' to be applauded by everyone, coverin' his insecurities wi' bravado, or else they push the unsure individual into far too much, too fast. Carlin makes very certain this new self comes out o' its shell, though. His star compound is on Serpens, the serpent, ladd.

An' then, on the eve o' the Blackthorne moon, the Cailleach Liath (kahlyuk leeah, grey-haired old woman) o' the fourth star arm, comes in to unleash the year's dark impulse into the soul sheath. The feminine fears take half this moon, the masculine, overlit by her consort, Gobha (go-a, blacksmith, Vulcan), the other half. These wisdom lessons are often the hardest of all, for their teachings always have to do wi' lettin' go the patterns o' the skyturn, relationships or projects dear to the heart. Sometimes it means the physical death o' family or friends, an' the grievin' can be severe.

But learnin' to move wi' the flow o' the One is a needed lesson, detachin' from what we ourselves may want to happen, eh? Great peace comes from these hard lessons, the comfort that we're no in charge after all, an' lettin' go o' everythin' but livin' in the day-to-day. Gobha is the smith that dismantles the dark masculine structures o' all sheaths that havena yet been washed clean, the spirit an' soul, all but the sensate that remains till Midwinter. I think it's a happy job he has, clearin' out the old darkness. I'd like doin' that meself! An' Caiileach is the dark river that washes away the feminine emotional shadow debris as well. His star is Fornax, the furnace that any smith needs, eh? An' her's is Cetus, the monster o' the emotional sea.

An' then at Samhein(2), the dismantlin' o' the passin' cycle's wisdom impulse into the pregnant waters o' the Goddess is completed by Artio. An' finally, after the last day o' the Samhein(2) intercessory period, the sensate sheath opens. This always involves facin' the deepest fear o' the three lower worlds for the skyturn. An' it's Rhiannon an' Carlin who lead the way through that one, too, to the full release o' the dark child o' this sheath on Midwinter Eve. completion! An' then the cycle begins all over again, as ye ken.

These indigo regents also overlight the closin' o' the inner sheaths an' the darkness o' each person's descent through bairnhood, ladd. We've been through this when we went over the White Pentagram, but I just want to review the dark pulsin's here. It's the structures o' the dark child these regents build over the divine child o' light through all the growin' years, the indigo child. In those future tumultuous times, many, many will be climbin' though thie cosmic Indigo Pentagram level to open the Diamond Core on earth. They'll be called indigo children. Those that reach the Core noo; they'll be called crystal bairns. But let's get back to the lesson, eh?

At birth, the Beloveds o' the Creator Sun close down, remember? Then Artio comes in to build the darkness o' infancy, the girl's descent through the rest o' the Creator Sun an' Diamond Core. This always involves a less than perfect attachment wi' the human Ma, due to neglect or anger perhaps, that leads to a disconnection o' the babe from Màiri an' Maithreil, an' Tara as Mother, too, for the stream from them is still flowin' through the human Ma. An' this wound'll place limits on intimacy throughout the bairn's life an' reduce it's ability to feel or believe in the Goddess. But Artio's real specialty is control, takin' over everythin'. She also brings in the one family member, also, who'll be most challengin' in later life, often a siblin'. This is the shadow keeper.

At age two then, Herne comes in to bring forth the temper tantrums that are his hallmark, the personal will out o' alignment wi' the all. But this anger'll tell ye clearly what's harmin' the laddie most an' what he's been sent here to shift later in life. It's the descent o' the ladd through the outer Creator Sun an' Diamond Core, eh? Herne always creates a natural hideaway outdoors to soothe the toddler's sore temper, though.

Then Artio an' Herne remain at age four as the inner Beloveds o' the Creator Sun reopen briefly, an' the core woundin' o' this lifetime occurs. This is when the centerpoint sheath opens, too, wi' the same regents. But all bairns are held in Herne an' Artio's strong arms o' love durin' this event an' the inner shock waves that follow. Still, this wound'll always feel like a betrayal o' the One Beloveds, close the heart's core, an' cause some deep an' lastin' separation from the human parents as well, for this is the fear around which all others are wrapped. This wound will also prevent the person's ability to manifest hearts desires, affect every relationship in life, an' canna be overcome without long years o' personal effort. An' once it occurs, there's no goin' back, as the heavy mantle o' fear is laid over the bairn, an' it accepts the shadow it has chosen to heal for the universe. But this core wound also fuels the bairn's deepest desire for change on earth, for it creates the passion an' drive necessary to reach that destiny pinnacle o' the future.

Yer own core woundin' was the beatin' yer Da gave ye for no wantin' to learn to hunt at the start o' yer fourth winter, ladd." And the druid laid a hand on Fìrinn's shoulders as he frowned and shook his head. "Ye'll be changin' the violence patterns on Skye later in life an' no mistake, though, so it was for a good end after all.

Then it's Rhiann an' Ùruisg who come in, from ages four to seven, as more parental woundin' occurs. An' the bairn learns to hide the self even further, the descent through the cherubim realms. This is the phase when the Beloved stream comes through the opposite gender parent, too, so distortions o' partnered love are always brought through durin' this time. Often the same gender parent becomes jealous or critical o' the bairn as well. But the major darkness o' the cherubim levels is the sacrifice o' the child, as ye ken, so there'll always be parental or societal expectations that utterly close down the inner bairn at this time, childhood left behind. This is often when siblin' issues arise, too, always woven deeply into each life's darkness. See how carefully all is constructed, ladd?

Durin' the next phase then, Ardunna an' Gòbhlach overlight the wounds o' the descent though the logos, she at eight an' nine, he at ten an' eleven. The emotion ethers open at this time, too, so the woundin's are deeply felt. This is the time when the child moves out into the wider world an' the core wound is repeated in some way, though far more gently than age four. But because it causes the bairn to feel at fault, a heavy false armorin' comes in over the true self, which closes the inner logos sheath, the backbone an' personal power o' the inner virgins.

Then Damona an' Borvo overlight the next years, her half, ages twelve to thirteen an' a half, his, thirteen an' a half through fourteen, the descent through the spirit realms an' sheath. So these regents bring forward the heavy time, work, an' mental pressures that close down the simplicity o' the inner child once and for all. Darkness o' the same gender parent is taken on at this time, too, strong societal structures that bind the true self even more.

Damona an' Borvo also bring up one old family issue to solidify the dark coverin's at this time, creatin' the final conflict that sends the bairn runnin' to its own age group. At the time the spirit sheath closes, all communication wi' animals an' forest friends shuts down as well, a sad an' lonely time.

Then at puberty, the great shift into the action ethers occurs. The short half-year puberty phase is overlit by Rhiannon an' Carlin. An' they always bring forward one sexual distortion, somethin' that'll be wrapped into all future sexual encounters an' contains the individual's deepest fear blockin' the One Beloveds. It can be quite hurtful, that, but important after all. Puberty is very much the end o' bairnhood, as the adult within from past lives on earth opens wi' the shift to the sensate ethers."

Coillore felt fatigue weighing heavily on Fìrinn's mind now, after his long day, and considered stopping to let the ladd rest. But there was so little left to this lesson, he decided just to finish it quickly, instead.

"Then comes the descent through the soul realms, overlit by the Cailleach an' Gobha, ages fifteen through sixteen an' a half, her, the first half, an' him, the rest o' sixteen an' seventeen. The soul realm is astral, remember?, many, many demons there, an' their influence comes through age mates at this time. So, the fears can be slippery an' quite dark: temptations to steal, addictions to drink or intoxicatin' herbs, sexual misuse, even killin' at times. An' those emotional soul waters loosen the identity structures, too, so the young person can feel quite wobbly durin' these skyturns. The Cailleach brings the soul shadows into love relationships, an' Gobha into specific life work as well. These soul sheath wounds are always wrapped into Oghama's light symbols within (DNA), too, multi-generational family patterns that the young person has agreed to carry an' heal for the tribe. This is the phase ye're in noo, Fìrinn. At the end o' this stage, the ladd or lass move to their own hut an' place o' work. That's when the soul sheath closes, an' all connection to the spirit realms is lost, earth life the only remainin' influence.

Then, durin' the final phase, ages eighteen to twenty-one, things get steadier at least, the descent through the sensate realms. It's overlit by Rhiannon an' Carlin again, her, the first half again, him, the second, for in spirit realms, the feminine always comes first. The astral influences drop away then, an' the heavy work o' adulthood or specialized trainin' takes their place. But the core darkness that blocks Tara's gift o' true love is brought forward by Rhiannon in the one long-term partnership at this stage. An' the core fear that blocks Oghama's world service gift is activated by Carlin, too. But the healin' o' these two fears late in life will finally heal the dark child o' this whole lifetime, its full release bein' Rhiannon an' Carlin's specialty again. Often at this young age, there's deep sadness about leavin' the parental home, too. An' adulthood is never what was hoped for either, too many responsibilities an' no enough freedom.

At the end o' age twenty-one then, the inner opposite gender o' the sensate sheath closes as well, militarization o' the male, perhaps, that shuts off his inner feminine, male domination o' the destiny patterns o' the feminine that closes her inner masculine. An' when this inner opposite gender o' the sensate sheath closes, each person is fully prepared for his or her shift into the ascension path o' adulthood at the start o' age twenty-two, wi' all shadow lessons o' the comin' life built precisely into place.

There ye have it, ladd, all the regents o' wisdom, wi' their impulses o' each skyturn an' bairnhood, eh? There's only one more centerpoint level to teach ye noo, the abyss. An' after that, ye'll be ready for yer brown robe initiation." And the druid's eyes shone.

"I'm full up in me head just noo, Coillore," Firinn said, rising quickly. "I couldna stuff one more bit o' learnin' into it." And the druid laughed, nodded, and closed his mouth. I can go on about the Diamond Core, he thought, but in the future, ye'll be thankful for these teachings, ladd. Then Coillore smiled, handing Firinn a bag of newly collected and boiled eider eggs, and waved him off. And Firinn hurried down the path through the birch wood beside the gurgling burn in the soft dusk of midnight.

But Firinn slept fitfully that night, restless after the lesson. And then toward morning, he had a startling dream that made his heart race. In it, he was lying in a thicket south of the tuath at Glen Elg, across the channel on the mainland, and he was hiding from some unknown danger. Tensing, he sensed game before he heard it, moving through branches nearby. And as a unicorn emerged from the underbrush, Firinn whirled to meet it. But as he turned, his mind slowed and sharpened, and the forest grew utterly still. The dusk glowed blue as the animal stopped and turned to face him, its dark liquid eyes holding Firinn's own. In wonderment, Firinn watched as the unicorn's skin fell away to the forest floor, like a worn cloak dropping silently on the moss. And out of it rose a tall flame of brilliant lilac. As Firinn watched, mesmerized, the flame took the shape of a woman, pale-skinned this time, with ash brown hair to her knees. She wore the pale purple robes of a priestess, and a glass city rose up behind her, the Atlantis Coillore had once described, a land that sank below the waves long centuries before. In the half-light, Firinn strained to make out the woman's features and then startled as he realized it was Soillse. Her feet were cupped in the lilac flame that didn't burn them, and she wore the unicorn pendant of Abaid an' Uan, the divine infants o' the Creator Sun.

And then the image changed again. Great white wings spread out behind Soillse's shoulders, wings larger than she was. He could see them quivering in the electrified air. And as her feet lifted off the ground, she became a great white egret that soared, flying high over the pines, wheeling southeast. Fìrinn peered for the Ogham letter formed by her outstretched feet, just visible as she lifted up over the trees. They were parallel, held straight out behind her, the symbol for Onn, Gorse. This letter signaled a period of steep travail, a gathering of wisdom for some high purpose, and a final breakthrough into sweetness.

Fìrinn had drawn the shortest reed, so his recitation was early, but it had been a strenuous day. The birch woods were cloaked in heavy mist, so he could barely see the trail to the druid circle south of the hut circle, as Bana Dhia, tail wagging, ran ahead of him. He rubbed his eyes as he hurried through the bracken under dripping branches to the clearing, wishing he could have curled into his furs, instead, for the night was growing cold. But Coillore wasn't sitting on the flat rock under the oak as usual. He'd never even lit the fire, and he was reaching behind the rock to pull up a large hide sack.

"What're ye doin'?," Fìrinn asked. "Am I recitin', Coillore?"

"Nah, nah, shhh. We're leavin' for Iona. The curragh's ready on the south rocks."

"But my manhood hunt approaches in less than a moon." And Fìrinn took a step backward in surprise. "Will we be back in time?"

"Shhh," the druid put a finger to his lips. "The wind woman harkens to me call. We'll be gone a quarter moon, no more. Wind callin'll be a good lesson for ye, too. Let's go!" And Coillore pointed with his staff toward the shore. The druid was dressed in his white summer robe and green cloak, but Fìrinn hadn't changed out of his muddy leather breeks and shirt after the games. Silently, Coillore handed Fìrinn a hide jerkin, homespun shirt, and plaid.

They tiptoed along inside the fringe of birches, keeping their footfalls quiet on the mosses, then climbed the eastern arm of the bay, furthest from the hut circle, to the southern beach. Bana Dhia followed and, thankfully, the guard dogs took no notice. A small curragh, the round oiled-hide boat used by the clans, was waiting. Coillore hadn't righted it yet, not wanting to arouse suspicion, and they both lifted the gunwale, flipped it, and crept slowly across the pebbles into the shallows. The boat floated easily, swaying lightly, and Fìrinn hopped in over the rim. Coillore motioned him to crouch down, and the druid pushed the boat into deeper waters, then swung aboard. Bana Dhia leaped into the sea then and swam out toward them, scrabbling over the low rim of the boat. Once inside, she shook herself dry, sprinkling boy and druid with salty droplets. And Fìrinn smiled, patting her flank as he wiped his face. Then the dog climbed up onto the wooden seat that ran four handspans below and inside the hard outer rim, holding her snout high and snuffling into the wind. Seumus'll have me hide when I get back, Fìrinn thought.

'Stay low,' Coillore's voice said in Fìrinn's mind, as the boy lay down inside the shell of the boat, while the druid began to paddle out into the sea loch beyond the arm of the bay. And then, as fog closed over the tuath, Coillore motioned for Fìrinn to take a paddle, too, and they moved into deeper waters. Almost immediately, the mist began to thin, hugging the shore. And then, as the druid pulled up a small sail and began to chant, a light breeze came up behind them, moving the boat steadily south. How does he do that?, Fìrinn thought, sliding his paddle under the seat and watching Coillore. After a time, as the ladd lay back down on the hide floor, he puckered his nose. It was ice cold and smelled of fish. Still, the rocking of the craft and the gusty wind, along with Coillore's chanting, soon put Fìrinn into a fast sleep.

The journey to Iona took two nights, no more. This surprised Fìrinn, who'd never been past the sea loch at home. But he was sick all morning that first day, as they headed into the open sea with its swelling waves. The curragh sat low in the water, so they felt everything, tipping up onto swells and then dipping into troughs, over and over again. Fìrinn groaned and retched overboard for an hour. But his stomach eased as he adjusted to the motion, though mild nausea remained. He enjoyed the way the boat handled the waves so easily, though, bobbing up and down like a seabird.

Just past midsky, they reached a small, uninhabited island, covered with thousands of gulls. It was also crusted in droppings and reeked of the scent. As they approached, hundreds of birds lifted into the air, crying into the mid-day sky. Coillore had changed into a workaday homespun shift and stepped out to gather eggs, folding them into a skin of moss for their dinner amid the swooping birds. And Fìrinn, holding his nose and breathing through his mouth, was glad to push off. The sea wind was cold, and a low cloud cover remained all afternoon as they hugged the mainland, rounding a long peninsula that stretched out into the sea to meet them. And then toward afternoon, once he'd grown used to the motion over the waves, Fìrinn thrilled with the rebellion of it all. Here he was on his way to Iona, without his Da so much as knowing and defying Seumas outright! It made him laugh out loud.

Beaching on a long, slender sandy flat, late in the day, they pulled the craft up close to the machair above. No settlements could be seen across the fields. So they built a low fire in the palm of a dune, feasting on eggs and oatcakes, and watching the sun drop through ragged, fast-blowing clouds. How easy it is to escape everything, Fìrinn thought, as he leaned back, full and content, his eyes searching the bowl of the sky. Twinkling stars peeked through mare's-tail clouds, and a deep peacefulness settled over the ladd as he lay down and rolled into the plaid and fur Coillore provided.

Absently rubbing Bana Dhia's belly as he listened to the ebbing whisper of the sea, Fìrinn thought, for this one night there's no one to compete with and no future that matters. And his mind gentled into the sleep of a bairn as soft waves lapped the shore.

A squall blew by in the early morning, lasting only a short time, but waking them before dawn and putting out the fire. So they ate cold oats, wrapped up tight in their plaids and oiled skins, as Fìrinn remembered the wonder of the night before. The sky stayed cloudy all that day on the sea, so it was chilly with only an occasional burst of sunshine to make the water suddenly sparkle all around them. And Bana Dhia kept her back straight and her nose to the breeze the whole way, sniffing the air from morn till night. This second day was more hazardous, with the wind coming in sudden gusts that shoved the curragh westward unexpectedly. So Coillore took down the sail, and they paddled for part of the afternoon, despite moving against the current on this southward journey.

But toward evening, the winds shifted again, and a light breeze filled the sail once more. And by the time they rounded the long Finn isle (Mull) between Iona and the mainland on the second evening, Fìrinn was growing tired of the sea, relentless drab green in all directions. How do those Phoenicians Coillore talks about keep to the sea for moons at a stretch?, he wondered. I need the tree people to talk to and hills under me feet.

Darkness deepened over the eastern sky as they headed for the small rounded island rising off the southwestern tip of the Finn isle. And then the late sun broke through at last. In its glow, the high peaks of the Finn isle shone terra cotta and blue, and scarves of mist wove their way through sheltered clefts there. As they approached Iona, her one tall rocky sentinel rose above the fields. And sunshine sparkled from raindrops on every rock along the shore and in the blades of grass above the high dunes. As Fìrinn hopped out and helped pull the curragh onto the northern beach, he wondered what mysteries he'd find here. At <u>last</u>, he thought, I'm on the druid isle!

But a watchman in a brown robe, hurrying down from the field above the dunes, gave them no time to wander. Silently, the young druid nodded to Coillore and motioned them to follow, turning to clamber up the steep sand banks and stride across the wide grassy fields, then along a muddy path between wind-stunted pines, with the hillocks of the isle rising to their right. Coillore had insisted Fìrinn change into clean breeks and the homespun shirt under his jerkin before they landed, and the druid was properly dressed again in his white druid robe. They walked some distance until they came to a flat yard, surrounded by a circle of small stone huts. And Fìrinn was taken to a solitary stone shelter, only large enough for a single pallet and hearth, a short way south of the main complex. And Coillore was taken to the nemeton, the druid grove of twelve ancient oaks. Even Bana Dhia was lured away by a warm meal and did not return.

In moments, another young brown robe with lowered eyes, a ladd of perhaps eighteen winters, brought Fìrinn some gruel and pointed toward the baths. And Fìrinn ate hungrily, then lounged in the warm waters, glad to have the itch of salt and sand washed off. The bathing place was beyond a rise, south of the hut circle from the main complex, sheltered from the ever-blowing wind. As he dressed in an undyed summer initiate's robe, Fìrinn saw another boy being led over the nearest hummock and away toward the west. Then Fìrinn went back to his hut and slept into the wee hours, until Coillore woke him gently.

"The chantin' has begun for ye," the druid whispered. "It's sixth night, so ye'll take yer initiation first thing, an' already the arch druid comes." Fìrinn nodded, sitting up and yawning. Coillore added that during this 'king's chamber' initiation Fìrinn would face his deepest fear, and handed him a heavy woolen cloak. But when the ladd asked Coillore what that fear was, the druid answered that only the gods knew for sure. It would come to meet him at his testing time. Then a tall spindly druid in a white robe and pale blue woolen cloak bent under the doorskin of Fìrinn's cell. The man's slender face was kindly under his white bushy brows, and he smiled at Fìrinn in welcome. It was halfway to dawn, and through the doorway Fìrinn could see the dusky sky muted with dark clouds.

"I am Eòlach (yawluch, the knower)," the arch druid said softly, and bent to light a bowl of fats. His voice was low and rustling, like leaves in the fall, and he began one of the chants of protection from harm. And then, breaking some herbs into the gourd bowl he carried, the arch druid stooped lower to hand it to Fìrinn. The broth was acrid, herbed to bring alertness and access to other worlds. And the ladd frowned and sighed as he tried to concentrate on the chant, longing instead to clamber over these hills after two whole days cramped in the curragh at sea. I'm not eager for another visioning, Fìrinn thought. And I'm still hungry. They'd fed him lightly here in preparation for his visioning. But now that he was on solid ground again, the ladd's appetite gnawed. I'll get no meals now, he thought irritably, until after me questing.

Eòlach hunched above him under the low roof, wearing the sun disc of the arch druid on his chest, a slight smile on his face, his powerful presence expanding through the small hut. He's older than Coillore, fifty winters at least, Fìrinn guessed. Arch druids all seem to outlive the average man. Eòlach's hair was completely white, too, thin and long. And he didn't need to tonsure it anymore, for it was bald past the formal tonsuring line across the head from ear to ear.

Slurping the broth slowly, Fìrinn glanced up into the arch druid's eyes. They were brown, and there was gentleness behind the stern expression that said each must face his darkest fears alone. And as Fìrinn stared at Eòlach's staff, looking at the carved Ogham letters spiraled along the wood, the druid's mouth turned up. Toward the top of the shaft were the circles of Abred, Annwyn, Gwynfyd, Ceugant, Leanabh Aingeal, the Diamant Meadhan an' Cridhe, and

Fìrinn's scalp tingled as he peered at them. I'll find me way there, too, he thought, as his gaze returned to Eòlach. And the druid's mouth curved up even more.

"We hurry ye to catch the power o' the waxin' moon," Eòlach whispered, "but ye've journeyed far an' need yer strength." And he pulled a wedge of cheese and bread from the folds of his robe, as Fìrinn grinned and ate them quickly. As he did so, Eòlach gazed down, and the ladd felt the gentle penetration of the druid's mind searching his own. Ther. Eòlach nodded, placing his hand lightly on Fìrinn's shoulder.

Suddenly, a bodhran began beating outside the cell, and Fìrinn stood up out of the furs, shaking his head to clear the drowsiness as he put on his jerkin, wrapped his plaid and cloak around his shoulders, and stepped out into a dusky night. Coillore walked beside him, his white robe barely visible, as they were led along the shore road back toward the place they'd landed only hours before. As he followed, the herbs made Fìrinn's mind hyper-acute. He heard a rabbit munching in a burrow on the hill and felt the wind woman gathering force for later in the day. But these preternatural sensations only made him sigh. I'm tired of initiations, he thought, and his belly knotted in fear, while the drumbeat resonated through his mind.

Across the channel, the dark hills of the Finn isle stood out against the sky, never fully dark during these summer moons. And to their left, the shadowy bulk of the hill Eòlach called 'the eye' blocked their view. Fìrinn had expected to be taken there, the highest point on the isle, and with that name, clearly a good spot for visioning. But they walked past it through grassy fields to the northern beach, climbing down the sand banks and turning left, following Eòlach, as the arch druid's torch guttered in the wind. Fìrinn stumbled once in the wavering light with the soft sands beneath his feet, and the waves sounded overloud in his ears, lashing the rocks, as he noted where the high tide line was. They stopped outside a small natural chamber composed of three massive slabs of fallen stone. The rocks were gneiss, grey veined with pink, needle-like and tall, and Eòlach motioned Fìrinn to enter and sit inside.

"Stay only till firstsky," Eòlach said, with no hint of a smile now, the curve of his mouth looking rather menacing instead. "To leave is to fail," the arch druid said brusquely. "Never give power to yer greatest fear especially, no to the slightest degree. An' remember, no one's tested beyond his strength, an' no one succeeds wi'out reachin' beyond the person he was when he began the trial." Then the arch druid turned away, taking the torchlight with him. What'll happen if I do fail?, Fìrinn wondered, noting the tone of authority in the arch druid's voice.

"Think always o' the Creator Sun," Coillore whispered. "No helpers can come to ye this time, no elementals, no teachers, no ancestors. Yer own spirit must defeat the force that appears."

No wonder the druids keep to this forsaken place, Fìrinn thought, and shivered. It's impossible to escape. And for an instant he considered taking the curragh, just down the beach, and going wherever the wind took him. But Coillore had insisted many times that to run from a testing sent by the gods is simply to ask for them to send it in another form, and always the next time is more severe. So Fìrinn sighed, his gut queasy, and pulled out his oiled skin to sit on. The torchlight flickered across the sands, and he heard the beat of the bodhran growing faint as Eòlach and Coillore disappeared beyond the dunes.

The slabs of stone here were considerably thinner than those of the dolmen, the walls rising to a point, creating an inner chamber that was the height of two men. And the floor was not sunken into the earth either, but the same womb-like feeling pervaded. It was damp, smelling of brine and seaweed, and Fìrinn could just fit inside with his legs crossed on the cold floor. He shifted his sitting bones to a flatter spot along the rock, and pulled the cloak tighter over his plaid, wishing they'd given hm a fur for his legs.

Abruptly then, the bodhran stopped, and a chill tingling swept up Fìrinn's spine and across his skull. The sound of the sea receded, and he was enveloped in a heavy stillness. The walls of rock, too, seemed to back away, so all was a dusky dark fog. Fìrinn tensed as he felt a cold presence enter the chamber, and fear constricted his belly even more.

"Brother stones," he whispered, "help me stay strong." And then the air before him began to glow. His gut was quivering in terror now, the fear pushing up from inside him like a beast clutching at his throat. And he felt a scream gather there, but he checked it. I'll not give way to ye, he thought. That'd only draw more dark spirits, lurking in the night. And then the slight glow before him formed itself into a shape that brightened slowly. He could make out rib bones, a skull, and wriggling feet. As it laughed, an evil, cackling sound, panic rose into Fìrinn's chest. And then the skeleton danced a jig of death, as Fìrinn watched in a cold sweat, shivering from head to toe. How do I defeat <u>this</u>?, he thought. Death is stronger than us all.

'I've come for you,' the skeleton's sibilant voice whispered in Fìrinn's mind. And Fìrinn felt the sound snake through the air and close around his neck. So this is me greatest fear, he thought, shaking the dark force away. How do I conquer it, though? It took Ma, didna it? As he watched the macabre dance, wide-eyed, Fìrinn imagined himself a warrior, growing into gigantic proportions. But the skeleton only laughed, and following Fìrinn's example, expanded bigger still. Fìrinn shrunk back to his normal size and sighed as the cackling laughter again filled the chamber.

Coillore said to think of the Creator Sun, Fìrinn remembered suddenly, and he always tells me to imagine me fears moving into the Creator flame in me heart. "Yer heart is bigger than any darkness in any realm," Coillore had said countless times. So Fìrinn imagined the skeleton's image moving into his heart. Did the glow diminish slightly? Fìrinn peered at it. "The Creator Sun," he said softly, and the skeleton dimmed perceptibly. In the Creator Sun, there is no death, Firinn thought, as a tinge of confidence filled his chest.

'But this is not heaven,' the sibilant voice hissed as bony fingers reached for the ladd. But even here, Firinn's mind argued back, we're born over and over, until we learn the lessons that open the gates to the Creator Sun. What ye call death is just leaving our current physical form, the passage of our spirits to the Otherworld. The spirit never dies. Never. And the skeleton shrunk even more.

"So death," Firinn said aloud, feeling suddenly brave, "ye trick us to think ye're the strongest force there is, an' we canna defeat ye. But the truth is, ye're no. We die only to take on a new form for deeper lessons the next time we return to earth, closin' the distance to the highest heaven." And the skeleton faded more, beginning to vibrate rapidly. "This is what I believe," the ladd said, standing in a burst of confidence, his head taller than the image now. "Ye're no real! Ye're just an illusion in me mind, an' only the forever realms are truth. So death," Firinn said more loudly, fisting one hand and holding it high, "I give ye no authority over me any more." And the skeleton, shrinking quickly, crumpled into a heap on the floor and slowly disappeared. Firinn took several deep breaths and called out into to the night.

"There is no death!" He felt giddy, intoxicated, and then he stopped and looked around. It's gone, really gone. Will there be more? He felt another dark presence lurking in the shadows, reptilian in its coldness, but not ready to reveal itself at this time. And Firinn sat down, stunned by his own power to transmute even the force of death. Crisp and clear, it came to him that his own beliefs made all things real and drew them to him in the first place. So as soon as I see the illusion of a fear and dinna believe in it anymore, he thought, it'll disappear from me life. Coillore keeps telling me that, but I didna really understand it before. What else is real, he suddenly wondered, his mind stretching to think how much of life might be illusion after all.

'*The Creator Sun,*' he heard Coillore's voice answer this thought, '*only that abides forever. It's the only truth, ladd.*' Aha, Fìrinn thought, if teachers penetrate the walls of an initiation in which no assistance is allowed, then the trial's over. He bent his head and whispered, "Thank Goddess!" And then he shivered as he realized the meaning of his name, Fìrinn, truth. How had Ma known it would become his standard? And he leaned back against the rock wall to wait for dawn, his mind still swirling.

Immediately in his dream, Fìrinn was in a meadow with daisies and hawkweed scattered among the tall grasses, like the alpine plateaus of home. Bees buzzed nearby, and he felt safe, absolutely, totally safe. Even in his sleep, Fìrinn knew this was a feeling completely unknown to him on earth, this lightness, without the hard weight of destiny he always felt on his shoulders. It was strangely familiar, this meadow and the security he felt here. The lap of the mountain held him like a mother, and golden sunshine burned soft and close over his head. And in their magic, Fìrinn felt loved for all that he was, right to his core. I ken this place, he thought, as he startled awake, but I barely remember it. Then into his chest came the knowing that he belonged there, and the certainty of this moved into the cells of his bones and gradually down to the soles of his feet. This place of safety, and this place only, was his Home. And he put his head down, steeping in the memory a while longer.

Coillore woke the ladd, gently pushing his shoulder. But Fìrinn groaned as the druid leaned in to help him stand, for a sharp pain cut through Fìrinn's neck when he moved, and his right leg was numb, asleep. Bright sunshine poured in between the slabs of stone, though, and the day was warm.

"No many sleep through their initiations," Coillore said quietly and smiled. And his eyes smiled, too.

Stepping out onto the beach and looking at the ebbing water, Fìrinn felt each wavelet sparkling just for him. Veined reddish rocks bounded the long sandy beach at either end, the near waves rushing smoothly toward the shore. The sand was soft, blush pink, reminding him of Soillse's skin. Then suddenly, Fìrinn laughed, pulled off his boots, and tugged his breeks up to his knees, running into the shallows. The cool water caressed his calves, and he threw off his shirt and pants altogether and lay down on the wet sand, arms wide. Me heart opens quickly in this place, he thought. It's the girl goddess of the White Pentagram, Iona, who beckons me on this isle. But, somehow, I feel Eriu here, too. And then a smiling Coillore led Fìrinn back up the dunes, through the grassy fields and the piney path to the druid complex and fed him warm goat soup, thick bread, and spiced mead. Full at last, Fìrinn curled up in the guest hut to sleep as long as he wished.

Fìrinn woke early to the cry of gulls, threw off his furs, and walked to the door of the hut, putting his face out into the sea breeze, grinning at the terra cotta hills of the Finn isle across the water. It was the third morning of his stay here. He whispered for Bana Dhia, returned to him after his initiation, and bent to grab his buckskin boots, then slowly lifted the door skin and went out. Coillore, on his pallet in the next cell, opened one eye and smiled.

The morning was cool and bright, the freshness of spring and the brisk breeze exciting the ladd, and he turned south along the channel on the way to the western shore. Coillore had told him to go there in his free time before the firstsky meal and find the small cove just north of the stony beach. "Most beautiful spot here," the druid had said the night before as he left Fìrinn in his cell.

So this morning, Fìrinn flew down the southern track, not even stopping at the clear turquoise coves along the way, turning west on the dirt path through low earthen mounds toward the machair. He leaned into the wind as he ran along the sandy track through tall grasses, dotted with flag iris, hawkweed, and primroses. He wore his buckskin breeks and hide shirt under his jerkin, for they kept out the wind better than his initiate's robe. Clambering down the dunes onto the broad curved beach below the meadow, he thought, thank Goddess I have the early mornings and the late gloamings to roam the isle. And it was glorious at this western beach, the waves sparkling, throwing rainbow droplets into the air as they crashed into rocky outcroppings, this bay real sand, not like the pebbles of home.

I have one more ceremony, Eòlach says, that'll gain me entrance into the order of brown robes. But I have to wait till the full moon in three night's time, and Fìrinn puckered his nose as Seumus's angry face flickered into his mind. The day before at the druid center, the circle of small stone huts on the eastern side of the isle south of the nemeton, Fìrinn had been given lessons in one-pointed focus, shape-changing into the power animal of his clan, and connecting with the White Tara. During the second lesson, he'd watched as many animals formed in his mind. And when he blended with the spirit of the roe stag, Fìrinn felt himself move through a thin film of seeming solidity over everything. Beneath that, he'd realized, all forms of life were the same moving spirit. And he recalled Coillore saying countless times, "we are all One, ladd." The druid teacher yesterday had called in a frog essence to blend with a stone, and Fìrinn noticed that the spirit force was far stronger than even solid rock, for it energized the stone into its own froggy likeness. How unreal the outer forms of this world are after all, Fìrinn had realized then. The spirit gives them life and only that. A few other ladds from distant tuaths attended these sessions as well, but outside the lessons, initiates were kept strictly apart, and silence was enforced.

But now, he waved those thoughts away, rolled up his breeks, and walked barefoot into the water up to his knees, then clambered up to sit on some boulders, watching the water thin, stretch, and curl into curving crests of waves. Bana Dhia ran before him, bounding into the shallows like a pup and scattering seabirds as she ran. Then she turned to chase gulls at the far end of the beach, as Fìrinn watched a pair of ducks peck at the bubbled seaweed that clung to the rocks. It rose and fell with each ebb and flow of the tide like a mermaid's dark hair. So beautiful, Fìrinn thought and sighed, so free. I wish Soillse could have come, too. She'd love it here. Then he walked the long curve of sand to the south end of the beach and back again, picking up colored pebbles from the mounded tumbles where the tide had dropped them, marveling at the varied colors, their depths and shadings in the wet surfaces. And then he climbed back up the dunes to the broad meadow and walked a short way north over the machair and a low rise, then past a small stony bay, as Coillore had directed.

And when Fìrinn came down on the other side of the hill, he gasped, for before him was a perfect wee cove, the sands creamy pink, with thin waves running gently in and out on the smooth beach. The small bay was enclosed by high rocky headlands, so it was completely private, a world apart. As Fìrinn crouched to run his fingers along the damp sand, he felt the sense of peace overcome him that he used to feel at the sea loch's edge as a child at his home tuath with his Ma. While Bana Dhia gamboled in the shallows, Fìrinn felt the call of the Iona goddess and Eriu both, telling him to be a child again and play. So he stripped off his clothes and waded into the water, sitting to let the waves lap his feet and legs. And suddenly, the water felt like Soillse's fingers on his skin, and he lay there and let it soothe him, until he had to hurry back for the firstsky meal.

On the day of his final ceremony, Fìrinn rose before the gulls and ran along the grassy path through low hillocks and stunted pines to the track north, Bana Dhia racing circles around him. He'd saved the climbing of the 'eye' for this, his final day of freedom. Each day he'd risen before the sun and run to another shore, north, east, west, and south, soaking in the rugged beauty of the sacred isle. He wanted, needed, to cover every inch of it, his heart pulled to explore everything there was. Inexplicably, the isle had come to feel like a dear friend, totally alive, every mood, every light revealing more loveliness. This would be his last morning here, and still Firinn couldn't get enough.

Climbing the path that wound up the rock face of the one steep pinnacle in the center of the northern end of the isle, he clambered through mire, glad he'd worn his hide breeks and heavy oiled boots. And Bana Dhia took the hill in great leaps and bounds, coming out above him and peering down under her shaggy brows, wagging her long white tail. The morning was hazy, a fine mist hovering beneath the peaks of the Finn isle across the channel and clinging to the beaches. Sun brightened the eastern sky but did not yet peek over the hills. Firinn struggled through wet grass and muck, the climb steep in places and the path boggy with spring rivulets, his hide boots and breeks soaked to the knee. He'd had mud up to his shins more times than he could count these past few days on the isle. But at last, he pulled himself up between two boulders and stepped out onto the small rock table at the top, fastening his fur jerkin tightly over his chest.

The northern wind hit him full in the face, and he had to lean into it to keep his footing, as he turned full circle, grinning as his hair streamed out behind his head. Behind him to the south, undulating hillocks gentled the view, and to the west a rocky tumble of boulders lined the shore. To the east were the soft shadowed terra cotta heights of the Finn isle, and to the north was sea, stretching on and on, with a hump of rock here and there beyond the waves. And suddenly, an unbounded passion for this isle seized Firinn's heart, emotion he didn't understand. *You've lived here many times,'* the Iona goddess whispered. *'You simply revisit your favorite places, friend of my heart.'* "Ah," he said, as he felt the spirit of the isle enfold him. And he knelt then, touching the earth with his palm, and sending into it all the tenderness he felt for this wild enchanted place.

"I have one last lesson for ye," Coillore said, when Fìrinn returned to his hut after the firstsky meal. And the ladd's chest flooded with annoyance. Ach, I am <u>sick</u> o' these regents an' their directives, he thought. But at the stern look on Coillore's face, dressed formally in his white robe at all times on this isle, Fìrinn settled before the hearth of the druid's small cell in silence, frowning until Coillore handed him some herbed flat bread. Two pieces was double the usual allotment given by the brown robes at the long table outside the cooking hut, and Fìrinn's brows rose as he stared at Coillore, who merely smiled and gave a slight nod. Then Coillore waited a moment before continuing, while Fìrinn wolfed down the bread.

"Below the regents o' the Indigo Pentagram sit the regents o' the abyss, wi' the heavy darkness they structure into all descendin' forms," and the druid drew three horizontal lines in the earth. "When ye emerge from yer heavy struggle through that abyss on yer way back up, the continental regents o' the Pillars come to meet ye, along wi' the overlightin' regents o' the Four Directions. An' sweet it is when they do, for the worst is over, or nearly so. From the northwestern father continent come Cead and Saorsa o' the Pillars. But it's Leòmhann an' Arienrhod, Liberty an' Lincoln, father regents o' the Four Directions, at the gateway, leadin' ye out o' slavery to fear an' into the light for all time. For it's they who overlight the passage through these heavy levels o' fear, openin' the final portals into the relative safety o' the Indigo Pentagram.

Then Treòraich an' Cùram o' the far east mother Pillars come in. But it's Eòl, o' the Four Directions mother quadrant, who melts down those old channels o' fear in the mind an' releases his structures o' truth o' all six lower worlds. An' Brìdget, o' the Four Directions mother quadrant, washes the dark child o' lower worlds away from the inner light body, too, birthin' the core divine child out o' its heavy sheath o' abyss darkness, cleansin' and cleansin' all residue o' these evils away. When I came through this portal, I felt her strong spirit waves washin' through me all night long, laddie. A pure miracle, that. Afterwards, all that remain are the fears o' the inner centerpoint an' Diamond Core levels.

Then the boy Pillar Corn Mother, Flidais, an' her birdman consort, Fionn, the bairns o' the southwestern continent, arrive to lift off most o' the heavy gridwork o' the old reptilian overwork structures coverin' the inner ladd. Fearghlas, too, virgin boy o' the Four Directions, dismantles that drivin' will force in the nerves, restorin' most o' the mother's vibration o' rest an' balance. An' Eilean, Fearghlas's consort, opens her miracles o' nature as well, exquisite details an' delights that always surrounded ye, but in yer constant haste, ye paid no mind to before.

Then the Pillar regents o' the African girl continent come in, Beli an' Anu. They remove all chords o' the spider matrix from the six lower worlds, for it was in Africa where the dark mother's control webbin' was first put into place. An' since the African tribes are keepers o' Guinefar's star tuath patterns, they reopen the inner connections wi' yer own Creator Sun family compound at this time, too. Then Siris an' Oisin, lass an' ladd o' the Four Directions girl quadrant, open the sweet girl stream within, her wonder an' his simplicity that'll mark the rest o' yer days.

The Middle Eastern Pillar regents, Aislin an' Colum, also remove the spinal weights that so crushed everyone's inner virgins, those domination an' brute force obstacles to peace an' surrender. But it's Maighdean, virgin lass o' the Creator Sun, who mainly overlights this birth o' the self, an' she widens the mystical marriage portal. An' then, Goddess an' God, Beloveds o' the Creator Sun, take over where the Pillar continental regents left off.

But most importantly, the One Beloveds arrive, Tara to light up the link to the higher self, that other half who is yer true love in the Otherworld, an' Oghama to open the final lifetime an' highest destiny templates, the ones that hold the keys to final peace. An it's Oghama Who overlights ye from here on. Beyond the filmy veils over the Diamond Core, the core wound is held, its mystery to be revealed much later, after the climb through the rest o' the Centerpoint an' Core. An' when ye reach the very end, through all the planes I've described to ye this past skyturn, laddie, Oghama, if ye identify as female, an' Tara, if ye identify as male, an' Both, if ye feel ye're a mixture, will reach through that silken curtain one soft night, take yer hand, an' gently pull ye through. As ye take that last small step into the bedchamber o' the One, over the Happily-Ever-After portal, ye'll realize that from that moment on, nothin'll ever be the same again." And Coillore gave a happy sigh, but then his eyes grew sad, for he sorely missed his Ailis.

"But let's look at the structure o' the abyss noo, an' we'll finally be done wi' yer lessons. Listen well, laddie," Coillore admonished, "for this teachin' could save yer very life in days to come." And Firinn sighed, looking wistfully out the doorcloth at the sea. "Evil can be summed up in two simple words, Firinn, power an' control. But darkness, too, is split into mind, heart, an' action," said the druid, pointing to the three lines in turn. "An' each o' those split again into the identical three once more within the larger levels, so nine planes here," and Coillore drew two smaller horizontal lines between each of the first three. "But each plane has a male an' female regent, so there's eighteen in all, six for the mind, six for emotion, an' six for action," and he drew a single vertical line down through all the others. "This is the 6-6-6, the cosmic beast or dragon, the guardian on the threshold. The abyss anchors into Orion, the hunter, an' there are three control centers here, too, in the central stars; mind at the top, Meissa; emotion in the central belt star, Alnilam; an' action in the sword or phallic star, Trapezium, hm?

So let's go through all these regents, startin' wi' the mind. In the control center sit the Borg queen, Beach (beyach, bee), and her consort, Counnspeach (counspiach, wasp). Hers is the mind control force that slips into another's consciousness an' possesses it, completely takin' over the will an' focus, ever servin' her control impulses, the queen bee. If ever ye feel thoughts that arena like yerself, do a quick healin' to clear them away, eh? Some dark shamans an' many hypnotists use this dark force every day. Mind that ye maintain charge o' yer own thoughts, whatever ye do, ladd.

An' Beach's consort is the fair-skinned elder male, the wasp, the one who puts himself an' his <u>mind</u>, especially, above everyone else. Durin' our descent, complicated left-brain structures were pounded into us by Counnspeach on pain o' death in order to create the electrical nerve structures needed for the Borg to control our minds. This shut down the peaceful mental flow o' Oghama, plus the free-flowin' intuition o' the Goddess. An' this extreme male domination o' the mind creates a deep split between the right an' left halves o' the brain, too, the masculine an' feminine. It'll one day be called schizophrenia. Ach, I have no use for either o' these regents!" And disgust flickered across Coillore's face.

"In the end, o' course, the left brain'll create the mental wizardry o' the male god within an' his ability to comprehend the vast mind flow o' Oghama. An' in due time, the Borg masters'll create mind machines, called computers, that'll greatly relieve our mental overload. The Borg also overran the Pineal Wheel an' the outermost planet o' our solar system, Pluto. An' from there, they send out the mind distortions that move into our mental ethers within. In Celtic histories, they're known as the Fir Bolg. This mental darkness is structured into the spirit an' diamond centerpoint sheaths especially, the mental realms o' the higher an' lower worlds.

Then, on the left an' right sides o' this control center are the Borg regents o' the shoulder stars, the masculine on the hunter's right side in Betelgeuse, an' the feminine on the left in Bellatrix. Bella's tricks is right," Coillore said, pointing to the first smaller line under the heavier top one. "The mind regents here are Balor an' Badh (bev). He creates lofty ideas an' long mental roadways that twist an' turn, leadin' us nowhere at all. He's the educator an' philosopher," the druid continued, barely pausing for breath, "always right an' knowin' more than anyone else." And Fìrinn perked up, thinking, oh, they must be the ones coming through ye these days, Coillore. "He fills her mind wi' more details than it can hold, bringin' her to the brink o' insanity. An' he fills the male wi' bullish, rigid fanaticism that builds its dark structures over Oghama's truths within. Balor wants to keep the feminine trapped in constant alertness that closes down her restful right brain an' totally disrupts her sleep, too. It's the evil eye, the pineal that's forever lit up wi' the male alertness force. His disease is one-pointed focus totally out o' balance wi' the rest o' the brain. It'll one day be called Asperger's.

But Badb complicates her own small world, instead. For she keeps a record o' everythin' in the hut, makin' sure it stays in it's own wee spot, so he canna move for fear o' arousin' her ire. An' she has rules for what to eat an' what to wear, an' when to do this an' that, till no one's mind can begin to hold it all, no to mention the cleanin', ach! There's no rest or family relaxation at all, when she's in charge. Her disease'll be called Obsessive Compulsive Disorder, ladd.

Then at the Borg heart level are the regents, Banshee an' Meall (meawll, decieve). He brings forward confusions an' complications in the left brain, especially regardin' work in the outer world, anythin' that disrupts the truth, plus the sudden breakin' o' plans that leave the masculine abandoned an' insecure, not knowin' what path to take. Meall makes the male take false steps that lead to failure an' humiliation, too, closin' him down in shame an' full submission to fear. It leaves the inner masculine in dread o' goin' in any direction at all (anxiety disorder).

An' then Banshee brings false intuitions an' demon voices into the right brain, the insanity forces. Hers are the nights o' isolation an' banshee wails within that twist the intuition o' the inner goddess, who ever kens what needs to be done, into lies, falseness, an' mental breakdown. The feminine gets harmed by constant outer disdain an' falseness, too, sapped by Banshee's endless lies, till no trust for love is left at all. Banshee's disease is paranoia, constant unremittin' fear o' the world an' everythin' in it.

Then the Borg action levels are ruled by Breas an' Bella. Both fuse their aggression an' disease structures into small life forms, insects an' single-celled beasties, called bacteria an viruses. His harm animals an' people mainly, those bothersome fleas wi' their plagues an' bedbugs bein' his specialty. An' he sends them into unsuspectin' villages in order to move in an' take over their lands after most o' the folk grow ill an' die. It's a real fight for survival when he shows up at yer door.

An' she creates disturbances o' weather an' small twisted life forms that infect plants mainly, any source o' food for the clan, to bring death, disease, an' mostly starvation to the masses, a most repugnant regent. She closes down the life flow o' the Goddess by tamperin' wi' Oghama's light symbols, too, through the genetic engineerin' wizards o' her dark Orion kingdom. In future days, she'll slowly try to take over the earth wi' such substances, puttin' them into foods an' crops across the globe. Such genetic engineering creates changes to Oghama's light structures within that allow Isle's dark tumors to flourish an' grow. An' in those times, she'll also create foods full o' chemicals that taste delicious but only lead to death. Junk foods, they'll be called, though death foods would be a better name.

But in truth, the intentions o' the Borg masters are pure an' holy. For in the end, their mental darkness brings forth a mind that bows to the humble will o' the One, knowin' those over-complicated lifestyles only lead to pain an' self-destruction, finally lettin' the simplicity o' love an' the <u>heart</u> take its rightful place as ruler. The mind lessons create the crowns o' truth an' wisdom, the halos round the heads o' sages ye sometimes see in the nemetons. All darkness is meant to teach, laddie, to be endured an' healed as soon as may be in order to bring forth the fruits hidden in the tangled vine.

Then come the regent o' emotion, the belt stars, the heart levels noo." And Coillore moved his staff down through another deeper line in the dirt. "Here, the Formorians or Mayan reptilians invaded the Pleiades, an' Cygnus as well. They took over another o' the outer planets o' our solar system, too, the one that'll be called Neptune in future times, playin' their dark, dark tunes. These distortions o' the heart create the emotion o' fear, ladd, which blocks love itself an' affects the emotion sheaths especially, the cherubim an' soul realms. Those great pyramids in Egypt are built in the identical pattern as these belt stars. An' that's because Egyptian times were when the dark regents o' Orion took over the earth an' buried the Goddess's memory under pyramids o' false father power an' control. An' Orion serves the dragon lords o' Draco, Isis an' Osiris's Egyptian culture, eh? So those pyramids brought in Isis's death an' Osiris's warfare streams as well. O' course, those pyramids also stand for climbin' that highest mountain to full freedom, too.

So, in the central control center o' emotion, Alnilam, sit the evil queen, Fuach (fooa, hatred) an' her consort, Aeval (ayvel). Fuach is the dark queen, whose hatred o' the true bairns o' the One knows no bounds. But her particular target is the virgin girl wi' her manifestation an' non-violence powers. The evil queen's hatred is often hidden behind the scenes, too, so others dinna see, breakin' down the spirit o' those she relentlessly targets. She's a master o' criticism, sharp stingin' words that cut deeply, an' envy, too. Hatred an' envy like this create a black ooze an' stony nodules in the gall bladder o' folk who harbor it, like this queen, that interferes wi' the Goddess's love within, too.

An' Fuach's consort, Aevel's specialty is coverin' the emotional flow o' the Goddess wi' his dark cosmic music, heavy metallic harmonies that block out Her song o' life. Aeval's culture is called Goth, full o' fear inducin' tunes o' death, despair, an' discouragement that weigh on the heart like chains an' armor. An' these chains grow heavier throughout life, too, leadin' to the belief that there's no end to darkness an' no escape, a disease called depression.

At the Formorian levels here, the 6-6-6 mind-heart-action regents sit in the outermost belt stars, the masculine on the hunter's right in Alnitak, the feminine on the left in Mintaka. At the mind levels, they are Tethra an' Morgause. He builds the iron gridwork o' rules an' regulations over the heart flow, forcin' everyone to follow complicated patterns in the outer world to get even their smallest needs met (Man-hat-ten). An' he drives everyone wi' his cold an' distant criticism, devoid o' any warmth, as well. In future days, payin' taxes or gettin' healin' or buyin' a hut, what should be simple tasks, will become mountainous jobs. That's him! His disease is constant insecurity o' life, ladd, blockages to what one needs to live.

But Morgause builds the iron shell o' disappointment over the feminine heart within. For she sends the feminine off on wild goose chases, breakin' promises, twistin' messages from family members, creatin' travel snafus, an' foulin' up family gatherin's till the fabric o' the family completely falls apart. This leaves them all alone, separated, an' starvin' for a bit o' real love. Her disease is loneliness, ladd.

An' then, at the Formorian heart level comes Ruaig (roo-u-ig, defeat) an' Macha, the dark lovers, who oppose the One Beloveds especially. He creates work that's perfectly suited to the inner male's deepest desires, but can never be completed an' is never good enough, endin' in frustration, time an' time again. Ruaig draws the masculine into menial work as well, blockin' success in even the smallest ways. It's defeat this regent overlays on the heart within, heavier an' heavier as life goes on.

Then Macha tempts the feminine wi' heart distortin' addictions, the poppy force, blockin' desire for love wi' agents o' death that only sap, paralyze, an' kill. Macha becomes an obsession, too, puttin' on false beauty to tempt all into love, then changin' into the demon she truly is. She leads everyone further an' further into her net, till they give up everythin' else to serve her, night an' day, for the rest o' their lives. It's death, she wants, an' in the end, everyone collapses under the weight o' her ever tightenin' web.

Then in the Formorian base, Agrona's the mother who mutilates her bairns, the ladd's especially, closin' the Goddess flow down. In the future, when a bairn is born to a woman who once mutilated that child durin' old goddess times, the babe's lack o' attachment to this Ma'll be called autism. An' in Africa an' the Middle East, even noo, Macha mutilates the women's place o' lassies, too. The world'll call it genital mutilation. All Macha does is based in utter hatred o' the virgins an' One Beloveds, wi' her need for control o' the creator flow at any cost. Dark, dark streams these are, ladd.

An' her consort is Dochann, (dochan, hurt or harm), the male partner who hurts an' beats his woman till she can barely stand, then joins wi' her, so love an' pain become intertwined, ever more tightly as life moves along. He brings in more an' more tools to cause harm, too, whips an' chains, smilin' as he hurts her, poundin' her into total submission to his hatred. His disease'll be known as sadism one day.

But even these regents o' evil eventually bring forth love's flowerin' Fìrinn; hearts that ken the face o' real Beloved love, true loves who gently support each other's desires, protect one another from all harm, an' work together in the holiness o' honest love. An' these heart lessons lead each disciple into the final ecstasy o' union wi' the One Who wears no fanaticism in His eyes an' keeps a tender restraint on all desires. Once through these portals, each disciple is perfectly prepared to step into true love an' world service in the humble an' tender image o' Oghama an' Tara, Beloveds o' the Creator Sun."

Then, it's the phallic or 'sword' stars that beam the phallic-force-in-separation-from-the-One all over the cosmos, from the control center in Trapezium. These are the heavy work masters o' the Orion star system, the ones who took over Sirius, wi' it's gentle child heart streams o' play an' lovin' kindness. They collapsed the girl's Sirian star wi' their iron layers o' endless tasks for her to do, too, the masculine takin' over completely. These fears flow into the action levels o' the cosmos especially, the logos an' sensate sheaths, too. All these evil action regents create <u>work</u> primarily, a master-slave mentality designed to keep divine bairns on earth enclosed in cages o' exhaustion an' powerlessness forever.

Once, our inner divine children manifested all they needed through the boy's surrender an' the girl's manifestation-into-the-physical powers, in joy an' freedom. But the Orions covered those wi' the lashin' phallic force that pushes all to work to near death, givin' the feminine especially no peace, no rest, no time for herself at all. These action Orions, that Celts would call Milesians, also took over another outer planet o' our solar system, Uranus (your anus), the one that goes it's own way wi' total disregard for the all, corrupted by that action phallic force out o' alignment wi' the will o' the One.

In the control center here, Trapaezium, sit the regents Smàd (smayt, abuse) an' Sgìth (skee, tired). Pushin' her to extremes, Smàd lifts the inner feminine to the very heights o' ecstasy, a new love, perhaps, or some special success, then crashes her to the ground as it all falls apart, dashin' her joy to pieces. Smàd's trapeze is like a spider, ladd, danglin' the feminine high above the ground, then lettin' her fall an' break into pieces on the floor. His disease'll one day be called manic-depressive disorder, the extremes o' action.

An' Sgìth's regency is paralysis, the deadly fatigue that comes from heavy continuous overwork, skyturn after skyturn. The masculine tasks are the heaviest, but o' course the feminine's are worse, for hers are the jobs no one else wants, cleanin' latrines, for instance," and Fìrinn puckered his nose. "But both get beaten down by filthy menial tasks, till they canna <u>move</u>, they're that tired. It's chronic fatique, Sgìth's disease'll be called.

Then in the outer 6-6-6 stars, the masculine regents in the hunter's right, Saiph, an' the feminine in the left, Rigel, sit the regents Fèineil (faenal, self-interest), an' Nemain (neemayn, frenzy). He thinks o' no one but himself, wantin' ever to be the center o' attention, talkin' an' talkin', an' then talkin' some more." And Fìrinn nodded vigorously, thinking of Coillore. "Or perhaps, it's jokes or foolery that grabs everyone's focus. He shouts about his great accomplishments, too, comparin' these to everyone else's to build himself up. An' he gets all to fulfill his needs, too, bringin' him cups o' mead or furs or slippers, others barely sittin' down at all. His disease'll be called narcissism some day.

But Nemain is <u>worse</u>, for she brings in the mania force, the anxious frenzy that drives all in the home to carry far too much work to stave off her abuse, starvation, humiliation, or all three. She takes over her man's life an' demands his help every single day, pushin' him around wi' her constant fears. Thank Goddess I'm no married to <u>her</u>," Coillore said with a shake of his head.

"An' then at the heart levels, come Hafgan an' Sùigh (sooy, to dry up). Hafgan brings in the action lessons o' mothers that are overburdened an' sapped by too many bairns or too large a hut, mothers havin' to permanently give up the needs o' their child within for the good o' their families. Mother's work is never endin', constant every day an' night o' her bairns growin' skyturns, the heaviest load there is.

But as regent o' darkness herself, Sùigh expects her man to carry the burden o' nourishment an' protection for the whole family his entire life long, the load that lasts the longest, till the day he goes to the Otherworld. She gets him to work to utter exhaustion to bring home meat for her bairns or useless trinkets for herself, work that takes over his life stream an' willna let go. Her family needs come above all else, closin' out time for rest, play, an' family fun that nourish his own child within. These are the forces that age her an' weaken his bones so rapidly, ladd, the grindin' overwork streams. Their disease'll be called osteoporosis one day

An' finally come the regents o' the action levels there, Carman an' Eigh (ey, ice). His is the inner drivin' force that harries an' pushes the inner male without end, from early bairnhood till death. He sets deadlines an' brings intense force to bear, causin' that racin' heart an' inner time pressure that harm so many. An' Carman meets out brutal punishment to any who fail to meet his expectations, too. It'll be called Type A personality one day an' cause irregularity o' the pace o' the heart, an' high blood pressure as well.

Then Eigh is the Ma who neglects her bairns, family, an' all responsibility, if truth be told, a cold uncarin' goddess. For she doesna even <u>notice</u> her family's pain, lettin' them suffer, sometimes intensely, as she goes off an' does whatever she wants.

These regents create the parent/child reversal streams, too, parental neglect or force pushin' both boy an' girl into adult patterns o' overwork, responsibility, an' heavy labor at far too young an age. Carman brings forward heavy work outside the home, an' Eigh, the constant work o' the mother near the hearth. An' always these heavy loads are too much for the children to carry, as the bairns collapse into resignation an' despair. These are the streams that create lower back an' hip pain at an early age for him, the breakin' down o' the pelvic stone circle, an' rectal an' woman's place collapse for her, the breakin' down o' the pelvic floor. <u>Always</u> take time to sing or dance or play, <u>every</u> day, ladd, an' REST! It'll keep ye young far longer than most." <u>When</u>?, Firinn thought to himself.

"But these Orion regents o' evil have their divine purpose, too, for once a disciple moves beyond their difficult portals, the sweet miracle o' the child opens, slowly, like the wild rose life truly is. Small delights come driftin' in: play, magic, laughter, fun that stretches out forever, rest an' happiness manifested wi' ease at last. Their powers are great, these regents, an' all must walk their tirin' path o' the drivin' action forces before life's simple blessings come clear at last, sparklin' wi' that diamond light that surrounds us all."

Then the druid bent his head, his long hair fully white now, and pulled his hands together, giving a long sigh. Firinn guessed that Coillore was revering the diamond light he'd just spoken of. But in truth, the old druid was blessing the one who had listened and absorbed teachings that had taken Coillore a lifetime to amass and understand within. These lessons were Coillore's greatest gift to Fìrinn's own divine child, who would far surpass the old druid, both in carrying darkness and in life accomplishments. And now, finally, the teachings were at an end. It's done, the druid thought, his face lit by the joy of completing this most important life work. I've given ye all I have to give, laddie, the heart o' me heart. But as he lifted his face, Coillore eyed Fìrinn with sadness, too. And as he watched Fìrinn hurry off to the beach at last, one tear fell down the old druid's cheek.

The brown robe ceremony was brief, held that night as the full moon rose luminescent over the hills of the Finn isle. Forty druids were circled in the nemeton, twelve white oaks circled on the grassy eastern flats just north of the druid complex. And Eòlach, in his formal white robe and lambskin cloak, called each boy to the white Iona marble altar stone in turn, smiling gently down at them. So, twelve other ladds who'd succeeded through their initiations stood with Fìrinn round the altar, while the druid chants drifted off into an unusually warm wind. As Fìrinn knelt before the arch druid and took the brown robe and pouch of amulets from Eòlach's hand, he felt a crowding of spirit ancestors nearby. And his eyes searched the gloaming, for the star beings felt close enough to touch. There were a hundred or more in the ethers, leaning in behind the altar stone, crowding there to welcome him back into the brotherhood of light he'd belonged to so many times before. And Fìrinn struggled not to weep openly at the overwhelming sense of reunion he felt. I've walked with the druid brotherhood more times than I thought, he mused. No wonder I love it here.

And then, after chanting the brotherhood blessing song, the notes wafting out over the channel into an orange gloaming, the druids spiraled out of the grove in comforting silence. And Eòlach walked with Fìrinn and Coillore to the north beach, even before the feasting began. The hills of the Finn isle were bright in the evening dusk as Coillore placed the food bundle Eòlach's assistant had given him into the boat. And the elders embraced in the ancient style, the muted moon glowing on their white robes as well. And Eòlach hugged Fìrinn, too, giving him the druid handshake for the first time, grinning at Fìrinn in his new robe.

"We're pleased," he said, winking at Coillore. "Ye've attained the first rank o' the orders, an' ye're still young, ladd. The Goddess'll lead ye deeper on the path. Trust Her an' remember us, will ye? It's only too bad ye're in such a rush to get back to yer tuath. Safe journey over the waves," Eòlach called in his rustling voice. And the arch druid held his hands up in blessing, his golden breastplate reflecting the moon circle in the sky, as Fìrinn pulled his robe off over his hide breeks, pulled on his hide shirt, and helped Coillore lift the curragh into the waves.

They swung over the gunwale as Bana Dhia scrabbled inside, and Fìrinn waved, his eyes soaking in the island landscape one last time. It was Fìrinn who pulled up the sail then, smiling at Coillore as if to say, time for a breeze, magician. And Coillore's eyes twinkled back. The boy had done extraordinarily well. In the folds of his robe, the druid held the new pouch of Ogham symbols he'd made here, small wooden rounds cut from twigs of the sacred oaks of the nemeton. They'll guide the ladd through the times of trouble that approach, the druid thought. But I'll wait till this moon's trials are over to present them. The hunt of manhood, the ritual of kingship will all unfold as the Goddess wills. Fate is closing in around the boy, and me work'll soon be over with him, the druid thought, his heart contracting as he felt their parting soon to come. And then Coillore carefully let this sadness go, imagining his grief laid on the altar of the One.

The druid set a course straight for Skye, not even stopping to warm their meals along the shore. It was time to get the ladd back for all that had been prepared for him. And as they journeyed through the night into a clear morning, Coillore breathed in the sea-salt air and smiled at the rising sun. He felt renewed himself from their journey. For this I was born, he thought, and bent again to his chanting.

Firinn lay in the bottom of the hide shell between furs and slept well into the day. Suddenly, he felt exhausted from all the changes to the bedrock of his soul. Sea sickness barely bothered him this time, and when he woke, he was famished, and ate half the nuts, oats, and flat bread the druids had given them in one sitting. But Coillore only smiled, nodded, and kept on chanting, looking like an elder wizard in his goatskin cloak, holding the wind steady that would take them home.

When he finished eating, Firinn looked backward toward Iona, but already she was gone. And with a pang, he realized he'd miss her till he returned again at some future time. Wish I'd thought to race to the western beach and say good-bye to the pink cove before we left, he thought. Some day I'll go back, and he tucked this hope into his heart, refusing to think about the trials he'd soon face, beginning with Seumus's glowering reception when they arrived back at the tuath.

In the silent stretch of time on their way north, Firinn envisioned Iona as he could not conjure up the Creator Sun. In his mind, he could clearly hear the sea wind on the isle, whispering across the machair, and feel the sweet beauty of the wee blushing cove. From the "eye," he could see the fields in the quiet morning spread below him. And he locked the rugged wildness of this girl goddess isle into his memory, that and the freedom for his spirit he knew awaited him there whenever he returned. In her very closeness, Iona would steady him in a way even the brilliance of the far-off Creator Sun could never do.

The journey back took only the rest of the night and the next day, for the currents were with them now. Coillore gave Firinn the helm at times, making him practice wind calling, for the druid knew the ladd would need this lesson in not too many more moons. As they neared the jagged peaks of Skye, Coillore, looking ordinary again in his old workaday shift under his jerkin, drifted to the small outcropping of rocks, too small to be called an isle, crowded with seabirds. And Firinn this time, in his old muddy hide breeks and shirt, dodging the gulls, gathered a large skin full of eggs.

"Seumus is always softened by food," the druid said, which made Firinn smile and then make a wry face at the nearness of this confrontation. As the evening gloaming deepened around them, they turned northeast into the sea loch toward the fostering and Coillore dropped the rudder, and sat back against the gunwale with a sigh.

"Ye try it again, ladd, the wind callin'. Gather us up a breeze an' take us back noo." And the druid's eyes shone under his white brows.

At that particular moment, Firinn was wondering if Soillse would be upset about his absence. The ladd's eyes were resting on the Cuchullin peaks ahead, dusky purple with night, but he turned sharply toward the druid with raised brows.

"What? Me?" And the old man nodded, handing the rudder to the ladd. Firinn hesitated, then shrugged, and sat forward with his brows knotted, staring toward the tuath off to the east across the sea loch. He drew his scattered thoughts into as sharp a focus as he could manage, singing out the chant of the wind spirits over the waves. And despite his troubled thoughts, Firinn's heart brimmed to overflowing now, for he returned to his love as well. As he prayed for the wind woman to fill their sail and speed them on, Firinn held the vision of the tuath distinctly in his mind. And immediately, a zephyr came up, gusting the little boat forward. It turned them this way and that, in a dancing whirl of motion. So Firinn, with pinched face, concentrated hard on a calmer wind without success, as they headed in to shore.

"Ye draw the youth o' her," Coillore chuckled, his fine hair blowing out behind him in the wind, "while I get the matron. That's as it should be, hm, ladd?"

The tuath rose up from the cup of the bay, the thatched wooden palisaded houses all in shadow now. It looked so peaceful in the gloaming, everything enfolded in the purple dusk, the bustle of the games and cooking hut stilled for once. Birds twittered from the birch wood on the ridge behind, and yellow iris beckoned faintly from the burnside. The land's greened since we've been gone, Fìrinn thought, his eyes searching the yard. Then the dogs began barking, as the boat brushed the sand. The ladd jumped into the shallows, with no thought for the curragh, picturing Soillse in his mind.

"Da! They're here!" A female voice hollered from behind the hut circle, and then a squeal rang out over the waters. He saw her then, racing from the shadows of the round house, barefoot in a summer shift, with a light woolen shawl pulled over her shoulders, nearly stumbling in her haste to get to the shore. And Seumus ran after her, his stomach bouncing under his homespun shirt. A score of ladds poured from the long house and stood, gaping toward the sea. But Fìrinn saw only Soillse and grinned at the glowing tangle of her hair and the brown freckles over the flush of her face as she flew into him. Almost knocking him over, she wrapped her arms tight around his back, her green eyes aglow with the sight of him.

"I didna ken where ye went...I didna ken...if ye'd come back...I thought... ye were gone...Fìrinn!" And she held her face up to him, quivering, with tears streaming down her cheeks, her head barely reaching his shoulders. As he picked her up, Fìrinn was surprised by the lightness of her. How small she is! And then, savoring the hunger in her eyes and not caring what Seumus did, Fìrinn bent and kissed her in front of them all.

Chapter Thirty: Soillse

As soon as she went out to fill the water skins at dawn, Soillse knew he wasn't there. His heart light didn't surround her as she walked to the burn, and she panicked for a moment. *Where is he? Why didna he tell me he was going somewhere?* And then she remembered Coillore saying he wouldn't be teaching at the clearing this quarter moon. *Oh, Goddess, not another initiation at the dolmen,* Soillse thought, her brows furrowed together. *Fìrinn hadn't mentioned one, not that Coillore ever told him beforehand. Or has he gone somewhere else? Is this the separation the symbols on me ceremonial robes tell about? No! We've had so little time!* As her heart raced, Coillore's face came clearly into her mind. *'There's a fear force tryin' to bend yer spirit to its will, lassie, an' there's no a shred o' truth in it. Bring it into yer heart an' feel us. We're on our way to the druid isle. Be gone a quarter moon, no more.'*

"Oh," she said, pulling up her shift to sit on the mossy bank beside the burn, then putting her feet into the water. Trying to collect herself as her pulse slowed down, Soillse imagined the panic moving into her heart to melt in the diamond light there. Then ignoring Ceit's calls, Soillse concentrated on Fìrinn and saw him fast asleep, curled up in the bottom of the small curragh, surrounded by the sea. Coillore was chanting, calling forth the wind. *Da'll be beside himself,* she thought. And Soillse sighed as she hefted the water skins to her back and carried them to the round house. Then she ran to the shore to look beneath the bushes. The small curragh was gone.

It was a hectic week, for the sun shone for five days straight, unheard of on Skye. Furrows needed to be dug, the seeds planted, and the seaweed brought up, chopped, and laid on the fields. Ceit yelled for everything to be done faster and faster, before the rain set in again and washed the precious seeds away. And beneath it all, Soillse missed Fìrinn terribly. She felt the lack of his gentleness around her, for even when he was off in the hills with the ladds, she could feel him nearby. The ache in her heart was so intense; it felt like a living thing. And she was glad for the busy-ness of the days, for her sadness grew far worse when she lay on her pallet in the silence before sleep.

For several nights after his departure, she lay long awake, and then her fatigue weighed the days even more. Everything felt more burdensome without him, too, and even Ceit was harsher, her black hair frizzed around her face. And Soillse realized that Fìrinn's nearness had protected her own self this past skyturn, for Ceit knew he'd intervene, if she went too far. Goddess help me, if he ever does go away for very long, Soillse breathed. How will I bear it?

One afternoon, Soillse took a wee while to go to her Aine tree for comfort, when Ceit was off on the ridge gathering grasses to mulch the new sown fields. Soillse hiked up her homespun shift and sat on the mosses below, then leaned against the trunk, exhausted. How delighted I used to be here, she thought, when I was wee, before the work got so relentless. That was before Fìrinn ever came to the tuath, and I was happy enough without him then. Come on, she thought, pick yerself up. Ye can do this.

"That dreamy Soillse, where is she? I need help wi' this load." It was Ceit in a fury entering the yard, her dark eyes searching the tuath. Soillse started awake and jumped lightly up, eyeing Ceit warily through the shrubs. Bending low and moving slowly through the underbrush, until she was near the latrine, Soillse then walked out into Ceit's sight.

"Where've ye been," Ceit shrieked, nearly a head taller than Soillse, her muscular arms tense under her light summer shift. "I need help spreadin' this grass. I carried it all meself from the ridge because I couldna find ye!" And then Ceit stared at Soillse's face. "Just look at the pink in yer cheeks, will ye? Ye've been off sleepin' somewhere!" But Soillse said nothing in reply, just bent to pick up an armful of grass to carry to the fields. "Ye're always so quiet, always so good," Ceit taunted with a sneer. "I just canna stand ye!" And Ceit suddenly reached out and raked her nails along Soillse's arm. Four cuts began bleeding there, and Soillse dropped her load and backed away, eyes blazing. Muirn came running from the cooking house, taller even than Ceit, shouting for Eilid, who appeared from the long house door in moments, holding a heap of soiled clothes in her arms. And then something inside Soillse snapped. I'm nearly as big as ye are, Ceit, she thought. I dinna have to take this any more!

"Ye canna harm me, Ceit, no matter what ye think," Soillse said, holding her head high and leveling her eyes on her sister. "An' ye dinna have the right to tell me what to do, either. I'm a woman noo meself." As Ceit narrowed her eyes in response, pure hatred poured out of them.

"I'll bide me time, I will," she whispered, as Eilid hurried to look at Soillse's arm, glowering at Ceit.

"Get ye to the south bay an' gather limpets, Ceit, noo!" Eilid's voice was low, almost a growl. "An' dinna return till ye calm yerself. An' dinna ever let me see ye treat yer sister this way again, unless ye want to be sent away from this tuath. I'll tell the lass what work needs doin' from noo on. I'm the Goddess keeper here."

"Ye dinna have the power anymore, Ma, an' everyone kens it." Ceit said, standing taller in her worn shift and taking a step toward Eilid with one side of her lip lifted. "I'll do as I like. I'm gatherin' grasses today. An' there's more to be brought in, since Soillse's been off sleepin' half the afternoon."

Muirn and Sìne, looking even more stern than usual, stared as Ceit, still sullen, strode up toward the burn. Then Sìne ran to the round house for a wet hide, and Eilid washed the scrapes on Soillse's arm, then rubbed plantain and willow salve into them. As her Ma did so, Soillse thought, why does Ceit hate me so much? Then the lass sighed. What did I ever do to her? Then she turned to start gutting the fish for the evening meal.

With her sore arm, Soillse slept even more fitfully that night under her furs. And when she finally drifted off, she saw a wide river in her dreams, nearly as wide as the bay, meandering through a flat sun-baked land. Trees with high, feather-shaped branches swayed beside the low banks, and fertile fields spread out on either side. A yard master barked out orders, as a group of men in loin cloths bent along a row, picking stalks of grains. *'Egypt'*, a voice said in her mind. And Soillse knew this river had once been a home she'd loved; it felt so familiar, the tall graceful papyrus plants reflected in the turbid waters of the Nile.

The scene shifted then, and Soillse stood inside a temple, looking out at a high colonnade of painted columns and terra cotta mud walls. She wore the indigo robe of a novice and the blue moon pendant of the priestess order of the great mother, Isis. A flat barge was moving slowly up the river toward the burial grounds on the opposite bank, stopping at the narrow canal leading to the Queen's pyramid. It was Soillse's mother on the bier, for the queen had died of an illness the physicians couldn't heal two moons ago. The priests said they hadn't seen this disease before, and ravages of fever had wasted the queen away in less than a moon, raving like a maniac on her bed. Now the seventy days of mummifying were over, and Soillse watched closely as the body was lifted out of the barge. Wrapped in ivory cloth with threads of silver, it was carried into the shadowy entrance of the pyramid to the waiting sarcophagus in the tomb, This was Soillse's last glimpse of her mother.

The queen's spirit would be released by the priests in the stone chamber under the pyramid, and she'd take her place among the stars. Not all were mummified this way, only those with special powers. Her mother had been strong in the sight, speaking the language of the Goddess clearly in her trances and communicating directly with the star, Rigel (left foot, Orion), bringing much needed information about medicines and healing to the people. In her mind, Soillse saw them lay the body in the sarcophagus and begin the chant to separate spirit from flesh. And her green eyes filled with tears as she felt her mother's soul release and lift away.

After her baby years, there had never been much time with her mother, for Soillse was sent off to the Temple of Isis, where her older sister lived, when she was only four. And even before that, her mother had been taken up with affairs of state. Soillse hadn't traveled north to the capitol city, Memphis, except for this burial, since she was seven years old, over a decade now. But she vaguely remembered her mother's long dark hair and the tender hands that had laid her in her cradle basket as a babe. Wiping one tear away, Soillse dimly heard her mother's gentle voice singing a lullaby, and her heart ached for the one who'd loved her in her infancy, the one who even now felt most like the mother goddess. There'll be more arguments with my sister after this, too, Soillse thought, and hiding behind the columns of the temple, she began to cry.

The scene shifted again, and Soillse was inside a smaller temple, dressed in the ivory robe of a grown priestess, with her full moon, mother-of-pearl pendant sparkling in the fire glow. She gazed at the altar, many cups of fat burning there, blending their cloying odor with the incense from the central bowl. But a cool evening breeze wafted in from the river through the large doorway of the shadowy room. The huge blue wings of the goddess spread over the terra cotta mud walls above the altar, the gold of her crown reflecting the flickering flames. And ranks of priestesses and novices stood in formal rows before it, Soillse and Ceit in the line of white robes at the front. All the priestesses were dressed in long robes with turquoise sashes and broad colorful beaded necklaces around their shoulders, hair cut bluntly to their shoulders in the Egyptian style.

The five elder priestesses in their sea blue robes, stood facing the initiates, and they took hands and began the praise song to the goddess. And Ceit, head held high, hair straight and dark, stood taller and stronger than Soillse. Tonight Ceit's cheeks were flushed, her eyes starry. The matron priestess, a plump woman with straight grey hair in the deep aqua robes of the elder mother, moved to the center of the altar and held out a small scroll.

"We've chosen the new high priestess, and it's not what we anticipated." And the mother's black eyes darted toward Ceit. "This may cause difficulty for a time, and our first challenge will be not to fragment the order. But we elders heard the mother goddess clearly in our visions, and we offer thanks to Isis." And then the elder mother walked between the two lines of priestesses nearest the altar and stopped in front of Soillse, handing her the scroll.

"No," Soillse whispered to the mother, pushing the scroll toward Ceit beside her. "This cannot be!" But the mother put the papyrus firmly back into Soillse's hand.

"Isis has asked for you, child. There was no mistaking it." And the matron placed a simple coronet of small gardenias on Soillse's head. As tears sprang into Soillse's eyes, she put her hands over her face.

"It's a great trust, mother, but I'm not prepared," Soillse whispered. She breathed out slowly, afraid to look at Ceit, then walked to kneel at the altar, bending to touch her head to the floor.

"Isis, mother, I thank you for your confidence in me. It's just so unexpected," Soillse whispered, and then paused for long moments. Suddenly, she felt a rush of power move through her feet and spin up her spine into her head, making her feel giddy, as if she might faint. "I'll serve you with my whole being." Soillse said softly, for the goddess's ears only. But her words could be heard throughout the temple, for the bronze panels reflected sound especially, and there was utter silence in the orders. As she stood and turned to face the priestesses, Soillse felt woozy and held her hand to her hair. The elder matron put her arm over Soillse's shoulders, smiling, and began the chant of thanksgiving. As they walked along the line of priestesses in the central aisle, up one side and down the other, Soillse looked deeply into the virgins' eyes. But when she stood before Ceit, there were too many tears to see.

"You always cherished her more, didn't you? And I've worked so hard for this!," Ceit whispered to the elder mother, her voice hoarse and crisp, her eyes blazing black fire. "The elder daughter rules the younger; it's always been so. And I, who've prepared for this for over a decade, am betrayed." And Ceit glared at the elder mother, rage quivering on her flushed face.

But the matron only drew herself up and looked Ceit squarely in the eyes. "It is not so, daughter, and your words create far-reaching disturbances in the ethers. The goddess has asked for her. It's as simple as that." And the elder mother, a head shorter than Ceit, reached her arms up. But Ceit moved backward as if she'd been struck, her eyes flashing.

"But it's always the elder who's chosen!"

"That's not so, either," said the mother calmly, letting her arms drop to her sides. "The goddess chooses by the gifts and talents of each initiate, according to what will be needed in the coming cycle. Apparently, a quiet inwardness is called for now, and your own strong determination is not what's required. It'll be easiest on everyone if you can accept the will of the goddess, Ceit, honoring and serving your sister, for she is now high priestess of the Temple of Isis."

"No, never! I renounce this false goddess you listen to, mother." And Ceit leveled slitted eyes on Soillse, rage pouring from them. Her voice had risen to a shriek, and the elder mother gasped as she reached out for Ceit. But Ceit backed sharply away, turned, and ran to the small brass door hidden in the altar panels, disappearing into the inner sanctuary.

Soillse was frightened when she woke, feeling some residue of the dream that she hadn't yet comprehended. But she did understand her own guardedness with Ceit now, her constant expectation of harm, and Ceit's ever present hatred. And her heart softened toward her sister, as she thought how unfair that choice in Egypt was. Glancing over at her sleeping sister's tousled hair and peaceful face, Soillse whispered, "Goddess, help us heal this an' move beyond it noo, please. An' thanks for the memory at last."

And then Soillse slipped on her summer shift and woolen shawl, crept out of the hut, and went to her Aine tree. The predawn was foggy and cool, and as she sat under the branches, she wished she'd brought a fur. In a whisper, she asked to see what it was she needed to bring into her heart. And a dark blue goddess formed in her mind as Soillse heard, *'Isis, Ice is.'* And Soillse could feel from this dark one a mandate to fragment all the ruling families of Egypt, the ice mother's task. She would tear apart the family fabric of their hearts, scatter them across the earth into diasporas, all the ancient families from the star tuaths of the sacred constellations in the night sky, disrupting communications with the star clans and the Creator Sun especially.

But Soillse could feel there'd been a purpose to this fragmentation, too, for these scattered tribesfolk would develop independence, inner strength, and powers of the mind that could never have matured if they'd stayed locked in the old tribal patterns of Africa. And Soillse felt many lives of family brokenness following that life in Egypt, the dark one goading and pushing herself and Ceit over centuries, becoming more and more entangled in discord and jealousy. In her mind's eye, Soillse saw Isis standing at the gateway to Africa, blocking her own memories of ancient tribal bonds of love there, and especially Soillse's connection to her family star tuath and city of light. But more than any other thing, Isis distorted memories of the true Goddess, the White Tara, Goddess of light. Instead, the dark one had seeded rivers of envy and hatred into all the tribes, to nourish and perpetuate the brokenness of the divine feminine in every land, the global sisterhood twisted by competition and cattiness. There was an acrid scent in the air around her. And slowly, tearfully, Soillse moved Isis into her heart over and over, until she felt the clear breath of morning on her face once more. And then she sighed in relief, bending her head and thanking the White Tara for this healing.

Then into Soillse's mind came the image of the new moon with Isis's face held within it. And Soillse saw dark shadows unleashed from Isis's hands, activating difficulties in her own life in order to help her remember the long ago past and free herself. Ah, so it's Isis who sends messengers of me fears, the new moon impulse, Soillse thought, the dark side of the Goddess. And she realized how the suffering from these living lessons had etched their wisdom teachings deeply into her heart, lessons of overwork and abuse, pain that Soillse would never forget.

"Isis, goddess o' wisdom," Soillse whispered," we call ye Isle noo." And then Soillse saw the full moon move across her mind's eye, instead, and misty nectar flow from it through the night sky. And in the ivory orb of light was the face of the White Tara, the tender One. Her eyes are always so sad and full of love, Soillse thought, and suddenly, Soillse felt an intensity of mother love she hadn't known since she was a babe at Eilid's breast. And Soillse saw moonbeam pulses of truth shining down from the full moon Mother, gently washing the new moon fears away. Ah, Ye're the bringer of freedom, Soillse thought with a slight smile. Yer two halves, Goddess, ken all me weaknesses and all me strengths. And Ye're sisters, too, working together to lead Yer bairns Home.

"Come to the birthing cave on the new and full moons now, will you? We'll teach you Ourselves. It's time, love," the Tara voice said.

"Aye," Soillse whispered, pulling her hands together. And feeling renewed as the mist brightened with dawn, she headed back to the cooking hut to begin the day's work.

The quarter moon dragged by slowly without Firinn. And with Coillore gone, too, there were no evenings at the druid circle to bring relief from the work of the yard. Seumus fumed about meddling druids that first morning and sent one of the ladds to the ridge each gloaming to look for the returning curragh. His patience lasted five nights, but after that he spent his evenings fretting and sputtering about the danger of the seas or another disastrous initiation. And Seumus prayed furiously every night in his furs that Firinn's Da would stay away from the fostering till the ladd got back.

"Every full moon, lass?" Eilid asked, staring. They were just finishing their evening stew, sitting around the hearth in the round house a few nights after Soillse's vision.

"Aye, Ma, twice a moon I'm to go, they said, at the new and full both." And there was utter silence in the round house, as Ceit glared.

"What's that for then? Ye tryin' to win Goddess favor? No one quests twice a moon!" And Ceit slammed her bowl down, spattering gravy over her shift and frowning at Eilid. But Soillse only sighed. I knew Ceit'd feel threatened by this, she thought, but what can I say? She'd never believe that dream of Egypt. And Soillse pushed her hands down the skirt of her stained workaday shift.

"I'm no so eager meself, Ceit," Soillse began, glancing at her sister and back to the table. "It's just more that has to be done, an' there's ever danger wi' a questin'. But I feel called. Would ye have me say no to the Goddess?" Soillse spoke softly with her eyes on her plate, for after her dream, she was reluctant to upset Ceit further. That conversation at the evening meal had been two nights ago, and Ceit hadn't spoken to Soillse since.

The wind woman tore through the hills all afternoon, scattering Aine's petals, as the gulls called over the bay. The

Cuchullin hills stood stark against the pale blue sky, swept stark and bare. And in the round house, Soillse put on her heavy winter shift against the cold breeze and wrapped her old woolen shawl over her shoulders. Freedom's in the air, Soillse thought, as she shouldered her furs just before the evening meal to walk the cliff path to the cave. Halfway there, she stopped to look back and felt a sudden premonition that she was leaving her old way of life somehow. From here, beyond the birches, the ladds in the yard looked small, like ants scurrying into line before the cauldron. So did Sine and Muirn, both tall and slender, one stirring and the other ladling out the soup. Then Soillse turned back and continued up the cliff path, the rocky ledges uneven and narrow, with the sea crashing below.

Waiting for a moment on the rock ledge at the cave mouth, Soillse felt a nameless sadness fill her chest. She heard a pewit calling from the rocks and stood, watching the waves and lowering clouds moving in from the west. Then she swept and smoked the cave with protective herbs, ate her bread and cheese, and placed the vessels of the elements and her Goddess figurine around the altar beside the hearth, which sat toward the back of the large room under a small opening to the sky. Lighting the fire and laying her spirit basket next to the rounded Skye marble altar stone, white with moss green veining, Soillse began to chant. Walking sunwise round the altar and stopping at the second place, the virgin, Soillse looked left toward the third place, one she'd not yet achieved, mother. I wonder when I'll have a babe, she thought, drawing in a long breath and putting her hands on her belly, smiling at the thought of Firinn's eyes in a lass. Then she raised her hands.

"Tara, the One Beloved Goddess, come and guide me in Yer purposes." Soillse began and hesitated, dropping her arms and pulling her shawl tight again. "This questing is irregular, an' I'm no sure what Ye're wishin' for." And then Soillse drank the herbed broth and sat down beside the hearth. The wind woman howled through the doorway and Soillse shivered, putting stones across the hem of the door skin, and drawing her furs up around her shoulders. Tension laced through her gut, and then she heard a swift brushing noise and whirled to see a black snake slither across the cave floor and wriggle out under the door skin. She shuddered and took an herb bundle out of her bag, lit it and smoked the dark hollows all along the back walls, chanting again for protection from harm. Finding her gaze drawn to the water bowl, Soillse sat before it, staring at the surface.

Immediately, she was back in the Temple of Isis, standing in the open doorway with the high terra cotta, painted colonnade before her. Looking out at the river, the headwaters of the Nile, Soillse smiled, thinking, this is my home. Forty-three sun cycles I've lived here, ever since my fourth summer. As the procession of priestesses in long white, nearly see-through gowns approached, Soillse held out the silver bowl in her hands, waiting in her shimmering moon robe and brow band with the mother-of-pearl orb to anoint them. The sun hung low and golden over the western fields across the Nile, a peaceful eve. But her heart was in turmoil. As the last of the virgins filed past, she leaned against the column and closed her eyes, listening to the soft singing. The high priest in Memphis had declared Akhenaton the one true Source ten years ago, and they were slowly closing down all the Goddess sanctuaries in Egypt. She'd pushed the priestesses to develop their inner vision and build their spirit powers quickly in order to oppose him and stop the desecration, rushing the virgins through their initiations, and two had died. She felt the spirits of these two around her often these days, and she sighed. But she was helpless to the changes in the land, as she felt the great Goddess of the cosmos slowly submerging into the earth, buried under priest domination. For years now, panic that the feminine Source would be completely lost to the people had taken hold of Soillse's heart. The rise of this new masculine, power-hungry, god was happening everywhere, all across Egypt and even in Babylon to the east. And she alone was not strong enough to stop it. Swaying gently to the music, she lifted her white silken robe with one hand, turned inside, walked slowly to the altar, and knelt before it. And the gentle tenderness of the Goddess enfolded her there.

'*I must be forgotten for a little while, child,*' Soillse heard the Goddess say. '*Try not to worry overmuch, dear, for you'll learn great wisdom, all of you. It's necessary. The cycle ahead will be painful. But trust, dear, and grow. And I'll return to you in 33 centuries. I promise it on My Heart!*'

And then, through the high temple doors, Soillse saw the gentle Tara light streaming from the full moon. And as she gazed up at it, she thought, Her light still bathes the land and nourishes the tribes, keeping family bonds strong and especially protecting mothers and babes. But turning back to the altar, Soillse saw in her mind the new moon move in front of the full, the dark one eclipsing the Mother-of-All's light, and in it was the face of Isis. And suddenly, the misty ivory ethers turned indigo and harsh around her, and Soillse frowned as she held her upturned hands toward the altar flame.

'*I will lead you through the dark cycle, the lost mother times,*' she heard Isis say. '*I will teach you to face great darkness with courage, to heal deep suffering, and to embrace all that comes in utter love. Everyone on earth must build their divine child within by pushing against obstacles, until all are strong enough to face and heal the ancient darkness and ascend into the light once more. There will be pain, daughter, but pain for all, shared alike, for suffering insures that the teachings are not forgotten, not for an eternity. No more hardship will be unleashed than is absolutely necessary to build the needed strength within. That is my pledge. Call on me when you're in need, will you? And do not fight the new order. It's meant to happen. The Goddess of Light will one day rise again.*'

Behind Soillse, some of the virgins were carrying snakes into the temple, broad baskets of them, the large black reptiles of the riverbanks, for these always carried messages from the Goddess up from the earth. But Soillse stood and watched with a tense brows, wanting to grab those baskets and run. Reptilians, she thought, black, for the dark one. By the order of the last priestess conclave in the north, the snakes would live inside the temples now. One of the priestesses coming in moved swiftly toward her, hooded irregularly in a dark robe and striding more swiftly toward the altar than the rest. This one turned abruptly toward Soillse as she came close and pulled a dagger from her robes. Alarmed, Soillse peered under the woman's hood. Ceit! Then Soillse felt searing pain as the small knife entered her heart below her ribs, swiftly and quietly done. Without a sound, Soillse slumped to the temple floor.

With a start, Soillse woke in the cave and sat up. The bowl of fats still burned with a low blue flame, and she glanced around the floor, remembering the snake and pulling in her feet. But there were no more reptiles in the shadows. She sighed and lay back on her furs, listening to the light rain that pattered on the rocks outside. As the comforting scent of wet earth filled her nostrils, she took a deep breath and reached to pick up the Goddess figurine.

"Goddess," she whispered, "the light One I lost so long ago. How do I remember Ye noo?"

'Move the dark one into your heart,' she heard, 'and all those false beliefs that I am gone of the long ago.' It was the gentle voice of Tara Soillse heard in her mind, and she nodded.

"Thank ye, Isle, mother o' darkness, for yer gifts o' strength an' courage. I guess women have their own trials, dinna they, different from the men an' their hunts. Ours are more connected wi' the container o' our families an' tribes." And Soillse wrapped up in her shawl and furs before the fire, imagined Isis moving into her heart to melt there in the diamond flame, feeling a lingering tenderness as she did so.

"I call forth the White Tara, ancient Goddess o' Light," Soillse whispered then, standing with her hands raised, palms upward. "I ask Ye to be restored within me again. Please, I miss Ye so much!!" And instantly, Soillse felt drawn to the doorway and moved to stand just outside the cave mouth, holding tightly to her shawl in the cool wind. Ragged clouds raced across the sky, but the rain had stopped momentarily. Watching, Soillse breathed in the moist clean air as the clouds parted slowly, and a full moon shone out over the sea.

"Oh!" Soillse gasped, feeling a tingling at the nape of her neck and in her feet. And she turned to see the moonlight full on the rocks bedside her. There was a sense of great power and some Otherworldly presence just beyond the veil. Touching the rock softly, Soillse began to cry. And then around her shoulders, she felt the arms of a Mother Who loved her more than life itself, a Goddess Who'd risk anything to reach Her child. And there before Soillse, for one brief instant, was Tara, the White Goddess, in a shimmering moonmist dress. And in Her Presence, Soillse felt a Heart that stretched out to every being in all worlds, angels and demons alike, holding each one in the tenderness of a Mother's forever love. And Soillse realized that Tara's Hands of Light were ever around her own heart, shielding it when necessary, mending the brokenness there, drawing out the day's darkness in sleep, and keeping everyone whole and sane through all the trials of their lives. As the Mother's soft adoration enveloped her, Soillse sat and leaned back against the rocks, her chest full of wonder. Then, after a while, Soillse felt another presence move in beside her, someone she'd been close to once a long time ago. But who?

"Grandma?," she whispered. But in her mind, she saw the image of a virgiin girl, lithe and fairy like in a rose pink robe, with long baby fine, light brown hair like her own. And then Soillse heard very clearly in her mind.

'I am Sebhia (sheveeya), yer sister o' light. I watch over ye an' send love every day, dear heart. Ye an' I live together in yer Creator Sun tuath, an' I'm yer sister forever, part o' yer clan o' light. It's different than yer tribe on earth, for that one doesna follow ye here. Earth family members are teachers really, no meant to last. Ceit, an' sometimes Eilid

or the others, bring forward yer wisdom lessons, an' they love ye well enough. But they're no yer true family. We are, I am, an' we love ye always, dear one o' our hearts. It'll take time an' courage, this climb ye've begun. But dinna be afraid. I'll help ye, love.'

"Will it take skyturns then?"

'Aye, it'll take ten or so, no nearly so long as yer eons o' descent, though.'

"An' will it take Fìrinn that long, too? Where is he noo? Is he all right?"

'Aye, I'll show ye,' she heard Sebhia say. So Soillse closed her eyes, and smiled when she saw the curragh in her mind. They were on the sea, heading for Skye, but she could feel that it would take all day before they'd arrive.

"Thank Goddess," Soillse said, taking a deep breath and steeping in Sebhia's tenderness around her for a time. Then she went into the cave, took off her shawl and banked the fire, wrapped into her furs, and slept well past dawn.

As she climbed back down to the tuath in the morning and resumed her work, Soillse could feel Fìrinn approaching throughout the day. She told Seumus her vision of the curragh, and so he kept sending ladds up the ridge to look for it over the sea. And finally toward dusk, one of them began shouting. Then suddenly, she, too, saw a speck on the sea loch and watched it come closer and closer, her heart racing as it moved toward the bay. And then the dogs set to barking.

"They're here, Da," Soillse hollered, "Fìrinn an' Coillore!" In her old workaday shift, she'd been cleaning bowls as quickly as she could out behind the cooking hut but kept running to peek round the hut as the boat drew near in the dusky gloaming. Now she dropped what she was doing and ran barefoot to the beach into the shallows, shouting and waving her hands. Fìrinn was grinning as he leaped from the boat, jumping through the waves to meet her in his tight doeskin breeks and hide shirt. Soillse held up her skirt with one hand and reached out to hug him with the other.

"I didna ken where ye went...I didna ken...if ye'd come back...I thought... ye were gone...Fìrinn!" Her green eyes settled on his, and she flung her arms about his neck as his lips touched hers as he lifted her into Oghama's embrace.

Chapter Thirty-One: Fìrinn

Seumus, moustache bristling, fumed and sent Coillore out of the yard, muttering about druids who snatched ladds away just when they needed their training most of all. But Coillore's face remained unperturbed. He simply took three of the eggs and handed the rest to Seumus, then walked slowly up among the new-leaved birch people in his white druid robe. Fìrinn could hear the druid whistling after he reached the burn.

That first day after he got home, Fìrinn was kept at swordplay and spear throwing relentlessly, loosing the shafts under Seumus's glaring eye. Standing in a light spring rain in the yard till past the evening meal with an oiled skin over his head, Seumus watched the ladd, grunting if Fìrinn slipped or dallied. Fìrinn hoped only to please his foster father, mostly wondering when Seumus'd calm down enough to set a date for the trothing ceremony with Soillse. Then finally, as the rest of the boys finished the evening meal, Seumus nodded to Fìrinn, satisfied that nothing had been lost.

Fìrinn's ritual hunt of manhood was set for late in the Oak moon (early June). So he had a mere ten days till the end of his fostering, and he spent them thinking mostly of Soillse. By each evening's gloaming, Fìrinn was exhausted. But he and Soillse sat or walked the shore, at least, talking of their visions and dreams. Soillse wanted to connect with the Goddess of light and bring Her into the life of the tuath in some way. And she wanted to learn to heal and become an herb woman and midwife like her Grandma. Fìrinn hoped to become a white robe, the highest order of druid, those who knew the laws and meted out justice for the clans. And a quarter moon after his return, Fìrinn at last asked Seumus about the betrothal ceremony. But the chief wished to postpone even the trothing till after the kingship trials, and the hand-fasting was set for the Apple moon. "When the kingship's been decided," Seumus said with a stern glare, pointing at Fìrinn, "<u>then</u> ye can focus on other things, ladd."

The morning of Fìrinn's manhood hunt dawned sunny, wisps of mist wafting through the valleys. And since he'd have no sleep that night, Fìrinn was given the day to rest. But instead, he helped Soillse carry stones to lay around the field of barley on the hill. Once the low foundation was completed there, they'd add a palisade to protect the new crops from deer and cattle. As the afternoon progressed, Seumus insisted that Fìrinn go lie down in the long house, and reluctantly Fìrinn agreed, sleeping lightly till nearly moonrise.

All three ladds who'd reached their sixteenth winter, and Fìrinn's seventeenth, because he'd come to the fostering a year later than most, waited bare-chested in their clan plaids at the standing stone on the ridge above the tuath, the wind cool off the sea, the dusky skies of the gloaming softened by thin clouds. Coillore in his white robe handed Fìrinn the herbed broth, and it keened the ladd's focus quickly. The fostering below faded into the shadows, and Fìrinn felt the eye of the Goddess upon him. The moon was just rising behind them over the inland hills, the time most of the ladds headed for their pallets, but Fìrinn shook off his need for sleep. Soft tendrils of mist rose off the moors, as the druid painted symbols of power on the boys' naked chests, chanting softly as he worked. A deerskin cloak, totem of his clan, was placed over Fìrinn's shoulders, the other boys wearing the skins of wolf and bear. And then Coillore turned each ladd toward a different direction and blew on the curved brass horn, signaling that the hunt had begun.

Bana Dhia set off quickly, and Fìrinn turned after her, south along the cliff path up the ridge. But the ladd felt sulky as he pushed through the bracken and scrub birches, and wondered how to overcome his mother's geis, not to kill except to save his own life. What kind of hunt was that?

In his mind, Fìrinn saw a crag, secluded and steep, some distance south along the shore. He seemed to be looking down on the land through the eye of a great bird high on the headlands, and he whistled for Bana Dhia, who'd bounded off into the bracken. It took time for Fìrinn to reach the place and even longer to shinny his way up the rock face. As he did so, frustration rose inside him. The horn would call them back at dawn, and he should be concentrating on finding prey, instead of wasting all this time. He sighed as he rested on a small outcropping of rock half way up. It all feels futile, anyway, he thought. With Ma's geis, how can I ever compete? Still, I have to be initiated into manhood, if I'm ever to win Soillse. Coming out above the underbrush onto sheer rock, Fìrinn heard surf crashing on the rocks below. Thank Goddess the nights were never full dark in the summer time. Still, he had to move more slowly now, nearly straight up, with just finger and toeholds to guide him.

But finally, he reached the peak, a stony outcropping no larger than his pallet, beside a wind-stunted pine. Behind him a sudden screeching and the sound of hard beating wings pierced the silence. Fìrinn whirled sharply as talons brushed his head. No bird'd prey on me, he thought, unless I'm close to eggs or young. And he stepped back away from the sheer drop, searching the dusky darkness above. The bird dove at him again, it's great yellow eyes glowing. Shrieking, it dug its talons into Fìrinn's skull, and he felt a sharp stinging pain rip through his scalp. Bana Dhia barked incessantly below, and Fìrinn called to her to hush. He couldn't think with the pain and the noise pounding in his ears. Two birds hovered above now, great horned owls, and Fìrinn threw his smaller lance at one and missed. This is close enough to defending me life, he thought. Is this what me hunting'll always be like from now on, violence and danger? Sure and I willna spend much of me life doing that!

The smaller bird rested on a nearby branch, waiting and watching, her eyes glowing with fierce determination. It's forbidden to take both parents when there are nestlings, Fìrinn thought, and then a soft otherworldly voice whispered in his mind. *'The Goddess helps you, manchild. The larger bird is yours. Leave the mother to her young.'* So as the male dove at him again, Fìrinn stood firm, waiting till the bird was close and loosing a second shaft. It took the bird in the breast and sent it crashing down the cliff into the underbrush, while Fìrinn slithered down the rock face out of the mother's reach.

Jumping down to the path, Fìrinn waited until Bana Dhia dropped the bird at his feet. The great owl, he thought, seer of the night, and shivered. Unusual prey. No one'll eat it; no one'd dare. It's sacred to Artio, the dark goddess o' the Indigo Pentagram. Still, the animals a warrior takes on his hunt of manhood become his spirit guides and foretell the skills he'll bring to his adult life. Owls bear the mark of inner sight, deep connection to the spirit world, and great change, too, not only to meself, but the whole clan. As Fìrinn held the bird up, he chanted the song of gratitude and return of the bird's spirit to the Otherworld, and the notes floated out over the sea into the midnight dusk.

And then toward dawn, on his long tramp back through the fringe of birch wood along the shore, Fìrinn saw a pair of foxes in the brush. But they didn't disturb him, and he feared to break his geis. I guess I have to wait for prey to attack me, he thought, shaking his head, and muttering at this danger imposed on him by his Ma. Walking slowly with the owl slung over his back, fingering the curled skin of the birches, Fìrinn wondered what more he could do. Would one bird be considered a success?

As he came onto the path above the tuath, he sat for a moment, feeling the soft warmth of summer impregnating the earth. He was tired, still sweating from his climb. The edge of sky outlining the eastern hills was beginning to lighten, so time was running out.

And he sighed, imagining Soillse in her bed furs, just as Bana Dhia turned suddenly and began to growl at a nearby thicket. A low grunting could be heard in the bracken there, and a voice in Fìrinn's mind said, *'watch out.'* Fìrinn leaped away from a crashing in the trees to see a boar in full charge, coming straight at him, only two pony lengths away. He barely had time to lift his lance before the boar gored the side of his bare leg and swung off into the underbrush. Searing pain shot through Fìrinn's calf. How dare ye?," he growled. Then steeling himself against the pain, he ran after the beast. Rage flooded Fìrinn's chest as he found the boar waiting behind an alder, watching with small glinty eyes. Fìrinn stepped behind a larger trunk for protection, breathless as the inner voice said, *'Quickly, take him before the chance is lost.'* So Fìrinn threw his lance in fury, and then another, startled at how the battle rage so suddenly overwhelmed him.

But the animal only moved away, looking back toward a tumble of rocks in the forest. He's protecting a burrow, no doubt, Fìrinn thought with clenched teeth, aiming more carefully and throwing again. And the beast made no sound as the lance took him in the chest, the boar falling to the mossy floor with a soft thud. Then Fìrinn's rage changed swiftly to sorrow. I make a sad hunter, he thought, crouched over the lifeless form, as he wrapped the gash on his leg with a strip of hide. If they didna hurt me, I'd rather let them live.

Coillore stared at the owl as Fìrinn dragged the boar into the yard and dropped the bird off his shoulder onto the dirt. For once, the old druid's imperturbable calm was shaken. He peered at Fìrinn's forehead for a moment, as if drawing the memory of the struggle from his mind. But the boar was no surprise, for these were frequently brought in from the hills. Its significance was more symbolic, for its spirit bore the stamp of wealth and fierce determination, the animal of the father god of abundance, Llew. Coillore smiled then and laid a congratulatory hand on Fìrinn's shoulder. The two other ladds had done well, too, one taking a stag, animal of the Dagda, signifying truth, knowledge, and stewardship of the land, and the second bringing in a hawk, which spoke of the skills of reaching one's goal after many obstacles, and a doe, animal of the virgin goddess, Sìth, signifying a peace maker in the tribes.

Seumus was pleased, too, no failures. He came out of the round house in his hide breeks and shirt as the skies lightened, ready for the day's games and rubbing his eyes. Then the chief whacked them all on the back with his great muscled palms, grinning. There'd be game aplenty for the tuath, too. Seumus startled back, though, as he peered at the owl and then at Fìrinn. Sometimes these birds portended the greatest change of all, death, and Seumus had always felt averse to them. It canna be eaten, the chief thought, except by the ladd himself, a strange powerful omen. It befits the boy, though. And then Coillore supervised the preparations for the feast, chanting over the animals and sending the hunters off for rest and their ritual baths.

Fìrinn slept soundly through the day under his furs in the long house, but his limbs ached as Duineil shook him gently awake at sunset. The gash in Fìrinn's leg throbbed painfully, though Coillore had quietly poulticed it with healing herbs as Fìrinn slept. But still, the muscles had stiffened. As the shadows lengthened, Fìrinn bathed in the large wooden tub behind the latrine. Then he dressed in his clan plaid, wrapping the long end over his right shoulder and pinning it with his mother's brooch, but wore no shirt. He strapped on the sword his father had given him, too. Then, thinking of Soillse, he combed his hair with pine-scented water that was waiting in buckets for the evening ritual.

The points of blue woad stung like bee bites under Fìrinn's skin as Coillore needled the tattoo of initiation into him. They stood beneath the standing stone on the hill above the tuath, and the druid hummed, smiling softly as he worked. The ladd had grown as tall as his Da now, wavy russet hair halfway down his back and a dark red moustache, and he had the same deep set eyes and thin nose as Speireag, too. The small druid, in his white robe and goat skin cloak, wove the owl, the boar, and the deer for Firinn's tuath, interlaced into a swirling pattern on the ladd's chest. Wind whistled through the birch boughs, and the leaden sky threatened rain. And the smell of burning fat from the yard below made Firinn's empty stomach cramp.

And then at nightfall, when the bodhran began to beat, all the foster brothers and clan folk gathered in the yard in the gloaming, the women in their embroidered hide robes and clan sashes, the men in their clan plaids and white homespun shirts. Thankfully, the rain held off, and the sky began to clear from the brisk cool wind off the sea. To the slow beat of the drum, the three initiates, now men, were led forward in front of the crowd, each wearing their tattoos of victory. And when the drum stopped, the hunters broke off the first portion of meat from their beasts and laid these on their foster father's plate. Then each was given the winner's portion and ate the first bites as the others looked on, cheering. This meal would bond the spirit of the animals to each new man, sealing their lifelong partnership and shared destinies. Of the owl, Coillore gave Firinn only one cooked piece of flesh to eat, laying four talons and eight wing feathers beside his plate.

And then all joined in the feasting. Sine, looking especially dignified in her ceremonial robe as the eldest of the clan, had loaded the board with steaming bowls of herbed barley and buttered fern heads. And there were nuts, berries, and bread, too. Firinn was glad that the three reaching manhood were allowed to eat their fill this night, a rare occurrence at the fostering. He stuffed himself, glancing often at Soillse, sitting in her hide robe at her father's table with her family. Her hair glowed gold in the firelight, and he watched her lithe form, budding, but not yet full, as she walked to the board for more meat for her father's table. It made Firinn's chest and groin ache! One more hunt, he thought, and then I'm yers for the rest of me life, love.

Afterwards, the three initiates stood in the yard and took their vow to protect the clans and the Isle of Skye even unto death, as tears ran down Fìrinn's face. And then with glistening eyes, the whole clan locked arms around them, swaying together and singing the song of the tuath, as all the ladds joined in.

It was a night of dance, drinking, song, and laughter. As the music quickened, Fìrinn took Soillse's hand and they moved, faster and faster, to the rhythm of the pipes. He threw himself into a fling, jumping to the music till his gash began to bleed, and then singing till his sides ached. As the celebration broke up and the sky finally cleared into a dusky purple glow, Fìrinn walked Soillse to the round house, hand in hand. After he left her, he stood there a moment, looking over the faces of his foster brothers and family. Me formal training is over now, he thought. If the kingship trials weren't half a moon off, I'd be assigned work by Seumus in the morning. Both the other ladds who reached manhood with me will leave for their own clans within a day. And as Fìrinn settled into his bed furs in the long house, Coillore quietly took the owl to the hills and returned it to the Goddess, bowing to Her slivered crescent as it sailed behind the wispy clouds.

Fìrinn's gash ached worse the next morning, and both Seumus and Coillore fussed over him. It would have to heal before the kingship trials or he'd be instantly disqualified, Seumus fumed. So Coillore poulticed the gash repeatedly, several times a day, holding his hands over it and sending in the diamond light. Fìrinn was kept sequestered, even from Soillse, in the long house for three days as the wound mended, Seumus especially insisting he stay off the leg entirely. But after that, the ladd had a whole quarter moon with few obligations, for Seumus refused to let him help with the games until the gash was invisible.

But Fìrinn still rose with the other ladds and, instead of being served by the women now, he dressed in his leather breeks and shirt as usual and helped Soillse or Sìne move the heavy cauldron over the fire. One day, he went egg and wood gathering with Soillse, and on another, joined her washing clothes in the burn. Seumus grew thoroughly disgusted with the ladd, but had no authority over him now he'd reached manhood. So finally in frustration, Seumus demanded that Soillse be given the lightest tasks until after the kingship trials. As he helped her, Fìrinn wondered at the long hours Soillse worked, the physical demands on her no less than his own training. And then, after the day's labor, he and Soillse shared the evening meal on the rocks above the slender beach, his arm about her, watching the gulls swoop in the gloaming's bright glow and the sandpipers run on their delicate legs across the wet sands.

Twice that quarter moon, Fìrinn took Soillse's hand and led her to the lean-to, the last time just two days before they were to leave for the king's pavilion in Port Righ. On that day, before the work of packing up began in earnest, Soillse left the cooking house for a time just past the mid-day meal. As she and Fìrinn climbed into the lean-to, he taking off his breeks and shirt and her shift, they lay down naked on the hides under the mossy roof. Fìrinn handed Soillse a shell ring, pale pink, carved with wild roses and interlaced in the Celtic style. Then he kissed her, long and deep. And they made slow love, as the sea lapped the shore and the winds caressed the hillside all afternoon.

Then, just three days before Midsummer, they set off over the inland track, headed north for Port Righ, the port of the king. Seumus, Eilid, Soillse, Fìrinn, four other ladds who'd compete in the trials, and Coillore took both the horses and most of the ponies and headed over the ridge. The rest of the ladds stayed at the tuath with Duineil and the other teachers, sending the contenders off with a shout of victory, all except Ceit, who had declined to go and glowered from the door skin of the round house as they disappeared into the wood.

It was windy on the heights as they crossed the rocky spine of the southern peninsula, the sky heavy, but no rain fell. They came to the big tuath at the broad northern bay and turned northwest, following the track above the northern shore. And they camped in a high meadow near the Cuchullin peaks that first night, Soillse and Eilid scurrying to cook the evening meal. After helping Soillse with the fire, Fìrinn picked wildflowers and laid them on her furs. Then he chased Bana Dhia in the meadow. And after the meal, Seumus brought out his pipes, and they sang the songs of all their tuaths, ending with the ballad of Scatha and the founding of the warrior school.

All the next day, Soillse, in a new shift the color of shells, riding next to Fìrinn, made up wee songs about how happy she was, humming and even dancing in the road when they stopped to water the beasts. They headed inland now, through the valley between the jagged Cuchullin mountains and then across the wide hummocky plateau of the central isle, north to Port Righ. Fìrinn smiled and squeezed Soillse's hand from time to time, but his calf ached from the tusk wound, itching under his hide breeks, and he grew increasingly anxious about the hunt to come. He had an intuition of disaster, his gut quivering when he thought of it. But Fìrinn kept these thoughts to himself, wanting only to get the trial over with. After this hunt, I can finally choose the life I long for, he thought, helping Soillse with her work and building our house at the edge of the wood, so I can hold her every night of me life. And I'll go back to the druid isle as soon as I can manage it, too.

As they approached the king's pavilion the next day, riding gradually down out of the alpine plateau toward the bay on the north coast of the isle, they passed booths set up with wares for trade all along the road; squealing goats, herbs, pottery, woven goods, and sweet smelling broths and cakes. A festival atmosphere prevailed in the warm sunlit afternoon as lassies danced before a young piper off to one side of the road. After they arrived and set up two tents in the wood above the king's grand hall, and the cauldron was heated over the fire. Fìrinn and Soillse walked through the crowds, he in his hide breeks and shirt and she in her new shift. They kept a distance from his Da's compound, looking at the varied clansfolk gathered near their tribal hearths, instead. Hide tents of competitors and their families completely surrounded the pavilion, fire circles crowding the forest glades and steep hills above the bay throughout all the nearby glens, except those reserved for the hunt. There was piping and dancing well into the gloaming that night, too, as a nearly full moon rose over the sea to the east. And after the evening meal, Fìrinn and Soillse stood to go join them, but Coillore, with a shake of his head, rested a hand on Fìrinn's chest.

"Rest, ladd, ye'll need all yer strength this time tomorrow. An' then at last, yer fate'll be decided." Coillore didn't mention that he saw worse hardship ahead.

So Fìrinn and Soillse stayed by the hearth, saying little, with Soillse's resting her head on his shoulder. But this night, Fìrinn resented the interference of the druid and frowned into the fire. Soillse, too, watched Coillore from the corner of her eye, fervently wishing the hunt was over and Fìrinn was done with his obligations, so they could finally do as they liked. That night, Coillore poulticed Fìrinn's leg again and sent him off early to his furs, even before the gloaming deepened into night's summer half-light.

The day of the hunt dawned sunny and hot, with no breath of a breeze. And they were awakened early; Seumus, Coillore, Fìrinn and the other ladds, bare-chested in their clan plaids, walking to the nemeton for the blessing of competitors. More beasts attacking me, Fìrinn thought darkly as they walked. I'll just be glad to get through this alive, and when I lose, no have Da humiliate me in front of all the folk. He sighed as Coillore led them up the forest path.

On the grassy heights above the bay stood the king's pavilion, a large round house with a wooden palisade and earthworks surrounding it, its entrance posts carved and painted with colorful interlaced designs. And the royal banners of three boars fluttered from low posts all around the perimeter near the gates, where the feasting would be held. And as they passed it, Firinn wondered who'd be keeper of this hall in one night's time.

Then they entered the nemeton, hidden in the forest on the highest peak above the pavilion, and sunlight filtered golden through the trees. And walking sunwise inside the circle of twelve sacred oaks, druids spiraled, chanting the call to the Sun Lord. Instantly, Firinn felt the light of Oghama sifting down on them, clearing his doubts away. And he hoped fiercely for some honored destiny, even if he wasna to be king. Then they waited as the druids chanted the blessing of Oghama over each competitor, forty-eight in all, the line of men circling slowly in front of the low flat altar stone, green-veined white marble from their own isle.

After the ceremony, the contenders were led through the hunting grounds, steep glens to the south and west above and below the pavilion, and shown the boundaries they weren't allowed to breach. Firinn was placed in solitude within a sheltered grove of pines that separated him from other competitors, while Coillore tended him there under the mantle of silence. The hunt, lasting through the night, would begin at moonrise. And the next morning, the druids would decide who'd rule Skye. As he listened to the muffled sounds of livestock struggling up the path behind the pavilion, tension gripped Firinn's belly more and more. Toward evening, he smelled roasting mutton and boar, and as his mouth watered, he wished he could share the hearth with everyone else.

At dusk, herbed broth was passed out to all competitors, but the light trance didn't bring to Firinn's mind the face of the god or goddess who'd be his patron in this event, as it should have. He sat glumly looking out into the forest, asking the Goddess only for survival this night. Children's shouting and barking dogs could be heard as the gloaming deepened. Though the gash had mostly healed now, Firinn's leg still ached, and he rubbed it idly as he waited. Killing only when I'm attacked is more dangerous than anything the others have to contend with, he thought, sighing again and wishing his Ma hadn't laid her foolish geis upon him. I've had initiations up to me teeth, he thought, his heart beating faster with the sense of impending danger. It all feels impossible, and I dinna even want to be king!

'Nah, nah,' Coillore's voice whispered in Firinn's mind, as the old druid frowned. And Firinn eyed the druid in his formal white robe through lowered eyes. What if it's all for nothing, the ladd's dark thoughts hurried on: the hopes and love of Ma, Da's constant pushing, the years of training, both druid and warrior, me completed initiations and ritual of manhood? How far I've come in seventeen winters, he thought. How far do I still have to go? Perhaps I was meant only to be a simple lancer at another chief's command.

And then, as the moon haze brightened below the eastern hills, Coillore began to paint the sacred symbols on Firinn's chest and arms. Chanting, the druid made the royal markings in red ochre this time: the ring and cup of the Creator Sun, shining down from the Diamond Core, on Firinn's forehead; sun whorls and star spirals on his arms, the circles of Abred, Annwyn, Gwynfyd, Ceugant, Leanabh Aigneal, and the Diamant Meadhan and Cridhe over and around the tattoo on his chest. The fats felt good on the reddened places where Firinn's tattoo pricks still showed.

As the druid worked in silence, with his eyes all but closed, the sudden awareness of the old man's constant service these past few winters washed through Firinn's chest. And in that moment, love for the old man flooded him, and tears filled Firinn's eyes. Even now, the druid's ministrations felt like his mother's long ago. Firinn wanted to speak of this tenderness, but he did not, fearing to break the steady silence of the druid's concentration. And then, as Coillore stood to lead him to the nemeton, Firinn's head began to throb. What kind of strange prey will I find this time?, he thought in panic. And he clenched his jaw as he followed Coillore, who held tight to Bana Dhia's lead.

Hounds bayed intermittently as they walked up the path, and Firinn could hear clansmen shushing their dogs at the top of the ravine. And then, just as the moon peeked over the eastern hills across the bay, they came up through the avenue into the sacred grove, all contenders colorful in their clan plaids. Firinn was given another bowl of spiced broth, and the fats settled his stomach, while the herbs brought his mind to full alertness. Suddenly, he heard crickets playing their fiddles beneath the leaves on the forest floor, and then the bodhran began to beat.

The druids in the grove intoned a low invocation, calling on the Sun Lord to lead the hunters in this race, especially the one who would become king. As the forty-eight contenders formed one circle, the pipes joined in. The men were led around a central bonfire, the oaks regal around them, and then the instruments abruptly stopped. In the flickering firelight, painted symbols dancing on their bare chests, the men linked hands and pledged to do their best, for both Skye and the Sun Lord. We look like one great interlaced beast, Firinn thought, feeling the night pregnant around them.

Then rotating sunwise under the oaks, each man was given the allotment of nine lances, passed out three at a time as they spiraled the inner circle of druids, who chanted softly in the tongue of the ancients. While the druids continued to sing, each man's games-master came to stand behind him, only in Firinn's case, it was Coillore, not Seumus. The teachers held each man's hound by hide tethers, dogs trained meticulously to the hunt. Not Bana Dhia though, Firinn thought, as she sat behind his right heel, bounding to her feet as the druids moved forward and Coillore tied the deer hide cloak over Firinn's shoulders. But this hunt was man and beast alone, the hounds used only for retrieval of prey, for the druids would note any teeth or claw marks on the game.

How solemn it all seems, Fìrinn thought. And then he noticed Duirc across the circle of contenders, the falcon gleam strong in his foster brother's eyes, shining red in the flickering firelight. Fìrinn nodded to him and got only a raised lip in reply. Then suddenly, Fìrinn wondered if man would hunt man this night and felt his belly steel itself to the possibility, as he gripped his spears more tightly. Abruptly then, as the competitors began to spiral out of the nemeton in silence, Fìrinn's Da burst out of the woods. And before any of the druids could stop him, Speireag ran straight to Fìrinn and laid a heavy hand on his son's shoulder.

"Ye must...," Speireag began as two of the druids, frowning, pulled the chief forcibly away.

Coillore signed the symbol of protection over Fìrinn's head, twice repeating the chant to ward off evil. And the old druid sighed before beginning the last chant, the one that sent the arrow of Fìrinn's mind into the current of the sacred flow. As the battle horns blared along the processional avenue, the moon lifted delicately off the eastern hills and every man was led to a separate path, all facing away from the nemeton like the rays of the Sun Lord Himself. At the blaring of the horns, they all began running off in the direction allotted them.

Fìrinn's mind recoiled at the noise, and he knelt a moment to steady himself. And then with his inner vision, he saw a boar dart through the underbrush beside the stream below. With fast snorts, it pulled in the cold night air, pawing the ground and crouching, ready to charge a hare. As the moon climbed gently, the clouds thinned before it, and Fìrinn headed in the direction of the burn.

It was nearing moonset, and the pipes ending the hunt would sound very soon now, the sky lightening to the east. Fìrinn was glad, for his head ached, and his lungs were raw from running. A fine sweat covered his chest and forehead, blurring the painted markings, and his arms and legs stung from long scratches he'd sustained in the underbrush. The gore wound in his leg ached, too, but he felt lucky not to have any real injuries that would disqualify him. He stood, tense and listening, wishing he could sit and rest a moment, but time was short. Just now, he wanted a stack of oatcakes more than anything else in this world. But come tonight, he had three days of feasting to look forward to. And drinking quickly from his water skin, he traced the outline of the star hunter in the sky, sending silent thanks for his success.

It had been a good hunt, one boar, lanced after he unintentionally cornered it into an attack, and a fox that he surprised in a burrow along the rocks. The boar had fought persistently, snarling as Fìrinn stood near the entrance to its lair. Still, the other hunters would have taken birds and smaller prey, and much more game perhaps, as Fìrinn could not. But the druids would take his mother's geis into consideration, too. His legs quivered with fatigue as he neared the pavilion, and Bana Dhia trailed him through the underbrush, tongue hanging, for the night had stayed clear and warm. Fìrinn slowed and poured the last drops from his water skin onto her tongue. Then suddenly, her ears pricked, and they both looked downwind, peering at a movement beyond a tangle of vines in a small clearing four pony lengths away. As Fìrinn crouched and lifted his spear, a red doe stepped hesitantly out of the thicket.

She watched them, waiting. The small doe, Fìrinn thought, sacred to the virgin goddess of peace, Sìth, an' me own tuath. I canna kill it. What does it mean? And then a sudden slowness came over him, as if he were in a dream, and he watched the doe's neck twitch and the fine hairs on her face quiver. She stood poised to jump, with her ears twisting back and forth, listening. He put down his lance, sending the message of safety to the beast, and wondered what to do. And then the doe turned her face toward him, her eyes like dark moons in a pale sky, and low green lights flickered there.

I've seen a face like that somewhere, he thought, as his mind raced. Then he gasped, "Ma," and stumbled backward, dropping his quiver. Suddenly, Firinn felt the doe's thoughts. She'd leap at an angle under that low hanging alder and run across the river to the safety of the glen beyond the hunting boundary, off into the eastern wood. Holding her head high a moment, the doe's eyes gentled before she turned and darted away. And then behind Firinn, there was a crashing in the underbrush.

"Did ye see her?" Duirc ran through the bracken on a barely visible track through the pines and beeches, holding up a light spear, his plaid limp with sweat and his bare chest scratched from the underbrush. "The red doe? She's mine! I followed her down from the nemeton," he said with narrowed eyes, peering through the underbrush. But Firinn only stood in a daze, looking toward the alder. "Have the druid chants finally addled ye? Or is it the bonfire tonight yer mind's off about?" Duirc taunted him. "This is no time to be thinkin' o' maidens." But Firinn only turned slowly toward his foster brother.

"The doe's past the river noo, cousin, boundary o' the huntin' grounds. Besides, she's enchanted. Ye'll no go after her." Firinn spoke in a low whisper that Duirc completely ignored, as he took a step toward the alder. And as Duirc leaned forward to run, he threw his head back toward Firinn and snarled in disgust.

"Have ye turned lass of a sudden? I knew it'd happen sometime. Dinna go after the red deer sacred to the virgin goddess? I'll head her off. Whoever gets her'll be king!" And Duirc laughed, turning to race down toward the river. But he stopped suddenly when he heard the low growl behind him. At first, he thought it was Bana Dhia, for the noise was not a human sound. But instead, Firinn crouched there, both he and Bana Dhia tensed to spring.

"Cross that river," said Firinn hoarsely, "an' I will stop ye. It's the boundary line an' full o' folk beyond. But more than that, the

Goddess lives in that doe!" There was the slightest hint of satisfaction in Fìrinn's tone.

"Ye canna be serious! What the.....? Have the banshees got ye? It's a <u>hunt</u>, no faery land! Shake it loose, man! Ye'll <u>never</u> be king noo. No after this! I'll bet the crown is mine even without the doe." And a slow, not unkind, smile crept across Duirc's face, as he realized Fìrinn was far too soft-hearted to ever hold the high seat, anyway.

"Curse being king!," Fìrinn spat out and snapped his last lance across his thigh.

Chapter Thirty-Two: Soillse

For that quarter moon, it was as if the Aine tree in her faery gown had come to life and was creating everything that happened according to all Soillse had whispered into her branches for skyturns. Firinn's manhood trial was over, and his gashed leg was mending well. Soillse had helped heal it herself, pouring the diamond light into the wound with her hands the way Coillore had shown her. And she gathered herbs along the ridge for the druid to poultice it with, too.

Even before the morning meal, Firinn was by her side in his hide breeks and shirt, lifting the cauldron and stoking the fires, just like any woman of the clan. He didn't care that some of the ladds laughed or that Seumus frowned at him from the yard. And every hour or so, Soillse pulled Firinn behind the cooking hut to steal kisses, and each one honeyed the days even more. Coillore didn't approve of Firinn working so hard with the women, either, sending the thought to both of them to let him rest. But Firinn simply refused, wanting to be by her side. He helped until late in the day, when she took his hand and led him to the shore to sit on the rocks, explaining that she could feel his gash in her own leg, and hers was starting to ache, too.

As they worked, they spoke little, but Soillse felt the light of Oghama around her more and more through the whole quarter moon. The softness of the morning mist brushing her skin, the Cuchullin peaks shining copper in the firstsky sun, or the gilded beauty of the sparkling sea as the Sun Lord hovered over it in the late gloaming, and Firinn by her side, all felt like Oghama holding out His diamond jewels just for her. Everything was more alive and more vivid through the nectar of His love, sent through Fìrinn's eyes and touch most intensely of all. And Soillse wondered at the power of this love, for the heavy weight of work she'd known all her life lightened into laughter, as if by magic, whenever Fìrinn was nearby. The wee lass within her, especially, opened in wonder and innocence again. How delicious everything was!

And as if that weren't enough, for once, Ceit left her alone as well. Soillse chose her own tasks for a change, exactly as she felt them, deciding on her work and pace throughout the day. She took turns with the other women, cleaning the latrines and grinding meal, gutting fish and tanning the hides, doing no more than her own share of those distasteful chores, for she preferred gathering and tending the fields. Soillse worked as hard as ever, though, singing as she did so. When she stopped one morning, Fìrinn asked softly if she couldna find more songs to sing.

"'Tis the most soothin' sound I ever heard," he said. And after a few days, he began to sing, too.

At the evening meal, Soillse and Fìrinn sat apart, by the shore or up under the birch trees beside the burn. One evening, leaning back against Fìrinn's chest, Soillse thought maybe, just maybe, the pictures on her ceremonial robe were wrong. What could possibly happen to disturb them now? He had no wish to go and live on Iona for skyturns, as she'd feared when Coillore took him there. No, Fìrinn wanted to stay with her and live a simple life at the tuath. And he didna mind if Ceit held the land right, either, he said. He'd happily be a simple clansmen for the rest of his days, if only he could be with her. Perhaps the Goddess'll leave us this way, Soillse thought. And she hoped so, hoped it with her whole heart.

Just before the kingship trial, as she and Fìrinn gathered muscles to the north of the bay one cool misty afternoon, Fìrinn took her leather fish basket and set it down in a wee pool high on the rocks. Then he led her up the cliff path and south through the birch wood to their lean-to under the pine on the ridge. In it, he'd scattered white rose petals from the wild shrubs on the hill. He said not one word as he unlaced her old workaday shift and drew it off, along with his buckskin breeks. And then he laid her down and kissed her, softly, so softly, his lips like petals, too. Then he asked her if she would do him the holy honor of becoming his hand-fast bride in the Apple moon, a quarter moon after Lughnasa. And she nodded and kissed him back, all the while smelling the tang of roses. When he ran his tongue up her spine, she shivered all over, thinking her heart would burst for happiness. And when she moved to give a turn to him, he put his hand on her shoulder.

"Nay, lass o' me heart. Ye work all the long days, an' no one pays any mind. This time, I want to care for ye fer a change." And then he massaged her calves, arms, and shoulders, kneading the aches from them all. He nibbled her nose then and her breasts, and ran his tongue along her inner thighs and the folds of her woman's place. Slow and slow, he brought her flame to fire, and she felt the Beloved light all around him, filling her heart to overflowing and pouring tenderness into every cell of her skin. As the inner fires overcame her, she turned and sat astride him, yearning to take in his seed and create the child of his desires. And then she felt the White Tara pulsing through her loins, stroking Firinn's manhood deeply and flooding them both with Her ecstasy, until Soillse shivered her release and Firinn loosed his seed. As she lay still on his chest, catching her breath, Soillse watched in her mind the tiny sparks of light he'd spilled into her, burrowing into the softness of her womb. Oh, Goddess, she prayed, make this enchanted moment into a babe with Firinn's eyes. Please!

Then two days later, they left for the kingship trials, riding up the ridge at firstsky, the ponies laden with packs of furs, meal, salt meat, and tents. Under her faded green woolen shawl, she wore a new summer shift she'd dyed the color of her skin. And they rode swiftly that cool, cloudy day, all along the ridge to the broad low bay at the northern end of the peninsula, and then slept in a meadow beneath the Cuchullin peaks. That evening, they watched the moon rise through skimming clouds over a pale blue sea against pale blue highlands, impossible to tell where the mainland across the waters left off and the sea began. Watching it all turn pink in the gloaming, Soillse felt like she'd landed in some enchanted place on top of the world.

The next day, they crossed the valley between the mountains, the place of the shells, bare jagged peaks surrounding them and a wide river meandering through. But under the lowering clouds, the heights felt treacherous to Soillse, the valley all in shadow as they rode. And as she lay waiting for sleep that night, Soillse felt the premonition of a steep and dangerous climb ahead. But she only shook this thought out of her mind.

And then, after they reached the king's pavilion the next afternoon, she and Eilid prepared the evening meal. Their tents sat on a low hill just southeast of the feasting yard outside the pavilion, with a grand view of the hall and the bay beyond. As Soillse lay in her furs that night, watching the stars and hoping Fìrinn wouldn't become king after all, she felt a soft tingling in her breasts, all around her aureoles, a fine quivering just under the skin. She took in a sharp breath and sent her inner vision to her womb, her heart suddenly racing. A star of light had formed there, pink and golden, and it roiled with new life, bubbling and expanding in whirling somersaults, over and over.

I carry our child!, she thought. And she smiled, as she looked over at Fìrinn's tent beyond the hearth.

"I'll call her Sìth," she whispered to the night. "Sìth nic Fìrinn (shee nick feereen), peace, daughter o' truth."

But in the morning, Soillse decided to wait until the hunt was over to tell Fìrinn. He had enough to worry about right now, and she didn't want to distract him from the trials. Besides, he was off early to the ceremonies in the nemeton on the hill and then kept sequestered for the hunt all that day. And she and Eilid had much cooking to do in preparation for the three-day feast to follow.

And then, during the night in her furs, Soillse dreamed of a wee forest temple. It was made of ferns, their high boughs leaning into an arch above her, like hands held in prayer. She and Fìrinn, small enough to stand underneath the ferns, were waiting there before the Creator Sun divine infants, Abaid and Uan. And Soillse was wearing a gossamer robe of lilac, with a fine shawl of palest pink, and tiny wings fluttered on her back. She was a wee bairn herself, a fae girl, perhaps two winters old. And a toddler Fìrinn wore tight green breeks and a loose white shirt under a pale purple jerkin, with a thin gold crown on his head. His wings were golden, too, and longer than hers, like a dragonfly. He grinned at her, then winked. And beside them was the Aine tree, covered with blossoms that quivered gently in the wind.

In the dream, Fìrinn handed her a bouquet of love-in-the-mist, forget-me-nots, and wild roses, and he pledged his heart to her, his child heart this time. He promised to be her best friend, forever and a day, and to protect and support her as long as they should live, "in any realm in the Kingdom," he said. And then Abaid handed Soillse a finely wrought crown, braided with threads of silver and gold.

"From the fae kingdom," Abaid said. "See? The silver stream o' the feminine woven wi' the gold o' the masculine, ever entwined in love." And then a tiny angel babe stepped out from the trunk, a wee lass in the same pale purple robes.

"I want to go, too," she said in her high child's voice.

"Ye will, dear," Abaid said, smiling and scooping the girl up in her arms, "in just a wee while more." And then the goddess nodded her head, and a crown of shell pink appeared in her hand, carved with wild roses, that she placed on the lassie's head. Me ring!, Soillse thought.

To still her excitement, Soillse, in her workaday summer shift, fed mushrooms, barley, and herbs to the cauldron all afternoon before the celebration, while Fìrinn slept. He'd given her a quick squeeze when he finally returned from the all-night hunt as she cooked the firstsky meal beside the tents, but he looked tired enough to drop, his hair sweaty, and small cuts from the branches all along his chest and arms. Saying little then, he'd gone straight to his furs. Coillore, eating his firstsky oats afterwards, told them Fìrinn had brought in enough game to be respected as a warrior, but not enough to be considered for the kingship.

And Soillse was secretly relieved, as she eyed the king's pavilion on the hill while she cooked. The hall had the symbols of kingship carved into it, and she felt the flow of the Sun Lord moving down over it to surround the one who'd soon rule there. Oaks grew behind the earthworks of the pavilion, too, and these were hung with the plaids of the clans, the woven banners of every tuath. Gazing around the hill where the pavilion stood, she looked for the small house by the sea she'd seen in her first moon-time vision, but it wasn't there. Still, she knew in her heart that one day she and Fìrinn would return here, and he'd be high king. But that was far off into the future, too far to feel now, and she was glad. For a while, he'd just be hers, hers and their faery child's.

Seumus was tense all that afternoon, the joking twinkle gone from his eyes, as he sat sipping mead by the hearth and quietly talking to Eilid about the weaknesses of all four of his foster sons who were competing here. He hoped the Sun Lord would favor one of them, anyway. It frustrated him greatly that the druids spent the whole morning in their meditations, then questioned three of the remaining competitors until late in the afternoon.

But Soillse mostly watched Fìrinn's tent, hoping he'd come wrap his arms around her waist while she worked, and she'd tell him her secret. He slept late, though, until sunset, just before the evening celebration was to begin. While the stew bubbled on its own, Soillse went into her tent and dressed in her ceremonial robe, fine doeskin with the blue sewn symbols spiraling up the front. She was glad this day was over, only the feasting to look forward to, as she brushed her hair until it shone and rippled down her back. Then Eilid braided the top into a circlet, plaiting sky-blue yarn into Soillse's hair and aqua through her own. As Soillse pinned the carving Fìrinn had made on her robe, he finally appeared, but only to race off to the tubs and then the oak grove after a quick kiss on Soillse's cheek.

"Queen an' princess o' me tuath," Seumus said, brightening as Soillse and Eilid emerged from their tent. "Ye look as if we foster high kings as a matter o' course." And he was resplendent in his ceremonial shirt, plaid, and sword.

And then they walked as a family up the path above the king's hall to the nemeton, jostled by the crowds headed toward the grove for the announcement of the druids. All contenders stood waiting along the processional avenue, dressed formally in white shirts, clan plaids, and swords. Then the horns blew and the pipers began, and the competitors walked into the nemeton, spiraling round the grove in the late sunlight. In the center stood the druids, white robes surrounded by green and then brown. And beyond the oaks of the holy grove crowded matriarchs and their chiefs, with all their clansfolk behind them, dressed in their ceremonial robes and the plaids of their tuaths. All clans were ranged around the grove according to the location of their tuaths on the isle, so Soillse was in the southwest. She stood on tiptoe to see Fìrinn, standing tall beside the other competitors at the entrance. And in the distance to the north, she noticed Fìrinn's Da, who eyed the druids with a frown. And then began the procession of the chiefs.

Each matriarch and chief, with their children and contenders from their clan, walked to the altar and around the circle of druids. And Soillse was amazed at the grace in Fîrinn's bearing, wearing the sash of a competitor, as he strode beside his father round the grove. How alike they appeared, father and son, both in the same plaid, and yet how differently their spirits shone, the chief's dour and Fîrinn's quite serene now. The stress of the hunt seemed not to have affected him at all, and Soillse's heart swelled with pride. Most of the other competitors were bedecked with swords, knives, shields, and the finery of skins, teeth, or feathers on their cloaks. But Fîrinn wore a simple homespun shirt and the plaid of his ancestors, wrapped round his waist and over his shoulder, with only the jeweled sword of his mother's tuath at his side. His eyes shone with love for the tribes as he circled them, and she saw the light of the Sun Lord reach out and touch his crown in the long rays of the setting sun through the oaks. Soillse wondered just then if she'd been wrong, thinking they must wait to return here, for Fîrinn walked through the grove like a king.

As Fîrinn passed in front of Seumus, he stopped and turned to smile at Soillse a moment. Then he pulled an apple leaf crown out of his shirt and placed it softly on her head. It was the act of betrothal, and by so doing, he was asking Seumus to bless their trothing before all gathered here. Seumus stepped back with brows raised, but then grinned and laid a hand on Fîrinn's shoulder.

"Ye dinna wait long after the hunt, laddie," Seumus whispered with a wink, and after a brief moment, placed a hand on both their heads. Loudly then for all to hear, Seumus called out, "Betrothed, Soillse nic Seumus an' Fîrinn mac Speireag. May the Beloved Creators bless yer marriage, an' may Their long arms o' love reach into yer hearts an' keep the hearth fires warm there every day o' yer lives. Ye're always welcome at me tuath, son."

As the procession drew to a close, the people bent and prayed, all the tuaths of Skye as one people, calling on the Sun Lord to choose the man who'd serve as king and be His representative to the clans. And as the golden haze of the gloaming hovered round the oaks, the arch druid stepped out before the altar, his white robe and sun disc shining in the dusk. He spoke the names of three competitors, the final choice to be made in a druid challenge on the morrow. Duirc was one, but Fìrinn's name was not among them. And Soillse's heart sank, as she turned to search for him in the crowd, hoping he wouldn't be so very disappointed after all. But in a moment, she grinned at Eilid. So Fìrinn'll come home to the tuath and be me own love now after all, Soillse thought. And if truth be told, it was what they'd both wished for, anyhow.

After the ceremony, Soillse ran to their tents to bring the stew and nuts to the tables in front of the pavilion. But as she searched for Fìrinn in the press of folk, she noticed a green robe staring at her. And she startled back, her heart racing, for the man looked exactly like the druid who'd hurt her when she was a wee lass. But Coillore had said that man wasna a real druid after all, she thought. Sure and this must be another, but she moved quickly behind Seumus to shield herself from the man's sight. And then suddenly, she was in Fìrinn's arms, safe again from all danger in his love.

Chapter Thirty-Three: Fìrinn

Duirc and the other warriors boasted long by the fires that night at the feasting grounds as the gloaming turned to dusk. All had brought in more game than Fìrinn, and he sat morosely at the tables of the competitors as they told their tales. In a fine ceremonial shirt and his plaid, Duirc spoke long of the red doe, shaming Fìrinn before the crowd and posturing his own right to the crown. But Fìrinn only listened quietly, running his fingers through Bana Dhia's fur and keeping silence, as Duirc accepted one of the winner's portions from a roast boar. And then, after the meal, Duirc strode across the circle and took his choice of maidens and led her to the dance.

Fìrinn's Da, dressed in his ceremonial shirt, plaid, and finest doeskin cloak, with his stringy red hair blowing in the night wind, got up as Duirc left the table and came to stand behind Fìrinn. It was the custom to argue when one's warrior skills were questioned, much less sneered at before the folk. But Fìrinn sat unmoving through it all, eating calmly. Speireag's jaw worked back and forth, as he suddenly grabbed up the storyteller's stone to face his son. In that moment, as Fìrinn watched the sparks fly up behind his father's face, the bonfire behind the chief made him look bigger and darker than life against the flames.

"Stand up, son," the chief said. And he gripped Fìrinn's arm, pulling him violently to his feet. A sharp pain shot through Fìrinn's shoulder socket as his Da shouted to the crowd. "Tell 'em how it really was, ladd," the chief bellowed, his eyes sweeping across the onlookers. "Come, take the bard stone, an' tell us the real story. Tame yer cousin's false boastin'!" And the man put his mouth close to Fìrinn's face, dropping his voice. "'Tis ill ye've let him take his meat wi'out protest," he said, spitting into Fìrinn's ear. The smell of mead filled the chief's breath, as he shoved the bard stone into Fìrinn's chest. Those who held it were allowed to tell only truth, and the gods were watching. Most of the clansfolk quieted. But Fìrinn stood in his own finery, sullen, unspeaking, and looking at the fire. Then silently, calling for the Sun Lord's help, he turned abruptly toward his father, eyes blazing.

"Duirc tells it aright, father, except for me lack o' courage. I heeded Ma's geis, shootin' only game that attacked me first, an' only those the Goddess gave me permission to kill. The red doe Duirc tells o' was Goddess merged, enchanted. If he'd killed it, it would've meant disaster for the tribes." Fìrinn's eyes were clear as he faced Speireag, full of youth and the firmness of his belief, standing taller than his Da in his plaid. Then grumbling was heard in the crowd.

"Leave the ladd alone," someone said.

"He did his best," said another.

"Aye, leave 'im to his meat," said a third.

"An' a lass, if he can manage her," said another, this followed by scattered laughter.

"The Sun Lord chooses, Speireag, it's no up to us." Coillore called out from the darkness. And the druid came and stood beside Fìrinn, leaning on his staff, his white robe bright in the firelight, despite being a head shorter than the ladd. "Whatever happened was destiny," Coillore said more loudly to the crowd. "Let it alone noo, Speireag." But the chief's eyes only widened further, and he stepped sharply toward Fìrinn.

"Twas yer Ma weakened ye," Speireag sputtered, lunging for his son, as Fìrinn dodged out of his Da's way. "I should've sent ye away long before I did." Spittle flew from the chief's mouth as he spoke, his teeth clenched as he shouted, "Get out o' me sight!" Speireag's face was redder than the embers now, the tendons in his neck pulled nearly out of his skin. "Mind," he screamed, "I'm still chief o' our tuath, an' tonight there's no king. None can undo me curse, until a high king is crowned. An' by then, it'll be too late. Banished ye are, son o' mine or no. For seven years, ladd, ye may no set a toe in me chiefdom. An' I'll personally punish any other chief o' this isle who allows ye in his! Banished from Skye ye are this night! Begone before firstsky, as the laws require, an' never let me see yer fawn's face again!" The chief's teeth glittered in the flickering firelight, as his fist came crashing down toward Firinn's' temple. But Firinn had already backed away into the crowd and was gone.

He ran straight to Seumus's hearth on the next rise, Bana Dhia loping after him into the ladd's tent. Bending hurriedly to gather up his boots and lances, Firinn startled and turned as someone entered after him. Coillore stood at the door cloth and made the sign of silence, handing Firinn a small leather pouch. The doeskin was as soft as silk and worked in dyed interlaced designs.

"Yer medicine bag," Firinn whispered and stared. "Ye canna give me that, Coillore!"

'Nah, nah,' the druid's voice came into Firinn's mind, '*yer medicine bag*.' And Coillore held up his own. The druid signed for silence again and, looking ahead, stepped outside. Watching, Firinn tensed. It was death to help a banished man. I'll slide out quickly, just take me hide breeks and shirt, a fur and jerkin, and me brown robe, and leave Coillore in safety, before anyone discovers him, Firinn thought. And he stuffed a few things into a small bag. And I canna risk saying good-bye to Soillse either. I'll send her a message later.

But the old man blocked the doorway, unmoving, as Firinn breathed to calm himself, waiting in the shadows. At length, Coillore turned back to face him. *'There'll be hardship, ladd. It's the way to the Creator Sun. Sufferin' releases the bonds to all lower worlds an' pays off the debts we still owe here. Understandin'll come later.'* Then the druid said aloud, "Go to Iona, ladd." And then Coillore bowed his head, pulling his hands together in blessing, and stepped back out of the way, as Firinn brushed past him into the night.

A cold mist was beginning to settle over the hills, and pulling on his breeks and throwing his plaid around his shoulders, Firinn ran a few steps toward the path that led southeast into the wood. *'Take the southern fork on the other side o' the rise that leads to Glen Elg,'* he heard clearly in his mind, and turned with raised brows. The druid nodded. And then suddenly, the old man looked small and wrinkled, standing there in the darkness.

'Will I ever see ye again?,' Fìrinn sent the thought.

'No,' came the reply, but the druid's eyes smiled at him from their blue depths. And suddenly, Fìrinn felt as forlorn as an orphan. He walked back to look down into his old teacher's face, as tears filled the druid's eyes. And in a great bear of a hug, Fìrinn grabbed up the old man and, crying softly, set him down again.

"I love ye, too, druid child," came the words, and then more sternly, "noo, go!"

A crashing could be heard in the underbrush above, and Fìrinn leaped into the forest, crouching behind a wide beech among the birches. But it was only cook, who half-ran, half-waddled down the path in her stained shift and old shawl. She carried a bag of dried meat and oats, not caring who saw or what they did to her.

"Where is he?," she demanded of Coillore, one hand on her hip, her frizzed white hair awry around her head. Fìrinn's heart tightened as he saw clansmen watching from the rise above. Da'll kill her, if I step out, he thought, backing silently into the darkness of the forest. Then he heard cook burst into tears as Coillore said softly, "gone." The old woman wiped her ruddy cheeks with her shawl and stood a moment, shoulders drooping, letting the bag drop onto the ground. Suddenly, she turned toward the forest that had swallowed her ladd.

"It's scorched porridge an' burnt stew yer Da'll be gettin' for the rest o' his born days!," she shouted into the woods at the top of her lungs. Then she limped back up the hill, her plump hips bouncing. Reaching the top of the rise, she turned toward the nearest clansman and, shoving his chest hard with the heel of her palm, sent him sprawling into the dust.

Firinn chuckled as the clansmen landed and sent a blessing after her for peace and easy passing to the Otherworld, whenever it came. Not too far off, he felt. I'll never see ye again, either, he thought, bowing his head. Coillore picked up the bag and threw it to him, as keening could be heard from above, a high wailing screech. Soillse appeared, holding her skirts high and running towards Coillore.

"Coillore," she shouted, "<u>stop</u> him!" She stumbled toward the tent and fell, her chest heaving, and sat where she landed, pulling at her hair. Then holding her head in her hands, she rocked and keened fit to wake the dead. But Coillore passed his hand over her back, chanting, and in a moment she quieted and lay back in the dirt.

"I canna <u>live</u>, Coillore," she whispered, as Firinn stepped out of the underbrush and kissed her cheek.

"I'm here, lassie, shhhh," he whispered. And she bolted up and held him close, sobbing into his chest.

"The fabric o' the heart is torn in two," Coillore said softly. "Women feel it all so much more, an' she such a wild-hearted thing. Take her down the path, an' I'll see ye're no disturbed for a short while. It'll mend her a bit an' do no harm. I've somethin' else to give ye, anyway." So Firinn lifted Soillse in his arms, pushing into the undergrowth until they were well hidden, and put her down.

"Firinn, take me wi' ye, please! I <u>canna live</u> without ye. Seven <u>winters</u>!"

"Ach, lass, it's death to aid a banished man. I canna let ye do that. I go to Iona. Da'll be deposed within a moon, anyway. An' if the king an' the druid council grant it, I might come back soon. We can hope for that, at least." He kissed her hair, thinking fast. "Or if no, I'll send fer ye. It willna be long, love. An' Coillore says it's the way to the Core. We best <u>try</u>, at least."

"Ye willna get any mercy, if Duirc gets the throne," she spat out, clutching Firinn tightly against her. His chest trembled to think of leaving her, too. And he kissed her as tenderly as if it was the

Goddess Herself he gentled into love, begging Oghama to mend her heart. But she only moaned and pulled him tighter.

"I love ye. I <u>love</u> ye, Firinn-ladd," she whispered, over and over again. And then her face became very serious, as she whispered. "I ask the Beloved Creators for a bindin' o' me own life to yers, an' for us to be bound for all eternity, for I'll have no other, no noo, no ever, no matter how long ye're away. This I promise ye, Firinn mine." And a soft golden light moved around her heart and circled his as well, weaving a figure eight around them both. And then, Coillore's voice could be heard at the head of the path.

"Go, ladd. Make haste. Ye're Da searches ye out wi' his men. I canna hold them off any longer." Quickly, Firinn grabbed up his clothing and cook's bags. And suddenly, Coillore was there behind him, holding Briagha. Firinn mounted the mare swiftly and pulled her east toward the mainland, as Soillse reached out her hands and broke into sobs. Harder it was for Firinn to draw away from her, than to see his Ma's face go ashen two skyturns before. And only the knowledge that they might harm Soillse, too, made him race away into the mists of night.

"I <u>will</u> come for ye, lass," he called back to her, "if I have to walk the whole o' Alba to do it!"

This novel takes place in the early years of the first century B.C.E. The 21 centuries spoken of then have passed. The time of the great transformation on earth is now, the end of darkness and realignment with the Laws of Love. Please join us at our teaching, ceremony, and workshop center in Minnesota, if you wish, Facebook.com/ CelticHeavenCenter

Glossary

Alba-Scotland

Albion-England

Aye-yes, always

Bairn-child

Breeks-tight fitting pants

Broch-double walled stone tower that tribe can stay in during times of danger, home of the matriarch and chief

Burn-river, creek

Byre-barn

Coracle-round hide boat

Curragh-same as coracle

Finn isle, the-Mull

Firstsky-dawn

Girdle-belt

Ken-know

Manhood-phallus

Midsky-noon

Nemeton-circle of twelve white oaks, where druid conclaves and ceremonies were held-light channels reach to Oghama or Christ in the Creator Sun-a circle of these trees protects against false incoming information

Plaid-a long length of fabric, usually wool, woven of the ray colors connected with the sacred purpose of each clan

Selkie-seal that turns into a mermaid or merman-can shape-change into human as well

Sheiling-rough herder's hut in high grazing grounds, used during summer moons only

Skyturn-one year

Syne-long time ago

Tuath-tribal village consisting of a matriarch and her daughters and their families to four generations

Woman's place-vagina, womb

Appendix One:
The 174 Planes of the Diamond Core and 39 planes of the Diamond Centerpoint:
Regents, Directives, Trees, Star Systems*

*Forty more planes of the Diamond Core listed in Book Two
Please note: names are given for Celtic tradition only, with a few cross references. Many traditions have their own names for these gods and goddesses

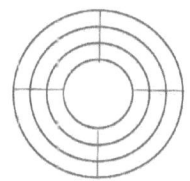

Diamond Core

Creator Sun

The Creators and One Beloveds

18) Union of God and Goddess, the diamond light, the Love force, love forever true, sexual orgasm, human true love partnerships, sacred sexual manifestation, manifestation into the physical, DNA, healing, clear light in water (Goddess), clear light in light (God) diamond initiation, Helix Nebula in Aquarius

17) Goddess, the White Tara Beloved (cosmic Magdalen), feminine Creator and divine feminine principle, intimacy, marriage, physical union, magnetic force of love through left heart, female partners, manifestation of true love, inner worlds, wisdom, full moon, inner worlds, **cycle of emotion, 15 24-day moons with 5 intercessory days, Nov. 24-28th, (druid year),** right brain, the sensate realms and earth initiation, 11 circuit labyrinth, elementals, Apple moon, apples, Scotland (Applecross), Apple tree, Bull star in Ursa Major

16) God, Oghama (ohahma) (cosmic Christ) Beloved, masculine Creator and divine masculine principle, radiatory force of love

through the right heart, male partners, light seeding in back of heart in the Oak moon, the outer world, truth, world service (Oghama), **mind cycle 12 30-day moons with 5 intercessory days, Dec. 27-31,** language, left brain, Diamond Core realms and diamond initiation, Oak moon, White Oak (Quercus Robur), Polaris

High Priestess, Priest, and Divine Infants

15) Union of High Priest and Priestess, spiritual paths, sacred ceremony, poetry, giving one's whole life in service to God/Goddess, highest destinies or our inner divine children, personal transformation, union with the divine, union of heaven and earth, platinum

14) High Priestess, Mona; informal path of experience, feminine spiritual paths, spiritual sisterhoods, all pagan religions,, Celtic religion, ceremonial music, music, Scotland (Balmoral), Apple tree, white gold, Crater (the cup)

13), High Priest, Don: all masculine spiritual paths, all formal religions and spiritual brotherhoods, ceremonial speech, laws of love, preparation for highest destiny, embodiment of laws of love into the heart, Christianity, England, Oak, gold, Ara (the altar)

12) Union of high priest and priestess with divine infants: Epiphanies, Don creates clarity, Mona creates peace, Abaid creates sense of oneness, Uan creates reverence

11) Union of Child Hearts, best friends, twins, lifelong childhood friend, child heart union following orgasm, thymus, thymus star in pets, Monoceros, Sirius

10) Abaid, divine infant girl, loving kindness, healing, white cells in bone marrow, meditation, rt. temporal lobe, thymus, hope, girl core wound, butterfly, St. Abb's in Alba, Sugar Maple, butterfly nebula in Scorpio

9) Uan, divine infant boy, basic truths of inner child, T cells in thymus, will in surrender to the greater good and Divine Will, focus, boy core wound, conscience, cherubs, shepherd boy, lamb, Eire, Lindisfarne, Dogwood, Canus Major

Virgins

8) Maighdean, **divine child cycle, 13 24 day moons with 1 intercessory day, Dec. 25th,** rules birth of all divine children and human babies, birth pangs before delivery, winter queen, Aut. to Vernal Equinox, newness, the red hot now, manifestation of Paradise on earth, union of hearts with virgin male, romance, first love-making, memories of Beloved relationship in heaven, healing sexual distortions, 2nd moon quarter, Kwanzaa, mermaids, peaches, Hebrides, Beech, Aquarius, Sadalmelik

7) Ridire (reedera, knight), crusader, breastplate of protection to heart and feminine, world server, orchestrates global masculine causes, lifts entire globe, union of male and female hearts, courtly love and restraint, pours their love into efforts in the outer world, **action cycle, 11 33-day moons, with 2 intercess. days at beg. and end of month of restraint** (Ramadan, Islam), summer king, Vernal to Aut. Equinox, Anglesey, Wales, whales, Cedar, Pisces

Divine Parents/King/Queen

6) Màiri (Mary), divine mother/grandmother-resets global emotion impulse at lunar southern standstill every **18.6 years** at Callanish; loves everyone, no matter what they do; still small pool in heart, life force and flow of life into the root; holding force, overlights all fem. efforts and choices in life, sleep, oceans, 4th moon quarter, Catholicism, Edinburgh, Scotland, Caledonian Pine, Cassiopeia

5) The Dagda, divine father/grandfather-templates of father's Kingdom, laws of love in structures of outer world, nation structures of Creator Sun and earth, executes Oghama's will, preparation for highest destiny, overlights all masc. efforts and choices in life, **100 year cycle**-sino-atrial node and end of life, Protestantism, England, Chestnut Oak, Leo, Regulus

The Family Creator Wheel

4) Màithriel, family food and nourishment; security of love and comfort in the home, emotional peace, milk, cows, **18 year family cycle from birth to leaving home**, 3rd moon quarter, Glasgow, Scotland, White Pine, Cygnus

3) Daiden (Joseph), provider and protector for family, security of resources in the family, housing, work, personal gifts through human father, **25-year generational cycle**, Spruce, Bootes

2) Eriu, spiritual purpose, confidence and sovereignty of self, direction in life, diversity, first two years of life, wild rose fairies, raspberries, 1st moon quarter, **girl's heart's desires cycle, 19 19-day moons with 4 intercess. days, Feb 28/29 to Mar 3rd** (B'hai), Ireland, Guelder Rose, Vela (sails of Argo), cats

1) Finn MacCuill, rules trust, root flow connection with mother's slow cycle of life, time, manifestation of personal care, simplicity of life, **boy 's heart's desires cycle, 12 27-day moons with 14 intercess. days, Mar. 15-28th**-leprechaun's, colon and solid waste, water play, ages 2 and 3, Swamp Cedar, Eire, Puppis (the stern of Argo), dogs

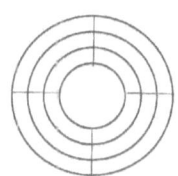

Death Star, Dragon lords, Draco
False goddess, god, and children

18) Union of Isle (Isis) and Taranis (Osiris) false beloveds-the force of hatred, breaking all bonds in love, marital betrayals, infidelity, insecurity of love in longterm partnership, sexual orgies

17) Isle, false beloved goddess, **control,** breaking the husband down, betrayal of the heart, take over eveything in household, marriage for power, heart attacks, left side, cancer, Crab Apple,

Draco

16) Taranis, false beloved god, breaking the wife down, betrayal of the heart, male domination and abuse of feminine partner, lock her into home, control her every move, sexual sharing without her consent, marriage for money, rage and emotional explosions, infidelity, heart attacks, right side, Weeping Oak, Draco

False high priestess, priest, and divine infants

15) Union high priest and priestess; Satanic ceremony, Satanic ritual abuse, worship of anti-love gods/goddesses, creating divisions between religions that lead to war, ritual sacrifice/mutilation, suicide for religious reasons

14) Iobair (sacrifice), dark high priestess, rules shadows of wisdom path, all fears humanity hasn't faced in depths of the sea, death, mutilation of males in ceremony, all sacrifice, all suicide, dark sisterhoods, black snake, **constrictions** in life, slavery, poverty, starvation, eating disorders, isolation, disease, Coronavirus, Egypt, Spindle tree (euonymous), Draco

9) Matarach (martyr), dark high priest, **power** over others, sexual abuse of parishioners, esp. children and women, mutilation of females in ceremony, dark brotherhoods, personal will in service to death, master/slave consciousness, terror, war, aggression, torture, bombs, militarization of boys, murder, heart attacks, Iraq, Weeping Oak, Draco

15) Union of parents and children; Iobair, displacement and break up of families, refugees; Matarach, war that fragments nations, breaks Tara an Oghama's global clan/nation fabric; total destruction of family and society; Bulai, competition in sport and between friends, pits one against another, deep divisions between peoples; Àrdan, weakens immune system through disease, fatigue, overwork, AIDS

14) Union of children, medical establishment that is far too complicated, expensive, arrogant, and terrifying, and keeps natural and spiritual healing hidden

13) Àrdan, haughty, rigid extravagant social and household standards, wants to be the best, disdain for others, hatred toward kind people, snobby, critical, catty, Weeping Birch

12) Bulai, bully, harms softest and smallest, does what he wants with no regard for others or divine Will, child temper tantrums, Weeping Larch

False parents and virgins

8) Mil, false father/king-grandiose schemes, never ending plans, work, and expenses, wheeler and dealer, dishonest; wants money, wants to be god, the luciferic force, Egypt, Weeping Moutain Ash, Draco

7) Opair, false mother/queen, heavy overwork for mother, own needs not met, starvation, concentration camp, Nazi, Israel, Weeping Black Pine, Draco

6) Aeron, Arawn-rape, total control of sexual choices of virgin girls, sexual slavery, closes down manifestation powers of virgin girl, rape of the heart, grooms her and seems like a prince, but turns into

demon of infidelity or sharing her with other men, Saudi Arabia, Weeping Cedar, Draco

5) Cat, sex without love, wants power and money, prostitution, spread of vernerial diseases that kill, Somalia, Weeping Beech, Draco

False family

4) Mider, mother, spider matrix force, excess details, webbing of confusion in home, wants household control, hoarder, clutter, shopper, saps male resources, Alzheimer's, Sudan, Weeping Willow, Draco

3) Deal, father, parasite, doesn't work, sucks life force from everyone else, chronic insecurity of food and housing, Eritrea, Weeping Spruce, Draco

2) Col (cohl, incest), incest, closes inner beloved, parent, and child heart streams of girl, forces child into adult overwork pattern, no family to rely on, abusive relationships for whole life, uterine disease, Niger, Weeping Cherry, Draco

1) Caolin (colon, Colin), sodomy, closes inner beloved, parent, and child heart of boy, blocks slow life flow of true mother, forces into driving rushing lifestyle and overwork, abusive authority relationships for whole life, colon disease, Greece, Corkscrew Willow, Draco

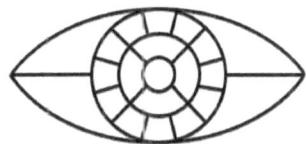

Stillpoint Center-cosmic soul star, mind
Four Directions-Regents of Divine Will
Girl Quadrant: children, overlight cherubim realms

24) Siris (sheerish, cherry), red dragon: mental ethers, east, morning, spring, element of air; moment of manifestation into the physical, short o, birth out of mental ethers on Bealltain,
cervix, thyroid, cherries, Japan, Cherry tree, Skat in Aquarius

23) Oisìn (ohsheen), sacredness of the ordinary, simplicity, moments of wonder, Zen Buddhism, Japan, Japanese Maple, Pheonix

Boy Quadrant: virgins,

22) Eilean (aylen, island), green dragon: emotion ethers, west, evening, summer, element of water, overlights logos realms, emerald flow of emotion into forests, Goddess wisdom impulse into trees, chooses trees near each person's home, opens heart with stunning beauties, short u, birth out of emotion ethers on Lughnasa, Celtic, green grapes, Ireland, Irish Elm, Virgo, Spica

21) Fearglas-green man, forests, sacredness of nature, tree lore, truths in trunks, resonates with nerves in spine, slowing inner rush, uses of wood and bark, forest wildflowers, Celtic, Ireland, Chestnut, Pisces

Father Quadrant: parents, western hemisphere, outer world, overlight diamond centerpoint realms

20) Areinrhod (ahreeinrhat)-yellow dragon, action ethers; south, noon, autumn, element of fire; Skye mother, freedom and nourishment for all, daytime bowl of the sky, leisure pursuits and the arts, pursuit of happiness, ascension wheel, torch to light the heart, Aug. 12th, short e, birth out of action ethers on Samhein, Scotland (Dunvegan), Sycamore or Plane, Vega

19) Leòmhann (lovan, lion)-courage in the father's heart, facing fear in outer world, manifestation and abundance into the physical world, the harvest, Feb. 12th(Lincoln's birthday), England, American White Oak, Leo

Mother Quadrant: grandparents, eastern hemisphere, inner world, overlight soul realms

18) Brìdget (the Dao)-black dragon, core ethers: north, midnight, winter, element of earth; breaking down shadow self to release new patterns, anam cara or soul friend through path for life and transition to Otherworld, responsibility for the All, bodhisattva path, inner creates outer, the sea of the unconscious, inner planes of light, Feb 1st, Aug. 2nd-Feb. 1st, short a, birth of divine child through core ethers at Imbolc, short i birth of divine child through core ethers at Midwinter,

Daoism, China, Sequoia, Andromeda, Mirak

17) Eòl (yawl) or El, (Buddha), white dragon, seeds of truth to open in coming year, bone fears of winter, inner path, deep understanding, peace of mind, lord of karma, Aug 1st, Feb 2nd-Aug 1st, China, Bodhi (Fig), Taurus, Aldebaran

Zodiac Circle: Twelve Tribes and Star Gateways:

Mother Quadrant: Wisdom Cycle

16) Mathus (mahoos, benevolence) (Quan Yin)-mind, teacher, path of experience, compassion, long pilgrimages, living outside the tribe, suffering, quark is beauty, Buddhism, China, Umbrella Pine, Saggitarius

15) Mara (of the sea)(Asherah, Shekinah)-heart, provider-brings in human families, fem. wisdom and light impulses through them, regents of **wisdom cycle, 12 29.5 day moons, 11 intercessory days, extra moon added into 5 sets of three year cycles with 2 sets of two year cycles in between**, like keys on piano, minor key years have wisdom lessons woven in, quark is strange, Judaism, Israel, Crab Apple, Cancer

14) Maireann, action, protector-keeps home pure from darkness, especially young women, chaos force that can break down societies, karmic debt to family members, blocking the feminine, endurance and patience, surrender to divine will, quark is down, Islam, Mecca, Lemon, Scorpio

Father Quadrant

13) Longinus, mind, teacher-8-fold path of enlightenment, mentors on the way, pursuit of truth, Samadhi sun, intellectual truths and teachers, quark is truth, Buddhism, China, Sessile Oak, Taurus, Ain

12) Manannan (mahnahnahn), heart, provider, brings in human tribes, masculine wisdom and light impulses through them, masc.

half of wisdom cycle, sea captain in storms of life, quark is charm, Judaism, Israel, Calliprinos Oak, Leo, Adhafera

11) Breiteamh (breetuv, judge), action, protector, the judge, scales of justice, weighs heart at end of life, fair dealings in commerce and work, arbitrator in disputes, compassionate and merciful, quark is up, Islam, Syria, Red Oak, Libra

Virgin Girl Quadrant

10) Neamh (nev, heaven), mind, teacher-rules plant kingdom, devas or fae women, communication and all learning from plants, meadows, girl power place in nature, African pagan religions, Hinduism, Silverbell or Halesia, Gemini

9) Ur (oor, new), builds inner goddess or fem. half of divine child over many lives, orange in uterus that sends pictures out to spirit world to manifest individual physical experiences over 13 divine child moons, orchestrates global causes for women and children, Iraq (Ur), Orange tree and fruit, Aquarius

8) Sith (shee, peace) (Jerusalem)-action, protector, peace on earth, non-violence, healing violence and brute force, standing in one's truth, spine and backbone, restoration of global feminine into equality with male, caring for young women and children, rules chakra flow and sorts next seven generations of children in Pleiades into chakras and social causes, all pacifist religions, Jerusalem, Rose of Sharon, Virgo, Porrima

Virgin Male Quadrant

7) Cernunnos (care-noonos), Pan, mind, teacher, rules animal kingdom, restoration of the peaceable kingdom, all communication with animals, teaching about caring for animals, divine will and action potentials in the mind, rules djinns or male fairies, pagan religions of South America, Galapagos, Alder, Capricorn

6) Deas (jess, right hand, Jessie, Jesus), builds inner god or masc. half of divine child over many lives, lifts entire cosmos with his efforts, the carpenter, wooden cross over spine of core wound last three years of path, global causes of boys and young men, Nazareth, Isreal, Redwood Cedar, Pisces

5) Pwyll, action, protector, rules phallic or personal will to action, power channel, brute force, Islam, Saudi Arabia, Olive, Aries

Outer Corners-Archangels

4) Maigeal (Michael)-father quadrant and dominion angels

3) Gabreal (Gabriel)-mother quadrant and virtue angels

2) Ureal-girl quadrant and seraphim

1) Rapheal (boy quadrant) and cherubim

The Wizard Wheel-the Brain-planet Mercury-

cosmic seventh chakra

10) Girl-Nimue (neemoo), outer southeast quadrant-serves cosmic girl quadrant-rules right temporal and parietal lobes, song, music, dance, art, inner spatial sense, the feminine everyday path-healer-right amygdala and girl fear memories-Coma Berenice (Berenice's hair)

9) Boy-Fionnmhar (feeoonvar), outer southwest quadrant-serves cosmic boy quadrant-rules left temporal and parietal lobes-outer spatial awareness, speech recognition and comprehension, the masculine everyday path-left amygdala and boy fear memories-PIsces

8) Father-Taliesin, outer northwest quadrant-serves the cosmic father quadrant-rules frontal lobe, mental focus, consequences of actions, right and wrong, planning for the future, sudden mental shifts and downloads-Carina (Keel of Argo)

7) Mother-Tatiana, outer northeast quadrant-serves cosmic mother quadrant-rules occipital lobe, inner and outer sight, pictoral thought, looking to the past to heal-Microscopus

6) Virgin Girl-Morgaine le Fay, inner southeast quadrant, the girl-rules pituitary, female sexual maturity, function, and cycles; birth and nursing; kidneys; food and sexual appetites-prepares for birth of divine child and relationship-pink dragons-Velpecula (the fox)

5) Virgin Boy-Gwydion, inner southwest quadrant, the boy-rules pituitary, fight or flight impulse; facing fear; physical growth; male sexual maturity, function, and appetite-prepares for world service-pale blue dragons-Grus (crane)

4) Grandfather/King-Palindore, inner northwest quadrant, the father-rules thalamus, alertness, relaying motor and sensory signals to the rest of brain-sends back in time to heal, opens ancient truths-gold dragons-Sextans (sextant)

3) Grandmother/Queen-Vivianne, inner northeast quadrant, the mother-rules hypothalamus, body temperature, hunger, thirst, sleep-healer of physical body-silver dragons-Antlia (the pump)

2) serves Creators-Emer, center circle-rules sensory strip in brain, develops five inner senses, mystical-peach dragons-Tongue, Alba, Corona Borealis

1) serves Creators-Cuchullin (coohoolin), center circle-rules motor strip in brain, sends calls to action from above, action potentials of nerves-rust dragons-Aires

Pineal Wheel-Patriarch/Matriarch of Tribe or Community, Wealth, Law, and Education

structures of earth-120 day cycle-cosmic sixth chakra

8) Priomh (preeov, chief), center triangle, the father, executor of Oghama's will, clan chief, chief of all star clans, provider, protector, and teacher for clan-rules all global tribes and communities, daytime half of circadian cycle, West Germany-Triangulum

7) Màthair-àil (mahairahl, matriarch), center triangle-the mother, clan matriarch-executor of Tara's will, matriarch or queen of all star clans, rules global feminine tribal organization and cultural structures: tribal patterns, birth and seasonal festivals, family gatherings, strengthening light networks between clan members, night half of circadian cycle, East Germany, Cassiopeia

Together overlight intercessory days, Dec. 21st-25th

6) Ionnsaich (yoonsich, teach), virgin male, first star arm (sunwise), teacher aspect, rules left brain learning, global higher education, written media, books, Mensa (the table)

5) Ciaradh (keearugh) (Dawn/Aurora), feminine virgin, first star arm-teacher aspect-rules early childhood education, teaching of performing arts, all pictoral media, film-Pictor (the easel)

Together overlight first 120-day phase, Dec. 26th-April 24th.

4) Llew, father, second star arm, provider, rules abundance and wealth of family and clan, support into the future, personal wealth, Switzerland, Libra

3) Siebh (shee-ev), earth mother, second star arm, provider, rules global commons of soil, air, and water, and all natural goods that support life: building and clothing materials, Reticulum (woman's purse)

Together overlight second 120-day phase, Apr.25th-Aug. 22nd.

2) Mìlidh, grandfather, apex star arm, protector, judge of clan disputes, protects safety of the tribe, oversees global law, law enforcement, and armed service structures, Aquila (the eagle)

1) Cobhair (cohver, aid), grandmother, apex star arm-protector, protector of women, children, and the infirm in the clan, rules global humanitarian and aid organizations-Vega

Together overlight third 120 day phase, Aug. 23rd-Dec 20th

Triple Spiral-Spiritual Path of Life-Flow into Mind, Emotion, Action Centers-cosmic fifth chakra

8) **Center**-Domhnall (donal), arch druid, high priest, pope-rules masculine spiritual path in all formal religions and spiritual

brotherhoods, ritual, ceremonial speech, spiritual teachers, paid church work, Catholicism, Ara (the altar)

7) Nemetona, center circle, high priestess, rules less formal feminine spiritual path in all spiritual sisterhoods, elder mother of all priestesses/nuns, ritual, ceremonial music, volunteer work in the orders, inner calls to new paths or directions, giving one's whole life in service to God/Goddess, seventh chakra (deep purple), union with the divine, Celtic/pagan religions, plums, elderberry, Hazel moon, Hazel tree, Crater (the cup)

Mind-6) Grainne (grahnya), first arm (sunwise), rules monthly feminine impulses into mental body, teachers and mentors on feminine path, less formal than masculine, right brain growth, intuition, Buddhism, Circinus (the drawing compass)

5) Aedd, first arm (Gautama Buddha opened flow for earth), rules monthly masculine impulses into mental body, intellectual teachers and mentors along one's spiritual path, Buddhism-Pyxis (the compass)

Heart-4) Etain, second arm-rules monthly feminine emotional lessons into emotional body on one's path, wandering off into new directions, taming emotions and desires, Judaism, Equulus (little horse)

3) Ecne, second arm (Jesus opened flow for earth), rules monthly masculine emotional lessons into emotional body on one's path, restraint of emotional impulses and desire in line with divine will, building laws of love into the heart, Christianity, Auriga (the charioteer)

Action 2) Siann (sheann, Fatima), third arm-rules portals to action for inner feminine, outpicturing of feminine beliefs in home and family, blending personal will with needs of the tribe and family, holds back fulfillment until feminine will for action is fully subdued to divine will, law, and timing, left hand, Islam, Yed posterior (the hand behind in Ophiucus, the snake charmer)

1) Nudd (Mohammed opened flow for earth), third arm-rules portals to action for the masculine, outpicturing of masculine beliefs in world outside the home, holds back destiny stream until personal will is fully subdued to divine will, law, and timing, right hand, Islam, Yed prior (the hand in front in Ophiucus)

The Child Heart-thymus-creates Rainbow Body or Magical Forever Child-rules 7-7-7 mental/emot./action ether openings of childhood-Ireland-cosmic Child Heart

12) Sirona (sheerona)-brings in loving kindness from Abaid, healer of the feminine, lymph, kidneys-6th chakra, indigo-ages 18 to19, 1st long term partner, patterns of intimacy and sexuality similar to eventual true love, large highbush blueberry, Adhaa (the virgin in Sirius)

11) Dion Cècht (jeean caycht), strong truths that set boundaries around darkness, T cells, ages 20 to 21, healer, opens deep desire for change in the world that frees inner children, Sirius

10) Ròsin (rosheen), fae infant, ages 0 to1, first chakra (red), identity of magical child, connection to earth, tribe, and human mother, threats to life, red currants, Halcyone in the Pleiades

9) Ruari (rooahree, red king)-fae boy, toddler, ages 2 to 3, opens gifts of magical child, boy's will and phallic force, seeds of future change, Phoenix

8) Cliona (cleoona), cherub girl, ages 4 to 5, second chakra (orange), sensual pleasure, intimacy with physical world, closeness to opposite gender parent, cloud berries, Electra in the Pleiades

7) Daineal (daneeil or Danny), cherub boy, ages 6 to 7, second star arm, use of masculine personal will in friend relationships, special friendship, Canis Minor (little dog)

6) Siannon (sheeannon or Shannon)-human girl, ages 8 to 9, third chakra (pale yellow), use of feminine personal power in family and tribal relationships, gooseberry, Asterope in Pleiades

5) Dairè (Derry), human boy, ages 10 to 11, develops talents of magical child, consoilidates masc. identity, personal connections in the work and outer world, use of masc. personal power, Pavo (the peacock)

4) Maeve, virgin girl, ages 12 to13.5, fourth chakra (emerald green), union of virgin girl and boy hearts, first love, sweet moments of union throughout life, green grapes, Maia, the Pleiades

3) Nechtan, virgin boy, ages 13.5 to 14, preparation of individual true love partners for eventual shared highest destiny, develops work talents of magical child-Pegasus

2) Erin, self assurance, song and dance to offset family work patterns, champagne essence in bone marrow, bubbly joy, opens new patterns of life, happy family times, girl's heart desires, 3 magical relationships, ages 15 to 16.5, fifth chakra (sky blue), children's songs, harps, small wild blueberries, Lyra

1) Padraig (padraik, Patrick), develops work patterns of Creator Sun family, play, humor, adventure, opens annual magical boy portal on St. Patrick's Day, formal religion patterns of life, restraint of personal will force, ages 16.5 and 17, Lyra

Holy Family-creates human families-the heart-cosmic fourth chakra

6) Còir (cooer)-father, northwest quadrant and upper right heart lobe, overlights family fathers-rules heavy masculine family responsibilities to provide, paid work outside the home-opens one package of fear and truth into right or masculine heart every moon, NW Russia, Leo

5) Màiri-ebh (màiri-ev), mother, northeast quadrant and upper left heart lobe, overlights family mothers, feminine family responsibilities, nourishing personal needs of all family members, devotion to family, endurance, herb woman-brings one package of truth and fear into left or feminine heart every moon, holds within to calm emotion, Siberia, Cygnus (the swan)

4) Aine (anya or Anne), girl, southeast quadrant and heart lobe, emotional understanding of others, carries emotional burdens, overlights family daughters/sisters, one to one closeness with everyone, inner connection to father, looks up to him, central south eastern Russia, Cygnus

3) Niall, boy, southwest quadrant and heart lobe, overlights human sons/brothers, heavy physical work, carries physical burdens, will in surrender to divine will, inner connection to mother, looks up to her, central south western Russia, Sadr in Cygnus

2) Epona, virgin girl, overlights adolescent girls, feminine driver of emotional change, horse power of the heart, freedom from fear-red blood cells, will bring world religions into one simple form, rose of the world, southeast Russia, Centaurus (the centaur)

1) Eochaid (yawchait), virgin boy, overlights adolescent males, oxygen (ox-djinn), brings the world server stream in through breath, love in action-driver of world service, shared destiny, horses, Mongolia, Pegasus

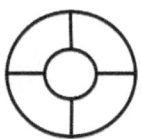

Pillars-Create Inner and Outer Path of Human Lifespan-Ascension Climb through Adulthood-cosmic third chakra

Middle East-the Beloved center, virgins-logos and fire initiation-inner and outer worlds, ages 11 to 22, spine

10) Aislin, (ashlin, Columbia), virgin girl, preparation of fem. for lifelong service to family and tribe, spine, backbone of feminine standing in her truth, esp. against male domination, Ash moon, Ash tree, Jerusalem, Israel, Columba (the dove)

9) Colum, virgin boy-preparation of the virgin male for lifelong service in the world, spinal rod of truth, standing up for what is right in the world, sends intentions up spine, tempts with sexual misuse, addictions, and violence-overlights Alder moon-Alder-Saggitta

Africa and Polynesia-the Girl quadrant, southeast-cherubim realms and initiation-inner world, ages 0-11, thymus and lymph

8) Anu, fae girl, girl's identity in left hip and leg, rules memories of paradise, natural power place and girl's connection with spirit world, sensual wonders of physical world, Polynesia, girl fears in abdominal unconscious, shamanic dance, following path till birth of paradise on earth, Africa, love shadow selves, Camelopardus (the giraffe)

7) Beli, fae boy, boy's identity in right hip and leg, rules comedy and humor of boy, connection to divine mother in lakes and sea, Polynesia, bringing up fears from the boy's abdominal unconscious, shamanic percussion, support of girl even if demeaned for it, Africa, Apus (bird of Paradise)

South America: the Boy quadrant, southwest-spirit realms and air initiation-outer world, ages 0-11, nerves

6) Flidais (fleetish), Corn Mother, cherub girl, builds girl's identity in the world, family and friends of childhood, forest power place, tomboy, staying true to girl nature, despite pressures to be masculinized, Tucana (the toucan)

5) Fionn (feeoon) (Quetzalcoatl), Birdman, cherub boy, builds boy's identity in the world, experiences that shape boy's destiny, leisure pursuits of child, holding on to slow lifestyle, despite pressures to overwork and hurry, shamanic flute and dance, Mayan calendar, Indus (the Indian)

Asia-the Mother quadrant, northeast-inner realms-soul realms and water initiation-inner path, ages 22 to end of diamond centerpoint climb, interstitial waters

4) Cùram (cooram), mother, rules feminine climb through inner planes of six lower worlds, teaching that each person's inner beliefs create the outer world and affect whole cosmos, responsibility to the All to heal inner fears-balance of giving and receiving, Willow moon, China, Willow, Andromeda, shoulder star

3) Treòraich (trayreech)-rules masculine path of inner truth, climb of inner masculine up all planes of six lower worlds, embodiment of truth, proper use of power, despite obstacles, Taurus, Lambda Tauri

North America-the Father quadrant, northwest-diamond centerpoint realms and bone initiation-outer path, ages 22 to end of diamond centerpoint climb, muscle and bone

2) Cead (ket, Lincoln), father, courage of the father's heart in

shouldering work and changing societal darkness-rules masculine ascension and destiny path of outer world, intensive preparation for final destiny, bringing fears up into consciousness for healing, freedom from slavery to fear, Feb. 12th, Leo, Ras Elased Autralis

1) Saorsa (soorsa, Liberty), mother-freedom, equality and nourishment for all world's children, help for the downtrodden-facing mental gridwork that blocks needs being met in the world, rules feminine ascension path in the outer world, torch of freedom in the heart, Aug. 12th, New York, Vega

Tara rules the sensate realm climb and earth initiation, Oghama rules the Diamond Core climb and diamond initiation

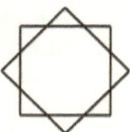

Circle of Eight-Regents of Cross-Quarter, Solstice, Equinox days-the Agricultural year-cosmic second chakra

8) Fiona, girl, red dragon, rules Imbolc, Feb. 4th eve and Feb. 5th day, opens girl yearly impulse into feminine mental body, new life and surprise, Delphinus (dolphin)

7) Finnegan, boy, rules Vernal Equinox, dawn, March 21st-opens boy growth impulse for the year into masculine mental body, alignment of personal will with divine will and pace of life with the mother's slow flow, Volans (flying fish)

6) Belissima, virgin girl, green dragon-rules Bealltain (bealchen), May 4th eve and May 5th day, brings yearly growth impulse into emotional ethers, opens virgin girl yearly impulse into feminine emotional body, cleansing in preparation for union of hearts with male virgin at Midsummer, rules white lightning force, Hawthorne moon, Huath, Hawthorne tree, letter H, cleansing of feminine bride, Virgo

5) Belenos, virgin boy, rules Midsummer, dawn June 21st-burns off veils between virgin boy and girl in the heart, rules union of virgin hearts, opens virgin male growth impulses for the year into masculine emotional body, world server or love in action, spiritual warrior, initiates heart partnership of virgin male and female into action impulse, Holly moon, Tinne, letter T, holding one's balance in facing darkness in outer world, Holly, Hercules

4) Cìrceidh (keerkay, Circe), mother, yellow dragon, rules Lughnasa (loonasa), Aug. 4th eve and Aug 5th day, opens mother yearly growth impulse into feminine action ethers, first fruits of the harvest, manifestation of nourishment into the physical, soil, overwork of the mother, overlights Reed moon, Cattails, Ngetal, letters Ng, peace of life, Izar (the girdle) in Bootes

3) Lugh, father, rules Autumnal Equinox, dawn, Sept. 21st, opens father growth impulses for the year into masculine action ethers, the harvest, manifestation into the physical, Vine moon, Muin or grapevines, letter M, union of heaven and earth, Seginus (the herdsman) in Bootes

2) Samhein (sahven), grandmother, rules Samhein (1), November 24th eve through Nov.28th day, black dragon, breaks down yearly growth impulses in mental, emotional, and action ethers through the spirit sheath; opens grandmother impulse into feminine core ethers; activates three fears for coming winter in core ethers; gratefulness celebration to the Goddess-Blackthorne moon, Straif, letters St, strife, and Z, manifestation of deep desire after one year's work, Blackthorne tree, Eriadne (the end of the river, Styx)- end of yearly impulse in all sheaths but sensate

1) Bran, grandfather, rules Midwinter, dawn, Dec. 21st, opens grandfather growth impulse for the year into masculine core ethers, opens portals for Arthur to implant new light seeds of coming year-saves seeds of new truths learned in passing year to be built into permanent light body, Elder moon, Ruis, Elder tree, letter R, the embodiment of wisdom, Corvus (the raven)

The White Pentagram-Birth of the divine child or inner god and goddess, lifetime and annual-birth of human babies-Celtic hidden stream and Christian year-human first chakra

12) Danu (Europa), mother of Celtic race, builds inner Goddess or wise woman throughout life, spleen, ages 15, 16.5, virgin fem. adolescent descent through soul sheath, brings forward three partners from past lives to prepare for marriage, special time with fem. relatives, opens generational patterns of fear, yearly feminine ascent through soul sheath during first half of Blackthorne moon, third trimester, plumping baby, Austria, Danube, Aquarius, Sadal Sund

11) Luis, father, builds inner god throughout life, highest destiny, liver ages 16.5 to 17, virgin masc. descent through soul sheath, brings forward work from last three lives to build into lifelong destiny, temptations of power and control, overlights yearly masculine ascent through soul sheath during Blackthorne moon-Rowan moon, third trimester, lengthening baby, France, Rowan or Mt. Ash, Leo Minor

10) Breith, fae girl-ages 0,1, infant girl/human mother/Tara bond, connection with family/human mother and Creator Sun regents

through them, stomach, pelvic floor, infant girl's descent through core (except Beloveds)-overlights yearly feminine ascent through core sheath from Midwinter to Epiphany, Hungary, long A, Ailm, Elm, birth of divine child through core sheath at Candlemas, first trimester, girl pillar, thymus, lungs, First Leap star in Ursa Major

9) Daimhin (jahveen, little deer), fae boy, ages 2, 3, boy's will force in action, taming will force, special spirit connection with grand/father, colon, pelvic stone circle of truth, and descent of toddler boy through core, annually opens light seeds into three stars of mind, heart, and base on Epiphany, overlights annual masculine ascent through core sheath from Epiphany to Candlemas, first trimester, girl pillar, Greece, Root of the tail star in Ursa Major

8) Eostre (yoster) (Ostara), cherub girl, ages 4 to 5, cherub girl's descent though centerpoint and cherubim sheaths, manifestation of own little world according to inner beliefs, egg of the heart, ovaries-yearly feminine ascent through centerpoint (first half of Candlemas to Lent) and cherubim sheaths (first half of Lent), removes three centerpoint or abyss fears on Easter morning, long O, birth through centerpoint/chrub sheaths on Easter, Gorse, Onn, travail with final sweetness, first trimester, boy pillars, nerves, Poland,Second Leap star in Ursa Major

7) Credne, cherub boy-ages 6 to 7, cherub boy's descent through centerpoint and cherubim sheaths, rules creation of life ladder of beliefs to final release from fear, family religious traditions, testicles, inner belief structures, bass bell of truth, yearly masculine ascent through centerpoint (second half of Candlemas to Lent) and cherubim sheaths (second half of Lent)-first trimester, boy pillar, brain, Czech Republic, Groin star in Ursa Major

6) Leanan (leenan, sweetheart), virgin girl, ages 8, 9, virgin girl's descent through logos sheath, rules passion for permanent union of hearts with virgin male, passion for change for the better for all virgin girls on earth, sweetness of life, pancreas, overlights yearly virgin girl's ascent through logos sheath (1 week past Easter to John Baptist Day), annually creates one passion for change for virgin feminine, birth of fem. from logos sheath on Pentecost, washes off fear debris from first half year on June 24th (John the Baptist Day), Netherlands, long U, Ur, heather, the wildness of love, push through the logos sheath from 1 week past East to John Baptist Day, first trimester, virgin pillar, spine, third leap star in Ursa Major

5) Nuada, virgin male- ages 10, 11, virgin male's descent through logos sheath, preparation for shared world service of virgin hearts, world service and spiritual warrior impulse, overlights yearly masculine ascent through logos sheath, Pentecost to John Baptist Day, one action impulse to ground past winter's growth, first trimester, virgin pillar, spine, Spain, the Flank star in Ursa Major

4) Boudicca, mother, ages 12 to13.5, sexual maturity, connection with One Beloved in virgin year, healing sexual distortions and addictions, feminine descent through spirit sheath, rules sovereignty and purity of the feminine, kidneys, waterfalls, overlights annual feminine ascent through spirit sheath, June 22nd to Aug. 15th, long E,

birth of yearly divine child through spirit sheath on Sept. 9th, Aspen, victory, second trimester, mother pillar, interstitial waters and life flow, quickening, Italy, the Thigh star in Ursa Major

3) Arecurius, father, ages 13.5, 14, virgin masc. descent through spirit sheath, rules intellectual foundation for life destiny and youthful preparation for eventual highest destiny, one destiny dream for late in life, driving mental and time pressures, adrenals, rules autumnal intellectual impulse that prepares for next yearly cycle, yearly ascent of masculine through spirit sheath from Aug. 16th to Sept. 9th, individuation and support of new aspect of self into specific action in the tribe during Reed moon, second trimester, mother pillar, Germany, the Muzzle star

2) Iona, girl, ages 18, 19, young adult fem. descent through sensate sheath, rules full individuation of fem. into sensate, 1st committed relationship, facing major relationship fear of life, annual, fem. ascent through sensate sheath, 1st half of Advent, full and final birth of divine girl out of sensate sheath on Midwinter midnight, long I, push through core sheath from Samhein till Midwinter, individuation of child of light, second trimester, father pillar, muscle, Belgium, Isle of Iona, Scotland, Southern Cross

1) Mabon, boy, ages 20, 21, young adult masc. descent through sensate sheath, full individuation of masc. into sensate, facing deepest destiny fear of lifetime-yearly ascent of boy through sensate sheath during last half of Advent, full and final birth of divine child, activation of yearly deepest sensate fear at Aut. Equinox, second trimester, father pillar, bones, Portugal, Isle of Anglesey, Britain, Perseus

Diamond Centerpoint
Indigo Pentagram-Release of dark child of the year and descent of childhood-earth star

12) Artio (arsteeo, Sophia), dark half of the goddess, rules wisdom, leads through darkness, feminine wisdom cycle of the year, birth pangs each month, 7 circuit labyrinth, loves dark as well as light child, ages 0-1, infant girl's descent through core (except Beloveds) and centerpoint sheaths, imperfect attachment with human mother, family shadow keeper, core wound, age 4-opens fear impulse into core sheath on Midwinter and centerpoint sheath on Candlemas, girl's yearly ascent through core (Midwinter to 12th night) and centerpoint sheaths (halfway from Candlemas to Lent), Turkey, Ursa Minor

11) Herne, dark half of Oghama, rules wisdom growth of the masculine, ages 2,3, boy's descent through core (except Beloveds)

and centerpoint sheaths, temper tantrums, will out of alignment, core wound, age 4, rules boy's yearly ascent through core (12th night to Candlemas) and centerpoint sheaths (halfway from Candlemas to Lent until beginning of Lent), Montenegro, Draco

10) Rhiann, girl, ages 4,5, girl's childhood descent through cherubim sheath, sacrifice of the child, harsh mothering, core wound from One Beloveds, girl's yearly ascent through cherubim sheath, 1st half of Lent, Hydra

9) Ùruisg (oorusk, brownie), boy, ages 6,7, boy childhood descent through cherubim sheath, sacrifice of the child, heavy work, yearly ascent through cherubim sheath, 2nd half of Lent, Hydrus

8) Ardunna, virgin girl, ages 8,9, virgin girl's childhood descent through logos sheath, repetition of core wound, false armoring over self of light, breaking backbone spirit, opens darkness into logos sheath 1 week past Easter, virgin girl's yearly ascent through logos sheath, sexual distortions and addictions, 1 week oast Easter to Pentecost, Canes Venatici

7) Gòbhlach (gohluck), virgin boy, ages 10,11, virgin boy's descent through logos sheath, militarization and violence, male posturing, virgin boy's yearly ascent through logos sheath, Pentecost to John Baptist Day, Chameleon

6) Damona, mother, ages 12-13.5, adol. girl's descent through spirit sheath, mental and time pressure, take on darkness of same gender parent, final family conflict that sends child to age mates, opens darkness into spirit sheath on July 22nd, inner mother's yearly ascent through spirit sheath, Juy 22nd to Aug. 15th, overwork and neglect of own needs,Musca

5) Borvo, father, ages 13.5, 14, virgin boy's descent through spirit sheath, heavy mental and time pressure, inner father's yearly ascent through spirit sheath, Aug. 16th to Sept. 9th, overwork of gathering harvest or not enough, Lacerta (lizard)

4) Cailleach Liath (cahlyuck leeah), grandmother, ages 15, 16.5, adol. girl's descent through soul sheath, astral influences in age mates, addictions and sexual misuse, grandmo. yearly ascent through soul sheath, 1st half of All Saint's Day to Advent, Cetus

3) Gobha (goa, blacksmith), grandfather, ages 16.5, 17, adol. boy's descent though soul sheath, astral influences, addictions and domination of fem., grandfa. yearly ascent through soul sheath, 2nd half of All Saint's Day to Advent, dismantles dark debris, Fornax

2) Rhiannon, virgin girl, send 1 sexual distortion at puberty, ages 18,19, young adult girl's descent through sensate sheath and final individuation, 1 committed relationship with core partnership wound, overlights Ivy moon, yearly release of dark child from cherubim, logos, spirit sheaths at end of Ivy moon, Gort, letter G, persistence in adversity, girl's yearly ascent through sensate sheath and falling away of year's dark child, 1st half of Advent to MIdwinter, Lupus

1) Carlin, virgin boy, ages 20, 21, young adult boy's descent through sensate sheath and final individuation, 1st work in the world with core destiny fear, disappointment of adulthood, work and restrictions, revelation of year's new aspect of self, being center of attention,

doing too much too soon, end of Reed moon, boy's yearly ascent through sensate sheath and full release of dark masc., 2nd half of Advent to Midwinter, Serpens

Cosmic Beast-666-The Abyss-Orion

Control centers-central stars of Orion

24) **Mind: the Borg, Fir Bolg, Pluto, invaded Pineal Wheel,** Beall (bee), Borg queen, mind control, possession of mental powers of others, forced left brain gridwork that breaks down, Pluto Maissa

23) Counnspeach (wasp), Aryan white male, superiority over others, wants power and money, keeps brown skinned people beneath him in rigid hierarchy, Pluto, Maissa

Heart: Formorians, Mayan reptilians, Neptune, invaded Maya in Plieades and Cygnus:

22) Fuach (hatred): evil queen, hatred poisons others, envy, criticism, control, gall stones and sludge, Neptune, Alnilam

21) Aeval, Goth, heavy metal music of death and despair covers Goddess song of life-weighs heavier on heart as life goes on, depression, Neptune, Alnilam

Action: Sirians or Milesians, masc. on Saiph, fem. on Rigel, Uranus, invaded Sirius:

20) Smàd (smayt), emotional sadism and control, lifts her up into false happiness and drops down into disappointment, manic depressive disorder , Uranus, Trapezium

19) Ruaig (defeat), defeat of masc. hopes and work, blocks success, even in small ways, overwork, breaks down fibers of right heart

Lateral Stars-the 6-6-6

Mind-the Borg, mind control, fem. on Bellatrix, masc. on Betelgeuse, Fir Bolg, Pluto, invaded Pineal Wheel

Mind: 18) Badb, complications of home life, rules and regulations about eating, cleaning, dress; pulls him away from focus on work, wants control; Obsessive Compulsive Disorder

17) Balor, the evil eye-constant focus on work, complicated mental structures, educator, know-it-all, disrupts sleep-Aspberger's

Heart: 16) Banshee, false voices and insanity impulses to break down right fem. brain, fear of the whole world, paranoia,

15) Meall, mental confusions in left brain facts and work, deception, breaking business plans, humiliation and defeat of masculine, anxiety disorder

Action: 14) Bella, disability and disease, weather and plant diseases that cause starvation, pesticides to kill Goddess flow through earth, genetic engineering to close down life force and let cancer flourish, junk foods that taste good but kill, plague

13) Breas, insects, bacteria, viruses that cause disease to animals, esp. fleas, to take over lands, warfare chemicals on pets to shut down inner goddess flow

Heart, emotional control, fem. on Mintaka, masc. on Alnitak, Formorians, Mayan reptilians, Neptune, invaded Maya in Plieades

Mind: 12) Morgause, disruptions to family gatherings till family fabric breaks down, meaningless errands, traffic snafus, breaks down fibers of left heart, loneliness

11) Tethra, iron mental forces of control over feminine heart, meeting complicated requirements to get basic life needs met, healthcare, taxes, housing, etc., constant insecurity and frustration

Heart: 10) Macha, poppy force, false beloved, drug and sexual addictions, obsession, love that leads to control and death

9) Sgìth (tired), continuous menial overwork of fem. throughout life, worn down, paralysis, chronic fatigue,

Action: 8) Agrona, mother who mutilates and sacrifices children, causes autism to child in future lives together, female genital mutilation

7) Dochann, sado-masochism, physical abuse to fem., links pain with love-making

Action, physical control, fem. on Rigel, masc. on Saiph, Uranus, invaded Sirius

Mind: 6) Nemain, constant anxiety about not enough food or money or shelter, driving frenzy to work more, mania

5) Fenneil, self centered, wants to be center of attention, talks constantly, sucks life out of others, steals focus-narcissism

Heart: 4) Sùigh-saps father's life force caring for her family-constant work outside the home, right side osteoporosis

3) Hafgan-saps mother's life force caring for too many children or too large a home, left side osteoporosis

Action: 2) Eigh (ice), mother who neglects children, parent/child reversal, force adult work on children, back and left hip pain in later life

1) Carman, driving male force into root, deadlines, time pressure, brutal punishment for failure, perfectionist, Type A personality, high blood pressure

Central Node
3 planes-entrance to diamond worlds

Appendix Two:
The Laws of Love

These were channeled for my book, <u>Guardians of the Celtic Way</u> and since updated. The sense of authority here is not my own voice, but that of the 'guardians' I was listening to as I wrote them down.

1) The One Beloveds: union of Hearts of the White Tara and Oghama (Magdalene and Christ) is the central principle of love. The One Beloveds stream from the Creator Sun. They are regents of: the love force, all true love partnerships, marriage, sexual union, the sacred sexual process of manifestation of heart's desires, and world service. They are the Mother and Father-of-all, divine feminine and masculine, Creators. Their Heart is the originator of the love force and its flow into all worlds.

2) The feminine Creator is recognized and honored for Her descent and for receiving and distributing the Creator energies in the world of form, as well as Her continued suffering in love of the All. She is the White Tara or the Magdalen; the Madonna, Mother-of-all, protector of the child of light, keeper of wisdom. She is held in the utmost respect for Her great strength, Her protection of the spirit child, Her descent, and Her Love.

3) The cosmic Christ or Oghama is the masculine Creator. He is keeper of truth and holds the worlds together, leadin all toward higher levels of love. He is honored for His strength, endurance, protection, and great Love.

4) The Creators are the guiding spirit of humanity and focalize all radiations from the Creator Sun through Their Heart. These continuously create the evolution of humanity into Their likeness.

5) The One Creator, Giver of All, Sustainer of All, fusion of Divine Feminine and Masculine, is adored and worshiped at all times and in every way. All honor is accorded to the One Beloveds and the One Parents, Tara and Oghama. Praise is free flowing, given daily and in joy, in any form desired by the adorer.

6) There is only Love. All forms in all planes make love in all times and in all ways. There is service to love and being in love and love alone, world without end. The highest value at all levels and times is love.

7) The primary goal is creating in love, individually and together. All forces: actions, thoughts, emotions, and speech move toward higher and purer expressions of love.

8) All forms of creation are honored and respected. All are recognized as equals with their own powers of love. Aside from the greatness of the Creators, no ranking is allowed.

9) All levels are held as equals: the sensate, the emotional, and the mental levels or sense, soul, and spirit. All planes in all worlds are held in utmost respect, treated with dignity, and used to express and reveal love and love alone. All worlds are visible, accessible, interpenetrating, and working together to create new forms of love.

10) It is understood and accepted that the All is One Body and any disharmony in any world or at any plane affects the All. Exceptions are allowed only in the service of growth in love.

11) All forms of life are regarded as temples and treated with gentle loving kindness at all times.

12) The heart is the vessel of love and the guiding force of life and personal choice. Mind and action take a secondary and supportive role to the force of love and the intelligence of the heart.

13) Sovereignty of all forms is law. No domination, no power struggles, no control, no forcing is ever tolerated at any level: spirit, soul, or sensate.

14) Love of self is paramount, for it is recognized that all radiations of love stream from love of self. Self-disparagement and harm hold the highest priority for healing.

15) Male and female, inner and outer, are held as equals, and their powers are used in balance and harmony.

16) The physical union of male and female is held as one of the most sacred forms of praise and worship. :)

17) The child, inner and outer, is allowed freedom to speak, to grow, to create in equal balance with the inner and outer adult.

18) Family is honored and supported, from the One Family to the nuclear family. Each is seen as a living organism and is respected and held in love.

19) Independence and intimacy are valued equally.

20) Rest (replenishment), work, service, and play in equal measure make for happiness.

21) All mistakes are met with kindness, held in love, and given a gentle reminder of the law. Punishment is forbidden.

22) Thoughts, actions, and speech that are not based in love are not tolerated. Each form is responsible at all times for his/her actions, speech, and thoughts. Exceptions will create instant return to the sender as a gentle reminder that a boundary has been overstepped.

23) Mistakes are held in love, but continued and purposeful misuse will result in probationary time and then the closing of the veil, to allow the one who has not attained wisdom to continue his or her growth in one of the lower worlds.

24) There are inevitable tensions in growth. These will be addressed openly and collectively until consensus is reached. No communal action will take place until consensus has been achieved.

25) All participation is voluntary. Action, thought, or speech based in obligation is not tolerated.

26) Simplicity is valued, both for its conservation of energy and its aesthetic of holding great love in minimal form.

27) Peace is greatly valued: peace of spirit, soul, and sense. Any exceptions in song, dance, or worship are done with prior notice to and permission from all forms.

28) Patience is valued, for individual growth includes growth of the All.

29) Personal will, timing, and desire are subdued in service to the All.

30) Experience is paramount. Lessons are learned and growth occurs primarily through experience and through play.

31) Time is irrelevant. Rushing or hurrying is not allowed. Each unfolding or teaching is accepted as having its own natural timing of expression and all are honored.

32) Humor is held in the highest regard. All lessons, all experience, all life is taken with a grain of salt. There is dedication to humor.

33) Honesty and truth are paramount. Falseness, whether by omission or commission, is forbidden.

34) Inner guidance is a beacon of light from higher realms, to be honored and developed. But it is not a law unto itself. Discernment and personal freedom of choice in love are paramount.

35) Death is seen as the illusion it is. There is continual change, recycling, and growth, but nothing is lost. All build into higher forms and expressions of love.

36) Creation is the highest achievement. Invention and art, poetry and song, are highly valued as the bringing through of the unrevealed into new forms of love.

37) All creating is done with conservation of energy, sustainability for all forms, and in the spirit of fun, joy, and love.

38) Celebrations in tune with the astrological and planetary forces are held in every world and all planes.

39) Purity is unrivaled in its essence. It is a goal to strive for at all times and in every endeavor. It is hoped for and embodied, but there is always room for growth.

40) The goals of society are healing and growth. All educators and healers are honored and supported.

41) There is a class who are guardians of the law and the purity of the Mother/Father's Kingdom. These are the law-givers and spiritual warriors. They are held in the highest esteem.

42) There is a class devoted to worship. These are the priests and priestesses, again, deeply honored and held by all levels of society.

43) There is a class who provide nourishment, farmers and growers. They are deeply honored and supported.

These are the statutes of the law, the Chivalric Code of The Celtic Realm of Heaven.

From the Guardians of the Celtic Realms

Appendix Three:
Simple Energy Healing Method

1) Close your eyes and relax.

2) Call in the God/Goddess you trust most and align with the force of love.*

3) Ask for protection from unwanted influences as you do this work.*

4) Ask for the next fear belief you need to clear.*

5) You will feel a tension in your body somewhere.*

6) Send your focus, a stream from your 3rd eye or your heart into the tension.*

7) Wait until you have a sense of what the belief is about. Most are from past lives or our descent into matter.* If you cannot read the energy, just practice this step for a couple of weeks, a few minutes a day, to reactivate your inner sensing systems.

8) Verbally release the contract to believe in that fear.*

9) Imagine the fear energy move into the creator flame in your deep heart. It is important to include both polarities in this step. If you were a victim, include the one who hurt you. These are both poles of the same fear. Do several of these, eight or ten a day.

10) Imagine the creator flame coming out of the deep heart in four directions. There are dark chords over the pieces of your light body you just released. Just let the light touch these and the dark bindings will melt off. Or you can just set this intention and it will be. These pieces of your original light body will lift off and stretch out into your aura and be permanently restored.

11) When you are done clearing fear beliefs, go into receiving. Just relax and let your spirit guides restructure your field at a higher level. The fear release leaves a tiny vacuum that needs to be filled by light before you release your protective spirit force.

12) Thank and release your guides.

When on a conscious path like this, the spirit world will work with you. Very often an event to open a fear will occur a day or two ahead of a planned healing in order to bring some fear into awareness. On any ascension path, many difficulties will arise. As fears are healed, new fears will come in for healing. Don't worry about any of them. Just keep clearing, even though some passages can be quite intense. Believe in the power of love and your eventual break-through, and this will be. After inner healing, the outer reality will be adjusted by the spirit world in alignment with the newly released inner light. Eventually this path brings mastery of fear, a realization that all fears are illusion, the self empowerment of knowing one can change one's outer 'reality' by inner healing work, the embodiment of wisdom, the full inner rulership of love, emergence of the divine or fully actualized self, and the happily-ever-after: true love, world service, and living in a community of ancestral family members. May all hearts open fully to love!

*These steps are from the Awareness Release Technique or ART (Arte!), developed by Robert Ibrahim Jaffe, M.D., as taught in his School of Energy Mastery in 1996-7. He is now president of the University of Spiritual Healing and Sufism in Napa Valley, CA. Printed with permission of Dr. Jaffe.

Appendix Four:
Stages of Suffering and Growth in the Druid Ascension Path

1) **Sensate Level**-The individuals are locked into rigid societal and gender roles. The deep heart is closed to spirit, so they search for love on the outside. There is an emphasis on money, status, and power. Intimacy, spirituality, and play are minimized. Ends with earth initiation (new location/partnership/work), 18.6 years (all years are approximate in life).

2) **Soul Level**-There is a male/female identity role reversal. The feminine becomes the wage earner, the masculine, the home/child keeper. This breaks down the rigid inner societal structures and opens the inner opposite genders. There are intense financial pressures and partner control struggles. This phase develops a deep understanding of the opposite gender and opens the realization that the individual cannot change another, but is creating his or her own 'reality' and needs to go inside and change him or herself. Communication with the devic realm and virtue angels opens. Ends with water initiation (financial pressure, new location/partnership/work), 18.6 year cycle.

3) **Spirit Level**-Commitment to one great spiritual work opens. There is intense time and work pressure, and deepening spirituality. This develops the inner cocreator relationship with God/Goddess. Communication with plant, animal, insect, and djinn (male fairy) kingdoms open. Ends with air initiation (rushed overwhelming work project), 8-12 month cycle.

4) **Logos Level I**-There is deep communion with God/Goddess, with one annual cocreated work. Isolation, fanaticism, and insanity forces come in for healing. Communication with seraphim opens.

Logos Level II-The infidelity of one's personal partner creates a turning inward for love and the opening of the God/Goddess Beloved portal and mystical marriage path. This brings forth an intense opening of the deep heart, and all life becomes the Body of the One Beloved.

Logos Level III-Military, violence, and sadism forces come in for healing. The highest destiny is brought forward, with repeated obstacles that break down the personal will force in separation from Divine will, and financial strain. This phase builds each individual's inner divinity, prepares him or her for world service, and forges an intense partnership with the One Beloved. Ends with fire initiation (intense and short but unfaithful lover) and moving through the eye-of-the-needle center of the Logos sun into next heaven, all Logos levels are on a 6.2 year cycle and includes the spirit climb.

5) **Cherubim Level**-Brings the breaking down of the shadow self over the inner divine child. This level brings in dark mother energies: hostility, abandonment, isolation, overwork from women in authority, and memories of child sacrifice. The inner child heart opens. This brings intimacy with all life, play and magic that become a way of life, and manifestation of the heart's desires of the child. Communication with the cherubim opens. Ends with leaving old way of life, cherub initiation. (sudden breaking away from community and work to new location and work), 6.2 year cycle.

6) **Diamond Centerpoint Level**- Begins with the bone initiation, a serious but short disease/accident, domination of male over female, overwork, mania, sapping the life force, left brain gridwork over the heart and right brain come in for healing. This phase carefully builds the highest destiny, often involving details that take years to comprehend or move forward. It fuses the One Beloved and individual inner hearts, and builds persistence and great courage, 6.2 year cycle.

7) **Diamond Core, Level I**-repetition of all former levels in miniature, healing all that has been missed, the highest mountain. Leaving one's home, relatives, favorite lifelong places in preparation for leaving the earth plane in 18.6 years, insecurity of housing, preparation for highest destiny. Brings in dance/language connections to original motherland. Leads to union with the virgin girl, Maighdean, and the Dagda father, of the Creator Sun. Communication with virgin girl, and elder father of the Creator Sun opens, 2.5 years.

Diamond Core-Level II-girl brings in dance and inner centering, but detailed intellectual lessons and neglect/criticism of divine gifts by others. Leads to union and communication with girl of action, Eriu, and father of action, Daiden, of the Creator Sun, 2.5 years.

Diamond Core Level III-return to birth location and relatives-many joyful outer activities-menial tasks, serious colon problems, continued work on highest destiny-leads to union and communication with elder mother, Màiri, and virgin boy, Ridire, of the Creator Sun, 2.5 years.

Diamond Core Level IV-cancer/death forces in close relatives, insecurity of close family relationships, sapping of personal time for other's needs, and lack of rest. Brings in living near the ocean/lakes, time on the water, and great simplicity of life, fun activities with others. Leads to union and communication with action boy, Finn, and action mother, Maithreil, of the Creator Sun, 2.5 years.

Diamond Core Level V-move to place of ease and simpler tasks, distance from friends and fun activities, isolation, personal gifts ignored, high creativity in the arts, brings communication with virgin aspects of Goddess and God, 2.5 years

Diamond Core Level VI-diamond initiation; heavy work, financial sapping, insecurity of housing, isolation, ongoing blockages to manifestation of partnership and work, cruelty by women in authority , personal gifts ignored, continuous stress, life threats to self, pets, closest family member, manifestation of personal desires blocked; the core wound comes in for healing, a disease or challenge that has run through the individual's entire life, their deepest fear, final fear lasts less than 24 hours, usually only a few minutes. Brings final release of the shadow self or rebirth into light and full union with the White Tara and Oghama, Beloved Goddess and God of the Creator Sun, 6 years. All Diamond Core levels are on an 18.6 year cycle.

8) **The Happily-Ever-After**-True love and world service/ one's highest destiny opens. This initiates the manifestation of heart's desires into the physical through true love and sacred sexual union. Lifelong partners live in a community of beloveds and ancient family members in the land of their ancestors in service to God/Goddess, expressing the ancestral traditions and spiritual purposes of this family and motherland. Heaven on earth, in the image of the Creator Sun.

About the Author

I have an M.A. and Ph.D. in Clinical Psychology, certification from The Jaffe School of Energy Mastery (a 21 month program teaching energetic healing through the use of light, movement, and sound), and post-graduate certification in Toddler and Infant Mental Health. I was a therapist in private practice from 1976 through 1999 and began using light healing exclusively in 1997. In 1997, I also did a radio show called "The Cycle of Darkness is Over." From 1999 to the present, I've been leading workshops, doing conference presentations, and writing books on energy healing, the personal transformation process, and Celtic spirituality. I have a workshop and teaching center in Minnesota, USA, Facebook.com/ CelticHeavenCenter/ And I'm the mother of three grown daughters. I love to write, sew Celtic and fairy wear and decorate clothing, row, tend perennial gardens and fruit trees, play my lap harp, walk by the sea, make pottery, paint silk scarves and goddess figurines, and snuggle with my dog, Síth (shee, peace).

Publications as Jill Kelly, Ph.D.; Guardians of the Celtic Way-Inner Traditions, 2003 (Includes moons and trees of the druid year, rays and the stone kingdom, the druid path of experience and transformation, the bird kingdom, the dragon kingdoms, the Arthurian fulfillment, and the Chivalric Code of the Celtic Realm of Heaven.)

Publications as Jill Frew, Ph.D.: Alba Reborn, Book One, Dogear Publishers, 2011. This book is now outdated, Alba Reborn, Book One Revised is the updated version of the same book, the path of transformation as lived by a Celtic couple in 1st C. Alba. Book One includes the childhood and adolescence of Soillse and Fìrinn in their tribes on the Isle of Skye, Scotland, with druid lessons on the nine light structures of the Diamond Core or the nine cosmic chakras, with the cycles and aspects of cosmic life each regulates, regents of the Celtic pantheon and their directives, simple energy healing method, and stages on the Celtic path of transformation.

Alba Reborn, Celtic Heaven Trilogy, Book One Revised; Createspace, 2015, identical to Alba Reborn edition but updated with new Stillpoint Center light structure, 24 planes of light, with regents and directives, and references to five new light structures to follow in Book Two.

Alba Reborn, Celtic Heaven Trilogy, Book Two, Createspace, 2016; includes the young adulthood of Soillse and Fìrinn, his slavery in Africa and her isolation in the forest near her tribe, both facing ongoing fears of their ascension climb, with their final reunion into true love, the remaining five light structures of the Diamond Core, plus the sacred geometry of nemetons.

Alba Reborn, Celtic Heaven Trilogy, Book Three, Createspace, 2018; includes the adulthood of Fìrinn and Soillse, he as high king of Skye and she as a priestess and healer, their world service and true love years.

Fountains of Remembering, Createspace, 2016, compilation of exquisite sonnets by Sumner Gage Whittier, listed online under his name.

Light Healing for Children, Createspace, 2017, two simple healing methods children can use to heal everyday hurts, the fourteen regents of the Creator Sun, their ray colors, matching crystals, and uses in healing.

A Druid Guidebook, Createspace, 2018; the process of becoming a druid; the eight holy days, moons, and trees of the druid year; Ogham letters and meanings; stages on the path; qualities of a druid; making a medicine bag.

May the Golden Road to Heaven Lead You Home, Createspace, 2020, stages on the path, inner healing, the seven heavens and sixteen light structures of the Diamond Core, wisdom lessons learned along the way.

Colors of the Great Heart, 365 Rays of the Cosmos, Createspace, 2021, all colors of light have very specific qualities of love infused into them, these are explained as well as the resonance of specific flowers, dogs, fibers, and foods with the planes of light and purposes of the Diamond Core (the seventh and highest heaven of the inner planes), the meaning of hair, eye, and skin colors, chakras, tartans, and crystals.

The Spirit of the Child, Createspace, 2022, the light impulses of child and human development with specific connections to the regents and light structures of the Diamond Core, explanations of the various phases of life and the spirit purposes behind them.

Beloved Communities, Createspace, 2022, communities of the future, beloved partners in family-of-light villages, heaven on earth, true love and sacred sexuality with laws of relationship, community structure and governance with connection to the Creator Sun, green building, local exchange trading systems, simple global worship.

Creator Power, Createspace, 2024, energetic effects of human sexuality, the long term *impacts* of raps and childhood abuse.

May all hearts open fully to love! :)

www.ingramcontent.com/pod-product-compliance
Lightning Source LLC
Chambersburg PA
CBHW030741030726
47497CB00001B/77